Praise for **The Killing**

'A very fine novel, which is more of a re-imagining of the
original story than a carbon copy – and with the bonus of a
brand new twist to the ending'
Daily Mail

'David Hewson's literary translation is far more than a cheap tie-in . . .
the book allows the characters more room to breathe . . . Hewson's
greatest achievement is that it's compelling reading'
Observer

'Not just a novelisation. Hewson is a highly regarded crime writer in
his own right; he spent a lot of time with the creators of the original to
ensure that he did not offend its spirit and mood, and he has provided
his own, different solution to the central murder mystery'
Marcel Berlins, *The Times*

'A fast-paced crime novel that's five-star from start to finish'
Irish Examiner

'The book is an excellent read in which the author manages to
dig deeper into the characters without having to rewrite their original
television characterisation. For those who haven't seen the series, this
is a very cleverly constructed and beautifully written crime drama;
for those who already know the ending, a new twist awaits'
Irish Times

'As gripping as the TV series.
It will keep you pinned to the very last page'
Jens Lapidus

'David Hewson should be commended for writing such a page-turner
of a book . . . *The Killing* has enough twists and turns to satisfy
not only any avid follower of the series but also readers that
are coming to it first time around'
www.shotsmag.co.uk

THE KILLING
II

DAVID HEWSON

THE KILLING II

BASED ON THE BAFTA AWARD-WINNING TV SERIES

WRITTEN BY SØREN SVEISTRUP

MACMILLAN

First published 2013 by Macmillan
an imprint of Pan Macmillan, a division of Macmillan Publishers Limited
Pan Macmillan, 20 New Wharf Road, London N1 9RR
Basingstoke and Oxford
Associated companies throughout the world
www.panmacmillan.com

ISBN 978-1-4472-1694-0 HB
ISBN 978-0-230-76175-9 TPB

Based on Søren Sveistrup's *Forbrydelsen* (*The Killing*)
– an original Danish Broadcasting Corporation TV series
co-written by Torleif Hoppe, Michael W. Horsten and Per Daumiller

The Macmillan Group has no responsibility for the information provided by
any author websites whose address you obtain from this book ('author websites').
The inclusion of author website addresses in this book does not constitute
an endorsement by or association with us of such sites or the content,
products, advertising or other materials presented on such sites.

1 3 5 7 9 8 6 4 2

A CIP catalogue record for this book is available from the British Library.

Typeset by SetSystems Ltd, Saffron Walden, Essex
Printed and bound by CPI Group (UK) Ltd, Croydon, CR0 4YY

Visit **www.panmacmillan.com** to read more about all our books
and to buy them. You will also find features, author interviews and
news of any author events, and you can sign up for e-newsletters
so that you're always first to hear about our new releases.

**Life can only be understood backwards;
but it must be lived forwards.**

Søren Kierkegaard

Acknowledgements

I'm once again indebted to a number of people for their assistance. Søren Sveistrup, the creator of the series, Susanne Bent Andersen and Lars Ringhof in Copenhagen were enormously helpful. I'm also deeply grateful to my editor Trisha Jackson in the UK and her colleagues at Pan Macmillan for their useful insights. As with the first book, all diversions from the original TV narrative should, however, be laid at my door alone.

David Hewson

Principal Characters

Copenhagen Police

Sarah Lund – *Former Vicekriminalkommissær (a post now known as Vicepolitikommisær), Homicide*

Lennart Brix – *Chief, Homicide*

Ulrik Strange – *Vicepolitikommissær, Homicide*

Ruth Hedeby – *Deputy Commissioner*

Madsen – *Detective, Homicide*

Svendsen – *Detective, Homicide*

Erik König – *head of Politiets Efterretningstjeneste (PET) the internal national security intelligence agency, a separate arm of the police service*

Folketinget, the Danish Parliament

Thomas Buch – *newly appointed Minister of Justice*

Karina Jørgensen – *Buch's personal secretary*

Carsten Plough – *Buch's Permanent Secretary, a senior civil servant*

Erling Krabbe – *leader of the People's Party*

Birgitte Agger – *leader of the Progressive Party*

Flemming Rossing – *Minister of Defence*

Gert Grue Eriksen – *Prime Minister*

Frode Monberg – *former Minister of Justice*

Danish Army

Jens Peter Raben – *former sergeant*

Louise Raben – *Raben's wife, an army nurse*

Colonel Torsten Jarnvig – *Louise Raben's father*

Major Christian Søgaard

Allan Myg Poulsen – *former comrade of Raben's*

Lisbeth Thomsen – *former comrade of Raben's*

David Grüner – *former comrade of Raben's*

General Jan Arild – *assistant chief of staff, army headquarters*

Gunnar 'Priest' Torpe – *former army clergyman, now a civilian pastor*

Torben Skåning – *former captain*

Frederik Holst – *army doctor*

Peter Lænkholm – *former lieutenant*

Others

Anne Dragsholm – *a lawyer and activist*

Stig Dragsholm – *Anne Dragsholm's husband*

Abdel Hussein Kodmani – *an Islamist activist*

Connie Vemmer – *a journalist, formerly a press officer with the Ministry of Defence*

One

Thursday 3rd November

11.42 p.m.   Thirty-nine steps rose from the busy road of Tuborgvej into Mindelunden, with its quiet graves and abiding bitter memories. Lennart Brix, head of the Copenhagen homicide team, felt he'd been walking them most of his life.

Beneath the entrance arch, sheltering from the icy rain, he couldn't help but recall that first visit almost fifty years before. A five-year-old boy, clutching the hand of his father, barely able to imagine what he was about to see.

Death was as distant to a child as a nightmare or a fairy tale. But here, in this solitary park trapped between the traffic and the railway line in Østerbro, it seemed to lie in wait like a hungry phantom, hiding in the shadows behind the gravestones and the statues, whispering the names carved into cold stone memorials lining the walls.

Brix, a tall and serious man, not given to fantasies or delusions, wiped his face with the sleeve of his coat. The familiar ritual of homicide was in motion. Officers in black uniforms tramped up and down the concrete steps carrying lights and equipment like stage-hands preparing for a performance. Radios crackled. Men asked predictable questions to which he gave predictable answers with a curt wave of the hand.

Mindelunden.

A haunting memory, a nagging fear that had stayed with him ever since.

'Boss?'

1

Madsen. A good cop. Not so bright but young and keen.

'Where is she?' Brix asked.

'The worst place. You want . . . ?'

Brix strode upwards, reached the head of the stairs, walked out into the blustery dark night. To his left the long line of commemorative plaques seemed to stretch for ever, name after name, one hundred and fifty-one, just a few of the partisans murdered during five years of Nazi occupation. There were many more, his father said that sunny day, May the 5th, half a century before, when every house and apartment put candles in their windows to remember those who'd died.

In his head he was back there on that sharp, still morning. Hat in hand walking to the statue of a woman holding her dead son, though the boy Brix could see little but the graves in front, line after line of tidy stone tombs, each with a commemorative vase, all beautifully tended as they would be, his father vowed, for ever.

On that far-off day the child that was Lennart Brix had his first encounter with the shadowy creature called mortality, came to understand that its grey, eternal presence would follow him from that moment on. It was still there in the bleak and visionless stone eyes of the woman cradling her lost child. In the names chiselled on the marble plaques. Death lurked like a feral animal, shrinking into the shadows of the little wood beyond the tidy, ordered graves, waiting for the opportunity to escape into the city at large.

'Boss?'

Madsen was getting impatient. He had every right. Lennart Brix knew where the worst place was and for all his years in homicide still didn't want to see it.

'We've got the husband. A squad car stopped him in a car on the bridge to Malmö. Covered in blood. Babbling like a lunatic.'

The Nazis seized Mindelunden when they took control of the neighbouring Ryvangen Barracks in 1943 as their grip on Copenhagen tightened. In the army buildings across the railway line they established a command centre. Here, on the flat land once used for parades and exercises, they walked partisan prisoners to the pistol firing range and shot them.

Madsen stamped his feet on the paving stones and blew on his hands.

'I guess that means half the job's done.'

Brix just looked at him.

'The husband,' the young officer repeated with obvious impatience. 'He's covered in blood.'

Two years before, when, half knowingly, they were stumbling towards divorce, Brix had shown his wife round Mindelunden. It was a futile effort to interest her in his native city, to keep her from flying home for good. She came from London, which meant she never fully grasped the context of the place. You needed to be Danish, brought here dutifully by a stern-faced parent for that.

The English knew the meaning of war but were naively, dangerously ignorant of the nature of occupation. For them, for the Americans too, conflicts happened in other places, broke out like remote wildfires then were stamped into cinders and ashes that stayed in foreign lands. It was different for the Danes in a way he could never explain. They had fought as best they could when the Germans rolled into Jutland in 1940. Then, for a while, quietly acquiesced in return for a semblance of normality, of sham independence in a Europe torn apart by war, a fresh cruel landscape which the Nazis seemed destined to master.

By the time Jews began to disappear and daring bands of partisans started to prick consciences attitudes were changing. Some fought back, paying the ultimate cost, tortured in cells in the Politigården, the police headquarters where Brix now worked, then driven to Mindelunden, tied to a stake in the ground against a grassy rampart made for targets that were not human, did not breathe.

He could still hear his father describing the scene in May 1945 when liberation came. The Germans had rushed to murder as many captives as they could in those closing months. Broken, rotting corpses lay half-buried in the bare fields, abandoned in the rush.

They didn't die easily and nor did the experience of occupation. That mixture of rage and grief and a secret sense of shame still lingered. As a child, shivering in front of those three stakes, preserved as memorials before the grassy ramp of the firing range, Lennart Brix had wondered: would he have had such courage? Or turned away and lived instead?

It was the question everyone who followed was bound to ask. But rarely out loud.

The bark of a dog broke his reverie. Brix looked at the forensic officers, white bunny suits, mob hats, marching grim-faced down the rows of graves, towards the space in the little wood where the rest of the team was gathering.

Perhaps, he thought, that moment fifty years before had marked him out as a detective. Someone who looked for reasons when none seemed easily available.

'Boss?'

Madsen's face was full of the prurient enthusiasm he expected of his men. They had to have the hunger, the need for the chase. Detectives were hunters, all of them. Some better than others, though the best he'd ever encountered was now wasting her life and her talents inside a border guard's uniform in a godforsaken corner of Zealand.

Brix didn't answer. He strode ahead, knowing this had to be faced.

A flat rectangle of grass muddy from the tramping of police boots, banks raised on three sides, tallest at the narrow end.

The floodlights were so bright it seemed a full moon had come to hover above them. Beyond their reach more men were starting to search patiently through the surrounding area, torches high in their hands.

Three gnarled stakes, replicas now, with the originals in the small Resistance museum in the city, the Frihedsmuseet. A woman was tied to the centre pole, hands behind her back, bound with heavy rope round her torso. Blonde hair soaked with rain and worse, head down, chin on chest, crouched awkwardly on her knees.

A gaping wound at her neck like a sick second smile. She wore a blue dressing gown slashed in places all the way to the waist, flesh and skin visible where the frenzied blade had stabbed at her. Her face was bruised and dirty. Blood poured from her nostrils, had dried down each side of her mouth, like make-up on a tragic clown.

'Fifteen to twenty wounds on her chest and neck,' Madsen said. 'She wasn't killed here. The husband called in to say he came home and found the place covered in blood. No sign of her. Then he took off in his car.'

He stepped forward for a closer look.

'So that's what a crime of passion looks like.'

The dog was getting frantic.

'Can someone get that animal to shut up?' Brix said.

'Boss?'

'Take the husband in for questioning. Let's see what he's got to say.'

Madsen shuffled on his feet.

'You don't seem so sure.'

'She's a lawyer. So is he. Is that right?'

'Yeah.'

Brix gazed at the torn and mangled body at the stake.

'Here?' he said, shaking his head. 'Of all places? It doesn't make sense.'

'Killing people doesn't make sense, does it?'

But it does, Brix thought. Sometimes. That was a detective's job. To winnow the logic from the blood and bone.

He couldn't stop thinking of the officer he'd lost, Sarah Lund, and how she was frittering away her life in Gedser. Brix wondered what she'd make of a scene like this. The questions she might ask, the places she would look. Something he'd encountered here fifty years before was supposed to give him that dread gift too, and had, a little. But it wasn't a talent like Lund's. He could speak to the dead, try to imagine their answers.

She . . .

The tall, severe chief of Copenhagen homicide wanted to be out of this place so much. It affected his judgement, his precious reason.

In some way he would never comprehend Lund could hear them speak.

'What do you want me to do?' Madsen asked again.

'What I just said. Bring him in.'

He went back along the narrow muddy path, through the field of gravestones, past the names on the wall, the statue of the mother clutching her murdered son, the memorial plaque with the patriotic verses of an awkward priest named Kai Munk, slaughtered by the Gestapo one dark January night near Silkeborg in Jutland a lifetime before.

Walked down the concrete steps, carefully, the way he had as a five-year-old child leaving this place feeling sick and giddy, aware that the world was not the safe and happy realm he thought, and that a shadow waited for him, as it did for everyone some day.

At the foot of the steps Lennart Brix looked right, looked left, made sure no one saw him. Strode over to the undergrowth next to the busy road, and did what he did all those decades before: vomited into the grubby bushes, strewn with trash, discarded bottles and cigarettes.

Then sat mute and miserable in his unmarked car, beneath the revolving blue light, listening to the sirens and the chatter on the police networks, wishing he possessed the faith to pray that Madsen was right. That this was a curiously violent domestic interlude to be swiftly and cleanly concluded.

A crime of passion, nothing more.

Two

Monday 14th November

7.45 a.m.   Gedser sat by the dull waters of the Baltic, a tiny town of eight hundred souls, most of them living off the ferry that came and went to Rostock throughout the day. When Germany was divided between East and West, the main smuggling activity was political refugees from the Communists. The twenty-first century had proved more enterprising. Drugs, hard and soft, human traffic from the Middle East and beyond. The nature of contraband had changed, and all the authorities could do was hope to hold back a little of the floodtide.

Sarah Lund, in her blue border guard's uniform, long dark hair tied up behind a regulation cap, had lost none of her powers of imagination and curiosity. After the disaster of the Birk Larsen case and the shooting of her partner Jan Meyer, she'd been fired from the Copenhagen police and offered this humble, poorly paid post in a backwater where she knew no one, and none knew her.

Had taken it with alacrity, settled into a tiny wooden bungalow which, even after two years, had no personal items inside it save for a few practical clothes and several photos of her son, Mark, now turned fourteen and living with his father outside Copenhagen.

Her life was in limbo, a dead, numb place though free, to an extent, of the nagging sense of guilt she'd felt in the city.

It was her fault the Birk Larsen case ended so messily. She was to blame for the fact that Meyer, an active, happy man, so in love with his family, would be confined to a wheelchair for the rest of his life.

And so she worked in Gedser and watched the trucks roll on and

7

roll off the massive vessels in the port, followed the expressions on the drivers' faces as they took the lorries out onto the quayside, became quickly proficient at spotting those with a nervous cast in the eye.

No one had caught more illegals in the previous year. Not that anyone was impressed. What did it matter? The challenge was to cross the narrow stretch of water between Rostock and Gedser. Once that was conquered they were on Danish soil and few, legal or not, would in the end be repatriated.

So she did her job as best she could. And between the ferries coming and going she read and wrote the odd letter to Copenhagen.

The week before she'd turned forty, marked the occasion on her own. Three cans of beer and a letter to Vibeke, her mother, telling of a fictitious party with her fictitious new friends. And bought herself a pocket radio.

Now, seated alone in the little cabin of the border office, rain coming down out of a flat dull sky, she listened to the eight o'clock morning news through her headphones.

'The future of the government's anti-terror package is in doubt . . .' the announcer began.

Lund's watchful eyes followed the departing ferry as it manoeuvred out of the dock and made its sluggish way out onto the water.

'. . . after the Justice Minister Frode Monberg was rushed to hospital with a heart attack. His present condition is not known. Parliament was due to debate the new anti-terror bill today. The Prime Minister, Gert Grue Eriksen, says Monberg's absence will not affect negotiations with the ruling Centre Party's coalition partners . . .'

Politicians, Lund muttered, remembering. They'd done Nanna Birk Larsen no favours. Just looked after themselves.

The suave voice of the Prime Minister filled her ears. Grue Eriksen had been close to the helm of Danish politics for so long that just the sound of him provided a picture: silver hair, beaming genial face. A man to trust. A credit to the nation.

'The anti-terror package is necessary in the present situation,' Grue Eriksen said in measured, confident tones. 'We're a nation at war with a vicious enemy so cowardly it seeks to make itself invisible. The fight against terrorism must go on, here and in Afghanistan.'

The illegals Lund had caught didn't look like terrorists to her. Just sad, impoverished foreigners who'd swallowed the lie that the West was a pleasant and generous land eager to welcome them with open arms.

Another news item.

'The suspect in the Memorial Park murder is still in custody. Little information has been released by the head of homicide, Lennart Brix, since the killing ten days ago. Sources within the Politigården suggest the man in custody, believed to be the victim's husband, will be released shortly unless the police make a breakthrough and . . .'

She snatched the headphones out of her ears. There was a truck in the queue for the next departure. That was why. No other reason.

It didn't matter that her shift had ended, or that her duty replacement was already marching towards the cab to deal with it.

Copenhagen was in the past. And so was police work. She wasn't happy about that. Or disappointed. It was how things were.

So she went to see the new man, talked about rosters and the latest bulletins from control. What the new anti-terror laws might mean for them. More paperwork probably, little else.

Then went back to the office to check out after a ten-hour shift, wondering whether she'd manage to sleep much when finally she got back to her little bungalow on the edge of this dreary little town.

There was a black Ford by the door. A parking badge in the front window that looked familiar: the Politigården. A man about her age stood by the door. Taller than Jan Meyer, more wiry. But with the same kind of clothes: black leather jacket and jeans. Same worn, pale face, short cropped hair and a couple of days of stubble.

Jan Meyer had pop eyes and big ears. This one had neither. He was handsome in an understated, almost apologetic way. Thoughtful behind the professional, distanced mask the job made him wear.

A cop through and through, she thought. He might as well have been wearing a badge on his chest.

'Hello?' he said in a bright, almost childlike voice as he followed her into the office.

Lund turned off her walkie-talkie, put it in the drawer. Got a cup of coffee.

He was in the door.

'Sarah Lund?'

The coffee tasted stewed as usual.

'Ulrik Strange. I've been calling you lots of times. Left messages. I guess you never got them.'

She took off her cap, let down her long dark hair. He didn't take his eyes off her. Lund wondered if she was being admired. That hadn't happened much in Gedser.

'There's coffee in the flask if you're feeling brave,' she said and filled out the night log: two lines, nothing to report.

'I'm Vicepolitikommissær . . .'

Details, Lund thought. They always mattered.

'You mean Vicekriminalkommissær?'

He laughed. Looked friendly when he did that.

'No. Things have changed in two years. Lots of reforms. Can't smoke in the building any more. We've got new titles. They dropped the word "kriminal". I guess it was thought to be a bit . . .'

He scratched his short hair.

'Judgemental.'

Cup of coffee in hand, he toasted her. Lund checked the entry in the log and closed the book.

'There's a case we'd like to discuss with you.'

She walked out to the clothes racks. Strange followed.

'A woman was murdered ten days ago. In very strange circum-stances.'

Lund got her plain jacket, blue jumper and jeans.

'I'll wait till you've changed.'

'Keep talking.' She squeezed behind the lockers and climbed out of the cold, wet uniform.

'You probably read about it. Mindelunden. A woman murdered in the memorial park. We'd like you to go over the case records to see if we missed something.'

'We?' Lund asked from behind the lockers.

'Brix asked for it. We need a new angle. He thinks you can give us one.'

Lund sat on her chair and tugged on her long leather boots.

'I can stay till midday,' Strange offered. 'Brief you here if you like.'

'I'm a border guard. I don't work murder cases.'

'We're pretty sure we've got our man. The victim's husband is in custody. We can't keep him for more than another day or so, not without charging him. You'll be paid for your time. It's fine with the people here.'

She got up, didn't look at him.

'Tell him I'm not interested.'

He was in the door, didn't budge.

'Why not?'

Lund stared at his chest until he moved then walked past and grabbed her jacket.

'Brix told me you'd say no. He said I should stress how important this was. That we need your help . . .'

'Well.' Lund turned to look at him. 'Now you've done it, haven't you?'

Strange clutched his coffee mug, lost for something to say.

'Make sure you close the door when you leave,' she added then walked out to her car.

When the call came Thomas Buch was alone in his MP's office in the Folketinget, bouncing a rubber ball off the wall. A habit he'd had since he was a kid. It annoyed people and so did he.

Some thought Buch an interloper, someone who'd only got into the Danish Parliament on the back of a better man lost to the nation. Buch was thirty-eight, had been a successful chief executive of a farming corporation in his native Jutland, outside Aarhus. Content with the countryside, running a company his family had built over the years until it employed more than four hundred people.

Then came the second Iraq War. Jeppe, his elder brother, the bright one in the family, slim, handsome, articulate, the media star who would soon enter politics, decided to rejoin the army.

Jeppe cast a long shadow. It seemed to loom ever larger after he was murdered by insurgents who attacked his unit as it delivered medical aid to a hospital on the outskirts of Baghdad.

For reasons Thomas Buch still didn't quite understand he agreed to fight the seat his brother had been promised in Parliament, exchanging the complexities of the Common Agricultural Policy for the intricate, prolix detail of Danish parliamentary law. Which was not so different, he discovered, as he gently prospered in the middle ranks of Centre Party MPs, tolerated mostly, suspected in some quarters, always thought of, he felt, as 'Jeppe's fat little brother'.

He missed his wife Marie who stayed at home in Jutland with their two children, hating the cynical, urban atmosphere of the city. But duty was duty, and the family company remained in good professional hands.

The idea of advancement within the rungs of government hadn't occurred to him. Overweight, with a gentle walrus face and wispy ginger beard, he was never a figure the media warmed to. Buch half hoped that once his present term had expired he could slink back to the quiet fields of home and become anonymous once more. In the meantime he would deal with what legislation came his way, the needs of constituents, the daily round of parliamentary duties.

And bounce the rubber ball against the office wall, always trying to judge the way it would respond to each careful change of angle. Watching that little object react to the tests he gave it helped him think somehow, and the call he'd had gave him plenty to consider. It was a summons, to an execution or an elevation.

A tie and a jacket were called for. So he bounced the ball one last time, judged precisely the way it would return from the wall, placed it in his pocket, dragged off his sweatshirt, and retrieved the best clothes he had from the little wardrobe by the window.

There was egg yolk on the tie. The one clean white shirt too. Buch scrubbed them but the yellow stain was persistent. So he found a black polo neck instead then walked out into the cold November day, crossed the cobbled space that separated the Folketinget from the Christiansborg Palace and walked up the long red staircase to the office of Gert Grue Eriksen, Prime Minister of Denmark.

The bungalow was bitterly cold however high she turned up the puny heating. Lund knew she wouldn't sleep. So she fried some bacon, burnt some toast, checked the train times.

Bus to Nykøbing Falster, then train. Two and a half hours. Regular departures.

Since the Birk Larsen case she'd scarcely been home at all. The city didn't frighten her. It was the memories. The guilt. In Gedser her life was bounded by the grey sea of the Baltic, the boring routine of work at the port, her lonely hours in the bare little cottage, watching the TV, messing round on the Web, reading, sleeping.

The city was different. Her life was no longer her own, became driven by exterior events beyond her control, full of dark streets she longed to walk down.

It was the place, not her.

You brought Meyer to that building late at night. You forced Bengt Rosling out of your life. Chased away Mark, his father too. Took all those wrong turnings trying to work out who killed Nanna Birk Larsen.

She hadn't heard that voice in a while.

Mark's photo was pinned to the fridge. She hadn't seen him in five months. He'd be even taller.

There was a sweatshirt she'd bought from Netto for his birthday. A cheap gift on her pathetic salary.

She ought to see her mother sometime. For reasons Lund didn't understand the war between them, once so heated and constant, had abated since the Politigården fired her. Perhaps Vibeke had found a strand of sympathy, of pity even, that her daughter had never noticed before. Or they were both just getting older, and lacked the energy to maintain the perennial bickering that had divided them for as long as Lund could remember.

A look at the calendar. Three clear days off work. Nothing to fill the time.

Lund picked up her laptop, looked at the news sites. Read what they had to say about the murder in Mindelunden. It wasn't a lot. Lennart Brix seemed better at gagging the media now than he was two years before, when half the politicians in the Copenhagen Rådhus were trying to avoid the fallout from the Birk Larsen case.

Brix.

He wasn't a bad man. Just an ambitious one. He hadn't fired her straight out. He'd offered a way to stay inside the police, if only she'd been willing to swallow her pride, say lies were truth, bury things that deserved to be left out in the harsh, unforgiving light of day.

She wasn't going to do this for Brix. Certainly not for his charming messenger boy, Ulrik Strange. For Mark maybe. Even for her mother.

But if she was going to do this, she'd do it for herself. Because she wanted to.

A reminder was blinking on the phone. The message: Mark's birthday was today.

'Shit,' she said, racing for the cheap sweatshirt, realizing the only wrapping paper in the house had reindeer on it.

While she bundled paper and tape round the gift she called home. Vibeke was out. Usually was for some reason these days.

'Hi, Mum,' Lund said. 'I'm coming back for Mark's birthday like I promised. Just till tomorrow. One day. See you soon.'

Then she got a battered shoulder bag, stuffed in the first clothes that came to hand and headed for the bus.

This was once the King's office, or so the secretary who welcomed him said. Palatial chairs and a large desk, signature Danish lamps. There was a view out to the riding ground where a solitary coach with two of the Queen's horses trudged round and round in the mud. The state of Denmark was mostly run from the buildings on the tiny island of Slotsholmen, once a fortress that was Copenhagen in its entirety. The Christiansborg Palace, the Folketinget, the offices of the various ministries . . . all these were crammed into a series of loosely linked buildings that sat upon the remains of the castle of the warrior-bishop Absalon, the roads and lanes that joined them open to the public, a reminder of the liberal nature of the modern state.

Buch liked it here mostly, though he wished Marie and the girls would visit more often.

He had his rubber ball in his pocket and briefly wondered what it would be like to bounce it off the panelled walls of the office built for the King of Denmark. But then Gert Grue Eriksen walked in and something on his face said this was not the moment. A government minister was gravely ill in hospital. The anti-terror bill stood beached in the Folketinget, caught up in the labyrinthine complexities of coalition politics. Grue Eriksen was the captain of the ship of state, charged with navigating a vessel that had many hands on the wheel. A short, energetic man of fifty-eight, silver-haired with a dignified, amicable face. He had been at the highest level of Danish politics for as long as Buch could remember, so much so that the man from Jutland remained a little in awe of him, like a child in front of the headmaster.

Nor was he one for small talk.

Brief greetings, the usual question about family, a shake of the hand.

'You heard about Monberg?' Grue Eriksen asked.

'Any news?'

'He'll live they say.'

The Prime Minister waved Buch to the chair in front of his desk then took the grand winged leather seat opposite.

'He won't be coming back to office. Not now. Not later.'

'I'm sorry,' Buch said with some genuine sympathy.

Grue Eriksen sighed.

'This is bad timing. We need this anti-terror package. And now we're trapped between right and left. Krabbe's so-called patriots in the People's Party. Birgitte Agger's bleeding hearts among the Progressives. Without some leeway from both the bill will fall. Monberg was supposed to deal with this.'

Grue Eriksen gazed at him expectantly.

'So, Thomas. What should we do?'

Buch laughed.

'I'm flattered you should ask me. But . . .'

He was not a slow man. Thomas Buch's mind had been turning all the way up the long staircase to Grue Eriksen's office.

'But why?' he asked.

'Because when you leave this room you will go to see the Queen. She must meet her new Minister of Justice.' Grue Eriksen smiled again. 'We'll find you a shirt and tie. And don't play with that bloody ball in her presence. Then you'll find some way to get our anti-terror package passed. We need a vote next week and right now this place is like a zoo. Krabbe keeps demanding more concessions. The Progressives will use any excuse . . .'

'I'm sorry,' Buch interrupted. 'But there's something I must say.'

Grue Eriksen went quiet.

'I'm honoured to be asked. Truly. But I'm a businessman, a farmer. I came here . . .'

He looked out of the window, back towards the Parliament building.

'I came here for the wrong reasons. It was Jeppe you wanted. Not me.'

'True,' Grue Eriksen agreed.

'I can't possibly . . .'

'You're the one we got. Not Jeppe. I've watched you over the years. Noted your quiet honesty. Your dedication. Your occasional . . .' He pointed at the black polo neck. '. . . difficulty with protocol.'

'I'm not a lawyer.'

15

'I'm not a Prime Minister. It's a job life gave me and I try to do it as best I can. You'll have the most skilled civil servants in the country. And my full support. If there's . . .'

'I have to decline,' Buch insisted.

'Why?'

'Because I'm not ready. I don't know enough. Perhaps in a few years, when I've been here longer. I'm not my brother.'

'No. You're not. Which is why I'm making this offer. Jeppe was a bright star. Too much so. He was rash and impetuous. I'd never have offered him this opportunity.'

Buch took a deep breath and looked out of the window at the two horses going round and round on the muddy riding ground, the coach behind them, the man with the whip in his hand. Held gently. Unused. But a whip all the same.

'I've staked my reputation, my premiership on this anti-terror package,' Grue Eriksen continued. 'You more than anyone know why it's needed. Knock heads together in those corridors across the square. Make them see sense.'

'I . . .'

'This is war, Thomas! We don't have time for faint hearts and modesty. They'll listen to you, in a way they never listened to Monberg. He was a journeyman political hack. He carried no moral weight.'

Grue Eriksen nodded at him.

'You do. I can think of no one better.'

'Sir . . .'

'You have the ability. I don't doubt that. Do you really lack the will? The sense of duty?'

Duty.

It was a hard word to sidestep.

The Prime Minister got up and stood by the long window. Buch joined him. The two stared out at the rainy day, the horses and the trap ploughing through the mud in the square beyond.

'I could appoint someone else from within the group,' Grue Eriksen said. 'But then the whole bill might be in jeopardy. Do you think that would be in Denmark's interest?'

'No,' Buch said. 'Of course not. The package we have is justified and necessary . . .'

16

'Then see it through for me. I will ask one more time only. Will you be our new Minister of Justice?'

Buch didn't answer.

'White shirt, conservative tie,' Grue Eriksen declared, calling for his secretary. 'We'll find you something for now. Best send out for more, Minister Buch. The days of polo shirts are over.'

Half jail, half psychiatric institution, Herstedvester lay twenty kilometres west of Copenhagen, a long boring journey, one Louise Raben had come to loathe.

She knew the routine. Bag through scanner. Body check. Permission slips.

Then she was through security, walking into the visiting quarters, wondering where he was, what he'd been doing.

Two years inside, every request for parole turned down. Jens Peter Raben was a soldier, a father, a husband. A man who'd served the Danish state for almost half of his thirty-seven years.

Now he'd become nothing more than a prisoner in a penal psychiatric institution, locked up as a danger to himself and the society he once thought he served.

Two years. No sign of the agony ending. If he'd been convicted of a simple crime – a robbery, a mugging – he'd be home now. Back in the army perhaps – and this was her secret wish, not that she'd voiced it to her father – finding a job in the civilian world. But Raben's mental state after he was invalided back from Afghanistan precluded the promise of freedom allowed to ordinary criminals. The idea of redemption was denied those deemed unsound of mind.

A terrible thought lurked at the back of her head more and more. What if they never let him out? What if her husband, Jonas's father, stayed in Herstedvester for ever?

Their son had just turned four. He needed a man around. They both did. She was young. She missed his friendship, his physical presence too, the warmth, the intimacy between them. The idea he might never return sparked thoughts in her head she'd never wanted to countenance.

If he didn't come back what price loyalty? Fidelity?

Louise Raben came from an army family, had grown up in barracks houses as her father worked his way up through the officer ranks. There were women who waited, and women who seized the opportunity to control their own lives. She didn't want to make that choice.

The guard walked her into the visitors' block. Outside she could see the prison wing and the hospital, a separate building, beyond it. High walls everywhere. Barbed wire. Men with walkie-talkies and guns. Then they let her into the private room, the one reserved for marital visits. Cheap wallpaper, a plain table, a sofa bed by the wall. And a man who was beginning to seem distant, however hard she tried.

'Jonas?' he asked.

She walked to him, hugged him. He kept wearing the same fusty clothes, a black sweater, threadbare cotton trousers. His beard was starting to go grey, his face was thinner. There was a strength to him that always surprised her. He didn't seem a muscular man. But it was there, inside him, visible in the blue-grey eyes that never seemed to rest.

Jens Peter Raben was a sergeant in her father's battalion. Someone his men trusted and on occasion feared. There was a fierceness and an anger to him that never waned, not that she felt it, ever.

'They had a party in day care,' she said, putting a hand to his cheek, feeling the bristles there. 'The other kids pestered him . . .'

'It's OK. I understand.'

'Have you heard from Myg?'

Raben shook his head. Looked a little worried at the mention of the name. Allan Myg Poulsen was one of his team from Afghanistan. Active in the veterans' club looking after ex-soldiers. That morning she'd called Poulsen, asked him to find a job for her husband.

'Myg says he could get you some work. Building. Carpentry. Find us a home somewhere.'

He smiled then.

'Maybe if you've got the offer of a job . . .'

'Maybe.'

He always seemed so peaceful when she saw him. It was hard to understand why every application he made for parole got turned down on the grounds he was too dangerous for release.

She'd brought some of Jonas's drawings, spread them out on the table. Fairy tales and dragons. Castles in the sky.

'Dad bought him a shield and a sword. He asked for them.'

Raben nodded, said nothing. Just looked at her with his lost eyes.

She couldn't return whatever it was he wanted at that moment. So Louise stared at the wall beyond the window and said, 'There's not much going on really. If it wasn't for day care. Living in barracks. It's not right . . .'

It was always her job to ask. She got up, pointed at the sofa bed.

'Shall we . . . ?'

'Let's wait for a while.'

He always said that of late.

Louise stayed on her feet, was determined not to cry.

'When do you hear about parole?'

'Very soon. The lawyer thinks my chances are good. The clinical director says I've made good progress.'

She looked at the wall again.

'This time they can't turn me down. They won't.'

The rain had started again. Other prisoners jogged past, hooded heads down, faces in the chill wind, bored, like him. Trying to fill the day.

'They won't, Louise. What's wrong?'

She sat down, took his hand, tried to see into his eyes. There was always something there she could never quite reach.

'Jonas isn't so keen to come here any more.'

The expression in his face hardened.

'I know you love to see him. I tried. He's four years old. You were abroad when he was born. You've been here half his life. He knows you're his father. But . . .'

These thoughts kept haunting her and they were so very precise.

'It's just a word. Not a feeling. Not . . .' She reached out and touched his heart. 'Not here. Not yet. I need you home. We both do.'

The sudden anger was gone, and in its place, she thought, came a little shame.

'Don't pressure him,' he said.

'I don't.' The tears were starting. She was an army wife, not that she'd ever wanted to be. This was wrong. 'I don't, Jens! But he's not a baby any more. He won't even talk about you. Some of the kids at day care have been teasing him. They heard something.'

The look on his face, torn between grief and an impotent fury, only made her want to weep more.

'I'm sorry.' She reached out and briefly touched his stubbled cheeks. 'I'll make it work. Don't you worry.'

'*We'll* make it work.'

She couldn't look him easily in the eye just then. He knew this so he took her hands, waited till she'd face him.

'I'll get out of this place, Louise. They've no reason to keep me any more. I'll get out and we'll be a family. I'll find a job. We'll get a house. It'll be fine. That's a promise.'

She tried to smile.

'I keep my promises,' he added. 'We'll be together so much you and Jonas will be sick of me before long. You'll miss the time you had together.'

Her eyes were closed. The tears wouldn't stop.

'You'll hate the way I snore,' he said, smiling, insistent. 'The way I smack my lips and get toothpaste all over the place.'

She laughed and didn't know if she meant it or not.

'I'm coming home,' he said, and she couldn't think of anything else to do except still his words and promises with a sudden kiss, hand to his head, a glance at the makeshift bed they put there for these visits.

'Please, Jens. I need . . .'

'Not here. Not this damned place.'

He held her hands. The same man she'd met all those years before when she was an officer's daughter, desperate to escape the tight, close circle of army life, certain she'd never fall for a soldier.

'When we're free I will . . .'

Jens Peter Raben clutched her to him, whispered private promises into her ear, made her laugh again.

Then, so soon, a knock on the door. Time had run out on them again.

Before she knew it Louise Raben stood outside Herstedvester in the rain, looking at the high walls and the barbed wire, wondering what a promise from jail was worth.

Brix was mulling over the latest interviews with Stig Dragsholm, the dead woman's husband, when Strange got back from Gedser. He looked up from the files.

'Sorry,' Strange said. 'Lund said no. She seems pretty settled down there.'

'Settled?' Brix asked, amazed. 'Lund?'

'You know her. I don't. She looked fine to me. How's it going?'

Brix scowled. Strange's phone rang.

'No,' he said. 'The chief's busy. Can I help?' An easy, confident smile. 'Lund? You changed your mind. I'm psychic. See.'

Brix snapped his fingers. Took the phone.

'If you still think I can help,' Lund said. 'I'm back today for my son's birthday. That's the only reason. I can go over some papers if you really want.'

'I wouldn't be asking if I didn't need you.'

A long pause.

'Why's that?' she asked.

She sounded the same as ever. Steady, monotone voice full of awkward questions.

'Get in here and let's talk.'

He heard the sound of a car horn down the line. Then, 'I've got to go.'

And the call went dead.

Strange looked at him.

'Is she coming or not?'

'In her own time. There never was any other. We're getting nowhere with the husband. I don't know if we're even close . . .'

He stopped. Looked down the long corridor, with its black marble walls and bronze lamps shaped like old-fashioned flaming torches.

Lund was walking towards them. Same steady stride, like a man, one with a purpose.

Two years. The office was changed completely. Gone was the little bunker where she'd huddled together with Meyer. The place was open-plan now. Lots of people. And the ones who'd remained probably didn't feel too warmly towards her judging by the glances she got as she walked through homicide.

The woman he'd exiled to Gedser came up and stood in front of him. Strange might as well not have been there.

'I'm not sure this is a good idea,' she said.

'Just read the files, will you? What harm can that do? I'll pay you. Every hour you're here. We'll need . . .'

She was doing what she always did. Looking round. Noting everything. Checking the changes.

'This place was better the way it was before.'

'I didn't ask for advice on interior decoration.'

Brix pointed Strange towards some desks.

'Show her around. Find her the papers.' He looked at Lund. 'Read every last one.'

She seemed content with that.

'After that,' he said, 'there's something I want you to see.'

'I said I'd read the papers. That's all.'

'I need . . .'

'One day. I go back to Gedser tomorrow.'

'A woman was killed, Lund. Brutally. There's something strange about it. Something I don't begin to understand.'

Her large bright eyes widened with outrage.

'Don't you have enough people here? What's so special about me you send your messenger boy all the way to Gedser?'

Strange had his hand over his mouth, stifling a laugh.

'You're here to see your family, aren't you?' Brix said with a faint, ironic smile.

Lund struggled for an answer.

'No matter,' Brix said. 'Just look at the files. And then Strange will take you for a ride.'

The Justice Ministry occupied a block on the north-eastern side of Slotsholmen, close to the Knippelsbro bridge. Buch returned there after the formal reception with the Queen in the Amalienborg Palace, and was not in the least surprised that the first call on his mobile was from his wife.

'Yes, yes, I shook her hand. I'm in the Ministry now. It's um . . . a . . .'

An office, he thought, much like any other.

'Whose Ministry?' Marie asked.

'Mine, I suppose. I've got to go.'

Then, still in the shirt and tie the Prime Minister had provided, he was guided round the department, introduced to staff high and low, and finally taken to a reception room where champagne was being served with canapés.

A dream, he thought. And soon, thank God, I'll wake up.

A young blonde woman by the name of Karina Jørgensen had guided him round the building.

Glass in hand, introductions seemingly ended, she led him into a small office with a desk and a computer. Buch sat happily in the chair, beamed at her and the few civil servants smiling indulgently around him.

The radio said his appointment had been 'unexpected'. Clearly these people felt the same.

'This suits me well,' Buch announced with a smile then picked up a pen on the desk, ready to wield it.

'That's my chair, Minister,' the blonde woman said. She wrinkled her pale face in puzzlement as she leaned over him to play with the mouse.

'What's this?'

There was a strange email on the screen. No subject. Just a link to a web page. And the message: *Keep trying.*

She clicked the link.

'Some idiot keeps sending us a stupid message. I don't know how it gets through. It doesn't go anywhere. Sorry . . .'

The blonde woman walked over and opened a pair of double doors that led into what looked like a gentleman's study from a country mansion of the kind to which Thomas Buch would rarely be invited.

Portraits on the wall of ministers who'd preceded him, all the way back to the nineteenth century. A table for meetings. A shining mahogany desk.

The place smelled fresh and new as if the cleaners had come in and removed every last trace of the unfortunate Frode Monberg.

Buch walked to the window. There he could see the traffic racing across the Inner Harbour, hear the horns of the boats, feel the city's pulse beating. Directly opposite stood the Børsen, the old stock exchange, with its curious spire of four dragons, tails entwined, fierce mouths agape.

'We've a few things left to change,' Karina said. Then, more tentatively, 'It's your choice to bring in your own assistant. Don't worry about me. The secretariat can reassign . . .'

'You know your way around this place?' Buch asked, still captured by the portraits on the wall, the fighting dragons, the smell of this new place.

'I've been here three years.'

'Then my first decision in office will be that you stay. If that's all right with you . . .'

She had a round, fetching face, very pretty, especially when she smiled.

'These things . . .' Buch slapped the pile of documents on the desk. 'I assume are Monberg's.'

'No.' A tall man of around fifty, with short salt-and-pepper hair and serious, dark-rimmed glasses, walked in. 'It's the negotiation process for the anti-terror package. Carsten Plough, Permanent Secretary.'

A firm shake of hands. Plough, Buch thought, was the epitome of every civil servant he'd ever met. Grey to the point of invisibility, polite, quick to smile, even quicker to look businesslike.

'Where are we with that?' Buch asked.

'Facing a deal with Krabbe and the People's Party. The Opposition won't play. But you can read all about that. It's in the papers.'

'I will,' Buch told him. 'But first you must know my opinion. We're at war. Whether we like it or not we have to find unity. Krabbe *and* the Progressives. I want to work towards a broad, inclusive agreement. War's not a time for party politics.'

Plough sighed.

'That's a fine sentiment. One Monberg shared. Unfortunately . . .'

'I'm not Monberg.'

Buch had stopped flicking through the papers on his desk. There was a set of photographs there in a folder. So bloody and brutal he thought this day had turned from dream to nightmare.

A woman in a blue dressing gown tied to a post, covered in blood, livid wounds on her neck, her torso. Close-ups of a pale face, dead but still full of shock and fear.

Plough stepped forward, hand to mouth, suddenly apologetic.

'I'm sorry. I passed on Monberg's files without checking.'

'The woman at Mindelunden,' Buch said, recalling the stories in the papers. 'Is this her?'

'Monberg took a personal interest. He asked to be kept up to date.'

'I didn't know that,' Karina said. 'He didn't tell . . .'

'He asked to be kept up to date,' Plough repeated, a little cross. 'I'm sorry. I can brief you later . . .'

'If Monberg needed to know, then so do I,' Buch told him.

He wasn't shocked by the sight of blood. Buch was a farmer at heart, a practical man, one who didn't shy away from harsh realities.

'Later,' Plough promised, then walked forward and shuffled the photos back into the folder.

Raben spent the day in the prison workshop, making bird tables for garden centres. Same design. Over and over again. He was getting good at it. Maybe good enough to get work as a carpenter somewhere.

At some point in the afternoon he was supposed to hear about the latest parole request. He waited till four then, bored, getting tetchy, he slid out of the side door, walked over to the wire fence that separated prison from hospital.

Director Toft, a pale, blonde woman, icily beautiful and aware of it, was walking along the path on the other side, headed towards the car park.

Raben went to the fence, put his fingers through the wire, waited for her to stop.

One of the guards had seen him, started yelling. Toft smiled, told the man it was OK.

Raben's heart sank. Kindness was usually reserved for bad news.

'How do you think it went?' he asked when the guard retreated.

'I can't tell you that. You should talk to your lawyer.'

'He won't be back till next week.'

She shrugged.

'Then you'll have to wait.'

Toft started for the cars again.

'This isn't for me!' he cried, following her on the other side of the fence. 'My wife's worried. I've got to call her. I don't know what to say.'

'Tell her the truth. You haven't heard.'

'I can get a job through the veterans' club. Somewhere to live.'

'I wish you'd said that before.'

'If it's bad, for God's sake tell me now.'

Toft stopped. Raben fought to keep his temper. This woman enjoyed the power she had over inmates. Liked to let them know that.

'You're approved as far as the medical staff are concerned. But that's not the end of it. The final decision rests with the Probation Service. The prison authorities. So nothing's definite.'

'And if they say no?'

'Then you wait six months and try again . . .'

Raben tried to see into her cold blue eyes, to make some kind of human contact through the wire fence.

'In six months I won't have a wife. Or a son. She'll give up on me.'

'You have to be patient, Raben.'

'I've been here two years. I'm fine. You said so yourself.'

Toft smiled, turned and walked away.

The guard started yelling again, ordering him back into the workshop.

'I'm fine!' Raben barked at her as she strode off to the psychiatric block car park.

'Raben!' The guard didn't sound too mad. 'A visitor wants to see you. Get in here.'

He stuck his hands in his pockets, went back to the door.

'My wife?'

'He says he's an army buddy. Myg Poulsen. Do you want to see him or not?'

Raben watched Director Toft climb into her flashy little sports car, drive out of the gates.

Allan Myg Poulsen. A skinny, brave little man. Raben couldn't remember what happened in that dusty, cold house in Helmand. Just the sound of weapons, of screams, the shrieks of the dying, the smell of blood.

But Myg was there. He was one of the damaged survivors too.

'I'll see him,' Raben said.

Lund read the files in the Politigården then, as the light was dying, Strange drove her to the dead woman's house. Anne Dragsholm lived in a detached villa in a dead-end street ten minutes from Mindelunden by car.

She walked round, documents in hand, talking mostly to herself.

'So the husband says he came home, found the place covered in blood. Got spooked and drove off?'

The house was cold, blocked from the outside world with Don't Cross tape, covered inside with all the familiar stigmata a forensic team left behind. It had been two years since Lund last saw a murder scene. Might have been yesterday.

'I'm glad you changed your mind,' Strange said. 'Really I am.

You're a bit of a . . .' He hunted for the right word. 'A kind of legend really.'

He was diffident, almost childlike in manner. Nothing like Jan Meyer.

'That's what they're calling it now?' she asked, trying to work him out.

'I was trying to be polite.'

'Don't bother. I didn't change my mind. I was coming anyway. Shouldn't we wait for Brix?'

'He's been delayed. He wanted me to show you around.'

He put on a pair of latex forensic gloves then handed a pair to her. It was like pulling on an old uniform.

'They were getting divorced,' Strange said. 'He'd had an affair with his secretary. The wife threw him out a month ago. She wouldn't talk to him. Hung up if he called.'

She followed him down the hall. There was a photograph on the wall. A wedding portrait. A pretty woman with long fair hair. She held the arm of a beaming man in a smart suit. They had lawyers' smiles, all well aimed at the camera. Then a later shot, with a young child.

'Where was the kid?'

'Daughter. At her grandparents'.'

Into the narrow kitchen. The walls by the room were covered with childish paintings. A dirty frying pan on the cooker. A dirty plate, a pen circle round it.

'At 7.41 p.m. she used her laptop to go on the Internet in here,' Strange went on. 'Opened a bottle of wine, looked at some estate agency sites, and took a bath.'

Lund kept following the details through the autopsy report.

'Was that her usual routine? Coming home late, taking a bath? Eating alone?'

'How would we know?'

'You'd ask the husband.'

'The husband isn't saying much. She was attacked before she got round to eating. In here. Then he took her into the dining room.'

They went through. Floor-length windows gave onto low trees just visible from some far-off street lights. A leather office chair was tipped on its side on the bloody carpet. A matching footstool close to it, a tall studio lamp by its side.

'She was stabbed twenty-one times,' he said, tapping the report. 'Once in the heart, which was fatal. We don't know what the weapon was.'

'A knife?' Lund asked.

She wasn't sure he appreciated that.

'More like some kind of sharp tool.'

He walked to a standard lamp near the window, kicked the on switch at the base. The detail came to life. A painting on the wall was crooked. Glass from some broken ornaments lay strewn across the timber floor.

Strange walked round the furniture to stand by the window.

'She was forced into the chair. The amount of blood indicates that.'

Lund was looking at the photos. There was a small cellophane wrapper near the body.

'Did he smoke? Did you find ash?'

'It's the wrong size for cigarettes. We don't know what it is.'

'Chewing gum?'

'We don't know what it is,' he repeated. 'The husband says he called round after midnight. He wanted to talk about selling the house. He told us he'd had a few drinks. More than a few from the blood test.'

'He was drunk?'

'Stinking.'

'Where was he beforehand?'

'With his girlfriend. He still had time.'

'What does he say happened?'

'She didn't answer the door. He saw the basement window was open. Got worried. Climbed in that way.'

'Didn't he have a key?'

'She'd changed the locks a few weeks before. And put in a new alarm.'

Lund went to the window, turned on the outside light. The garden led down to scrubby woodland. There was the sound of a train. One of the lines running out through Østerbro. Maybe the same one by Mindelunden where she was found.

A rap on the door behind them. Brix was there.

'Dragsholm must have been really scared of him,' he said. 'She'd fired her old security company, hired a very expensive one in its place. They'd ordered new sensors for the garden.'

Lund nodded.

'She was scared of something.'

'It's good to see you,' Brix added. 'I'm sorry. There was never time in the Politigården to say that.'

He took a deep breath, like a man facing a difficult decision.

'If there's nothing more here shall we look at the place we found her?'

They had no idea how the killer had brought Anne Dragsholm to Mindelunden. The place was locked up at night, but scarcely secure. Open ground close to the centre of the city. Anyone could get in, from any number of directions, if they tried.

Strange turned on his heavy police torch and they walked across the spongy long grass of the old firing range towards the three bronzed stumps rising from the soil against the ramp behind.

Brix seemed oddly silent.

'Anne Dragsholm was entitled to half her husband's money and half the firm they owned,' Strange said.

'What's her connection to this place?' Lund asked.

Brix broke his silence.

'We can't see one. It's pretty clear he broke open a wooden door on the gardeners' entrance and dragged her through there. Why . . .'

Lund opened the forensic file again, got Strange to shine his beam on it.

A woman of forty or so, in a bloody blue dressing gown, slumped dead on the ground, strapped to the centre stake. In a sacred place like this it was a kind of blasphemy.

'The husband's no idiot,' Strange said, pointing at the body in the photos. 'We think this is a diversion. He's making it look like the work of a lunatic. What else . . . ?'

Lund walked off, not listening, threaded her way through the stakes, backwards and forwards. Brix followed, gloved finger to his cheek.

'What are you thinking?' Brix asked.

She peered at him, wondered at the odd look in his eye.

'I think this is a mistake. I'm wasting your time. You know what you're doing. Why ask me?'

'Because I thought you might have an opinion.'

'No,' she said, handing him the file. 'I don't.'

'Sleep on it. Let's talk tomorrow.'

'I don't have any ideas.'

'Maybe they'll come.'

'They won't.'

'Call me if they do. If not, that's fine too. As things stand I've got to release the husband tomorrow. We don't have enough to charge him.'

'Right.'

Lund checked her watch.

'I need to see my mother,' she said. 'Can one of you drop me in Østerbro? It's not far.'

Brix nodded.

'All right. But I want you to meet someone first.'

From the moment he saw Erling Krabbe and Birgitte Agger sit down around the conference table, Thomas Buch knew his first meeting as Minister of Justice would not be easy.

The dragons across the street, on the spire of the Børsen, were like this. Entwined with one another, yet in constant conflict, teeth bared.

Krabbe was a tall, skinny ascetic man who looked as if he spent too much time in the gym. His grandfather had been a famous partisan during the Second World War and was lucky to survive, not make his mark on the wall at Mindelunden. Krabbe now headed the nationalists of the People's Party, compared on occasion by the left to the Nazis themselves. Unfairly, Buch felt. They were against immigration, suspicious of foreign culture. Inflexible, often caustic in their language. But because of this they never prospered greatly. What little power they possessed came from the necessities of coalition politics. Government in the Folketinget was never entirely in the hands of one party. Concessions were needed for any difficult legislation.

Birgitte Agger was no minority party leader seeking crumbs from the table. Fifty-two years old, a career politician who'd clawed her way to the leadership of the Progressives, she was the soft left's principal hope, an elegant, carefully manicured chameleon who could flick from policy to policy in tune with the popular sentiment. The polls had her neck and neck with Grue Eriksen. She saw herself as Prime Minister in waiting. Any negotiations over the anti-terror bill were, Buch knew full well, only to be carried out in the context of her greater ambitions.

He thought again of the writhing dragons beyond the window.

The government was trapped between Krabbe and Agger that moment, one accusing Grue Eriksen of weakness, the other of an attack on long-established civil rights. The details of the bill – tighter border controls, more money for the security services, longer detention without charge for terrorist suspects – were the battleground for these two, each seeking victory through a surrender on the part of others.

'Scarcely a minute goes by without another Islamist extremist group making its presence known . . .'

Krabbe was midway through a rant against what he saw as the infiltration of Danish society by foreign influences. 'They want to overthrow our democracy and replace it with the brutality of the sharia . . .'

'We already have laws to deal with anyone who incites violence,' Buch noted patiently.

'They're not enough.' Krabbe was immaculate in blue shirt and blue tie, short hair neatly trimmed. He looked like a grown-up Boy Scout seeking the next challenge. 'These people want to take us back to the Middle Ages.'

'This is ridiculous.' Agger got her case, ready to go. 'If the People's Party wants to start locking up people for their thoughts that's their problem. We all know why we're here. It's the stupid war. If it weren't for that . . .'

'It is a stupid war,' Buch told her. 'I agree. I've good reason to.'

The two of them went quiet. *Jeppe*, Buch thought, and reminded himself this was not a trick to try too often.

'But it's the war we have. The place we start from, like it or not. We all know we need tighter border security. More resources for the police and the intelligence services.'

'A ban on these damned Islamists,' Krabbe broke in.

'See?' She got up, patted Buch on the back. 'Good luck. The old man didn't do you any favours, did he? Monberg looked ready to crack the last time I saw him. You're being asked to square a circle here and it can't be done. Tell Grue Eriksen to go back to NATO and tell them to get the hell out of there.'

'When we can,' Buch answered, 'we will. But not now. If you were sitting in his office, you'd be making the same decisions.'

She laughed.

'We'll see. Goodbye, Krabbe. Back to your fantasies of a little Denmark that never existed.'

Then Agger was gone.

Erling Krabbe poured himself some more coffee.

'I'm sorry if I was too frank for you. But it had to be said. We've got to protect ourselves. Think of New York. Think of London and Madrid.'

'Think of Oslo and Utøya,' Buch replied. 'Everyone was rushing to blame the Muslims then, weren't they? Instead it turned out to be a lunatic called Anders Behring Breivik. Norwegian born and bred. One of . . .'

He stopped himself. *One of yours.* Which was deeply unfair. Krabbe had some ludicrous ideas and a few deep-rooted prejudices. But he was a parliamentarian through and through.

'One of what?' Krabbe demanded.

'One of ours.'

Buch got up from the table, made one last effort. He'd gone through the briefings from Politiets Efterretningstjeneste, PET, the police security and intelligence service, charged with protecting domestic security.

'If PET wanted the measures you suggest they'd be asking for them. And I'd place them on the table. But they're the experts and they don't. I can ask them to tell you why if you want.'

Krabbe waved him away.

'I know why already. We're all too frightened of these people. Afraid that if we stand up to them they'll scream prejudice. My grandfather fought the Nazis for this country, risked his life . . .'

'A scare campaign doesn't do you any harm when the polls look bad either. Does it?'

Buch had to say it. Krabbe's pomposity was too much.

Krabbe got up, put on his expensive jacket, smoothed down the sleeves.

'Agger's not backing you under any circumstances. That means the only way you can get a majority is through me. Count the numbers. I have.'

'Erling . . .'

'I want an answer by seven o'clock this evening. Talk to the PM. He understands the situation.' Krabbe raised his empty cup in a toast. 'Even if you don't.'

He gazed round the office, smiled at the portraits on the wall, looked Thomas Buch up and down in a way that made him feel more than a little out of place.

'Nice coffee, Buch. Good day.'

Back in the Politigården Lund was getting the stares again. From the ones who knew her. And the ones who'd only heard. Svendsen, the surly detective she'd once threatened with a gun, marched past, folders in hand, giving her the coldest look she'd seen in months.

Lund smiled at him, nodded, said, 'Hi!'

Then Brix whisked her into an interview room. A short, elegant woman in a business jacket and skirt sat at the table, talking on the phone. About Lund's age, but with the air of management: expensive clothes, a fetching, smiling face, dark hair carefully cut into the nape of her neck. Perfectly ironed white shirt.

And perfume.

In her winter jacket, jeans and red sweater Lund felt uncomfortable.

'This is Deputy Commissioner Ruth Hedeby,' Brix said, guiding her to a chair. 'She wants to listen.'

Hedeby shook her hand.

'I've heard a lot about you.'

'I can imagine.'

'Mindelunden's a national monument. I want this cleared up. It's been ten days and we still don't have it nailed.'

'Charge the husband then.'

'We don't have enough.' Hedeby folded her arms. 'Any ideas?'

'I can't find fault with the investigation. The forensic evidence seems clear . . .'

'Yes. But what do you *think*?'

Lund glanced at Brix. He was waiting too.

'I don't think he killed her.'

Hedeby closed her eyes for a moment and sighed. Not the answer she wanted.

'I could be wrong,' Lund added. 'I doubt it.'

Hedeby toyed with her wedding ring then asked, 'Because?'

She flicked through the files on the desk.

'It says it's a crime of passion. But the body was dragged from the house, taken to Mindelunden—'

'To divert the investigation,' Hedeby said. 'To make us think it was the work of a lunatic. Forensics said his clothes were covered in her blood. How . . .'

'Let's hear what she's got to say,' Brix suggested. Hedeby glared at him. 'If you don't mind.'

Lund looked at them and wondered: who was really the boss? In terms of rank it was Hedeby. But Brix came with friends, influence. Had done from the outset of the Birk Larsen case. Still kept those links she guessed.

'Anne Dragsholm was afraid of her murderer,' Lund said. 'Had been for a while. Her husband had a motive. He was manipulative, but we've no record of violence. She never complained to us about him. I think . . .'

She paused. Hedeby's bright and hungry eyes were on her.

'I think he wanted to make a statement by placing her body where he did. On the stake in Mindelunden. It's too significant to ignore. Too . . . horrible to be an impulse, something that occurred to a man in the middle of a drunken fight.'

Ruth Hedeby folded her arms.

'He was trying to say something?'

'Exactly.'

'Then he failed, didn't he? Otherwise we wouldn't be here trying to work out what?'

'True.' Lund pushed back the file. 'Unless the real murderer's waiting for his moment.'

'Why would he do that?'

'I don't know. What did the woman do before she married?'

'Quite a bit.' Brix opened a second file. 'Anne Dragsholm was thirty-nine. College education finished in the US. Worked for charities and NGOs in Africa and Asia. Did some legal duties for Amnesty and the Danish Army. Never anywhere for long.'

'What was her role in the military?' Lund asked.

'Legal adviser. Sent to the Balkans, Iraq, Cyprus and last of all to Afghanistan.'

'Does she still have army contacts?'

Brix went through the papers.

'Doesn't look like it. She makes a monthly contribution to a veterans' club. A thousand kroner. That's generous.'

A knock on the door. Brix went to get it leaving Lund alone with Hedeby. The deputy commissioner was tapping the table with her finely manicured fingertips.

'I'm just guessing,' Lund said.

'You always were from what I hear.'

Lund didn't like that.

'If I'm right there's something you haven't found. You need to go back. To the house. To the park. To the places Dragsholm went. You need to look properly . . .'

Hedeby was staring straight at her.

'You think so?'

'I said I'm guessing.'

'And you think it would have been different if you were still here?'

'I've no idea. I came because Brix asked. I'm sorry if I've disappointed you somehow . . .'

Brix walked back in, hands in pockets.

'The husband just confessed. To murder and the disposal of the body.'

'Did he say why he took her to Mindelunden?' Lund asked.

'He confessed,' Hedeby yelled and slammed her fist on the table. 'God knows we've been trying to get that out of him for long enough.'

'Congratulations.'

Lund got her bag.

Hedeby was on her feet talking about lawyers and charges and court appearances.

'You had me worried for a moment there,' she said with a sharp glance at Lund then left the room.

Brix sat down at the table.

'Thanks for coming all this way. I'll arrange a day's payment like I said.'

'Don't bother. It was just a few hours. I did nothing. I've got to see my mother anyway. It's why I came. I'll get a taxi. Don't worry about it.'

He didn't move.

'Congratulations,' she said again.

'Svendsen got it out of him. You never liked him much.'

'He didn't listen. He didn't do what I told him. Oh, yes. He's a thug too.'

Lennart Brix got up, shook her hand, then went and opened the door.

'Thanks anyway,' he told her.

Raben met Myg Poulsen in the same visiting room. The sofa bed had changed position. Another prisoner had received a visitor. The place smelled of sweat and quick sex.

Poulsen was a little man with a miserable pinched face. Recovered from his wounds mostly though he walked with a limp. Back in army camouflage fatigues. He threw his arms round Raben, embraced him, laughed.

'I'm sorry I don't come more often.' He didn't look Raben in the eye when he said that. 'Lots of work with the veterans' club. And things . . .'

His weedy voice trailed off into silence.

'Louise said you could help me get a job.'

'I can try.' Poulsen pulled a note out of his pocket. 'I don't know if it's any help. They're looking for a carpenter. The boss was in the regiment. Maybe he'll bend the rules a little for one of his own.'

He handed over a name and a phone number.

'Retired sergeant. God, did I have to listen to some war stories to get that. There'll be some work in a couple of months.'

'Does he know where I am?'

'He knows. He's helped us before. Get Louise to call and he'll send the paperwork.' A pause, as if he was scared to say something. 'You're ready now, Jens? You're better.'

Raben pocketed the note.

'I'm better.'

'We help each other, right? That's what it's about. The club can help you find somewhere to live. I'll get Louise some details before I go.'

He was looking askance again, fidgeting the way he did when they were getting ready for a mission.

'Go where?' Raben asked in his sergeant's voice, the one that couldn't be ignored.

Poulsen wriggled on the seat.

'Back to Afghanistan. I'm with the team that leaves next week. Six months. Looking forward to it. What's there to do for the likes of me here?'

'Where?'

'Helmand. Camp Viking to start with. I'm just a squaddie. How should I know? I only asked a couple of days ago. It's fine. No problem.'

Raben got up, stood in the way of the door.

'Last time we met you said you were out of all that.'

'I have to go.'

Poulsen started to walk past him. Raben took hold of his arm. The little man snatched it away, didn't look so friendly any more.

'What is it, Myg? What did you do? Maybe I can help . . .'

'You're a nutcase,' Poulsen snarled. 'How can you help me?'

'I don't remember what happened. I know it was bad . . .'

'You know jack shit! Keep it that way.'

Poulsen's pale face was going red with fury and fear.

'All that crap's done with, Raben. Buried. If people come asking questions . . .'

'What questions?'

'Best you didn't know.' His shrill voice rose. 'Guard!'

'Myg . . .'

'Guard! Get me out of here!'

Raben took hold of him again. The little man wriggled out of his strong grip.

'I can get you a job,' Poulsen yelled at him. 'That's it. But you start opening your mouth and the whole deal's off. You don't drag me down with you again. Not going to happen . . .'

The door was open. The guard was there, swinging his stick. Raben let go, watched Myg Poulsen hurry out of the room.

He knew something. So did Raben once. The truth was still there. He understood that. It rumbled round the back of his head like an angry dumb monster lost in the dark.

Her mother's flat in Østerbro was full of memories, few of them pleasant. Not now. Mark was there, tall and handsome, happier than he'd ever been with her. She'd not been a bad mother. Just failed to be an actively good one. So he'd settled with her ex-husband, got more money spent on him than she could ever have afforded on her present salary. And he'd hate Gedser, with good reason.

Fourteen candles on the cake. Vibeke, her mother, happy too, with what looked like a new boyfriend in tow. Lots of relatives with names she struggled to remember. They sang Happy Birthday, watched as Mark bent down to blow out the candles on his cake.

He was kind enough to wear the blue Netto sweatshirt she'd bought him, put it on the moment it was out of the terrible wrapping. A nasty, cheap thing and one size too small.

The boyfriend was called Bjørn. He was a rotund, balding cheerful figure, mid-sixties she guessed, happily recording every second of the party on a video camera. When the candles were out Vibeke clapped her hands and they all fell silent on command.

'Since you're here,' she declared in a ringing, happy tone, 'Bjørn and I have an announcement.'

Her mother was blushing. Lund wondered when she'd witnessed this before.

'This darling man has been foolish enough to propose to me,' Vibeke said, beaming like a schoolgirl. 'What could I say?'

'Only yes,' Bjørn answered with a grin.

'So I did. I won't wear white. There's going to be no fuss. There. That's it.'

She hesitated, then added, 'On Saturday. *This* Saturday. You'll all get invitations. Who said old people couldn't be impulsive?'

There was an astonished silence then a ragged burst of applause. Lund found herself giggling, hand over her mouth.

Mark came over.

She stroked his chest, laughed at the ridiculously tight sweatshirt.

'I'm sorry. You grow so quickly.'

'Don't worry.' His voice was deep and calm. She could scarcely believe he was the same troubled kid who'd lived with her here for a while during the Birk Larsen case. 'It's nice you're back. When do you have to leave?'

'In a minute.'

'Gran said you were here for a job interview. You might come and live in Copenhagen again.'

'No. How are things?'

'Fine.'

There was disappointment on his face. She was back with the twelve-year-old Mark for a moment. Once again she'd failed him.

He took her by the arms, kissed her once on the cheek, said something sweet and terribly grown-up and understanding.

Vibeke was crying out fresh orders to eat more cake.

Lund's eyes strayed to the floor. There was something there. A scrap of cellophane next to the wrapping paper ripped off the gifts.

Same size as the unidentified, half-torn piece they'd found in Anne Dragsholm's house.

Ruth Hedeby had hated it when Lund told her they all had to look harder. But really that was what the job amounted to. Looking. Never turning away, however hard that might be.

Lund bent down and retrieved the cellophane from the floor. On the table above was a plastic case by Bjørn's busy video camera. A new cassette waiting for its turn.

She put the wrapper in her pocket, walked out into the corridor, got out her phone.

It took two calls.

'Strange here.'

'It's Lund. I can't get hold of Brix.'

'Is this important? I'm busy.'

He was in the street somewhere. She could hear the traffic.

'It's about the Dragsholm murder. That piece of cellophane . . .'

'I thought you were done with this.'

'He filmed the whole thing. Unless you think the husband's capable of that you've got the wrong man.'

Strange didn't answer.

'I want to visit the house again,' Lund said. 'OK?'

A long, miserable sigh.

'Give me an hour.'

'What's wrong with now? Strange?'

'An hour,' he repeated and then the line went dead.

Behind her the guests were singing again. She had a horrible feeling she was expected to join in.

The Ryvangen Barracks stood in a triangle of land where the railway lines in Østerbro forked north out of the city. Louise Raben and her son Jonas had lived there with her father, Colonel Torsten Jarnvig, for almost a year since the money ran out for the flat that was meant to be a family home. Raben had never lived in it. He'd been confined to Herstedvester on psychiatric grounds not long after his return. There'd been a violent incident no one fully understood, a court case, an indefinite sentence.

So she and Jonas moved to Ryvangen, temporarily, or so it was supposed. She still wanted a home of her own. A life outside the close-knit community that was the army. But that wasn't possible. His release date got put back constantly. She didn't have enough money to pay for a place herself. So she and Jonas took the one spare room in her father's quarters. It was modest, but not as rudimentary as the accommodation she'd once shared with her husband in a sergeant's flat.

Jarnvig was a solitary man, dedicated to the army. His wife, Louise's mother, had long since fled, hating military life. Now he was barracks colonel, officer in charge.

Louise loved her father though she saw too much of him. In his own way he was trying to take Raben's place, nagging her to find a local school for Jonas, to convert the basement, make two rooms so they had more space. Late that afternoon, seated at the dining table, picking at a sandwich, he was back with the same song.

'You have to enrol early to get the best school. It's important . . .'

Jonas was sitting on the spare room floor. He had the latest toy that Christian Søgaard had given him. Søgaard was a major, a handsome, confident, strutting man, her father's number two. He hung around the house a lot, smiled at Louise, patted the boy on the head. Gave him toy soldiers, with guns and uniforms. Jonas loved them, liked to sit next to Søgaard who laughed as he shouted, 'Bang, bang.'

That afternoon Jonas had got into a fight at kindergarten. Another kid had teased him about his father. Søgaard had gone to pick him up, intervened, taken him home.

Louise knew what Søgaard really wanted. So, she suspected, did her father. Army marriages fell apart in all the usual predictable ways. Absence either sealed or broke them. Raben's disappearance into the maw of the Danish psychiatric penal system was worse, even, than his six-month postings to Iraq and then Afghanistan. At least with them she knew when he was supposed to come home. Unless it was on a hospital stretcher or in a coffin.

'The school depends on where we're living, Dad. Jens should be released soon. He can get a job. Myg says there's work on building sites. Carpentry . . .'

'And you'll leave us? The infirmary loves you. We need you here.'

She was a nurse in the barracks hospital. A good job. Lousy pay. But she felt wanted, appreciated, and that mattered.

Jarnvig picked up his mug of coffee.

'You really think they'll let him out?'

'Why not? He's better. There's no reason to keep him in that place. You'd know if you met him.'

'And if he isn't? You've been waiting two years.'

'I know how long I've been waiting. I've counted every day.'

'You keep putting things off. It affects you. It affects Jonas . . .'

She always thought her father a handsome man. Tall, straight-backed, confident, honest and decent. She was fifteen when her mother walked out, took a plane to Spain to find a new life on her own. The pain of her loss was still there, for both of them.

'Jens is Jonas's father and I love him. If that's a problem for you I can move out right away.'

He took a bite of his sandwich then flicked through some papers on the table.

A knock on the door. Said Bilal. One of the younger officers. The new breed. Danish-born Muslim, son of immigrant parents. Dark-haired, dark-skinned, no friends she knew of. If he smiled she never saw it.

He stood helmet in hand, full combat fatigues, stiff and upright.

'Major Søgaard said you wanted an update on the loading sched-ule. '

'Later,' Jarnvig said and didn't look up.

'There's a lance corporal I need to talk about . . .'

'Later. Thank you.'

'He's not a happy soldier,' Louise said when Bilal left.

'So what? Soon he'll be in Helmand. They do it because they have to. We shouldn't expect a song and dance.'

She went back into the spare room and joined Jonas and Christian Søgaard on the floor.

'I want to show Dad my new toy,' Jonas said, 'When can we see him?'

She kissed his soft fair hair.

'Soon.'

Søgaard's attention was more on her than Jonas, and in a way she didn't mind. He was a good-looking, attentive man. For two years she'd lived like a widow or a virgin. It felt fine to have someone around who gave her an admiring glance from time to time.

'How soon?' Jonas asked.

'Very,' Louise Raben replied without the least hesitation, returning Christian Søgaard's smile.

Carsten Plough loathed change deeply, which meant that he also hated the arrival of a new minister. It was like marrying a stranger. A civil servant never knew what he was letting himself in for.

'Where is he now?' Plough whined to Buch's secretary.

'I don't know.'

'He needs to start behaving like a Minister of the Queen.'

'Well Buch's new to it all.' The strange email they kept getting had come in again. 'He's only been here since this morning.'

'It's amazing how much damage you can do in one day. He's lost Birgitte Agger completely. Now Krabbe thinks he can walk all over us.'

She tried the link again. 'What in God's name is this?'

Plough came and stood behind her.

'An email from the Finance Ministry. It's their turn to organize this Friday's drinks. Probably someone's idea of a joke.'

She tugged on a strand of blonde hair and chewed on it. 'I'm sure they sent the invite for the drinks earlier. And that address isn't in the directory.'

Footsteps at the door. Buch marched in. Blue sweater, clashing purple shirt, no tie.

'Krabbe's here already,' Plough said. 'Where've you been?'

'Out. It was supposed to be seven. I hate it when people are early. Come . . .'

Seated at the conference table, Erling Krabbe looked triumphant.

He got up, shook Buch's hand, almost warmly. Smiled at Plough and Karina.

'I was a bit forward earlier. I'm sorry. Long day. Headache. Forgive me. Now. To business . . .'

'The situation's very simple,' Buch interrupted cheerily. 'Neither now nor in the future will we compromise our constitution's protection of basic democratic values.'

The lean politician looked at him, wide-eyed.

'No threat, no scare campaign, from you or from the terrorists, will change that position. Do I make myself clear?'

'Very,' Krabbe said with a curt nod. 'So the government thinks it will be best served without us?'

'Not at all. Though that's your decision. I would have to explain the basis of our position if you do quit, of course.'

Buch placed his briefcase on the table and retrieved a set of documents.

'I'm no historian or lawyer. But I have consulted both on your suggestions. As far as I'm aware a Danish government has only once before prohibited a legal association for no other reason than its views. Here . . .'

He passed Krabbe the papers. Plough shuffled over, looked, groaned. Photographs from the Second World War. Nazi soldiers on the streets, rifles extended, bayonets raised, fearful crowds watching them.

'It was in 1941. When we outlawed the Communist Party. The Wehrmacht forced our hand on that occasion. I don't need to tell you where that led. Your grandfather doubtless mentioned it.'

Krabbe threw the pictures onto the table.

'There's no comparison.'

'I've experts on constitutional law who'll swear otherwise. You'll find their statements in there if you're interested. Feel free to share all this with your colleagues . . .'

'Don't insult me.'

Buch's big right arm cut the air between them.

'Truly, Krabbe, nothing could be further from my mind. The question is very simple. Does the People's Party wish to be part of a broad agreement and introduce the kind of legislation the security services are asking for? Or do you want to stand alone with an opinion that hasn't been voiced since the Nazis ran Copenhagen and treated us like slaves and puppets?'

'Minister . . .' Plough began.

'No.' Buch smiled at both of them. 'He can answer for himself.'

43

'This is pitiful,' Krabbe said, heading for the door, leaving the documents on the table. 'You're out of your depth, Buch. My mistake was failing to realize quite how much.'

'I can't stay here all night,' Strange grumbled. 'Get to the point. Why would he film it?'

They were back in the Dragsholm house walking round the living room. All the lights on. Grey shadows of trees at the end of the garden. From somewhere the rattle of a train.

It was seven fifteen. She should have phoned her mother to say she'd be late. But Vibeke looked so happy with Bjørn she probably never noticed.

'You said the bloodstains show the woman was stabbed first then forced into that chair.' Lund looked at the leather executive seat still turned sideways on the floor, tipped over the way it was found. 'What if you're wrong? What if she was in the chair first and stabbed there?'

Strange frowned.

'You're losing me. If it was a crime of passion . . .'

'You make the theory fit the facts, not the other way round.'

He looked chastened. She picked up the file, scanned through the autopsy report, the photos of the cuts all over Anne Dragsholm's neck and torso.

'There was one deep stab wound to the heart,' Lund said. 'They think that was a knife. The other wounds were different. More shallow. Rough-edged.'

'We don't have any weapons.'

'You mean you haven't found any.'

'Yes,' he said mock patiently. 'That's what I mean.'

'What did Svendsen squeeze out of the husband? Did he say how he killed her?'

'A knife. He threw it away somewhere.'

She stared at him.

'Somewhere?'

'I wasn't in the interview.'

'But it wasn't just a knife, was it? Why didn't Dragsholm defend herself? Why are there no wounds to her arms?'

Thinking. Looking. Imagining.

The old habits were coming back. She could dream her way into a crime scene sometimes. Almost be there as it happened.

Lund looked at the leather chair. It had strong shiny metal arms and a firm base. The red stain at the edge of the left arm had taken on the sheen of the metal as it dried.

She set it upright, did the same with the footstool. Then grabbed the tall metal studio lamp and placed it in front of both, aimed the lamp straight at the chair back, found a socket, plugged it in, turned it on.

The lamp was very bright. The beam fell straight on the chair back. It looked like a scene from an interrogation room. The kind of set-up a thuggish cop like Svendsen would have loved if he was allowed one.

'You're making this up,' Strange said, sounding a little in awe of her.

'Correct.'

She pulled back the foot stand, set it by the lamp.

'He sat here. Shone the light in her eyes. Tortured her first of all to get her talking. When he'd got what he wanted he took out a knife and stabbed her straight through the heart.'

Strange shook his head.

'She was in the middle of a divorce. Why would someone hold a kind of mock interrogation . . . ?'

'Nothing mock about it. He came in here with a purpose. This was what he wanted. Intended all along.'

The light caught a set of bookshelves against the back wall, behind the chair.

She went along the rows slowly, methodically. Titles on law. On history. Travel and the military.

'They checked everything in the room, Lund. They wouldn't have missed anything.'

'That's right. They never do.'

A small statue stood tucked between a set of heavyweight legal volumes. Half their size. Nothing special.

The classical figure of justice, a blindfolded woman holding the scales.

Something odd about it.

The statue was bronze. The blindfold silver, like a chain. It was

45

loose. Separate. She took the thing in her gloved hands, turned it round. Something was hidden away behind the back, chinking against the stand.

Strange came and joined her.

'What's this?' she asked.

Hanging on the chain was a piece of shiny metal, hidden behind the statue. It looked like an oblong crudely cut in half. The severed edge was sharp and stained with blood and tissue. A line of crosses were stamped into it. Near the edge a single word, 'Danmark'.

'A military ID,' Strange said. 'A dog tag.'

'This is what he used to cut her. It's broken in half.'

He didn't answer.

'Strange . . .'

'They do that when a soldier dies. When they send his body back from battle. They break the dog tag. It's kind of a . . .'

'An army ritual,' she cut in. 'Have you got an address for this veterans' club Dragsholm used to give money to?'

'We need to call Brix. He'll want forensic back here.'

She waved the bloodied metal fragment in his face.

'You mean the people who missed this?'

'Yes but . . .'

'I want to see this veterans' club she gave money to.'

'Lund! I've got things to do . . .'

'Do them later,' she said, then placed the dog tag in a plastic evidence bag and put it in her pocket.

Another night in Herstedvester. Raben pacing the corridors, not talking much to anyone, wondering why they wouldn't allow him a phone call home.

Louise was slipping from him. There seemed precious little he could do.

So he pestered the guard again, asking for a permission slip for an extra call.

'Tomorrow,' the man said. 'The warden can look at it then.'

'Tomorrow's too late.'

The guard was hefty, foreign.

'You're out of calls, Raben. You shouldn't have made so many.'

'It's important.'

Director Toft was a couple of doors along talking to one of the prisoners. Raben walked up, interrupted, asked her if the warden would see his call request.

The icy, beautiful smile.

'Raben!' the warden called down the corridor. 'Time to get in your cell.'

'I got a visit from an army buddy,' he said, not moving. 'I'm worried about him.'

'Why?' she asked.

'He's not well. I think he might harm himself. I need to talk to him. And my wife. She can help.'

'I'll tell the warden you say it's urgent.'

'It *is* urgent.'

'I'll tell him that.'

Footsteps behind. The burly guard was coming for him.

'There's something else we need to talk about, Raben.'

'Can't I call first?'

'No. The Probation Service rejected your application. Usually they take a week or so to consider our recommendation. But . . .' She shrugged her slender shoulders. 'They just turned you down flat. I don't know on what grounds . . .'

He was short of breath, struggling to think.

'When I do know I'll tell you. I'm sorry.'

'What?' He could hear the guard getting closer. 'What is this?'

She was walking away. Six months more in this prison and she broke the news in a moment.

'Toft! I completed the treatment. I did everything you asked—'

'I don't know why.' She barely turned as she pulled out the keys for her flashy sports car. 'When I do—'

'I've got a young son. A family.'

'In another six months you can apply again. Keep up with the treatment—'

'For fuck's sake, woman, what do I have to do?'

The guard was by his side, fists bunched, smiling, looking for a fight.

'Step away from the clinical director,' he ordered.

'I didn't touch her.'

The big man took his arm. Raben was fit again now the wounds were healed. Strong and well trained. He turned, pushed the guard hard in the chest, sent him scuttling down the corridor, falling on his backside.

Toft looked as if she was enjoying this. Arms folded, blank pale face focused on his.

'You need to remain calm,' she said.

'I am calm. I just don't understand.'

Noises behind. The guards had a routine. Never pursue a fight on your own. Some of the men in here were big and trouble. Get backup. Wait for the moment.

'I'm not a psycho. Not a paedophile or a criminal.'

The guard was back, stick in hand, beating it into his palm.

'Get away from her, Raben.'

'I didn't touch her! I won't . . .'

'We can't help you if you won't help yourself,' Toft said calmly.

'The shit you bastards feed me . . .'

Then came the fury, the same red roar he'd felt in Iraq, in Afghanistan. The bellow of rage and violent fury they wanted, trained and encouraged in him.

He'd picked up a table and barely knew it. Was swinging it in front of him, walking towards the foreign guard.

Dark skin the colour of the Helmand mud. He saw it everywhere when he was out on patrol, not knowing whether they were meeting friend or foe.

One quick dash and he launched the table in front of him, aiming for the man, screaming.

Hands came from nowhere, knees jabbed, feet kicked, fists flew.

Jens Peter Raben was on the floor getting smothered and beaten by their flailing arms.

Someone took his legs. Another turned his screaming face hard into the tiles.

Toft's words, spoken in that flat, refined tone he'd come to hate, hovered somewhere above him. He looked up, saw her, blue eyes focused.

'Medicate him,' she ordered. 'Put him in the room.'

Strong arms dragged him screaming, kicked and forced him into the solitary cell, lifted him onto the metal table, wrapped the leather straps round his struggling body as he cursed and spat at them.

A hypodermic stabbed into his shoulder. Memories of another place, a different kind of violence swam into view.

Jens Peter Raben wondered if he'd ever escape this nightmare, find refuge and peace at home with Louise and the little boy who scarcely knew his face.

Wondered what he might turn into – return to – if they never let him out. Thought of Myg Poulsen too, the scared little soldier who'd been with him in Helmand when the walls of their small, shared world began to tumble into dust.

Poulsen never wanted to go back to war. There was only one reason he would. He was too scared to do anything else.

Then the chemical bit, hard and loud and rushing. After that he didn't fight against the leather straps or think much at all.

Plough remained as furious as his tightly reined civil servant's temper would allow. Then, ten minutes after Erling Krabbe stormed out of Buch's office, he was back on the phone, meekly offering his party's support for the bill with a few minor amendments.

'And yet,' Buch said, once the call was finished and he was packing his things for the evening, 'you don't look happy, Carsten.'

'I'm not. In no way can the law of 1941 be compared to the People's Party suggestions. Next time I would appreciate it if you asked my opinion first before consulting any legal experts.'

'You're right. I'm new to this job. Allow me a little latitude, please. Also I'm a politician. I want to get my own way.'

Plough appeared to have summoned all his courage and strength for an argument. Buch's immediate apology threw him.

'I understand that, Minister, but in future . . .'

'First day!' Buch patted him on the arm. 'It didn't go *too* badly, did it?'

The large man from Jutland had a pleasant smile and knew when to use it.

'I wasn't saying that. There are ways of doing things. Ministerial ways . . .'

Karina marched in from the office.

'You need to look at this. Both of you.'

'No,' Buch replied, gathering his things. 'There's a reception at the Polish Embassy. Sausages . . .'

'I've cancelled. Please . . .'

She looked close to tears, and she was a strong, confident young woman.

'PET are on their way,' she said, walking back to her desk.

The two men followed. She sat down in front of the computer. A video was on the screen, paused. A house in darkness, lights on inside.

'What is this, Karina?' Buch asked again.

'An email we kept getting. It's coming from an address in the Finance Ministry. A fake. The link wouldn't open till seven thirty. It's . . .'

She took a deep breath and hit the play button.

'See for yourself.'

The screen jerked into life. A light came on. A woman appeared in an upstairs window, towelling her hair as if she'd just come out of the bath. There was the sound of anxious shallow breathing from the camera. The lens followed her through the windows into the kitchen. She drank a glass of water, appeared to look at something then walked away.

'This is all very well,' Buch said. 'But the Polish Embassy . . .'

'Forget it,' Karina insisted.

The sound of footsteps, the camera moving closer. The woman chopping vegetables on a board in the kitchen. Her hair's wet. She's wearing a blue dressing gown. She hears something, stares through the windows, lets out an unheard cry, drops the knife.

Rapid movement, the sound of glass breaking.

Then forward an unknown amount of time. A close-up. She's in a chair by a lamp, still in the blue dressing gown. Blood pours from her nose, one eye black and bruised, a cut above the brow. The robe is down close to her breasts, above it cruel slashes streak her skin through the flesh.

She looks torn between fury and defiance, stares into the lens.

'My God,' Carsten Plough murmured and pulled up a chair.

Buch moved closer and as he did the lens pulled back. They could see the ropes around her torso. In her left hand a sheet of paper. Her bloodied, frightened face turns to it and, in a broken, tremulous voice she begins to read.

'I accuse the hypocritical Danish government and the infidel Danish people of crimes against humanity.'

The sheet of paper shakes. Her eyes move to the camera seeking pity, a response, receive nothing.

'The time has come for Allah's revenge. The Muslim League will punish the sufferings Denmark has caused . . . in Palestine, Iraq and Afghanistan.'

Wet hair down on her naked shoulders, head shaking, tears starting to streak the snotty gore that runs from her mouth, her nose, she half cries, half whispers, 'I plead guilty. My blood will be shed. And many will die along with me.'

The camera zooms in. Her face in terror and agony.

'I haven't done anything . . . I've a little girl . . . For the love of God . . .'

Closer still, closer. Bloodied mouth, bloodied teeth, a scream, a frozen image. Then silence.

On the screen. In the room.

Karina got up, excused herself, strode quickly out of the office.

Thomas Buch sat down heavily beside her desk.

This was the same woman in the photograph he'd seen in Frode Monberg's file.

Anne Dragsholm. Buch had learned one politician's trick. He was now good at names. He would not forget this one easily.

The veterans' club was in Christianshavn, not far from the former military area that had turned into the hippie free state of Christiania. Strange drove, looking grumpy all the way.

'What's wrong?' Lund asked as they passed Slotsholmen, still lit, and then the Knippelsbro bridge.

'You.'

He was nothing like Meyer. No sense of jocularity around this man. He seemed decent, quiet, responsible. She liked that, up to a point.

'I'm sorry if the work's getting in the way of your social life.'

He looked at her, frowned. Maybe there was a note of humour in there somewhere.

'It was a joke, Strange.'

'I don't live and breathe the police. I've got things to do. Haven't you?'

She didn't answer.

'I mean,' he went on, 'you came back to Copenhagen to see your mother. Not stick your nose in a murder case.'

'Brix asked me.'

'To read the files.'

'Which I did.'

'And here we are. Out on a call.'

He had an unusual face. Very alert, younger than his years yet mature in its intensity. Good-looking but careworn.

'You don't have any authority here, Lund.'

'Brix asked me . . .'

'When we get there you stay in the car unless I call for you.'

'Don't be ridiculous.'

He didn't like that. Strange checked the traffic, pulled into the side of the road, cut the engine.

'You stay here until I say otherwise,' he repeated. 'Agree to that or you can get out now and find your own way home. Which is where you should be by the way. Not out here in the pissing rain with me.'

He folded his arms, waited.

'You'll come and get me?' she asked.

'When I'm happy it's safe.'

'I'm not a child, Strange! I had your rank once.'

'Once.' His acute eyes looked straight into hers. 'And then what happened?'

He waited. She wasn't going to rise to that bait. Not with a stranger. Not with anyone.

'Doesn't matter,' Strange said quite gently. 'People talk. What do you expect?'

'You don't know the half of it.'

'Want to tell me?'

The silence again.

'Good. Because I don't want to hear.' He started the car. 'I'm the cop here. Not you.'

Without waiting for an answer Strange started the car, pulled out, back into the evening traffic.

The rain was coming down in vertical stripes as he drove into the empty car park behind a derelict block next to one of the pedestrian lanes leading into Christiania.

'I checked the club. It's got ten, eleven thousand members all over

Denmark. The secretary's called Allan Myg Poulsen. He's got a room near the office. Number twenty-six.'

'He's still a soldier?'

'I don't know.'

'Served in Afghanistan?'

Strange didn't answer.

'Dragsholm was giving these people money. Every month,' Lund said. 'You have to find out why.'

'I'll ask.' Strange turned off the engine, took the keys, opened the driver's door. 'Wait here until I get back.' He turned and looked into her face. 'Is that understood?'

Lund saluted and pulled the most severe face she could muster.

Watched him get out of the car, walk along the line of doors, find the communal entrance to the building and go in.

Swore and said something caustic and deeply unfair.

He'd get kicked for bringing along a civilian. Maybe. Or perhaps he was just making a point. Jan Meyer always felt challenged around her, which she never fully understood. He was a good cop, bright and imaginative. He learned quickly too. From her mostly.

She watched a light go on in the building ahead.

Strange was different. A lot more sure of himself for one thing. She wanted to hear him talk to someone. Judge how he threw questions at people.

Most of all she wanted to do that herself. There was a smell, a feel, a taste to a murder inquiry. Lost in Gedser, looking for pathetic illegals trying to smuggle their way into Denmark, she'd forgotten what it was like. Now the scent was in her head again and she liked it.

'You need me, Brix,' she whispered in the passenger seat of the black unmarked squad car.

I can look, she thought. I can see.

There was an iron walkway on the first floor at the side of the building. Lund ran her eyes along the metal grating. A heavy padlock chain. Broken.

As she watched a figure in black, hooded against the foul night, walked out from the main body of the block, hands in pockets, head down, marched quickly towards a set of the stairs at the end.

Hunched, in a hurry, trying to shrink inside his black winter jacket.

Lund rolled down the window, shouted, 'Hey!'

One word and then he began to run.

She was out of the vehicle without thinking.

A single exit through a covered car park. Lund broke into a run, went after him, yelling all the time.

Beyond the lee of the block the squall hit her, heavy and icy. He was heading for the gates to Christiania, crude paintings of joints, peace signs, hippie symbols.

Inside the free state. No cars any more. A warren of buildings, groups of people shuffling through the night.

There were only two people running here. He was the other one.

She pushed on, careered through lazy, grumbling crowds, through the dope fumes, past the makeshift cafes. Music on the air, stupid laughter.

Pusher Street. Crowded with curious tourists and local buyers meandering among the busy stands.

Dope stalls lined with trays of hash, suspicious eyes watching her as she careered up and down, torch out, high in her hand, the way only a cop did.

One more brief glimpse of the fleeing hooded figure. Then he was gone. Lund tried to follow, found herself lost in the alleys and dead ends of Christiania, had to take out her phone to work out where she was from the map.

Then made her way back towards the veterans' club, found the normal streets with cars and people carrying shopping bags, not joints.

Was halfway there when someone leaped out from the side of the road, took her arm.

'Jesus,' she gasped, and then saw Strange's worried, puzzled face.

'You know that bit where I said stay where you are?'

'There was a man running away from the building. I called and he couldn't wait to get away. Something's wrong.'

He leaned back against the grey brick wall behind him, rain streaming down his face.

'Isn't it?' she asked.

'Search me. I barely got inside before you started yelling. Then I came after you. What else was I supposed to do?'

'Find Myg Poulsen?'

He shook his head.

'Do you really want to be a lone cop shouting out your existence to a bunch of dope dealers?'

'I'm not a cop,' Lund said. 'You said so.'

She walked back towards the apartments and the veterans' club.

Was inside before he caught up.

The door to Poulsen's room was open. The place looked empty.

'I'd got this far when you started squawking,' Strange said, catching her up. 'Maybe I should call control . . .'

'And say what?'

She walked in. A chair was overturned. It looked as if there might have been a struggle.

Nothing more here. She came out, went down the corridor. The door ahead had a painted sign, 'Veterans' Club'.

Chairs. A table tennis table. A cheap computer. A kettle, some mugs and a gas hob.

'They really know how to live,' Strange said. 'Maybe we can look at the books. See where Dragsholm's money went.'

He had his torch out, was nosing round. Lund found the light switches, turned on every one.

A line of big, powerful fluorescents came to life. The place was a dump, dusty and bare.

At the end of the room opaque plastic sheeting blocked off a corner. For painting maybe. Or building work.

Lund walked closer. A red stain was smeared against the inside.

She didn't wait for Strange who was still poking round the desk.

Strode over, threw back the plastic sheeting with her arm, looked.

A man upside down, feet held by a rope round an iron beam above.

Blood seeped from his slit throat, formed a dark sticky pool on the floor.

Lund got out her torch, looked more closely. Was aware Strange was closing in behind her now, muttering curses under his breath.

She still had the forensic gloves she'd used in Anne Dragsholm's house. Lund took them out of her pocket, pulled them on, crouched down, went close to the corpse strung up in front of her, swinging slowly side to side like a sick pendulum.

Used a pen to stretch out the object hanging round the dead man's neck.

Silver chain, blood sticky along its length. A piece of metal sawn in half.

A dog tag, the edge feathered with scarlet tissue, sharp and rough and used.

Standing next to Myg Poulsen's body slowly dripping onto the hard cold floor, Strange called Brix.

Lund listened. The conversation seemed protracted.

'What is it?' she asked when he came off the phone.

'He's coming with a team.'

'What else?'

He was looking at her. Puzzled. Interested too, she thought.

'The terror alert's gone from yellow to red. The government's received some kind of threat. It's to do with the Dragsholm woman. Says she's the first.' He paused, looked at the dead body strung up from a hook in front of them. 'Just the first.'

Lund turned three hundred and sixty degrees on the balls of her feet, taking in the grubby, bare room. Not a lot else to find here, she thought. Not without forensic help. The man she'd pursued into Christiania must have fled by the back stairs, onto the walkway.

She should have caught up with him. Not that she had a gun. Or anything else.

'You knew it wasn't the husband all along, didn't you?' Strange said.

'Didn't *you*?' she replied.

It was a mistake to think that crimes were inherently complex. They stemmed from the simplest of urges: fear, lust, envy, hatred, greed. It was the job of the police – her job when she was allowed it – to try to peel away the layers of deceit, the fabric of lies that hid this simple fact.

'Statistically you look close to home,' Strange said.

Lund thought of the dog tag on the statue by the books. The torn piece of metal round the neck of Myg Poulsen. Both were fakes. She was sure of it. No numbers, just a line of crosses from some kind of amateur machine.

'First you have to look,' she said.

Ten minutes later there was a noise at the door. Brix was there, and with him a sight she thought she'd never witness again: grim-faced officers ready to work as many hours as the chief needed. Men and women in white suits, white boot covers, mob caps.

A case under way.

Three

Monday 14th November

6.52 p.m.   Brix took them outside, talked in the blue flashing lights of the police vans. A video had been streamed on an Islamist website earlier that evening after an email from a bogus address was sent to the Ministry of Justice. It showed a bloodied Anne Dragsholm being forced to read out a promise of more attacks against 'infidels' in Denmark.

There was a news blackout but details were already leaking out to the media. PET were taking charge of the domestic terrorism side of the case. The murder investigation would remain with homicide for the moment. The formal announcement of the move to the highest terror alert would be made any minute.

They went inside and Strange took over.

'The dead man's Allan Myg Poulsen. Thirty-six, unmarried. Professional soldier. He's been based in the Ryvangen Barracks for ten years. Moved between there and the veterans' club. Quit the army for a while two years ago but re-enlisted last month. Stayed here sometimes. In the barracks when he was on duty.'

Army recruitment posters on the wall. Photos of men on duty in distant, dusty locations.

Poulsen's well-used military boots were on a newspaper on the floor, next to them a brush, a can of polish. By their side was a scattered pile of leaflets in what looked like Arabic: images of a bloody sword wielded by a shrieking warrior.

'We've got a search in hand for the man who ran off,' Strange went on. 'Lund didn't really see him.'

'It was dark,' she said. 'He could run. He went straight into Pusher Street. Young and fit.' She looked at Strange. 'About his height and build.'

'Any witnesses?' Brix asked.

'A door at the back looks forced. Maybe the killer was waiting for him.'

Lund stared at the dirty boots and the polish. Brix was watching her.

'I wouldn't expect a soldier to start something without finishing it,' she said. 'I'd work on the idea Poulsen was sitting here when someone came through the door.'

'No sign of a struggle,' Strange added.

Lund walked back to the body. The two men followed her.

'He was tortured,' Strange said. 'All those cuts . . .'

The wounds were much like those on Anne Dragsholm. Methodical slashes.

'He must have known the building was derelict. Took his time here.'

'The murder weapon . . . ?' Brix began.

'He was slashed with the dog tag to begin with,' Lund said. There was a wider, deeper wound to his chest. 'He used a knife at the end. We've got to get people searching the vicinity. Get into Christiania. He knew his way through there. Look at how he got in here. It's not easy. Maybe he wasn't on his own. Except . . .'

'What?' Strange asked.

She bent down and looked at the dark pool beneath Poulsen's torn corpse.

'I'd guess this is an hour or two old,' Lund said.

'We need to speak.' Brix glanced at Strange. 'Alone.'

A crowd was gathering by the gate. Locals, photographers, reporters waving voice recorders. The rain was steady and relentless.

'I only saw one but there might have been others,' Lund told Brix. 'What did PET say?'

Hands in pockets, long face, he walked her to the edge of the building.

'I guess they were taken by surprise,' she added when he didn't answer. 'We need to start from scratch. I want those leaflets translated. If you can get me a copy of the video I'll take a look at it straight away . . .'

Something was bothering her.

'The soldier had been dead for a while. So why did he come back? He was looking for something. Let's check the files, the computer . . .'

'Lund,' he said with a long, pained sigh. 'You're not on this case. I asked you to read the files. That's all.'

She shook her head.

'What do you mean? You sent Strange to Gedser to get me.'

'To take a look. Give an opinion. Nothing more.'

She didn't get angry often. But it had been a long day. No sleep. A visit from a stranger when she came off shift. Mark's almost forgotten birthday. Her mother getting married.

But, more than anything, two bodies. Bloodied dog tags. A mystery begging for an explanation. Hers.

'You knew it wasn't the husband, Brix. Cut out the games, please.'

He didn't like that.

'Then why did he confess?'

'To get that pig Svendsen off his back. He's a lawyer. He knows you had no case. He's probably getting ready to sue you right now . . .'

'The case may have changed,' Brix cried. 'Your record hasn't. Two years ago I had to fight to keep you out of court. You didn't obey orders. You threatened a colleague with a weapon.'

'Yes. Svendsen. I told you. He wouldn't listen.'

'They haven't forgotten in the Politigården. They're not likely to. Your negligence . . .'

'I was fighting everyone. You included . . .'

'Meyer won't walk again. Or work. Do you think he blames me? Or you?'

That was too much. She prodded the chest of his expensive black winter coat.

'I think he blames all of us. I know it.'

'Have you asked him recently?'

He knew all the right questions. Meyer's shooting weighed on her conscience every day. Of course she hadn't.

'What do you want?' she asked.

'A reason I should trust you.'

Lund stuffed her hands in her pockets, wondered what she'd do if she went back to Gedser. How she could get a case like this out of her head.

'I made mistakes. I wasn't the only one.'

She looked up into his grey, unsmiling face.

'If I could change things . . .' There was no way to tell if she was getting anywhere with this man. 'But I can't.'

She looked at the flashing blue lights, the officers checking out the yard, the white suits going to and fro.

'This is what I do best,' she said, for him, and for herself. 'This is the only thing I do and I'm good at it. That . . .'

She stabbed him again in the chest with a firm forefinger.

'. . . is why you summoned me here. Not because you wanted me. Because you need me.' Lund pulled out her phone, looked at the time. 'I can still catch a train back to Gedser if you want . . .'

'I'll call them in the morning,' he said quickly. 'We'll borrow you for a while. A couple of days to start with.'

She nodded.

'Are we agreed?' he asked.

'Same rank as Strange,' she said, and it wasn't a question. 'Whatever it's called these days.'

'Vicepolitikommissær.'

'I want ID. I want that video. I want everything.' She smiled at Brix. 'And I want him to do as he's told.'

'Don't screw up this time,' Brix grumbled. 'What am I letting myself in for?'

'I'll do my very best,' Lund said, nothing more.

Thomas Buch called home, wondered what people were saying, thinking in distant Jutland. Told his wife to kiss the girls goodnight. Then sat down with Erik König, the head of PET, and Ruth Hedeby, the deputy commissioner of police, wondering if this day would ever end.

König was an ascetic-looking man, a little too intellectual to be a police officer. Mid-fifties, grey hair carefully tended, rimless spectacles, he came in first, sat down first, treated Hedeby, a quiet woman, as a subordinate from the outset. With some reason. PET handled internal security issues such as terrorism. The police answered to them, always.

'The video was on a server in London,' König said. 'The site had a Danish address. We've closed it naturally.'

'Did many people see it?' Buch asked.

'Quite a few.' König took out some documents. 'The link you received was sent to other ministries, to the media here and internationally. We have . . .' König took off his glasses and polished them with his handkerchief. '. . . a situation on our hands. I think it's safe to say that.'

'Quite,' Buch agreed. 'Any idea who sent the emails?'

He frowned as if the question were too obvious.

'Of course not. Spoof addresses, sent through proxy servers. The website was a forum for fundamentalists. That's our most promising lead. As I said it was registered in Denmark.'

Carsten Plough, taking minutes, lifted his head and asked, 'By whom? When?'

'Six months ago. We're trying to trace the domain holder.'

Buch nodded.

'And this Muslim League?'

König almost seemed to resent such questions.

'New to us. It may be an existing group working under a different name. The number of individuals involved in these organizations is tiny. They work hard at making themselves seem bigger than they are.'

'The woman?' Plough asked.

'She's the victim from Mindelunden,' Ruth Hedeby replied. 'Anne Dragsholm. A lawyer.'

'And now there's a second death?' Buch asked.

'It was discovered while the video was going online,' Hedeby continued. 'A soldier. Allan Myg Poulsen. Thirty-six.'

She handed Carsten Plough a file.

'A soldier?' the civil servant asked. 'A lawyer? Where's the connection?'

'Poulsen served abroad, in Iraq and Afghanistan. The woman also worked there, briefly, as a military legal adviser.'

Plough passed the file across the table. Buch glanced at it, then at her.

'You're saying they're symbolic targets because of their connections to the army?'

'Precisely,' König agreed, taking over again. 'This is a clear act of retribution, planned in advance with some precision it appears . . .'

'Yet it took us by surprise,' Buch interrupted. 'How am I to explain this to the Prime Minister? To the public?'

Ruth Hedeby leaned back in her chair and was silent. König was on his own.

'It's an unusual case,' he insisted. 'There was no indication of a terrorist connection in the murder at the memorial park. The police assumed it was the husband. He confessed, didn't he?'

They looked at Ruth Hedeby.

'He withdrew that earlier this evening,' Hedeby said quietly. 'Perhaps the questioning was a little . . . robust.'

'Had we heard earlier there was a dog tag in Dragsholm's house . . . ?' König added.

'Nobody's trying to pin blame here,' Carsten Plough said. 'How do we solve this? Where do we go from here?'

König nodded in agreement.

'The threat appears to be against the military so we'll issue a warning to all barracks. Increase the level of security at airports, train stations. The usual places. I don't want the media writing about the second victim. Let's keep a lid on this for now.'

Buch was aghast.

'Keep a lid on this? There are two people dead in Copenhagen. A terror plot's been hatched under our noses without you even noticing. People are entitled to hear what's going on. We'll inform them, responsibly, accurately, with as much as they need to know.'

'Minister, that's not really how things are done,' Plough said.

'So I see. We've had a group of terrorists working inside this country for weeks, months . . . And now they're here and we've no idea who they are or what they're doing. König?'

The PET chief squirmed on his seat.

'You report to me directly, I believe? Good. Then tomorrow, when you have the time, tell me why we appear to be in the dark.'

'Minister . . .'

'Is there more I need to know?'

König said nothing.

'Good.' Buch glanced at the door. 'I must talk to the Prime Minister. Keep me informed.'

They walked out in silence, leaving Buch with Plough and Karina Jørgensen.

'Protocol,' Plough began.

'That's a word you use a lot,' Buch said brusquely. 'I'm not much interested in hearing it now.'

Karina had brought him a tie. She wanted him to wear it for the meeting with Grue Eriksen.

'Frode Monberg was aware of the Dragsholm case,' Plough explained. 'But none of us thought it would develop into such madness.'

It was a circuitous stroll from the Ministry of Justice round to the old palace where the Prime Minister's office was based. Enough to get soaked.

'Is it still raining? Do I need an umbrella?' Buch asked.

They looked at one another.

'What's so funny?' Buch asked.

'You don't need to walk outside any more,' Karina said, and gently took his arm. 'Shall we go?'

She led him into a corridor he'd thought a dead end. Found another junction, opened doors he'd never known about, punched in codes, walked on. Through the winding maze of private passageways that bound the government offices of Denmark on the island of Slotsholmen she led him, crossing buildings, passing the breadth of the Folketinget, until, untouched by the weather or even a hint of a chill draught, Thomas Buch reached the Christiansborg Palace itself and found himself outside the office of the Prime Minister.

There he was received for the briefest of meetings, one shorter than his walk through the maze itself.

Domestic terror, Gert Grue Eriksen emphasized, was Buch's responsibility. Then he looked at his watch, talked of appointments with foreign dignitaries, smiled and waited for him to leave.

Back in the Politigården Brix briefed the night team: search the area, interview anyone living in the vicinity. Check any CCTV cameras around. Poulsen was a loner who often stayed on his own in the club. No visitors seen or recorded.

'What about PET?' Strange asked. 'Can't they give us a list of suspects? They've got to have them.'

'PET will get back to us in due course. Find out about the victims. Their past, their military records. Is there a link between the Dragsholm woman and Myg Poulsen? Let's try and understand why these two were picked.'

Lund sat at a computer going through the video of the woman strapped to the chair. The office was open-plan now, not the warren of little cubbyholes she was able to hide in with Meyer. She didn't like it.

'Check out the veterans' club,' Brix went on. 'They'll have a database of soldiers. Let's see if anyone's been snooping. If they're looking to attack someone else it makes sense they'll follow the same path.'

Lund took her attention away from the computer monitor, watched Brix for a moment. He was different from how she remembered. Not quite as sure of himself. There was always something secretive to the man. But now she wondered if he looked a little vulnerable.

'The dog tags were forged,' he continued.

The photo collection was building on the walls. The woman at the stake, in the chair from the video. Fresh pictures of the murdered Poulsen. His death had been even more cruel, more agonizing than hers. This was a showy act of brutality. Someone was being taught a lesson.

Lund went back to the video, started it again. The woman in the blue gown, face covered in blood, mouth a shriek of fear and agony, reading out the ludicrous statement the man behind the camera – it had to be a man – had given her.

'Sarah Lund is here to assist us,' Brix announced.

Her head went up. She wondered why he needed to say this.

'Some of you may know her.'

They turned and looked. Mostly strangers. She was glad Svendsen wasn't among them. Lund didn't regret pulling a gun on him, not for a moment. He'd begged for it.

'I expect you to welcome her,' Brix concluded.

'Right. Let's get started.' Strange walked in front of them. Officer in charge. 'Any questions?'

Brix left him to brief the team in detail then came over to Lund's desk.

'Work alongside Strange. You report directly to me.'

She kept looking at the video.

'Lund? Did you hear me?'

'The Muslim League. Why've we never heard of them?'

'It's not unusual. They invent a name for the cause. We've seen it before.'

'What about the website?'

'Nothing new. PET are looking into it.'

'They only tell us what they want. And then when they feel like it. They think they're better—'

'Please.' Brix stood over her. 'Don't start.'

'An observation,' she said with a smile, got up and pulled on her jacket.

Strange came back. Brix returned to the team.

'We need to talk to people at Poulsen's barracks in Ryvangen,' she said. 'That's all the family he had from what I can see.'

'Makes sense.'

He was staring at the desk. The nameplate there was his. She'd placed her coffee cup on some papers, left a big stain over a forensic report. He picked it up, frowned. Put the pens she'd moved back into their holder.

Lund took out her gum, considered sticking it very visibly under the desk, thought again and deposited it in the bin.

He pointed to the other half of the desk.

'That's free. This,' he said, 'is mine.'

'It's just a desk, Strange. It's not like . . . your own little country or something.'

He leaned down, ran his finger along the middle.

'It is now and that's the border. Nothing crosses it.'

Lund retrieved her pens, her coffee cup, laptop, keys and a pack of tissues, half open. Got them over the line. Tidied them as much as she felt able.

'Just a desk,' she said again.

There was a red and white Danish flag on a little stick. A hangover from a party perhaps.

With a grave face Strange picked it up, placed it next to the pen tidy that marked the edge of his zone, folded his arms, stared at her, eyes narrowed.

Lund saluted, walked round and took her seat.

Then Brix was back. Something in his hand. An ID card. They'd used her old photo. Lund looked at it: an unsmiling woman with large eyes and long dark hair staring into the camera as if hunting for something that was just out of reach. She hadn't changed much in two years. Not that she'd checked. She still hated the picture.

New title: Vicepolitikommissær. Whatever that meant.

'And you need to carry this.'

Brix handed her a standard-issue police handgun, Glock 9-millimetre compact. The kind Meyer liked so much he always swaggered round with it on his belt, even in the Politigården.

'Strange can show you where the lockers are. The place has changed since you were last here. We're more . . .'

Brix was looking straight into her face.

'More what?' Lund asked.

'More professional,' he said then went to talk to someone else.

'Are we going?' Strange asked.

She couldn't take her eyes off the gun in its black fabric holster. Lund didn't like weapons. They always seemed an admission of defeat.

Strange stood there, arms folded again, that same half-comic, half-bossy look on his face.

'I'm coming, I'm coming,' she said, and stuffed the Glock into her bag alongside the tissues and the packets of gum.

Colonel Torsten Jarnvig sat on the sofa in his private quarters watching the TV news as his daughter ironed and tidied away clothes behind him. The heightened alert was already in place at Ryvangen. The barracks had systems, procedures, a chain of command, from Jarnvig to Søgaard, then to subordinates like Said Bilal.

The army was a world in miniature separated by ranks and established hierarchies among officers and men. Jarnvig had worked inside these boundaries all his adult life. Without them, he knew, nothing functioned.

Thomas Buch, the new Minister of Justice, was on TV, an unlikely-looking politician: overweight, with a straggly beard, wayward brown hair, and a puzzled, ponderous manner.

'Both victims have been stationed abroad by the army,' Buch said to the forest of microphones. 'It's possible their murders were in retaliation for our part in the war against terror.'

The phone rang. An old, familiar voice. General Arild, one of the assistant chiefs of staff from headquarters in Aalborg. A dry, hard man, once Jarnvig's comrade in the field.

'Are you watching the news?' Arild asked.

'Of course.'

'And?'

'We've guards on all entrances and triple shifts in the grounds.'

'They're cowards. They won't dare attack you from the front. Confine men to quarters as much as possible. Try to restrict family movements outside.'

Jarnvig watched his daughter working patiently at the ironing board. She'd spent much of the day in the barracks infirmary dealing with medical supplies for dispatch to the front in Helmand.

On the TV the politician was making promises.

'The police and PET are working with the other intelligence agencies as part of the investigation,' Buch told the cameras. 'That's all I can say at present.'

Louise stopped what she was doing, walked into the room, watched the news next to him.

'It'll be done,' Jarnvig told Arild.

'You've got eight hundred men going out to Afghanistan next week. That's what matters most. I want them ready for combat the moment they land.'

'I understand . . .'

'No distractions,' the general ordered then hung up.

Thomas Buch was trying to leave the pack of reporters. One of them was getting pushy, shouting at him.

'Why's this such a surprise, Buch? Shouldn't the agencies have had warning?'

The fat man smiled. A politician's expression.

'We're looking into all aspects of the matter. Thank you.'

'And the terror package?'

Buch's mask slipped. He was lost for words. And so he turned and walked away.

'What's going on, Dad?' Louise Raben asked.

Jarnvig picked up his phone and a set of keys.

'There's a terrorist alert. Have you heard from the prison?'

She looked shifty.

'We went there. They wouldn't let us see Jens. I don't know why. The probation service turned him down. I don't think he . . .'

'What?'

'I don't think he took it well.' She stood in front of him, didn't move. 'What's going on?'

'They think someone's targeting soldiers. I don't know any more. It's best you stay inside the barracks for now. You belong here. Jonas too.'

'No.' She shook her head. 'I've got to see the lawyer tomorrow. Back at Herstedvester.'

'Why?'

'To file a complaint. Toft said Jens was fit, recovered. There was no reason he shouldn't be released. If I do nothing it's another six months before he can apply again. I don't know if I can . . .'

Her hand went to her dark, untidy hair. He remembered when Louise was young and so attractive. The belle of every officers' ball, glamorous and careful with her appearance. Now her beauty lay hidden under the cares of motherhood, the worry of dealing with an errant husband lost in the prison system, serving an indefinite sentence for a crime no one understood, least of all him.

'If the probation service ruled against Jens it had to be for a reason.'

'Then I want to know it,' she insisted. 'Herstedvester said he could go. Why should the prison department in Copenhagen block him? It's not right.'

Raben was discharged from the army after coming back from a difficult tour in Afghanistan. A few weeks later he seized a civilian in the street, took him to a deserted wood, beat him unconscious. A threat to society, the court said. Not that Louise could ever see that in him.

'Be patient,' Jarnvig said. 'If you have to wait six months we could redecorate the basement, make it liveable. Jonas can have his own bedroom. You can enrol him for the school . . .'

She had a sharp and rebellious look sometimes. One she'd inherited from her mother. Jarnvig knew it only too well, understood when there was no point in arguing.

'You don't care whether Jens gets out or not. You never wanted a common soldier for a son-in-law, did you?'

Jarnvig couldn't find the words. There was a rap on the door. Major Søgaard, briefly catching his eye then smiling at Louise.

The tall blond-haired officer stayed there. This was to be private. Jarnvig walked over, listened as Søgaard whispered in his ear.

'Good God . . .' the colonel whispered. 'Do they know who did it?'

Søgaard shook his head, waited for orders, left when none came.

Torsten Jarnvig looked around his comfortable little house. He served wherever they sent him, had spent time in the Balkans, Iraq and Afghanistan himself. Knew what it was like to lose men. But not here. He never expected the war to come home.

'Dad?' Louise asked, looking concerned. 'What's up?'

'Have you seen Myg Poulsen recently?'

She was back sorting through Jonas's clothes.

'No. Jens did yesterday. He was going to find him a job.'

Jarnvig went back to the dining table, took a seat, looked at the dispatch papers there. Eight hundred men headed for Afghanistan on a six-month tour. And now there'd be a military funeral for one of their own before they left.

'Dad?' she asked again. 'What's up?'

Strapped to the bed in solitary, light on, Raben stared at the ceiling. Then the door opened and Director Toft walked round, tight sweater, tight jeans.

He stifled what he wanted to say.

Sorry if I'm keeping you from your boyfriend.

'How are you, Raben?'

'I'm sorry. It was stupid. I don't know what came over me.'

He was tied down by his wrists and ankles. Could still get his head up. And plead.

'Can I talk to Louise?'

'She came to visit you. Jonas did too. Obviously . . .' Toft smiled. '. . . that wasn't going to be possible.'

Did she enjoy hurting him? Or was this part of the cure? He didn't know. Didn't care. Just wanted to be out of this hell. To be home with his wife and son.

'I told her what happened. I made sure the boy didn't hear.'

Raben kept his head upright until it hurt. The pain seemed right. Something he was owed.

'Are you ready to go back to your cell?'

'Jonas came?'

'He did. He's a lovely little boy.'

'I need to talk to Louise.'

'One thing at a time.'

'What does that mean?'

His voice was too loud and he knew it.

'It means you have to earn things. You have to learn there are consequences to your actions.' She paused. 'You have to go back on your medication.'

'I don't want you doping me up.'

'If you don't do what I ask I can never get you out of here.'

'There's nothing wrong with me!'

That long pause again.

'Do you remember what happened in Afghanistan? What you did when you came back? All the wild stories . . . ?'

They weren't all wild, he thought. *Just things they didn't want to hear.*

'There's . . . nothing . . . wrong . . . with . . . me.'

'You took a stranger hostage. Here, in Copenhagen. Almost killed him.'

That episode was still a blur.

'It was a mistake. I've paid for it.'

'Not until I say so.'

'Please . . .'

'The police want to question you about Allan Myg Poulsen. I think they should wait. You're not fit.'

He let his head fall back on the hard prison bed. Gave up. That's what they wanted.

'Why would they want to talk to me about Myg?'

'Our number's on his mobile phone apparently. He came to visit you this afternoon, didn't he?'

'So what?'

She watched him very closely.

'Poulsen was found murdered this evening. I'm sorry.'

Raben's mind began to race. The way it did when he got angry. Really angry. The red roar.

'What happened?' he asked as calmly as he could.

'I'll tell them to come tomorrow. That's all I know.'

'What . . . ?'

'Tomorrow. You're not fit now.'

She checked her watch, frowned at the time.

Sorry to keep you, he wanted to say.

Lund sat in the front of Strange's unmarked car chewing on a piece of gum. She didn't miss cigarettes any more. That craving was gone anyway. He drove patiently, carefully, taking a call on his earphone, talking quietly to the other end.

The Politigården had translated the leaflets they found next to Poulsen's body. They said, 'Fight for God's cause. Kill those who place others next to God.'

'What does that mean?' Lund asked.

'Something from the Koran apparently.'

'Anything else?'

'They're trying to trace where they were printed.'

She was going through the papers Brix had given her on Dragsholm's military background.

'OK,' Strange said. 'Since we seem to be colleagues now it's time for a proper introduction. My name's Ulrik.'

He took his hand off the wheel, held it out. Long fingers, delicate almost. As if he played the piano, though that seemed unlikely.

'I've worked in the Politigården for just over a year,' Strange said with the kind of smile he might have saved for a job interview. 'I got divorced not long before that, which is OK, all friendly. I've got two great kids and they're cool with it. As cool as you can expect anyway.'

'I don't really need—'

'It's hard for them when you break up. But best in the long run, for everyone I think. I like football and opera, up to a point. When I was at school I loved camping and birdwatching and orienteering. All that outdoor stuff. But now . . . the time . . . the time . . .'

'Sarah,' Lund said and shook his hand very quickly. 'Take the next left turn. Poulsen was decorated.'

'How about you?'

'I was never decorated.'

'I meant—'

'I know what you meant. There's nothing to tell.'

He looked at her, frowned.

'Everyone's got something to tell.'

'You've been to Gedser. You've heard the office gossip.'

'I don't listen to that shit.'

'And I don't talk about it either.'

He went quiet.

'We can chat about everything else,' Lund suggested. 'Football. Opera. Camping.' She laughed. 'Birdwatching.'

'Now you're taking the piss.'

'No I'm not. Anything else. It's not that I don't want to talk to you.'

'So long as it's about the case.'

He went quiet for a moment. She'd offended him and wasn't sure how.

'Next left?'

A sign appeared: Ryvangen Barracks. Lots of soldiers at the gate. They had rifles.

'I'll go with that,' Lund said.

Ryvangen had been in the hands of the military for more than a century, a mixed collection of buildings, barracks, officers' training grounds. It took ten minutes to get through security. Lund used the time to think about Mindelunden, less than a kilometre away.

A busy railway line separated the barracks from the memorial ground, but it wasn't impassable. Not to a soldier. A childhood memory told her the two were once linked, which was why the Nazis who occupied these buildings used the former practice ranges to execute their prisoners.

Coincidence. Probably.

Once inside she felt she'd entered a different, foreign world. Groups of armed troops ran in formation through the rain. Camouflaged lorries and all-terrain military Mercedes G-Wagens flitted everywhere. The buildings were mostly a bastardized version of Brick Gothic, dun-red, four-square, angular, imposing.

She was unsure of their jurisdiction here. The army had their own police force. To add to the confusion Lund didn't know precisely where the Politigården's writ ended and PET's began. But two murders had been committed, both in the city, not behind these high wires.

Homicide was her territory again. Anyone who trespassed on it had best beware.

They met in the office of Colonel Jarnvig, camp commander from what she could gather, early fifties, a tall, ascetic man, not happy they were there. With him was Major Christian Søgaard, a cocky-looking blond officer with a grizzled hunter's beard. Both wore camouflage uniforms, a few medals, epaulettes. They shook hands but it was Strange they looked at mainly. This was a man's world.

They sat opposite Jarnvig at his desk while Søgaard stood stiff behind as if to attention.

'I know what this is about,' the colonel said. 'Myg Poulsen. I got a call.'

'Who from?' Lund asked straight out.

'Aalborg,' he said, as if that answered everything.

'Who in Aalborg?' she persisted.

'Aalborg's army headquarters,' Strange explained. 'Brix was going to tell them. Procedure . . .'

'Procedure,' Jarnvig repeated.

'What was Poulsen's connection to the barracks?' Strange asked.

'Lance Corporal Poulsen did service here for many years,' Jarnvig replied. 'He was a good man. A brave and dependable soldier. We're deeply distressed by this news.'

'How long was he in?'

'He came in as a conscript then signed up,' Søgaard said. 'Saw service abroad. The usual places.'

'When did you last see him?'

'Yesterday morning at roll call. He joined up again a month ago. He was due to go out to Helmand with the new team in a week.'

'Isn't that unusual?' Lund asked. 'To leave the army then come back?'

'Not really,' Søgaard answered with a shrug. 'Some of them moan like hell when they're in. Then when they're out they realize it wasn't so bad after all.'

'How was he killed?' Jarnvig asked.

Strange was about to speak when Lund said, 'We can't go into the details.'

'Would I be right to assume his death is connected to the terrorism alert? Is he one of the two victims they're talking about?'

Jarnvig wasn't going to let this go.

'Possibly,' she said. 'Did anyone threaten him? Is that why he signed up again?'

'He signed up because he wanted to come back,' Søgaard said with a bored sigh. 'He didn't mention any problems.'

'Have you received any general threats?' Strange asked.

A grim laugh from Jarnvig.

'We get it all the time. Kids. Lunatics. Troublemakers. Phone calls and emails every day. But nothing from the Muslim League.'

Lund kept quiet. So did Strange.

'It was on the TV news,' the colonel added. 'I heard the name there.'

'We'll need a printout of all the threats you've received,' Strange said.

'And Allan Myg Poulsen's personnel file,' Lund added. 'Anything that relates to his period of service.'

Jarnvig thought about this.

'Søgaard will give you what we're able to release.'

'I want it all,' Lund said, and tapped her finger lightly on the desk.

Jarnvig shook his head.

'He was a soldier. Anything that doesn't touch on national security you can have. That's as far as I can go . . .'

'This is a murder inquiry. We're police.'

'And this is an army barracks. I've eight hundred men about to go to Afghanistan and risk their lives for their country. Nothing leaves this place if it puts them in jeopardy for a single second. What I can give you Søgaard will provide. Now . . .'

He got up from the desk, held out his hand. Strange stood up straight away, took it.

Another former soldier, Lund guessed. Denmark had conscription. It was hardly surprising. That deference to your superiors never really disappeared.

'If you don't mind I'd like to inform my staff personally,' Jarnvig said.

Lund took out a picture of Dragsholm, smiling, recent.

'Do you know this woman?' she asked.

'No,' Jarnvig said without the least hesitation.

'Her name's Anne Dragsholm. A military legal adviser. Perhaps she did some work inside Ryvangen.'

He passed the photo to Søgaard who looked at it and shook his head.

'We'd like to talk to someone who knew Myg Poulsen well,' Strange said.

Jarnvig nodded.

'I understand. His company commander can show you around.'

He passed over a card, told Søgaard to do the same.

'It's important the police understand our position. This case poses uncertainty and worry. It's the last thing my men need before a tour of duty. All communication on this matter must go through me or Major Søgaard. I want that clear now.'

'Sure,' Strange agreed straight off.

Lund picked up the photo of Anne Dragsholm and said nothing.

Poulsen's company commander was Lieutenant Said Bilal, a young, gloomy-looking officer, Danish-raised from his accent, but with immigrant parents judging by his looks.

Bilal took them to the barracks room Poulsen shared with seven other men when he was on duty. Bunk beds, a few personal belongings. It was almost as bare and characterless as the veterans' club where he died.

'Most of the men are at home now,' Bilal said as he led them in.

He pointed out a single top bed near the window.

'This was his bunk.'

Then a tall metal locker.

'This was his locker.'

Lund opened the door. Clothes, shoes. Underwear. Photographs of women in bikinis.

'Did you know him well?' Strange asked.

'Not very.' Bilal stood by the bed, erect, moody. He had very dark hair and the face of a bored teenager. 'Nobody did. He didn't mix much.'

'Kept the veterans' club going, didn't he?' Lund asked.

Bilal nodded.

'He liked to do things for people who'd left, I guess.'

'When did you last see him?' Strange went on.

She went back to the cupboard, sorting through the things there.

'Roll call yesterday morning.'

'Later?'

'No. They had the rest of the day off.'

Strange kept throwing questions at him.

'When did he volunteer to go back to Helmand?'

Bilal thought for a moment then said, 'Last week. Not long after he signed up again.'

'Was it a sudden decision?'

'I don't think so.'

Strange's phone rang. Lund went through a sheet of appointments: training, medical, briefings.

A name had been scribbled in for that afternoon.

'Who's Raben?' she asked.

Bilal looked round the room, out of the window, didn't meet her eyes when he said, 'I don't know.'

'It's not someone in the camp?'

'I said. I don't know.'

Strange finished the call.

'They've found the printers. The leaflets were delivered to a bookshop in Nørrebro. We've got a name. Aisha Oman.'

'Anything else?' Bilal asked.

'No,' Strange said.

Lund closed the locker door.

'Brix says we should take a look,' Strange told her.

'Fine,' she said, then stood in front of Said Bilal, smiled at him, said very politely, 'Thanks for everything.'

It was just past ten in Buch's office. Karina had sent out for some Japanese food. Two dirty plates and a couple of sets of discarded chopsticks littered the table alongside the rising piles of documents. Buch had called home, confirmed a security detail had been placed around his family. Not that his wife liked that at all.

And the anti-terror package – the very measure he wanted dealt with – was back in limbo. Buch's first hope was that the news of the attacks would bring Krabbe and Agger back in line with the government's position. He was beginning to realize how naive some of his firmly held backbench opinions about national unity seemed once they were viewed from the perspective of government.

'They're both saying they back the general position . . .' Karina began after coming off the second of two long phone calls.

'To hell with the general position. Will they vote for the package?'

'They want to be informed about the case, Minister.'

'Oh for pity's sake, call me "Thomas".'

'I can't,' she pleaded. 'It's not right. And you shouldn't call Plough "Carsten" either. It makes him uncomfortable.'

Buch finished the last piece of sushi.

'Do you want me to order some more?'

'No. That would be greedy. Why is everyone around here so uptight?'

That brought a mischievous glint of amusement to her eyes.

'This is the civil service. It's the way things are.'

'Call me Thomas when no one can hear.'

'No. Sorry.'

'Ridiculous. So they won't make a statement of agreement tonight?'

'Not until they've heard from you.'

He balled up his napkin, threw it very carefully at the bin in the corner, was pleased to hit it dead centre first time.

'Plough was right,' Buch said. 'They're just waiting for an excuse to play politics. Krabbe will demand something new. Agger too, or else she'll try to damn us somehow. I'll try again. See if I can dredge up a sense of decency in them.'

That made her laugh, which pleased him. She seemed too young to be working such long hours.

He called Krabbe.

'You wanted to be informed.'

'How bad is it?'

'At the moment I wouldn't like to say. It's important we show a united front . . .'

The trill of another phone. He looked up. Karina was holding her mobile.

'A moment,' Buch said and put Krabbe on hold.

'The police have found out who set up the website for the video,' she said.

He nodded, went back to Krabbe.

'Let's meet tomorrow morning and I'll brief you as much as I can.'

'Why not now?'

'Because I'm busy. Wouldn't you expect me to be?'

'We're not going to get on, are we?'

That offended Thomas Buch.

'I hope so. For everyone's sake. How about eight? I'd like Agger to be there.'

'Eight,' Krabbe said and the line went dead.

A terraced building across the Lakes, close to the Dronning Louises bridge. The usual pizza and kebab shop on the ground floor. Flats above and behind, probably fifteen or more in the whole block.

They worked their way door by door up to the second floor.

'Where's the bookshop?' Lund grumbled.

A woman came up the stairs. She was young, Middle Eastern-looking with a purple hijab.

'Hi,' Lund said, taking out her ID. 'We're looking for Aisha Oman.'

A young man behind her was carrying a baby. Husband, Lund guessed.

'You've come to the wrong place,' he said. 'We live here.'

'She owns a bookshop.'

The man thought for a moment, then said, 'Try the ground floor. Behind the pizza place. Someone keeps books there I think.'

'Who?' Strange demanded.

'Kodmani. I haven't seen him today.'

'What about his wife?' Lund asked.

'She died a couple of years ago.'

Lund looked at Strange.

'I thought you tried that door.'

'I did. No one answered.'

She walked downstairs, found the bell push, pressed it once, waited for a couple of seconds, then kept her thumb on it, listening to the weedy trilling from behind the door.

Nothing.

They stood back. Lights on inside. Music coming from somewhere.

Lund looked at Strange. Raised a dark eyebrow. Waited.

Watched him kick down the door, go in yelling, handgun raised.

This, at least, he seemed good at.

The place was brightly lit, the walls covered in exotic tapestries, repeating oriental patterns, beaded curtains dividing off the space between dining room and a small tidy kitchen.

Footsteps. The gun twitched. A tall, heavily built man with a thick black beard came out from behind the beads, started yelling at them, a foreign tongue first, then Danish.

'My children are asleep. What is this? What do you want?'

A young boy, no more than eight or nine, stood behind him, clinging to his father's white robe. A girl, a year or two older, was further back, glaring at them, her pretty face full of hate.

Strange told the man to hold out his arms, patted him down.

'Are you Kodmani?'

'What do you want?'

78

He was still playing with a prayer bead as the handgun dodged around him.

'Don't be afraid,' Lund said to the two kids. 'Go back to bed. There's nothing to worry about.'

She looked at the man.

'Kodmani? Help us here. We've no business with your children.'

He calmed down a little at that, told them to go back to their rooms.

These big old houses, she thought, looking around. They seemed to run on and on for ever.

'Three months ago you ordered some leaflets in your wife's name,' Lund said once the kids were out of earshot. 'Why did you do that?'

He puffed out his chest. Like the men in Ryvangen, Kodmani didn't think women should be asking questions either.

'Do you have a search warrant? I know my rights—'

'Where were you earlier today?'

'I want to see a lawyer.'

'Why?' Strange asked. 'What did you do wrong?'

'I know my rights.' He was wagging his right finger at them, the way men did in the suicide videos she'd seen. 'I know you can't just break in here . . .'

Lund looked at the oriental carpet and the way the wiring ran around it. Some of the cabling was amateurish, tacked along the skirting board.

Then it went down. Somewhere close to where Kodmani had quite deliberately stood.

'Move away,' she ordered.

He didn't shift.

'Move!' Strange yelled.

Kodmani got off the carpet. Lund dragged it aside.

A full-length trapdoor replaced the flooring all the way into a disused chimney breast. She took hold of the handle, lifted it.

'That's my storeroom!' Kodmani shouted, getting angry, scared. 'You can't go down there. I want to see a search warrant.'

Lund found a light switch, walked down a set of modern metal stairs.

It was warm and fusty and smelled of damp. One big bare room with pipes and discarded tools. But there was a faint light coming from behind another set of beaded curtains.

She walked through.

A desk. A fish tank. An angled lamp. Boxes and boxes of freshly printed leaflets and posters. Piles and piles of a book with the title *Al Jihad* in English.

Rack upon rack of computer equipment, boxes, wires, what looked like a discarded satellite dish, and one large monitor.

She sat down in front of it, found she could place the image of the screensaver. Mecca during the Haj. Thousands and thousands of pilgrims milling around the black and gold cube of the Kaaba.

Lund edged the mouse on the desk, brought the screen to life.

A single window, a browser. Anne Dragsholm on the screen, reading out the last words she'd ever utter.

Back upstairs, she nodded at Strange.

'Do you have any relatives who can look after your kids?' Lund asked Kodmani.

'Why?'

The man in the long white robe didn't look so confident any more.

'Because I don't think you'll be seeing them for a while.'

Tuesday 15th November

7.43 a.m. The sound of morning traffic. Stale city air. It took a moment to realize where she was. Then Sarah Lund walked into her mother's tiny bathroom and got ready for the day.

Mark was gone, along with every shred of wrapping paper. He was a teenager who tidied up now. How things had changed.

Vibeke was still in bed. Strange called as Lund got some coffee and toast.

'His name's Abdel Hussein Kodmani. A widower. Moroccan.'

She went into the spare room. There were still some clothes from two years before. Shirts, jeans and the Faroese sweaters she'd grown to like. They hadn't followed her to Gedser. Looking at them now she couldn't remember why.

Strange was going through tedious details.

'Kodmani's lived in Copenhagen for sixteen years. He was running the website that hosted the video.'

I guessed that, she almost said.

The sweaters once meant something. Promised a life she'd never have, out in the rural wilds of Sweden with Bengt Rosling, pretending to be someone she wasn't.

Lund picked up the heavy, thick-knit jumper. It didn't feel quite right yet. Too many associated memories. So she got a plain red one instead and climbed into a pair of clean jeans. They still fitted. Gedser hadn't changed her really.

'The police say Kodmani has been working under several aliases.'

'Does he have a record?'

'Not a thing. The school says he's a good father. Very picky about the details of his kids' education. Most of the Muslims there think he's a bit nuts.'

Lund didn't say anything.

'What are you thinking?' Strange asked.

'Who says I'm thinking anything?'

'I can tell.'

'I was just thinking . . . if you're running a terrorist cell, do you pick someone to front it who's nuts?'

'Yeah, well,' Strange said a little testily. 'That was all the good news. Here's the bad. PET want a meeting. They're pissed off with us. They'd had their sights on Kodmani for a while. We picked him up while they were waiting for some big fish to arrive.'

'How the hell were we supposed to know that?'

'Ask them. We've got to be there at nine.'

Then he was gone.

Vibeke came in. She didn't look as welcoming as the day before.

'You're not going to stay in a hotel tonight, are you?'

'I don't want to disturb you. I don't know what kind of hours . . .'

'You won't bother me.'

It was a bright, pale day. Vibeke's street was by the railway line running to the Ryvangen Barracks, then Mindelunden across the tracks. In a way this case felt local.

'You can have the key. I'm at Bjørn's place most of the time anyway. We can talk about Saturday later.'

Lund packed her bag, got her jacket.

'What about Saturday?'

Vibeke folded her arms.

'I'm getting married, remember?'

'Of course I remember!' Lund lied. 'I meant . . . what about Saturday, here?'

'Bjørn's relatives will be staying over. We've more than thirty people. Let me get you a spare key.'

She went to the table and found one on a short ribbon.

'You will have time for dinner with us, won't you? I want you to get to know Bjørn. He's lovely. So kind and funny.'

Lund took out a plain elastic band, pulled her hair roughly into place behind her neck, didn't bother looking for a mirror.

'I'd like to get to know him. Maybe not now. I'm going to be busy. I want to see Mark too.'

'You surely have time to eat!' Vibeke took a deep breath. 'Bjørn has a very pleasant friend. Much younger than him. It would be nice if you could meet him.'

Lund's fingers fumbled with the elastic band. She kept quiet.

'Well,' Vibeke said. 'I suppose it doesn't have to be right now.'

There was a sound outside. Lund looked. Strange's black police car was up on the pavement by the bench seats near the trees. He was out by the driver's door, honking the horn. A touch of Meyer there, she thought. About time.

'I've got to dash,' she said. 'I'd love to have dinner with Bjørn and you. Sometime.'

Vibeke was at the window.

'Who's that man?'

'The key, Mum.'

'Oh.'

She handed it over.

'Sarah. I heard the news. I know I can't ask you . . .'

'You can't.'

'I said! I know!'

Lund was bad at these moments. She hadn't appreciated quite how awkward they were for her mother too.

'Don't worry,' she said and briefly touched Vibeke's arm.

Brix sat silent throughout the meeting with Erik König in an interview room at the Politigården. The grey man from the security agency was clearly determined to make them feel as small and as guilty as possible.

'You've jeopardized an investigation we've had running for months,' the PET man declared, tapping the table with his trimmed fingernails.

'We were faced with a situation. We dealt with it,' Strange replied.

'This has done us incalculable damage.'

'If you'd been watching him for months why didn't you know something was about to happen?' Lund asked.

No answer.

'Or did you?' she persisted.

'You know I'm not going to discuss matters of national security. You stick to your job. Let us do ours. And don't get in our way.'

Strange was getting mad.

'Don't try and pin the blame on us. We've got two corpses in the morgue. What are we supposed to do? Twiddle our thumbs until you decide to say something?'

'This is an unfortunate outcome,' Brix intervened. 'Let's accept that and work out where we go from here. At least we've got our man.'

König snorted.

'No you haven't. Kodmani's got an alibi, and since we've been watching him we know it's watertight. Even if he didn't . . . he's a troublemaker. He doesn't have the guts to kill someone. They're pulling his strings. He's just an idiot they used . . .'

'He must know something,' Lund said. 'Do you have other leads?'

König took off his rimless glasses, played with them.

'We've inquiries to make. I want you to focus on Kodmani and any followers he might have.' Glasses back in place. Cold grey eyes on Brix. 'Is that agreed?'

Beyond the window, shapes moving. Guards from the adjoining prison, walking Kodmani to a room in the Politigården.

'Good,' König said without waiting for an answer. 'Let's see how he interviews.' He cast a glance at Strange then Lund. 'And you.'

Breakfast in Thomas Buch's office. Birgitte Agger and Erling Krabbe around the table with coffee and pastries. Buch pacing the room, going through the morning coverage. Plough making notes.

'What's happened with the man they arrested?' Agger asked.

'It takes time,' Buch replied. 'They'll interview him this morning. Let's leave the police and the security services to do their work, which I will follow. And concentrate on ours.'

He sat down, showed them a front page: Anne Dragsholm's bloody face from the video.

'We need to announce a united front about the anti-terror package. The public expects a response. So do the vicious bastards behind this. The answer for both is the same. We're resolute. We shall not be moved. Denmark is an open, democratic nation. We'll guard our borders, redouble our security. But we will not change who we are.'

Agger scowled.

'Save your speeches for the press. Why were we taken by surprise in the first place?'

'The police believed the Dragsholm woman was murdered by her husband,' Carsten Plough broke in. 'We had no way of knowing there was a connection to terrorism.'

She was unconvinced.

'You have PET. That's why they're here. Anything else you need to tell us?'

'No,' Buch said. 'We need to stick together. If we let them divide us—'

'I said this would happen!' Krabbe cried. 'You've allowed these people to come here, to behave as they wish. To poison our way of life . . .'

Buch took a deep breath.

'We're here to discuss a piece of legislation. Not a criminal case under investigation.'

'Two people are dead, Buch. A fundamentalist is in custody. Save your breath. We won't vote for this package as it stands. It's cowardly and insufficient. These people are murdering innocent Danes.'

Buch fought to keep his temper.

'I'm the Minister of Justice and I don't know who these people, as you call them, are. Why are you so sure?'

'Who else could it be? And when he's found guilty—'

'May I make a suggestion?' Plough interrupted. 'We're discussing these matters in ignorance. Let's give the police a chance and meet again in the evening. Then, hopefully, we'll know more.'

'Play for time all you like,' Krabbe said then shuffled his papers and tucked them into a briefcase. 'The facts speak for themselves.'

Birgitte Agger waved at him with her fingers as Krabbe left.

'That silly little man thinks he's got you on the ropes, Buch. The trouble is he's right.'

'We should be above politics on this. Why . . .'

She was laughing, at him.

'What is it?'

'Nothing's ever above politics.' She finished her coffee, got up from the table. 'If you alter one word of the present agreement you can count us out.'

'That won't happen,' Buch insisted. 'I'll call you later to confirm.'

'One word . . .'

And then she left.

Silence for a while and then Plough said wearily, 'You're going to have to rewrite the package and give Krabbe what he wants.'

Buch blinked.

'What?'

'He's under pressure from his own party to win something. Agger's got no reason to give you a break. So she'll dump you. Even if it's over a comma. She's planning it already . . .'

Buch bristled.

'You know that, do you? For a fact?'

'No,' Plough said patiently. 'But I'm right. You'll see.'

Lund looked at the Moroccan man across the table. He now wore a blue cotton prison suit. His beard was freshly combed. He seemed calm, earnest. Resigned even. A man in the hands of enemies, in his own eyes anyway. He had someone from one of the left-wing legal practices by his side.

'My client will cooperate,' the lawyer said.

'He can tell us what he knows about the Muslim League then,' Strange began.

'I only heard about it yesterday,' Kodmani answered. 'When all you people started shouting at me.'

'Their video was on your website,' Lund pointed out.

The lawyer broke in, reading a statement on Kodmani's behalf.

'My client sells and publishes books to spread the word of the Koran. Under the law he enjoys both freedom of religion and speech—'

'Won't get that back home, will you?' Strange cut in.

Behind the one-way glass Brix and König were watching. Lund wondered how they'd take that.

'My client offers the website as a literary platform and an international forum. He's not responsible, legally or in any practical way, for everything that's uploaded there. He knew nothing of the video and has never incited anyone to commit a terrorist act.'

Kodmani's eyes were closed. He appeared to be praying.

'Nice try,' Strange said. 'We've been all through that little office you hid downstairs. We know what you were up to. The videos. The leaflets. Incitement—'

'There's nothing there that's illegal,' the Moroccan insisted.

'We found your leaflets at the second murder. Your website was used for a video of a woman about to be killed in cold blood.'

'I didn't know . . .'

'That's not good enough,' Strange said, voice rising. 'You've got an alibi. We don't think you murdered anyone. But you're involved. Either you talk now or . . .'

'It looks bad,' Lund added, staring straight at him across the table. 'You can see that. It looks very bad.'

The man was kneading his hands. The lawyer leaned over and whispered in his ear.

'We'll have to foster your kids if you go to jail,' she went on. 'They'll try to find a Muslim family. No guarantees. Maybe—'

'I didn't know!' Kodmani screamed. 'OK?'

Lund folded her arms, kept watching.

'He got to me through the website. He emailed me.'

'Who did?'

The man in the blue suit looked ashamed to be talking to them.

'He called himself Faith Fellow. He seemed . . . a good man. Someone who liked what I was doing.'

'A fan?' Strange asked.

'Maybe. He said he had a religious video he was making. He wanted to upload it somewhere everyone would see it. I told him OK. Gave him a password. Suddenly . . . it turned up there last night. I didn't know what it was.'

'We need the emails he sent you,' Lund said.

Kodmani laughed.

'I don't keep emails. They all get deleted. Properly. For good. Do you think I'm stupid?'

Strange pushed his notepad to one side.

'Tell me this isn't a fairy story. Who do you think this Faith Fellow is?'

'I don't know! If criminals get hold of my leaflets . . . that's not my fault. You can pick them up at public libraries. Like I told you. They're legal.'

The lawyer was looking smug.

'I don't expect you to like me,' the Moroccan said. 'We're on different sides. But . . .'

The wagging finger came out and it pointed at her.

'I didn't break your laws. You've no cause to keep me here.'

The lawyer looked at his watch and started to pack his things.

'We're counting,' he said. 'Hold my client one second more than you're entitled and we're in court.'

Lennart Brix wasn't interested in the Moroccan's faceless email correspondent Faith Fellow.

He passed Strange a list of Kodmani's religious contacts and customers for his books along with the addresses of those who'd registered with the website.

'I want them all questioned. We found blood on some barbed wire on the way out of the veterans' club. No match with anything on the DNA records so far.'

'What was he looking for in the club?' Lund asked. 'Why did he go back?'

'I don't think that's much of a priority. Is it?'

'But why—?'

'Not a priority,' Brix repeated and walked off.

She got her bag.

'I'll be gone for an hour or so,' she told Strange.

'Why?'

'Myg Poulsen visited an army buddy yesterday. He's called Raben. He's in Herstedvester. I put in a request for an interview but the medical staff wouldn't allow it.'

Strange watched her sifting busily through the papers on her desk.

'Brix told us to focus on Kodmani.'

'Why would he upload a video like that onto his own website? He's a fanatic. Not an idiot.'

'So you want to talk to Poulsen's army buddy?'

'Just a thought.' She smiled. That seemed to work on Strange. 'I've got something to do on the way. It might be more than an hour. More like two. Or . . .'

The pen she liked had strayed onto Strange's half of the desk. She reached out, caught the edge of a cold cup of coffee, sent it tumbling, spilling brown liquid all over his papers.

Ulrik Strange blinked, said nothing.

'I'll call,' Lund said, then grabbed the pen and hurried out.

Meyer still lived in the same place on the edge of Nørrebro. Lund parked the car in the road, looked up the drive. Saw the garage. Doors open. No motorbike there any more. But the DJ turntables were visible at the back, now gathering dust.

The rain was holding off for the moment. He was in the yard playing with two of his three girls. Beautiful kids with blonde hair, taller than she remembered, running round and round Meyer's shiny powered wheelchair.

There was a baseball net on the wall. Full size. Not like the little one he had in the office they'd shared.

He was grabbing the ball from them, bouncing it on the hard, uneven ground, popping it up towards the net. His arms looked more muscular than before. She didn't want to think about that too much.

Lund stayed behind the wheel and watched.

He hit the net twice, shaking with laughter. Then let the girls get the better of him, prodded, cajoled, persuaded them until, finally, they got three scores.

Her heart felt as if it might tear in two as she watched him hunch over, bury his pop-eared head in his arms and pretend to sob, shoulders heaving, a faint, pathetic cry reaching her ears.

She'd seen this for real, in hospital when she tried to drag him back into the Birk Larsen case one last time, and brought from Meyer an animal howl that haunted her even now. Lund couldn't believe she'd acted like that. Meyer had screamed something about how she couldn't connect with anything, anyone close.

Mark, the young Mark, not the fast-growing, calm, intelligent teenager who now lived with his father, had said it too.

Mum, you're only interested in dead people. Not me.

That wasn't true. It couldn't be. It was just . . .

Meyer had stopped playing with his girls. He was looking out from the yard, down the drive. Towards the road. He'd been a good cop, better than he knew. She'd taught him how to look.

And now there was a solitary car parked outside his house in this quiet corner of Nørrebro. Of course he'd see.

See her.

She thought of what Brix said. *Priorities.*

Wondered what she'd say to Jan Meyer after all this time. The things she should have told him in hospital. The words that had run through her head during so many sleepless nights in her lonely bed in Gedser.

I'm sorry I failed you. I wish to God I could make you walk again. Help you be whole. The good, funny, intelligent man you were.

One other refrain that kept going round and round.

For God's sake, Meyer, if I could take your place I would . . .

She looked up the drive, wondered if he realized who she was.

The kids were getting restless. One of them stole the ball from him, yelled something, started playing again. In an instant Jan Meyer was back where he wanted to be, inside their game, their world.

Lund had the courage to walk that short distance up the drive. She didn't doubt that. But she didn't have the right.

A young girl's happy squeal. Meyer's rough, joking voice came to her through the window.

Another time, she thought and drove away.

The red and white Danish flag was at half-mast over the main barracks building in Ryvangen. Louise Raben placed two white lilies alongside the bouquets at the foot of the pole and wondered what to do, who to call.

That morning she'd made an effort. Tidied her hair the way she used to when she was first married. Put on a smart navy wool coat over her white nurse's uniform. It was important not to let go. Even if there was no one there to see.

When she walked away from the flagpole she found Christian Søgaard staring at her from the other side of the road. Khaki uniform, blond hair, beard carefully trimmed. A handsome man. If he'd turned up at Ryvangen earlier her father would have pushed her in Søgaard's direction. She didn't doubt that. Didn't mind the idea too much either. It was too late, but . . .

He was tall and strong and persistent. An officer born and bred, from an upper-class family with a long military tradition. Not a working-class boy like Jens from a grim Copenhagen suburb.

She walked over. He smiled.

'Did the police find anything?'

'Not that we know of,' Søgaard said. 'Were you and Myg friends?'

'He served with Jens. They were.'

She shrugged.

'I'm just an army wife. I don't get to share in those relationships.'

'It's best sometimes.'

'Because we're not up to it?'

'No. Because you're not there when . . . things happen. It's hard to explain.'

'Jens can't even remember what happened. Even harder for him.'

Søgaard nodded. A wry smile. A man, not an officer. Or that was what she was supposed to think.

'They come back sick sometimes. Delusional even. Sometimes you see things and . . . I don't know.' He took off his black beret, ran his fingers through his perfect hair. 'Maybe it's best you tell yourself they're not real.'

Major Christian Søgaard rarely had this problem she suspected. He looked like a man in control.

'Everyone's in shock,' he added. 'I hope the police can sort it out quickly. We really don't need this. I'm sorry to hear they turned down your husband again.'

She stared at the cold ground.

'Yes. Well . . .'

'Your father says you're redecorating the basement. You're going to stay on for a while.'

'For a while. I left a list of vaccinations in the infirmary. If you could . . .'

'Sure, sure, sure.' He looked as if he was one step ahead of her already. Usually did. 'If you want some help with the decorating. It's kind of . . .' He hesitated. 'A hobby. Yes. A hobby.'

Christian Søgaard was stumbling for once. She liked that.

'What's a hobby?'

'Painting. Fixing things up.'

Louise Raben put her hands on her hips, raised an eyebrow.

'It's been a while,' Søgaard added. 'But if you tell me what you want. I've got some . . .'

He gestured with his arms.

'Some brushes?' she suggested.

'Brushes. That's it.'

It was a stupid joke and it made her laugh. Not much else had recently.

'I'll bear that in mind,' she said and took out her car keys.

'Going somewhere?'

'To see Jens. If they'll let me.'

But Director Toft wouldn't countenance it.

'I can't,' she said sitting primly in her antiseptic office in the medical wing at Herstedvester. 'He was very difficult last night. The rage. The delusions . . .'

When he came back from Afghanistan he was raving about nightmares, about monsters, things he thought real that couldn't be. Now, Toft said, that had changed into an obsession that he was being kept in jail for reasons no one would tell him.

'It's very simple,' she explained. 'If he does what we ask. Takes his medicine. Learns to control his temper and his fantasies, then . . .'

'He's been fine for months. You said so yourself. You told us he was ready for release . . .'

'The Prison Service makes the final decision. Not us.'

'Why's this happened? When he was making such good progress?'

Another time she might have cried at a conversation like this. Not now. There was a distance between the two of them, one that had grown slyly, like a tumour, over two years. Louise could look at Jens the way she looked at one of her own patients in the Ryvangen infirmary: dispassionately. And this she hated.

'I don't know,' Toft said. 'Let's hope it's not a total relapse. He has to learn to cooperate. I felt he was improving . . .'

Director Toft was getting bored. Her day ran on precise appointments. Judging by the way she kept looking at her diary another was on the way.

'Your husband was very badly wounded in Afghanistan. The physical hurt's ended. But the mental . . . He doesn't remember what happened to him. Let's not forget he took a complete stranger hostage thinking he was an army officer from Helmand. When in fact he was . . .'

A librarian from Vesterbro. How many times did they have to say that?

'He can't differentiate between what's real and what's not. We can't release him safely until we're sure he's over that. Let's see how things stand in a week.'

'A week? We've got a meeting with our lawyers. I have to make decisions about school. Where we're going to live.'

Toft leaned back in her chair, almost yawned.

'Your husband needs rest. He can't deal with that now.'

Louise Raben was ready to scream.

'Punish him if you like! But why punish me? Why hurt his son?'

'We're trying to help. He needs to understand that. So do you.'

'All Jens needs is his family.'

There was no point in begging. Or threatening. Nothing would move these people. Nothing . . .

'I'll see what I can do,' Toft said, checking her watch. 'But he must cooperate. Without that . . .'

Lund went through security at Herstedvester. A woman was leaving as she came in. Someone she'd seen before. Pretty, pale face, worried. In pain.

The barracks, Lund thought. She was there. And if she was visiting Herstedvester . . .

'That's Raben's wife,' Director Toft said, noticing Lund's interest. 'I just told her she couldn't see him. Now I'm supposed to let you in there.'

'I won't tell,' Lund promised.

She never took an instant dislike to anyone. But if she did this slender, glacially elegant woman would do.

'It's a bad time to question him. We had trouble last night. Can't it wait?'

Lund had visited Herstedvester a few times in the past. It was the principal penal psychiatric institution in the country and housed some of Denmark's most dangerous criminals. Two separate buildings: one for medical staff, one a high-security jail. Toft took her over to the prison, walked her down long yellow corridors, past iron doors, a guard with them all the time.

'I won't be long. Why's he here?' Lund asked as she waited for another heavy security gate to be unlocked.

'Not long after he got back from his last tour in Afghanistan he abducted someone in the street. He said he thought the man was a former officer. Someone Raben thought . . .'

'Thought what?'

'I don't have the exact details. The man had never even been in the army. Raben seized him, took him to some woods, tied him to a tree. Beat him to a pulp trying to make him confess to something . . . I don't know.'

Another long corridor, another door.

'The court decided an indefinite term here was the best sentence. He'd been discharged from the army for unacceptable behaviour. He was delusional . . .'

Toft looked concerned for a moment.

'We send them out there and expect them to do whatever's needed. But when they come back we don't really give a damn, do we? I want this man better. He's got a nice wife. A child. They need him and he needs them. I thought . . .'

'Thought what?'

Toft stared at her. There was doubt in the woman's face, and Lund guessed that was unusual.

'I thought we were there. I recommended him for release last week. But the Prison Service turned him down.'

'Why?' Lund asked.

'I don't know yet. It's their call. All I have to deal with is his mental state. They have broader considerations. And now . . .' She folded her slender arms. 'Now we're back where we began.'

They stopped outside a cell. The guard opened the small metal shutter on the door. Lund peered through. He was there waiting for her. Thin, alert face, searching blue eyes, dark stubbly beard. An unremarkable man. One who'd disappear easily in a crowd.

'Careful with your questions,' Toft told her. 'We'll have a guard with us. If Raben starts getting upset I'm bringing it to an end.'

The room was cold and tiny with a single opaque window. Raben stood by it, looking at the light outside as if he craved to see the grey sky for himself.

'Myg wanted to help me,' he said. 'He had a job. Carpenter. I could do it. I could get out of this hole.'

He came and sat down at the table.

'Was he nervous? Did he seem afraid of something?'

'Afraid? Myg wasn't easily scared. He served with me three, four times. No. He wasn't afraid.'

Lund waited.

'He seemed a bit uneasy. Maybe he was in trouble. We were men, not officers. Sometimes we did things they didn't like.'

'Such as what?'

'Just little things. Showing . . .' He said the words very carefully. '. . . insufficient respect.'

'Just that?'

'I don't know if he was in trouble or not. I shouldn't have said that. What happened?'

Toft was staring at her.

Lund said, 'Someone cut him with a fake dog tag. Then strung him up by his legs, head down.'

Raben's eyes widened.

'Does that ring a bell?' she asked.

It took a while but eventually he shook his head and said, 'No.'

Lund looked at her notepad.

'He hadn't served abroad for two years. The last tour was the one where you were wounded. A month ago he re-enlists. A week ago he volunteers for Afghanistan. Why did he suddenly want to go now?'

'He said he wasn't happy here. I think he was bored. Myg did a lot of work for the veterans' club. He was a good man. But . . .' Raben's face broke into a brief smile. 'Who wants to spend their time trying to help wrecks like me? He was a soldier. I guess he wanted to feel the buzz again.'

'All the same . . .'

'I really don't have anything else to tell you. I'd like some peace now.'

'This was good, Raben,' Toft said, getting to her feet. 'Thank you.'

'I need you to look at this.' Lund picked up her bag and took out the photo she'd shown Søgaard. 'This woman's called Anne Dragsholm. She was a legal adviser to the army. Was she connected to Myg Poulsen in some way?'

Raben was staring at her. Blue eyes very open and interested.

'Why's that important?'

'She was murdered two weeks ago. There's a connection between her death and Myg's. I'm trying to understand what it is.'

Raben thought for a while.

'I don't know her,' he said, pushing the photograph back across the table. 'If Myg did he never mentioned it.'

Jens Peter Raben didn't look in the least delusional, Lund thought.

'You're quite sure?'

'I don't know her,' he repeated. 'What else can I say?'

That was it. Toft was getting anxious. And Raben was saying nothing more.

Lund gave him a card.

'If you think of anything . . .'

He turned to Toft.

'I'm sorry for last night. It was stupid. I don't know what came over me. I want to cooperate. Just tell me what to do.'

Toft smiled at him.

'Good. First it's medication. We'll take it from there.'

She stood up. They all shook hands. Then the two women left.

'That was a surprise,' Toft said outside. 'I got something out of him.'

'Lucky you,' Lund said and watched the guards start the long, slow process of letting them back into the grey world outside.

In the car park she called Strange. He had teams of men pulling in Kodmani's contacts. More than thirty were in custody already, their names culled from customer lists and other databases.

'And?' she asked.

'Where do we begin?'

'You find out where they were yesterday afternoon for one thing.'

A long pause on the line.

'I wasn't being literal,' Strange complained. 'Yes, we're checking their alibis. They all look OK to me. These are small fry. All mouth and not much else. They came in like tame sheep. If they were real terrorists we wouldn't be able to pick them up this easily.'

He hesitated then asked, 'How about Herstedvester? Did this Raben character come up with anything?'

'Probably not.'

'Sounds like we're pretty much in the same boat, doesn't it?' He had a chirpiness about him at times. 'Here's one thing for you. Remember the foreign-looking officer we met at Ryvangen?'

'Remind me.'

So many men in uniform. They began to run together after a while.

'Bilal?' Strange said. 'Myg Poulsen's company commander? The one who showed us his bunk?'

'What about him?'

'He's in Kodmani's customer file. Bilal bought a lot of rabid Islamic literature from him. A hell of a lot. Nasty stuff too.'

'I'll pick you up,' Lund said.

Thomas Buch was on the phone arguing with Krabbe again when Karina walked in. The look on her face made him cut the call.

'What is it?' he asked.

'I don't know. I just heard Agger's called a press conference of her own. About the anti-terror package. Did we get an agreement or something?'

Buch grabbed his jacket.

'No,' he said.

They went through the maze of corridors, into the committee rooms of the Folketinget, found Agger close to her office. She didn't look pleased to see him.

'I was going to call you, Buch,' she said, suddenly flustered.

'But you didn't.'

She was smartly dressed, plenty of make-up. Looked young. Looked ministerial. Ready for the TV cameras.

'What's going on, Birgitte?'

'We're out. You'll have to make do with Krabbe, I'm afraid.'

'But—'

'We've discussed this at length. We no longer have confidence in you.'

'One day in the job and I'm suddenly incompetent?'

'You deceived me.'

Buch's eyes narrowed with astonishment.

'Come again?'

'I know about the memo.'

'What memo?'

'The memo PET gave Monberg. Warning him the first killing was connected with terrorism. Not a domestic murder.'

Karina shook her head and said, 'I never saw that and I was his personal secretary.'

Agger laughed, shook her head.

'Oh please. I've got a copy. Dated, stamped, signed. You're not going to hide behind us, Buch—'

'How many times? I know nothing about any memo!'

Agger stared at him, still amused.

'In that case, it's even worse, isn't it? Excuse me. I've a press conference to attend.' She put her hand to his arm for a moment. 'Don't worry. I won't tell them that last part. You can save that for the inquiry. And there will be one. That I promise.'

Back at Ryvangen Barracks, in the midst of the military, Lund felt a little less out of place this time round. She and Strange had got through security on the gate without much in the way of argument, found Said Bilal working on an armoured vehicle in one of the depots.

'Got a moment?' Strange asked.

'The colonel's at a meeting in town,' Bilal said and went back to the equipment.

'It's you we want to talk to.'

He stopped at that. Put down the spanner he was wielding, climbed down from the ramp. Stood half to attention, staring at Strange, not at Lund at all.

'Do you know Abdel Hussein Kodmani?' Strange asked.

Bilal hesitated then said, 'No.'

Strange pulled out a file.

'So how come you've bought so many books from him? Thirteen over three months. You want the titles? *Al Jihad. Radical Islam.* Not exactly comics are they?'

Bilal was looking round to make sure no one was listening.

'I bought them off the Internet. I don't know who from.'

Strange just looked at him.

'I haven't broken the law, have I?'

'Why did you get them?' Lund said.

'What's this to you?'

'Just tell us,' Strange demanded. 'You're a serving soldier. What are you doing with this shit?'

Bilal glared at him.

'I want to know who these scum are. I want my men to know too.'

He started to walk to the doors. They followed.

'You're a Muslim yourself,' Strange said.

'So what?' He wasn't worried. 'I was ordered to buy those books. Ask Colonel Jarnvig. The army paid.'

He stopped by a group of soldiers near the sliding doors. There were weapons on the ground, mostly disassembled. Heavy mortars. Night scopes. Armaments she could only guess at.

Bilal bent down, looked at some of the men working.

'If that's all, I'm busy.'

Lund walked up, pointed to the knee of his camouflage uniform. It was wet. Red.

'I think you're bleeding,' she said. 'Where were you last night?'

'Here. OK?'

'I don't know,' Lund answered. 'Did anyone see you? That would be OK.'

'We're flying out next week!' he yelled. 'How can you come in here, wasting our time?'

'I want a blood sample,' Lund said. 'Do you consent to it? Or do we have to go about this the long way?'

For the first time he looked worried.

'I want to see the colonel. I'm not saying anything until he's back.'

Strange walked up, stood close to him, looked into his dark eyes.

'This isn't about Colonel Jarnvig. It's about you.'

A call from Herstedvester. The meeting with the lawyer and her husband was back on.

Now they sat in the same small room, with the little sofa and its crumpled cover, listening to the solicitor spell out what they already knew. Nothing could be done until another six months had passed.

'Do as they say,' the lawyer insisted. 'Take the medication. Follow the programme.'

'He's been doing that all along,' Louise said with a sigh.

'If there's a repetition of last night you're talking a year or more. That's before they even consider you.'

'It won't happen again.' He took her hand, squeezed it, made sure the man saw. 'I promise. I want to go home. I'll do whatever they want.'

The lawyer was getting sick of this case, she thought. Too much work. Not enough money.

'Can we have some time alone, please?'

When the man was gone she held Jens's arm, looked into his clear, intelligent eyes.

'I'm really sorry about Myg. But I need you now. Jonas too. Let's not forget—'

'How is he?'

'He's fine. He wants to see you again.'

Raben was smiling. He looked so very normal most of the time.

'You have to focus on this, Jens. It's the most important thing there is. We've got six months. Let's use them. Should I find a different lawyer?'

He'd drifted already. His eyes, his thoughts were somewhere else.

'Jens? Do we file a complaint about the Prison Service? What are we going to do?'

He shrugged.

'We wait. What else can we do? I've got to see the medics. Toft said so.'

'But . . .'

He looked as if he was getting bored with this.

'They'll only let me out of here when they want to, Louise. It's their decision. Not ours.'

She had to fight to keep her temper.

'You have to convince them you're well!'

'I'm doing the best I—'

'It's not enough!' That hurt him and a part of her didn't mind. 'I've had two years of this. All these decisions. Where's Jonas going to go to school? Where do we live? How do I pay for things? I can't . . .'

He reached out and touched her dark hair. Didn't notice it was different at all, she thought.

'I know I screwed up,' he said. 'I'll make it right for you. For Jonas. I promise.'

Then he kissed her once on the cheek, hand briefly at the nape of her neck.

'Toft wants to see me. I have to go.'

'What is this? Jens? *Jens?*'

Raben got up, went to the door, walked out, didn't look at her again.

*

A short walk down the prison corridor to the medical office at the end.

A blue-uniformed guard. A male nurse in white who checked his name then got two red capsules from a jar.

Raben didn't hesitate. Took them and the offered plastic cup of water. Put the pills in his mouth, drank.

The guard marched him back towards the cells.

It was time to leave the prison quarters to see Toft in the psychiatric wing.

Almost.

'Can I get a shower?' he asked.

'You want to look good for the ice queen? Too classy for you.'

He sighed.

'Two minutes,' the guard said.

Raben gave him a wry salute, went to his room, got his washbag, walked to the communal shower.

It was empty. He closed the door, went to the basin, spat out the two tablets he'd kept under his tongue, rinsed his mouth with water from the tap.

The door wouldn't lock. So he got the mop from the corner, jammed it as hard as he could against the handle, turned on the shower to make some noise, put his head under the lukewarm water.

Months before he'd secreted the tools under a drain cover, wondering if he'd ever need to use them. A wrench and a heavy spanner stolen from the workshop. A torch he'd taken when a guard wasn't looking. All wrapped in greasy oilcloth to keep out the moisture.

Raben got on his knees and ripped up the grimy metal cover. They were still there, still in good condition.

The guard banged on the door. Yelled, 'Raben?'

'Two minutes you said.'

'Get on with it.'

He ran to the door, got the mop out of the way. Just in time. The guard was testing the handle. When he opened it Raben was there, damp hair, damp towel, the tools and the torch inside his washbag.

The guard barked at him to get his jacket. It was raining outside. Then he got on his radio, announced Raben was leaving the prison block, headed for the short walk across the grass.

From one locked door to another, behind the high walls, the electric fences of Herstedvester. Cameras watching him all the way.

They were so sure of themselves, of their security, they'd let ordinary prisoners – and Raben was one – walk across on their own. Where was there to run? How?

'Thanks,' Raben said as the guard let him out.

The rain was cold and icy. The night black.

Ordinary.

No one called him that in Afghanistan. He was a leader, someone who'd been through *jæger* training. A hunter. A lone wolf when he wanted to be.

The tools were under his jacket now. He stepped out into the dark.

Anywhere else and Lund would have bundled Bilal straight into the car and taken him down to the Politigården. But this wasn't her territory. They were inside the army barracks, possibly beyond their jurisdiction. Strange didn't seem to know either.

Hierarchies.

No one was moving until the surly, silent company commander had seen his superior. So twenty minutes after they confronted him in the depot, Lund and Strange found themselves facing a furious Major Søgaard.

'Bilal has nothing to do with the killing,' Søgaard insisted, as the young officer stood rigid to attention in the corner of Jarnvig's office. 'I can assure you—'

'We're not asking for character references,' Strange broke in. 'If he doesn't start talking we're booking him . . .'

'We have to wait?' Lund wondered.

At that moment Jarnvig stormed in. He looked even angrier than Søgaard.

'I told you,' the colonel bellowed, 'that all communication had to go through me or Søgaard here. How dare you—?'

'What's wrong here?' Lund asked. 'Two people dead. One of them's your own soldier. Bilal's been buying fundamentalist literature from a website connected with their murders. He's got blood on his clothes . . .'

'There's an explanation,' Jarnvig began.

'Let me hear it from him. He can talk, can't he?'

Jarnvig glared at her. Women didn't answer back much in his world.

'OK,' she went on. 'I'm starting to get this now. He . . .' she nodded at Bilal '. . . can't talk until you let him. So tell him to speak. Let's hear it.'

He thought about this for a long moment, stared at the man in the corner, stiff to attention, hands behind his back, then nodded.

Eyes straight forward, focused on nothing, Bilal spoke in a bored, plain monotone.

'Lance Corporal Myg Poulsen was under my command. I was concerned about his state of mind. I went to see him in the veterans' club to see if we could sort things out.'

Then he looked at Lund and Strange.

'I could see someone had broken in before me. The door was open. So I walked in. The place seemed empty. Then I saw him hanging from the ceiling. There was blood everywhere.'

'And then you ran?' Lund asked.

'I heard you arrive. I didn't know who you were.'

'You didn't think of calling the police?'

He glanced at Jarnvig.

'My first duty's to the barracks. To the men here.'

Strange laughed.

'That's a hell of an explanation.'

'What had Myg done?' Lund asked. 'His . . . state of mind . . .'

Bilal went quiet again. Looked at Jarnvig. The colonel nodded. And Lund swore under her breath, none too quietly.

'We had a serious security breach,' Bilal said. 'It's possible . . .'

He stopped.

'I'm one minute from dragging you into the Politigården,' Lund told him.

'Our chief of security had reported an illegal entry into our network. The log files showed Myg Poulsen had accessed confidential data from the operations database . . .'

Lund stared at Jarnvig.

'About what?'

'He'd downloaded a document.'

'And?' she asked.

'It was a list of soldiers in a team. The men he'd served with the last time he was in Afghanistan. Two years ago.'

Lund folded her arms, looked at Strange, waited for a question. She was starting to like this man but he wasn't much help here.

'Poulsen probably needed the list for the veterans' club,' Bilal suggested.

'Couldn't he have just asked for it?' Lund wondered.

He stared at the floor.

'We'll need DNA,' Strange said. 'If you'd come out with that fairy story yesterday we might have believed it.'

Lund swore again and wandered over to the wall of Jarnvig's office. It was covered in photos. Afghanistan she guessed. Men in a dry, sparse country, with weapons and military vehicles.

'I'm telling the truth,' Bilal said behind her back.

'I can vouch for that,' Jarnvig intervened.

'There's a surprise,' Lund murmured.

She liked looking at photographs. They told stories. Complex ones sometimes. There were scores here, overlapping, held in place by pins.

'After you left last night Bilal came and told me all about this,' Jarnvig added. 'I immediately contacted PET and gave them a full explanation. They accepted it absolutely. You can't march in here and threaten my men. I won't . . .'

Lund closed her eyes, wondered if she could believe what she was hearing. Turned slowly round and stared at these men, colonel, major, lieutenant. A tidy little trinity of power who had no intention of talking to lowly civilian cops like her and Strange.

'PET,' she said, 'deal with security. We investigate murders. That man . . .'

Strange was on the phone already.

Jarnvig strode over.

'If you'd done as we agreed and come through me or Søgaard you'd have known all about this. You're at fault. Not us.' He smiled, not pleasantly. 'As I think you'll soon appreciate. Goodnight. See yourselves out.'

The three soldiers strode from the room, in strict, hierarchical order.

Strange came off the line.

'So what does Brix say?' Lund asked.

'Special Branch have arrested three people connected to Kodmani. He wants us back. He's not sure why we're here in the first place.'

'Really?'

Ulrik Strange shrugged and went to the door looking a touch

bemused. Lund followed, but not before she'd carefully removed the photograph she wanted and moved another into its place.

Raining again outside.

'I've never worked with PET before,' Strange said. 'Is it always like this?'

'Like what?' she asked, pulling out her phone when they were clear of the building and any nearby soldiers.

'One-sided.'

'No. It isn't.'

She got through.

'Send two officers to Herstedvester,' Lund told control.

She retrieved the photograph, handed it to Strange and said, 'Bottom left corner.'

There was frost on the car. They weren't far from the depot where Bilal was working. He was back there now. Watching men work on the mortars.

'What exactly am I supposed to see?'

He wasn't slow, she thought. Just unobservant at times like most of them.

'Next to Myg Poulsen,' Lund said, pointing a finger at the photo. 'That's Jens Peter Raben. His friend. The one I visited today in Herstedvester.'

'So what?'

Control were taking for ever. She wondered why.

'Anne Dragsholm?' Strange asked.

'Looks like her to me. But Raben said he never knew her. I didn't believe him then . . .'

Control came back.

'Yeah,' Lund said. 'There's a detainee there. Jens Peter Raben. I want him brought in for questioning immediately.'

She tried the car door. Locked.

'Bring him straight to an interview room. Strange?'

He was staring at the photo as if he was still struggling to understand.

'Strange?' she said again.

'The door?'

'Oh.'

He got out the remote, unlocked it, handed her the photo. They got in.

Lund was still on the phone. Control wouldn't let go. She listened, cut the call, took a deep breath, performed the childish faux head butt of the dashboard that Mark liked to do when she said something stupid.

Strange was staring at her.

'We're not going back to the Politigården,' Lund said.

'Where are we going?'

'Herstedvester. You know? The high-security psychiatric prison that no one's ever escaped from?' He looked at her, face blank, truly a touch out of his depth, she thought. 'Well Jens Peter Raben just broke that record. He's gone.'

Four

Tuesday 15th November

7.52 p.m. It took them thirty minutes to get there. Strange drove carefully even when he was in a hurry.

The place was lit up like an ocean liner travelling through the night. Sirens wailed. Dogs barked. Prison officers and police were combing the areas inside and out, hunting for the missing Jens Peter Raben.

Lund found the head of security, watched some of the CCTV sweeps from his office by the gate.

'He was supposed to see the clinical director. We let them walk from the block to the medical wing. It's not far.'

The man tapped the screen.

'It's secure. We've never had a break before.'

Lund folded her arms and looked at him.

'Raben's no normal squaddie, you know,' he said as if it were an excuse. 'If anyone could get out . . .'

'What's so special about him?'

'You work it out. He climbed into a sewer. Opened the manhole.'

They went outside. It was freezing now. Mist on their breath, on that of the dogs working the grounds.

'Do you know how far he's got?' Strange asked.

'He's on foot. We knew he was gone straight away. It's as dark as hell out there and he's on his own. No sign of a car outside. He must be nearby.'

Three officers stood around an open manhole cover. One was going down it. Hesitantly. She wondered whether to join him.

She bent down and, with her gloved fingers, picked up the wrench that was next to the manhole.

'Yours or his?'

No answer.

'I want to see his cell,' Lund announced and walked back to the prison block.

They had a lockdown. Men were banging on their cell doors, shouting happily. Someone was finally free.

She got a guard to show her Raben's tiny room. It was more human than she expected. The walls were covered with drawings, childish, those of his son she guessed. One subject only: soldiers and war. Men in green, smiling, raising weapons. Dark helicopters with the Danish flag dropping men from a plain blue sky. A camouflaged fighter raining bombs on screaming villagers in turbans, waving weapons as their world exploded in blood.

A photo of Raben with a boy of two or three, blond-haired, fetching, staring up at him adoringly. Taken in the interview room here, she thought. Another, older picture: Raben and his wife. She looked so much younger, beautiful, not careworn at all. There was a date on the back. Five years before. Raben looked drawn and difficult even then.

Lund sifted through the drawers, opened the three paperback books he owned, all military thrillers, flipped the pages. Went to the wardrobe. Another picture there. Black and white. Raben with his wife maybe ten years ago. Both of them young, happy, her head on his shoulder, his cheek to her hair. In love. The photo shouted it.

A noise. Lund looked. Strange was at the door.

'They're still searching the sewers,' he said. 'This one's smarter than they think.'

' "No normal squaddie". What does that mean?'

'I checked his record. He'd done some training with the Jægerkorpset.'

Jæger. Hunter. Lund had heard the term. It was shorthand for a shadowy kind of hero. Special forces. She didn't really take much interest in military matters. Never found the need.

'So?' she asked.

'You could drop those guys anywhere and they'd get through. That's what they're taught. Ultimate survival. Never stop. Never give up. He's going to be a bastard to catch.'

Lund couldn't take her eyes off the black and white photo. Raben seemed so happy, so young in that. Not innocent. Not quite.

'Were you a soldier, Strange?'

'For a while. I did my duty.'

'You were a *jæger*?'

He threw back his head and laughed. It was so spontaneous and funny she almost did too.

'Are you kidding? Do I look the hero type? I'm not macho enough for those guys. Even if I wanted to be. Which I don't.'

She took one last scan of the room.

'From what I remember,' Strange added, scratching his crew cut, 'you never tell anyone you were in special forces. So maybe Raben was.'

Lund looked at him. Waited.

'And maybe I was too,' Strange added, catching on. 'Except I wasn't.'

She was back going through Raben's clothes.

'What are you looking for?'

'Something that tells me who he is. Why he'd break out.'

'They turned him down for release.'

'Yes. And one day we'll find him. And he'll be back here for years. For a smart man this seems very stupid. Or desperate.'

So many paintings on the wall and all of them by his young son.

'Raben's thrown away everything. Why?'

'Brix is asking for us.'

'Is the medical director here?'

'She is. But Brix wants a report. PET have arrested three—'

'Brix can wait.'

Director Toft's file on Jens Peter Raben seemed remarkably slim for a man in open-ended custody.

'He was considered for parole but the Prison Service turned him down,' she said. 'I guess that caused a relapse . . .'

'Of what?' Lund asked.

'Post-traumatic stress. As I said he was involved in an incident in Afghanistan. It's not uncommon sadly. But Raben's case was extreme. He could be violent, delusional, obsessed—'

'What kind of incident?'

Toft shook her blonde head.

'There are rules . . .'

'You just told me we've got a very dangerous man at large. He's probably headed for Copenhagen. If you conceal anything . . .'

Toft sat back in her chair. This was a new experience and she didn't like it.

'Some of his comrades died in an attack in Helmand. He held himself responsible. In one way his amnesia spared him some grief. In others, it made it worse.'

Strange asked, 'How?'

'Because he didn't know what really happened. So his mind invented fantasies to fill the vacuum. Sometimes he'd think people here were soldiers. Dead ones. He'd scream at them. Attack them if he had the chance. I told you. Before he was committed he took a complete stranger hostage. Almost killed him. I'd hoped we were over that phase . . .'

Lund pushed a photo in front of her.

'Tell me about Myg Poulsen.'

Toft nodded.

'Raben wanted to call him for some reason. He said he was worried.'

'Worried about what?'

She thought about this.

'He said Poulsen might harm himself.'

'And you didn't think that was important?'

Toft laughed.

'Raben was delusional. If I believed everything he said I'd be as sick as him.'

'What about her?' Lund placed the woman's photo on the table. 'Anne Dragsholm. Lawyer. Adviser to the military.'

Toft shook her head.

'Raben hadn't talked about the war for months. He was focused on the future and his family.'

'Could he have been in touch with this woman?'

'I don't think so. I vet all contacts. What is this? Look, I'm sorry he's escaped. But that's all this is. Someone who got out of here . . .' She looked puzzled, lost for a moment. 'I should have realized he wasn't doing as well as I thought. You need to see something.'

She went to a filing cabinet, retrieved a disk, slotted it into her laptop.

'This was what he was like when he first came. He spent three weeks in solitary before we could even consider treatment.'

Lund and Strange walked behind her desk. It didn't look like the man she'd met here only the day before. Raben was thinner, with a full beard and greasy, unkempt hair. Dressed in a sweatshirt and tracksuit bottoms. Cursing, screaming. Right arm in a cast but he still tried to hammer the walls with his bare fists until they bled.

Then he picked up the one chair in the bare room and began to beat at the lens, bellowing with fury.

'Most of them don't even notice the camera,' Toft said. 'It's supposed to be hidden. Raben . . .'

The video came to an end. She closed the screen.

'I think he saw through everything. Me included. If anyone was going to escape it was him.'

They were outside again by nine. Just as many officers and dogs around.

'We need the area searched,' Lund ordered. 'I want visits to his family and friends. Keep them under surveillance. He got out because he wants to talk to someone.'

'He's a missing convict, not a suspect,' Strange said. 'Let's not get this out of proportion.'

'Listen—'

'No, Lund. You listen. Raben was photographed with the two victims, but there's nothing to tie him to their murders. He was locked up in this place when they happened. He can't have—'

'He knows something. He lied about Anne Dragsholm and then clawed his way out of here.'

He opened the car door, signalled for her to get in.

'There's not a phone call or a visit from anyone who looks remotely suspicious. Brix says they've got more on Kodmani. We have to question him again. Just get in, will you?'

She stayed by the door, furious.

'Raben could have escaped from here a long time ago. He's smart enough. He was a *jæger*, wasn't he?'

Strange groaned.

'I wish I'd never said all that.'

'He could have got out whenever he wanted. So why now? Why this moment? Will you at least admit it's worthy of investigation? I'm trying to help you here.'

'Help me?' His passive face lit up with astonishment. 'I've got rank, Lund. They didn't give me that as a favour.'

She held out her hand.

'Give me the keys. I'm driving.'

'It's my car . . .'

She came and stood next to him, hand out, like a mother demanding something from a disobedient child.

'Give me the keys.'

He shoved his hands in his pockets, wouldn't move.

'We can stand here all night if you like,' Lund said.

Nothing.

'All night. I promise—'

'Dammit,' he swore, then walked round and climbed into the passenger seat.

It took six phone calls before Louise Raben found a lawyer willing to listen. Most didn't take on hopeless cases. This one at least seemed willing to consider it.

'He hasn't any previous convictions,' she said, listening to him wriggle on the line.

'Let me think about it,' the man said.

'He's a good husband. A loving father. They treated him terribly. I don't know—'

'I said I'll think about it. Call me next Monday . . .'

'I can call you tomorrow.'

'I'm busy for the rest of the week. Get me the papers. We'll talk on Monday. I don't normally take on soldiers' cases. I don't think they should be over there.'

Another time she'd have bitten his head off. Jens didn't start that war. He was a soldier. He went where they sent him. But now . . .

'Jens didn't like it either.'

On that fragile lie she ended the call, closed her eyes, said a small prayer.

When she looked up her father was in the living-room doorway.

'Dad.' She ran to him. 'I think I've got us a new lawyer. A good one this time. We've got grounds for appeal.'

He didn't look his usual self.

'I promised to send him all the papers.'

'Louise . . . there are some people here.'

Two men had moved behind him. Police in their blue uniforms.

She was an army wife. Could scent bad news on the wind, in people's eyes.

'What is it?' she whispered.

Then sat at the kitchen table and listened.

One cop spoke for both of them.

'He'd been planning this for some time,' he concluded.

'When did he escape?' her father asked.

The man nodded at her.

'Just after your daughter's visit.'

All three of them stared at her.

'I didn't know. That's the truth.'

'Louise . . .'

She ran to the sink, stared at the black night, tears blurring her vision.

'Dad! Don't you believe me?'

'There was no one waiting for him outside,' the cop added. 'We don't think he had help. But if you've got any idea where he's heading you should tell us. He's dangerous—'

'No he's not!' she cried, turning on them. 'That's the point. If you'd let him out. Let him come to me and Jonas—'

'Your husband's an escaped felon,' the cop said. 'We're treating him as a risk to the public and himself. If you know where he is—'

'She's no idea,' her father broke in. 'They didn't let my daughter see him much. When she did get in he wasn't exactly . . . communicative.'

Louise Raben wiped her eyes and glared at him.

'We need a list of his friends. Relatives. Places he liked to go.'

'I'll talk to my daughter. We'll be in touch.'

The man in blue got up, came and stood next to her.

'If you hide anything you're breaking the law. You could go to jail too.'

'She knows nothing!' Jarnvig yelled at him. 'Just go, will you? Can't you see we're shaken up by this? We thought Jens was coming home.'

The second cop, the silent one, got up and shuffled over.

'We'll be back for that list in an hour,' he said. 'If you don't have it I'll wait.'

Then they left.

Dishes in the sink. Washing to do. Jonas had broken his lunch box. She couldn't get it back together again.

'Want me to help with that?' her father asked.

'No.'

She went and sat at the table again, struggled to put the plastic fastenings in place.

'This is all wrong.'

'Louise . . .'

'He said he'd resumed the treatment. All he wanted to do was come home.'

Her father took the lunch box from her, snapped the lid back in. She couldn't begin to make sense of what she'd heard.

'Whatever he's done, there must be a reason. Jens wouldn't just run off . . .'

He took her hand.

'But he did.'

A bright spark of anger.

'Just like that? No reason? The way Mum did? That's what you said then, didn't you? And that wasn't true? Was it?'

He didn't like it when someone answered back.

'No. She left me. She hated . . .' He nodded towards the barracks outside. '. . . this. The army life. So I suppose she came to hate me too.'

'She had her reasons.'

'They were her reasons, not mine. I never understood them. How she could leave me, yes. But not you. Never you. I can't begin . . .'

The words failed him. Torsten Jarnvig was staring at the door. She turned. Jonas was there. He looked tired, close to tears.

'Mum?' the boy said in a clear, hurt voice. 'What's happened?'

She was there in an instant, scooping up his little body in her arms, holding him, feeling his warm cheek against hers.

'Nothing, darling,' she whispered. 'Nothing.'

'They were talking about—'

'Nothing,' she murmured and hugged him so tight he couldn't say anything at all.

A cold damp night. Frost on the ground, on the trees of this dead land at the edge of Copenhagen.

Jens Peter Raben was finally free.

After he'd emerged from the remote disposal plant he'd broken into the staff offices, stolen some clean clothes, jeans, a sweater, a khaki hooded jacket, dashed into the woods, washing himself with the frosty dew on the trees, trying to get rid of the stink, then changed.

The plant was empty. No car to hotwire. Not even a bike.

So he ran down the track, a steady jogging pace for twenty minutes or more, until he found a main road busy with night traffic, trucks and cars.

Soon it started to rain. Then the rain turned to sleet. Two hours after he'd slipped out of Herstedvester he found himself approaching a petrol station surrounded by woodland.

He stopped in a clump of conifers by the edge, tried to fix in his head what he was doing.

Training.

It didn't all happen abroad. Often they'd run manoeuvres in Denmark, on terrain much like this. Hide and hunt sorties. Stay out of sight, cover tens, hundreds of kilometres with no money, no obvious form of transport. Emerge at the other end, carry out the assignment.

He didn't fail then. Didn't intend to now. But that was practice, for a purpose. One the army supplied. Now he was on his own. A solitary man with a mission he'd yet to discover.

Even in Afghanistan, on the odd lone assignment, he'd never been completely alone. The army came with you. Whispered comforting promises in your ear.

Not now, by this deserted petrol station on the icy outskirts of Copenhagen.

Raben checked for the positions of the CCTV cameras, pulled the hood down as far as it would go, then walked over to the toilets. Got some water to drink. Broke open the lock, jammed the door, stripped off, washed again. Sniffed. Tried to believe the smell of the sewer was gone.

A car pulled in. Long black Volvo estate. Raben angled himself so he could see better. A man about his own age got out with two boys, filled up, went into the kiosk.

Time to get to the Volvo, close enough to see the keys were in the dash. He was about to get in when he heard the kids' voices.

They were heading back, laughing at the sweets they'd got out of their father.

Raben went straight to the bucket, picked out the squeegee, started sponging down the windscreen, taking off every speck of dirt, every leaf.

The driver came up, gave him a filthy look. The kids got in the back doing the same.

'Here,' the man said and gave him a twenty-kroner coin.

Raben took the money. If it weren't for the kids he'd have seized the keys so easily.

'I really need a lift into the city,' he pleaded.

'I'm not going there.'

'Can I drive with you anyway? If I can get to a station—'

'No.'

The man's head was down, his eyes on the ground. Raben knew this look. It was the one he got from employers after the army kicked him out and he was forced to go round begging for work. It said: *I know you exist but I wish I didn't. This is not my business and never will be.*

Another car had pulled in, quickly refuelled. The woman driver was walking back towards it. Raben strode over, asked for a lift.

'Don't worry. I'll behave. I just want to . . .'

Not a word. She was scared. Running behind the wheel, starting the engine, pulling out.

Raben looked back to the kiosk. He was out in the open, had taken down his hood without thinking. They could see his face. Two cameras on him at that moment, maybe more. The attendant was on the phone.

It wouldn't take the cops long. The training seemed lost to him. It was all so distant it seemed unreal.

He walked inside, took the mobile from the hands of the kid behind the till, put it in his pocket.

'Give me all the cash you've got,' Raben ordered. 'I don't want to hurt you.'

Couldn't have been more than nineteen. Jonas might look this way one day.

'Please, kid. Don't screw around. Just give me the money.'

'We don't have much. People pay by card.'

He pushed the till open. Raben snatched the few notes there.

'And your car keys.'

'I don't have a—'

'You're in the middle of the woods! You don't walk.'

'My dad brings me,' he said in a low, petulant voice.

Raben wanted to hate himself but didn't have the time.

'I need to get out of here.'

The kid reached down behind the counter. Raben was too slow to stop him.

Came up with a leather fob and a single key on it.

'The manager keeps an old wreck out the back for emergencies. Here . . .'

Couldn't move for a moment for the shame.

'You'd better go, mister,' the kid said.

'Sorry,' Raben said, then walked out, found a beat-up old Ford out back, got it to start on third go, saw the fuel gauge go up to half, then turned out and slowly, carefully drove towards Copenhagen.

He'd got a phone and a few hundred kroner. A car he could drive for thirty minutes in safety, no more.

Back in training, charged with getting across country and committing a fake hit somewhere he didn't even know, this would have counted as cheating.

Right now it felt that way too.

Buch stood in Grue Eriksen's office watching the TV. The lead story was the probable collapse of the anti-terror package. And him.

'Newly appointed Minister of Justice Thomas Buch failed in his attempt to win a broad agreement on the bill which the Prime Minister says is vital for national security.'

'Ha!' Buch pushed out his big chest and laughed.

'The Opposition accuses the government of withholding key evidence about the two murders, believed to be acts of terrorism.'

Birgitte Agger came on, expression set to outrage.

'In a memo, PET specifically warned the Ministry of Justice there were terrorist links. The government did nothing,' she insisted.

'I knew nothing of that memo,' Buch grumbled. 'I told her . . .'

There was frost on the circle, frost on the grand grey buildings all around the island of Slotsholmen. Karina had walked Buch through the maze of corridors once more. But he was learning the private way from his office opposite the Børsen, through the Folketinget, across the second-floor pedestrian bridge into the Christianborg Palace. Next time maybe . . .

'Why didn't you see this memo?' the Prime Minister asked.

He seemed more puzzled than disappointed.

'Monberg removed it from the file, and some other material too it seems. Birgitte Agger's fully aware I never saw it.'

Grue Eriksen took his leather chair, beckoned Buch to the seat opposite. Creaseless blue shirt, maroon tie, every silver hair in place . . . Buch knew he could never be a politician like this.

'Why on earth would Monberg tamper with the records?'

'It was just before he fell ill. We don't know.'

The Prime Minister looked baffled.

'This is quite extraordinary. And improper . . .'

'He never said anything?'

'Monberg never spoke of the case in my presence. Why do you think he would?'

Buch struggled for an answer. Krabbe was right: he was out of his depth in some ways.

'I assumed . . .'

'You should never assume anything,' Grue Eriksen said with a laugh. 'I know everyone thinks I'm the boss here. But really I'm the face on the packaging. The details I have to leave to ministers like you. If I'd known there was a hint of terrorism I'd have convened a formal meeting with the Opposition parties and briefed them instantly. That's their right. And our duty. We may have to give them that now . . .'

'Of course,' Buch agreed.

Grue Eriksen scowled.

'I don't believe this is about national security for one minute,' he said. 'It's politics. Agger wants to smear us any way she can.'

Grue Eriksen got up and put on his jacket.

'You need to limit the damage, Thomas. Put a lid on the whole matter. Bring Krabbe round. We can deal with Agger.'

'Of course.' Buch had no idea how he could achieve either. 'It's a shame Monberg hasn't regained consciousness. If we knew his side of things it would be easier.'

Grue Eriksen shook his grey head.

'Don't bring Monberg into this. He's still in a coma. Do a deal with Krabbe. Close the murder investigation. Then no one will listen to Birgitte Agger's bleating for a second.'

Grue Eriksen looked at the clock.

'I've got to go.' He rose from the chair, came over and shook Buch's hand very warmly. 'I'm sorry for this baptism of fire. I'm sure you'd no idea what you were letting yourself in for. I certainly didn't.'

Outside, in the chilly corridor, waiting for Karina to turn up and take him back to his own office, the phone rang.

Buch looked at the number and felt his heart leap.

Home.

'Are the girls asleep?' Buch asked.

A stream of complaints rushed out of Marie. About the security around the house. The way he didn't call when he'd promised.

'I'm sorry I never said goodnight to them. Something came up . . . Slotsholmen. Politics. Work.'

The one question he didn't want.

'I don't know when I'll be home, love. There are problems here. Maybe a crisis. I don't know . . .'

To his surprise she offered to come and stay in Copenhagen for a while. He thought about this, but not for long. He wouldn't have time to see her. Things would only feel worse.

'Let's talk about this later,' he said and felt an immediate stab of guilt.

That was a politician's answer, not a husband's. And it seemed to come so very easily.

Brix was striding down the corridor towards the homicide detectives' office, a box file under his arm, Lund telling him what she knew. Not that he showed much interest.

'Raben denied he'd met Anne Dragsholm.' She showed him the photo lifted from Jarnvig's office. 'But we found this.'

The chief was in a casual shirt beneath his customary charcoal suit. As if something had disturbed his ordered life.

'Raben was in a team called Ægir. They went out two years ago on a six-month tour.' She pointed at the picture. 'That's Raben, Myg Poulsen and the Dragsholm woman in the same shot.'

'So what?' Brix asked. 'Where's the connection to the Muslim League?'

'Someone got into the barracks database using Myg Poulsen's password. They took a list of Team Ægir's members.'

Brix walked into a side office. Strange was waiting there.

'We need to find Raben,' Lund insisted. 'He knows what this is all about.'

Silence.

'Am I wasting my breath here?' Lund asked, hand on hips.

He looked at her, pulled a sheet of paper from his file, passed it over to Strange.

'PET have arrested three more suspects connected to Kodmani,' Brix said.

'Raben—' Lund repeated.

'Forget about Raben for a moment. When PET were searching Kodmani's home they found a key to a post office box in Vesterbro. It's registered in Kodmani's name.'

He took an evidence bag out of the box file: a silver dog tag, no name, just crosses where the numbers should be.

'The contents speak for themselves. I don't think we need worry about escaped soldiers.'

A noise at the door. Erik König in a blue suit, raincoat over his arm. He shook Brix's hand, called him "Lennart". Smiled for a second or so.

'You two are going to throw this at Kodmani,' Brix said. 'We'll watch.'

He stayed in the observation room with Erik König, following the interrogation through the one-way glass.

Kodmani in a prison suit, trim beard, face impassive. Lund and Strange across the table.

'You sympathize with the Taliban,' Strange said, pointing a pen at him.

'The Afghan people have the right to defend themselves against foreign aggressors. You would, wouldn't you?' Kodmani smiled. 'Unless it was the Nazis. Took a while then, didn't it?'

Brix watched for his officers' reactions, knew König was doing the same. Strange took a deep breath, looked ready to get mad. Lund sat still, arms folded, not saying a word.

'Is it OK to kill Danish soldiers?' Strange asked.

'What do you expect? You're at war. You kill us too. Kill women and children . . .'

Strange opened Brix's file. Took out the evidence bag.

'Is that why you collect dog tags?'

'What?'

'You heard. These were in your post office box in Vesterbro.'

Kodmani glanced at the tags and shook his head.

König came close to Brix.

'He looks a good man,' the PET chief said. 'The other one seems to have lost her tongue.'

'Give it time,' Brix suggested.

Strange persisted.

'You registered the box a month ago.'

Strange picked up the bag.

'These tags are identical to ones that were left at the murder scenes.'

The man in the blue prison suit looked scared then.

'I've never seen these things before.'

'Then why were they there?' Strange asked.

'I don't know—'

'What was the post office box for?' Lund asked. 'You kept those flyers at home. You work with email . . .'

No answer.

Strange scattered some photos across the table.

'Take a look at what you did. Don't deny it. I want to know who you ordered to kill these people—'

'I didn't order anyone to do anything!'

'Look at this, damn you.'

Crime scene shots. Anne Dragsholm's body tethered to a stake in Mindelunden. Myg Poulsen upside down bleeding onto the floor of the veterans' club.

Kodmani was swallowing, didn't like this.

'Faith Fellow told me he needed a post office box,' he said. 'I never used it. He did—'

'Bullshit!' Strange barked at him. 'You were the recruiting sergeant. You picked the men. I want to know who.'

Lund leaned forward. She looked as if she was getting cross, and not with Kodmani.

'Why would anyone need a post office box?' she asked.

Strange was on a roll.

'You take what you can from living here and preach to us about injustice. Then let these other mugs do your dirty work for you—'

'What language did Faith Fellow write in?' Lund asked.

'Come clean, damn you!' Strange shouted.

Kodmani sat back, confused, scared. Two sets of conflicting questions.

'You run an interesting line in interrogation, Lennart,' Erik König said quietly. 'We're under the spotlight here. If there's a screw-up someone's going to pay and it won't be me.'

Lund persisted.

'Did he write in Danish? In English? In Arabic?'

Strange was still ranting.

'Shut up for a moment, will you?' Lund barked at him. 'What did Faith Fellow write, Kodmani? What about Raben?'

Brix was watching König when that name came up. Noted the PET man's visible reaction.

'Did he mention someone in Team Ægir called Jens Peter Raben?' Lund asked. 'This is important. If we're to believe you . . .'

Kodmani's arms wound more tightly round his prison suit.

'I'm not answering any more questions.'

'You haven't answered any in the first place,' Lund said. 'Who's Faith Fellow? What do you know . . . ?'

König tapped Brix's arm.

'Perhaps it would make more sense if we handled the questioning from now on . . .'

Brix walked out, opened the door to the room, waited for her to fall silent, then nodded. The interview was at an end.

He went with König to a quiet place, a circular vestibule in the warren of black marble corridors that ran through the Politigården.

'We'll keep Kodmani and the three men you found for now.'

'I meant that about the interrogation. We can't . . .'

'This is a murder investigation. I'm sure you've got better things to do.'

König put on his raincoat, glanced at him.

'Remember what I said. Cases like these make and break careers. Be careful who you choose to keep around you.'

'Lund's temporary. She used to work here—'

'Thank you,' König said curtly. 'I know who Lund is. Her reputation precedes her.'

A precise, meticulous man, he pulled out the white cuffs of his shirt so they showed from the coat.

'I won't interfere with your investigation. Yet. But she was thrown out of here for a reason.'

He patted Brix lightly on the arm.

'You're taking quite a risk. I hope you think she's worth it.'

Lund stayed in the shadows, listening to the two men talk in low voices around the corner. Brix knew she'd be eavesdropping. That was why he'd taken the man from PET where he did. The Politigården was built for conspiracy. She'd fallen victim to it once before. Never really learned to play that game.

So she went back into the interview room where Strange sat silent, going over his notes, avoiding her.

Brix returned.

'I'm sorry,' Lund said. 'I didn't mean to break it up like that. I just think—'

'I want a word with Lund on her own,' Brix said.

Strange got up from the table, took his pad and pen.

Stopped, looked at the tall man in the suit.

'I just want to say I'm with Lund here,' Strange told him. 'I don't see how the dog tags could have been planted on Kodmani. But . . .'

Brix did not want to hear this. Strange knew and didn't care.

'If it hadn't been for Lund we'd never have got this far. If she feels this strongly about Raben then maybe we should be checking him out.'

Then he left.

Silence between them. That was rarely good.

'I said I'm sorry.'

'I heard.'

'If you want me to go back to Gedser—'

'I'll tell you when that happens, Lund. Just try and keep a handle on your temper in future, will you?' He hesitated, as if thinking about whether to say what was on his mind. 'Especially when we've got PET watching.'

*

Back at the desk she shared with Strange she started going through the files they'd got from the barracks and PET again. He was trying to track down more information on Jens Peter Raben.

'He robbed a petrol station near the Herstedvester,' he said coming off the phone. 'Stole a car. Could be anywhere by now.'

'If he's a *jæger* won't he be good at this?'

'I said he trained with them. He wasn't one of them. If he was . . .'

Strange stamped his finger on the list for the Team Ægir tour.

'His name wouldn't be on here. Jarnvig wouldn't feel he owned him.'

'Any friends?'

'Myg Poulsen and a lawyer they just fired. We need one of your bright ideas.'

'Somebody from Ægir can tell us about him. And the victims.'

He looked at the papers strewn between them.

'Five hundred names or more. We could start at the barracks tomorrow.'

He passed over the sheets.

'I'll follow up on Raben,' Lund said. 'You see if you can get something out of the army.'

'Sure.'

He got up, took his windcheater and scarf off the rack.

'And thanks,' Lund said. 'For . . .'

Thanks were never easy.

'For what?'

'Sticking up for me.'

He looked surprised.

'We're partners. We watch out for each other, don't we?'

'True.'

That quick, bright smile.

'Besides, you weren't going to stop, were you?'

'Is that a problem?'

'No.' He looked embarrassed for a moment. 'I wish we hadn't met like this.'

It seemed an odd observation.

'How else . . . ?' Lund asked.

'I don't know. Maybe . . .' A finger in the air. 'Birdwatching. That's it.'

She found herself laughing.

One of the uniform officers came in and called him over.

'Sorry,' he said. 'I'm meeting someone. See you tomorrow. Phone if something important turns up.'

Lund didn't watch him go. She concentrated on the papers, the work. Not Ulrik Strange, a passably talented police officer with a curious, warm side to him.

It was just an accident that, as she got up for her jacket, she turned to look at the corridor outside. Saw him there with a blonde woman, back to the glass, Strange's arm round her shoulders.

He gave his companion the briefest kiss on the cheek then they left.

One of the young officers came in with some photographs. Raben at the petrol station, begging desperately for a lift.

'They said he was trying to get back to the city,' the detective told her. 'We've got the car. It was abandoned in Enghaven park.'

The name of the place gave her a jolt. Nanna Birk Larsen had been held captive just a couple of streets away.

'So he's here,' Lund said.

'Somewhere,' the young cop agreed.

Fancy restaurants and sex shops. Run-down alleys and the grimy, twenty-four-hour bustle of the meat-packing district. Vesterbro was a bustling inner-city suburb of neon-lit streets, family enclaves, small immigrant communities. A useful warren in which to hide.

Raben knew it well from his youth, though now he had no friends, no family there. This was good. The police would know too so they'd have no idea where to look for him.

The church was sturdy Brick Gothic with a tower by the side. The industrial buildings of the meat-packing district were just two streets away. At night some of them gave over their upper floors to discotheques and clubs. Or so he'd read in the papers. This was all new to him, beyond the tastes and the pocket of a soldier with a family.

Head down, hood around his features, he found his way to the side door, let himself in.

The familiar old smell. Polish and damp. The same chill air.

A figure was at the altar, arranging some flowers. Raben pulled down his hood, stopped on the threshold.

He recognized that burly shape.

'We're closed,' Gunnar Torpe announced in that strong, musical voice Raben had heard every Sunday, almost without fail.

Priest. That was the one name they used for him. Raben was never sure they needed men of God on the battlefield. But at least this one could fight when needed.

'Come back tomorrow,' Torpe said as he glanced up at the crucifix above him.

The building seemed bigger inside than out, with white walls, a few paintings, silver candelabra and lamps. A long way from the dusty tents in Helmand where Torpe used to preach his sermons.

Raben closed the door.

The man in a priest's robe turned and looked at him sharply.

'I said tomorrow!'

The scruffy figure walked forward into the dim light above the nave.

Torpe stood frozen beneath the painted statue of Christ, gazing at him as if a corpse had risen from the grave. Stocky as ever, with the muscular build and aggressive stance of a soldier. Grey hair perhaps a little longer. Face pugnacious, judgemental, unforgiving. An Old Testament pastor.

'Long time no see,' Raben said in a steady, confident voice.

The churchman stayed on the steps to his altar, hands on his waist, saying nothing.

'I need your help, Priest. That's why you're here, isn't it?'

Torpe had a room at the back of the church. A shower. Some food. A fresh set of clothes. Good clean ones this time.

'I've got some communion wine if you want it, Jens. It's not bad.'

'No thanks.'

The priest had left the interior door open for some reason. Raben nodded back towards the body of the church.

'You like it here?'

'It's a nice little parish. People don't have much money. They've got a lot of faith though. Suits me.'

Raben pulled on a heavy sweater, wondered about the other smell. Candles. That was it. They seemed to be everywhere, little flames flickering in the chilly airy interior.

'Do you see any of the old team?'

'No. Why would I?'

Raben said nothing.

'I heard about Myg. I don't know what you're up to.'

'Some things never change,' Raben said and smiled.

Torpe stared at him.

'They told me you went crazy. Threatened some poor man off the street. Didn't know what you were doing . . .'

Raben nodded.

'They were right.'

Torpe came and stood in front of him. His face was an odd mix. He'd seen action. Fought fist fights with his own soldiers from time to time. Liked a drink too. But there was always a distanced, dreamy quality to him. Something spiritual he called it.

'Do you know what you're doing now?'

'I know what I'm not doing. Sitting in a cell while all hell breaks loose.'

'Be careful, Jens. Think of your wife and son.'

'I do. All the time.'

He picked up the clothes Torpe had given him.

'There's someone I need to talk to.'

Torpe was silent. Scared maybe. Which wasn't such a bad thing.

Raben came close, looked him in the eye.

'I don't know who else to ask. Or trust.'

He glanced at the empty dark nave.

'This is sanctuary, isn't it?'

Torpe stood rigid, unmoved.

'Isn't it, Priest?'

'Raben—'

'I never needed you much in Helmand. I need you now.'

Wednesday 16th November

8.45 a.m.   Lund picked up Strange from his apartment. Sharp winter day. Frost on the cobbled street and the cars parked outside the sterile red-brick building close to the water.

He'd been on the phone already. No sign of Raben anywhere in Copenhagen. Search warrants were being issued for more people associated with Kodmani. The three in custody were still being held.

They sat in the car, Lund waiting. When he said nothing she asked, 'What about Ægir?'

He looked pale, tired. His hair was still wet from the shower. She could smell aftershave. Too much of it.

'I do get time off. I was a bit late last night.'

'Out on a date?'

He'd bought a cup of coffee from the bread shop opposite the block. Asked her to hold it, looked at her.

'It's called life,' Strange said, rifling through the pockets of his winter coat. 'You should try it some time.'

'Team Ægir—'

'Ægir was two years ago. There's a new name for each tour. The soldiers who were on Ægir are all over the place. Some have left the army. We know Raben was there. Myg Poulsen. Dragsholm obviously had contact with them. That's as much as I know right now.'

He groaned.

'I don't suppose you've got paracetamol or something?'

'Do I look like a chemist? It's not my fault you're hung-over and . . . whatever.'

'Forget the whatever, will you? She's just an old friend. No need to get jealous.'

She snorted. Said nothing.

'What did you get on Raben then?'

He'd found a pack of pills somewhere deep in a pocket. Took back the coffee and popped a couple.

'He's thirty-seven,' Lund began.

'I knew that.'

'Been in the army most of his adult life. Rank staff sergeant. Trained at the school in Sønderborg. Tried to join the Jægerkorpset. Did some time with them but never made the grade.'

'Doesn't mean he's a pushover.'

'I never thought that,' she said. 'I'm just giving you the facts. He was mainly stationed with the armoured infantry. Decorated several times. Two years ago when he was out there with Ægir he was badly wounded and sent home.'

Strange gulped at the coffee and let out a gentle, self-pitying moan.

'Got discharged for some reason. They thought he was getting better but something snapped. He took a stranger hostage. The court sent him to Herstedvester.'

'Most of that I knew.'

'Don't take out your hangover on me. He's got a wife, Louise. A son, Jonas.'

'So?' Strange asked.

'Her father's Jarnvig. The camp colonel. Raben's his son-in-law.'

Suddenly he looked interested.

'What is it?'

He stroked his crew cut, massaged his brow as if that could get rid of the pain.

'If I was a colonel I wouldn't enjoy a sweaty sergeant marrying my daughter. I'd want her to do better than that.'

Another swig of coffee. He was recovering, she thought. Very quickly.

'Jarnvig was battalion commander with Ægir,' Strange said. 'Small world, huh?'

Lund shook her head.

'That can't be right. Jarnvig denied knowing Anne Dragsholm. She was there as a military lawyer. He must have met her.'

'Maybe . . .' he said swinging his hand from side to side.

'Jarnvig was with Ægir? Why the hell didn't you tell me that earlier?'

He smiled. It was a declaration: better now. Amusing too, not that she was letting on.

'Because,' he said, 'you were too busy being jealous. Are we going somewhere? Or do we just sit in this car park all day long?'

Ryvangen Barracks were little more than five minutes away across the railway tracks. They found Jarnvig in the main office building. Shirt and combat trousers, both khaki, a dark look on his face that didn't bode well.

'You told me you never met Anne Dragsholm?' Lund said, following as he walked from one floor to the next.

'I didn't,' Jarnvig replied without even looking at her.

Strange tagged on behind.

'How that's possible?' she asked. 'Dragsholm's on a photo in your office. She was there during the Ægir tour. You were the battalion commander.'

He stopped, folded his arms.

'That photo was taken at Oksbøl before deployment. Not Helmand.

I'd like it back by the way. You should consider yourself lucky I don't lodge a complaint. I don't like people stealing from my office.'

'She's been murdered . . .'

Jarnvig set off downstairs. The two of them followed into a bright lobby with pale-blue walls and classical statues of Greek and Roman heroes.

'Maybe Dragsholm was there to lecture on law and war,' Jarnvig said. 'We want to keep within the conventions. I never saw her. I can assure you she was not with Ægir.'

Jarnvig stopped in the middle of the central atrium, by a towering full-length figure of Hercules with his club.

'Check with Army Operational Command if you won't take my word for it. I know my advisers. She was never one of them. I trust that's all . . .'

He started to walk off. Lund was on him straight away.

'I'd like to hear about your son-in-law, Jens Peter Raben.'

Jarnvig stopped outside the door to the gym.

'Why?'

'He was invalided home. Everyone thought he'd be fine. What happened?'

The army man walked back to face her.

'What have our private lives to do with you?'

'There are some coincidences . . .' Strange began.

'I don't give a damn about your coincidences. One of my men's been murdered. We've got a terrorist threat to deal with. And you're asking me about Raben?'

He was getting mad. Enjoying it. Lund wondered if this was part of the training. Just blank out the doubts with a sudden, all-consuming fury. Maybe that made life easier.

'You do your job and we'll do ours,' Jarnvig barked, pointing a finger in her face. 'I don't want you wasting our time here any more.'

With that he walked straight into the gym.

Outside Strange called Operational Command, spent five minutes getting through to someone who could talk. They said Dragsholm was only at Oksbøl for a legal seminar.

'Jarnvig could cause you a lot of problems for stealing that photo, you know,' Strange added.

'I'll try not to let that keep me awake at night.'

'Jesus!' He was the one getting mad now. 'Don't you get it? Brix stuck his neck out for you. Hedeby could chop it off. So could that bastard König given half a chance.'

They got back to the car. Strange put a hand on the roof, wiped his brow again.

'Feeling better?' she asked.

'Yes.'

'I'm so pleased.'

'Can we go and pick on Kodmani now? You know, the one who had the dog tags? The one who hates us?'

Lund wasn't listening. Louise Raben had walked out of the infirmary opposite. White nurse's uniform, pale-grey sweater. Talking to one of the soldiers.

'You do it,' she said. 'I'll get a cab and catch up with you later.'

'Lund? Where are you going?'

Louise Raben had gone back inside. Lund worked her way through the army vehicles, past the red and white Danish flags, and followed.

Erik König came to the Justice Ministry first thing.

'Kodmani is behind a network called Ahl Al-Kahf,' the PET man said. 'It means the seven sleepers. It's based on an old legend, about seven men oppressed by pagans who are sent to sleep in a cave, waiting for the moment to wake and take vengeance on their enemies.'

Buch toyed with his coffee and pastry. He felt tired, grumpy, out of sorts. He missed home, his wife, the girls. The sky and fresh air. All his life now seemed bound up in the winding corridors of Slotsholmen. And Grue Eriksen had been proved right. Later that day he was to be dragged in front of the Joint Council and asked to explain why a warning about a terrorist threat appeared to have escaped him.

'We have three suspects in custody. There are more to come.'

König seemed more a civil servant than a police officer. Quiet, calm, determined. Worried. Much like Carsten Plough who sat opposite him at the desk in Buch's office. Buch was glad Karina was around. She brought colour, life and a touch of rebellion to this dry, humourless place.

'So you think the case is pretty much solved?' Buch said.

'Yes,' König insisted. 'The evidence is incriminating.'

'And the threat?' Plough asked.

König shrugged.

'The threat's always there. We'll never lose it entirely. But with this we remove an entire level of their structure. It'll take them years to rebuild. Give us a little more time, Minister, and you can announce this.' König paused, smiled. 'I'm sure that will be helpful.'

Plough stared at him.

'How did Birgitte Agger get hold of a confidential memo you wrote?'

The PET man bridled.

'Not from us, that's for sure. Have you looked for a leak here?'

'For pity's sake, man,' Buch said with a long, deep sigh. 'Why so touchy? I need to understand the course of events. What did my predecessor know? What action was taken? And why?'

König was sweating.

'The woman was in the army. The possibility of terrorism was apparent. So we sent Monberg a memo.'

Buch nodded.

'And you didn't think it sufficiently important to make sure I knew about it when I arrived here?'

'It was in the file, wasn't it?' König said instantly. 'I hardly think it's our job to decide your reading list.'

'Dammit,' Buch roared. 'I'm facing a Joint Council later. They'll want to know why I was in the dark about a possible terrorist threat that you were aware of for nearly two weeks. I would like some clarification. What did Monberg tell you?'

'He was very concerned, naturally.'

'So why didn't PET inform the police?'

König bridled.

'We were investigating terrorist activity. Domestic security is our responsibility. Not theirs.'

'But murder is! Why keep them in the dark?'

König hesitated, glanced at Plough.

'That was Monberg's decision. He thought it was too . . . risky. He felt certain information might compromise national security.'

Buch's walrus features creased in disbelief.

'Here we go again.' His fat forefinger jabbed across the desk. 'If I find you're lying to me, you will earn the privilege of being the first man I fire. What information?'

König suddenly looked terrified.

131

'It wasn't my decision—'

'What information?' Buch demanded.

'I don't know,' König said. 'Monberg said he'd get back to me with an explanation. The next thing I know he's in hospital. These are unusual circumstances I'll admit . . .'

Buch tapped his pen on the desk, exasperated.

König looked around the office.

'I'd suggest, Minister, you're more likely to find the answer here. Not with us. And I do not lie. To you or anyone.'

'I'm glad about that,' Buch said. 'I had to fire fifty people in one day back home. It wasn't pleasant.' He put the cap back on his pen. 'Though here . . . in Slotsholmen . . .'

He gazed at the dry, humourless man in front of him.

'Perhaps it wouldn't be so hard after all.'

Twenty minutes later Plough had people dredging the email archives. Karina was going through the paper files.

Buch waited, bouncing his little rubber ball off the wall.

'Monberg had a lot of the files shredded,' Karina said. 'I can only see two left.'

'Birgitte Agger's got a point,' Buch said, and launched the ball at the wall again. 'Monberg didn't take the threat of terrorism seriously. Or at least if he did he never told anyone. Just as no one told me.'

'I was Monberg's Permanent Secretary from the moment he came here,' Plough complained, looking at another stack of Karina's papers. 'He was a very careful man.'

'He kept a terrorist threat to himself,' Buch cried. His attention dropped. The ball flew off to one side, bounced off a portrait of a predecessor from the nineteenth century then disappeared beneath the chairs.

'Will you please stop doing that!' Plough cried. 'You're damaging the walls. This is a historic building. It's got protection.'

'It's a bloody ball,' Buch muttered.

A lost ball now and he couldn't be bothered to get on his hands and knees to find it.

'Monberg must have had his reasons,' Plough suggested.

'Then tell me what they are . . .'

Karina had gone quiet as she read through something from the files. Both men stopped bickering, realizing this.

'Perhaps I can,' she said quietly.

132

Buch came over and looked at the papers in her hand.

'This was listed for shredding too but the office hadn't got round to it.' Karina showed him. 'Monberg requisitioned some records on Anne Dragsholm. From the Ministry of Defence. He asked for personnel reports. Anything she'd written for them.'

Plough was fiddling with his glasses, fussily furious.

'He couldn't do that without my knowledge. All such requests must go through me. This is quite unheard of.'

'Well he did,' Buch pointed out. 'Can you get me those reports? Could I kindly see what he saw?'

'I'll call someone in Defence. Karina? Get the minister ready for the Joint Council. Run through the possible questions.'

'I can deal with questions any time,' Buch snapped. 'It's answers I'm short of.'

Plough hurried through the door.

Karina stared at Thomas Buch.

'I'm sorry,' he said. 'I hate being in the dark. Was I a bit harsh with him?'

'Plough's quite a sensitive soul in some ways, I think.'

'I'll buy him a hot dog,' Buch promised.

'You need to practise these questions. If you don't Birgitte Agger will rip you to pieces.'

The ball was under the sofa. Buch couldn't take his eyes off it. She saw this too.

'Not now,' Karina said, getting up and kicking it out of sight.

A bearded man in a wheelchair pushed himself slowly up the aisle of Gunnar Torpe's church. The morning sun streaming through the stained-glass windows was unforgiving. His face was pasty, sick and sad. His green parka worn and dirty, his hair badly cut, not recently washed. But his face still seemed young, optimistic even. Naive.

He moved slowly through the gap between the pews, towards the figure in the Lutheran robes and ruff at the end.

'Grüner,' Torpe said. 'Thanks for coming.'

'That organ needs playing.' He looked around. 'Where's the choir?'

'The choir isn't coming.'

'Why not?' David Grüner picked up the folder on his skinny, useless legs. 'I brought my music.'

'Someone's here to see you.'

Torpe walked to the church doors and locked them. Raben emerged from behind the pulpit.

Grüner's arms gripped the wheels of his chair, turned them slowly. Raben smiled, held out his hand, waited.

'Stranger,' the crippled man said.

'We're never strangers, David. We couldn't be.'

Grüner laughed. So did Raben, though more easily. In the pale winter light under the dome their hands met.

A few minutes of small talk and silence. Raben sat on a pew. Grüner fidgeted in his wheelchair. His legs were so skinny. But there was life, a little laughter in his face.

'The work's boring,' he said. 'But it's the best I can get. With these . . .'

He slapped his legs.

'Beggars can't be choosers. Or I'd be a real beggar. And that's not on . . .' His eyes went to the mosaics above the altar: a gold Christ with his disciples. 'I'm a bit choosy. Priest lets me play the organ here. So he should. I'm good at it.'

'How's your wife?'

'She's fine with it now. Got a job in a supermarket. Between the two of us we're doing all right.'

'And the baby?'

Grüner laughed.

'The baby? He's two and a half. Not a baby any more.' The smile disappeared. 'Nothing stays the same. Except me.'

'Don't—'

'You know the stupid thing, Raben? If I could walk I'd go straight back in there. Serve again. For all the shit and the pain. It's what we do, isn't it?'

'I guess . . .'

'When he grows up the kid wants to have a wheelchair.' Grüner laughed again, spun round on the spot. 'Just like Daddy. Got a beautiful boy. A loving wife. Got my music. A crappy job. Could be worse.'

He leaned forward, put his arms on the pew.

'When did they let you out?'

'They didn't. I walked.'

He got up, stood over the man in the wheelchair.

'Did Myg look you up? There's something happening.'

'Jesus . . .' Grüner wouldn't look him in the eye. 'They'll lock you up for ever now.'

'I was there for ever anyway.'

His voice was too loud. Raben could hear it echoing through the cold body of the church.

'Raben—'

'Myg's dead. That lawyer woman too. Don't you see the news?'

'Yes. But Myg and me didn't exactly exchange Christmas cards.'

Raben bent down, took hold of the arms of the wheelchair.

'What's going on?'

'Who says anything's going on? There are some terrorists—'

'You believe that?'

Grüner looked at the mosaics.

'I don't know what to believe. Maybe it's the will of God . . .'

Raben could feel his temper rising and couldn't stop it. He bent down, spoke fiercely in Grüner's ear.

'God didn't string Myg upside down and let him bleed to death. He visited me the day he was killed. He was worried about something—'

'Don't stir up that old shit!' His voice was so loud it silenced Raben. 'It's dead. Keep it that way.'

His hands went to the wheels. Raben held them, locked them.

'I don't know what happened, Grüner. I don't remember—'

'Let me go, dammit.'

'What do you know?'

He was still strong, fighting as hard as he could to get free.

'I don't know shit!'

The crippled man's torso lurched forward. The wheelchair overbalanced. In one slow movement David Grüner tumbled face first onto the hard marble floor.

Raben tried to cushion the fall, caught most of it. Kicked the chair upright, struggled to drag Grüner back onto the seat.

'Get your fucking hands off me!'

His voice was almost a falsetto. It rang shrill around the nave.

Raben stood back, held up his arms. Waited.

Something on the floor. Sheet music. He bent down, picked it up, placed it on the crippled man's withered legs.

'You're crazy,' Grüner grunted and started pushing himself towards the doors.

Raben strode past him, unlocked them.

'If you want to talk to me call Priest. OK?'

No answer. He watched as the man who was once one of his strongest, bravest soldiers wheeled himself down the disabled ramp, moved off into the busy street.

Gunnar Torpe stayed behind in the nave.

'What did he say?' he asked when Grüner was out of sight.

'Nothing. I need to get hold of the others.'

'How can you do that? I don't know where they are.'

'You've got connections. Use them. Get me some addresses.'

The phone he'd taken from the kid at the petrol station was useless. They'd be listening.

'I need a mobile. I've got to talk to Louise, tell her why I broke out.'

'Tell me,' Torpe said. 'I don't understand.'

'In time . . .'

Still Torpe found him a spare phone. And a copy of the morning paper.

'You're news.'

Bottom of the page. Stock army photo. A story about his escape.

'It says you're dangerous, Jens.'

'I can read.'

'The best thing you can do . . .'

Raben thrust the paper back at him.

'Don't shop me. That wouldn't be a good idea.'

'Why shouldn't I?'

'Because this is about us somehow. About what happened. About . . .'

Sometimes it came back as a dream, as a nightmare of sound, of blood, of screams. But what was real and what fantasy Raben never understood.

'Do you know what happened in Helmand, Priest?'

'I wasn't there, was I? I just heard the rumours when they got you out of there. I know three good men never came back, and those that did weren't the same. Sometimes you have to think about the future, not the past. Sometimes . . .'

Raben's hand went to his shoulder. A friendly gesture. At least it was meant that way.

'I tried that and they wouldn't let me. Myg's dead. So's the lawyer. Someone's got a list. I need it too.'

Louise Raben was in the infirmary talking to a sick soldier, someone clearly suffering from serious wounds. She didn't want to leave. Lund didn't give her any choice.

Outside in the cold, she stood shivering in a skimpy coat over her white nurse's uniform. Grey sky. Men in khaki everywhere.

'I told you everything I know. Why can't you leave us alone? I didn't help Jens escape. I wish to God he hadn't . . .'

Lund pulled the photo out of her bag. It was crumpled now and had a coffee stain on it.

'This is Anne Dragsholm. The woman murdered in the memorial park. Your husband knew her.'

She looked at the photo, shook her head.

'Well I don't.'

'Was Jens worried about something?'

Louise Raben started to walk back towards the office block where Lund had confronted her father earlier.

'Myg had just been killed. The parole board had turned him down for release. What do you think?'

Lund kept up with her, wouldn't let this woman go.

'That's why he escaped?'

She blinked, looked close to tears, said nothing.

'How long have you been married?'

'Is this important?'

'I'm trying to understand, Louise. I don't think your husband wanted to break out at all. He's worried about something. I need to know what that is. How long have you known him?'

They stopped in the cold road.

'I don't know . . . fourteen, fifteen years. It's six since we got married.'

'How did you meet?'

'I visited my dad in the barracks. Jens gave me a lift into town. He'd just started here.' She hesitated. 'I was always going into town back then. This place . . .' She briefly looked around her. 'It was like a prison. My mum had left us. She couldn't take it.'

'And then you got together?'

137

'No. Jens joined the army because he bought all their promises. See the world. Become a man. Achieve something. And he did. It was what he wanted.'

Lund waited.

'I didn't plan to be a soldier's girlfriend. I certainly didn't want to be an army wife. I told him.' The shortest of laughs. 'Some things you can't stop, can you? Doesn't matter how hard you try.'

'What happened?'

'After the Ægir tour we'd agreed. He was going to leave the army. Get a civilian job. We'd move to the city and Jonas would go to school there. Then . . .'

Anger and grief in her pretty, pained face.

'They got ambushed and cut off from the rest. Afterwards they flew Jens to a field hospital and put him on a flight home when he was fit enough. I went and sat by the bed. It was weeks before anyone even knew if he'd survive and then . . .'

'Then what?'

'He wasn't the same man,' Louise Raben said in a blunt, flat voice.

Lund fumbled for her card, handed it over. 'If he contacts you it's important you let me know. For his sake too.'

Louise Raben stared at the piece of paper.

'The border police at Gedser?'

'My number's on the back.'

'You've got terrible handwriting.'

'I know.'

'He was their sergeant,' she said. 'Do you know what that means? He felt responsible. Still does somehow. The army . . . I grew up here. I'm still a stranger, an outsider really. It's hard to understand sometimes . . .'

'Call whenever you want,' Lund said and started for her car.

'Wait!'

Louise Raben was thinking about something.

'That woman in the picture. I think maybe she visited Jens when he was in hospital. Not long before they threw him out of the army. I saw her there. Lots of people came to see him when he was recovering.'

'What did they want?'

'I don't know. He was sick. He couldn't really remember what happened. That wasn't his fault, was it?'

'No,' Lund said. 'Do you know what he did?'

'Nothing bad. He was a soldier. He did his duty. Whatever they told him.'

Lund took out the photo again.

'You saw this woman in the hospital?'

'I think so.' Louise Raben shrugged her shoulders. 'It was two years ago. I'm not sure. I'm sorry. I've got to pick up my son . . .'

Lund called Strange for an update when she was gone.

'We've got an email Kodmani sent,' he said. 'He was inciting his followers to continue the war on Danish soil. We're pulling in everyone he's been in contact with . . .'

Lund closed her eyes, listened to the sounds around her: heavy vehicles, men marching, barked orders. Louise Raben felt trapped in this place, wanted so much to escape it. As did her husband, or so she thought.

And now he'd done something so stupid he wouldn't be out of jail for years . . .

'Anne Dragsholm visited Raben in hospital when he got back from Afghanistan,' Lund told him. 'Louise Raben recognized her. I think Dragsholm wanted to question him about what happened over there.'

'Why would she want to do that?'

'You'll have to ask someone in the army.'

He laughed.

'Oh no. I'm not banging my head against that brick wall again.'

'This is a double murder case. We can talk to them as much as we want. Find out what Dragsholm was doing for the army when Raben was in hospital. She went there for a reason.'

A deep sigh.

'And in the meantime you'll be doing what?'

'Talking to Dragsholm's husband.'

'Not a good idea. He's suing us for wrongful arrest. Also today's her funeral.'

'I'll be discreet.'

That silence of his again.

'Strange?'

'It's OK. I was just trying to imagine what that was like. Listen to me. PET want to hold a press conference about the investigation. We're going public with these arrests. König thinks the terrorists killed Anne Dragsholm. And Myg Poulsen. They say . . .'

Lund took the phone from her ear. Louise Raben had stopped some way along the road. She was talking to Søgaard, the big, self-assured blond major. Smiling, face lit up, eyes sparkling.

'Lund? Lund?'

Strange's tinny voice squawked at her.

'Did you hear what I just said? PET think this is about the Islamists. Brix says so too.'

She cut the call and put the phone back in her pocket.

Then it must be true, she thought.

The training was so intense it never left you. Jens Peter Raben had gone undercover in Iraq, in Afghanistan. In other places the Danish public weren't supposed to know about. And now he was hiding in plain sight in Copenhagen.

Hood up, hunched over, with the gait of a sick and shorter man, he'd hung around Østerport Station for the best part of an hour. Jonas's kindergarten was nearby. Louise had to come here sooner or later.

Amidst the pushbikes and scooters, hidden by the iron railing, he watched her emerge from the subway, cross the street, walk the short distance to the nursery. Then return with Jonas back along the road, not smiling, not talking.

After two years of incarceration, first in hospital, then, after a brief spell of freedom, in Herstedvester, Raben found this grey and open world a strange and foreign place. It looked bigger. So did Jonas.

Louise wore a black coat and a pink scarf. He was in a blue anorak with green mittens. Feeling awkward, looking sullen. Louise was having to drag him along by the hand. He dropped his lunch box, deliberately. She picked it up. He let go of his mittens. She said something and got those.

They crossed the road.

Behind the railing Raben was no more than ten metres from them now but if they saw him, doubled over, hood down, looking like a cripple, they'd never know.

See but be unseen. Move like a ghost, swift and invisible.

The hard-taught lessons kept you alive when others perished.

Louise was on the phone, dragging Jonas by the hand along the other side of the railings. Still hunched over, hidden in the shadows, Raben began to walk.

All she had to do was turn into the entrance, get into the darkness of the stairway down to the metro. Then he could glide towards her, say something briefly, look to all the world like a stranger asking directions.

Two men in uniform by the subway entrance. Raben's head went down further, he turned his back, stopped, coughed, kept out of sight.

Chance gone.

Then, through the iron railings, he saw the blue uniforms again. The cops were stepping into a white marked car, one talking on the radio. Raben watched it set off into the traffic, heart lifting, wondering if he could catch up with Louise down the steps.

Put his hood down. Walked out, looked, saw nothing.

A cry, young and angry.

In front of Raben was a single green mitten. Beyond it Louise was dragging Jonas to a military Mercedes G-Wagen.

Christian Sögaard stood by the vehicle, holding the door open, waving them in.

Jonas screamed something at him. Louise stopped, looked up at Søgaard and smiled.

Something cold and furious held Jens Peter Raben where he was.
Training.

The head rules the heart. The head keeps you alive.

He stepped behind the station wall, peeked round the corner. Watched his wife and son climb into the khaki Mercedes.

Was close enough to hear their voices. Søgaard's officer's boom.

'I'm sorry I couldn't drop you off. Tomorrow should be fine. Jonas . . . sit in the middle. Five minutes and we're home.'

We're home.

He was too cold, too tired to get mad. So Raben did what he was supposed to. Tried to plan.

Went back and picked up the mitten. Bought himself a coffee from the Irma supermarket by the station and stood in the shadows behind the railings, sipping at it.

After a while the phone he'd got from Torpe rang.

'This is Grüner.'

'What's up?'

He could hear sounds behind Grüner's worried voice. Traffic in the open air somewhere. Not the job Grüner got in an underground garage. That would have sounded different. Raben tried to picture him trapped in that nightmare, all day, some nights too, locked up with the petrol fumes, dreaming of music. Hell came in different shapes and sizes.

'I'm sorry I got mad with you, Jens. I was scared. That lawyer woman came asking questions a few weeks before she was killed.'

'What about?'

'You really don't remember, do you?'

'I told you—'

'Lucky man. Come and see me at work.'

Grüner gave him an address in Islands Brygge across the water.

'Half an hour,' Raben said.

'No. I don't start till four. Give me a couple of hours and then . . .'

The funeral was at Solbjerg Park in Frederiksberg. Lund stood and listened to a distant church bell as she watched the small group of black-clad mourners gathered round the grave.

She'd seen Stig Dragsholm briefly in the Politigården on that first day when he was a suspect. Not long after Svendsen had managed to bully a confession out of him. He was a tall, good-looking man with the trim, honed appearance of a fancy lawyer. No one talked to him much as his former wife was buried. No one walked away from the grave by his side.

She stepped across the grass and stopped him close to the car park.

'Sarah Lund,' she said, flashing her card. 'Police. I just want to ask a few questions . . .'

He stared at her, incredulous, then shook his head and walked off. Lund followed.

'I wouldn't bother you today if it wasn't important.'

Dragsholm got out his car keys. She heard the locks click on his Volvo, got in front of the car door.

'I'm worried that other people are going to die. That your wife's not the last.'

He brushed her out of the way, climbed in, sat behind the wheel. Stared at the dashboard. Didn't make a move.

Lund walked round, opened the passenger door and got in.

He was crying. She let him get on with that for a while.

All the other mourners were gone. Another funeral was getting under way, pale coffin being carried across the grass. It was an endless procession, one Lund knew well by now.

Dragsholm got out, stood by the front of the spotless saloon. She joined him. After a while he started to walk round the sprawling cemetery. Lund kept up.

'Why did you confess?' she asked when they were away from the car and the grave.

'That pig of a policeman kept screaming at me. I just wanted him to shut up. I knew I didn't kill Anne. She knew it too. That's all that matters.'

He looked at her.

'Besides. I'm a lawyer. I was going to tear your case to shreds once I got out of that stinking hole.'

'I'm sure,' Lund agreed, and felt happy Svendsen had departed on holiday the previous night. 'Did she talk about what she did with the army?'

'Not much.'

He looked round the cemetery. The vases. The bouquets, huge and plentiful for recent burials, smaller for earlier ones. Some graves unattended, forgotten completely.

'Did she ever mention Myg Poulsen?'

'They asked me that already. The answer's still no.'

'Jens Peter Raben?'

'No.'

They came close to the next funeral. Someone was weeping very noisily by the grave.

'I wanted her to find another job. Anne enjoyed the army. I think she liked the idea she was doing something confidential. Something she couldn't talk about to me.'

'Even with you being a lawyer?'

A glint of resentment in his bleary blue eyes.

'A boring commercial lawyer. I earned ten times what she did. But she always said she got ten times the satisfaction. And then she got fired.'

'You're sure?'

'That's what she told me.'

'Why would they fire her?'

'She had an argument. There was a row over an investigation she conducted. She wouldn't talk about it. Not in any detail. I think she crossed the wrong people.'

He stopped, looked back at the car. Was getting a grip on himself, Lund thought. He'd be gone soon. This part of his life would start to slip away into the hazy, distant place that was the past.

'Anne could be a real tiger. Once she got her teeth into something she never let go.'

'What kind of thing?'

'There was an incident in Afghanistan. Two years ago. She wouldn't say any more than that. I have to leave now—'

'So the army asked her to investigate?'

Dragsholm shook his head emphatically.

'No. That was the problem. Anne heard something. She looked into it on her own initiative. She wasn't supposed to go there. She was very keen on . . . human rights. That's where I wanted her to work. She really cared.' He shrugged his shoulders. 'I don't so much. It's a job. But she had this sense of justice.'

'What did she find out?'

'There was an ambush. The army had an inquiry when it was over. They didn't believe the story the soldiers told them.'

'Anne looked into that?'

'She represented the men who survived. Conducted their case. Lost it, and she never liked that. So she kept on asking questions.'

Lund felt stupid, and deceived.

'Let me get this straight. She was the lawyer who represented the men who came back from Team Ægir?'

'Ægir.' He nodded. 'That's right. She thought they'd been badly treated. Anne hated anything she saw as a miscarriage of justice. In the army. Out of it.'

'I'm sorry we made it so much worse for you,' Lund said and held out her hand.

He didn't take it.

'I made it worse, didn't I? Running away like that. Getting in the car.'

'Why did you?'

'I was terrified. I'd been drinking. Didn't think straight. There was so much blood. I thought maybe it would be me next.'

She didn't say anything.

'I'm not like her,' Dragsholm muttered. 'Anne had courage. She'd stare down anything. I'm just a coward and I know it.' Briefly he shook her hand. 'Was it these terrorists the papers are talking about?'

'I can't talk about the case.'

Dragsholm stared at her. A smart man, she thought.

'No,' he said. 'I didn't believe that story either.'

He walked off to his car. Lund phoned Strange.

'I asked around at the Operational Command,' he said. 'They're looking at what happened in Helmand.'

'Forget about that for now. Have you got the list of men from Ægir?'

He took a second or two.

'In front of me.'

'Does it break down who was in Raben's group?'

'I can work that out.'

'Good. We need to talk to them.'

'Kodmani—'

'PET can waste their time on him. I want to see one of those soldiers.'

The Joint Council met at short notice in a small committee room in the Folketinget. All the party leaders with their advisers, a hand-picked number of journalists in attendance. Agger was at Buch's throat from the off, demanding an explanation for the apparent slip-up over the terrorist threat.

'Monberg took his decision out of consideration for national security,' he pointed out.

'Are you saying we couldn't be trusted?'

Buch rolled his eyes in despair. Carsten Plough was seated next to him, twitching uncomfortably at the polite aggression building up in the room.

'What about Ahl Al-Kahf?' Krabbe asked. 'Is it true that members of this disgraceful organization have been arrested?'

'A number are being interviewed . . .'

Krabbe leaned forward and spoke loudly into the microphone.

'Let it be noted that this is one of the groups the People's Party wants proscribed.'

Buch smiled, waited till they were all looking at him.

'The anti-terror package which will be put to Parliament next week will include measures against all the groups which our security agencies believe merit action. If Ahl Al-Kahf fall into this category, their name will be on the list. If not—'

'You're wriggling, Buch,' Birgitte Agger interrupted. 'Your predecessor thought this was an act of terror. So why did the police spend ten days questioning the victim's husband?'

A good question. Thomas Buch closed his eyes and wondered what the kids were doing at home in Jutland.

'Frode Monberg cannot be here to answer for his actions for reasons we all know. However I am able to share something.'

He nodded to Karina who walked round the table handing out copies of a single-page document.

'I'm circulating this in confidence and with some reluctance. This document remains classified information and must not be shared with others, including the press. When you read it—'

'Games, Buch,' Agger said.

'When you read it . . . You'll see that Monberg was advised that any open investigation might reveal information which would compromise our military strategy in Afghanistan, thus endangering the lives of Danish soldiers.'

Agger passed the sheet to her assistant.

'So you say.'

'No. So our own security advisers say. Do you doubt their motives too?' Buch asked. 'As you appear to doubt mine?'

'Don't bring up your brother again—'

Buch's fist slammed the table.

'My brother's been dead six years! Nothing I can do will bring him back. But if I can save one Danish family the pain we went through I will—'

'Then bring them home,' Agger yelled and regretted the words the moment they'd left her lips.

'They're there,' Buch said, sensing triumph. 'Whatever you feel about the war *they are there*. So tell me. If this memo had fallen on your desk. If you'd read what it said. That to talk about this case would expose our brave men and women to mortal peril . . .'

Agger's mouth was a thin line of fury. She snatched at her remaining papers. A few fell on the floor.

'Would you have gone ahead and revealed it anyway?' Buch asked. 'Never mind the cost?'

No answer. She got up, stormed off. All eyes fell on him.

'If there are no more questions . . .'

It was aimed at Krabbe only and he shook his head.

'Then,' Thomas Buch added, 'I will withdraw and resume my duties.'

'Damn, what a team!' Back in the Ministry, Buch beamed at Plough, blew a kiss at Karina. 'Did I go too far? I'm not mentioning my brother again. I'd never have brought him into it if she wasn't alluding—'

'She asked for it,' Karina declared. 'Bloody cheek. There's something we need to talk—'

'We could still report her for making a classified memo public,' Plough added hopefully.

'Magnanimous in victory!' Buch declared. 'Forget it. Anyone fancy a hot dog? I'm buying.'

Neither rose to the offer.

'We still need to find out how Agger got hold of the memo,' Plough said. 'Someone's stirring it here.'

The phone on the desk rang. Karina took it.

'It's the Prime Minister,' she whispered, hand over the mouthpiece.

'Get someone onto that,' Buch told Plough.

'Thomas!' Grue Eriksen sounded happy. 'Congratulations. I hear it went quite well.'

'I've got good staff here.' He nodded at Plough and Karina. 'They prepared me well. The credit's theirs in all honesty.'

'You're too modest. Now concentrate on the bill. Feed Krabbe a few crumbs. Let's get it out of the way.'

'I'll do that. Prime Minister?'

But by then Grue Eriksen was gone and Carsten Plough was opening a bottle.

'Krabbe's going to demand you put that organization on the banned list,' Plough warned.

'Ha! I just saw off Birgitte Agger, the Wicked Queen of the North. I'm not in the mood to start cutting deals with little people now, am I?'

Plough laughed, said, '*Skål.*'

'Karina?'

She'd gone to the office. When she returned she closed the door behind her.

'Send some bottles to the Ministry of Defence too,' Plough ordered. 'Agger's not going to get anywhere with her inquiry now. She wouldn't dare.'

'There's something you need to see,' Karina said, placing a leather desk diary on Buch's desk. 'I found it when I was going through Monberg's private documents before the meeting. I can't believe I never saw it before.'

'Just put all that stuff in a box and send it to his home,' Plough said and poured more drinks. 'Here. You deserve one too.'

'I don't want a drink. Will you please listen to me? Monberg kept a private diary. I didn't know. It was just him, and his thoughts.'

'So what?' Buch said.

She took a deep breath.

'I read a bit. It seems he knew Anne Dragsholm personally. He was meeting her. Recently.'

She opened the pages of a small brown leather diary. Plough put down his glass. Buch finished his. The two men came and looked.

'This is her mobile number. The last time they met was in a hotel the weekend before she was murdered.'

Buch leaned back against the wall and closed his eyes. The sweet taste of victory was gone.

He looked at Plough, tapped his finger on the page.

'Check this out,' Buch ordered. 'I'm going for a walk.'

Eight o'clock, a pitch-black November night. Jonas in the front room of Jarnvig's barrack house playing with his toys. A plastic tank, three soldiers, a gun, a warplane.

Louise Raben watched him from the doorway. These first few years were so important. They would shape the rest of his life. And what did he have? An absent father. A mother who spent her days fighting for his release. And the men around him . . . soldiers too. Jonas was growing up in a world coloured khaki, filled with the sound of army vehicles, of boots on concrete, of shouted orders, hierarchies and obedience.

The idea of freedom would never occur to him. It barely occurred to her any more. She loved her father. He loved Jonas. If you had to live in a cell this was, at least, one that had some comforts.

But it was still a prison, with no hope of release. Jens was now a criminal twice over, not just a dangerous, deranged ex-soldier. When he broke out of Herstedvester their chances of escape had dwindled to nothing. The police would catch him. They'd put him away for years. Jonas might be in his teens before his own father was able to sleep in the same house.

Could he wait? Could she?

Louise Raben was thirty-four. She missed her husband. Missed his company and his touch. The physical rush of being with a man. And he'd never reach for her in prison again. Not on the makeshift sofa in the area they set aside for married couples. She knew that now.

A part of him had died in Helmand. There were hard decisions ahead. Not for Jonas but for her.

'Mum?'

He had Søgaard's plastic plane in his hands, was fiddling with the toy bombs set under its wings.

'Can we have dinner soon?'

'In a minute. When I'm done with the washing.'

'I've been fighting.'

Her heart fell.

'At school?'

'No! Here. With my soldiers. My men.'

'Fighting who?'

'Ragheads!' he cried.

She didn't laugh.

'Don't use words like that. You spend too much time with the soldiers.'

'I'm going to be one when I grow up. Like Dad. Like Granddad. I'm going to be a major like Christian.'

'Are you?'

She knelt down and watched him playing with the plane, making it climb and dive in his hand, growling violent bombing noises from his little throat, caught in the grip of a child's vividly unrealistic imagination.

'Listen, Jonas. How would you like to have your own room?'

He looked at her, smiled, nodded.

'We could make it really cosy with all your toys. You wouldn't have to listen to Mummy snoring all night.'

'You don't snore!'

'Shall we do that?'

The plane came up to her face. He peeked from behind it and said, 'Yes.'

'There's a school near here.'

'Am I starting school soon?'

She looked around at the barracks house. It wasn't so bad. Life here was safe. Predictable. What choice was there?

All the same her voice was getting weak and she could feel the tears pricking at her eyes.

'Yes. Soon.'

'Is Daddy going to have his own room?'

Footsteps at the door. Her father stood there, looking at the two of them.

'One day. Let's get some dinner, shall we?'

She got up.

'Jonas,' Jarnvig said. 'I've got something of yours.'

The boy dropped the plane and came to him.

'One green mitten.' Jarnvig held it in his hand, looking down at the boy. 'You must have dropped it.'

'When?' Louise asked.

'I don't know,' Jonas said.

'It's got his name tag.' Jarnvig showed her. 'One of the men found it by the main gate.'

'We didn't come in by the main gate. Søgaard gave us a lift.'

He held the mitten in front of her face.

Louise sighed.

'You, young man, need to be more careful in future. Instead of dropping things everywhere . . .'

Jonas went back to the toy plane and the bombing noises.

'I'm going to get changed,' Jarnvig said heading upstairs.

She waited for him to leave. Then looked more closely at the mitten on the table.

Jonas never had a name tag. He couldn't have left it by the main gate.

And it was scarcely a tag at all. A shred of white cotton, probably ripped from a handkerchief. A name written in leaky ballpoint, 'Jonas Raben'.

It was a childlike scribble, one she recognized.

Strange was out somewhere when she got back to the Politigården. No answer on his phone. Lund went through some files, avoided Brix and Erik König who was hanging round the place looking desperate. Word had filtered through from Slotsholmen that the politicians were unhappy PET had kept the terrorist dimension to the Dragsholm case to themselves. König's job might be on the line, which would only make him more desperate to shuffle the blame elsewhere.

Finally her phone went.

'You always moan if I go somewhere without telling you,' she pointed out before he could say a word.

'I don't believe it. Still jealous?'

'You wish . . .'

'I do. For your information I've been trying to find someone who served with Raben. It's not easy. They seem to have spread themselves out since Ægir.'

'And?'

'I was thinking of pizza tonight. Quattro stagione or margherita?'

She liked pizza but she wasn't going to tell him.

'Do we have someone to talk to?'

'I'll come and pick you up.'

She waited outside the Politigården. Was glad to see his plain black car pull up. Strange jumped out, opened the door theatrically as he ushered her in.

'Pathetic . . .' Lund muttered as she took the passenger seat.

'You first,' he said getting behind the wheel. 'Was Dragsholm the unit's lawyer?'

'I think so. We need to confirm it. Where are we going?'

'Not far. David Grüner. Conscript soldier served with Raben's men. He was a promising pianist before he joined up. Degree in music.'

They started to cross the harbour.

'Now he's a car park attendant in Islands Brygge. Stuck in a wheelchair. He'll be at work till ten.'

They stopped at an office block near the metro station. Lund got out, looked through the door.

'Are you sure this is the place? It looks empty.'

'His wife said it's here. And wives never lie. You try inside. I'll see if there's another entrance.'

She took the nearest door into the cavernous building.

A bored security guard stopped her before long. Lund flashed her ID, mentioned Grüner's name and the car park. He took her to a door by the lifts. They were out for maintenance so she had to walk.

Two floors down. The smell of engines and dust.

A sign for the office. Followed it.

The petrol stink was stronger here and it seemed raw somehow. The desk in the tiny room was empty. The computer screen contained nothing but musical notation.

She looked along the corridor. A figure in jeans and a khaki winter jacket shuffling along, back to her.

No wheelchair.

'Hey!' Lund shouted.

He turned.

Bearded, angular face. Muscular frame.

Couldn't think for a moment.

'Raben? *Raben?*'

He flew off through the far door, out into the car park.

She could run. But not like that. All she saw by the time she got there was Strange's black car wheeling down the ramp.

Lund ran out into the open space between the lanes and flagged him down.

'What?' Strange said, winding down the window.

'Raben's here. Grüner isn't. What the hell's going on?'

The smell of petrol was getting stronger. Lund looked back along the length of the car park. A Renault van was parked near the end, doors open, lights on.

She walked towards it. Strange followed.

'Call Brix,' she said.

'For what?'

She swore, got to the Renault, looked inside.

A dog tag, shiny new silver, severed in half, was hanging from the driver's mirror.

'For that.'

He still didn't call. Strange was looking at the seat. There was a phone there.

She went to the back of the van, threw open the doors. It was full of empty plastic carboys. No need to pick them up. The smell told her what they must have contained.

'Did you call Brix yet?'

He was still by the car door.

'You need to see this,' Strange said.

'See what? Where the hell is this man?'

Lund walked back anyway. The phone on the seat had lit up. There was a clock on the screen. Seconds. Ticking down.

Only five left. She watched them feeling stupid and powerless.

'What is this?' Lund asked as the numbers hit zero.

Strange looked round.

'I don't know . . .'

It was the softest of explosions, like the first yawn of a waking giant.

Lund turned, looked at the air vents. Stayed rooted to the spot till Strange's powerful arm took her and his urgent shrieks burst into her head.

'Run,' Strange yelled as the fiery cloud broke free of the metal grates and burst into the concrete tomb around them.

So run she did.

Five

6.34 p.m. Brix came with a fleet of vehicles from headquarters. By then Lund and Strange had pieced together some of what had happened. David Grüner was due to come on duty at four that afternoon. The van with the phone was his. It looked as if someone had attacked him as he was getting out with his wheelchair, forced him into a small room in the basement and locked him in there.

Brix listened to them as they walked through the car park. The alarms were still ringing. Fire officers were cleaning up everywhere. Foam and water ran around them. The place stank of bitter, chemical smoke.

'Do we have any witnesses?' he asked.

'The CCTV was turned off just before Grüner arrived,' Strange said. 'It registered as a fault with the security company. They were due to come and look at it this evening.'

'We should have known,' Lund murmured.

'How?' Strange asked. He turned to Brix. 'We found the van. He'd set up some kind of timer to do with the phone. We couldn't do anything before the thing went off.'

Brix looked at the ceiling.

'The sprinklers never came on?'

'They got turned off too,' Lund said. 'This is really good. If you think a fanatic walked straight out of a mosque and . . .'

She stopped when she saw Brix's face. Took a deep breath. Wished she could get the stench of that small room in the basement out of her nostrils, the image of it out of her head.

'Do you want a look?' Strange asked. 'It's not . . .'

He glanced at Lund.

'I never saw anything like it,' he added.

The chief went first in his grey wool coat.

'He'd poured petrol round Grüner. Probably over him too from what forensic seem to think,' Strange continued as they went down the narrow steps.

The smell of smoke and something worse was growing all the time. Lund's stomach turned. She knew what that other reek was: burned meat.

More officers, some in white suits, others in face masks wandering the length of the corridor, checking with torches.

'The phone in the van was linked to a detonator on the firebomb underneath the wheelchair,' Strange went on. 'So he could call from outside and start the sequence.'

Lund shook her head.

'Why couldn't he detonate it direct?'

Strange shrugged.

'I asked forensic that. They said he needed the second phone to be close.' He pointed to the low ceiling. 'We're underground, remember. Grüner was tied up, gagged. The wheelchair was chained to a radiator. Poor guy couldn't move, couldn't shout. Just sat there waiting.'

Strange pulled two white cotton masks out of his pocket, passed them to Brix and Lund. It didn't make much difference to the smell.

'What do we know about him?' Brix asked.

'David Grüner,' Lund chipped in. 'Twenty-eight years old. Army veteran. Served with Raben in Ægir. Worked here for a year after being invalided out of the army. Wounded in action.'

The team in white suits brought out a blackened wheelchair, a body in it so badly burned it looked barely human.

Brix got closer, looked at the sad, charred figure. It seemed melted to the metal frame of the chair. Something black, like a misshapen necklace, sat round his neck.

'His legs were shot to bits in Afghanistan,' Strange added.

'Is that a car tyre?' Brix asked.

Strange bent down and took a closer look.

'They used to do that in South Africa to traitors,' he said. 'We found the severed dog tag in his van. It looks like the same set-up.'

'If we'd been briefed when PET knew this was on the cards . . .' Brix complained.

Lund just looked at him.

'What?' the chief asked.

'He turned off the alarms. The CCTV. Wired up a phone to set off a firebomb. Besides . . . we've picked them all up, haven't we?'

'Only takes one,' Strange suggested.

'I need to make a call,' Lund said and walked back along the corridor.

She found a utility room on the floor above, threw up in the basin. Was swilling out her mouth when Brix came in looking for her.

He waited as she spat a couple of times into the sink and wiped her mouth with a tissue.

'I should have known,' she said again when she got her breath back. 'As soon as I saw Raben I should have done something.'

'You did all you could.'

'If we'd been half an hour earlier. Fifteen minutes—'

'Lund—'

'I screwed up. Again.'

She got another tissue, wiped her mouth once more, threw it into the bin.

'You can't blame yourself . . .'

She turned and stared at him.

'That's three dead. And we still don't have a clue . . .'

Lund went for the door.

'Where are you going?'

'Back for another look.'

Twenty minutes later Erik König arrived. Brix briefed him at the end of the corridor leading to the room where Grüner died. The PET man didn't seem keen to go any further.

'They used tyres like that in South Africa,' Brix said. 'Strange said it was for traitors.'

'From what I recall it's more specific than that. They used it on informers. But how could a crippled ex-soldier inform on anyone. Over what?'

Lund was back near the site of the explosion, patiently going through items on a trolley.

'I hear there were witnesses,' König said, watching her.

'Raben was here.'

'Is he a suspect?'

Brix frowned.

'If he is it's just for this. We've got the severed dog tag, just as we had for the first two killings. We know Raben wasn't responsible for those. He was in Herstedvester.'

König couldn't take his eyes off Lund.

'So she uncovered all this?'

'Pretty much. She asked Strange to track down someone from Raben's team two years ago. It would have been useful if she'd told me first.'

'None of this means Kodmani's innocent.'

'Maybe not,' Brix said, watching him. 'Soldiers stick together. Perhaps Raben was looking for help. Or offering it. I think . . .'

Lund was sifting busily through the pieces in front of her.

'It's probably best if I take her off the case.'

König shook his head.

'Why would you want to do that? I know what I said yesterday. But—'

'I dragged her back here. It wasn't her idea. There's an obsessive side to her. I—'

'You don't like the idea you can benefit from using it?' König smiled. 'Don't worry, Lennart. We all have a twinge of conscience from time to time. Here are two good reasons for keeping her where she is. I'd like to know what she thinks of this Faith Fellow Kodmani mentioned. Let's keep an open mind there, shall we?'

'And the second?'

'Kodmani's asked to be questioned again. He says he's something of substance to tell us. On one condition.'

He nodded at the woman along the passageway.

'He'll talk to her and no one else.'

König looked at his watch.

'I have an appointment at the Ministry,' he said.

'I gather they're not happy.'

No answer.

Brix watched him go. Then he walked over to Lund. She was with Strange, looking at an evidence bag and juggling a call at the same time.

He waited.

'My mother's getting married on Saturday,' she said when she came off the line. 'She wants me to go round to Bjørn's.'

'Who's Bjørn?' Brix asked.

'Her boyfriend,' she said as if it were obvious. 'I need to go home and change. The smell . . .'

'Sure.'

'Any news about Raben?' she asked.

Brix shook his head. Her phone rang again.

'Cake?' Lund said. 'OK. I'll buy cake. Come again?'

She put the phone in her pocket and sighed.

'What is it?' Strange asked.

'Bjørn has a nut allergy. Where do I buy a cake that doesn't have nuts?'

'Lagkagehuset,' Strange said. 'You just have to ask. "Cake without nuts, please."'

'I know how to buy cake,' Lund said very slowly.

'Get it later,' Brix ordered. 'Kodmani's got something to say. And he wants to say it to you.'

Lund's large, all-seeing eyes stared at him.

'Cake shops don't stay open all night, Brix.'

Strange got her jacket, held it for her, arms open.

'We'll stop along the way.'

Raben lurked among the curious bystanders gathered in a huddle in the rain to watch the emergency services go in and out of the office block in Islands Brygge. His hood was well down. His jacket was grimy. He could have been one more drunk or homeless hobo living on the edge of the city. Someone people noticed but never went near.

And so he could watch as they carried out a stretcher, on it a bent shape wrapped in a shroud of black plastic.

Raben hung around, thinking, wondering. Then she was out again. The woman cop. Striking more than pretty, her hair looked a little lank and her bright eyes shone with a relentless curiosity.

She was peering at the crowd. Smart enough to know he might hang around. Raben pulled his hood down further then slunk off towards the bridge and Vesterbro.

Twenty minutes striding through the drizzle and he was back in Torpe's church telling him what had happened.

The priest looked scared.

'You don't know who was on that trolley,' Torpe said. He was in jeans and a sweatshirt. Civilian clothes. 'Maybe David wasn't the victim.'

Raben sat on the hard pew, cold, hungry, miserable. Lonely too. He wanted to talk to Louise. He wanted to have Jonas sit on his knee.

'It was him.'

'Maybe it was an accident—'

'Grüner's dead. Why can't you face the truth? There's something going on here. Something bad . . .'

Torpe, a strong man, looked ready to weep. He half-fell onto the pew ahead and put his hands to his face.

'Pull yourself together, man,' Raben ordered.

'David had a wife and child!' Torpe barked at him, bleary-eyed. 'So do you. Think about them . . .'

'Did you find the others?'

'What others? Don't you remember? Myg's gone. David now. Apart from you there's only one left. Lisbeth Thomsen.'

That wasn't right.

'No. What about HC? He got back OK. I heard he was a bit crazy—'

'HC died in a car crash last year. It's just you and Thomsen.'

Raben swore, lifted his eyes to the altar. Looked at the figure on the cross, understood nothing.

'Where's Thomsen?'

'I heard she left Copenhagen a while back. You know what she's like. Never happy unless she's on her own . . .'

There was a sound at the door. Someone rattling the handle. Raben was on his feet in an instant, fists ready.

'No, no,' Torpe assured him. 'It's Louise. She called when you were out. She said you gave her a sign. I told her I didn't know where you were. It didn't matter. She wanted to come anyway.'

'They'll be following her.'

Torpe scowled at him.

'Do you think she doesn't know that?' He beckoned to the side room. 'Go in there. Let me check.'

Raben didn't move.

'I won't let you down,' Torpe said. 'I never did that in Helmand, did I? Why would I start here?'

When Raben had gone Torpe went to the front door.

'Jonas?' She was on the phone, talking in a motherly voice bordering on the cross. The priest nodded towards the back of the church. 'Do as the babysitter says. Go to bed. I'll be home soon.'

Torpe checked outside, saw no one, let her in then went into the rooms out the back.

When Raben came into the nave she didn't rush towards him.

'Who knows you're here?' he asked.

'Nobody. I told the babysitter I was visiting a friend. They had a car follow me.' She paused. 'I went into a bar in Vesterbrogade. Got out the back.'

He came close. Wondered whether to try to hold her. Louise didn't move, wasn't smiling in the wan street light from the high church windows.

'I've been phoning everyone trying to find you. The priest couldn't lie to me.' She seemed as stiff and cold as a stranger. 'Why did you escape? Why couldn't you wait?'

'Myg and Grüner have been murdered.'

She shook her head, retreated from him as he tried to touch her.

'Grüner too?'

'Tonight.'

'Why—?'

'I don't know why! They were scared. They remembered something from Helmand. I can't—'

'What are you talking about, Jens?'

There was a note of anger in her voice he hadn't heard before. Louise had always sided with him. That mattered.

'Something happened out there—'

'They went through all that when you came back. There was an inquiry. I know you were sick—'

'Something happened. I never told you the truth. None of us talked about it.'

'What?'

He shook his head, wished, more than anything, he could answer that question.

'I don't remember. It's just a mess . . . We went into a local house. There was an officer there. We got hit. A bomb. Next thing I'm in an army hospital back home. But it happened. It's in . . .' He tapped his skull. 'It's in here somewhere. Myg knew. I think Grüner did too. I could see it when I talked to him—'

'You spoke to Grüner?'

'I thought it was just something rotten in my mind. It was me somehow.'

He looked at her. Wondered about the expression on her face, where he'd seen it before. Remembered. She was a nurse. It was the way she looked at sick people.

'I wasn't dreaming,' Raben said, trying to take her hands. 'It was real. I wasn't crazy. They knew that when they locked me up . . .'

She retreated from him.

'Jens! You kidnapped a stranger in Vesterbro. You said he was an officer from the army. You threatened to kill him.'

Raben couldn't think of a thing to say.

'He was no one,' Louise said, coming a little closer, but still not touching him. 'Someone you saw on the street. You were ill. Maybe still—'

'I'm not sick now,' he insisted. 'They're not taking me. If I don't find out what's going on they'll let me rot in Herstedvester for ever.'

'No . . .' She took out her phone, held it out for him. 'This has gone too far. I want you to call the police. Give yourself up. You do this.' She waved the mobile. 'Don't make me.'

He closed his eyes, felt a bitter note of laughter rise in his throat.

'We can explain it somehow,' she went on. 'All you need is time. Do what Toft says. Take your medication.'

He didn't get mad. He wouldn't allow that.

'Louise,' he said, and before she knew it, took her arms. 'Don't you see?'

Her eyes were glistening. He hated it when she cried.

'I did all that. I did everything they wanted. They still didn't let me out. They've got a reason.'

She snatched her hands from his, swore bitterly.

'Two years I've waited for you. On my own. Talking to doctors and lawyers. I feel like a widow . . .'

'I did what they asked,' he said again very slowly.

'You broke out of jail. You robbed a petrol station. What chance are we supposed to have?'

'Someone killed Myg. Then Grüner.'

'I want you home . . .'

The heat, the fury came anyway, unbidden.

'Do I wait ten years in that cell then?' Raben roared. 'Let my son forget me? Wait until you run off with that slippery bastard Søgaard?'

Another curse, she turned away and walked towards the door.

They always talked, too much sometimes. Friends before they were lovers. She was the best companion he'd ever known. More than a wife. Always would be, or so he'd thought.

'I'm sorry,' he said, catching up with her. 'I'll sort it out. I promise. I know what I'm doing.'

She didn't walk off.

'Help me, Louise,' Raben pleaded. 'There's something wrong here. Really wrong.'

'Jens. We're little people—'

'You're not little to me. You're the most important thing in the world. You and Jonas.'

Her bright eyes flared.

'Then why—?'

'Because I want to be home. With both of you. If I just sit back and wait . . .'

He'd got her attention, finally.

'You'll stay in jail,' she said. 'I get the message.'

'No.' He held her. 'I'll be like Myg and Grüner. Dead.'

She looked round the church, then at him.

'There's only two of us left,' he said. 'Lisbeth Thomsen's the last. She's left Copenhagen. There'll be a personnel file in the barracks database.'

'Jens—'

'I've got to warn her. Take this.' He gave her Torpe's spare phone. 'I'll get another from somewhere. I'll call you tomorrow morning.'

He put a hand to her forehead. It was cold, like her.

'I've got to go, love. They'll be looking for me here.'

'Go where?'

'There's a city out there,' he said, nodding at the door. 'A million places.'

'Who are you?' she whispered, stretching out of his grip as he tried to hold her.

'I'm Jens. I'm who I always was.'

She stared at him and didn't say a word.

'Kiss Jonas for me.'

At that she let him come close and briefly plant his lips on her cheek.

This, he thought, was all the intimacy they had left. Everything else had been stripped from them.

Jens Peter Raben walked her to the church door, watched his wife leave. There'd be a doorway to sleep in somewhere. A place to hide in the dark.

Karina had been through more of the diary.

'I can't see any way Monberg and Dragsholm knew each other personally. PET don't believe it either.'

'König kept this whole case to himself for no good reason,' Buch muttered. 'Am I supposed to take his word on it?'

'PET monitor ministers. You do know that?'

'I'm sure they've got photos of me eating a hot dog. Listen. We know the two met at a hotel the weekend before she was killed. Why?'

She checked the diary. Monberg was speaking at a seminar on human rights. It was arranged by Amnesty. Dragsholm was on the organizing committee.

'Did they spend the night together?'

She shook her head.

'How would I know? I was there in the afternoon. I never saw her. I'm sure they weren't having an affair. I think I'd have noticed.'

Plough came in looking glum. He had a fresh folder. More photos sent direct from the murder scene in Islands Brygge.

'Who is it this time?' Buch asked.

'A former soldier from Ryvangen. He was an invalid who served with Myg Poulsen.'

The photographs were so disgusting Karina couldn't look. A crippled man incinerated in his own wheelchair. Buch could just about make that out.

'The Prime Minister wants a meeting with you and the Minister of Defence,' Plough said.

Buch was barely listening.

'We need to know what connects Monberg to Anne Dragsholm. We've got to find out if Monberg withheld information for personal reasons.'

Plough stared through the rainy windows. He seemed embarrassed.

'There's something you should know. I wouldn't ordinarily intrude into the private lives of ministers.'

Silence.

'Out with it,' Buch ordered.

'For the last few months Monberg acted strangely at times. He cancelled meetings where his presence was needed. It wasn't like him. He always had a plausible excuse if I asked—'

'Get to the point,' Buch ordered.

Plough took off his glasses.

'I'm afraid he wasn't always where he said. He lied . . .' The civil servant looked visibly hurt. 'To me. I wondered if he was seeing someone.'

He coughed.

'Without his family's knowledge as it were.'

'You mean he had a bit on the side?' Buch demanded.

'If you wish to put it that way—'

'And it was Dragsholm?'

'I don't know who it was. Sometimes he stayed at a hotel in Klampenborg. She didn't live far away. He could get back into the city easily too I imagine.'

'PET never reported any of this,' Karina said. 'Monberg was a responsible man. If any of this related to a case he was handling he would have mentioned it.'

Buch took a bar of chocolate out of his pocket and broke it over the photos from the crime scene. Karina declined his offer of a chunk.

'Monberg was the Minister of Justice,' he said. 'If anyone knew how to avoid PET who better—?'

'I think it's best you don't mention any of this when you meet the Prime Minister,' Plough suggested. 'Monberg has lots of friends in government. The Prime Minister. Flemming Rossing, the Defence Minister, has been close to him for years as well. It's a sensitive matter. We can't just blurt this out.'

'I'm not in the habit of blurting,' Buch objected.

The two of them were silent.

'Am I?' he asked.

Lund questioned Kodmani in the same interview room, taking control from the outset. Strange grabbed a chair in silence, pulled out a notebook and a pen.

Kodmani stared at him.

'I said just the woman.'

'It doesn't work like that,' Lund told him. 'My colleague's just going to . . .'

Strange bent over the notebook, pretended to lick the tip of the pencil.

'Take notes,' she added. Then to the man in blue, 'You want to tell me something.'

Kodmani held his hands together, stroked his long black beard.

'I want to tell you all I know about Faith Fellow. This is the truth.'

'I hope so.'

'It is the truth. Those people . . . those friends of mine you arrested. They've got nothing to do with this. You should let them go.'

Strange grunted. Lund kicked him under the table.

'We don't cut deals. We arrest who we suspect. If they're innocent they'll walk free.'

He seemed to accept that.

'I know I made a mistake, lady. I know I'm going to pay for it. But it should just be me. No one else.'

'What mistake?'

He leaned back, folded his arms in front of his chest.

'Faith Fellow came to me through the website. I thought he was genuine but now . . .' He sighed. 'He played me like a fiddle. Told me what I wanted to hear. I was a fool. He seemed to understand me. My faith, my politics, my hatred for—'

'I'm not writing this bastard's life story,' Strange said and put down the pencil.

Lund picked it up and placed it back in his hand then put a finger to her lips. Kodmani watched. He seemed to like this.

'I thought I could trust him,' the Moroccan went on. 'He seemed so ... convincing. He asked me to set up a post office box for his donations. Then he wanted to know how he could upload a video to my site.'

'Did he ask you to kill a few people too?' Strange said without taking his head up from the pad.

Lund glowered at him.

'He never asked me to do anything that looked bad,' Kodmani replied. 'There was nothing like that. I'm not a warrior...'

He leaned forward, gazed at Lund.

'My only crime is it made me feel good. At first. When I saw your people were dying too. It was like you were being punished for once. I felt vindicated...'

'And then?' she asked.

'You showed me those photos. I knew we were going to pay for this.'

She shook her head.

'What do you mean?'

He laughed.

'I thought you were smarter than them. But you just see what you want to see. These murderers aren't my people. They're someone else. Someone who hates us.'

'Who?'

'You're the police, aren't you?' he said with a sneer. 'Go find out. I didn't kill anyone. None of the people I know would. But this Faith Fellow...'

'What language did he write in?'

'English mostly. Arabic sometimes.'

A sudden look of disgust.

'That was to impress me. He wasn't good at it. I think he knew that. I asked him one time where he came from.' Kodmani shrugged. 'He never answered.'

'Did he write about an army squad? About Anne Dragsholm?'

'No.'

He was drying up.

'There must be more, Kodmani...'

'He was a man who sent me emails. Got me worked up. He knew what he was doing. The words Faith Fellow used...' Kodmani glanced at Strange. 'They were very precise and brief. Like a man in authority.'

He leaned forward again, anxious suddenly.

'He sounded like a soldier. Yes. He was a soldier.'

'Oh come on,' Strange snarled. 'How can you possibly know that?'

Kodmani glowered at him.

'She asked me the questions. Not you.' He looked at Lund again. 'Faith Fellow's a soldier. I'm convinced of that. Or maybe—'

'Maybe?'

'Maybe he used to be.'

Just like last time Brix and König watched through the glass. They met with Lund and Strange after the interview was over.

The PET boss looked more miserable than ever.

'I'm not putting Kodmani in the clear yet,' König said. 'This whole story about Faith Fellow sounds like a fabrication to me. What does he have to back it up?'

'He says Faith Fellow's the one behind the Muslim League,' Lund pointed out. 'The video, the army connections, the dog tags. We've got nothing that points towards Kodmani's own people.'

'Nothing,' Brix agreed. 'We need to focus on Ryvangen and find a motive.'

'What motive?' Strange asked. 'Kodmani's got one. If one of his people didn't do it . . .'

Lund turned on König.

'Tell us what you know about Raben's squad.'

The PET man didn't like being pushed.

'They were a solid team. Raben had been their leader for two years. They served in Iraq. Good record. Same in Afghanistan.'

'What did they do?' Lund asked.

'They were soldiers,' König replied, as if that said everything. 'Front line. Plenty of combat experience. On the last mission the squad got hit in a suicide attack.'

'Where are the rest of them now?'

Strange checked his notes.

'Poulsen and Grüner are dead. A third soldier was killed in a car crash last year. That leaves Raben and a woman. Lisbeth Thomsen. She left the army after she came back. No one knows where she's gone.'

'Wait,' Lund cut in. 'Dragsholm wasn't part of the squad. She was just connected to it. Is that right?'

'Yes,' König agreed. 'Anne Dragsholm represented all five surviving soldiers at the inquiry.'

'Inquiry into what?'

'Their last mission. Why it went wrong.' He hesitated for a second. 'What happened.'

Brix stared at him.

'What did happen?'

König was wriggling.

'Some local civilians said Raben and his team murdered an Afghan family in their home. That was why they were attacked. It wasn't the Taliban who tried to kill them. It was the villagers themselves.'

'And?' Lund asked when no one else did.

'The judge advocate cleared them completely.'

'Wait, wait, wait.' She wasn't going to let this go. 'I talked to Dragsholm's husband. There was an argument. She felt the army as good as fired her.'

König shook his head.

'Maybe she told him that but the fact is she resigned. We've got her letter in the files.'

There was a knock on the door. Ruth Hedeby asked to see König outside.

'I still can't see this,' the PET man said before he left. 'Kodmani told us he thought Faith Fellow was from the military. Let's say that's true. It's someone who came back from Afghanistan. Why would he want to take revenge on his own comrades? No . . . It doesn't work.'

He left it at that and walked out.

'What's a judge advocate's report?' Lund asked when König was gone.

'It's an inquiry to see if a military crime's been committed,' Strange explained. 'Raben and his team could have been prosecuted if it went against them.'

Lund looked at Brix.

'I want a copy sent to my address as soon as you can get it.' She picked up her bag. 'We need to find Lisbeth Thomsen. And . . .'

'Lund,' Strange said.

There was something else she couldn't remember.

'The cake,' he said patiently. 'You need to deliver that cake you bought.'

*

168

Brix went next door, summoned by a phone call from Ruth Hedeby. She'd been talking to Erik König, smiled at him as he went out.

Then she walked round the table, kneading her hands. Brix buttoned up his jacket.

'What's wrong?' he asked.

'I see you decided to keep Lund after all.'

Brix thought of all the answers he could give. How König had asked for her. How she'd been two steps ahead of everyone else.

Instead he said, 'Is that a problem?'

'No, Lennart. Not if you don't care about what happens to your career.'

He walked to the window, looked out at the movement in the offices across the way.

'You're discussing my future with Erik König? I find that faintly insulting. From what I hear in the Ministry he's got a sight more to worry about than—'

'I talk to the Ministry!' Hedeby cried, looking up at his craggy, unsmiling face. 'Not you.'

Brix said nothing.

'Oh I know, Lennart. You've been hanging around all the corridors that matter for years. You're not just chief of homicide, are you? There are friends everywhere.'

He did smile at that.

'I'm a social animal. You of all people ought to appreciate that.'

'If anyone's under pressure in the Ministry it's Buch himself. Have you seen him on TV? Fat ball of blubber—'

'What's going on? I've a right to know. If you or König know something . . .'

Ruth Hedeby reached up and adjusted his silk tie.

'You're an arrogant bastard.'

'I think you may have mentioned that once or twice.'

Her hand ran across his perfectly ironed white shirt.

'I've got some free time this evening. Shall we meet up later?'

She watched him anxiously.

'Best be your place, Lennart. We don't want to be disturbed, do we?'

Still he kept quiet.

'I'll take that as yes,' Hedeby said. 'Ten o'clock. I'll bring the wine.'

'No.' Brix looked startled. 'My wine please.'

She raised an eyebrow.

'It's better,' he said.

Buch was getting to grips with the inner maze of Slotsholmen so he made this journey on his own. The bright-red hot dog smothered in fried onions, sliced gherkins and remoulade sauce had long disappeared by the time he finally found the footbridge over to the Christianborg Palace. Buch was wiping his greasy fingers on his suit trousers as he walked into the Prime Minister's office.

They were watching the TV news. The third murder. The media even had a name, David Grüner, and the fact that he'd served at Ryvangen.

Grue Eriksen and Flemming Rossing were deep in conversation when Buch turned up. Rossing was a dapper man, always perfectly dressed, with a striking craggy face dominated by a Roman nose and hair reminiscent of an eagle's smooth, trim feathers. He raised an eyebrow as he caught Buch surreptitiously rubbing his hands on Grue Eriksen's curtains.

'Dining out again?' he asked.

'Just time for snacks at the moment.'

He'd never much liked this man. On the few occasions he'd needed to ask questions of the Minister of Defence Rossing had seemed dismissive, as some of the old guard of the party did. They saw him as an upstart, riding on the shoulders of his dead brother. Nothing Buch could do would change that.

'Like the two previous victims,' the TV continued, 'Grüner was the victim of ruthless violence.'

'Where do they get all this stuff?' Grue Eriksen complained. He looked deeply, personally hurt. 'What about the poor man's wife?'

Buch took the seat opposite them by the window. In the ring outside, beneath the dim street lights, a solitary horse was trotting round in the rain tugging a coach on which a uniformed man sat buttoned up against the weather.

'She was informed very quickly,' Buch replied. 'I made sure of that. This was a major incident in a public place. We can't keep it quiet.'

The Prime Minister looked dissatisfied with that answer. An aide came and gave him a phone. He walked to the window and started to speak in a low, inaudible voice.

Rossing got up, shook Buch's hand.

'I wish these were more pleasant circumstances.'

'Am I late for something?'

'Just catching up on events.' He smiled, a practised gesture, friendly without much warmth. 'So many since you took office. Holding up?'

'I can cope,' Buch answered.

'That's the spirit.' Rossing slapped him hard on the arm. A male gesture he might have learned from the military. 'You're doing fine. Monberg . . .'

The mention of an old friend made Rossing's face seem more human.

'I think he would have been pleased to know you've taken over from him. Besides . . . If the pressure made him sick before, what would it have done to him now?'

'Let's get started,' Grue Eriksen announced, coming off the phone.

Coffee and very fancy pastries from a woman aide and then they were left alone with their papers.

'Police and PET are onto it,' Buch said after he briefed them on the state of the investigation.

'This is going to take some time?' Grue Eriksen asked.

'Looks like it.'

'We don't have time,' Rossing grumbled. 'These bastards know we're struggling to reach an agreement on the anti-terror package. We can't wait for Agger to see reason. She's sniffing votes here.'

Buch took a deep breath and said, 'She's taken an inflexible position I agree—'

'Inflexible?' Rossing cried. 'That woman will do anything to score a point. It doesn't matter how low the blow. We have to come to an agreement with Krabbe and the People's Party immediately. If that means banning these obscure little pests they hate so much then . . .' He sighed and opened his hands. 'What choice do we have? Let's cut the deal and have done with it.'

'It's not as simple as that.'

Both men stared at Thomas Buch.

'Sadly . . .' he added, 'we picked up these extremists because PET were watching them. But there's no direct evidence they were involved. We can't place a single individual we've arrested anywhere near one of the crimes.'

'Thomas . . .' Rossing began.

'We've got just about every known militant in Denmark in custody. And still there's another murder. To ban them because of this case alone would be ineffective and wrong.'

'Caution and patience are fine and dandy for peacetime,' Rossing observed, with a caustic note in his voice. 'If that were the case now I'd agree with you.'

'So could I,' Grue Eriksen added. 'We have to show firmness.'

'We have to demonstrate justice,' Buch objected. 'If we ban these people and then find ourselves forced to admit they're entirely innocent—'

'They're not *entirely* innocent, are they?' Rossing noted. 'PET wouldn't be watching them if they were.'

'Other matters are clouding the picture and they may have nothing to do with this Kodmani creature and his sorry followers.'

Grue Eriksen put a thoughtful fist to his chin. Then Rossing did the same. Buch felt once more like a schoolboy called to the headmaster's study, this time with the head prefect listening too.

'It seems Monberg knew the first victim, Anne Dragsholm, personally,' he said, watching their faces, seeing no reaction at all. 'He kept it a secret.'

'How did he know her?' Rossing asked. 'What do PET have to say?'

'PET knew nothing—'

'Monberg's a friend of mine,' Rossing cried. 'One of the most decent men I know. I don't have to listen to office gossip—'

'This isn't gossip, I'm afraid. We found his diary. We know they met. We know they had discussions about . . .'

Rossing threw up his hands in despair.

'If this was of no interest to PET then it's of no interest to us.'

'Thomas,' Grue Eriksen cut in. 'Is there something you're not telling us?'

The carriage outside was wheeling off the ring. The rain was coming down at forty-five degrees. Too much even for one of the Queen's riders.

'I've told you everything I know at the moment.'

'Good,' the Prime Minister replied. 'Let's leave PET to get on with their work while we focus on ours. We need this package through the

Folketinget. Perhaps it's rash to accuse this particular organization. But we've all read the kind of filth they propagate.'

'It may be vile. It's not illegal.'

'These people are reprehensible and hostile to everything we stand for,' Grue Eriksen interrupted. 'If Birgitte Agger wishes to complain when we take action against them let her do it. I don't think the man on the street will give her the time of day.'

'The law—'

'The law's what we make it!' The Prime Minister didn't look quite so avuncular at that moment. 'I want you to agree to Krabbe's demands. Put some more names on the banned list. He's got us by the balls and he knows it. Seal an agreement with the People's Party so we can announce it as soon as possible.'

Buch was quiet.

'Can you do that?' Flemming Rossing asked.

'A broad agreement would be better.'

'A broad agreement's impossible!' Grue Eriksen cried. 'Surely you can see this by now. I know you're new to government. But . . .'

He waited for a response, knowing none would come.

'That's that then,' the Prime Minister declared, bringing the silence to an end.

After the news from the Politigården Colonel Jarnvig called Søgaard and Bilal together for a briefing. The three men sat in his office looking at the transport schedules and the plans for troop movements.

'This next dispatch has enough problems as it is,' Jarnvig grumbled. 'We don't need more. What's the mood?'

'Not good,' Søgaard admitted. 'We've introduced some new briefings on security measures, here and abroad. Some of them will still try to opt out.'

'They'll have to explain that to me first,' Bilal said.

'Me too,' Søgaard added. 'But they've got the right to refuse combat service and some of them will. Not many maybe but . . .'

Jarnvig frowned.

'If a man's too scared to fight I don't want him there. What else can we do?'

'We've invited the soldiers and their relatives to a meeting,' Søgaard said. 'Bilal will talk to them tomorrow.'

'They're going to ask about Grüner now,' Bilal said. 'What am I supposed to say?'

'Tell them the truth,' Jarnvig replied. 'This is a temporary and untypical situation. It won't last. We'll get things sorted out.'

He looked at them in turn.

'We're soldiers. We serve. We manage the hand we're dealt and we don't ask questions. That's our duty. They know that. Don't they?'

'They know it,' Bilal said with some force before Søgaard could answer.

'Good.'

The dark-haired officer didn't move.

'Grüner was in the same team as Myg Poulsen. The woman who got killed, the legal adviser, was something to do with them too.'

'What are you saying?' Jarnvig asked.

'People are going to talk.'

'Let them,' Søgaard cut in. 'That can't be helped. We're hiding nothing here. The police—'

'We'll give them all the help they need,' Jarnvig said. 'If they ask for a file they get it. Just make sure you tell me first.'

Bilal stood up, arms obediently behind his back. He didn't look satisfied.

'What about Raben?' he asked. 'He was squad leader. He broke out of Herstedvester—'

'Why in God's name are you bringing up Raben now?' Søgaard barked at him.

'He's going to come looking for his old comrades,' Bilal replied. 'He'll be fishing round here before long.'

Søgaard laughed.

'If he's stupid enough for that I'll throw him in a cell myself.'

Bilal didn't speak.

'Well?' Jarnvig asked.

'I saw Raben in the field. He's good. If he doesn't want to be caught we won't even see him. He's got friends inside here—'

'If you're worried about my daughter's loyalty, Bilal,' Jarnvig interrupted, 'then say it.'

The young officer stayed silent.

'Good.' The colonel nodded at the door. 'That's all.'

Louise walked in before they could leave.

'Do you have a moment, Dad?' she asked.

'Not now. I'll see to it that the furniture's cleared out of the basement tomorrow. You can start working on it then.'

She shook her head.

'I heard about Grüner. He was in Jens's squad too. What's going on?'

'I don't know.' Jarnvig couldn't stop himself from looking at her. 'The police told me Jens was there just before Grüner was killed tonight. They're looking for him.'

'Oh, for God's sake! You don't think—?'

'I don't know what to think. The police are going to be keeping an eye on you and Jonas.'

'They've been doing that already. I'm not a criminal.'

He put on his beret, picked up his papers.

'But your husband is, Louise. That's not your fault. If Jens contacts you it's important you let me know.'

Bilal and Søgaard stood at the back of the office, silent, staring at their feet. Listening to every word.

'Louise?' Jarnvig asked again. 'Did you hear me? Will you agree to that?'

Then she looked up into his face, nodded, said, 'Yes. Sir.'

It was the voice she used when she was a rebellious teenager. And it meant nothing then either.

'Good. We've got to go. There's a couple of dirty shirts in the drawer from the gym. Can you wash them for me?'

She saluted him. Then them.

Torsten Jarnvig muttered something and left with his officers.

The shirts were where he always left them. In a basket by the side of the desk. She looked at the computer there. He never remembered to log out and it was ten minutes before the system did that automatically.

Louise Raben sat down. Hesitated for only a moment then started to type.

He was camp commander. Had access to files she'd never see in the infirmary. Lisbeth Thomsen was in there somewhere. All she had to do was find her then get out without leaving a trace.

Lund hadn't let Strange into the bakers on the way back from Islands Brygge. She just knew he'd have an opinion about which was the best cake to buy. Would probably be right too. Cakes weren't her thing. So she picked something chocolate. Everyone liked that.

After she'd changed into fresh clothes her mother set about dissecting it with a large sharp knife.

Work intruded always. Lund soon found herself standing in the living room of Vibeke's flat in Østerbro taking a call from forensic who were being evasive about reports.

'I want them by the morning,' Lund said. 'That's that.'

She wasn't much interested in a lecture on the laws of physics. Or eating really.

Bjørn and her mother sat on the sofa with a pot of coffee picking at the cake and looking at paperwork for the wedding on Saturday.

'Thanks,' Lund said and ended the call. 'I'm sorry, Mum. All yours now.'

'Take a look at this,' Vibeke said.

It was a printout for a table setting. More than thirty people, all named, all placed.

'We've decided to have a traditional horseshoe setting.'

Bjørn nodded.

'That's the nicest,' he said.

'I'm sure it is,' Lund agreed, wondering what they were talking about.

'There's nothing else traditional about our wedding!' Vibeke declared happily.

She'd never seen her mother this content, not for years anyway. Back when Lund was a quiet, solitary child with two parents who seemed to love one another.

Bjørn was a touch on the podgy side and quite bald. More like a grandfather than a stepfather, she thought. A few years older than her mother. It was hard to judge. Lund found it natural to peer at strangers and try to understand them, to see behind their facade. But those close to her were always more opaque somehow.

'This cake's very good,' Bjørn said, helping himself to a third slice.

'You see where you're seated?' Vibeke asked, pointing to the sheet.

'Can't I be next to Mark?'

'We'd like you here, please.' That motherly voice had resumed its natural, hectoring tone. 'Bjørn's cousin's in town on his own because his wife's ill.'

'He's a country boy,' Bjørn said, then started coughing. 'Someone has to look after him. Excuse . . .'

His hand was over his mouth. Crumbs of chocolate cake flew into the air.

'You're welcome to bring someone,' Vibeke added. 'If you must.'

Lund shook her head.

'Don't you have a boyfriend?' Bjørn asked. 'Pretty young thing like you. If old folk like us can manage it—'

'Sarah's taking a break,' Vibeke broke in, then patted his knee as the coughing fit resumed.

Bjørn's face was going red. Lund could see the label for the cake. It was on her side of the table. The ingredients . . . She reached over and slyly dislodged the paper from the wrapping, crumpled it and slid the screwed-up label into her pocket.

'I was taking a break too,' he said, his voice hoarse all of a sudden. 'But then your mother came along and made me think better of it. Did she tell you how we met?'

Lund's phone trilled. Vibeke scowled. It was Strange. He said he was passing on his way home. He was outside and had something.

'How?' she asked, coming off the phone.

'Yesterday . . .' he crooned to the tune of the old song then kissed Vibeke on the cheek.

'It's a second-hand shop,' her mother said. 'Very good quality. Not charity rubbish or anything . . .'

'Of course not,' Lund agreed.

'I was looking for a coat.' He paused and punched his chest with his fist. 'A good brand. Then—'

The doorbell rang. Lund excused herself and got up to answer it, trying to ignore the sound of coughing growing louder from behind.

Strange stood by the door dripping rain onto the floor. Two folders in a plastic bag.

'I found the judge advocate's report like you asked. And a file on Lisbeth Thomsen.'

She took them.

'Any clue where she is now?'

He shook his head. Strange looked tired for once.

'She sublet her flat a year ago. Every three months she comes back for mail and to collect the rent. That's all I know.'

Lund flicked through the judge's report.

'Maybe she wants to be on her own,' he suggested. 'She trained with special forces too, alongside Raben. If she wants to hide—'

'Why should she do that?'

He looked at her.

'You went all the way to Gedser, didn't you?'

'That's not the same . . .'

A sound behind. Vibeke was helping Bjørn towards the door. He looked awful, breathless and sweaty. For one dreadful moment Lund thought he might throw up on the spot. She stepped aside and let them through.

'We've got to go,' Vibeke said. 'Bjørn's feeling unwell.'

'I'm sorry . . .'

His eyes were puffy. A nice man, he seemed more embarrassed than troubled.

'Are you sure there were no nuts in that cake?' her mother demanded.

'I . . . well . . . I asked.'

Strange coughed into his fist and looked at the floor.

'Gluten does it to me too,' Bjørn said quickly. 'It's nothing at all. I'm used to it. Goodnight . . .'

Hand on the railing, he went down the staircase very carefully.

Vibeke stayed.

'And you are . . . ?' she asked suspiciously, eyeing Strange from head to toe.

He held out his hand and smiled. She took it and a conversation ensued so genial and easy Lund felt an intruder to be witnessing it. In a few short sentences Strange covered the weather, best wishes for the impending wedding, and an assurance that the fated cake was indeed entirely free of nuts, or so the bakers had said.

Vibeke would have stayed longer if Bjørn hadn't started bleating between coughs from downstairs.

She gave Ulrik Strange a look Lund hadn't seen since her teenage years, when a boy called, one Lund hated. It said: what a nice young man.

'I can hardly believe you're a police officer,' Vibeke said, bidding them goodbye. 'You should see some of them. They're animals . . .'

Strange saluted. When her mother was out of earshot Lund said, 'I think I'm going to be sick now.'

'It's not the cake, is it?'

'You've no idea whether it's got nuts or not.'

He shook his head.

'I was backing you up. That's what partners do, remember?'

She waved the reports at him, ready to go back inside.

'I've asked Colonel Jarnvig to come in and talk about it tomorrow,' Strange added.

'And there's still no news about Raben?'

'No.'

'OK. See you in the morning.'

Strange didn't move. He was no longer quite so confident.

'I like cake,' he said. 'With nuts. Without nuts. I'm . . .'

He stamped his feet.

'My car's way down the street. I had to plough through the rain to get here. I'm cold.' He peered round, into the empty flat. 'You've got coffee too?'

'Anything else?' she asked.

'Cake and coffee will be fine for now, thanks.'

There was a glint of hope in Strange's eyes. It made him look young and rather innocent.

'Goodnight,' she said and closed the door.

Thursday 17th November

9.03 a.m.   Louise Raben took her father's car to the kindergarten. Close to Østerport Station the phone rang.

'Go out towards Dampfærgevej. The ferries. Use the big car park.'

It was just a few minutes away.

'You've got transport?' she asked.

A pause.

'Priest lent me his car. Did you find anything?'

'I've got some documents. There was a file on Thomsen. Just her Copenhagen address.'

'She comes from Hirtshals.'

'There was nothing about that.'

'She had an uncle in Sweden. He lived on an island.'

Louise took the printouts out of her bag and spread them on the passenger seat, scanned them when the traffic came to a halt.

'Thomsen used to go there on leave,' Raben said.

So many papers. Everything in army language, curt, concise, blunt. On the third page she saw a few lines.

'There's a note here. The uncle's dead now. She got leave for the funeral. A place called Skogö.'

'That's it. She used to stay in his shack.'

The car park was half empty. She drove slowly up and down the lanes.

Towards the docks there was a grey Renault. A large silver crucifix dangled from the rear-view mirror. A man in a baseball cap was huddled behind the wheel, barely visible.

'Pull into the next bay on your left,' Raben said. 'They're watching you. Black Saab, fifty metres behind. Two men, one with a beard.'

'Jens . . .'

She did what he wanted then looked in the mirror. The unmarked police car rolled past. One of the men inside was speaking, trying not to look at her.

Jens had ducked beneath the dashboard as they approached. All they saw was an empty car. He always said he was good at this. She didn't doubt it. Didn't want to know what else he excelled at either.

'I don't want you involved,' he said, coming up from behind the wheel as the black car disappeared round the corner.

'So why did you ask me to raid the barracks computer?'

'I'll call you when I can.'

'Jens!'

She wanted to get out, walk over, throw open the door of Priest's car and scream in his face.

But she couldn't. It was easier to say it into an invisible microphone, knowing the words would travel the few metres between them unseen, in a metallic voice that failed to disguise her pain.

'I can't take this any more. I'm thirty-four years old and I want my life back.'

'Listen . . .'

She could just make out his hawk-like eyes fixed on her from the car across the way.

'No, you listen. I've decided,' she said. 'I'm not moving from the barracks. The army's going to be our home. They'll keep me on at the infirmary. I need the money. Some stability.'

'Don't do this to me . . .'

She felt herself getting mad.

'To you? *You?* What about me? What about my son? I've waited two years and now you've run away like a thief.'

'You're my wife.'

'I'm not your bloody slave! I won't wait for ever. I'm human. Not made of rock or something . . . Oh fuck it.'

She got out. Determined to say this to his face.

Goodbye. The end. She couldn't finish a marriage she'd treasured over the phone.

The engine of the grey car came noisily alive. Tyres screeching, it wheeled away as she approached, back towards the city.

Louise Raben glanced round. No black Saab. Maybe they'd gone anyway which seemed odd.

'Jens?' she said into the phone.

But the line was dead.

Jarnvig turned up at the Politigården in uniform. They took him into the same interview room they'd used for Kodmani: the colonel in the middle, Strange and Lund either side of the table.

Lund pushed the judge advocate's report towards the army man.

'This says something about civilian casualties. What was that about?'

'The usual.'

'The usual? The usual what?'

'It's a war. People die. We try to avoid collateral damage as much as we can but . . .' He sighed as if this were all tedious. 'We're fighting in towns and villages. In people's homes sometimes. They don't wear uniforms. They look like everyone else. It could be a kid carrying an IED. A woman.' He stared at them. 'A police officer.'

'I appreciate that. But in this specific case . . . was it true?'

'No. There was a thorough investigation. It cleared the squad of any wrongdoing. The complaint came from a village that was involved in the opium trade. There was the question of government corruption. It's a complicated situation . . .'

An officer came to the door and nodded at Strange. He left.

'So you don't believe the allegations?' Lund asked.

Jarnvig gave her a filthy look.

'Not for one minute.'

She picked up a passage in the papers.

'The report says—'

'I didn't come here to be treated like a criminal.'

Jarnvig seemed bolder with Strange out of the room.

'You haven't seen how I treat criminals,' Lund replied with a smile. 'We're trying to get to the bottom of three murders, Colonel.'

'I lost that many men, all of them from Ryvangen. Dead in some Afghan hellhole.' He pointed at the papers. 'I think you'll find that in there as well. We took it seriously.'

Lund sat back, looked at her empty coffee cup. She'd meant to bring Strange a piece of cake but forgot.

'And you think someone from Afghanistan has come all this way to take revenge?' she asked.

'You tell me. We try to build bridges over there. We don't want a battle with the entire population. But someone could still bear a grudge. We're not universally popular, in case you hadn't guessed.'

'What if it's one of your own? Someone within the ranks who sympathizes with the Taliban?'

Jarnvig laughed at her.

'You really don't know anything about the army, do you?'

'I'm doing my best to learn.'

He leaned forward, rapped his strong finger on the table.

'We're a family. We look after our own. We don't murder them.'

A memory. A word. *Stikke*. Grass. Informer. Grüner with the tyre round his neck. Something older too. During the Second World War with the Resistance growing. When the Nazis occupied the Politigården itself and a few brave Copenhagen police officers risked their lives to fight them from within.

Some of those wound up on the stakes in Mindelunden where Anne Dragsholm's corpse was tied almost seventy years on.

'What if someone betrays the tribe?' Lund asked. 'If he's a *stikke*? What happens to them?'

Jarnvig stared at her.

'I've no idea what you mean. Do you honestly think a Danish soldier is killing his comrades one by one?'

'I'm trying to keep an open mind. How about you?'

Strange came back in. He was waving a piece of paper in his hand.

'The very idea's insane,' Jarnvig said then got up from the table.

Khaki uniform. Three silver pips on his epaulettes. Monarch of the little kingdom of Ryvangen.

'Thanks,' Lund said and held out her hand. 'That's all for now.'

'What is it?' she asked when Jarnvig was gone.

'Lisbeth Thomsen's living in Sweden. An island called Skogö. Two hours north of Malmö.'

He was getting his jacket. She did the same.

'She's staying in a house that belonged to her late uncle. Someone's going to talk to the Swedish police, tell them we're on our way. My car. I just filled it up.'

'That's good,' she said. 'I'll drive.'

He looked puzzled.

'Why? Oh!' His stubbly face brightened. 'It's the cake.' He looked at her bag. 'You brought me some.'

Lund said nothing.

'You promised.'

'I'll buy something along the way.'

'I don't drive and eat.'

'I said I'll drive.'

'Oh no. Your mind wanders. I've noticed.'

'I'll get you some cake,' she insisted. 'You can eat and watch me drive. Can we go now, please?'

Thirty minutes later they were across the Øresund bridge, through the checkpoints, into Sweden. She drove carefully, responsibly. Never breaking the limit. Never taking her eyes off the road.

There was one reason only: Strange would be on her in an instant if she started speeding or getting a little careless. He was a very precise and proper man. Almost puritanical in a way.

Lund still found time to watch the Swedish countryside go by. She knew this drive so well. Two years before she'd been about to take it one last time, abandoning Denmark for ever for a new life with Bengt and Mark. Her life as a Copenhagen cop would have been over. Instead she'd be a lowly civilian with the Swedish force. A good mother to her son. A loving partner to Bengt Rosling.

Then the Birk Larsen case intervened and exile to Gedser. Everything changed. Except her. She could still taste the anger that old self had felt as the search for Nanna spiralled into confusion and finally madness.

She had regrets. About Jan Meyer mainly, and the mistake – her mistake – which left him in a wheelchair. But those few slip-ups apart she felt sorry for nothing. Given the chance again she would attack the case with the same determined vigour. And hope for some better breaks.

'Lisbeth Thomsen was a volunteer,' Strange said as they passed solitary woodland, naked trees, brown grass, signs showing leaping deer, the odd ramshackle wooden bungalow. He was going through the files again, slowly, page by page, line by line.

'I take it you weren't.'

He laughed out loud.

'Volunteer for something? You've got to be kidding.'

She turned and smiled at him. He was looking a little guilty.

'I told them I had a bad back.'

'Did you?'

'No. But I was scared. Didn't work. They checked with the doctor so I ended up in a muddy field, full kit, running up and down like a madman, messing round with rifles and stuff. I think they were getting their revenge.'

'Come on. You're a man. You must have loved it.'

His head went from side to side.

'It wasn't so bad. I thought I'd join the police for a while. I did a whole summer in the Politigården after college. Work experience. You were there.'

Lund's foot came off the accelerator. She looked at him.

'What?'

'Couple of years older than me. You were a real cop. I was just a cadet. So you never talked to me. I wasn't important enough.'

'Even eighteen, twenty years ago, there were quite a few women in the police. I think.'

'It was you, Lund. You were scary even then.' He hesitated, licked his lips, thought about whether to say it. 'Pretty too. In uniform. Apart from that you haven't changed much actually. Me . . .'

He ran his hand over his cropped hair.

'I've aged.'

'Bullshitter,' she muttered.

'Believe it or not. I did a summer in the Politigården. I saw you a couple of times. Then I went and did my army service. I didn't have anything else to do. Actually . . .' He seemed to be going back to something he'd never thought about much. '. . . when my time was up I stayed on for a few years. There was a freeze on recruitment in the police. The army's all right. I know that Jarnvig character comes across as an ass. But . . .'

'But what?' she asked when he said nothing.

'It's hard to explain if you've never seen it. The army's about loyalty. About duty. About looking after each other. And not having to think much. Just do as you're told.'

She wondered about this.

'Does that mean he'd lie if he wanted to protect someone?'

'Maybe,' Strange said.

He tapped on the map that sat between them.

'You're going the wrong way. We should be on the E6.'

'No. This is quicker.'

'The map says—'

'The map's wrong.'

He wouldn't give up.

'Well I think—'

'I don't give a damn what you think. I used to drive up here all the time. I had a Swedish boyfriend.'

'Oh,' he said, as if he understood something.

Lund kept driving. Kept thinking. Strange was an easy man to be with.

'I bet he was called Nilsson,' he said. 'They're all called Nilsson. Also—'

'He wasn't called Nilsson.'

'Johansson then. Or Andersson—'

'It doesn't matter what he was called!'

He picked up the map and looked at it again.

'Why didn't it work out?'

'It just didn't.'

He kept quiet. Waiting.

'I was about to move to Sweden when . . . a lot of things happened.'

Strange looked at her and shook his head.

'I can't see you holding hands in the forest. Playing a guitar. Mind you . . .' He pointed at her jumper. She'd got out one of the old patterned pullovers from the Faroes. They seemed to fit her mood now. 'You've got the sweater for it.'

185

She didn't want to laugh. Didn't want to like this man really. Lund had married a cop once and that was one of the biggest mistakes she ever made.

But he was wry and funny and charming. She was glad he was there.

'Very amusing.'

'I like the sweater. It's got character. It says something.' He scratched his stubbly chin. 'I'm not sure what . . .'

'Has someone warned the local police Raben may turn up?'

'That's unlikely, isn't it?'

She looked at him, raised an eyebrow.

'You don't think I'm very good at this, do you?' Strange asked.

'When did I say that?'

'You don't need to. I can see it in your face.'

'Don't look then.'

She made sure they didn't talk much after that. An hour later they were on the ferry. Twenty minutes more and they were on the island of Skogö, parked outside the harbour where the ferry docked: fishing boats and dinghies.

They got out, looked around. Strange had finished the cake she'd bought him without spilling a single crumb. Lund wondered how he'd managed that.

'Do you think they have bears here?' he asked, suddenly as excited as a school kid on a trip. 'I've never seen a bear. I mean, not outside a zoo.'

She stopped, folded her arms, looked at him.

'I'll find out where Thomsen is,' he said sheepishly, and went off to talk to a cop chatting to a fisherman by the quay.

Lund watched him go. Her mind wandered. So she never saw the farmer's truck drive last off the ferry. Or the figure in a grubby parka slipping from behind the hay bales in the back, crouching furtively behind the harbour wall until he reached the cover of brambles and shrubs at the edge of the long, shallow bay.

Buch was out of options. He called Plough and Karina into his office.

'The Prime Minister wants us to accept all the demands of the People's Party. Every last one. We need an agreement on the anti-terror package today—'

'Impossible,' Plough interrupted. 'This is all far too hasty.'

'I'll decide what's possible or not. Just write it up, will you.'

'How?' Plough asked. 'Do I hand them a blank cheque?'

Buch appreciated this man. Admired him in some ways. But his obsession with detail . . .

'You wanted this agreement, Plough.'

'Not at any price. There are too many loose ends.'

'And,' Karina cut in, 'you're against the kind of blanket ban Krabbe's demanding.'

'It's not up to me! It's a political decision. Above my head.'

'You stood up for something, Thomas.'

'Yes. I did. And I lost. These fundamentalists have done themselves no favours. The kind of material they've been handing out—'

'Who says the fundamentalists have anything to do with it?' she asked.

'Who says they don't?'

Buch had thought about this overnight. Had scarcely slept. He hated the idea of giving in to Krabbe. But there seemed no alternative.

'We can't prove that Monberg and Anne Dragsholm were having some kind of relationship. It's just gossip and I'm not having my arse hauled over the coals for that again. Let's just do as we're told.'

A knock at the door. Erling Krabbe looking triumphant.

Buch smiled as broadly as he felt able.

They went through into the meeting room. Krabbe had a hand-written list of amendments on a sheet of paper. He took off his jacket and read them one by one. Bored, Buch went to the window and watched the dragons wrestling across the road.

'You talked to the Prime Minister, I gather,' Krabbe said without lifting his head up from the table.

'I did.'

'So all of these organizations will now be proscribed?'

'They will.'

Krabbe tapped his finger on the paper.

'Not quite there yet. Your draft says, "Organizations said to encourage or incite to terror . . ."'

'You've had all the time in the world to come up with amendments,' Plough pointed out.

Buch thought he'd never seen him so furious.

'True,' Krabbe said, grinning at him. 'But I only just thought of this one. It ought to read, ". . . incite to terror or any other subversive activities".'

'Then we'd have to define what subversive means,' Plough objected.

'I know what it means,' Krabbe replied. 'Don't you?'

He scribbled the changes on a fresh piece of paper then passed it over.

'So now we're back to where I was when I finished negotiating with Monberg. A pity he couldn't have dealt with it.'

'I couldn't agree more,' Buch replied, straight-faced.

Krabbe didn't notice the edge in his voice. He didn't notice much, it seemed to Buch.

'Monberg put in a lot of effort on this, you know,' Krabbe said. 'He only cancelled one meeting.'

He was remembering something.

'It was the day all those leftie protesters turned up outside the home of the Minister of Integration. That gave us something to talk about at the next session.'

Buch sat down, put his big fist under his chin and listened.

'You need to know who your enemies are,' Krabbe added. 'Send me the finalized agreement. I'm open to the timing of the press conference. You tell me.'

Then he left.

Plough was muttering mild obscenities under his breath. Buch got up and walked into the office to tackle Karina.

'Monberg cancelled a meeting on 7th October. Do you have any record of where he was going instead?'

There was a mountain of post in front of her.

'No. Why?'

'That was one of the days he checked into the hotel in Klampenborg. He was about to finalize the deal with the People's Party. It must have been important if he ditched Krabbe . . .'

She was going through his diary.

'He had a doctor's appointment that day. Nothing else.'

'Get me Erik König. PET was expecting trouble then. They were watching out for all the senior ministers. If Monberg was in a hotel with Anne Dragsholm it should be in their report.'

'Is this really necessary?'

She looked pale, worried. Too much work, he thought. Too many long hours.

'Yes, Karina. It's necessary. That's why I'm asking.'

The local police chief they met at the ferry was a cheery, rotund man with a beard and the ruddy complexion of a fisherman.

'Welcome to Skogö.'

He spoke very slowly, as if he expected them to struggle with the language.

'We're a small and very quiet island. Nothing much happens here, you know. But if it did—'

'Where's Lisbeth Thomsen?' Lund asked.

'She lives on the other side. We're saving you the journey. Someone is picking her up.'

One middle-aged police chief. How many other officers could there be?

'We think she could be in danger.'

He laughed.

'No. Skogö's the safest place on earth. Besides, Lisbeth was a soldier. She can handle herself. You should have met her uncle. The stories about him—'

'What does she do?'

'Mainly,' the Swedish cop said, waving to a woman who greeted him as she wheeled her bike onto the outgoing boat, 'she keeps herself to herself, like most of us here.'

'When she's not busy doing that?'

'Then she's working in the forest. With the trees.' He made a chopping motion with his arms. 'Cutting them down.'

He thought of something else.

'And hunting too. Fishing. She's very capable. She lives out there on her own. Fends for herself. Come!'

He climbed into the back of Strange's black police car.

'I will direct you to our police station. You will like it, I think.'

They set off from the harbour. It seemed a pretty, sleepy place.

'You may get a visit from someone called Raben,' she said, turning to look at the officer in the back.

'Oh, we know all about him. Your people in Copenhagen sent us some information. Via our computer.'

'He's a very capable man,' Strange said.

'As are we,' the Swedish cop said. 'As are we.'

He sat back and beamed at Lund as they went past some boats and a few restaurants.

'So,' he asked. 'Do you like fishing?'

'We're not here for the fishing,' Strange said.

The Swede was still smiling.

'Really? I thought that was why you came.'

Winter woodland. Bare trees, damp earth. Raben was back in his early army days, staying low, listening, looking.

One mile from the harbour he stopped a woman hanging up washing, smiled, mentioned Thomsen's name. Got a rough location.

The island was small, sparsely populated, linked by narrow, muddy tracks. Everyone knew everybody. There wasn't such a thing as an address. Just a cabin in the woods.

Down the road, the woman said.

So he smiled again, said thanks, walked far enough down it to lose her then ducked back into the trees.

After a while he heard the sound of a chainsaw. A clearing emerged. A single-storey bungalow, stone-faced with a red roof.

Lisbeth Thomsen was a loner even when she was the only woman in an eight-strong strike team combing the badlands of Helmand. It didn't surprise him to find her in the backwoods of Sweden living like a hermit.

There was a garden near the back door. No flowers, just tidy lines of winter vegetables. Raben wanted to walk straight in, grab her by the arm, tell her to run. Just two of them left now. If he could find her, so could someone else.

Instead he edged cautiously round towards the sound of the saw. She was there, in a khaki jacket and heavy trousers, knife on her belt, black hair still short and mannish. A powerfully built woman, capable and strong.

The chainsaw was tackling a pile of logs. Thomsen was slicing them the way another woman might slice bread.

Some things don't change, Raben thought and wondered where to begin.

Was still wondering when a figure emerged from the road. Blue uniform, cap with a badge, white visibility markings on the jacket.

Swedish cop.

Raben fell back into the forest, watching every move.

Thomsen killed the saw. The man's voice was loud and officious.

'The Danish police have called about you, Lisbeth,' he said. 'You've got to come in for questioning.'

Thomsen uttered the kind of curse he'd often heard before, not usually from a woman.

'Where the hell do you think you're going?' the cop asked as she walked back to the house.

She waved the saw at him.

'Do you want me to bring this?'

Then she kept walking.

'Now don't you go running away,' he shouted. 'I'm not too good on my pins these days and I don't want to be chasing you.'

She swore again. The cop did a passable impression of Munch's *Scream*, his hands over his ears, mouth wide open.

'You Danes have potty mouths,' he said.

She almost laughed. That, Raben recalled, was as much as anyone got.

Then Lisbeth Thomsen stowed the chainsaw in an outside shed, and walked off with him.

A few seconds later a car marked 'Polis' went down the road.

She lived alone. The place was empty.

Raben got up, walked to the back door. Tried it.

Open.

A little island off the coast in Sweden. No one locked their homes. Why would you?

He stopped, forced himself to think.

Maybe they'd want to search her place.

Maybe she'd forget something and make the cop come back.

Maybe . . . someone else altogether would come along.

Stay hidden.

Observe.

Two perpetual commandments. But the first took precedence over the second, always.

Jens Peter Raben wasn't ready to be seen yet. That could only mean capture or worse. So without looking back he took to his heels, fled back into the forest, determined to stay invisible for a while.

He'd time, for now anyway. Thomsen would return, he was sure of it. In an hour or two he'd feel safe enough to work his way to the cottage and wait for her. Until then . . .

In his jacket were a couple of muesli bars and a bottle of water. There were a few of the last tart autumn lingonberries among the vegetation on the forest floor. Some edible mushrooms if he felt desperate.

Survival was easy so long as you stayed on your own.

The police station looked like an ordinary residential home: white-washed, two storeys, with a balcony at the front. Strange didn't go in. He muttered something to Lund about bumpkins and checking out the island.

'Not for bears, I hope?' she said too loudly.

'Bears?' The old cop stood on the front step, stamping his feet. 'We have no bears round here. This isn't the north, you know.'

'I want to see if they've really been looking for Raben,' Strange said to Lund, ignoring the Swede. 'He could have walked in here under their noses and they'd never know.'

'OK,' she agreed and gave him the car keys.

Thomsen was sitting at a desk in front of two very old portraits of the King and Queen of Sweden, a moose's head and a stuffed salmon. She was a tall, athletic woman with short dark hair, an unsmiling though handsome face, a gruff manner.

'I've got things to do,' she said. 'And this is Sweden. Why am I being summoned by the Danish police?'

Lund sat down. So did the chief of police, who then lit a foul-smelling pipe and listened.

'Don't you watch the news?'

'No,' Thomsen relented. 'I just have a radio. I heard about Myg. And Grüner.'

She didn't look Lund in the eye as she spoke.

'Any idea what's going on?' Lund asked.

'None.'

'Have you received any threats?'

Thomsen laughed. Not for long.

'Of course not. Why would someone threaten me?'

This was going to be slow and difficult.

'Have you had any recent contact with anyone from Ægir?'

'I live in a shack in the woods. On my own. I like it that way. I haven't seen anyone from the army in two years.'

'It wasn't just soldiers who died. Your lawyer was murdered. Anne Dragsholm.'

Lund placed the woman's photo on the table.

'Did she try to contact you?'

'No,' Thomsen said straight away and barely looked at the picture. 'Can I go now? I've got work to do.'

'What happened? In Helmand?'

'You've come all the way from Copenhagen to ask me that? Why don't you talk to someone at Ryvangen?'

'I have. I want to hear it from you.'

'We lost three good men. It's all in the report.'

'All of it?'

'Yes!'

'Whatever's happening is connected to your squad. I'm trying to understand.'

The Swedish policeman took the pipe from his mouth and tapped out the stinking ashes into a tray on the desk.

'I think you'd best answer, Lisbeth. Tell the lady what she wants to know. Then we can all go home.'

'What's there to tell? We were on a patrol. A long way from base. We stopped for a break. When we came back Raben said he'd got a call on the radio from another Danish squad. They were under fire. Trapped not far from the river. We knew we were the nearest team.'

For the first time Lund saw some emotion in her face. A nervous, twitchy fear.

'They were in the Green Zone. Enemy territory. We couldn't leave them there. So we tried to cross the river. The bridge was mined.'

Her eyes turned dark and distant.

'Bo was sitting right across from me. Rifle between his legs. He got the barrel up his throat when the explosion hit us. We lost the armoured vehicle. We were cut off from the rest of the platoon.'

She was looking around the room, lost in the memories.

'Couldn't raise anyone on the radio. There was a village half a kilometre across the bridge. That was where the squad was. Raben decided to go there and help them. Wait together.'

'And then?'

Thomsen sniffed, stared at Lund.

'That was the last I saw of them. He wanted me to get Bo out somehow.' A sour, sarcastic look marred her face for a moment. 'I was the woman, wasn't I?'

'You did your best, Lisbeth,' the cop said. 'Didn't you?'

'Best wasn't good enough. I carried Bo to the next valley. Five, six kilometres. He was dead by the time they picked us up.'

Lund said, 'But you saw your team later? At base? They must have told you what happened.'

'It's in the report. They were hit by a suicide bomber. Two more died. Raben and Grüner were badly wounded.'

'The local tribe said there were civilian casualties too. They accused Raben's team of atrocities.'

Thomsen's steely eyes fixed on her.

'You believe that?' she asked.

'I don't know. I'm asking you.'

'Half the people out there hated us. Half of them said they were on our side. The trouble was you never knew which half you were talking to. And they changed, one day to the next. I don't know anything about atrocities.'

'Someone's mad enough about what happened to be killing members of your team.'

Lisbeth Thomsen's fist thumped on the table.

'I'm sick of this crap. We lost three soldiers. Friends of mine. Good men. Husbands and fathers. We were cleared!'

'Thomsen—'

'No! I won't hear it. Raben, Myg, Grüner . . . they put their lives on the line. While people like you sat in your comfy offices in Copenhagen wondering what to have for lunch. Don't talk ill of them. Don't you dare.'

'OK, OK.' Lund closed her notebook, not that she'd finished with the questions.

'No,' Thomsen bawled. 'It's not OK. We risked our lives in that hellhole. And when we came back they wanted us to answer for it.'

'Calm down, Lisbeth,' the old cop advised. 'The lady has to ask her questions . . .'

'There was no patrol,' Lund said.

Thomsen's eyes narrowed.

'What?'

'The official report said there was no patrol under fire.'

'Raben told us,' Thomsen yelled, banging the table again. 'He took a radio message—'

'There's no record of any Danish team, any NATO unit, in the area at the time,' Lund insisted. 'Apart from yours.'

'Enough.' Thomsen folded her arms. 'Are we done now?'

'This is for your own protection. I think you know it too. That's why you're hiding here.'

The Swedish cop was becoming ever more interested.

'Hiding here?' Thomsen cried. 'It's where I live.'

'Skogö's not much of a place for a handsome young woman,' the Swede began.

'It's where I live, old man. I enjoy a little peace. At least I used to. Are . . . we . . . finished?'

Lund shook her head.

'No. I'd like you to look at some other photos.'

She spread out the pictures on the desk. The Swede came over and looked hard at them. So did Lisbeth Thomsen.

Anne Dragsholm, slaughtered, tied to the stake in Mindelunden. Myg Poulsen upside down, cut to ribbons in the veterans' club. David Grüner burnt to a cinder in his wheelchair.

Lisbeth Thomsen stared at the photos, was for once lost for something to say.

'We don't want anything like that in Skogö,' the cop said. 'You will help this young woman, Lisbeth. For the sake of your uncle, God rest him. Your own sake too.'

He shivered.

'Now,' he added, pointing at the pictures. 'Put those away please.'

Ninety minutes to the press conference and Erling Krabbe was demanding another meeting. Buch remained in his office, dithering. Vacillation was out of character and he didn't like it.

Phones ringing, he paced the floor. Another time he'd have got out the little rubber ball, bounced it around, trying to think.

But that was in the past. He could judge the way that little toy returned to him from the wall. Mostly anyway. The world of government had no such certainties. It was more grey, shifting and slippery than he'd ever guessed.

'Krabbe's getting impatient,' Plough said, holding out the phone. 'He's every right to expect a briefing beforehand.'

Buch waved away the phone.

'Not now.'

'What am I supposed to tell him?'

'Say I'm on the phone to PET.'

Karina walked in, a large white padded envelope in her hand.

'What does König say?' Buch asked.

'I haven't spoken to him.'

'I asked! Give me his number.'

She was in a sober black business suit, long blonde hair carefully combed, no make-up, no smile on her face. Something was wrong.

'Out with it,' he said.

'Dragsholm wasn't having an affair with Monberg,' Karina said.

A glance at Plough, something apologetic in her eyes.

'I was.'

Carsten Plough groaned. Buch was lost for words.

She played nervously with her hair, took a seat at the desk.

'The night he met Dragsholm I was in the same hotel. Monberg was giving a talk in the afternoon. He asked me to come to discuss some work.'

'Karina,' Plough intervened. 'Before you go on. You have to understand this is now a disciplinary issue. You have rights—'

'Oh don't be so damned stuffy, Carsten! You want the truth, don't you? We had a fling and then I finished with him. He asked me there. I thought he was trying to change my mind. It wasn't that. We met in the bar, after he'd seen Dragsholm. He seemed very downcast. He was drinking too much. I was worried about him.'

Karina placed the white envelope on Buch's desk.

'He had this with him. I didn't see what was in it. Then he left.'

'Did you see Dragsholm?' Buch asked.

'No. He never mentioned her. I'd no idea he knew her.'

She hesitated, trying to find the right words.

'Something was wrong. I thought at first he was miserable because I'd finished with him. It wasn't that. He never came near me again, not until the night before his heart attack.'

Her pale finger tapped the envelope.

'He wanted me to post this. So I did. That was the last time I saw him. Now it's been returned. He sent it to a dead address. He must have known that would happen.'

Buch picked open the envelope and took out a blue folder.

'He got that at the meeting with Dragsholm,' she added. 'I'm sure of it.'

Plough came to look over Buch's shoulder.

'It's the judge advocate's report into an incident in Afghanistan,' Karina said. 'Dragsholm must have given him a copy. There's a list of the soldiers in the squad that was under investigation.'

'Poulsen, Grüner . . . These are the men who were murdered,' Plough said.

She got up and stood behind him, pulled out a single sheet.

'If you look in the margin of the covering letter Monberg's scribbled something. A request for the case to be reopened.'

Karina folded her arms.

'You don't need to go through the motions of a disciplinary inquiry. I'll resign. I don't want to make a fuss. Carsten . . . I'm really sorry I let you down.' She tried to smile. 'Things just happen sometimes. Slotsholmen's like that for some of us. Not you, I know. But when you get so close to people all day, all night. It becomes . . . unreal.'

She murmured a second apology, turned and walked out of the office.

Plough's phone was ringing again.

'It's Krabbe. The journalists are turning up. What should we do?'

Buch was scanning through the report.

'Monberg left us this for a reason. We need to know what it is.'

'The press conference! Monberg's report can come later. You have to deal with this now.'

'How?' Buch asked, staring at the neatly typed sheets of the judge advocate's report, and Monberg's scrawl in the margin. 'Without knowing . . .'

Bilal arrived in Jarnvig's office to report back on the meeting with soldiers and relatives, stood rigid in front of the colonel's desk as Jarnvig browsed through the messages on his computer.

'Tell me it went well,' the colonel ordered.

'Five men want out of the team. They're upset about what happened to Grüner and Myg Poulsen.'

'That happened here. Not Helmand.'

'They say they want to be near their families. Leave it with me. Everyone's got till nine tomorrow morning to think it over. I'll work on them. If they won't go I'll find five others.'

Jarnvig was running idly round the computer. He'd looked at a report from headquarters the previous day and needed it again. So he went to the recent documents list.

The first file there had Lisbeth Thomsen's name on it.

He'd never looked for that.

'Did you come in here last night?'

Bilal frowned.

'What?'

'Did you come in here and access Lisbeth Thomsen's file?'

'No.'

'Do you know if Søgaard did?'

'I can ask the security officers to look into it if you like.'

'Don't bother. Forget I asked.'

Bilal didn't move.

'I said forget it,' Jarnvig repeated.

He left. Jarnvig opened the file. Thomsen's full personnel record. Relatives. Service details. Training. Contact addresses.

Footsteps. Bilal marched back in without knocking on the door.

'I just talked to the security officer.'

Jarnvig's temper was rising.

'I told you there was no need.'

'There is now,' Bilal said.

The basement of the colonel's house was big. A living room, two bedrooms off, a bathroom. Perfect in most ways, Louise Raben thought. Only stubbornness had kept her out of here before. Jonas would have a room of his own finally. Something he deserved.

Christian Søgaard turned up unasked. Blue sweatshirt, army trousers. Blond hair in place, a strong man, always smiling. For her.

'You don't have much furniture,' he said, looking at the chairs and tables waiting to be moved into place.

'Give me time.'

They lugged an old sofa into the main room. The house was on a slope so there were windows on one side of the basement, looking out onto the trees behind the parade ground, the railway beyond, and in the distance the green space of Mindelunden.

She walked into the smallest room.

'Jonas is staying with a friend,' she said. 'I'm going to paint this. It's his.'

Red. He'd picked the colour. One wall done already.

'I told you I like painting,' Søgaard said.

Louise laughed.

'You don't really.'

'I do.' He grinned. 'Besides I need a break from barking orders at sweaty men.'

He had a reputation around the barracks. Good in bed some of the women whispered after drinks. But lately he'd been more circumspect. Christian Søgaard was on the promotion ladder and determined nothing would hinder that.

He walked around, adjusted some of the plastic sheets, looked at the paint pot, stirred it with the stick she had.

'Good work. You just need a man's touch.'

He walked over, came up to her, peered into her face. Then took a very clean and freshly ironed handkerchief from his pocket and dabbed delicately at her right cheek.

She almost retreated. But he must have had a reason. And she liked the feel of a man so close.

'There,' he said and showed her the white fabric. A red stain. She'd got some paint on her face.

'Thanks, Christian.'

No one had touched her gently in two years. Jens hated the hard sofa in the prison marital quarters. On the rare occasion he did want her it was quick, almost brutal. One more duty.

Still she took the handkerchief from him and tried to clean up the rest herself.

'There's a bit left,' he said after she'd rubbed around her cheek for a while. 'You can't do everything on your own, can you?'

No answer.

'I can't anyway,' Søgaard added.

In civilian clothes he looked different. There was no badge, no uniform to proclaim his rank. He was just a nice man trying to summon up some courage.

'I'm very grateful,' Louise said. 'For your . . .'

She didn't have the words either.

'Just say when you need me.' Søgaard was trying to cover up her embarrassment. 'I'm happy to come and give you a hand. You know if—'

Quick footsteps on the stairs. Torsten Jarnvig marched in, long face furious.

'When did you see him?' he barked at his daughter. 'Was he here? At the barracks?'

She looked at Søgaard.

'I'd better be off,' the major said.

'Stay here,' Jarnvig ordered. 'This concerns you too. Louise, I want the truth.'

She didn't retreat, didn't look away.

'Jens wanted to know where Lisbeth Thomsen was living. He's worried for her safety.'

She looked at the half-painted walls, the mess on the floor. It wasn't a home. Not yet.

'So I got it from your computer. He said it was important.'

'When did you let him into the barracks?' Jarnvig demanded.

'I didn't, Dad. He's never been here.'

He didn't believe her. She could see that. Louise took one step towards her father.

'I told him to give himself up. I told him . . .' Her eyes stole towards Søgaard and she wished they hadn't. 'I said if he couldn't do that we were finished.'

She glared at her father.

'There. That's what you wanted to hear, isn't it? Are you happy now?'

'Where is he?'

'I . . . don't . . . know.'

Jarnvig turned to the man beside him.

'There's been a break-in. At the munitions depot.'

Christian Søgaard changed, became a soldier once again.

'What?'

'Someone who knows our security procedures got in. They made off with five kilos of plastic explosive.'

Jarnvig looked at her. So did Søgaard.

'Jens wasn't here. I'm telling you. Dad . . .'

The more Lisbeth Thomsen wanted to leave the little police house on Strogö, the more Lund was determined to keep her close. They'd

200

spent almost two hours going over the same questions again and again.

'I'm sorry,' Lund said when the woman started demanding the Swedish cop let her go. 'I think you're keeping something from us.'

'I want to go home.'

The door opened. Strange walked in, nodded to Lund for a private word.

They went outside.

'I've been trawling round this place for ages,' he said. 'I can't find anything that suggests Anne Dragsholm was here. If she was no one saw her.'

'What about Raben?'

He shook his head.

The Swedish cop came outside, chewing on his pipe, eavesdropping.

'We haven't seen anyone suspicious,' he announced. 'And we would. We have very good eyes, you know.'

'You wouldn't see this one,' Lund said with a sigh.

'Good . . . eyes,' he repeated, pointing to his own. 'I think we should drive Lisbeth home. I'm sorry you had a wasted journey. Would you like to buy some fish to take back to Copenhagen? Swedish fish is so much better than Danish . . .'

Lund marched back into the office. The two men followed. Hands on hips, she looked at Lisbeth Thomsen, a tall, strong woman in tough country clothes.

'No. She's coming with us.'

'I'm not going to Copenhagen!' Thomsen cried. 'This isn't a police state . . .'

'You have papers?' the old cop asked.

'We'll get you some papers.' She nodded at Thomsen. 'You can pick up some things first.'

'Call Brix,' she told Strange. 'Tell him we're bringing her in.'

'What the hell is this?' Thomsen yelled then spat out a flurry of curses.

The cop didn't look impressed by that.

'Maybe they're right, Lisbeth,' he said. 'You seem jumpy to me. There's a ferry in forty-five minutes. I think it's best you go with them.'

'No.'

He put down his pipe. Folded his arms, looked at her, not blinking, not moving.

More curses and then she went to the car outside.

Through the dead woods, Lund driving the black Ford from the Politigården, Strange in the back next to Thomsen.

Lund's phone rang.

'Someone tried to call,' Brix said.

'We're bringing Thomsen in for her own safety. Two hours. Three at the most.'

'We talked to her tenant here. A week ago he got a call from the tax office. They were threatening action for unpaid bills. Demanding he call them the next time Thomsen turned up. They wanted to talk to her.'

'And?' Lund asked.

'We talked to the tax people. No one's made any enquiries about Thomsen. Someone's on her trail. Maybe you're not on your own out there.'

Then he was gone.

Timber country. The track wound deeper into the tall fir forest, the winter foliage blocking out the light. Lund turned a corner, hit the brakes.

The way ahead was blocked by a pile of felled tree trunks. They'd been stacked by the side of the road. The ropes that held them had been broken or cut, spilling timber onto the muddy lane.

They couldn't go on.

'Does this happen a lot?' Strange asked.

'No.' Thomsen seemed worried. Scared too. 'Let's turn back. I don't need any things. Let's just get on the ferry.'

Strange took off his seat belt, opened the door.

'I'll check it out.'

'No,' Lund told him. 'Get back in. We'll go.'

'One minute. I want a look around. If there's someone here . . .'

He looked at the spilled trunks, walked behind the main pile, stepped into the forest.

Then wheeled round, gun in hand, as if he'd heard something and ran into the trees.

'What was that?' Lund asked.

'I didn't hear anything.' Thomsen sounded anxious. 'Let's just go, can we?'

'I can't leave him here. Stay where you are. I don't want to come looking for you twice.'

'No!'

Thomsen's strong hand was on her shoulder.

'Something happened in that village. I heard rumours. It's all about that.'

'About what?'

'I wasn't there. It was gossip.'

'Like what? Tell me.'

Her eyes were wild with fear.

'And end up dead? Like my buddies? Get me out of here!'

'Did they tell you civilians were killed?'

'Raben's men didn't do it.'

Nothing more.

'Lisbeth. I'm trying to help.'

'You don't understand.'

'Tell me.'

'It's the army,' Thomsen said in a low, tense voice. 'Sometimes you get men who drift in and out. You never speak to them. You never know who they are. They're like ghosts. They do things the rest of us can't.'

'Who killed those civilians?'

'Some fucked-up Danish officer who went crazy. He was there. He called them in.'

'No,' Lund insisted. 'I read the judge advocate's report. There was no officer.'

She laughed in Lund's face.

'I said you wouldn't understand. He was there. We all knew there were guys like that around.'

'Doing what?'

Thomsen's eyes stayed on her.

'Whatever they wanted. We have rules. They don't. They can go anywhere. Kill or bomb or bribe or . . . It's war. It's not us against them. It's dirtier than that.'

'This man—'

'They called him Perk. I don't know if that was his real name or not. I never saw him.'

'Perk?'

'Myg Poulsen and Grüner told the judge. Raben couldn't. He

didn't remember. It didn't matter. Nobody believed them. It was just a whitewash. We all knew it.'

'The lawyer?' Lund asked.

'She believed them from the start. She came to see me a month ago, asking if I'd testify and help reopen the case. For God's sake—'

A sound. A man's voice. Angry, scared, she wasn't sure which.

Strange was shouting warnings. Somewhere not far away in the wood.

'Stay here,' Lund told her and got out of the car.

The first shot sounded when she reached the trees.

It was dark beneath their cover. She remembered a night in Copenhagen. A warehouse. Jan Meyer bleeding, unconscious on the floor.

She'd left him too.

Another shot.

Lund ran.

After a minute there was a clearing. She didn't take out her own gun. Never thought of that.

There was a canvas structure on stilts ahead. A watchtower.

A figure at the top of the ladder, moving down, hand over hand on the rungs so quickly.

'Strange! *Strange! For God's sake!*'

He got to the ground just as she turned up.

Someone had been there. Wrappers on the forest floor: muesli bars, an empty water bottle, some lingonberry branches.

'Raben was here,' he said. 'Jægerkorpset. They can live off nothing and you never get to see them.'

'Ulrik?'

He looked at her, puzzled.

'What happened to "Strange"?'

'Don't you ever run off like that again.'

He grinned.

'Sorry, Mummy,' he said and gave her a little salute. 'But I heard something. Where's Thomsen?'

'Don't you ever . . .' she repeated.

A car door slammed hard behind them.

Before she could say a word Ulrik Strange was running back to the blocked road, faster than Lund ever could.

*

Thomsen flew into the forest the minute Lund was out of sight. Ran the half kilometre to her bungalow in the woods.

She had the red Land Rover in the drive. A boat. Could get to the mainland easily if she needed. Stay out of sight until the storm – whatever it was – had blown over.

All her outdoor gear – food, a compass, more knives, a rifle – stayed in a cabinet by the sink. Thomsen raced to it, got the door half open.

Stopped.

Wires inside. They were never there before. A pack of stick explosives taped to the stock of the rifle.

Clumsy, she thought. Even the Taliban could do better than this.

A sound at the door. A tall figure. She shrieked, looked for a weapon and then he was on her, hand over her mouth.

Thomsen stared into his cold eyes.

Raben, hood down, breathless.

'You scared the living crap out of me,' she whispered. 'Why in God's name . . . ?'

'I saw you running,' he said. 'What's wrong?'

'What are you doing here? There are police from Copenhagen. They want to take me back. They say . . .'

He was staring at the half-open cupboard.

'Have you been in here?' Thomsen asked.

'No.'

She gestured at the door. He knew about these things. Raben bent down, opened it very carefully.

The wire was a simple trigger, mechanical not electrical. It ran back to the explosives and ended in a physical detonator.

'That's a blind,' he said. 'Too easy. There's got to be something else.'

He shoved a chair against the cupboard door to stop it moving, glanced around, took her arm.

'Car keys?'

She nodded at the table. Raben took them.

'Let's go,' he said.

They edged out of the cottage. Raben got down on his hands and knees, checked underneath the Land Rover, then opened the bonnet gingerly and looked there.

Nothing.

An engine was gunning somewhere. Fast and urgent.

'Where . . . ?' Thomsen asked.

He put a finger to his mouth, guided her into the shelter of the low conifers.

They watched. The black car with a Copenhagen plate slewed to a halt in the mud outside the bungalow door. The old Swedish cop climbed out, looked round. Two figures, Lund and the man she came with, emerged from the other side and went straight through the door.

'We've got to warn them,' she whispered.

'They can look after themselves,' he said through gritted teeth. 'We need to get out of here.'

'You don't know—'

Finger to lips again. She went quiet. He was the boss in Helmand. The boss now.

The Swedish cop strolled leisurely inside too. He'd never see a bomb, not if it jumped up in the street and said hello.

'I don't like this . . .'

Raben ran, got into the battered red Land Rover, hit the ignition, beckoned.

Decisions.

Back in the army they were easy. You did what you were told.

Lisbeth Thomsen dashed out from the trees, leapt through the passenger door he'd kicked open. Was struggling to hold on to the cold metal dashboard as Raben floored the accelerator. They slid and swerved across the mud, headed back into the forest, over the roughest track he could find.

Twenty minutes later Skogö's two police Volvos stood outside Thomsen's cottage. Strange had retrieved the black squad car from the mud where it had stuck when they tried to give chase. It was just before seven in the evening and Lund was furious.

'Where could they go?' she asked the Swedish cop again.

'You keep asking me this. I'm telling you the same thing. This is a small island. Just forest and a few houses. And then the sea. They won't get onto the ferry, I promise you that. In the morning, when it's light—'

'The morning could be too late,' she said.

'We've got twenty thousand hectares of forest and Lisbeth Thomsen probably knows every tree. She's been coming here since she was a little girl. A good kid. In the morning—'

'You told us Raben wasn't here.'

'And I was wrong,' he said very patiently. 'We've got Bertil and Ralle looking for them too.'

Lund wanted to scream.

'I asked for backup.'

'They're on their way. From the mainland. A couple of hours maybe. I've asked my brother-in-law too.'

'He's police?'

'No,' he said as if puzzled by the question. 'He's a fisherman. How many policemen do you think we need on Skogö? If you'd told us you were going to let Lisbeth go we'd be better prepared—'

'She ran,' Lund pointed out. 'Raben's here. Someone else maybe . . .'

Strange came out from the cottage, frowned when he saw her.

'I don't want anyone inside until bomb disposal turn up,' he said.

'If there's a bomb why would we go inside?' one of the men asked.

'I'm going to go mad in a minute,' Lund muttered just low enough so only Strange could hear. 'What's in there?'

'Someone's been having fun. The doors are flimsy. The windows were open—'

'We don't usually lock our doors in Skogö,' the old cop butted in. 'What's the point?'

'The point,' Strange said, 'is someone booby-trapped the place.'

'No one from Skogö,' the man replied. 'I'm sure of that. This Raben character of yours, perhaps?'

'He was in jail when the first two were murdered,' Lund muttered.

Strange was looking at her.

'What is it?'

'Raben could rig up something like that. It's crude but—'

'You're wrong.'

She started to walk round the cleared patch of ground beyond the cars. Strange followed, hands in pockets.

'If Thomsen had gone for her rifle she'd have been blown to bits, Lund. There's about a kilo of explosive stuck in there.' He sighed. 'Brix is going to be so pissed off about this.'

'Never mind Brix. I'm pissed off. Worry about that.'

'What are you looking for?'

It wasn't that he was slow. Strange was . . . not tuned right some-how.

'He leaves a sign,' she said. 'Remember?'

They got to the end of the clearing. Lund got out her torch, shone it around. Eventually it fell on an outside tap near the vegetable patch. Something was dangling from the top.

Strange came and looked. Shining in the beam was a severed dog tag on a silver chain.

'Maybe Raben made the roadblock,' she said. 'He didn't booby-trap the cottage.'

'Why . . . ?'

'He's their squad leader. He feels responsible. He wants to save the last one left. And himself. Where the hell are these Swedish hicks for God's sake?'

She stomped round in the dark. Found nothing more. Then they heard the roar of an engine. Something stormed down the track, four bright lights on the grille, the same on the roof. A huge all-terrain truck, open-backed for the forest.

'This is my brother-in-law and his mates,' the old cop said proudly. 'Now we have the big Datsun we can go anywhere.'

'Ja,' the driver said, grinning as he hung out of the door. 'We found Lisbeth's little toy stuck in the mud. They must be on foot. So . . .'

He clapped his hands.

'Anyone here want a ride?'

Lund climbed into the open back, Strange beside her, clung on to the rail, and they lurched into the dark forest.

Thomsen knew these woods, understood how few tracks crossed them, how easy they would be to find. So when they abandoned the Land Rover the two of them ran through the stark upright trees, crossing the rough forest floor as best they could in the weak moon-light and steady rain.

She had a boat. It was the last option open.

They passed the spilled, felled trunks, passed the forest watch-tower. Thomsen screamed, went down hard on the ground.

'Come on!' Raben roared, and it was just like the old days. Them against the world.

When she didn't move he came back. She was whimpering, clutching her ankle in pain.

Soldier down. The response was automatic.

He crouched next to her, lifted the leg of her khaki trousers. Brambles had torn the skin. A livid bruise was emerging.

Raben ripped the fabric with his knife, cut a strip, bandaged the wound.

'How far to the boat?'

'A few minutes. That's all.'

'Who was in your cottage, Lisbeth?'

'I don't know. I haven't seen anybody.'

She looked at him.

'It wasn't there when the police took me in. It can't have been.'

He tied the makeshift bandage too tight. She put her hand on his, made him loosen it a little.

'That woman came to see me, Jens. The lawyer. She asked me to testify again. She wanted to reopen the case.'

'Why? What did she say?'

Thomsen got up, tested her leg.

'She said she'd uncovered some new information. She wouldn't say what.' Thomsen held his arm and he didn't know whether it was to steady herself or not. 'What happened in that village, Jens?'

'I don't really know. What else?'

'Nothing. Did you do something wrong?'

His voice rose.

'I can't remember, dammit!'

'Who was Perk?' Lisbeth Thomsen asked in a quiet, scared voice he'd never heard before. 'Was he real . . . or . . . ?'

'Perk! Perk! I don't know.'

He let go of her, squeezed his eyes tight shut.

'I remember the screams. The stink of something burning. The kids trying to . . .'

He stopped.

'To what, Jens?'

His mind had strayed somewhere it hadn't been in a long time. A dark place, full of mysteries.

'It was Perk. That was what he called himself. He murdered them. I remember that.'

She looked round the forest. No lights. No sound. Raben should have been doing that. But just then . . .

'Did any of them survive? Is someone here, looking for revenge?'

Lights in the distance. A big vehicle, fast-moving.

He seized her arm.

'They've found the Land Rover. They won't be long. Come on.'

She tested the leg. Put weight on it. Didn't wince at the pain.

'Can you run?' he asked.

'I can try,' Lisbeth Thomsen answered.

Louise Raben sat on the chair in her father's office, Jarnvig and Christian Søgaard opposite, and wished she could find the will to laugh at their stiff pomposity. It was ridiculous. She was a nurse, not a soldier. They'd no right to interrogate her like this.

But she went along with it because she had, in truth, little choice. It was close to nine in the evening. The barracks were on a high security alert. Jonas was at his friend's house for the night. Jens was God knew where.

And besides . . . she liked to watch Søgaard, wriggling by her father's side, too scared to show any support, too interested to abandon her.

'Why did he need these explosives, Louise?'

'I told you. Jens never asked about explosives. He never came here—'

'You used my computer. You got Thomsen's file.'

'Yes! I did!'

'You took the codes to the ammunition depot.'

'No, no, no.' She shook her head. Wondered why she didn't have the energy to cry. He could make her weep. He did it to her mother from time to time. 'I never took any codes. I wouldn't know what they looked like.'

'He told you—'

'He didn't! Jens was never here. I looked at the computer after you left. I got Thomsen's file and printed it out. I don't know anything about your explosives. Jens doesn't either.'

She leaned forward, looked at him, wished he would believe her.

'He was worried about Thomsen. He wanted to find her. There's something funny going on. Don't you know that?'

'So you did meet him. Where?'

'It doesn't matter.'

He got up, went to the window, hands on hips, face white with fury.

'Of course it matters! He's an escaped criminal and you're an accessory.'

She grabbed his phone from the desk, held it up for him.

'Go on then. Call the police. It's your duty, isn't it? That's always more important than family.'

The hurt on his face was immediate and real.

'I'm sorry,' she stuttered. 'It was in the car park near the Oslo ferries. The police followed me there. If they'd had half a brain . . .'

'So he called you beforehand and you agreed to meet? Even though you'd promised to tell me—'

'He's my husband! I've got duties too.'

'Do you have any idea where he is?' Søgaard asked gently.

'No.'

'Louise . . .' His voice was close to wheedling, his face full of sympathy. 'We need to deal with this.'

'I don't know,' she repeated slowly.

There was a knock on the door. Said Bilal entered, looked at Louise, kept quiet.

'You can talk, Bilal,' Jarnvig told him.

'The police forensic people are all over the munitions depot. They say it wasn't the colonel's code used to gain access. It was a different one. It's not on our list.'

'How can it not be on our list?' Jarnvig roared.

'It's some kind of master security code. I don't know any more than that.'

Louise sat back, looked at her father, raised an eyebrow.

'The police want to speak to you, sir,' Bilal added. 'They've found explosives identical to ours on an island in Sweden. In a house belonging to Lisbeth Thomsen.'

Her father dismissed Bilal, waited till the young officer was gone.

'Where did he say he was going?' Jarnvig asked.

'He didn't.'

'But he was asking about Thomsen's house in Sweden?'

She didn't answer. Jarnvig muttered something foul under his breath and left. After a while she got up to go.

'Louise.' Søgaard was next to her, strong hand on her arm. 'Jens is sick. He needs help. More than we gave him. I'm sorry. If they've found the explosives at least he can't cause more trouble.'

'That wasn't him. How many times do I have to say it?'

'You're going to need to convince the police of that.'

'Fine. Maybe they'll lock me up too.'

He shook his head.

'I'll have a word with your father. They don't need to know everything. It won't be as bad as . . .' He grimaced. 'As this.'

'Really?'

'If it's any consolation he's kicked my backside much harder than that. Many, many times.' Søgaard looked into her face. 'He's the colonel. He's here to look after us. I guess he feels that responsibility twice over when it comes to you. He means well.'

'He means to keep me here for ever.'

'Is that so bad?'

'I've got a husband . . .'

'He ran away from you. I don't know . . .' He was so good at this, she thought. 'I don't know how any man could do that. But he did.'

His hand was on her arm. Fond and protective. Søgaard was predictable, safe, strong, and happy to show it. So unlike Jens who kept his emotions and his thoughts close and tight inside.

'Goodnight,' she said and walked straight back to the house, down to the basement, to sit on the sofa and stare at the bare walls.

After a while she got up and sorted through the rubbish bags out the back. The phone he gave her was there, underneath a discarded pizza box.

She called the number she had, listened to the message.

Unavailable.

He could be in Sweden, she thought. Jens was chasing Lisbeth Thomsen, determined to find her. He would too. But he didn't have those explosives. She felt sure of that.

The old cop was good in the forest. He was hunting Lisbeth Thomsen and Raben the way he tracked deer.

Deep in the woods he found a scrap of khaki fabric stained with blood.

'Someone fell here and cut themselves. Not long ago. They can't be far away.'

'There's a path over there,' said one of the locals.

'Going where?' Lund asked.

'East,' the cop said. 'Towards the harbour. If they go there we'll have them.'

'And they know it.' She was getting sick of this. 'What about the other direction?'

'That's a caravan park,' said the local. 'But it's closed for the winter. No one comes to Skogö when it's cold. Though the fishing's—'

'Is there a harbour there too?' Strange asked.

'Just a landing stage.'

Lund looked at Strange.

'There was an outboard engine in front of Thomsen's house. In pieces. Some buoys and a rod,' she said.

'Everyone goes fishing in Skogö,' the cop said. 'Why wouldn't you?' He took off his cap and scratched his grey hair. 'Lisbeth has a boat, of course.'

Lund was striding back to the truck already. The cop was on the phone to the coastguard.

'If they put to sea . . .' she began.

'Then,' the cop said, catching up with her, 'we're in trouble.'

A thin low mist was starting to roll through the trees. Raben was in front, Thomsen limping behind on her bad leg. There was a hut in the woods then, fifty metres away, a jetty, little more than a line of planks running out over the still, black water. A white dinghy at the end, the engine hooded, prop out of the water.

She stopped him by the hut. Arm on his.

'Everyone knows I've got a boat here. They'll bring in the coastguard.'

He nodded at the sea. The mist was getting thicker all the time.

'Come on,' he said in his old military voice. 'We can run rings round these people.'

'I left my best outboard at the cottage. I don't know if the thing on this works. Jens . . .'

He looked into her bloodless, strong face, and thought to himself: we could be on exercise now. In Canada or Jutland. Part of the never-ending game.

'They're not here yet,' he said. 'It's time to go.'

There was a tarpaulin by the jetty. She turned from him and dragged it away. Beneath was a scarlet kayak, a paddle in the bows.

'Row north with this. I'll go the other way. The coastguard will follow me. They'll hear the engine.'

'We stay together.'

'Listen to me for once!' Her voice was too high. He looked back into the woods. 'You're an escaped criminal. I'm not. The police will let me go. They'll throw you back in jail.'

'They need to catch me for that,' he said, trying to grab her shoulders.

'We're not in Helmand any more. This is your one chance. I can talk to them. You can't.'

Raben nodded.

'Nice try,' he said, pushing her towards the boat. 'We're going together.'

'OK!' Too loud again. 'But we need some fuel. There's a jerrycan in the shed. You get it. I'll prep the engine.'

Breathless, exhausted, he hesitated.

'Just do it, will you, Jens? I'll be on the boat. I can't exactly run away, can I?'

He watched her walk to the end of the jetty then he went back into the woods. The door was at the back of the timber hut. The chain was off, padlock on the ground.

Raben pulled gingerly on the handle, looked round as the gap opened, took out his torch, ran the beam around the interior.

On the floor was a canvas bag with Danish army markings. Wires from the flap to an unseen detonator that had to be hooked to the wooden door he was now opening.

His fingers let go. His feet took him swiftly backwards, hand shaking, the torch beam quivering in the night.

From the jetty he heard a sound. Something moving in the water. An oar maybe.

Raben ran.

The dinghy was edging slowly away on the black water.

She was a couple of metres off already, oar in hand, trying to get away without his hearing.

'Lisbeth!' he yelled, running, still some way short of the planking. She heard, looked up.

'Take the kayak, Jens,' she shouted. 'Like I said. It's best . . .'

'He's here! Don't . . .'

214

She was in the back, starter rope in hand. Jerked it once.

'Don't start the . . .'

Jerked it twice and then the world lit up in a ball of fire, its breath warm and rank, chemical and wet.

The force of the blast blew him off his feet and, for a long moment, took away his consciousness. When he came to amidst the clearing mist and smoke, panting, mind racing, he was face down in the shallows by the jetty, water against his cheek.

He crawled to his knees, wiped at his face. Could taste something. The torch in his hand moved, ran across shattered timber and wreckage. Found his own reflection in the water.

A familiar face, tired, unshaven, lost. Scarlet with blood like a murderer.

Raben bent down, washed himself, checked again.

It was worse.

Looked again.

She was floating no more than an arm's length away. Or her torso was. Khaki jacket shredded, naked flesh torn beneath, savagely cut off at the waist where . . .

He didn't want to see it. Couldn't.

Panic was for others. Never him.

Raben crossed to the far side of the jetty, washed his hands and face in the cleaner water there. Climbed into the red kayak, pushed it out onto cold and gentle waves, got in and began to pull on the paddle.

After a minute the mist swallowed him. But through it there was faint light ahead, the moon. Soon, if he kept a straight track, there would be land.

Noises behind and lights. A siren. Shouted voices.

Raben stabbed the paddle into the water and fell into a rhythm, first one side then the other.

He was the last one alive now. A final target in the sights of a ghost who'd emerged from the nightmare of Helmand two years before. A phantom with a name.

Perk.

The press conference was assembled in the room beyond Buch's office. Fifteen minutes after it was supposed to start Buch was still behind his desk, trying to track down Gert Grue Eriksen. Ruth Hedeby had called with the first reports of the incident in Sweden. The last thing Buch wanted at that moment was to face the press.

'We can't wait any longer,' Plough said. 'Krabbe's going frantic.'

'Why can't I speak to the Prime Minister?'

'He's on a plane,' Karina said. 'Coming back from Oslo.'

'Dammit. This is going to be on the news before I can raise it with him. Isn't it?'

Ear to her phone, she nodded.

'The Swedish police are putting out a statement. If . . .'

The door opened. Krabbe stormed in.

'What in God's name is happening?' he bellowed. 'We've got every political hack in Copenhagen out there and you're keeping them waiting.'

'I'm sorry, Krabbe. Something's come up.'

Krabbe stood over Buch, threw his long arms in the air and laughed.

'Oh for God's sake. What game are you playing now?'

'I can't tell you. But believe me, it's important and unavoidable.'

'So important you'll put off our deal for it? I don't believe Grue Eriksen would want that.'

Buch was growing tired of this pompous, small-minded man.

'Neither of us wishes to make a hasty decision—'

'Stop this now! I know you don't like this compromise. I also know Grue Eriksen ordered you to accept it. Our country's waiting for us to take action.'

Buch wanted to scream.

'Oh please. We don't need the histrionics. There's no audience for you here but us and frankly we're tired of it.'

The door opened. They could hear the low grumble of the hacks in the conference room beyond.

Krabbe's voice turned to a whisper.

'The Prime Minister gave you your orders. I want a damned good explanation for this nonsense. Either that or I walk straight out there and tell them this administration's rife with incompetence and useless at making the decisions this country needs.'

A press officer put her head round the door and announced the reporters were demanding an explanation.

Vacillation. Thomas Buch loathed it.

'Last chance,' Krabbe said. 'You should put on a tie for pity's sake. I won't say—'

'Oh shut up,' Buch spat at him then marched into the conference room, aware Krabbe was rushing to keep up behind, walked to the desk and the line of microphones.

'I'm sorry for the delay,' Buch said as a beaming Krabbe raced into the seat beside him. 'It's a busy day in the Ministry of Justice. The government is pleased to present the new anti-terror agreement which we have reached with the People's Party.'

A sea of faces, a few them familiar. Thomas Buch never cuddled up to the press. It seemed tacky.

'Terrorism has sadly become a fact of life,' he said, improvising all the while. 'It's the duty of the government, any government, to ensure the security of the nation under all circumstances. As much . . .'

Plough was at the back of the room, listening intently.

'As much as we can. These threats must not force us to compromise our democratic values. To forget who we truly are. A generous, open, liberal country, offering justice to all. We must protect these freedoms and fight the dark forces who wish to destroy them.'

'Quite,' Krabbe said too loudly by his side.

'Since the recent killing of Danish soldiers on our native soil the need for such vigilance seems more urgent than ever before. Before we discuss the package itself Erling Krabbe will say a few words.'

Buch sat down, unable to think about anything but Sweden and Frode Monberg. Krabbe fiddled nervously with his tie. This was the most important single victory his party had won in years. He was bound to make the most of it and he did, grinning as he recounted how difficult the negotiations had been, the way the People's Party had to stick out for 'the right agreement' in the face of opposition even – at this he glanced at Buch – from those in the heart of government.

'Nevertheless I applaud the administration for finding the courage to take the bull by the horns,' Krabbe declared. 'For discovering its spine when the Opposition lost theirs. The People's Party . . .' His nasal voice took on a distinct whine. '. . . makes a point of guarding our freedoms. We will not be trampled by medieval fanatics . . .'

Buch watched the men and women in the audience, noted the disquiet on some of their faces.

'. . . Nor stand idly by while plots are hatched by parasites from Muslim schools and organizations paid for by the Danish state . . .'

The reporters weren't watching Krabbe at all. They were staring at Buch and he knew the question they wanted to ask because it was the same one running through his own head: why are you quietly listening to this nonsense? Is this what you feel too?

'. . . We shall take the most severe measures against the groups involved,' Krabbe said in a voice so strident it sounded as if he were at a party meeting of his own. His skinny fist thumped on the desk. 'Those who seek to undermine our cherished Danish principles will find they have made implacable enemies. They shall not steal our identity from us. They shall not stamp on our traditional Christian values . . .'

Buch couldn't look at them any more. So he gazed at the silver water jug on the desk and saw his own miserable, podgy walrus features staring back at him. The face of a farmer, not a politician. Back in Jutland, managing the estate, a man who said what he thought, not what he felt people wanted to hear. He liked that.

'. . . And now . . .' Krabbe had uttered a couple of sentences Buch hadn't even heard, and he was glad of that. 'The Minister of Justice will give a summary of the anti-terror package we have agreed.'

Buch couldn't take his eyes off the reflection in the jug. He thought of his wife, his girls. Of Jutland where decisions seemed so simple, where good and bad, right and wrong, were as easy to spot as a sick cow or a field that needed fertilizer.

The silence continued. He could feel the heat of their stares.

A hand jogged his elbow and it took him a moment to realize it belonged to Erling Krabbe.

Jolted awake, Thomas Buch took one last look at his face in the shiny metal and knew what he had to do.

'Well, this is no good,' he said standing up.

His arm had nudged the jug. Falling it caught two full tumblers. Water, glass and metal tipped sideways as he got to his feet.

'I'm sorry,' Buch announced. 'This has to come to an end.'

They were so shocked that for once no one asked a question.

'That's it.' He clapped his flabby hands. 'Meeting over. I can't go into details.'

Krabbe was on his feet, mouth flapping, trying to speak.

Buch did his best to look serious and formal.

'You will have to excuse me, ladies and gentlemen. I have urgent business to attend to. Good night.'

And with that he strode out of the room.

An hour later Gert Grue Eriksen was back in Slotsholmen marching into Buch's office with his grey security men struggling to keep up.

Plough was in the middle of explaining the disciplinary procedure for Karina's dismissal. Buch didn't want to hear it.

'I'll leave you,' the civil servant announced then closed the door behind him.

Grue Eriksen was still in his coat.

'I haven't been here since Monberg's fiftieth birthday,' he said, walking round the office. 'These portraits of your predecessor should remind a Minister of the Crown of his responsibility.'

'They do,' Buch confessed. 'I know this doesn't look good. But if you'll bear with me . . .'

The dapper man with the silver hair turned and stared. The genial uncle was gone for good.

'Are you even faintly aware of the repercussions of your actions?'

'I'm aware of the consequences of bad laws.'

'This is a crisis of some magnitude now, one of your making.'

'It would be wrong to put forward the anti-terror package in the belief it somehow relates to the murder cases. Monberg—'

Grue Eriksen waved at him to be silent.

'Don't try and blame Monberg. I can't believe you're still peddling this rubbish.'

Buch was determined to keep his temper. He went to the table, found some of Plough's papers.

'It's not rubbish. I wish it were. We've got written proof. Here . . .'

He held out the documents. Grue Eriksen didn't move to take them.

'Very well,' Buch said. 'Let me tell you what we know. Monberg met with the first victim. She was a lawyer. She wanted Monberg to help her reopen a military case. An inquiry into an atrocity.'

'What has this—?'

'The soldiers who were murdered were all involved in that inquiry. They were witnesses. Their squad was accused of killing civilians in Afghanistan.'

Grue Eriksen seemed to soften a little. He came to the table and looked at the papers there.

'The squad were cleared but their story about an atrocity was dismissed as a fantasy,' Buch went on. 'The lawyer wasn't happy with that judgment. She gave Monberg the case file. Five days later she was murdered.'

'How did you get hold of this material?'

Buch shook his head.

'I don't understand that either. Monberg had it posted to an address he knew didn't exist. He did that knowing it would be returned here. It turned up just before the press conference.'

Grue Eriksen was sifting through the other documents.

'I begged Krabbe to give me a little time but he wouldn't wait. He wanted his moment of fame.'

'He's got that, hasn't he?'

'Monberg should have raised this case with the civil servants, with Plough, the moment he came to know of it. But he didn't. I need to understand why.'

The Prime Minister sat down, put his head in his hands.

'I know he's too ill to talk to anyone,' Buch went on. 'But when he's well we must ask him what this was all about. It raises so many questions. I can't put legislation through the Folketinget without knowing more. Birgitte Agger will crucify us—'

'Monberg didn't have a heart attack,' Grue Eriksen said wearily.

Buch took the seat opposite him, put a hand to his chin, waited.

'He took an overdose. He'd been depressed for a while. His marriage was on the rocks. I think the strain of government—'

'I should have been told.'

Grue Eriksen nodded.

'You should. I'm sorry. His wife's devastated. Monberg's a good man at heart. We agreed to give the press a different story for the sake of both of them.'

Buch groaned.

'Wonderful. That makes life even more interesting.'

'You seem to be coping, Thomas.'

'You seem surprised.'

Grue Eriksen nodded.

'I am, to be honest. Most men would buckle under.' He shuffled the papers again. 'What on earth was Monberg up to? Why was he sticking his nose into an old military investigation?'

'I can't begin to imagine.'

'You're right. We need to know,' the Prime Minister said earnestly. 'You've got to find out. Look into it. Mum's the word. This woman murdered. Two soldiers—'

'Three.'

Grue Eriksen stopped reading the papers and gazed at him.

'What was that?'

'Three,' Buch repeated. 'Another member of the squad was killed in Sweden this evening. We're still getting details. They were coming in when Krabbe demanded I play second fiddle at his damned press conference.'

Buch had no idea whether Grue Eriksen had heard the news already or was simply taking it in his stride.

'I came here to haul you over the coals, Minister Buch. It seems I owe you an apology instead. You did the right thing. I'll talk to Krabbe. He's a little man, and all the smaller because he doesn't know it.'

'He really mustn't rant like that in public. Not while I'm around.'

The Prime Minister got up from the table, slapped Buch on the shoulder.

'I'll fix Erling Krabbe.' He pointed at the documents on the table. 'You must get to the bottom of these.'

Lund stood amidst the stench of explosives and blood, trying to still her fury. The forestry truck was parked facing the sea, all lights blazing. More Swedish officers were arriving by helicopter from the mainland. Men in uniform, forensic teams. Figures in plain clothes who didn't speak much at all. The whiff of terrorism always brought them running.

And Lisbeth Thomsen, an odd, evasive woman, was dead. The phlegmatic Swedish cops Lund had regarded as bumpkins were slowly picking pieces of her out of the water, a few with tears in their eyes.

Strange was on the phone to the Politigården again. Brix by the sound of it. Lund didn't have the temper or the patience to deal with that.

'How were we to know she'd run off?'

He was doing his best but it was a ridiculous question. Thomsen was a soldier too. She'd take every opportunity. Lund would have realized this if she'd stopped to think. But all she could see was Strange blundering into the woods, gun out, stumbling towards whatever lay out there.

Perk.

A ghost.

There were shadows like that everywhere. One of them had taken Jan Meyer and left an empty husk in his place. That guilty memory weighed heavily on Sarah Lund, always would. It had sent her scuttling into the dark forest after Ulrik Strange, a decent man, a father too.

She'd never thought about Lisbeth Thomsen for one moment. Now she couldn't get the woman out of her head.

'There's no trace of Raben here,' Strange barked into the phone. He was getting angry. That never worked with Brix. 'Maybe he's got another boat . . .'

The white suits were turning up. One of them berated the old island police chief for picking up something Lund didn't want to look at and gently placing it on a plastic sheet by the jetty.

'We're looking,' Strange went on. 'So are the Swedish coastguard, the police, the navy.'

He came off the phone, walked back to her.

'PET want a meeting first thing tomorrow. Brix says someone broke into the barracks in Ryvangen and stole five kilos of explosive. It looks like the type he used here.'

'Perk,' she said and it wasn't a question. Lund had told Strange what Thomsen had said. It still sounded wrong.

He frowned.

'Soldiers . . .'

'What is it?'

'Sometimes they go a bit crazy. They invent stuff here.' He tapped his own cropped skull. 'Heroes and villains. Crazy things.' He sighed. 'I served with a guy in Iraq who never went anywhere without going through his little rituals. When he ate breakfast the salt and pepper had to be in the right place. If you spilled something only he could wipe it up. There was a way he had to hold his rifle. Go to the latrines. If he didn't do it right he was a mess and—'

'Did it work?' she asked.

'I guess. He's stuck behind the counter of a bank now. I used to hear stories like that. About shadow units. Faceless guys who could come and go as they pleased. They weren't true. They were just part of the game. Thomsen knew that. She was leading you on.'

'I could have stopped her. If—'

'No!' It was one of the few times she'd heard him raise his voice. 'Enough of this. They've found a bag in the shed. Raben rigged something there—'

'Raben was in jail when Anne Dragsholm died. And Myg Poulsen.'

Strange was getting mad with her. This was new too.

'He was there when David Grüner was killed. He's in this some-how.'

She turned and walked off into the trees.

'Lund?' he cried. 'Sarah?'

Away from the water the smell receded though the familiar clatter of a murder scene – male voices, officers lugging gear and lights – never left her. She'd brought it to Sweden now, the little island of Skogö, a place that never deserved it, a woman, Lisbeth Thomsen, who didn't either.

Ulrik Strange could argue all he liked but it was their failure – *her* failure – that did this, nothing else.

Six

8.04 a.m.   First thing the following morning Lund and Strange found themselves back in the Politigården watching Brix, Ruth Hedeby and an anxious Erik König in a meeting room across the corridor.

The TV news was still calling it terrorism. Four victims now, and the police and PET had no clue who was behind the Muslim League. Strange turned off the set.

'What the hell are they going on about?' He nodded at the three people talking earnestly just a few metres away. 'Why aren't we in there too?'

Lund had the latest reports on her desk. Hadn't read them much. She was thinking of Gedser, the easy blank days. Trying to pick up illegals as they turned up on the trucks. Something told her she'd be back there before long.

'Will you please speak to me?'

Strange had drawn up a chair. He didn't tire much, she thought. Or perhaps he always looked this way: nervously active, always waiting for the next lead, the next place to go.

'What do you want me to say?'

'Anything! We can't give up now. We're on to something here.' He looked at her very directly. 'You're on to something.'

'No we're not. All we do is find the bodies.'

This was so like the Birk Larsen case. Seemingly obvious one moment, baffling the next. She and Meyer struggled with that because, as he yelled at her from his wheelchair in the hospital, everyone lied to them. Politicians, school kids, teachers, even family and police looked after their own interests, not those of a murdered teenager. They failed back then, Meyer said, because they weren't connected. To each other, to their families, to the need to deliver an explanation, however inadequate, to Nanna's grieving, raging parents.

It didn't feel so different now, not that Ulrik Strange could appreciate that.

'We're running round and round the same rooms,' Lund whispered, 'when the one we want's locked up somewhere we can't see.'

The door to the office opened. König walked in, followed by a scowling Hedeby and Brix.

Meeting over, the PET chief marched straight over to them.

'This incident in Afghanistan,' he said. 'We don't know what happened for certain. It seems some fundamentalist group there has decided these soldiers were guilty, whatever the judge advocate's report says.'

Lund took a deep breath and kept quiet.

'The evidence is clear,' König went on. 'The websites. There were threats, fatwas, against the soldiers and the system that exonerated them. This is the focus for the inquiry from now on. Whoever deals with it.'

Hedeby listened, arms folded, not looking at anyone. Lund knew what was coming.

'This hasn't gone well,' the deputy commissioner said. 'I'm asking Brix to restructure his team from today.'

Strange leapt to his feet.

'What?'

'You can take a few days off . . .' Hedeby began.

Lund didn't listen. She'd been here before. So she looked at the gathering collection of forensic photos on the wall. Grüner's incinerated skull, locked in a charred scream. Lisbeth Thomsen's severed torso. Anne Dragsholm pleading for her life into a camera. And Myg Poulsen's dog tag, filed to a sharp edge, covered in his blood.

'We're making progress,' Strange objected.

'You let your witness go!' Hedeby shouted. 'When the killer was in the area.'

'She ran off! We could hardly put her in chains.'

Hedeby's voice was turning shrill. She didn't like it when someone argued with her.

'You knew some religious fanatics were out to kill that squad, Strange. You fouled up. Don't try and pretend otherwise . . .'

So many photos. Lund scanned them, wondered why they said so little. Once, when she was here full time, she could look at these things, use her imagination, see a narrative begin to emerge.

'This is outrageous,' Strange howled.

'Will you all shut up?' Lund yelled at them. 'I'm trying to think.'

They went quiet at that. Then Hedeby said, 'You can both go home.'

'What if it's someone else?' Lund said, not moving an inch. 'What if it's not the fundamentalists who want to get rid of the squad?'

She got up, walked past the pictures of the dead.

'This is all so . . . symmetrical. So logical. Do terrorists work like that? Do they have a list? Like a business plan?'

'What are you saying?' Brix asked, interested, even if König and Hedeby were sighing at one another.

'Imagine we're supposed to think this.' Lund turned, peered at him. 'It's all manufactured to make us believe a myth. The flyers, the video, Faith Fellow, the Muslim League. That stooge Kodmani.'

'What in God's name is she talking about now, Brix?' Hedeby moaned.

Lund looked at her.

'Think about it for a minute, will you? Dragsholm wanted the case reopened. She asked Thomsen if she'd testify.'

Hands on hips, staring at the photographs. Running through the possibilities. Imagining.

'Someone doesn't want this looked at again.'

'Like who?' Hedeby cried. 'They're all dead! Apart from Raben, and Herstedvester's a damned good alibi.'

'The explosives were stolen from the barracks,' Strange cut in. 'The detonators were the same as the army use. Could a bunch of Muslim lunatics do that?'

König was staring at his feet.

'We don't even know if there was an incident in Helmand,' Hedeby said. 'Or whether Dragsholm was going to get it reopened.'

'But we do,' König said quietly. 'There was talk of a fresh investigation. I only found out last night from the Ministry. This is a political issue now. I'd suggest we all tread carefully.'

226

Lund struggled to keep hold of her temper.

'It's about four murders!'

'There's nothing to link what happened in Helmand to the killings,' König insisted.

Brix shook his head, amazed.

'Really? It would explain a lot.'

'The army doesn't slaughter its own!' the PET chief cried. 'I'm telling you.' A glance at Hedeby. 'I'm telling all of you. We need to look at the Muslim League. Pick up Kodmani's associates.'

'We've got them all,' Lund retorted. 'It didn't help Lisbeth Thomsen.'

'The army doesn't—'

'We're talking one man,' she cut in. 'Maybe one soldier, with a motive. He's got a name. Thomsen told me. Perk—'

'I don't have time for this nonsense.' König picked up his briefcase, glared at Brix. 'I expect to be briefed when you've restructured your team. I want—'

'You can hear it now,' Brix said casually. 'Lund and Strange continue to work on the case.'

Hedeby and the PET man stopped on the way to the door.

'Excuse me?' she asked.

'I'm the head of homicide. I decide who works for me. These two officers know more about the case than anyone. It would be rash to remove them from it and ask a new team to start from scratch.' He smiled, briefly, almost warmly. 'I'm sure you understand.'

Hedeby looked ready to argue for a moment. Then she said, 'On your head be it.' And they walked out.

Lund got her jacket.

'Ryvangen,' she said.

'Don't give them any reason to complain,' Brix told her.

'We need to find Perk.'

A couple of uniform men were bringing someone into the interview room opposite. It was Louise Raben.

'What's the wife doing here?'

'She met up with her husband yesterday,' Brix said. 'Who's Perk?'

'How's that possible? Aren't PET supposed to be watching her?'

'I don't know. She's admitted she told him about Thomsen's place in Sweden. Perk—'

'Perk's a ghost,' Strange cut in. 'Raben invented him.' He hesitated, looked at Lund. 'He's crazy, isn't he? Maybe Raben's Perk. Have you thought of that?'

'I have actually,' she conceded. 'Get your coat.'

It took three hours in the dim moonlight to navigate the kayak across the narrow strait from Skogö to the mainland. Another hour to find his way to Priest's car hidden in the forest near the ferry harbour. Daybreak saw Raben driving back towards the long slender arm of the Øresund bridge, eyes drooping from exhaustion as he watched the crucifix swinging from side to side from the driver's mirror.

By ten he was in Vesterbro, in the aisle of Torpe's empty church. The priest wore a blue work shirt, jeans and a foul temper.

'You can't stay. The police have been here twice. Louise called. They know you spoke to her. They've taken her in for questioning.'

There was a copy of the morning paper on the pew. A photo of Lisbeth Thomsen, younger, prettier, happier. A headline: *Fourth Danish victim dies to the terror campaign.*

'I'm out of money. Can you lend me some?'

'For what?'

'Just a couple of thousand.'

Torpe nodded at the door.

'Get out of here and rob a gas station or something. That's what you do now, isn't it?'

Torpe was muscular, strong. But he'd never been a real soldier.

Raben walked up to him and he looked scared.

'This has got to stop, Jens. You're the last one. Give yourself up. At least you'll stay alive.'

'Will I?'

'Yes. Talk to the police . . .'

He was exhausted, bored with these arguments. Torpe was a priest. He was supposed to help.

'Are you going to give me some money or not?'

'Turn yourself in, man.'

Raben sighed, looked at him.

'You don't get it. Thomsen said the lawyer woman wanted to reopen the case.'

'What case? What are you talking about? You're sick. You don't know what's real and what isn't.'

'I lost three men in Helmand! Don't tell me I dreamed that.'

Torpe said nothing.

'She knew something, Priest. She'd found out . . . I don't know.' Raben jabbed a finger at his own forehead. 'Whatever's stuck in here.'

'Give yourself up.'

'Do that and they're all dead for nothing. Me too probably. Don't you get it?' He picked up the newspaper, showed it to the stocky man in blue. 'The lawyer didn't talk to me about terrorists. Just what happened.'

Torpe looked nervous, shifty.

'She came to you too. Didn't she?' Raben said.

'I never met her. You're crazy. You need help. I heard all those rumours. There was no officer. They checked—'

'They covered it up.'

'You've got a wife and son. Think of them.'

'I just saw Lisbeth Thomsen blown to pieces. Don't tell me to turn the other cheek. It's too late for that. I want some money, dammit . . .'

The older man was walking for the door. Raben moved quickly, grabbed him by the waist. Torpe's arms went up, a gesture of surrender.

There was a wallet in his back pocket. A thousand, barely more.

'I need the PIN for your cash card.'

Torpe glowered at him.

'Can you hear yourself? I don't use a cash card. I'm a man of God. I live on the charity of the congregation.'

Raben walked over, grabbed the copper donation jug.

'I'll take it from your boss then,' he said and seized the few notes and coins inside.

Thomas Buch sat in the back of his ministerial car listening to Plough read out an editorial from one of the morning papers. It was damning. Buch was castigated for his unpredictable behaviour at the press conference.

'Erling Krabbe is telling people he's washed his hands of you,' Plough added. 'A few of your parliamentary colleagues are saying the same.'

'What's Grue Eriksen saying in public?'

'That he expects an explanation.'

'Don't we all?' Buch murmured, watching the suburb of Valby roll past the window. He'd asked for a meeting with Karina at her home. Plough didn't like this idea. She was now a file for the personnel department. No longer an aide to a minister.

'I talked to the Ministry of Defence,' Plough added. 'They say there's nothing to connect Monberg to the Helmand case.'

There was a tone to the civil servant's voice that Buch was beginning to recognize. It indicated he had more to say.

'Well?'

'I've been wrong about Monberg before. He wasn't always entirely frank with me, as you know. This business with Karina . . .'

'I need to see her. Don't start.'

'Please don't say anything that will complicate the process.' They were stopping outside a modern block of apartments in a quiet street. 'You'd best go in by yourself. It wouldn't do for me to be . . .'

'Involved?' Buch asked.

'We shouldn't be discussing this.'

'Oh for God's sake, Plough. All she did was go to bed with the boss.'

'A Minister of the Crown!'

'A Minister of the Crown,' Buch repeated in a sarcastic sing-song voice. 'What does it matter?'

'How do you know there's not more to it?'

'You just don't want to hear about Monberg's sex life.'

Plough nodded vigorously.

'On balance I'd rather not.'

The block seemed to stretch for ever. He looked up the number. Found the place, a ground-floor flat. Karina appeared, smiled, let Buch in then led him into a bright, sunny room. There was a double bass parked against the wall, a laptop on the table. Newspapers everywhere, a few toys, piles of folders and a half-eaten apple on the floor.

A nice place, Buch thought. It carried the feel and smell of family and he missed that.

She left him for a moment. He plucked a string on the bass and listened to the pleasant sound it made. Then looked at the papers on the table. A double-page spread, his miserable face taking up most of it. The headline: *Paralysis in the Folketinget.*

Karina came back with a child in her arms. A beautiful girl of three or so. She placed her daughter on the sofa and asked her to read a book.

'The nanny's helping move a few things,' Karina said as a dark-haired young woman appeared carrying some boxes. 'Lotte! Just a minute . . .'

They both disappeared to the back of the flat.

Buch stood in front of the little girl, bowed and said, very seriously, 'My name is Thomas Buch. Good morning, Madam.'

She giggled, bowed too.

'My name's Merle Jørgensen.'

'Merle. One of my favourite names.'

'Mummy said you were funny.'

'Merle!' Karina cried as she marched back in.

'No, no,' Buch insisted. 'I am funny. I like funny things. The world needs them.'

Lotte the nanny came and took Merle by the hand. It was time for kindergarten.

Her mother waited till they were gone then said, 'If it's about my resignation . . . I'll do whatever the Ministry wants. I won't cause trouble. Will I have to talk to the police?'

'I didn't know you had a daughter.'

She saw the newspapers on the table and closed the pages.

'I never told them at the interview. I'm sorry. I have to go to the post office.'

She walked around the room, picking up bills and letters.

Buch went over to the bass and plucked the string again.

'So her father's a musician?'

'No. That's mine. Please don't mess with it. Do you want a coffee?'

'You don't have to make coffee for me any more.'

'I never had to in the first place. Merle's father's a lawyer. He decided he preferred earning lots of money in Dubai to being here with us.'

'I don't want you to resign, Karina,' Buch said straight out. 'There's no good reason. I would like you back in the office, please.'

She seemed surprised.

'I'm saying this for entirely selfish reasons,' he added. 'You're good at your job. I'm not.'

'Did you talk to Plough? I misled you. And him.'

'Plough doesn't think you've done anything wrong.'

He knew the look he got then. It said, 'Oh please . . .'

'Carsten could do with a roll in the hay too,' Buch added.

She didn't laugh.

'I'm pleading, Karina. I need your help.'

'No.'

'I've got to find out how Monberg's involved in all this. Do you have any idea why he wanted to hide his discussions with Anne Dragsholm?'

'I would have told you!'

'Why all this secrecy?'

She shook her head. Lifted up the bills and letters. Time to go.

'Why did he try to kill himself?'

That stopped her.

'What?'

'I only found out last night. That was another secret he wanted to keep. It wasn't a heart attack. He took an overdose. Maybe he had a bad conscience about something.'

She sat down, looked shocked.

'I don't know what to say. Monberg tried to kill himself? Why?'

He'd upset her now and Buch regretted that.

'I haven't a clue,' he said. 'Please change your mind . . .'

'There are some things in the office. I'll need to pick them up.'

'Say hello when you do.'

His phone rang. It was Plough, sounding even more anxious than usual.

'The Minister of Defence has called a meeting.'

'What about?'

'They didn't say. This afternoon.'

'Tell Rossing I don't have time for mysteries,' Buch said and ended the call.

'There's only one soldier left now, isn't there?' Karina asked as he walked to the door.

'Yes. And we've no idea where he is. Or . . .' This last seemed most puzzling of all. '. . . why he's running.'

'You'll find out, Thomas. Whatever other people think.' Her eyes strayed to the paper. 'You'll get there.'

'Call me when you come in,' Buch repeated then went outside and waited for the car.

It was parked at the far end of the street. Carsten Plough, he guessed, had no intention of seeing his former colleague eye to eye. Not if he could help it.

The munitions depot in Ryvangen. Wooden crates with army stamps on the side. Racks of plastic boxes. Paperwork on noticeboards. Colonel Jarnvig and Said Bilal met them at the door, both dressed in green camouflage fatigues.

Bilal had his passport with him, and a list of vaccinations.

'Are you looking forward to it?' Lund asked trying her best at small talk. He was a surly young man maybe a year short of thirty, cheerless, forever on duty, she thought.

'I'm a soldier. It's what I do. I don't go out for another month anyway. Admin work to do here.'

Lund thought of her own son, Mark. He'd been talking of joining the army one day. It would pay for his college education. He spoke of the decision as if being a soldier was just one more job, like that of an accountant, a lawyer, a doctor . . .

Torsten Jarnvig was every inch the army professional. She couldn't imagine him as anything else. But Bilal seemed so young, so unformed and lacking in personality, he might have been anything.

The world had changed. War once seemed something extraordinary, antiquated. A relic of a past that would never return. A memory for your parents and grandparents, of Nazis in jackboots stomping around the streets of Copenhagen in front of mutinous crowds of Danes.

Now it was ubiquitous, never-ending, a stream of constant bloody pictures on twenty-four-hour TV. A kid coming out of school would flick through a careers brochure full of weaponry and planes and battleships without a second thought. Conflict was part of the everyday world in a way that would have been unthinkable two decades before. Bilal's attitude was natural. It was her own discomfort that was out of sorts with the times.

'Myg Poulsen worked here,' Jarnvig said as they walked down a long corridor towards a cavernous room at the end. 'He had a key. It's possible he had access to some kind of master code. They were both used to get in.'

'Possible?' Lund asked straight away.

'The code wasn't allocated to any one individual,' Jarnvig said testily. 'I can't tell you any more than that.'

233

Lund shook her head.

'Don't you cancel a code when someone dies? Isn't that the most basic . . .'

Jarnvig didn't like the question.

'I told you. It was a generic code, part of the system. No one imagined anything like this could happen.'

'Security's about dealing with the unimaginable.' Strange's eyes didn't leave the colonel's face. 'You're sloppy here. When I picked up the judge advocate's report I didn't see a single guard in this area.'

'I didn't realize you were an expert on army security.'

Strange stood his ground.

'I did my time. I know sloppy when I see it.'

Bilal retreated, watching his superior with interested, keen eyes.

'We're preparing for a mission,' Jarnvig said, fighting to stay calm. 'The depot's locked electronically. Only seven people know the customary access codes.'

'One of them being a dead man. And whoever killed him,' Lund chipped in. 'Except maybe he didn't know that code at all. Great. What time was the break-in?'

Bilal checked his clipboard.

'According to the log files the outside lock was disengaged at 0:39. Just after midnight. Then again at 1.04 on the way out.'

Jarnvig led them into the main depot room. A vast hangar-like structure full of uniformed men working silently on crates and boxes and pallets. Gun barrels lay stacked like drain pipes waiting to be laid. A Mercedes all-terrain vehicle stood on jacks in the corner.

There was a cage at the end. It was open now and suited forensic officers were working inside.

The colonel led them through. A heavy padlock sat on the cement floor ringed with black ink.

'Poulsen dealt with ammunition and explosives,' he said as they entered the cage, Bilal last, hands tucked dutifully behind his back. ' The key was for here.'

'You couldn't just find this place with a key and a lock code,' Lund pointed out. 'He must have—'

'We've put together a list of civilians who know their way around the barracks,' Jarnvig broke in. 'It runs to several hundred. Contractors. Other visitors.'

Lund walked around, staring at the green metal boxes and the impenetrable stamps they carried.

The code still bothered her.

'If it was generic,' she said, 'a civilian technician might have known the code. Right? Or someone from another barracks? Army headquarters?'

'We don't know where the code originated,' Jarnvig said grimly. 'I can't keep repeating this. Lisbeth Thomsen was a good soldier. How did she die?'

'Someone set booby-traps for her. One of them worked.' She watched him. 'They got a chemical stamp in forensic overnight. She was killed by your explosives. From this depot.'

He didn't like that.

'We're giving you all the cooperation we can . . .'

'Maybe you never noticed anything because he's one of you,' Strange said.

'There's a hole in the fence! Why would one of our own need to do that?'

Strange peered round the cage.

'Could be a diversion. Whoever got in here knew this place. Knew what he was looking for.'

Jarnvig struggled for an answer.

Lund said, 'I want the names of every officer, every soldier in the barracks with general access.'

'That's three platoon commanders. Two officers. Poulsen—'

'Poulsen's dead! What about you?'

'Of course I've got access. I'm the camp commander. Why are you wasting our time—'

'Wasting your time?'

Brix said to keep it cool. Brix wasn't here. If he was he'd be as annoyed by this arrogant, dismissive man as much as she was.

'I think we need to continue this conversation in the Politigården, Colonel,' Lund said.

'Why?'

'Because that's where we take people for questioning.'

Jarnvig looked around at his men, his equipment. This was his castle, Lund thought. His kingdom. That was why she wanted to see this man without the protection he felt he was owed in this place.

'I'm too busy.'

Strange walked up and stood next to him.

'You can come willingly. Or we can arrest you.'

'This is an army barracks—'

'This is Denmark,' Lund interrupted. 'Will you kindly get in the car?'

The men stiffened to attention as Jarnvig walked out of the Ryvangen munitions depot and marched in silent fury to the black Ford.

A report from PET was waiting when Buch and Plough arrived back at the Ministry of Justice.

'König says they're still extending their investigations into the Islamic groups,' Plough explained, scanning it as they walked to Buch's office. 'It's his belief the murders are in revenge for an atrocity the fundamentalists say occurred in Helmand two years ago.'

'Yes, yes. I know that. But is there actual evidence to support any of this?'

He passed Buch the skimpiest of files.

'You should ask him. They've nothing connecting Monberg and Anne Dragsholm.'

The civil servant coughed into his fist. Always a sign he was about to say something awkward.

'König's complaining about a lack of cooperation with the police,' he said.

They got to the top of the stairs, two doors from the minister's quarters.

'That's a bit rich, isn't it? PET told the police nothing for nearly two weeks.'

'Let me look into it. I've posted the vacancy for your new personal secretary. I know of two possible candidates—'

'I don't want a new secretary,' Buch said, trying hard not to sound petulant. 'I want Karina . . .'

He stopped. Flemming Rossing was standing outside his office looking nervous in a long raincoat.

'Do you have a moment?' the Defence Minister asked. 'I came over specially.'

'You caught me at a bad time, Rossing. Let's talk later, shall we? I'll get my secretary . . .'

236

Rossing smiled. That beak-like nose, those keen, avaricious eyes. He looked, Buch thought, like a raptor considering its prey.

'You don't have a secretary. Word gets around . . .'

'Two minutes. That's all.'

But by then Flemming Rossing was already walking into the office, past the long window and the writhing dragons.

'The Prime Minister briefed me,' Rossing said. 'We need a chat.'

Buch sat down. Rossing stayed by the window, walking to and fro. Carsten Plough had once again vanished.

'I know Monberg's a friend of yours,' Buch declared. 'You may not like what's coming out. I'm sorry but we've got to get to the bottom of this.'

'I remember when I was first appointed,' Rossing said, smiling at the portraits behind the desk. 'You're nervous. You want everyone to like you. Especially the Prime Minister. It's like going back to school and being made a prefect all over again.'

'No one ever made me a prefect. More to the point I'm really very busy . . .'

Rossing pulled up a seat.

'There's no connection between Monberg and the military case. I know.'

'Well, if you know—'

'There's something you have to understand. Frode had been under terrible pressure for a long time. The negotiations over the anti-terror package. Problems at home. May I?'

Rossing poured himself a glass of water without waiting for the answer.

'He always had an eye for the women.' Rossing nodded at the office outside. 'You've got an empty desk to prove it. Then he was approached by Anne Dragsholm. They knew each other from years ago.'

Buch glanced at the dossier he'd got from Plough.

'There's no mention of that in PET's report.'

'Frode was Dragsholm's lecturer at university. They had an affair. He was already married. There were children. So he dumped her.'

He sipped the water. Hesitated as if wondering how far to go.

'I don't think Frode was in touch with her since. He'd talk about his . . . dalliances with me from time to time.' Rossing's aquiline face hardened. 'I hated all that. He tried to make it sound like a confession but it was nothing more than boasting. Then Dragsholm turned up again wanting some help. So he met her . . .' He raised the glass in a bitter toast. 'For old times' sake.'

Buch asked, 'Is there a point to all this?'

Rossing's light-blue eyes lit up with fury.

'Monberg didn't give a shit about this case. He wanted Dragsholm back in bed. That was all there was to it. When she was murdered he went frantic. I never saw him so bad. A few days later he cracked up and . . .'

Buch thrust his hands into his pockets and waited.

'I had lunch with him a couple of days before. All he could talk about was how his life was one long series of mistakes. All his achievements . . .' His free hand swept the office. 'Here. They didn't mean a thing. I was busy. I didn't want to hear about one more grubby little affair, thank you. And then—'

'So it's just a squalid little sex scandal? Best we forget about the whole thing?'

The blue eyes were fixed on him.

'I wasn't saying that. I know everything's got to come out into the open. I just don't think we need it now. You'll damage him. The government. Give that bitch Birgitte Agger all the ammunition she needs.'

'Four people are dead and you're asking—'

'I'm not asking anything. You're the minister. It's your decision. Monberg's nothing to do with that case. Drag him in and all we'll get is pointless dirt. Think before you act, Thomas. Please.'

He finished the water, put the glass on the table. Picked up the PET report, flicked through the pages, then put it back.

'It would have helped if you'd told me this before,' Buch said.

'How?'

'I would have been prepared.'

'I doubt that. I mean no offence. We're ministers. We're not here to know everything. We exist in order to make decisions. Good ones, hopefully. Though few remember those.'

He got up, patted Buch on the shoulder.

'Only the bad,' he said then left.

Jarnvig looked smaller once he was sat at a table in a Politigården interview room. Lund, leaning on the radiator by the window, could

238

scent something on him. An uneasiness that wasn't there behind the barrack walls.

'Yesterday you said no civilians were wounded in that village.'

'That's true,' he agreed.

'I talked to Thomsen before she fled with Raben. She told me a different story.'

'No. We heard that fairy tale. The judge advocate looked into it. All those rumours were proved to be false.'

Strange sat relaxed on the black bench seat, watching Jarnvig perched at the desk, rigid as ever.

'You lost three men from that squad,' he said. 'Maybe you weren't as focused on the truth as you might have been.'

'It was the judge who cleared them. Not me.'

'Give us the process.' Lund put her hands flat on the table, looked at him with her big bright eyes. 'I'm curious. I'm a civilian remember. A woman. I don't understand your world.'

'Ask me a question and I'll answer,' Jarnvig replied dryly. 'If I can.'

'When the squad was flown back to the camp what did they tell you?'

'You know this! They claimed they'd received a call from a patrol under fire outside our control zone. It was an area where the Taliban held some control.'

'Some?'

'Some,' he repeated. 'It's Afghanistan. There are no borders, no front lines. They said the call came from a village. When they got there they found one officer, Perk. He'd been under fire and wanted help.'

'What else?'

'They said Perk had taken refuge in a house. They were under siege for forty hours without radio contact. We'd no idea where they were. The helicopter that picked up Thomsen looked but it was impossible.'

Jarnvig sipped at the coffee Lund had given him.

'A few of the local tribesmen claimed later something happened to the family in the house. They were looking for money.'

Lund asked, 'What did they say?'

'They said the Danish officer killed the family. Father, mother, two, three children, I don't remember. No one was quite sure. It was ridiculous.'

'You went to the village and asked?'

'It's Afghanistan! We did what we could. We got to the house for a while. There'd been an explosion. We could see that. No one knew anything about a message from a missing squad.' His eyes darkened. 'Except Raben . . . There was no record of any troops in the area. No bodies . . .'

'Thomsen had heard of someone called Perk,' Lund pointed out.

Jarnvig leaned forward and slammed his fist on the table.

'There was no officer called Perk. Do you think I didn't look? Raben's my son-in-law. I never liked the man but for my daughter's sake I wanted to see justice done.'

Strange shook his head.

'Why would Raben lie? Why would the others? They told you the same story.'

'That adventure cost three lives. Raben was always headstrong. Never took orders easily. He was trying to be a hero maybe. Perhaps he wanted to shift the blame.'

'What about the family?' Lund asked. 'Someone lived in the house, didn't they? Did you find them? What did they say?'

'No. We were told they'd fled.'

'Everyone?'

'Everyone.'

Lund flicked through the papers.

'You were officer in command. Did you check this all yourself?'

'Not personally,' Jarnvig replied, as if this were somehow beneath him. 'I wasn't in camp when it happened. But I was briefed fully on my return. It was clear—'

'Stop!' Strange ordered. 'You weren't in camp?'

'No. I was at a security council meeting in Kabul. My second-in-command kept me posted.'

Lund asked, 'Names?'

'Captain Søgaard. He's a major now, of course. I came back two days after they got Raben and his men out of there. Søgaard gave me a full report and I—'

'That's all for now,' she said.

'What?'

'That's all.' Lund beckoned to the door. 'You can go.'

Brix was hovering in the corridor as Jarnvig left. Lund watched the two of them pass each other. Not a word spoken, plenty of eye contact.

'Jarnvig's going to be stirring it,' Strange said. 'We weren't supposed to rock the boat.'

That stray thought she'd first recalled the day before returned as she watched the man in uniform walk out of the building. The Politigården wasn't always a stranger to the military. During the German occupation the Nazis had occupied the place, running the Danish police officers who remained in post. Some of the Danes had crossed the line, brought in partisans for questioning. She knew the rumours. The stories of a ghost in the basement, close to the rooms where the Germans and their local allies beat and tortured suspects then shipped them off to Mindelunden to die tied to a stake on the shooting range.

And some of those turncoats died themselves, assassinated by the partisan gangs.

Stikke.

Mown down outside their homes, shot on the bus as they went to work.

War wasn't always a foreigner. For some it was a familiar, everyday thing, part of the landscape, like bad weather or disease. A shape in the shadows she'd simply been lucky to avoid until now.

'Where's Søgaard?' she asked.

'I've left four messages. He never gets back.'

'Is that so?' Lund said.

Buch got Carsten Plough to check out Monberg's past the moment Rossing was gone. Then he put on his heavy winter jacket and abandoned Slotsholmen for the pleasures of the hot dog wagon in the square across the bridge. Copenhagen looked normal here. People going about their lives, unaware of the feverish activity in the grey buildings of government behind them. Denmark had been run from this small island for centuries, ever since a warrior bishop called Absalon built his castle there. In an idle moment as a new MP Buch had visited the remains of the fortress deep beneath the Christianborg Palace. Slotsholmen had been a magnet for power for more than a millennium, and with that he guessed came rumour, scandal and scheming.

When he got back he found there was a little progress.

'I think he's right,' Plough said. 'Monberg was a visiting professor when Dragsholm was at university. They could have had an affair. Afterwards she did some work overseas then applied for a job in the army.'

'Do we know they had an affair?'

The civil servant shrugged.

'We don't bug bedrooms. Do we? Well, not a minister's. I hope you weren't too rude to Flemming Rossing. He's not a man to cross.'

Karina was walking into the office carrying her daughter in her arms. The little girl was wrapped up for the cold in an all-white wool coat and pretty hat.

Buch bowed and said very grandly, 'Merle Jørgensen. Thomas Buch and his dragons welcome you.'

She chuckled and said, 'What dragons?'

Buch gestured to the window and the spire of the Børsen.

'They're not real,' the girl announced in that sparky kid's voice that denoted a playful argument.

'Who knows what's real and what's not?' Buch asked.

'Grown-ups do . . .'

'If only . . . I have to phone someone.' He looked at Karina. 'Can we talk afterwards?'

He called Rossing.

'If this is another argument,' the Defence Minister said when Buch got through.

'No arguments. I've been thinking about what you said. I'm new to this kind of responsibility. You should forgive my naivety at times.'

Rossing said nothing.

'I lost perspective,' Buch continued. 'You're right. We need to think of the bigger picture. I'll tell the Prime Minister we must let sleeping dogs lie. The murder investigation will continue its course. But Monberg need be no part of it.'

'I'm pleased we see eye-to-eye finally. You're a good man and you'll make a fine minister. We should talk more often. Frankly, as we have.'

Plough was waving at him from the door.

'Dinner,' Rossing went on. 'That's the thing. There's a French restaurant I know. Why not tonight?'

242

'I've plans, thank you,' Buch lied.

'Not another bloody hot dog I hope.'

'Another night. I promise.'

Plough was waving desperately. Buch said goodbye to Rossing then went into his office. Karina was in a chair, her daughter by the window waving to the entwined dragons.

'Monberg is connected to the military case, Thomas.' She looked apologetic at saying this. 'Dragsholm contacted him to complain about errors in procedure.'

Plough stood by the door, listening. She took some documents out of her bag.

'The investigation ignored the statements made by the soldiers. Monberg knew this was the case—'

'Karina,' Plough interjected. 'We know all this. If you've come back to try to reclaim your job—'

'Give her a chance,' Buch ordered.

'At first I found nothing,' she said, pointing to the documents. 'Then I looked in the system and cross-checked the soldiers' names with the files we keep here.'

'You no longer have access to the computers!' Plough complained.

Buch stared him into silence.

'The case went through the Ministry of Defence,' she carried on. 'But Monberg attended a meeting about an individual soldier.' She found the sheet. 'Jens Peter Raben, after he was committed to Herstedvester.'

'The one who's on the run?' Plough looked shocked.

'Him,' she said. 'There are no minutes of the meeting. If it wasn't for the line in Monberg's diary I wouldn't even know Raben was involved.'

'Karina,' Buch began. 'This is all very well . . .'

'Defence Minister Rossing instigated that meeting. I remember taking the call. He was very insistent.' She shrugged. 'Monberg wasn't looking forward to it.'

Buch rubbed his chin.

'Rossing assured me it was nothing more than an affair. He *assured* me.'

'Then he lied to you.'

Plough was tut-tutting.

'He lied!' she repeated. 'What else explains it?'

The two men looked at her in silence.

'What else?'

'You've told Rossing you won't pursue this,' Plough said. 'It would be unseemly if you went back on your word.'

'Unseemly?' Thomas Buch roared. 'I was buying time, you fool!'

The quiet civil servant cowered at the volume of his voice.

Karina's little girl wasn't giggling at the dragons any more. She was staring at him and she looked scared.

'I'm sorry,' Buch said, more quietly. 'I'm really very sorry indeed.'

The police drove Louise Raben home after they finished the interview. It wasn't generosity. The two detectives then set about searching her rooms in Jarnvig's barracks house, taking what they wanted. She sat at the kitchen table. It was the last room they looked at. One man went through the drawers. The other had her diary and her bag.

He was a cheery, bald man of forty or so. Persistent. Not in a hurry.

'Is this your address book?' he said, taking it out from the bag.

'Yes. You won't find anything in there.'

He put it in his case anyway.

'You'll get it back.'

Jonas walked through the door and stood by the table, staring at them balefully.

A forced smile broke on Louise Raben's face. This was what mothers were meant to do. Stay bright and cheerful.

'Hi, darling.' She stroked his brown hair. He didn't smile. 'Did you have fun?'

The tall cop with the address book winked. Jonas stared at him, then the other one.

'They're helping Mummy clear up,' Louise said. 'Nearly done. They're leaving now.'

'Sign here,' the man said and gave her a form.

While she was doing that he bent down and looked at Jonas's rucksack.

'Nice bag. Did your daddy give you that?'

'No he didn't,' Louise snapped, close to breaking.

The second cop had got hold of the laptop and was putting it in a plastic bag.

'Why are they taking our computer?' Jonas asked.

'They're going now. Aren't you?'

'I want the computer,' Jonas whined.

'It's all right, darling.' She stroked his hair. Again no smile. 'They just want to borrow it. We'll get you a PlayStation soon. OK?'

They went not long after. She got Jonas some food. He didn't say much, however hard she tried. She'd always thought families fell apart in a flood of screams and shouted accusations. But they didn't. It happened like this, in silence and unspoken fears.

After a while he walked away from the food, went to the living room and turned on the TV.

The buzzing noise of a phone near the cooker. She looked around, made sure no one was looking.

The police had taken her mobile. She knew they'd do that so she'd slipped the sim into a spare handset and hid it in the stove hood. They weren't having everything.

'Louise? Hello?'

'It's me,' her father said. 'I think you'd better come over to my office right away.'

The grey-faced priest, Gunnar Torpe, was in Jarnvig's office when she got there. Louise Raben had not met him much. Never liked him when she did. She could never work out which he truly was: a man of God or a man of war. Torpe was a bachelor, almost too covetous of his role with the troops. When they went to war he was there. When they left he always seemed a touch resentful at seeing them return to their families. Jealous. That was probably unfair, but true, she thought. It was there in his restless, angry eyes.

'Jens is sick,' Torpe said, getting to his feet. 'Terribly sick.'

She didn't take the seat he offered. Just stood and watched him, arms folded, under the observant gaze of her father.

The army was run by men like these. They always knew best.

'We need to get him some help,' Torpe went on in his sing-song priest's voice. 'We have to get him out of harm's way before he does something really stupid.'

'Did you visit him in jail?' she asked, not kindly.

No answer. She knew he'd never been to Herstedvester. Jens had mentioned it.

'I did,' Louise told him. 'Week in, week out. I saw him getting better and better. And still they wouldn't let him go.'

'He needs help now,' her father said. 'Call him. Say you want to see him. Let the police do the rest.'

'Just hand him over?' she cried. 'Send him back to jail?'

'He's not right in the head,' Torpe pleaded. 'The things he says . . . don't make sense.'

'Myg dead,' she said. 'Grüner. Now Lisbeth Thomsen. This lawyer woman. What does make sense?'

'He's the last one, Louise . . .'

Torpe had a soldier's hands, but he used them like a priest. Now they were pressed together as if in prayer.

'I did try to call him,' she said. 'He doesn't answer.'

'Try again,' her father demanded.

She left them in the office. Stood outside in the corridor, watching the activity in the yard beyond. Men in green combat gear lugging equipment, mortars, rifles. Another tour of duty on the way.

'Where are you, Jens?' she whispered. And then, so softly she barely heard herself, 'Where am I?'

Torpe's church wasn't far from the rough quarter of Vesterbro. Sex shops, half-hidden brothels. Drug dens. Hookers on the street.

It wasn't hard to find the kind of business Raben wanted. A couple of conversations with men near the meat-packing halls. A phone call. A nod. An address.

The place turned out to be an abandoned garage not far from the Dybbølsbro bridge. Scaffolding held up the interior walls. There was a stink of open drains. A rusty green VW camper van was parked by the half-arch windows at the end.

He was big with the face of a boxer: scarred and ugly. Leather jacket. Heavy physique that spoke of body-building and pills.

Raben looked at him and thought about it. Some men learned to fight in jail. Some got better teachers.

The thug opened the back door and unwrapped a roll of old carpet. A tiny arsenal sat there. Small-bore pistols. Service revolvers. Semi-automatics.

Most looked like adapted replicas, dangerous, useless to him.

Raben's face must have spoken. The thug brushed aside the cheap fakes and pulled out a black Neuhausen. Swiss semi-automatic. Old but good.

'That came from the army,' he said. 'Best weapon I got. I can get four thousand euros for that in Spain.'

Raben felt it. He knew this kind of gun. Had used it in anger.

'How much are you good for?'

'About six hundred,' Raben answered.

The man with the boxer's face stood over him and grunted.

'Six hundred? You can't buy an air pistol for that.'

The magazine was missing. He stuffed the gun into his belt.

'Did you hear me?'

So much training it came as second nature. The bigger they were, the easier they came down.

Raben jabbed his boot hard into the guy's shin, pounced when he yelled, took out the leg, jerked him off balance, pushed as he went over. The weight did the rest. Down the man went, cropped skull hard on the cement floor.

Dazed, bleeding, yelling.

Raben checked he was stunned, kicked him in the head once for good measure, ran his hands over the leather jacket.

The magazine was there. This was his gun. Raben slotted it in place. Kept the weapon on the grunting figure on the ground, ran over his jacket again. Took the phone. Took the wallet, checked it. A thousand, that was all.

They never carried much. It was a risky profession.

He'd got his head back now. Was staring at Raben from the hard ground in a way that said: *I will remember you.*

'I need it,' Raben said.

The gun came up. The man looked scared. He was meant to.

'Get in the van,' Raben ordered. 'Drive away. Don't think about me. Don't talk about me. Pray we don't meet again. Because if we do . . .'

He jerked the weapon towards the VW. The thug with the bloody boxer's face struggled to his feet, waddled to the open door, climbed in, drove off.

When he was outside in the street the phone Torpe had given him rang.

'Louise?'

'I think my dad knows about this number.'

'Did Priest tell him?'

'They're worried about you, Jens.'

'Do the police know you're talking to me?'

'I don't think so. Are you OK? Priest says you're safer if you give yourself up. He says—'

'I know what I'm doing. We can't talk now.'

'Jens!' Her voice was close to breaking. 'For God's sake . . . we both—'

He cut the call and put the mobile in his pocket. Looked round at the sex shops and the sleazy corners of Vesterbro. A couple of shady men in black were talking surreptitiously by the corner. As he watched a young and pretty mother pushed a pram past them, along the line of hookers in miniskirts gathering for the day's trade.

Life went on regardless.

The duty officer at Ryvangen said Søgaard was in the shower after a workout. Lund asked for directions and went straight in.

The place stank of sweat and cheap body cologne. The air was damp and steamy. She walked past a line of red lockers, past naked men clutching towels to themselves.

One finally plucked up the courage to challenge her.

She pulled out her police ID, looked past him.

'I want Major Søgaard.'

No one spoke. There was laughter from the end, the sound of showers.

Lund walked on, stopped at the very edge.

Some of them were out and shaving, dog tags round their necks. Søgaard was still amidst the steam. He didn't try to cover himself like the others did. Maybe he thought he had something to be proud of.

Lund glanced, covered a yawn with her hand.

'Yes?' Søgaard asked, coming out to look at her, naked except for the silver dog tag round his neck.

'We've been leaving messages for you all morning.'

'This is my last full day with all my officers. It's a busy schedule.'

'I want to talk to you about what happened in Afghanistan.'

He didn't move.

'Do we do it here?' she asked.

'I was going to go for a shit,' he said, pointing to one side. 'Do you want to come in there for that?'

'Get your clothes. Or I'll drag you down to the Politigården right now.'

'My schedule—'

'Fuck your schedule,' Lund snapped, aware that the men around her were starting to watch, amused. 'Outside now or you're in my office for the rest of the day. You choose.'

She waited by the front door of the building, watching the soldiers go to and fro in their armoured vehicles.

Søgaard didn't rush. Twenty minutes later he was there, immaculate in dress uniform, blond hair dried and perfect beneath a dark beret.

'This is a waste of my time,' he said before she could speak. 'I know no more than Colonel Jarnvig.'

'Well, that can't be right, can it?'

He didn't like being questioned. Especially by her.

'Why's that?'

'Jarnvig was in Kabul. You were in the camp. You must have witnessed the soldiers' statements.'

He laughed at her.

'Civilians. You really have no idea what it's like, do you?'

He started walking towards a Mercedes troop carrier. Lund went with him.

'Enlighten me.'

'I can't tell you anything you don't already know.'

'The soldiers mentioned an officer called Perk.'

That stopped him. Søgaard looked her up and down.

'Yes,' he agreed. 'They did. They'd been under fire. Three of their comrades were dead. Raben and Grüner were so badly wounded we didn't know if they'd live. They rambled on about lots of things—'

'Perk?'

'There was no officer out there. No squad under fire. Nobody called Perk.'

He leaned against the vehicle and peered into her eyes.

'No distress call either. Raben should have confirmed with the camp before going in. He broke procedures. It wasn't the first time—'

'You don't like him, do you?'

Søgaard hesitated.

'He used to be a good soldier. Maybe he got promoted above his temperament.'

'How do you know they didn't kill this Afghan family?'

'Because I went there. I led the operation that got Raben's squad out of the shit.'

He wanted to leave it at that.

'You were the first to get to this village?' she asked.

'The first from our side. Correct.'

'And you saw nothing significant?'

'I guess it depends what you mean by significant. We picked up three dead soldiers and the rest of them wounded or shell-shocked. Does that count?'

'Civilians—'

'There were no civilians. Dead or alive. There were maybe six or seven houses in the place. All empty. One had taken some kind of hit. The Afghans walk away if there's trouble. Usually they never come back.'

Someone was shouting for him from across the road.

'And a few months later they pinned some more medals on you and made you a major?'

He didn't like that at all.

'Was that a reward for the mission?'

'We saved them, didn't we? The ones who were still alive.'

An open-top G-Wagen turned up. Søgaard climbed in.

'If something happened in that village it was your responsibility, wasn't it?'

'*If* something happened. But it didn't. War's a dirty business. We die. The enemy die. People who get caught in the middle die. We're out there to get blood on our hands so you don't see any on yours. End of story.'

'This is about four murders, Søgaard.'

'Good luck with it,' he muttered then made a circular waving gesture with his hand and the vehicle lurched off.

Lund stood in the road and watched, ignoring the procession of vehicles behind Søgaard's, all honking at her to get out of the way.

She took out her phone and called Strange in the Politigården.

'I want Søgaard's alibi checked. Where was he? Who did see? What did he do around the time of the killings?'

'OK,' he agreed. 'Brix has got some records from the army. All officers stationed abroad in the last ten years. There's no one called Perk.'

'There's got to be.'

'Let me finish. Some recruits were trained by a lieutenant they used to call Perk.'

'And?'

'His real name's Per Kristian Møller. He was with Ægir.'

The line of army vehicles was getting frantic. Lund could barely hear in the cacophony of horns. Slowly she stepped out of the road and walked to her car.

'Any idea where he is now?' she asked.

A moment's silence.

'Working on it,' Strange said. 'Give me an hour.'

By late afternoon they'd traced Per Kristian Møller to a house in an expensive tree-lined street in Frederiksberg, west of the city, not far from the cemetery where Anne Dragsholm was interred two days before. His mother Hanne was home on her own. The light was gone. A log fire was blazing in the living room as she took them through her son's army career, sifting through a few of the belongings he'd left behind.

'These,' she said, showing them a holiday photo, mother, father, strong young son, by the beach, 'were Per Kristian's favourite sunglasses. Won't you sit down? My husband's abroad but I'll do all I can to help.'

She was a plump woman, forties. Not much older than Lund herself. Long hair, fashionable clothes, a young face though lined.

'When did your son die?' Lund asked.

'In the month of May. Two years and six months ago.'

'In May?'

'Yes. May the 13th. In an explosion.'

She ran a hand through her long brown locks.

'I wouldn't forget that, would I?'

Then she walked to the wall and put the picture back in its place, next to a portrait of him in uniform, smiling for the camera.

'Let's leave her in peace,' Strange whispered. 'This guy was dead three months before Raben's squad got hit.'

Lund looked at him and shook her head.

'I tried to talk him into doing something else,' Hanne Møller said, arms folded, eyes on the wall. 'He was an only child. I never wanted to let go. It was ridiculous. The army was his life. It was all he ever wanted. To do his duty. To be a good citizen.'

A weak smile.

'Then they made him a lieutenant and we hardly ever heard from him after that. Until they phoned and told us what had happened. We buried him in the church down the road. He sang in the choir when he was little. He's still close to us. He's still ours.'

'I think we should go,' Strange whispered.

Lund struggled for something to say.

'It must be a comfort,' was all she could manage.

Hanne Møller tried to keep smiling.

'Is this about the investigation? That lawyer who was here. A woman. She was asking the same questions you did.'

'Was she called—'

'Dragsholm. Anne Dragsholm. I saw the dreadful news about her. So . . . horrible.'

She went to a line of keys on the wall by the refrigerator.

'I showed her his belongings. I suppose you'll want to see them too.'

They followed her into a wooden shed at the back of the house. A jumble of boxes and cases, shelves and bags under three harsh fluorescent tubes.

'We kept all his things. I insisted on it.' She opened a box and took out a football and a pair of boots. Probably for a kid of twelve. 'Everything.'

Then she walked up to some suitcases.

'Every time we're about to throw something out we have second thoughts. I know it's silly.'

'What did Dragsholm ask for?' Lund asked.

'The documents concerning his death. In case we were entitled to compensation.' The smile left her face. 'I had to go to the kitchen to take a call. When I came back she was just going through his things. Very rude if you ask me . . .'

Lund had picked up a school satchel. It was empty save for dust.

'Like you,' Hanne Møller said with an edge.

'Why was she doing that?' Strange asked.

'She wouldn't say. She asked me a lot of questions. Funny questions. About the funeral and all . . .'

'What about the funeral?'

'She seemed concerned that we hadn't seen him.'

'Seen him where?'

'In his coffin.' She glanced around the shed as if she regretted bringing them here, starting this conversation. 'We wanted to. We asked. But they told us we'd better not. For our own sake. He died in an explosion . . .'

'They never let you see your own son?'

'No.'

'Whose decision was that?'

'Captain Søgaard. And the priest. They were polite . . . But very insistent. I don't think they would have let us even if we'd pleaded. It was as if . . .' She looked ready to cry and Lund didn't want that. 'It was as if he belonged to them. Not to us any more. But it was a beautiful funeral. They were very kind. Do you want to see a photo of the grave? We put fresh flowers there every week.'

'Please,' Lund said.

She walked back to the house and left them.

'No.' Strange wagged a finger at her. 'I'm not going along with this. She's upset. Let's not make it worse—'

'Dragsholm was here. Are you asleep?'

'He died three months before the incident happened!'

'And Søgaard swore he never knew an officer called Perk. He's covering up—'

'Perk's dead. He was in the ground before any of this started.'

She liked Ulrik Strange but he could drive her mad sometimes.

'When will you learn to ask questions?' she demanded. 'They wouldn't let his own parents see the body.'

'Because he'd been blown to bits!'

Lund was thinking.

'We need permission to dig up the coffin and see what's inside. That bastard Søgaard might have put rocks in it for all we know.'

'You're kidding?' Strange said, too loudly. 'This is madness.'

'We have to exhume the coffin. If you can't see that, Strange, what are you doing in this job? I mean . . .'

Lund stopped. Hanne Møller had come back so quietly neither had noticed in the midst of the storm between them.

She looked older. Angrier.

'I want you to leave,' she said in a cold, hard voice. 'I want you to get out of my house now.'

'There's something wrong here,' Lund said.

'Leave!' Hanne Møller yelled at them.

Gunnar Torpe was in his priest's robe, the black surplice, the white ruffed collar. The last parishioner had gone. He had accounts to complete, people to visit. One final turn around the church. He walked through the darkness, locked the main doors. Came back and nearly tripped over the figure crouched in the dim recess at the end of the pews.

The priest almost jumped out of his skin when he saw who it was.

'Jens?'

Raben stayed in the faint illumination of a security light. He felt dirty, worn out and angry.

'I never really believed in God,' he said in a low, hard voice. 'I had to listen to all that shit you used to throw at us. We didn't have any choice, did we? But it all just seemed so . . . unreal.'

The heavy Bible was in Torpe's hands. He looked as if he didn't know whether to stay or run.

'So where is he?' Raben asked. 'What does he do when he watches us going through all this crap? Laugh himself stupid?'

He got up and stared at the altar, the figure on the cross.

'Maybe they should invent a pill. A shot that gives you faith. I'd take it. Would you like that? Would it make you happy?'

The stocky, middle-aged man said nothing. Raben walked past the old stone font, confronted him. The gun he'd stolen was in his right hand.

'Tell me the truth, Priest. Did you talk to Louise?'

'I went to Ryvangen. I pleaded with her. We want to help you, Jens. She needs you more than ever.'

'Why?'

'Because she's your wife and she loves you.'

'Really?' Raben said and loathed the harsh tone in his voice.

'She does, though God knows you're testing her. And I don't know how long she'll wait.'

Raben wasn't sure why he was putting himself and Torpe through this. The decision was already made. It wasn't easy. He'd seized the gun thinking there was something he could do with it. But what?

He put the weapon on the wooden cover of the font.

'You'd better take this. I don't want it.'

Torpe moved quickly and grabbed the pistol.

'I need to change,' he said. 'Come with me.'

Raben followed into a side room, watched him go through another door, talking all the time. Of God and family and faith. Of truth and honesty and a dim and elusive thing Jens Peter Raben didn't understand at all. Something called justice.

It was a tiny office. A desk. A computer. A diary. Some religious books. A noticeboard on the wall.

As Torpe found some civilian clothes Raben looked around. Cards for plumbers and roofers on the noticeboard. Flyers for supermarket offers and concerts in Vesterbro's little square.

A name caught his eye. A business card more sober than the others.

Holding his breath he unpicked the drawing pin that held it to the crumbling cork.

Anne Dragsholm, Lawyer. A work number. A mobile. An office address in Kongens Nytorv.

Truth, Raben thought. It was what you made of it. One man's lie was another's creed. It depended where you stood.

'Priest!' he said clutching the card, trying not to sound angry, sure it wasn't working. 'Dammit, Priest! She was here. Dragsholm. What the hell . . .?'

He opened the side door, walked through. Gunnar Torpe was out of his priest's robe. He wore a khaki jacket that could have been from the army. His face was set, his eyes determined. In his right hand, fully extended, sat the black military Neuhausen.

'Do what I say or I swear I'll fucking shoot you,' Gunnar Torpe spat at him. 'Do it, Raben! Hands behind your head!'

'You were never that good—'

'It only takes one bullet and I do the world a favour.'

The barrel came closer, grazed the skin of Jens Peter Raben's temple.

And then he did as he was told.

A grey slab in the cemetery, clean and recent. The name Per Kristian Møller. Two dates separated by twenty-seven years. A simple inscription: *Hvil I fred.*

Rest in peace.

It was just after eight. Lund was guiding the forensic team she'd brought in. Her mother was on the phone.

'You promised you'd give me a hand, Sarah. The wedding—'

'Something came up. There's still time.'

'You forgot, didn't you?' Vibeke cried.

'Of course I didn't forget. How could I? I'll come in the morning.'

'Tomorrow's the wedding!'

'Mum, I can't talk now. I'll call you. Bye.'

They had digging equipment and lights by the grave.

'Have you done this before?' she asked Jansen.

A good man. He'd stuck his neck out to help her during the Birk Larsen case and escaped the fallout somehow. Now the ginger-haired forensic officer squinted at the headstone and the ground in front. They'd moved a fresh bunch of flowers. The grave was framed by a low bush hedge.

'Couple of times.'

'How deep is he?'

'Two metres or so.'

'Is the coffin still intact?'

Jansen folded his arms, stared at her. He was rebellious, mischievous at times, and didn't suffer stupid questions gladly.

'We left the X-ray vision goggles back in the Politigården. Ask me . . . Hey!'

One of the men was digging up the low hedge.

'Leave that,' Jansen ordered. 'It's someone's boy. Let's have some respect, please.'

Strange had been on the phone for the best part of fifteen minutes. Finally he came off the call. He looked tired and miserable.

'We've got a big problem here,' he said, taking Lund to one side. 'We can't get a warrant right now. The judge wants to know more.'

'Oh for God's sake. *I* want to know more. That's why we're doing this.'

'We need better reasons,' Strange said patiently. 'Let's talk to Søgaard and the chaplain again. The priest knew them all. Raben, the squad.'

His voice fell.

'The mother just turned up too.'

'Talk to her,' Lund ordered.

'No.' He didn't look happy saying this. 'You're dead smart, Lund. I'm with you most of the way. But not this. We've no right to do this. The mother's cut to pieces. We can't—'

'Where is she?'

'There,' he said, nodding at the grey church at the end of the cemetery.

Hanne Møller was yelling at the priest when Lund walked in.

'I want those people out of there,' she screeched. 'I won't have anybody digging up my son.'

Lund walked straight up.

'Can we speak, please?'

'No! I won't change my mind. That's my son's grave.'

The priest quickly made himself scarce.

'There may have been a mistake,' Lund said calmly.

'You've no right to do this.'

'We have to be certain it's really him in the coffin. I need your permission.'

Hanne Møller gazed at her in anger and despair.

'I promise we'll do this with all due respect and care.'

'Why wouldn't he be in the coffin? What do you mean?'

'We think he was seen three months after he was reported dead. Some soldiers witnessed an incident in Afghanistan. The officer there was called Perk.'

'You mean he's alive?'

Her voice was strident and full of pain.

'I don't know,' Lund admitted. 'It's possible he was involved in a crime. The killing of civilians—'

'Per would never do such a thing!'

'With your permission we can start immediately. Otherwise I'll be forced to go to court, which will only prolong matters. Please. If you—'

'What kind of monster are you?' the Møller woman screamed. 'Do you have no feelings at all?'

Lund fought to keep her temper at that accusation. It brought back memories, of Jan Meyer, furious in his wheelchair, saying much the same. She had feelings. She did care. That was why she put herself and others through these ordeals on occasion. To find the truth, to end the pain.

'I know how this must seem . . .' she began, trying to stay calm.

'Lund?'

One of the uniform men was at the door.

'I'm talking,' she said.

'Brix is here. He wants to see you.'

Hanne Møller glared at her in silence. Lund went outside to the cemetery. No one was working any more.

Brix stood by the grave, stony-faced in his heavy winter coat.

'We didn't talk about exhumations,' he said when she turned up.

'The family never saw the body. Søgaard stopped them. So did the priest.'

'That's not a good reason to dig up a grave.'

He looked angry. Maybe Ruth Hedeby had been on his case again.

'The army's the key here. Not Kodmani's fanatics.'

'You can't exhume a coffin without a relative's consent or a court order. Do you have either?'

Her hands went to her hips. She stood in front of him, not moving, shining eyes fixed on his face.

'That coffin went into the ground without a single relative seeing inside. I don't even think there is a body—'

'Why would they bury an empty coffin?'

'To get Perk off the hook! He was there in Helmand, three months after he was supposed to be dead and buried here.'

He nodded at the team.

'Send these people home,' Brix ordered then walked off towards the gate back to the road.

Lund raced after him.

'Wait! Brix! Hear me out!'

She grabbed his arm. Wondered at her own sudden anger. A long day. So many things happening. And her mother getting married . . .

Brix stared at her hands until she let go. They were alone, out of earshot of the others.

'You asked me here for a reason, didn't you?'

'I thought so.'

'You wanted me because you didn't think Strange was up to it. Or any of the others. You knew—'

'Don't tell me what I think.'

'You knew all along this wasn't what it seemed.'

He folded his arms, said nothing.

'Why drag me back from Gedser if you don't trust me? There's something going on here . . .'

Footsteps. Brix put a finger to his lips. It was Strange.

'I got through to Søgaard in the end. He says he's too busy to answer any more questions.'

'Is he?' Lund said, not taking her eyes off the man in front of her. 'Have him brought into headquarters. Arrest him if you have to.'

'And the priest?' Brix asked.

Strange looked at his notepad.

'Torpe's not in the church. Not at home. We're looking.'

Brix was thinking.

'We waited and Grüner died,' Lund said. 'We waited and Lisbeth Thomsen got blown to pieces, almost in front of our eyes.'

'The mother could sue us,' Brix said.

'Not if we're right. And if we're wrong blame me.'

'I don't like this . . .' Ulrik Strange began. 'That woman's in a bad way.'

'Get Søgaard in,' Brix ordered. 'Find this army chaplain.'

A glance back at the lines of grey gravestones.

'I'll talk to the mother,' he said.

Two plain-clothes detectives picked up Louise Raben as she walked into Gunnar Torpe's church in Vesterbro. She had Jonas with her. No babysitters around that night. The talkative cop was young and friendly. He let Jonas sit on a pew playing with his toy soldiers then took her to one side to talk.

'You knew he was here?' the cop asked.

'I didn't know anything. Jens has been hanging round Vesterbro. It was a guess.'

He didn't believe her.

'You talked to Torpe?'

'Yes! He came to the barracks. He'd met Jens. He said he was sick and needed help. Can we go now?'

'Would he be mad at the chaplain for trying to bring him in?'

She folded her arms, bored with these stupid questions.

'They're friends. They served together.'

The cop's face said: unimpressed.

'Would your husband harm him?'

'Not so loud!' she hissed, indicating the boy playing.

'The priest left in a hurry,' the cop told her. 'He missed a parish council meeting. He left this place unlocked. He was seen with someone who looked like your husband. We're concerned for his safety.'

'Jens wouldn't harm him.'

'Any idea where they might go?'

'How the hell would I know?'

He didn't seem so friendly any more.

'You were in contact when he was on the run. I could bring you in and charge you for that.'

She looked at Jonas. Wondered what would happen to him.

'Jens would never dream of harming Gunnar Torpe. Hurting any of the men he served with.' A bitter thought. 'He was closer to them than his own family.'

The man was running out of questions.

'If he contacts you again and you don't tell us we will arrest you.' He glanced at Jonas. 'That wouldn't be good for the kid.'

'I'm so glad you've got our best interests at heart.'

The cop scowled.

'I don't think you're taking this seriously.'

'Four people my husband knew are dead. Jens is the only one in his squad still alive.'

The man looked at his colleague by the door. He was ready to leave.

'What do you think?' Louise Raben threw at him before he could go.

A moonlit night. Hareskoven, the Forest of Hares, north-west of the city. Nature trails and bike tracks, a fast road by the edge.

Raben behind the wheel. Gunnar Torpe in the passenger seat, the gun held low and as steady as the ride allowed.

'Where are we going, Priest?'

'To Heaven or Hell. I told you that often enough. Just drive, will you?'

The woodland was ahead. No traffic to speak of.

'Your sermons were always a pile of shit. What did Dragsholm say? Why did she contact you?'

The silver crucifix was still hanging from the driver's mirror, swinging with the motion of Torpe's car. It had taunted him all the way back from Sweden after Lisbeth Thomsen died.

'She was going to reopen the case,' Raben said. 'She knew we got stitched up . . .'

The gun rose above the dashboard. Torpe indicated a side road.

'Turn left there.'

Raben kept driving.

'Turn left, damn you!'

The cold barrel was against his temple. He slowed, braked, moved carefully onto the exit. Little more than a dirt track winding into a patch of tall, spare conifers.

Much like the island in Sweden where Thomsen died.

The lights of the city were gone. There was nothing but the dark, the slender trunks of the trees and the sparse winter vegetation between them. Torpe pointed to a parking space filled with wood chippings, slammed his hand on the dashboard, said, 'There.'

Raben did as he was told then cut the engine.

'Leave the keys in the ignition,' Torpe ordered then waved him out.

Cold night, promise of rain. Owls hooting, animals scuttling through the ferns and bracken around them. Raben had learned the phases of the moon years ago during covert training. Had been deprived of the ability to see them locked in his cell in Herstedvester. Four nights of freedom . . . This was waxing gibbous, bright and getting brighter. He saw more than most men. More than Gunnar Torpe ever would.

'Move away from the car.'

Raben took a step.

'Further! Further!' The priest was waving the gun like a child playing with a toy. 'I know what you're like. We all did. You stay clear of me. OK? Now walk.'

'I was a soldier,' Raben said slowly, edging into the wood. 'That's all.'

'One of the best and one of the worst.'

'Who said that?'

'Søgaard. Everyone.'

'What is this, Priest?' Raben asked, half-turning. The gun kept bobbing behind him.

Torpe was a big man. He'd served. He'd fought. But he never spent time with the Jægerkorpset and it showed in his nervousness, the shaking fingers, the cracked tone in his booming voice.

A false, modern electronic sound rang out over the gentle noises of the forest. Raben glanced backwards. Torpe had his phone out, holding it with his gun hand, was clumsily punching the keys with his free fingers.

'It's all going to come out,' Raben said. 'Doesn't matter how hard you try to hide it.'

'All what?' Torpe sneered. 'You don't even remember. You're a crazy man.'

The phone went to his ear. The gun was back on Raben and steady.

'Hello?' Torpe said, back with that lilting priest's voice he used in church. 'Is that the police? My name's Gunnar Torpe. I'm in Hareskoven. I want to report an assault.'

Raben stopped. They were maybe thirty metres from the car.

'It concerns a former soldier you're looking for. Jens Peter Raben. He drove me into the woods and threatened me with a pistol.'

'Oh for fuck's sake . . .' Raben began.

The gun was on him, straight and firmly held.

'No,' Torpe went on, in a voice that sounded scared and maybe was. 'I don't know where he is. I ran away. I'm waiting by the main path, near the nature trail signs. You can find me there.'

The phone went back in his pocket.

'You should have shopped me in Vesterbro,' Raben complained. 'We didn't have to come all this way—'

'I know you!' Gunnar Torpe roared. 'I know how sly and hard and bitter you are, Raben. I don't want that near my church. I'm going back to the city now and when they find me gone they'll flood this place and flush you out like the animal you are.'

'I never meant you harm.'

'You don't know what you're doing.' Torpe shook his grey head.

'Go back to Herstedvester. Stay there till you're well. Hope your wife still loves you . . .'

'What did Dragsholm want?'

The black handgun pointed at a path into the trees.

'Go that way,' Torpe ordered. 'Run!'

Raben looked at the narrow track, sniffed, took a step closer to the man in front of him.

'I don't know a thing,' the priest cried. 'Stay back!'

'She saw Myg. Grüner. Thomsen . . .'

Raben kept walking. Torpe was edging backwards now, towards the car.

'Get away from me.'

'She wanted them to testify against the officer. Against Perk.'

'I buried Perk three months before!'

Raben kept coming. The gun was up at his face. Torpe couldn't see but he was backing straight into a tree.

'Don't make me do this.'

His back hit the trunk. Cornered.

'Don't make me!' Gunnar Torpe bellowed.

The barrel was cold against Raben's forehead.

'Do it then, man of God,' he said and laughed as Torpe pulled the trigger. Then clicked and clicked again.

Raben took a handful of shells out of his pocket and held them in front of the stupefied Torpe.

'You don't think I'd give a man a loaded gun, do you?' Raben asked slowly, taking the weapon from the priest's shaking fingers then feeding the shells into the empty magazine. 'Even an idiot like you?'

The barrel rose again, straight in the terrified face of Gunnar Torpe.

'I want to know what Dragsholm uncovered, Priest. I want to know why she reopened the case.'

Two hands on the weapon, feet splayed, ready to shoot. Torpe looked ready to piss himself.

'She asked me to testify! I'd heard them talking about the officer. About Perk.'

'You knew all this was wrong and still you left me rotting in that hole—'

'What could I do? I was the chaplain. I didn't know a damned thing.'

His hands went up. A gesture of surrender, not prayer.

'I asked Søgaard what was going on,' Torpe said.

Moonlight played along the barrel. The priest fell against the trunk, slumped to his knees.

'What did he say?'

'He said it was bullshit. Perk wasn't there. The judge advocate's report—'

'He said I made it up.'

'They investigated!'

'I was locked up for two years. Filled with their stinking dope. Cut off from my family. I was a soldier. I fought for this country—'

'Don't blame me!' Gunnar Torpe was a sorry heap at the foot of the tree. 'Talk to Søgaard. Colonel Jarnvig. The others at the barracks. I didn't put you in that place.'

'No.' His boot came up, caught Torpe hard in the gut. The older man screamed like a hurt child. 'But you left me there.'

Raben stepped back, glanced at the moon, listened. No cars yet. Only the owls and the night animals.

'Forgive me.' Torpe was on his hands and knees. The crucifix round his neck was loose and hanging down to the dank earth.

Raben kept the gun on him and it never shook.

'Think of your wife. Think of your son.'

He laughed.

'What about my soul, Priest? Shouldn't I think about that?'

Raben lifted the gun. Looked around. Started to plan.

'No need for an answer,' he said and walked back to the car. One glance behind. Gunnar Torpe amid the pine needles and rotting leaves. Head to the ground. Bent as if in worship.

He was glad Torpe left the keys in the ignition. It made life easier. Not that he needed any help. Raben was relishing his freedom. Starting to follow strategies. Tricks designed to keep a man alive in a world that was hostile.

Søgaard.

An ambitious, ruthless officer intent on clawing his way to the top. Raben remembered that much from Helmand. But not much else. He needed answers and he knew where they lay.

*

264

Søgaard was in the interview room by the time Lund and Strange got back to the Politigården. Same uniform, same smug, arrogant face.

'This will go further,' he said before she could get out a word. 'You're in the way of an army mission.'

'That's terrible,' Lund said. 'You said you didn't know any officer by the name of Perk.'

'I didn't,' he said calmly. 'I still don't.'

'Per Kristian Møller. Everyone called him Perk.'

'Not me.'

'He was on Team Ægir. As were you.'

'We've got around seven hundred and fifty men and women scattered across Afghanistan. Some specialists too. Am I supposed to know them all?'

'Oh come on, Søgaard,' Lund said, laughing. 'They made you a major. And that's the best you can do?'

'Perk was a nickname. I didn't know the man personally . . .'

Strange sat to one side, hands clasped, watching.

'But you and Torpe attended his funeral in Frederiksberg. Why?'

Søgaard's blue eyes lit up with a sudden anger.

'Because we were on that flight home from Helmand. It was our job.'

Lund nodded.

'And you made damned sure no one saw his body.'

'You bet,' he agreed. 'Møller died in an explosion.' He leaned forward and stared into her face. 'Ever seen one of those?'

'Yes,' she answered straight away. 'In Sweden. I saw Lisbeth Thomsen cut to pieces, just a few minutes after I talked to her. I saw David Grüner burned to a cinder in his wheelchair too. Don't give me this shit—'

'Perk's head was severed from what was left of his body!' Søgaard yelled. 'I've seen worse. I doubt the parents have. What's this about?'

A knock on the door. An officer there calling for Strange. He walked out and left Lund on her own with Søgaard.

She wasn't going to get anything out of this man and she knew it. That made it all the more important to try.

'You must have been surprised when Raben and the others said they met a man called Perk. Given he'd been dead for three months.'

Søgaard shrugged.

'Not really. The rest of their report was fantasy too. I buried Perk. How could—'

'Who else saw him? Who declared him dead?'

Søgaard broke into a huge grin, looked at her, shook his head.

'This is ridiculous! What are you playing at?'

'Why was there no autopsy?'

'We were at war. In Afghanistan. If you'd seen what was left of the man—'

'There are rules in battle, aren't there?'

He was still smiling.

'That's what you think when you're here,' he said in a quiet, steady voice. 'It helps you sleep at night, I imagine. Don't worry.' He winked. 'We won't disturb you with the truth.'

'You're a Danish citizen. The law—'

'Perk killed himself,' Søgaard said. 'Either that . . .'

He went quiet.

'Either that or he was messing with an IED for some reason. Or making one for all I know. He'd been on duty with one of the covert teams. Gone a bit funny in the head they said. It happens. Sometimes we don't notice till it's too late. I don't know what he was up to. That wasn't my business.'

'He was Jægerkorpset?'

'You know I won't answer that. My guess is suicide. We'll never know. For the sake of the family—'

'Don't give me that. We're about to open an empty coffin. Do yourself a favour and tell me the truth now.'

He didn't speak for a second. Something in his eyes worried Lund.

'You're digging him up? You're insane.'

The door again. Strange there.

'Lund,' he said. 'We need to go back to the cemetery.'

The forensic team had taken the coffin into one of the outbuildings. The duty pathologist was the same bearded, middle-aged man she'd worked with on the Birk Larsen case. The one who gave her the recipe for cider she'd never get to make in Sweden.

'Hi, Lund,' he said, beaming as she came in. 'Nice to see you again.'

The coffin was on a wooden trestle in the middle of the room surrounded by cops and forensic men treading on the earth fallen around it. The lid was open, the contents clearly visible.

'Caucasian male. Late twenties I'd say. The femur indicates he was about six feet tall. He's had some very rough treatment. Definitely consistent with an explosion. Bit of a mess really. Reminds me of when I was doing some work in the Balkans—'

'No,' Lund said. 'You can't be sure it's Møller.'

'We'll need to run some tests, I agree.'

'It's not him! They could have put someone else's body in his place. There's no proper autopsy. No death certificate we'd recognize—'

'What's that?' Strange said, pointing to something beneath the bones and the decaying flesh.

One of the assistants reached in and pulled out a piece of camouflaged fabric. It was ragged at the edges and burned. A piece of army uniform. A fragment of a stencil on the charred fabric, '369045–9 Per K'.

Lund waved it away.

'That doesn't mean a damned thing! We'll have to take a DNA test. What about his teeth?'

She put her bare hands inside the coffin and started to look.

'Cut it out!' the pathologist yelled and snatched her fingers away.

Her eyes were ranging round the room so quickly she couldn't focus on anything. Until she saw Brix and she knew that look, had seen it before.

'This can't be Møller,' she insisted. 'Søgaard and the chaplain wouldn't let his own family see the body. Why would Raben know the name of a dead man three months on?'

Brix said nothing. Strange said nothing. The pathologist was staring at his feet.

'I'm not crazy!' Lund said in a shrill high voice that sounded too close to a shriek.

A good minute and no one spoke. Lund could see Hanne Møller hovering outside the door.

'I want those forensic reports as quickly as possible,' Brix said. 'Do this quietly. We've caused enough trouble as it is.'

'Brix!'

The expression on his craggy, unemotional face stopped her.

'We're going back to headquarters,' he said. 'You two can come in my car.'

One last story before bed. Jonas was on the sofa, head on her shoulder, listening to tales of warring dragons, unimpressed by her feeble jokes. She stroked his soft brown hair, reached for the duvet.

'Time to go to sleep. Soon we'll have your bedroom finished. That will be nice, won't it?'

He raised his small head and she found herself held by the force of his eyes. It was hard to deceive a child. Cruel somehow.

'Why are they chasing Daddy?'

'It's a game.' You had to lie, she thought. Especially when you didn't know the truth yourself. 'He's playing hide-and-seek. Just like you do at kindergarten.'

The boy pulled himself from her and laid his head on the pillow by the sofa's arm. He'd been sleeping here for almost a year since they returned to Ryvangen from the rented flat she could no longer afford on her nurse's wages. Not for much longer.

'Did he do something wrong?'

'No. They just want to find him. And when they do we can visit him again.'

His blue and white cotton pyjamas were getting too small. He needed new ones. More expense, and she didn't want to bother her father again. This limbo was squeezing the life out of them. It couldn't go on.

'Did you like that new scooter Major Søgaard bought you? Shall we try it out tomorrow?'

A scowl on his young, unformed face. Jonas said nothing.

'Sleep tight, darling,' Louise whispered, then kissed his warm forehead and tucked the duvet round his small body.

Her father was in the kitchen eating a sandwich. Combat dress, boots. Scanning some papers on the table.

'They found the priest,' he said as she came in. 'He says Jens took him to some woods at gunpoint. Threatened him.'

She put an anxious finger to her lips then closed the doors that separated them from the room where Jonas was supposed to be going to sleep.

'Torpe's OK,' Jarnvig added. 'Jens beat him up a bit. Threatened him with the gun.'

'Why would he do that?'

Her father stared at her, the way he did when she was a mildly rebellious teenager, unable to comprehend something he found so obvious.

'Because he's ill. Face it. I came back to check you were OK. It's best you and Jonas don't leave the barracks for now. Until they have him in custody.'

He dragged his beret out of his pocket, pulled it on his head.

'Is that an order?' she asked in a bitter, sarcastic voice.

'It's a father's request to his daughter. I'm worried about you. About Jonas . . .'

'I want to know what the hell's going on, Dad. Myg, Grüner. Thomsen. That woman lawyer. These explosives getting stolen. You and Søgaard getting taken in for questioning.'

'Nothing's going on.'

'And now Torpe tells this tale. I don't believe it.'

'You never do,' he said quietly. 'That's the problem. It's just a routine investigation—'

'No!' Her voice was loud, enough to wake Jonas but she didn't care. 'That's not true. Jens told me. He said something bad happened in Afghanistan. It's all come back somehow . . .'

Jarnvig stood in the doorway, silent.

'Tell me,' she pleaded.

'There's nothing you want to hear.'

'Tell me!'

'Three men died.'

'It wasn't that.'

'Three men died because Jens screwed up. He was their leader. He got it wrong. I'd feel bad in the same situation. We all would.'

'So that's it? He's doing all this because he feels guilty?'

'It's time you realized there are sides to your husband you don't know,' Jarnvig said simply. 'Sides we see that you don't. He's not—'

'Not what? The son-in-law you wanted? Just an ordinary boot soldier, not an officer you can take to the mess and get drunk with?'

'There are things I can't say—'

'Or daren't?'

She turned her back on him. Looked at the packing cases for the move downstairs, to the basement Søgaard had so carefully worked on in his free time. Ryvangen was a prison, a pleasant one most of the time. And they were busily raising the walls.

'I think you should leave now,' Louise Raben said.

Jarnvig was angry with her. That didn't happen often. He walked into the room, took her by the shoulders, made her look him in the face.

'You hit Mum once and she left,' Louise said in a calm voice full of intent. 'Same goes for me.'

'I was a good husband! I didn't choose to go to war one month after you were born.'

'There weren't wars then. And neither did Jens. You sent him.'

'No! He had a choice. He volunteered.'

Memories. A tearful farewell. Jonas tiny in her arms. The feeling of loneliness already starting to well up inside.

'He wanted to go, Louise. He was desperate. He begged me. Begged me not to tell you too.'

'You're lying.'

'Call me anything but that.' He took his hands off her. 'I've never lied to you. Jens wanted to go. I tried to dissuade him. He wouldn't hear of it. He said it was . . . his duty.'

The tears were coming and she always hated that.

'Jens isn't the man you think . . .' he said, taking out a handkerchief, offering it to her.

'Just go, will you?'

Still he stood there.

'Get out of here!' she bellowed.

Jonas was by the connecting door when Torsten Jarnvig walked out. Louise knew he'd be there somehow. That was the way things worked these days.

The truce with Rossing hadn't lasted. Just before nine the Defence Minister had called Buch demanding to know why the police were exhuming the coffin of an officer killed on service two years before.

'There are eleven thousand police officers in Denmark,' Buch replied. 'I confess I cannot tell you what each and every one of them is doing at this moment.'

The conversation went downhill from there.

Afterwards, thinking logically, the way he did when he was deciding where the farm cooperative's milk and pork and eggs would go to market, he tried to set down what they knew.

'Rossing called a meeting with Monberg. We know that Jens Peter Raben was on the agenda.'

Plough had been rummaging through the files. He had one piece of paper connected to the meeting.

'According to this,' he said, 'the reason was to discuss the prevention of crime among demobilized soldiers.'

'Why are there no minutes?'

'They were alone. I was busy working on the detail of a bill that day.'

'You weren't invited. Admit it.'

'No. But that's not suspicious in itself. Also Monberg had a bee in his bonnet about cutting the cost of the Prison Service. I imagine having fewer soldiers . . .'

Plough was starting to look agitated.

'If Monberg knew about the military investigation and failed to inform the police when Dragsholm was killed,' he said, wandering round the room, 'this is most serious.'

'Have the police and PET told us any more?'

'At the moment they're bickering over the exhumation of that soldier. Extraordinary! Digging him up like that. König's furious. He says it was quite unnecessary . . .'

'I want to know what Monberg was told. Every last detail. And talk to Karina. She'll be outside. I asked her to pop in once the nanny had picked up Merle.'

'You asked her to visit again?' Plough said very slowly.

'I did. To thank her. And to beg her to come back to work.'

'No!' Plough looked mortally offended. 'She can't do that. There are disciplinary proceedings. I've posted the vacancy.'

'Well cancel it.'

'She slept with the minister!'

'Well she won't sleep with me, will she?' Buch passed over his own phone.

'No.' Plough shook his head. 'I won't. Even I have limits, Buch. You've transgressed them once too often.'

Then he briskly walked out of the room.

*

Karina was sitting primly in the lobby. Casual jeans she would never have worn to work. The same smart jacket though and pink scarf.

Caught. Plough cursed his luck as he stomped out of Buch's office.

'Hi,' she said and smiled as if nothing much had happened.

He didn't walk off. It would have been rude.

'Thomas said you wanted to see me.'

'So I gather.'

'Do you?'

'No. It was his idea. He never told me until just now.'

She stood up, gave him that little shrug and smile he'd come to know so well over the last few years.

'OK. I get it,' she said and started to walk for the stairs.

Close by the banister she stopped.

'Plough. I want you to know . . . I really enjoyed working here. I learned so much. From you mostly. I don't think there's anything you can't untangle in this place. Drafts. Memorandums. Intergovernmental dialogues.'

'Thank you,' he said with a smile.

She laughed.

'It's a shame you're such a pain in the arse when it comes to people. And going home at night.' Karina folded her arms then came and stood in front of him. 'I wore out three nannies because I had to be here every day meeting your . . . your *impossible* demands. And even that wasn't enough, was it? No . . .'

'This is government,' he said, trying not to look offended. 'The Ministry of Justice. Everything must be done properly.'

'Plough's way. The only way. I was never good enough. And just to rub it in I slept with Monberg. That must have hurt—'

'It did!' Plough retorted in a high voice close to falsetto.

'I'd just been through a vile divorce. My personal life was hell. But you never asked, did you?'

He stuttered for an answer, failed to find one. Karina was angry, upset, with him, no one else. She was voicing all the hidden thoughts people were supposed to keep locked inside them, and this naked act disquieted him deeply.

'You never asked how I was and meant it. Never . . .'

'This isn't right,' he muttered and marched back towards his office.

To his dismay she followed, in full flow with no sign of the fury abating.

'You're so bloody prudish. So very proper. The moment something human happens, when there's no rule, no regulation to run up
against it, you're floundering. Are you ashamed of me? Is that it?'

'You deserved better!' he cried and was glad he'd finally said it.

That stopped her.

'So much better, Karina. There was a bright career ahead of you.
I could see that so clearly. And you ruin it for . . . what? A creep like
Monberg. After all we've worked for. After all I taught you. Gone for
a moment of—'

A clap of hands so loud it sounded like a small explosion. The
two of them turned and saw the large, happy figure of Thomas Buch
filling the door of his office.

'Loud voices and frank exchanges!' he declared with a grin. 'I
think I'm back in Jutland amid sanity. Thank God for that.'

He marched straight up.

'However there's no time for this nonsense. Karina, you're rehired.
Plough. Fix it. I just called Monberg's wife. Good news . . .'

He raised a single finger to the ceiling.

'Our dear friend, my predecessor, has today regained consciousness. His condition's stable. With prior permission visitors are
allowed.'

Karina said something under her breath. Plough stayed silent.

'We must talk with him as soon as possible,' Buch added.

'I'll call the hospital,' Plough said, taking out his phone.

'Let's make sure we get to him before Rossing. Karina? Get me an
update on Raben from our system. And find out where the police
and PET stand.'

That deafening clap of his large hands again.

'What are you hanging around for?' Buch asked. 'Hurry up!'

Karina put a hand on his arm.

'I didn't say yes, Thomas.'

He laughed, a booming noise that echoed off the white Ministry
walls.

'You didn't say no either. Up Karina a grade, Plough. Give her a
rise. Come on!'

Then he was gone, a large man in a shapeless blue suit waddling
down the corridor back to his office.

The two of them stood in silence for a while.

'You've a nanny?' Plough asked eventually.

'Yes!' She didn't meet his eyes and that was rare. 'Carsten . . . I didn't mean to hurt you. I just needed to say those things.'

'You did. I understand that.'

'Forget about the grading and the rise.'

Plough gazed at her and fiddled with his glasses.

'The minister asked for it. If the minister says—'

'Fine, fine, fine.' She patted his arm. 'Let's get on with it, shall we?'

Brix's office, close to midnight. The reports were in from forensic. Ruth Hedeby was going through them.

'DNA will take a couple of days,' Brix said.

She gave him an incredulous stare.

'Don't waste money on those. The army gave us his dental records. The pathologist checked his teeth. It's him. No question.'

Brix knew that.

'This is either going to be Lund's funeral or yours.'

He stood by the window saying nothing.

'Is anything I said unclear?' Hedeby asked.

'How many mistakes are we allowed?' he wondered. 'If we get it right in the end?'

She threw the report on the desk.

'We're not getting it right, are we?'

Hedeby came and placed her hand on his arm, looked into his face.

'PET have got sight of Raben.'

Brix's eyes narrowed.

'You mean they've caught him?'

'No. König wasn't exactly forthcoming. We're going to talk again tomorrow.'

'If they know where Raben is . . .'

Her fingers brushed dirt from his collar.

'Don't go too deep. Talk to König. Be cooperative.'

Lund was silhouetted in the office opposite.

'To think you could be so wrong,' Hedeby said. 'Does she interest you, Lennart? Is that it?'

He wished he could find the energy to laugh.

'She sees things we don't. Even when we walk straight past them.'

'It's up to you,' Ruth Hedeby murmured, then ran her fingers down his arm, briefly, lightly touched his hand. 'But I think you'd best do it now.'

Lund knew what was coming the moment Brix walked through the door. When he asked for her gun and ID she handed them over without a word. The weapon she didn't miss. The Politigården card . . . was different.

'I'll tell Gedser you can resume your work there.'

Strange was watching them.

'Release Søgaard,' Brix told him. 'We don't need him any more.'

Lund watched him go out into the corridor and start the call. Strange came over, sat on the edge of the desk. She got her things. The bag. The dark jacket. The pack of chewing gum half-hidden among the strewn papers.

'Do you want a ride home?' he asked.

She shook her head. It was hard to take her attention away from the pictures on the wall. There was something unfinished here and the incomplete always infuriated her.

'Thanks for the help,' she said.

'I'm sorry . . .'

She'd left his desk a mess. Lund kept finding stray packets of gum. She didn't remember buying them all. Or scattering them round like this. Everything seemed so chaotic. Strange, a fastidious, careful man, did well to tolerate her.

'You were good to work with,' she said.

'Shall I call you tomorrow?'

She just smiled as she got up to go.

'Give your mother my best wishes for the wedding.'

'I will,' she said and kept walking.

'Lund!'

He strode to the door, opened it, always polite, she thought. Nothing like Jan Meyer.

'What?'

'If it means anything I think you're right. Not about the coffin. That was really stupid. But there's something . . .' He glanced down the corridor, towards Brix quiet on the phone. 'Something stinks around here.'

'No need to call,' Lund said and briefly smiled. 'I'll be back in Gedser on Monday.'

'I'll miss you,' Strange told her, with that look again, the one that made her feel awkward.

She ducked under his arm and walked down the corridor, past Brix without a word, out to the spiral staircase, and then the rainy night.

Seven

Saturday 19th November

9.03 a.m.   Erik König looked more and more like a man under unbearable pressure. A man, Brix thought, with secrets too.

'Raben abandoned the chaplain's car two kilometres from Hareskoven. He stole an old Volvo nearby. We picked him up around two in the morning. Kept watch.'

'Kept watch?' Brix asked.

'We were lucky to get sight of him. He's tired. Desperate. Got his guard down. A good Jægerkorpset soldier would never—'

'He wasn't Jægerkorpset though, was he?' Brix asked gently and enjoyed the PET man's discomfort. König had kept them in the dark from the start. Brix wanted to let him know this was over.

'Close enough. He slept for three hours in a lay-by. Now he's near Ryvangen Barracks, in a side street on a housing estate.'

'Bring him here when you pick him up.'

Ruth Hedeby stared at the plain grey desk and said nothing.

'Raben's the last one in the squad,' König replied. 'We know where he is. We know we can stop him doing any further harm.'

'Bring him in!' Brix demanded.

'No.' König took off his wire-rimmed glasses. 'If the Islamists have been tracking the squad he's the next potential victim. Raben stays free, under surveillance.'

'As bait?' Brix asked.

The PET man leaned back in his chair and frowned.

'There's a limit to how many religious lunatics we can arrest. Sooner or later one of them is going to put his head above the parapet.'

'We can help with surveillance,' Hedeby suggested.

König had the coldest and most insincere of smiles.

'We're better equipped for this kind of work. Besides, after that farce with Lund—'

'That's dealt with,' Hedeby said briskly.

'I'm sure the Ministry will be pleased to hear that. They're looking for scapegoats. I'd like you to look at these . . .'

He pulled a sheaf of photos and identity documents from his briefcase and threw them on the table.

'They're refugees from Helmand, living in Denmark for the last couple of years. They might be after revenge.'

Hedeby passed the pile to Brix.

'I want them watched,' König added. 'A few questioned.' A dry laugh. 'No one need be exhumed.'

Brix didn't look at the photos.

'How did a refugee from Helmand break into Ryvangen Barracks and steal explosives with a current security code?' he asked. 'How's it possible they've access to military records—?'

'Lennart.'

There was a hard, scolding note to her voice, one that silenced him.

'I'll leave that to you to find out,' König said. He glanced at his watch. 'I've got a meeting at the Ministry.'

Then he was gone. Hedeby looked at Brix across the table.

'I can't protect you from yourself,' she said quietly. 'Someone's going to pay. One way or another.'

'König's thrashing around in the dark trying to save his own skin.'

'You dug up a dead soldier for no good reason. I'm struggling to make sure no one but Lund picks up the blame. Try and help me, will you?'

In the adjoining office Strange was interviewing Gunnar Torpe. Brix leaned on a filing cabinet and listened. Lund had never said Strange was a poor cop. It wasn't necessary. Brix could read the occasional impatience in her eyes.

'Why did Raben take you to the woods at gunpoint?' Strange asked.

Torpe sat pale and tired in a chair.

'How am I supposed to answer that? Maybe because he's sick. Here . . .' He tapped his forehead. 'Crazy. Delusional.'

'He must have had a reason.'

'Crazy people don't need them. I tried to reason with him. To get him to think about his wife and son.'

'What did he say?'

'It was just . . .' Torpe shrugged. 'Crazy stuff. War does strange things to people. They don't know the difference between right and wrong sometimes. Between what's real and what's not.'

Strange placed something on the table.

'We found this in the office in your church. Anne Dragsholm's business card. What was it doing there?'

'Raben must have dropped it.'

'Did you know her?'

The priest twisted on the chair then said, 'Raben asked me that too. I never met her. I never saw that card before. Can I go now? I've got a committee meeting.'

Brix took a deep breath, stared at the lean officer seated in front of Torpe. Waited.

'OK,' Strange said. 'We'll probably need to get back to you later.'

'PET have located Raben,' Brix said when Torpe had left. 'They've got him under surveillance.'

Strange scratched his cropped hair.

'Surveillance? We need him brought in.'

'We do as we're told.' Brix passed him the names and photos König had given Ruth Hedeby. 'I want every last one of them checked out. Bring in any that are marked. Some are outside the city. You've got some driving ahead of you.'

'Lund thought we need to check out the chaplain. So do you—'

'Lund's not here any more.' Brix tapped the papers.

Strange frowned.

'So what are we supposed to say if someone calls up and wants to speak to her?'

'Tell them the truth. She's gone to a wedding,' Brix said.

Men and vehicles. Loading orders and schedules. Torsten Jarnvig felt he'd been watching these rituals all his adult life. Dispatching men to uncertain fates in Bosnia, the Middle East and now the bleak and distant provinces of Afghanistan.

Most came back.

Most unharmed.

Not all.

Christian Søgaard had been round to see Møller's mother. An initiative of his own. Jarnvig hadn't asked for it.

'She's livid,' he said. 'Who wouldn't be? She says she's going to sue the police for trespass. For pain and suffering.'

The two men were walking from the main headquarters building towards the car park. A security barrier rose as they approached. Men in combat fatigues saluted.

'I spoke to Gunnar Torpe,' Søgaard added. 'He's very upset.'

'You've been busy.'

'The police were on your back. I didn't think you needed to be bothered. It was welfare. I usually look after that on my own.'

Jarnvig raised an eyebrow.

'Welfare? This is welfare?'

'What's Raben going to do next?' Søgaard asked, avoiding the question. 'He seems desperate. I've told everyone to keep their eyes and ears open when they leave the barracks.'

He hesitated.

'That means everyone,' Søgaard repeated. 'How much does Louise know?'

'Enough,' Jarnvig answered, watching a line of trucks roll past. 'Until this happened I thought he was one of the best soldiers I ever had. Brave. Intelligent. Resourceful.'

Torsten Jarnvig thrust his fists deep into the pockets of his fatigues.

'Didn't like him much. But when everybody else gave up Raben just kept going.'

'A pity he couldn't take the pressure,' Søgaard said. 'I always thought there was something brittle about him. Ready to snap.'

Jarnvig stopped and looked at him.

'How very observant, after the fact. Did we get to the bottom of that story of his?'

'Damned right we did,' Søgaard replied straight away.

'You were certain?'

'One hundred per cent. It was bullshit. He was covering up for his own mistakes. Why?'

Jarnvig didn't answer.

'It's not easy when these things turn personal,' the younger officer added. 'The past few days have been tough. I could relieve you. Maybe you and Louise and Jonas could—'

'Could what? Go on holiday? That won't be necessary.' Jarnvig cast his eyes around the red-brick buildings of the barracks. 'This place is good enough for me. Louise grew up with the army. It's good enough for her too.'

'What I meant was—'

'No,' Jarnvig said and left it at that.

The artificial beach of Amager Strandpark in November. Stained concrete shiny with winter rain. A few children wrapped in thick anoraks, struggling against the wind, their faces hidden inside tightly drawn hoods.

Louise Raben watched her son zigzagging on his little scooter across the dun slabs by the grey sea, beneath the grey sky, no smile on his face, no expression there at all.

Slowly he scooted back to her. They stared at the empty beach.

'Are you hungry?' she asked.

He didn't eat enough. He didn't do anything much except play with his toy soldiers, slaughtering fantasy enemies in his head.

Jonas took a sandwich then she watched as he pushed the little scooter towards a group of kids who had ignored him before and doubtless would now.

Children had their own rules, their own sensibilities. They suspected anyone who stood out. And Jonas, in his loneliness and misery, always did.

While he was wheeling down the sea wall she walked slowly in his wake. A figure emerged from a metal shelter, gestured.

Green jacket, pale-grey hood. Beard and watchful eyes.

Her heart fell. She wanted to flee and would have if she didn't know he could always outrun her.

'We've only got a couple of minutes,' Raben said, dragging her back into the dark of the shelter.

'Jens—'

'Listen to me!'

His voice sounded fragile and broken. His eyes were as wild as she'd ever seen. She wondered whether to feel afraid. For herself, for Jonas.

'You've got to leave the barracks,' he said, clutching at her cold fingers.

'You followed me here?'

'It doesn't matter.'

'What's wrong with you? Why did you treat Gunnar Torpe like that?'

'I didn't do anything to him!' High, fractured, his voice echoed round the darkness of the shelter. 'They're lying to you.'

'You hit him. My father said—'

'He's lying too.'

She took one step back. The hood came all the way down. He looked so hurt and vulnerable.

'No,' Louise said. 'He told me about what happened in Helmand. How you feel guilty.'

He shook his head.

'It's not that.'

'What is it then?'

'They're covering up for something an officer did.'

'Who?'

'I don't know. I don't remember it all. Maybe Søgaard . . . Maybe others.' His eyes wouldn't leave her, and they had the expression she'd learned to hate. That of a soldier hunting his prey. 'Maybe your father.'

'My father's a good man. He tried to help you.'

A sound outside. A kid going past kicking a can. Raben recoiled from her, fell against the wall, hand going to his belt. She saw the gun there, the fear and tension in his eyes. Found she had no feeling for him at that moment but contempt.

'I don't believe this,' she said, glaring at him. 'Two years I've waited. Two years I've looked after our son. And look at you. Cowering like a thief . . .'

The kid with the can was still outside, making a din kicking it against the wall.

'Get hold of that woman from the police,' he ordered. 'Sarah Lund. I called the Politigården. She's at her mother's wedding. You've got to go there. Tell her to check—'

'Is it true you volunteered for active service? Abroad? When Jonas was born?'

His face could change so rapidly. From the hard, unfeeling coldness of a warrior, to the boyish gentleness she'd once loved, all in an instant.

'Who told you that?'

She took a step towards him, looked up into his pained, pale face. Knew she wouldn't leave this place without an answer.

'Is it true?'

A moment of hesitation. His eyes pleaded with her.

'Can't you see what they're trying to do? They want to separate us. They want to lock you inside the barracks for ever.'

She turned her back on him, watched the kid with the can wander away.

'It's not what you think,' Raben said, placing his arms around her shoulders.

There was no colour in this world, she thought. Not for her. Not for Jonas. They deserved better. There was a limit to the sacrifices you could make.

'I've been a soldier since I was eighteen,' he went on, still clinging to her shoulders. 'It's all I've ever known. The things I've seen. The things I've done . . .'

'My father's a soldier. A good man. Ordinary like the rest of them . . .'

'I wasn't like him. There are things you shouldn't know.' He tapped his lank, greasy hair. 'Things here. I didn't deserve Jonas. I didn't deserve you. He was so pure. I wasn't. I thought if I stayed I'd poison you both . . .'

'Let go of me,' she said as his grip tightened on her jacket.

'I've changed.' His fingers still held her. 'All I want is to come home and be with you. To learn to be a good father. A good husband.'

Her blood began to boil. He no longer held her in an embrace. It was as if she belonged to him. As if he'd captured her.

'I've heard that shit too often, Jens. And where are we now? How many years in jail? How many visits am I supposed to make a week and I still can't even drag you into bed in that stinking little room? Fuck it—'

'Louise . . .'

Half an order, half a plea. His arms wound round her more tightly.

Through the door a tiny figure flew, screeching curses too old for a child to know. Jonas was on them, little arms beating at Raben's legs, little feet kicking at him.

'Let Mummy go! Let Mummy go!'

Raben retreated, fell back against the grille and the leaden light outside.

Crouched down, looked at the child, young face full of fury, tears in his eyes.

'You've grown, Jonas,' Raben said. 'It's me. Daddy.'

He smiled. Jonas didn't.

Raben's hand went out to the toy soldier sticking out of the boy's jacket pocket. Retrieved the figure. A warrior with a shield and a raised sword.

'What's he called?'

'Mummy,' Jonas said, wheeling his scooter to her side, 'I want to go.'

She took the boy's hand and led him to the door. Stopped there. Looked around. In summer this place was full of happy voices, kids playing with their parents, running, laughing, feeling alive. Jonas had never known that. Nor had she. Raben had fled from them through some inner fear he'd never been able to share. And now she hated him for that too.

'Don't ever try to see us again,' she said, aware of the spiteful fury in her voice. 'I mean it . . .'

'Louise?'

He could turn on the charm when he wanted, like a naughty child caught stealing. But she'd been tested, so many times.

'Never again,' she said and walked out into the first few drops of winter sleet starting to fall from the heavy sky.

Jonas tugged on her hand. He was pointing at the man hiding in the doorway. In Raben's hand was the toy soldier, shield raised, sword at the ready.

'I'll buy you a new one,' she told her son and dragged him to the car.

It took a lot of arguing to get permission to visit Monberg in a private room in the Rigshospitalet. But Karina won through in the end and accompanied Buch in the car from the Ministry.

They stopped in the corridor outside.

'You don't have to come in if you don't want to,' he said. 'If it's embarrassing.'

The remark seemed to puzzle her.

'Why would I be embarrassed?'

'Well . . .' Buch struggled for an answer.

'Let's go in, shall we?' she said and led the way.

Frode Monberg was in a bed by the window. Unshaven. Looking tired and pale. As a backbench MP Buch had never mixed much with ministers. Now he could see Monberg was a handsome man, with a narrow, smiling, genial face, a mop of unruly brown hair and lively, roaming eyes.

Buch stepped forward and placed a box of expensive chocolates on the bed.

'Karina,' Monberg said warily. 'My successor. Congratulations, Thomas. I hope you're having fun.'

'It's good to see you. How are you doing?'

No tubes, no wires. The monitors by the bed were switched off. This was a man in recovery. Barely sick at all. And yet behind the bright facade there seemed something gloomy and desperate about Frode Monberg. The politician's smile vanished much too quickly.

'I'm OK.' His melancholy brown eyes roved over Buch's huge frame. 'It seems quite a storm's been brewing while I've been in here.'

He looked at Karina.

'And how are you?'

She nodded, said nothing.

'It was good of you to take the job,' Monberg added, turning back to Buch. 'You must have wondered what the Prime Minister was thinking. But now . . .' He patted his chest. 'I can take better care of this old heart.'

He moved to put the chocolates on the bedside table.

'I doubt I'll be allowed things like this for a while. The doctors . . .'

Karina folded her arms. Buch said nothing. Monberg's face turned sour again.

'So. It gets around.'

'I took over your job,' Buch said. 'I had to be told. It's not general knowledge. It won't be. Don't worry.'

'Don't worry?' His voice became fragile and old. 'That's easy for you to say. I was sick for ages. No one noticed. No one cared. You're stuck in that damned office, day in, day out. Nights too. It all . . .'

His eyes turned briefly to the smartly dressed blonde woman by his bed.

'It all becomes unreal after a while. You find yourself doing things you'd never dream of. I don't want my family to suffer any more. You hear that?'

'Of course,' Buch said. 'I guarantee it. We just want to talk about that old military case. The one you were looking into. Before . . .' He nodded at the bed. 'You know. The Dragsholm woman.'

'There's nothing to tell,' Monberg said too quickly. 'Anne came to me with this odd story. She wanted me to look into it. A favour for an old friend.'

'And?' Buch asked.

'We had a meeting. Talked about the past. She was going through a divorce. I think she was getting a bit . . . obsessive. She gave me a folder when I was leaving. The case seemed to mean a lot to her. God knows why. I never got to look at it, of course.'

Buch took a deep breath, folded his arms, said nothing.

'Why do you ask these questions, Thomas?'

'You already knew about the case before she came to you. You sent that envelope to a dead address for a reason. Please. Try to be clear on these things. The Defence Minister called a meeting about a soldier.'

Karina extracted the papers from her bag. Buch showed them to the man in the bed.

'A certain Jens Peter Raben.'

Monberg took the documents, did no more than glance at them.

'I'm still a bit hazy about some things.'

'Let's dispense with this nonsense,' Buch said, aware his voice was rising. 'Just tell me what you and Rossing spoke about at that meeting. It's important.'

Monberg shrugged, got a pair of reading glasses from the table, scanned the papers.

'This was ages ago.'

'You withheld information about a serious military investigation! You kept it hidden from the police, from PET, from your own civil servants.' He pulled up a chair, got close to the bed. 'Why? What are you and Rossing hiding?'

Monberg turned to Karina, pleaded for her help. She kept quiet.

'Why did you have a meeting about Raben?' Buch persisted. 'What did Rossing say to you? Why were no minutes kept?'

'What is this, Buch? What are you going on about?'

'You met with Rossing. Later Dragsholm raises the case with you. But you never let on. Never told the police or PET, even when she was murdered. I need to know—'

'If you've come to blame me for your screw-ups you can get out of here now,' Monberg barked.

'What did Rossing say at that meeting?'

A noise at the door. A woman in a dark-blue suit. A doctor by her side. Monberg's wife. Buch recognized her.

'Visitors again, Frode?' she said, rushing to his side, kissing his head as Monberg scowled like a child. 'That won't do.' She stared at Buch. 'I appreciate your concern. But the doctor needs to examine my husband.'

Monberg held up the papers. Karina took them then went to the window and began to sift through the get-well cards.

'This kind of pressure isn't good for him,' the wife added.

'I'm supposed to rest,' Monberg agreed.

Karina nudged Buch. One of the cards was from Flemming Rossing. A bunch of roses on the front. A standard handwritten greeting inside, then a scribbled addition – *It was so good to see you better, Frode. We are brothers always.*

Buch read it and nodded.

'I believe the minister's about to leave,' Monberg noted.

'Yes,' he said. 'Get well soon, Frode.' He threw Rossing's card on the sheets by Monberg's knees. 'All of your friends want to see that.'

Outside in the corridor, breathing in the hospital smells, listening to the beeps and whirrs of the machines in the wards around them, Buch waited for Karina to catch up with his furious pace.

'Rossing got there before us, didn't he?' he snapped when she reached his side.

'He knew what you were going to ask. And what he was going to say.'

'Shit,' he muttered. He couldn't take his eyes off her. 'What's Monberg like? Really?'

'Witty. Funny. Charming.' She thought about it. 'Weak.'

'We need more options,' Buch said, and tried to imagine what they might be.

'Here's an idea,' Karina said as they sat in the back of the ministerial car, trapped in traffic on the way back to the Ministry. 'Why not issue an apology for the exhumation of the soldier?'

Buch grunted something wordless and looked at the crowds of shoppers beyond the window. Ordinary people with ordinary lives. He envied them.

'Thomas,' Karina went on. She always used his first name now, when they were on their own. He liked that. 'It'll take off some of the pressure. Krabbe's getting impatient. He's pestering Plough for an urgent meeting.'

'Plough can tell Krabbe to go and sit outside the Prime Minister's office, begging for an audience with him if he wants.'

'An apology would go down well.'

Buch kept several packs of chocolate biscuits in the back of the car, in the small cabinet where others stored booze. He opened the nearest, offered it to Karina, took two when she shook her head.

'How can I say sorry for something I never knew about?'

'You're the minister. It happens all the time.'

'That doesn't mean I like it. Whose idea was it to dig up this poor bastard anyway?'

'A policewoman. She was fired.'

'That was quick.'

'She had history. Remember the Birk Larsen case a couple of years ago?'

Buch shuddered.

'That was horrible.'

'She solved it. Got fired after that too.'

Buch looked at her, interested.

'There was a possibility a few local politicians were involved,' Karina went on. 'She wouldn't let go of that either. If you put out a statement you could mention this wasn't the first time she ran into disciplinary issues. Say something like . . . we expect all officers to uphold the fine traditions of the force.'

Buch stared at her.

'OK,' Karina agreed. 'That's not your style. I'll leave the wording to you.'

'What's her name?'

'Sarah Lund.'

'I want to talk to her.'

She burst out laughing. The thought that he could amuse this sharp, intelligent woman cheered him somehow.

'You can't possibly talk to her! She's just been booted out of the force.'

'I'm the Minister of Justice. I can talk to anyone I like. If this Lund woman solved the Birk Larsen case she can't be stupid. Maybe she knows something.'

He offered her the biscuits again. This time she took one.

'If you do that you'll compromise your relations with the police.'

'And haven't they been forthcoming! No. If Monberg won't speak to us we'll have to try another avenue. Get me Sarah Lund, please.'

'Thomas,' she said, and her voice was that of a mother scolding a child. 'If they find out you could be in big trouble.'

'Oh for pity's sake. If I don't get to the bottom of this I'm out on my ear anyway. Let's not pretend otherwise, shall we?' He tapped her bag. 'You're very good on the phone. Find me this Sarah Lund please. We'll go there straight away.'

A Danish working-class wedding. A hotel banqueting room full of friends and relatives. A happy couple. Soft music. A civilian registrar pronouncing the familiar refrain, 'I now pronounce you man and wife. You may kiss the bride.'

Bjørn, a playful little man, full of good humour and mischief, grinned like a wicked pixie and did as he was told.

Lund was glad her cake hadn't poisoned him much. He was nice and her mother was finally happy after so many years of solitary bitterness.

So she stood in the best dress she had, purple silk, applauded them both, smiled at Mark, tall and handsome beside her.

All the world moved on. Everything shifted with the times. But not her. She was in the same place she occupied two years before, after that black night when Meyer was shot and everything unravelled in her life. That was why she took so much awkward guilty comfort in the sight of her mother like this, consumed by the smothering bliss, the contentment that came from giving one's life selflessly to another, burying an individual identity in a shared love that would whisper the perpetual lie 'Now you're safe for ever.'

This was a sacrifice she could never make and those who knew her understood. Mark was no longer the surly teenager who once snarled, 'You're only interested in dead people.'

He still thought that, she guessed. He was just too kind to say it.

It was a fine banqueting hall in Østerbro. Marble walls and the scent of too many bouquets. When the applause faded Bjørn clapped his hands and declared, 'Now let's have something to eat and drink, please. Then another drink! Then another!'

Her mother was in a green silk dress she'd made herself. She looked so perfect, so complete, Lund felt the tears start to well in her eyes.

'You can tell Bjørn used to be in the Home Guard,' Mark chuckled by her side.

'Oh yes,' she said, watching a couple of men in regimental blazers embrace the old man and slap him on the back.

Vibeke came over, hugged them both, kisses on the cheek, arms round each.

'This idea about me making the toast . . .' Lund began.

'Nothing to it,' Vibeke said quickly. 'A short speech for your mother's wedding. Small price to get rid of me.'

'I've never been much good at speaking.'

'All the more reason to keep it short. There has to be time for dancing. Next you'll tell me you're no good at dancing too. And I know that isn't true.' Vibeke's joyful face became serious for a moment. 'I remember you when you were Mark's age. I know you can dance, Sarah.'

'Wife! Wife!' Bjørn's squeaky voice rose above the hubbub. 'We've got to have our pictures taken.'

Still she didn't move. The two of them stayed where they were, mother and daughter. Mark retreated as if seeing something.

'But I won't make you,' Vibeke said quietly. 'I've tried so hard over the years to force you to be someone you're not. I'm sorry. I just wanted . . .'

Lund threw her arms round her mother, brushed her lips against Vibeke's warm and powdered cheeks.

'You are who you are and I love you for that,' her mother whis-

pered into her ear, then fled back into the crowd as if terrified by this
sudden outburst of intimate honesty.

A hotel worker in a white shirt appeared with a small bell in his
hand.

'You ring this for attention,' he said, as if she'd never been to a
wedding before. 'The presents are on the table. Along with the
flowers. Oh, and the bouquet that came for you.'

'Who sent me a bouquet?'

'Search me,' he said, pointing at one particular bunch of flowers.

Three red roses in cellophane amidst the stacks of gaudy boxes.

'Everybody . . .' the photographer announced. 'Take your places,
please.'

Bjørn in the middle, Vibeke and Lund on either side. She remembered her own wedding, recalled how a nagging question had dogged
her even as she posed for the pictures: could it last?

This one would. A peace had been declared. Vibeke's long and
sorrowful years of loneliness, a war of a kind, was over.

Mark knelt in front. Lund found her hand straying to his soft hair,
stroking it, was pleased when he smiled, didn't recoil as once he
would.

Ten minutes later, everyone seated round the table, watching
the first course come out from the kitchen, the singing began. Wedding tunes with ridiculous words, half chanted, half bellowed from
the lyric sheets that sat next to the menu. The wine was white and
lukewarm. She'd been deliberately seated next to a bachelor cousin
of Bjørn's, an accountant from Roskilde whose principal topic of
conversation, between the choruses, concerned the future of double-
entry bookkeeping.

Lund didn't touch the drink. She felt heady enough as it was.

The man appeared sufficiently cognisant to notice the subject
bored her.

'You're a police officer?' he asked.

'Sort of.'

'I heard they dug up a dead soldier. It was in the papers.'

Lund changed her mind, gulped at the too-sweet white wine and
said, 'Really?'

Then, before he could utter another word, rang the bell.

Vibeke was on her feet. The hotel man was back by Lund's side.

'I'm sorry,' he said. 'Someone's here to see you. She says it's important.'

A blonde woman in smart office clothes was standing just outside the door. She nodded when Lund looked.

'I've been looking forward to this speech,' Vibeke declared, rising to her feet. 'So . . .'

Lund slid back her chair and started to leave the table.

The woman at the door introduced herself as Karina Jørgensen from the Ministry of Justice.

'A toast!' Vibeke ad-libbed behind her. 'Cheers!'

Lund followed into the serving area.

'This conversation happened by accident,' the woman said. 'There'll be no record of it. You won't inform anyone in the Politigården.'

They went downstairs. White tiled corridors. The smell and noise of a kitchen nearby.

There was a large man at the end, next to a woman folding tablecloths. He had a phone in one hand and a chicken leg in the other. The half-gnawed leg got thrown into a bin as she approached. Then the phone went into his pocket.

He wiped his hands on the nearest napkin then shook hers.

'I'm Thomas Buch. Minister of Justice. For now anyway.'

Lund said nothing.

'Karina says we met here by coincidence.' He had a genial face with an untidy brown beard. 'Some coincidence, huh?'

'My mother just got married upstairs.'

'I know. The truth is I'm in dire need of some answers. And I think—'

'Look. If it's about the exhumation, I'm really sorry. It was my mistake. Don't blame Brix or Strange . . .'

He waited until the waitress disappeared.

'Do you know about the accusations against Danish troops in Helmand?'

'A bit.'

'Did you see any indication that civilians might have been murdered by our own soldiers? Any—'

'Like I said. You should call Lennart Brix or Ruth Hedeby. They're in charge now—'

'I'm not sure about that. And I'm the Minister of Justice. There's a suggestion an individual officer was involved in an atrocity. Do you know about this? Did you see evidence that someone was trying to cover it up?'

Lund shook her head.

'That story came from a soldier who was mentally disturbed. There probably wasn't any officer.'

The big man stuffed his fists into the pockets of his trousers and didn't move.

'So why did you go to all the trouble of digging up a soldier?'

'Because I screwed up. I don't know anything. I've got to get back to the wedding. I'm sorry.'

'What about the squad leader, Jens Peter Raben?'

'I thought he knew something but . . . he's mentally ill. He had good reason to escape. He'd just been turned down for parole.'

'By whom?'

'By the Prison Service. The medical director said he was fit to go but . . .'

Buch glanced at the blonde woman.

'Herstedvester gave him a clean bill of health?' he asked. 'And the Prison Service blocked his release?'

'That's right. He was desperate to get out. His marriage is falling apart. Probably has by now.'

Buch put a finger to his mouth, thinking.

'Bear with me a moment.'

He turned to the woman.

'Monberg was working on a bill about the Prison Service, wasn't he? When was that abandoned?'

She thought for a moment.

'Just after he met the Minister of Defence.'

'Quite. Get Plough for me.'

A broad smile, the big hand again. Lund took it.

'Thank you,' Thomas Buch said. 'And congratulations on your mother's wedding.'

'What's this about exactly?'

His finger went to his bearded face again. Another wry smile. Then a wink.

'Enjoy your day, Sarah Lund,' Buch said as he waved goodbye.

Bjørn was in full flow by the time she got back to the wedding.

'Vibeke,' he said, standing next to her, reading from his notes.

'You make me so happy. I just want to sing and dance and make speeches, all the time.'

Lund walked to her seat saying a silent prayer this wouldn't happen.

Then thought about the man she'd just talked to. Thomas Buch was the Minister of Justice. And he was in the dark too, just like her.

'Sometimes,' Bjørn went on, 'I wish we'd met earlier in life. But then we wouldn't have been ready for one another. So I'm glad I walked into the second-hand shop that Tuesday in May. And walked out with the woman who would one day be my wife.'

Lund ignored the dubious jokes of the man next to her, stared at the presents and the three red roses.

No one sent flowers to a solitary daughter at her mother's wedding. Even the cheapest bouquet a delivery company would handle.

The guests were getting up. Glasses in hand. Bjørn was making a toast.

'Long live the bride!'

As Bjørn bent down to kiss Vibeke, Lund crossed the room, found the bouquet, picked out the white envelope tucked into the top.

She was aware of the silence, of the fact they were all watching.

The hotel man was going past with a fresh bottle of wine.

'Who brought these flowers?' she asked.

'A courier,' he said with the same dull tone he'd used before.

A scribbled message inside.

Tjek hundetegnet – Raben.

Check the dog tag.

Vibeke was watching her, smiling but tense. She rang her knife against her wine glass and stood up.

'Now that we're all gathered together I'd like to say my piece too. Before Sarah . . .'

Lund picked up her little toastmaster's bell.

'Dear Bjørn . . .' Vibeke began, then stopped, watching as her daughter approached.

Lund came and stood by her. So many years of difficulties between them. So many arguments and tantrums. And now she would fail her mother one more time, on her wedding day.

Something changed in Vibeke's face. She smiled. Lund placed the bell by her plate, embraced her, kissed her on both cheeks and got the same in return.

294

'What is this?' Bjørn asked, a faint note of outrage in his voice. 'You can't walk out on your mother's speech! What kind of guest leaves before the wedding party has begun?'

Lund wiped something from her eye.

'That's exactly what my daughter's doing, Bjørn,' Vibeke said in a voice that was close to rebuke. 'And it's OK.'

'OK?' he asked, wide-eyed.

Lund said nothing, just started to slip from the room.

'Yes!' Vibeke said very brightly. 'It's very OK. The women in this family are busy and have minds of their own.' She slapped him on the back. 'Get used to it, boy. And try to keep up.'

Lund marched out of the room. There was laughter behind. Nervous, perhaps. Laughter all the same.

They'd talk about her but they always had.

Then her mother's voice, strong and forceful boomed at her back.

'Now, dear Bjørn. Where were we?'

She didn't listen any more. She walked down the stairs, and knew exactly where she had to go.

Hanne Møller was clearing out her garage. She had a photograph in her hands, a wistful look in her eyes.

Lund walked in, a worn blue donkey jacket over her purple wedding dress.

'I came to apologize. I know the police said sorry too. It's not enough. I wanted you to hear it from me.'

She could see the photo. A handsome young man in an army beret, smiling for a standard portrait. Hanne Møller put it back in the box.

'I realize I can't put it right,' Lund continued.

'No,' the woman said in a low and bitter voice. 'You can't.'

'I need you to understand.' One step closer. She wasn't leaving until this was said. 'I had to be certain.'

'And are you?'

She picked up some of her son's clothes and placed them in a black rubbish bag.

'I'm certain he's dead. I'm sorry. But there's something we still don't know—'

'Just go, will you?'

Lund looked around the garage. Wondered.

295

'I need you to listen.'

Hanne Møller's voice rose and it was full of pain and anger.

'Why do you never leave when I ask? Why do you keep coming back here? Haunting me?'

'Because something's wrong. I think you know it too.'

'Do I?'

She was holding a sweater. Blue military wool. Or part of a school uniform. They looked so similar.

'It's about your son's dog tag. The chain the army gave him with the metal name tag on it.'

Lund found herself gesturing awkwardly with her hands to describe the thing. From the look on Hanne Møller's face this wasn't necessary.

'Do you know where it is?'

'Why's a piece of metal important?'

'They give the dog tag to the next of kin. Did you get it?'

'I asked,' the woman said, shaking her head. 'They never found it.'

'But you got his other possessions?'

The woman gestured at the box.

'No. These were what he'd left at home. We got nothing. Just a body they wouldn't let us see. Why do you keep asking these questions?'

Lund wondered whether to say it. But Hanne Møller was owed something after the debacle in the cemetery.

'I think someone found your son's dog tag. I think he used it to take on Per's identity. And then cover up an atrocity.'

'Per was a good boy,' his mother said in a soft, hurt voice. 'I never wanted him to go into the army. When he was little there were no wars. I thought he'd be a teacher. Or a doctor. But then he grew up and the world was different.'

She stared at Lund.

'It was as if it was just another choice. Go to work in a school. Go to some country he'd barely heard of and fight a war none of us understood. I never imagined for one minute he'd wind up in a uniform. We need soldiers, I suppose. But not Per. He was too gentle for that.'

Lund stayed silent, thinking of Mark.

'You think you can guide them towards something good,' Hanne

Møller added in that same soft, pained whisper. 'But you never know what's waiting out there. Not really.'

'I'm sorry for the hurt I caused. It was stupid of me. I won't bother you again.'

Lund walked towards the garage door.

'Wait a moment,' the woman said. 'There's something you need to see.'

She went to the corner and dragged out another box.

'I thought it was a mistake. Maybe it is. But it still bothers me.'

'What does?'

'Now and then things turn up. As if Per were still alive. Here . . .'

She pulled out a sheaf of opened envelopes.

'Letters. The last one was a few weeks ago. Look.'

Lund took it.

'When they started I thought . . . I dreamed maybe he was still alive,' Hanne Møller whispered. 'But he's not, is he? And then that woman came along. And you . . .'

Receipts mostly. Posted long after Per K. Møller died in an explosion, suicide maybe, in Helmand more than two years before.

'It is a mistake, isn't it?' the woman asked.

'Probably,' Lund said. 'Can I keep these?'

Just before six Buch was back at the Rigshospitalet determined to take a second tilt at Frode Monberg.

The reception desk was empty so he walked straight in. Found Monberg in white pyjamas, seated on the edge of the bed reading a newspaper.

'If you must come,' Monberg said, 'you should ask in advance and do it during visiting hours.'

Then he got up from the bed, walked to the window, put on a dressing gown. He still hadn't shaved. He looked gaunt and worried.

'I've nothing more to say to you, Buch.'

'There's not much I need to hear. I know it already.'

Monberg turned and grinned. It wasn't a pretty sight.

'Oh, do you?'

'Pretty much. You were preparing a bill. You'd promised to cut the cost of the Prison Service. It was in the manifesto.'

'There was too much overcrowding. Why does this matter?'

'And you wanted fewer mentally ill criminals locked up, didn't you?'

The thin man glared at Thomas Buch and kept quiet.

'You'd asked for every case to be reassessed, and parole for all those who weren't perceived to be a threat to society.'

'Digging through old files is a job for civil servants. Not ministers.'

'One of those who was going to be set free was Jens Peter Raben. A soldier. A man who claimed to have witnessed an atrocity committed by our own forces in Afghanistan.'

'I don't remember . . .'

Buch took a step towards him.

'Don't lie to me. Rossing came to discuss Raben's case with you. And then, for whatever reason, you abandoned your proposal entirely. Nothing came of it.'

Monberg nodded.

'True. There were other reasons for that.'

'I won't disturb you any longer,' Buch announced, and headed for the door. 'This is a matter for Plough and the legal team now . . .'

'Buch!'

He stopped.

'For God's sake will you listen to me?' Monberg pleaded.

Buch came back and looked at the skinny, stricken man by the side of the bed. He wanted to feel a sense of guilt for punishing him like this. But it was hard.

'What do you plan to do?' Monberg asked.

'That depends on you. I don't want to punish anyone. I just want the truth.'

'Rossing was adamant Raben shouldn't be released. All the reports from the hospital said he was fine. But Rossing regarded him as a security issue. He said it was against the national interest to release him. He had to stay in Herstedvester.'

Buch almost laughed.

'The national interest? What does that mean? We don't lock up our enemies unless they give us reason. Why should we do it to our own soldiers when they've fought for us, for their country?'

'Rossing didn't elaborate and I didn't ask.'

Buch raised a finger, pointed it at the frail man in front of him.

'Jens Peter Raben was aware something had gone terribly wrong in Afghanistan. Rossing wanted him locked up because he feared the political fallout if that were made public. That's not the national interest.'

'I don't know about any of this! Rossing asked for my help. He told me what to do.'

'And then Anne Dragsholm wanted to reopen the case.'

Monberg scowled, went to the bed, started to tidy the sheets, turned his back on the big man throwing questions at him.

'What did Dragsholm say? What had she discovered?'

'I can't go into these details . . .' Monberg muttered and began to reshape his pillows.

Buch lost it.

'Dammit!' he roared. 'Do you think you can hide in this place for ever?'

His arm shot to the door.

'People are dying out there! And you . . .' His finger stabbed at Monberg's haggard features. 'You're the one they'll set up to take the blame. Not Rossing. They'll condemn you as a sick lunatic the way they condemned Jens Peter Raben. Can't you see that?'

Frode Monberg gripped the end of the bed, fighting for breath. Fighting for some courage too.

'I only came into politics to do something. To serve.'

'So tell me,' Buch begged.

The thin man hesitated, took a deep breath.

'She said she'd found proof the soldiers were telling the truth. There was a massacre. A Danish officer was responsible. It was an injustice Raben had been locked away like that.'

'How did she know?' Buch asked.

Monberg closed his eyes, looked like a man on the edge.

'Because she'd found him.'

'Found who?' Buch demanded.

'The one who did it. She knew who he was. She wouldn't say. She was too frightened. I was in the government, wasn't I? I don't think she really trusted me.'

Buch didn't say the obvious: Dragsholm was right.

'That's all I know,' Monberg added.

He turned from Buch, looked out of the window.

'What the hell am I going to do? It just gets worse and worse.'

'You tell the truth, Frode. That's all.' He put a hand on Monberg's shoulder, was shocked that he felt little there but wasted muscle and bone. 'Tell the truth and everything will be all right. I promise. The Prime Minister's behind me all the way. He asked me to get to the bottom of this. We'll back you, I promise.'

Frode Monberg turned and glared at Buch, said nothing.

A rap at the door. Karina.

'I'm sorry,' she said. 'Excuse me. But I have to talk to you. It's important.'

'Two minutes,' he told Monberg. 'Then we'll work out what to do.'

The lean man glared at him.

'You're an infant, Buch. Rossing won't say a word.'

Karina was still bleating.

'Two minutes,' Buch repeated.

'You can't make him,' Monberg said and there was fear in his eyes. 'You don't know. He's not like me. Not like any of us.'

Out in the corridor, Karina dragging him away from Monberg's room, Buch was finally beginning to feel he'd made a breakthrough.

'Thomas . . .'

'I got him to talk. He confirmed what we guessed. We need to get PET over here right away.'

'Will you listen to me?' She dragged him into an alcove. 'Monberg's not your problem now. It's Krabbe.'

Buch took a deep breath.

'What's the Boy Scout up to now?'

'He's demanding your resignation.'

'Oh come on.'

She looked miserable and that wasn't like her.

'Krabbe's given the Prime Minister an ultimatum. Either you go or he withdraws his support for the administration. He wants your head or he could bring down the government.'

'No, no, no.' He couldn't get the conversation he'd just had out of his head. 'Listen to me. Monberg has confirmed he spoke to Rossing. That he kept a Danish soldier in Herstedvester at Rossing's request. This is what matters now.'

She folded her arms and gazed at him.

'Let's get to the truth and then everything will work out,' Buch insisted. 'It usually does. Come . . .'

He led her back down the corridor.

'You can hear it for yourself.'

'This is serious,' she replied, following him.

'Everything's serious. It's just a matter of degree.'

He marched back into Monberg's room. A nurse was changing the sheets. The bed was empty.

Buch looked at the nurse.

'He said he wanted a bit of exercise,' she said with a shrug.

'And you let him go?'

She bridled.

'This is a hospital. Not a prison.'

Buch swore, went back into the corridor. Monberg had to have turned left. If he'd gone the other way they'd have seen him.

'Thomas . . .' Karina bleated.

'Not now.'

He wasn't a nervous man. Anxiety wasn't in his nature.

'Thomas! You need to call the Prime Minister.'

'No!' He was shouting at her and he regretted that. 'We've got to find Monberg. Don't you get it?'

'Tell me,' she said and folded her arms.

'I pushed him, Karina,' Buch said quietly, almost to himself. 'I pushed him very hard.'

She watched, listened, then walked in front of him, scanning the rooms left and right.

'Frode?' she cried, and got no answer.

Jarnvig's house in Ryvangen Barracks. The basement was almost finished. Painted by Christian Søgaard, bright wallpaper in Jonas's new room. A cot bed, a small yellow chair, a standard lamp, a little desk. It was the first time he'd ever had any space of his own. Louise watched her son standing by her father as Jarnvig placed a poster of fantasy warriors on the space above the bed.

'Is it level, Jonas?' he asked when the picture was in place.

'Yes, Grandpa. Like that.'

Jarnvig turned and grinned at him, took some drawing pins out of his pocket and stuck the poster to the wall.

'Right then,' he said, patting the boy on the head. 'It looks smashing, doesn't it? All yours now.'

'You have to knock before you come in,' Jonas told him.

'Sir!' Jarnvig said with a salute and a click of his heels.

Jonas did the same. The two of them laughed. Louise Raben saw this and felt both happy and sad.

Then she walked back to the kitchen and started to clear up.

Her father followed.

'I'll leave you to it now,' he said. 'It looks nice down there. This was always a bachelor place before. Now . . .' A foolish grin. 'It feels like I've got a family again.'

'Thanks for helping, Dad.'

'What else can I do? I said some stupid things yesterday. I'm sorry. It gets to me too. I hate . . . I hate seeing you like this.'

She took off her rubber gloves, came and touched his cheek.

'It's all right. I've been an idiot, haven't I? I always thought for ever meant for ever. That's stuff for kids, isn't it?'

'Sometimes,' he agreed. 'Come to the cadets' ball. I'd like that. You could be my guest.'

She remembered them from when she was a teenager. All the young soldiers aching to dance with an officer's daughter.

'I'm too old and fat for that.'

'Nonsense. You're neither. It would do you good.'

'I should be with Jonas.'

'Jonas is OK. I can get someone in to babysit. It's you I'm worried about. Come on . . .'

She ran a cloth across the sink. The gold band of her wedding ring was by her watch next to the tap. She always took it off to wash up.

For ever.

Pipe dreams for children. She'd stuck by Jens through more than most women would bear. And got what in return? A coward who ran away to fight in the Middle East the moment she had a child. A criminal fleeing from everyone.

'Just a couple of hours,' he pleaded. 'We can leave when you like.'

She couldn't take her eyes off the wedding ring. Once it had seemed so important. A symbol of something they shared. Now it was a relic, a bitter reminder of everything she'd lost.

'Of course,' Jarnvig said. 'I understand. It's up to you.'

He laughed.

'But I always loved to watch you dance. You thought you were no good at it. You'd no idea . . .'

Louise folded her arms.

'So what time are you going?'

Jarnvig clapped his hands, his face wreathed in the kind of delight she hadn't seen much in recent years.

'As soon as you've picked the right dress. So God knows . . .'

One hour later, outside the wire fence of the barracks. Raben was in the second car he'd ripped off that day, slumped in the driver's seat, hood round his face. Door open, ready to flee at the first sign of trouble.

A good place. A clear view of Jarnvig's house. Lights on. Toys just visible in a downstairs window. The sight made his heart ache. For what he'd lost. For what he had to recover.

The door opened. Torsten Jarnvig walked out in full dress uniform. Black jacket and gold epaulettes. White shirt with bow tie. A long Mercedes limousine was waiting.

Raben knew this routine. It was the ball for the new intake of cadet officers, in a hired hall near Kastellet. Men like him were never allowed near. They just had to imagine the music, the cackle of laughter, the odd drunken jape. To grit their teeth and hope these raw, green youngsters didn't get in the way of fighting, of staying alive, once the unit hit the hard terrain of Helmand.

Officers had their place. But it was men, ordinary soldiers, enlisted squaddies, little in the way of education and social background, who decided whether the battle was won or lost. Their blood, more than any other, that was spilled on dry, foreign soil.

He watched Jarnvig get to the car, throw a cigarette in the gutter, look around, wondering what he thought of this man. The commanding officer. Louise's father too. Raben never really understood if he was family or just one more soldier waiting for his orders. Perhaps Jarnvig struggled with the same conflict too.

The door to the house opened again and Raben's thoughts froze, the breath caught in his mouth. Louise was walking out. Fur stole, scarlet silk dress. Hair perfect. Face pale with make-up. Ready for the cadets' ball, the officer's daughter all the junior men would dream of.

And yet she'd ignored every one of them and picked him instead.

She walked slowly down the steps. Reluctantly, Raben thought. As if a decision had been made.

Jarnvig held open the limousine door. A uniformed soldier sat

303

erect at the wheel. Louise got in, looking ahead all the time. She'd slipped back into their world now. And he wasn't, never would be.

Raben watched the car move slowly to the guardhouse, the men salute as Jarnvig and his daughter were driven out of Ryvangen.

Then slowly, carefully, he took his stolen Peugeot into the road behind them, following from a safe distance, wondering what to do when they were there.

In the back of a cab, on the way into the city from Mrs Møller's house, Lund called Strange.

'You don't sound like you're at a wedding,' he said.

'I need you to check something.'

'You're off the case.'

'I need you to check something,' she said again, impatiently.

'I'm in Helsingør.'

Forty minutes north of Copenhagen by car.

'What are you doing there?'

'PET want us to drag in every last Afghan in Denmark. I'm with an interpreter at a refugee centre. Waste of time. Let me step out-side . . .'

She waited. The car was getting stuck in night traffic. Her mother's flat might be half an hour away like this.

'So what's up?' Strange asked after a while.

'Someone used Per K. Møller's identity. His dog tag is missing.'

'They're fighting a war, Lund. Things get lost.'

'It's not just that. Someone's been buying things using his name. In the last few months. The letters have been coming back to his mother.'

'Oh.'

'You need to talk to the priest again. And Søgaard. Run Møller's name through the credit agency system and see if anything else turns up.'

'I'm in Helsingør, remember? Talking to people who hate me.'

'Fine. Get in the car and come back. You can do it in thirty minutes if you put your foot down.'

'I've got work to do! It's going to be a couple of hours.'

He went quiet for a moment.

'Have you told Brix about this?'

'Not yet,' she admitted. 'I will. Honest.'

That long pause again.

'Please tell me you're not going to do something stupid.'

'Like what?'

'Like . . . I don't know. Going off on your own again. That never works out well, does it?'

What do you care? she thought. You're just another cop they gave me. One who's not so good at the job. Too nice for it in many ways.

'I'm not going to do anything stupid,' Lund said, and realized she didn't want to hurt his feelings. 'But thanks anyway.'

That was it. Rain now. Cars in slow-moving lines ahead of them.

'I want to go somewhere different,' she said to the driver. 'Vesterbro. How long?'

He laughed. Shrugged.

'You tell me,' the man said with a chuckle. 'You're sure?'

'Yes. I'm sure.'

Cutting through Indre By in the city centre the cab turned down a narrow lane and knocked a cyclist off his bike. The inevitable argument ensued. The cyclist, a big man, plenty of beer inside him, reached inside the taxi and stole the keys.

She waited a couple of minutes watching the two men dance around each other in the street. Then she left her card on the dashboard and told the driver she'd stand witness if he really wanted someone to testify how bad he was behind the wheel.

It was a short walk back to Nørreport Station. From there the trains ran in all directions. She could be in Vibeke's apartment in a few minutes, calling her mother, trying to make amends for walking out of the wedding. Or she could head out to Vesterbro and try to find the priest, Gunnar Torpe.

Normally it would have been an easy choice. But Strange's closing words bothered her. It wasn't stupid to chase things she didn't understand. This was what she did. Who she was. And besides . . . what was it to him? A decent, half-competent cop who seemed to have stumbled into the police because he was sick of being a soldier. Ulrik Strange didn't look much like a man with a career. He'd fallen into what he did and that was never the case with her.

Lund walked into a cafe opposite the station, bought herself a cappuccino and a sandwich.

Strange was so unlike Jan Meyer, a man she'd found amusing and infuriating at the same time. There was a seriousness to him. A sense of solitary devotion and duty, one that seemed strengthened by his self-awareness. He knew he was struggling with this case. That was why he clung to her, listened to her, did as she asked, even though they were both, nominally, equals in rank until Brix kicked her out once more.

She sipped her coffee slowly, took time over the sandwich. Looked at her watch. Quarter to eight. If Strange had done what she asked he'd have been back in the Politigården by now chasing the leads she'd suggested. She could call. But that would be checking. It might annoy him and she didn't want to do that.

So she finished her drink, walked to the metro, went down the stairs, looked at the two platforms, one leading to home, the other to Vesterbro and Gunnar Torpe.

It wasn't much of a choice at all.

Thirty minutes later she was in the church. The place seemed deserted. The only lights were on the altar. Three gold candelabra on a white cloth in front of a painting of Mary weeping over the dead Jesus.

Lund walked down the aisle, looked around. There was a noise from an open door to the right. A dim light beyond there.

'Hello?' she shouted, and found herself hearing Jan Meyer's voice out of nowhere. That rough, familiar cigarette-stained croak. It said, *You're not going to go in alone again, Lund? And without a gun?*

These were the tricks your head played sometimes. She went to the door and cried, 'Anybody there?'

No answer. She pushed it open.

'Hello?'

Her voice sounded musical in the echoing interior. It was dark in the room. She found a switch, turned on the single bulb. Jumped back with shock when the first thing it threw at her was a tiled sink stained with splashed blood.

Hand to the pocket. Nothing there but a phone.

'Shit,' Lund whispered and did what came naturally. Walked on.

A second room. In semi-darkness this time, since there was a window to the outside, and a street lamp leaking its wan light through the glass.

A familiar shape, both obscene and holy, in the centre. A figure, arms outstretched like a crucified man, tethered to an iron bar strapped between two tall wooden candle holders.

Gunnar Torpe, face bloodied, in a combat jacket, black tape over his mouth.

Lund walked to him, snatched the tape away. Blood poured from the priest's mouth. His head went down. His eyes were closed.

She got to his arms, removed the fastening there with one hand, supporting him with the other. Right arm first, then the left. A heavy man. She struggled as she let his body fall slowly to the hard concrete floor.

He was breathing. Just.

Phone.

Lund called control.

'Sarah Lund. Send an ambulance to St Simon's Church, Vesterbro. Tell Brix. I just found the priest. He's still breathing but . . .'

Something glittered near Torpe's body. She looked. A dog tag cut in half, blood on the sharp severed side.

'You need to be quick. Tell . . .'

A sound nearby. Footsteps at the back of the room.

Lund looked at Torpe. At the blood. Fresh. At the wounds. So many, so livid.

A shape. A hooded man, head down, crossed briefly in the light from the window, ran out towards the rear.

'Tell Brix I'm in pursuit,' she said then left the bleeding priest and raced for the door.

An hour they'd been looking. An hour wasted. The hospital administrator, a bad-tempered woman, was with them.

'How can you lose a patient?' Buch demanded.

'How can you walk in here and berate him without his permission or ours?' the administrator demanded. 'This is outrageous. I don't care who you are. It doesn't matter—'

Her phone rang.

They were on the third floor. Intensive Care. No sign of Monberg. No one had seen him anywhere.

Buch watched the way her face changed. He knew what bad news looked like now. There'd been so much of it of late.

'What is it?' he asked when she put the mobile in her jacket pocket.

'I think we need to call the police.'

'I'm the Minister of Justice!' Buch bellowed. 'The police answer to me.'

'Fine,' she grumbled, and led them to the end of the corridor, through what looked like a storage area. No rooms. No wards. Just equipment and boxes.

'Patients aren't allowed here,' she said. 'Under no circumstances . . .'

There was a service lift. With his bulk and the two women it was just about full. The administrator pressed the button for the ground floor. Said nothing more.

After a while the door opened. Three men in green overalls, bent round something.

Buch pushed through.

Monberg lay on the floor face down. A pool of scarlet blood ran out from his haggard features. His smashed spectacles lay by his side. The red stained his white pyjamas. His eyes were open and looked puzzled. In some cruel way more alert than they ever had been in life.

'Jumped from the third floor just now,' one of the men said.

'Patients are not allowed . . .' the administrator began.

Karina had turned to the wall and was sobbing.

'There'll be an inquiry,' the woman added.

'You're sure he jumped?' Buch asked.

No one answered.

He got up, took hold of one of the men by the shoulders. Got a filthy look in return.

'You're sure he jumped?' Buch repeated.

'I was down here sweeping up,' the man snapped back at him. 'I saw him standing there. Smoking a cigarette. Then he saw me. Got on the railing.' His hand pointed up the winding staircase. 'I heard him screaming all the way down.'

'You're sure?' Buch asked again but quietly.

'I don't think I'll forget that in a while. Would you?'

Ten past seven. The meat-packing district was coming to life. Trapped between the railway lines and Vesterbro, it was the place that fed much of Copenhagen: butchery wholesalers, fish companies, bakers, grocery firms crammed into low metal buildings ranged across a sprawling industrial estate. Then, in the evening, another side emerged. The spare space, on the first floor, sometimes the ground, opened up to the night crowd, with bars and tiny restaurants where the glittering party types flocked to dine and drink near the rows of cattle carcasses and trays of freshly gutted salmon.

Lund chased the distant hooded figure out from Gunnar Torpe's church, saw him dash left at the Bosch sign above a fashionable organic hangout.

Still she ran and ran, arms pumping, breath coming in short, rhythmic gasps. Brix could deal with the priest. Lund had the man in her sights and nothing else mattered.

She rounded the Bosch sign, scanned the square ahead. Warehouses and commercial outlets. Vans loading. Taxis turning up with women in garish dresses out for the night.

A hooded figure disappeared into the building in the far right corner. Lund set off, ran through the half-open doors behind him.

An empty loading area. Forklift trucks parked for the morning. Steam rising from grates in the grey concrete floor. An iron staircase winding up to the timber ceiling.

A sudden noise. Lund jumped. It was the thump of a sound system from the floor above. Loud, rhythmic disco music. The sound of laughter, squeals of delight.

One door open ahead. She walked on. Found herself back in the chill night. A yard full of black rubbish bags, pigeons pecking at the waste.

The place was empty.

She called Brix, heard the sigh in his voice as he answered.

'Lund. I'm busy. I'll call you back.'

'The priest—'

'What about him?'

'You didn't get the message?'

'I told you. I'm busy.'

'I found him half-dead in his church. I called control. Told them to get an ambulance there. To tell you—'

'What in God's name are you doing?' he yelled. 'You're supposed to be at a wedding.'

'Someone ran from the church when I got there. I'm trying to track him. He's in the meat-packing district.'

She glanced around. So many buildings. But there was broad open space between them. If she got lucky . . .

'He can't be far away. Send me all the backup you can spare. We can isolate this place—'

'Stay where you are,' Brix ordered.

She could hear him snapping his fingers at the officers around his desk. *See* him doing that.

'We're coming. You're unarmed. I don't want you going near—'

'Talk to the priest. Get us an ID. He saw him.'

'Lund?' His voice was back to a bellow. 'How many times do I have to say this? You're off the case. I don't want you anywhere near.'

'I'm here. You're not.'

A hazy shape moved across her line of vision. A hooded figure racing out of the empty loading bay towards the building opposite.

'Just move, will you?' she said and put the phone in her pocket.

She saw him push through a plastic ribbon curtain, the kind they used in the loading areas. Lund walked towards it, got the raw, sharp smell of freshly slaughtered meat in her face and the chill of refrigeration.

Went through. The place ahead was in darkness. Her fingers fumbled on the brick wall, found switches, flipped them. Bright fluorescent tubes burst into life, crackling, flashing, sending their blue-white light everywhere.

Through the next ribbon door. Sides of bloody red beef hanging from hooks on the right. Naked dead pigs, as bare and pink as gigantic babies, ranged on the left, snouts up to the ceiling, eyes closed.

Line upon line of dead flesh set against white-tile walls. Lund caught sight of herself in a shiny metal door. Black donkey jacket, purple wedding dress. Gunnar Torpe's blood on her chest.

Walked on.

A cutting room now. Tables like the morgue, clean and shiny. Saws and electric knives. The stench of blood and severed tissue.

She walked through slowly, moving the wheeled cutting slabs out of the way.

Looking. Listening.

Another room ahead. A handle turning. Lund got to another set of plastic ribbons then saw it coming. A trolley laden with rubbish bags and cartons, flying through the grey sheeting, straight at her.

She caught the metal frame with her hands before it could strike, took the blow, rolled with it, fell backwards, half into a bloody gutter

310

stinking of disinfectant, turned on the ground, trying to see, to judge if he was coming for her.

Just the trolley.

She got up, started running. A corridor. Long enough so she could see him. A man. Not big, not small. Not broad, not skinny.

Unremarkable.

They usually were.

He scooted right at the end, scattering bins and pallets as he fled, throwing shut an iron rollaway grating behind him.

She ran too quickly, slipped on the greasy floor, took a hard fall into a waste bin, smashed her head against the metal side. Stumbled upright, ran on.

A staircase leading towards the light and the noise and the people.

Night in the meat-packing district. No one came to buy dead cow or fresh fish. They were here to party, and Lund was fighting her way through them, pushing, scrabbling, staring everywhere.

Kids and their stupid music. A relentless, idiot beat. They screamed as she spilled their hundred-kroner cocktails, fell silent when they saw her, bloodied and furious, clawing her way through their party dresses and designer denim.

Looking.

A shape far ahead. The one hooded figure in the place.

Lund raced past a psychedelic purple light, got blinded for a moment, refocused, saw him escaping by a distant door.

A bare narrow corridor. Empty and dimly lit. Offices maybe. Closed for the night.

He had to be exhausted. She was.

One door at the end. She opened it and found the cold wet night blowing in her face.

The roof. One floor up. Somewhere not far away the sound of sirens.

And nothing.

Nothing.

Lund started to turn. Saw the briefest shadow sweeping through the air. Felt something hard and cruel connect with her neck, send her stumbling towards the roof edge, then over, feet turning as she fell into empty space, drop like a stone onto what felt like corrugated plastic.

Her head felt loose, her mind ranged. She hadn't fallen a full floor. That was impossible. She was alive, conscious, could think. There was another part to this structure. He'd sent her flying onto that, not the ground which would surely have killed her.

Face side on against the sheeting, blood trickling into her eyes. She couldn't move. Could barely breathe.

A sound. Footsteps on metal stairs. Slow and deliberate. Getting closer.

'Not yet,' she whispered, willing her dead limbs to move.

A crazy memory. Her mother at the wedding. The stupid songs. Mark laughing, behaving like the responsible, careful adult she'd never been herself.

Then, so quiet only she could hear, 'Not now.'

He was there and she knew it. Knew too that if she had the strength she'd turn and stare him in the face.

Another sound, one too familiar. The slide of a semi-automatic pistol racking the first shell into the chamber.

One last sentence in her head.

Let me see you.

But she lacked the strength and the means to say it.

Only her eyes could move at that moment. So she kept them open and looked ahead. At the black Copenhagen night, and the bright-red neon Bosch sign of the restaurant on the corner.

Waiting.

The office in Slotsholmen, the evening news on TV, the little rubber ball bouncing against the wall, back and forth.

The only story was Monberg's death. Plough was pacing the floor, tie undone looking distraught. Karina moped around as if she took some responsibility for what had happened.

Buch threw the ball again, misjudged the way it would come back, watched it fly off behind the sofa.

He'd disabuse her of that notion soon enough. He'd badgered Monberg. No one else. And now the TV news knew too. They were reporting that shortly before he killed himself Monberg had been visited by his successor, and a confrontation had taken place.

Karina, shirtsleeves rolled up, perspiration on her brow, came over and turned the TV to mute.

'The Prime Minister's called a meeting with Krabbe and Rossing. You're not invited.'

Buch went to his desk, pulled out another rubber ball, bounced it against the wall. Monberg's photo was on the TV. Back when he was minister. A good-looking, confident politician. Nothing like the man who succeeded him. Frode Monberg liked to tell everyone how he dined in all the finest places, Noma across the harbour, and Søren K in the Black Diamond Library that sat by the water in Slotsholmen. Thomas Buch wanted nothing more than to sit a short distance away from Søren K, in the garden near the Jewish Museum, close to the statue of Kierkegaard, the Danish philosopher who gave the Black Diamond restaurant its name. No fancy food. A sandwich. A hot dog. He was happy like that, would have been content to stay a foot soldier in politics until his early retirement.

But then Grue Eriksen called, just the previous Monday. And everything changed.

'Thomas!' Karina said in that matronly, scolding voice. 'Will you please stop behaving like this? If you hadn't pressured Monberg he'd never have admitted anything.'

'If I hadn't pressured him he'd still be alive.'

'You don't know that. He'd already tried to kill himself once. Flemming Rossing was in there before you. How do you know he didn't say something?'

Buch didn't answer.

'How hard did you lean on him?' Plough asked.

'He did what was necessary,' Karina retorted.

'You don't know that,' Plough said. 'What happened? Exactly?'

The ball went to the wall, came back. The fat man with the walrus beard said nothing.

'This mess is Monberg's fault,' Karina insisted.

Plough dragged his tie away from his neck and threw it on the desk. In a man like him it seemed an act of rebellion.

'You don't understand the politics of this. The way things connect.'

'I understand we've got to focus on the meeting with Grue Eriksen!'

Buch kept throwing the ball. He hated this stupid habit as much as they did now. But it was hard to stop.

Plough's phone rang. He answered it.

Karina came over and stood next to Buch.

'From what I gather Krabbe and the Defence Minister will take over responsibility for the anti-terror package. They're going to

313

sideline us completely. So we'll never get to the bottom of this. You'll be paralysed. Or fired. Dammit, Thomas! Will you at least say something?'

Marie, his wife, had been phoning his mobile. He hadn't the heart to answer.

'The meeting's started,' Plough said, coming off the phone. 'We should wait and hear what they have to say.'

Karina glared at him.

'We've got to stop this! The Prime Minister hasn't a clue about the games Rossing's been playing.'

The TV was murmuring in the corner. A familiar voice. Buch abandoned the ball and turned up the volume. Rossing was there, smart suit, black tie, being interviewed outside the Defence Ministry before going to meet Grue Eriksen.

'I'm shocked by the loss of a good colleague,' he said to the camera with a stony face. 'Frode was a great political personality. A man who made an enormous personal contribution to Denmark. Above all, a very dear friend.'

Buch turned up the volume to make sure the row between Karina and Plough didn't catch fire again.

'It's a great loss,' Rossing went on. 'Especially at a time like this, when our country faces serious problems.'

The ruse didn't work. Plough was taking aim at Karina again.

'Don't defend Monberg!' she yelled at him. 'He doesn't deserve it.'

'I want to know what happened,' Plough barked back. 'You should know. All things taken into consideration—'

'What happened?' She slammed her fist on the table. 'What happened is the damned coward killed himself because he couldn't face the consequences of his own actions. Impeachment. Shame. Don't blame me. Don't dare blame Buch. Blame the man himself.'

She pointed at the TV.

'Blame Rossing. His fingerprints are all over this. For Christ's sake, Plough. I'm sorry I offended your puritanical sensibilities by sleeping with the man. Doubly so now. But don't make that more than it was. Nothing to me. Nothing to him either. It just happened. The way it does between normal human beings, not robots like you.'

The pale civil servant looked dumbstruck. No words. No answer at all.

314

Buch threw the ball away, turned off the TV and said to both of them, 'I want you to call in the press. Straight away.'

'The press?' Plough gasped. 'Please tell me this is a joke.'

'Just do it,' Buch ordered.

The curtains were closed to keep out the black night. The Prime Minister, Flemming Rossing and Erling Krabbe alone. No civil servant to keep minutes. No pens, no notepads on the table.

'Here's the truth,' Krabbe began. 'You've got much better candidates than Buch. You should never have appointed him in the first place.'

'He's an honest man,' Grue Eriksen noted. 'Intelligent and hardworking. Lacking in experience. But . . .' He smiled at the thin, dour man across the table. 'We all are until it happens to us.'

'He's unfit for the job,' Krabbe insisted. 'Now there's all this publicity about Monberg, too. What the hell is going on?'

'Leave Monberg out of it,' Grue Eriksen replied. 'Buch's my minister. Get off his back.'

Krabbe bridled.

'If you want my support you're going to have to listen to me.'

'We are,' Rossing broke in. 'I told you already. We can alter the anti-terror package to accommodate the People's Party. We'll proscribe the organizations you want—'

'Buch must go,' Krabbe insisted.

'Will you listen for once?' Grue Eriksen barked. 'I decide the ministers in this government. Not you. Buch got the sharp end of the stick. There were irregularities on Monberg's part he never knew about and neither did the rest of us.'

'What irregularities?' Krabbe demanded.

'You don't need to know. Now he's dead . . .'

Flemming Rossing coughed, glanced at Grue Eriksen, and said, 'Frode wasn't quite master of the situation. Let's leave it at that.'

Krabbe threw up his skinny arms in despair.

'Every day there's a new surprise. When's it going to stop? Rumours about this. One of your ministers killing himself. Buch flapping around like the fat idiot he is . . .'

A man in a grey suit walked in, whispered in Grue Eriksen's ear.

'And now!' Krabbe's whiny voice was approaching falsetto. 'There's

315

talk about some old army case. What the hell's that about? Did the Islamists do this or not?'

Grue Eriksen got up and turned on the TV.

'Let's do the deal on the anti-terror package,' Rossing went on. 'Get that out of the way. It'll bring you closer to government. You can learn from us. Things will settle down. I guarantee it.'

The news came on, a caption: *Live from the Folketinget*. Buch on the screen, blue shirt open at the neck, looking tired but determined. A line of microphones pushed into his face.

'These are very critical questions which must be faced,' he was saying. 'I will demand a report from the Defence Minister concerning a military case which may be connected to the recent murders.'

'Fuck,' Flemming Rossing murmured.

'It seems,' Buch went on, 'the Defence Minister has withheld important information from the police in order to cover up his own negligence. My predecessor Frode Monberg confirmed my suspicions before he died. That's all I can say at present.'

A fusillade of questions shot from the unseen faces in front of him.

Grue Eriksen watched the impromptu press conference end in chaos.

'Is that what you mean by settling down?' Erling Krabbe piped up.

Madsen was in the first car to get to the meat-packing district. He briefed Brix as they walked through the nightclub full of sullen, puzzled people, then out to the roof.

'Lund chased him through the warehouses, then the club, then out here,' he explained. 'She didn't even have a gun. Crazy cow.'

They stopped by a line of metal steps leading to a level below the roof.

'As far as we can work out he hid behind the door and slugged her when she came out.'

Brix stared at the drop.

'Did Gunnar Torpe say anything?' he asked.

'He was unconscious by the time we got there. Really badly cut, like the others. With a dog tag by the looks of it.'

Madsen looked at the crowds of clubbers getting ushered from the building.

'He died in the ambulance. Never recovered consciousness.'

Forensic officers were working the steps, brushing for evidence, taking photographs.

'What did Lund say?'

'She didn't see his face. She wants us to look for the dog tag belonging to the soldier she exhumed. It's missing.' Madsen shrugged. 'Seems crazy to me.'

'Usually does. How is she?'

'Stubborn.'

The older man glared at him.

'Tough as old boots. She wanted to walk to the ambulance. I think a stretcher was . . . beneath her.' Madsen scratched his head. 'She had some crazy idea that the guy was about to shoot her then changed his mind.'

Brix looked interested.

'I don't think so,' Madsen went on. 'There were people coming out of the club by then. They knew something was happening. He just legged it.'

'And Møller's missing dog tag?'

Madsen stared at him.

'What about it? We've got another murder. We've got an officer almost killed.'

'Just look into it, will you?' Brix ordered.

A black car flew into the loading space below, blue light flashing. Strange was out of the driver's door straight away.

'Where's Lund?' he shouted.

'On her way back to the Politigården from hospital,' Brix called down to him.

'Is she OK?'

'Yes,' Brix answered. 'Shaken but . . .'

Strange didn't stop to listen. He got behind the wheel, slewed the car across the wet concrete, disappeared the way he came.

Brix watched him go, nodded to Madsen to get on with it.

Then called Ruth Hedeby.

'We need to talk,' he said.

Half an hour in Casualty then back to an interview room in headquarters. A wound above her right eyebrow. Bruises. A thick head. And questions. Lots of questions, none of them the ones the young detective who was with her thought of asking.

'Are you sure you didn't see his face?'

She sighed.

'If I saw his face I'd tell you, wouldn't I?'

'There must have been something special about him. The way he dressed—'

'Black anorak. Hood up. Is this the best line of questioning you've got?'

'I learned from you, Lund!' he cried, a little hurt.

She looked at him. A cadet she'd mentored a few years before.

'You always said to keep asking.'

'I did,' she answered. 'And you should. But sometimes there's nothing to say.'

'You told me,' he said, pointing an accusing finger, 'I was supposed to be part of a team.'

She nodded.

'You are.'

'But not you?'

Before she could answer the door opened and Strange strode in. He looked pale and worried.

'Are you all right?'

Lund got up. Her hand went to the wound above her eye.

'Fine.'

Strange nodded at the officer. He left straight away. She went back to the seat, quietly cursing the bruises and the pain.

'OK,' Ulrik Strange declared. 'You should not be here. I'm driving you home. Is there anyone I should call?'

She sipped some of the lukewarm coffee they'd brought her.

'No. I'm not going home.'

'For God's sake. Will you stop being the hero?'

'I'm not! My mother's getting married. Some wedding guests are staying over. I don't want to see them like this.'

She put her head on the table, closed her eyes.

'I can sleep in one of the night rooms here. Get me a bed. Find me a cell if you like. Won't be the first time.'

'You're a complete pain in the arse.' He got up. Put a gentle hand on her shoulder. 'Come on. We're going now.'

Head on the table, eyes barely open, she glowered at him.

'I used to pick up my kids and sling them over my shoulder

when they did this shit to me,' Strange said. 'Don't try it. You won't win.'

'Sleepy,' she whispered.

'You're leaving this damned place. Even if I have to carry you.'

Lund didn't budge.

He bent down, whispered in her ear. His breath was warm and smelled of liquorice.

'Even if I have to carry you,' Strange repeated.

Madsen had contacted Møller's mother by the time Brix got back to the Politigården. There was a message for him with one of the uniform men on the desk: someone had misused her son's identity.

'Also . . .' Madsen went on.

Ruth Hedeby was wandering down the corridor ahead, looking to avoid him.

'Later,' Brix ordered and followed her.

'Ruth,' he said when they got to her office.

She turned on him, finger jabbing in his face.

'What the hell was Lund doing in that church? If I find you've gone behind my back—'

'I didn't know she was there. She told Strange. Wanted him to look. He was in Helsingør—'

'The woman's a liability.'

She walked off to her desk. Brix took her shoulder.

'Lund's the only one who's seen this right from the start. It's nothing to do with terrorism. We've got to get König in here and find out what he really knows.'

She sat down. Brix took the seat opposite.

'We need to start afresh—'

'König's got problems of his own,' she broke in. 'The Minister of Justice called a press conference this evening. He's making accusations against the Defence Ministry and demanding PET look into them. Meanwhile Raben's parked outside a hall in Østerbro where the Ryvangen cadets are having their ball. Do you feel a spectator in all this?'

'Ruth—'

'PET will decide what to do. We just sit back, listen and take orders.' Her acute, dark eyes fixed on him. 'That means you. That means me. That means Lund too.'

He got up, closed the door.

'We can't go on like this.'

That irked her.

'There's a dividing line, Lennart. Work and pleasure. We agreed that from the start. Don't pretend otherwise.'

'That's not what I mean.'

'What is it then?'

'If you don't trust me any more.' He hesitated, made sure she understood. 'After all we've done together.'

Ruth Hedeby's mouth dropped. She looked younger. Looked vulnerable, and a part of Brix said he shouldn't pull a trick like this.

'Then really,' he added, 'what's the point?'

'How can you use that against me?'

'I'm not.' He put his feet on her desk, leaned back, stifled a yawn. 'I can work round König. We don't have to sit here like junior partners waiting on their lead.'

'Listen—'

'König's had us running all over Denmark chasing immigrants who don't know the first thing about these murders. Was that out of incompetence? Or did he have a reason? I'm not asking you to step out of line. I'm demanding you do your duty. *We* do it.'

She was wavering. Torn.

'I want Lund back and I want a free hand,' he said.

'You're a bastard.'

He smiled.

'Sometimes. But not now. They're jerking us around. I know you hate that as much as I do. So . . .'

'Let me think about it,' she said.

'Ruth . . .'

'Enough. You've got work to do, haven't you?'

The cadets' ball was in a whitewashed army hall close to the Kastellet fortification near the waterfront. Lights in every window, a string quartet, young men in fine uniforms, girlfriends on their arms.

Torsten Jarnvig had an unexpected guest: Jan Arild. Once a fellow lieutenant in the Jægerkorpset in Aalborg, now a general at army headquarters. A short, stocky, sly-looking man a couple of years older than Jarnvig. With his fine ginger hair, ruddy complexion and sharp features he'd earned the nickname 'Fox' back then. Appropriately,

Jarnvig thought. They'd served together, in hard times on occasion. Arild was a survivor. An important man now, in dress uniform covered with ribbons of service. He held divisional responsibilities over Ryvangen. It was important to cultivate him. And never call him Fox again.

So Torsten Jarnvig smiled and laughed at his bad jokes. Didn't complain when he smoked at the table even though it was frowned upon. Didn't mention his poor manners, or the coarse way he'd whistle at anything, his own crass remarks or a woman walking past.

Instead Jarnvig looked at his daughter and raised an eyebrow. He wanted her to know this offended him too. Wanted her to understand it was one of the burdens of being Colonel of Ryvangen.

'I could tell you stories about me and your old man,' Arild said and nudged Louise's elbow. He didn't notice when she shrank from him. 'Places we were never supposed to be. Doing things they'd never want to hear about in Geneva . . .'

'Jan,' Jarnvig began.

'See! I'm still Jan.' He leaned forward. 'Not so good here, you know.'

'General . . .' Jarnvig said with a sigh.

'Things we never talk about,' Arild repeated. 'That's the way of the army.'

Arild admired the couples on the floor. Let loose a low wolf whistle at a woman in a low-cut red gown.

'I gather the only surviving member of this renegade squad of yours is your own son-in-law,' he said, still eyeing the dancer. Arild stubbed his cigarette into the smoked salmon on his plate, glanced at Louise. 'Never works when men and officers meet outside duty. They know their place. We know ours. What do the police say he's up to?'

'I really don't know much about it,' Jarnvig replied. 'We've more important things to focus on. How was . . . how was the hunting season?'

Arild scowled.

'I don't have time for that. If Raben attacked the army chaplain he must be quite mad, don't you think? A lunatic.'

Louise stared at him.

'What?' Arild asked. 'Did I say something out of place?'

She was about to speak when Søgaard turned up at the table. A bright smile broke on Arild's face. He got to his feet, shook the new-comer's hand briskly.

'Major Christian Søgaard,' Arild cried. 'Behold the future.'

'I believe,' Louise broke in, 'Major Søgaard was about to ask me to dance.'

She got up, took Søgaard's arm and pushed, half-dragged Søgaard to the floor.

Arild scowled at Jarnvig.

'Spirited young woman. Do you think she'd feel the same if she knew about our little games together all those years ago?'

'I did what I was told and so did you.'

'A man should know his duty,' Arild agreed and lit another cigarette. 'Even better if he doesn't need to be told. PET's about to pick up that renegade of yours. They've been following him for a while.' He tapped his sharp nose. 'That's confidential. Keep it to yourself.'

'Why are they waiting?'

'Because they hope to pick up the killers, of course. If he's stupid enough for PET to track him down I can't see a bunch of Muslim fanatics having much problem, can you?'

Jarnvig's phone rang. The music was too loud. He walked out, went down the hall, found an empty room. White walls, a glittering Murano chandelier.

The call was from Bilal, on security duty outside the ball. Gunnar Torpe was dead. A policewoman had been attacked.

Jarnvig leaned against a wall and closed his eyes.

'What are the police telling you?'

'Not much,' the young officer said.

'Leave it with me.'

He pocketed the phone, wondered what to do. Looked up and saw Jens Peter Raben by the long curtains. He was as filthy as a tramp and had a pistol in his left hand, the barrel pointed at the floor.

'Do as I say, tell the truth,' Raben ordered. 'That's all I ask. Then you can go back to the ball and push Søgaard at my wife again.'

'How the hell did you get in here?'

'The way I was taught. Your security stinks.'

'I just got a call to say Gunnar Torpe's dead. They found him murdered in his church this evening. And someone attacked that policewoman, Lund.'

Jarnvig watched him. He was used to judging soldiers. He knew when they were scared and lying. He knew when they were just scared.

'Wasn't me,' Raben said.

'Maybe not. I know you didn't start this but by God you're not helping yourself or Louise any more.'

'I'm staying alive,' Raben barked back. 'I'm the only one who managed that. I need to see the personnel files.'

'It's the cadets' ball,' Jarnvig said, spreading his arms wide. 'They keep old records at Holmen now, in the personnel office.'

'I need—'

'PET know where you are. They've been following you all along.'

'Bullshit.'

'It's true,' Jarnvig insisted. 'They let you stay loose because they hoped you'd bring these terrorists out into the open.'

'What terrorists? You don't believe—'

'Do everyone a favour and give yourself up.'

'I need those files.'

'Are you listening to me? PET are here tonight. They know you're inside. If you got this far it's only because they let you. Be smart for once.'

Raben checked the gun, the magazine.

'Oh for God's sake,' Jarnvig cried. 'Don't make it worse. I'll come with you. I can speak up for you—'

'Speak up for me?' Raben yelled and the gun came up a fraction.

'If you give me a chance.'

'The same chance I had before?'

The scruffy man with the unkempt beard, grubby clothes and scruffy hair seemed so far from the immaculate soldier who'd taken Louise down the aisle. Torsten Jarnvig had been proud that day, even if he had his misgivings.

'I was coming home,' Raben said in a low, bitter tone. 'I had two weeks to go. Then I was back with Louise and little Jonas. Out of the army. A new life. A new home. And now . . .'

The gun shook in his fingers.

'It's been two years of hell and it's never going to end, is it? You could have given me a chance back then. You could have investigated Perk—'

'There was no Perk, Jens. You ruined everything. For yourself. For Louise and Jonas.'

'I told the truth! Priest knew it too. Why would he lie? Or the others? I tried to stop him.'

'Who?'

'Perk! He had the officers' academy badge tattooed on his shoulder.' Raben tapped his temple with his free hand. 'I can see him now.'

'You said the man you attacked first of all was Perk—'

'I know what happened! I know what I saw.' He glared at Jarnvig. 'You were my commanding officer. You should believe me first. Not PET. Or whoever's spinning these tales. To hell with it . . .'

He went for the door.

'Stop.'

Raben had his fingers on the handle.

'They're looking for you, Jens. I told you. Go that way.' He pointed to a side exit. 'There's a corridor. It leads out into the garden. Keep your head down.'

The man in the grimy clothes stared at him.

'Just do it will you?' Jarnvig pleaded.

Raben shambled off. With trembling fingers Torsten Jarnvig lit a cigarette, looked at himself in the mirror as he smoked it.

Halfway through a man marched in. Dark suit. Earpiece. PET. Had to be. Said Bilal was behind him.

'The toilets are at the end of the hallway,' Jarnvig told him. 'Show him, Bilal.'

The man looked the colonel up and down, checked the room, the curtains, everywhere, then left.

Torsten Jarnvig finished his cigarette and went back to the ball.

Jan Arild sat on his own, furious, his vulpine face flushed with booze and anger.

'That was a long call,' he said. 'Any news?'

'No,' Jarnvig said. 'Just personal.'

Arild folded his arms, watched Louise still on the dance floor in the arms of Christian Søgaard.

'Now that,' he said, 'is a couple.'

Thomas Buch was starting to know too well the labyrinth of corridors from his office opposite the twisting dragons to Grue Eriksen's quarters. So when he was summoned he broke recent habit, got a coat, walked outside, behind his own ministry past the little square where he used to eat sandwiches by the statue of Søren Kierkegaard, ambled to the Christianborg Palace through the cold damp night.

Along the way he called home. He and Marie had married when they were nineteen and Buch was still working on the farm, learning the business. They seemed to have been together for ever but that night, in the chilly Copenhagen drizzle, she felt distant from him. She hated the city, the noise, the commotion. He no longer noticed. There were other, more pressing matters. The conversation was difficult and trite, which was less than she deserved. He'd abandoned her in a way, and the pressing questions Monberg had left hidden in his papers meant Thomas Buch barely had time to feel regret.

The call ended outside the imposing facade of the palace. Buch walked in, went upstairs. The Prime Minister didn't look too mad. But he was.

'I had no choice,' Buch said, taking a seat opposite the silver-haired man behind the vast shiny desk from which he ran the nation. 'I wanted to prevent—'

'Be silent, Thomas, and listen to me for a moment.' Grue Eriksen leaned back in his chair, put his hands together. 'I didn't hesitate when I appointed you. Nothing in your past suggested you'd be rash enough to stab your own government in the back.'

'You didn't hear me out . . .' Buch began.

'You called a press conference without my knowledge. Accused one of your own colleagues of criminal behaviour. These accusations cannot be retracted . . .'

Buch shook his head.

'I've no wish to retract them. The facts—'

'I've worked with Rossing since he first entered politics. I know him. I trust him.'

'Then let me ask him some questions, in front of the Security Committee. That's all I want.'

'You've backed me into a corner, haven't you?'

'It's important we get to the bottom of this!'

The Prime Minister leaned back in his chair and muttered a quiet curse.

'And there I was thinking I was raising a simple farm boy to Minister of State. You learn more quickly than I thought. And a few tricks I'd rather you'd missed. Do you realize what you've started?'

'Tell me,' Buch answered miserably.

'A witch-hunt, one I'm now forced to play out in public. If there's something amiss it's got to come out. In the open. For all to see, whatever the damage.'

'Transparency is all I ask.'

'But if this is nothing but gossip and speculation,' Grue Eriksen added in a cold and vicious tone, his finger raised, his eyes blazing, 'I will send you back to Jutland to sweep up cow shit for the rest of your life.'

The Prime Minister glanced at his watch.

'You can go now,' he said.

Back in the office Plough and Karina were dissecting the latest news from the Politigården.

'They found the priest badly injured in his own church in Vesterbro,' Plough said. The tie was gone, the jacket too. He was changing, Buch thought. Maybe they all were. 'Gunnar Torpe. He died in the ambulance. A former field chaplain attached to troops from Ryvangen. He was in Helmand at the same time as Raben. That's five dead. Six if we count Monberg.'

'Monberg killed himself,' Buch snapped. 'The hospital porter saw him jump. Did the priest have a dog tag?'

'Yes.' Karina sat on the edge of Buch's desk. Jeans and a shirt. She looked tired. A little dishevelled for once. 'It seems Lund interrupted the murder.'

Buch blinked.

'The woman we met at the wedding?'

'Her. The priest was with Ægir. He knew the first victim, Dragsholm. She'd visited him. Maybe all the victims knew what really went on in Afghanistan.'

Plough shook his head.

'We know what happened. Nothing. The army investigated. An official inquiry. It said Raben's claims were nonsense. Just a way of shifting the blame.'

He threw a report in front of Buch.

'Read it for yourself. Nothing points towards the killing of civilians.'

'Things get covered up sometimes, don't they?' Buch asked. 'If there was an atrocity they'd have good reason.'

326

Plough tugged at his open shirt, as if struggling to come to a decision.

'There must be someone inside the Defence Ministry who bears a grudge against Rossing.' He looked at Karina. 'Can you think of anyone he's fired recently?'

Buch grinned with surprise.

'That's the spirit,' he said.

'But it isn't.' Plough looked offended. 'It's petty and dishonourable.'

'We need to get close to the police and find out what they uncovered about this officer,' Buch added.

Karina frowned.

'Not easy. They've taken Lund off the case. It's being run by PET.'

'And what do they say?'

'They're still chasing what we told them about Monberg. König doesn't think it's relevant to the investigation. They feel . . .'

She was reluctant to say it.

'They still think we can solve this by locking up every last Muslim we can find?' Buch asked.

'Pretty much.'

'And these clowns are running the show? While Lund's fired?'

'König's a very experienced officer,' Plough said carefully. 'He's very . . .'

'Very what?'

'Very well connected.'

'I think we need to make some calls,' Thomas Buch said, waving at the phones. 'Let's get busy.'

Thirty minutes later Erik König was back in an interview room in the Politigården. It felt, Brix thought, a little formal, and he was happy with that.

'Don't you think it's odd no one ever found Møller's dog tag?' he asked.

König laughed.

'Not really. The man was blown to bits. How many pieces do you expect them to pick up?'

'You've had us chasing Islamists for days, Erik. Up and down the country. But there's nothing, not a thing, that indicates fundamentalists are behind these killings.'

'Only the video and the material we found at Kodmani's.'

'Faith Fellow planted that on him. And we don't have a clue who he is.'

'Speculation—'

'Why aren't we investigating the army and Ægir?' Brix asked. 'Do they have some kind of immunity?'

'Stop this. I won't answer to you, Lennart. We're PET. We never have.'

'I want Raben brought in here for questioning. If you know where he is fetch him now.'

The PET man took off his rimless glasses, polished them carefully with his handkerchief, placed them back on his face.

'That's not possible. He's got away from us.'

'You've lost him?' Brix roared. 'If you were one of my men—'

'I'm not. We're looking. We'll find him. When we do . . .' König sat back in the hard interview room chair. '. . . I'll let you know.'

Brix threw up his hands in despair.

'Lennart.' König leaned on the table, looked him in the face. 'Do you honestly think that if I knew there was something to hide in that barracks I'd be sitting here, lying to you?'

Brix didn't answer. Hedeby came in.

'I just had a call from the Ministry of Justice,' she said. 'Monberg told Buch he knew the first victim, Anne Dragsholm. She'd found the officer Raben talked about. The one responsible for the massacre. They want a full investigation. By us.'

She sat down next to König, very close, looked into his grey, emotionless eyes.

'Us,' she repeated. 'And if anyone stands in our way they want to know.'

'Do they indeed?' the PET man said and got up, put on his coat and left.

Ruth Hedeby watched him and didn't say a thing. That took guts, Brix thought.

'Thanks,' he said.

'Don't thank me. Thank the Ministry. They're even more pissed off with PET than they are with us.'

'There's the question of staffing—'

'I don't want Lund back. We're on thin ice as it is. The answer's no.'

Her phone rang again. She looked at the number.

'Dammit. Don't these Ministry people ever sleep?'

Brix watched her take the call, followed the expression on her face.

'Minister Buch . . .' she said quietly. 'It's not normal for a politician to become involved in personnel issues here.'

The response was so loud and furious Ruth Hedeby held the phone away from her ear.

When it was over she said, 'I'll see what I can do.'

Brix sat and waited. When she stayed quiet he said, 'So you told them Lund wasn't coming back?'

'No,' she said haughtily. 'But they found out anyway.' She glared at him. 'I wonder how.'

He glanced at his watch and said, 'Search me. I'm going home. We can put everything together in the morning.'

'Lennart!'

He stopped at the door.

'For God's sake keep an eye on her this time. If you can. She scares the living daylights out of me.'

'I'll tell her.'

'No.' Hedeby got up and pulled her coat around her. 'No need.'

Lund didn't object when Strange drove her to his flat. The last thing she wanted was to bump into a bunch of happy, drunk guests from her mother's wedding.

The place was barely furnished, the way Danish bachelors liked. Two bedrooms, the second with a couple of single beds for his kids when they visited.

They sat next to each other on the low sofa, opposite one of the giant TVs she hated so much. He had a menu for pizza from a place round the corner.

'Number thirty-eight,' she said.

He was on the phone to them already.

'Number thirty-eight,' Strange said in his calm, genial voice.

'With extra cheese,' she added.

He sighed.

'With extra cheese. Same for me. No cheese.'

The hospital had given her something for the wound. She was pouring some fluid onto a piece of cotton.

'How's your head?' he asked.

'I took some pills.'

She dabbed the cotton onto her forehead and missed.

'Let me,' Strange said and tried to take it from her.

'I'm not an invalid.'

'You can't see what you're doing. Is it so hard to be helped?'

She let him take it. Sat there like a child as he brushed back her hair, looked carefully at her face.

'It's not so bad. You won't even get a scar.'

'Wonderful.'

'You're a tough old bird.'

'You're too kind.'

He dabbed at the wound with the cotton. She gasped.

'I know. It stings.'

'Why am I here? I could have stayed in the Politigården.'

'You could have put yourself up in a hostel too.' He looked round the room. 'It's not so bad is it? No dirty underwear on the floor. No porno mags lying around. And I wasn't expecting you. Give me a break.'

There was a photo on the low table by the sofa. Black and white and old. A tall, upright man in uniform.

'Your father was a soldier?'

His face turned grim and she couldn't guess why.

'Uniforms run in the family. Army usually, not always. That's my grandfather. He was a policeman. That's the old uniform. Didn't I tell you?'

'No.'

'Well he was. In the Politigården during the war.' Strange stopped and looked at her. 'He was working with the Resistance. The Germans found out. Someone, some *stikke*, informed on him. My father said he died with all the other heroes at Mindelunden. Tied to one of those stakes I guess. I don't know why I keep that picture really. Such a long time ago. There's enough shit happening now without worrying about yesterday.'

She pulled back from him, picked up another photo of a man in uniform, army this time, more recent but still old.

'Is this your father? He looks just like you.'

'Soldiers you see. There's something in our blood. We're born to serve.'

He laughed, looked vulnerable at that moment.

'I'm not like you. I'm best when I'm part of the pack and someone's telling me what to do. I guess I inherited that—'

'What happened to him? Your father?'

Strange stared at her.

'Who said anything happened to him?'

'It's an old photo. If he was still around you'd have a recent one.'

'Good God. You're a piece of work. Do you ever stop?'

'Not really. If you don't want to tell me—'

'He quit the army. My mum nagged him to leave. He bought a franchise for some stupid insurance agency with his pay-off. Was never going to happen. Remember what I said? We're born to serve. Not lead.'

Something on his face made her wish she'd kept quiet.

'We didn't know he was going bust. I'm not even sure it would have made a difference. I was only nineteen. That summer I was in the Politigården. When I thought the police uniform was for me.'

'How long will the pizzas be?'

He frowned at her.

'You asked. You've got to listen now. Only polite.'

'Strange—'

'I came home one day. He was hanging in the garage. I remember seeing the shoes first.'

'I'm sorry. I shouldn't have said anything.'

Strange scratched his stubbly cheek.

'You can't stop yourself. Besides, why not? You weren't to know. I hated him for that. For years. Then, when I was looking to come out of the army, my wife started giving me the same line. You're bright enough. Start your own company. Get a job in management. Be your own man.'

He brought the cotton wool to her face and dabbed again.

'That was enough to get me to re-enlist. I know who I am. I like being told what to do. By you. By Brix. Suits me. You're brighter and you know it.'

'I never said that.'

He laughed.

'You think you need to? You've got a face like an open book.'

'I've got a face like a football.'

'Still nice to look at.'

It had been so long since she'd had a conversation like this.

'I don't understand,' Lund said.

'What?'

He went back to working on her bruises and cuts.

'Why he didn't pull the trigger?'

He took away the cotton wool.

'Sarah. You don't know what happened. Don't worry about it.'

'I know. I heard. The gun . . .'

'There were people around.'

'He had time. He made a decision. I could feel it.'

'OK.' He put down the bottle and the swab. 'Listen to me. This won't happen again. You will not run away from me—'

'You were in Helsingør!'

'You could have waited.'

'Well I didn't.'

'Next time I'll make you. That's a promise.'

It was her turn to laugh.

'A promise? What am I to you? Just a crazy woman you fetched back from Gedser because Brix told you to . . .'

He put his hand on her arm. Then his fingers ran to her cheek, brushed back her hair, gently stroked for one brief moment her lips.

She didn't know what to do. Her head still hurt. She ached all over.

He moved towards her. She recoiled but just a little. So he persisted, tried again, got the meekest of pecks on her cheek, as much as she'd allow.

'This is a hell of a time to hit on me,' Lund whispered.

'When's a good one?'

He was so close, so full of a quiet and caring interest in her. Lund leaned towards him, tried to remember the last time she kissed a man.

The doorbell rang.

'Dammit,' Strange muttered. 'That was quick.'

He got up and a part of her was relieved. When he returned he looked grumpy.

'It's for you.'

Ruth Hedeby was outside in a heavy wool coat looking as if she'd rather be somewhere else.

'I'm sorry for the intrusion, Lund. I won't take much of your time.' She had an envelope in her hands. Opened it. There was Lund's police ID inside. 'Lennart . . . Brix can fill you in on the details. We were a bit rash, it seems.'

Hedeby handed her the ID, a sheaf of new reports from PET and the Politigården's own team.

'There are developments in the case and a change of attitude in the Ministry of Justice.'

She glanced at Strange.

'We'll see you both tomorrow,' Hedeby said then walked to the lift.

'Wait,' Lund said.

Hedeby stopped.

'I want your guarantee I can stay on the case until it's closed.'

'My guarantee?'

'Yes. It's my case. I work with Strange. We handle it together. OK?'

'If the two of you can get along—'

'I want no restrictions. I don't want PET or anyone else telling me what to do. All the officers involved in Ægir are to be questioned. And maybe . . .'

'Maybe what?'

'Maybe something else I haven't thought of yet.'

Hedeby walked back, faced Lund.

'Let me make the position clear. This is not my decision. The Ministry want you back on the case. I don't know why. I don't want to know. But if you say that's how it is then so be it. The shit won't land outside my door.'

'Good. And stop the tail on Raben. I want him in for questioning.'

'PET have lost track of him. We've no idea where he is.'

Lund shook her head.

'No idea . . .'

'I'm sorry. König screwed up. On lots of other things too. The Ministry notice these things. Let's make sure they don't turn the heat on us, shall we?'

The lift came. Hedeby stepped in and left.

'Where am I supposed to sleep?' Lund asked.

'In one of the kids' beds. Don't you want your pizza first?'

'Save it till tomorrow.'

She waved the sheaf of documents at him, then wandered into the little bedroom, closed the door behind her and started to read.

Eight

8.10 a.m.   Brix let Strange brief the team the next morning, Lund listening near the door. After more pills her head didn't hurt so much. The wound over her eye was swollen but behaving. She stood at the back of the room, casting her eyes across the latest intelligence reports on the board, listening but not much.

They'd barely talked. Strange went out and got coffee and warm pastries from the bakery across the road then, in silence, drove her to the Politigården.

'Lund never saw the man's face,' he told the group of detectives assembled before him. 'We're working on the idea he was one of Team Ægir's officers. There were twenty-eight in all. I want every one considered a suspect. Get them in for questioning. I don't care where they are or what they're doing. If the army kick up a stink let me know.'

Lund marched into the middle of them, stirring her cup of coffee back to life.

'They never found Møller's dog tag either,' she said. 'We've reason to believe someone used his identity. There's a list of bills . . .'

She went to the table, picked up the papers she'd got from Møller's mother.

'These are all items ordered in his name. After he was dead. I want them checked. Anne Dragsholm found out who the officer was. The one who called himself Perk. That's why she was killed.'

Lund looked at the line of detectives in front of her.

'If a woman lawyer can find him so can we.'

They went off. Brix waved to her. He had something in his hand.

335

'This is PET's report on what happened outside the cadets' ball last night. They saw Raben go in. Never saw him come out. He abandoned the car he stole.'

She scanned the document.

'You look better than I expected,' he said.

'It says Raben's wife and Torsten Jarnvig were there. He must have talked to one of them.'

'You don't know that.'

'Then why did he go? How did he give PET the slip?'

Brix didn't like being contradicted. It showed on his craggy face.

'What about this row between the ministers?' she asked. 'Which one do I talk to first?'

'Who said anything about getting involved in Slotsholmen?'

'It's all the same thing,' Lund said, baffled that he couldn't see this. 'We have to . . .'

The door opened. Christian Søgaard was marched in by two uniformed men. He stared at Lund, gave her a furious, bitter nod as he was walked off to an interview room.

'Do we know anything about this man?' Brix asked.

'Born soldier,' Strange said. 'Tough guy or so he thinks. If there's a fight somewhere he's up for it.'

'That narrows it down,' Lund said, still going through the papers.

Søgaard was moaning even before they started.

'This is outrageous.' He sat slumped in his combat fatigues. 'We're sending a new team to war. And here you are screwing around—'

'You do want to know who killed your men, don't you?' Strange interrupted.

No answer.

'You turned up late for the cadets' ball,' Lund said. 'Why was that? Where were you between five and nine?'

Søgaard blinked.

'You're watching us now? Do you really have nothing better to do? While these terrorists—'

'Forget about that,' Strange told him. 'We were being led up a blind alley. Where were you?'

'One of my officers asked for a talk. He was uncertain whether he wanted to go.' A sour smile. 'Worried about leaving his family behind.'

'You talked him round, I bet?' Strange asked him.

'That's my job.'

Lund passed over her notepad.

'I want his name and address.'

Søgaard scribbled something on the page.

'You'd better get a move on. He's off to Helmand for six months.'

'We will,' Strange said. 'Don't worry. According to the phone records you called Torpe, the priest, not long before he died. Why was that?'

'I had nothing to do with what happened to Torpe.'

'Frightened he was going to tell tales?' Strange went on. 'He knew everything, didn't he?'

'There's nothing to know. Raben had attacked him. Torpe was scared he'd come back. I told him not to worry. That you people had the case in hand.'

He stretched out his feet, banged his big boots on the floor.

'More fool me.'

Lund took back her notepad.

'Anne Dragsholm had been in touch with Torpe, about what happened in Helmand. Raben's accusations. The ones the military tribunal rejected.'

'Really?' Søgaard shrugged.

'That case bothered you,' Strange said. 'You called Raben unpatriotic and cowardly for saying those things. It's on the record.'

'What if I did? His fairy tales damaged us. He should have taken responsibility for his own failings. Not tried to blame some imaginary officer called Perk.'

Lund checked her notes again.

'You like his wife,' she said. 'What's your relationship with her exactly?'

'What's that got to do—?'

'You took her home last night. You danced with her at the ball. She looked as if she was with you. So—'

'So?'

'How long have you known her?' she asked. 'What's the deal? Did Jonas just get a new daddy? Has Colonel Jarnvig finally got an officer for a son-in-law, not a scruffy lowlife from the ranks?'

Søgaard waved away the question and stared at the wall.

Strange had more papers.

'According to army records five years ago you had three cadets tied to a tree on a training ground in Jutland. You left them there overnight. Middle of winter. Freezing cold.'

'You have been busy, haven't you?' Søgaard sneered.

'You said they'd been disloyal. Is that an approved punishment, Søgaard? Did you make a habit of it?'

'I train them for battle,' the army man yelled at him. 'When we're out there anyone can take a shot at us, put an IED by the side of the road. We have to trust one another or we're dead. If I have to strap a mouthy cadet to a tree to teach him that lesson I'll do it. He'll thank me one day.'

'Not all of them,' Lund said. 'Raben's got as much field experience as you have. Was that the problem with him and his squad? They didn't toe the line. They let you down by accusing an officer of killing civilians when really they should have kept their mouths shut?'

Strange pulled his chair closer to the man in the combat fatigues.

'Which if you think about it gives you and your fellow officers quite a motive to shut them all up. Especially when a civil rights lawyer comes knocking and says she knows who impersonated Perk. Who killed those people.'

'Bullshit,' Søgaard replied. 'You're dancing in the dark. I'm not talking to you clowns any more. Not without an army lawyer here.'

Strange laughed.

'We could have got you Anne Dragsholm if she wasn't dead. I'll put you on the request list. We've got twenty or thirty of your mates coming in here soon. Maybe we'll stick you in the same hole and let you swap war stories.'

Christian Søgaard closed his eyes, leaned back in the chair and yawned.

'For an innocent man you don't have much to say,' Lund noted. 'Do you?'

He smiled at her, a sour, confident face, and kept quiet.

Ryvangen Barracks was in the semi-organized chaos that came with any new troop deployment. Trucks moving everywhere, teams of men handling pallets, weaponry and vehicles. Raben's wife was in a white nurse's uniform with a pink sweater against the bright, cold day, helping with the medical supplies, sick of the young cop called Madsen who kept badgering her.

'Let me get this straight,' he said, following her as she walked from the infirmary to a green army truck, her arms full of medication boxes. 'You left the ball with Søgaard? You were with him afterwards?'

'He gave me a lift home. That was all.'

'Did he seem different?'

She gazed at him, puzzled.

'No.' She handed the boxes to a woman soldier. 'This is for the armoured vehicles. Bandages, painkillers, morphine. The usual . . .'

'And the day Grüner was killed?'

'Why do you keep asking me the same questions? I already told you. Søgaard gave us a lift back here.'

'And after that?'

She ordered the woman soldier to get more supplies.

'After that I've no idea. Maybe he drove to Sweden to deliver some explosives. Or went down the mosque to say his prayers.'

Madsen didn't appreciate the joke.

'Look,' she said. 'I told you all this. He helped us with some decorating and after that he talked to my father. I don't know what you think he did but really . . .' She put her hands on her hips. 'This is pretty ridiculous if I'm honest.'

'And you didn't see your husband last night? At the ball?'

'Oh God.' She wanted to scream. 'Of course I didn't. How could Jens possibly be there?'

'He was,' Madsen said, and left it at that. Then he shook her hand the way the police always did. 'If anything comes up I'll let you know.'

She didn't like being left in the air. A car drew up. She saw who was getting out and bristled at his presence. Her father was wandering across to the warehouse with a clipboard. Louise walked over and said, 'I need the keys to the storeroom. I want to get some of Jonas's things out for him.'

'I'm busy right now.'

'It's a key, Dad.'

He frowned.

'I said—'

'Never mind. You've got a visitor. That idiot from last night.'

Jarnvig peered at the long black army limo and the wiry figure climbing out of the back. General's uniform, flat cap, long raincoat with gold epaulettes.

'I can't believe you used to be friends with a moron like that,' she added.

'Dammit,' Jarnvig snapped, reached into his pocket and gave her the key. 'Best leave us.'

Arild wanted a meeting in Jarnvig's office. When they were alone he looked around, scowled at the meagre, bare room.

'If you'd listened to me years ago you'd be doing better than this, Torsten. You're too wedded to your men. You could have made general if you'd wanted.'

'I'm happy here. I like it.'

'Do you like having the police poking round the place day and night? I got a call from PET. The Politigården say they're now focusing on Team Ægir. It's nothing to do with terrorism apparently. This is all down to us.'

'So I gathered,' Jarnvig replied.

'They've put this damned woman back on the case. What's she called?'

'Lund.'

'What's so special about her?'

'I don't know,' Jarnvig admitted. 'She seems . . . determined. She asks good questions too. A few I'd like answers to if I'm honest.'

'Don't be ridiculous! She's pointing the finger at some of our best officers. They're not murderers or terrorists.'

Jarnvig wondered why Arild had come. It wasn't just for this casual conversation.

'I've told everyone here,' he said. 'We'll do all we can to cooperate with the police. It's in our interests this is cleared up as quickly as possible. Just as much as theirs.'

Arild laughed.

'Is it just the police you're helping, Torsten?'

'I'm sorry . . .'

'PET tracked Raben to the ball last night. He was in the building.' Arild's vulpine features narrowed and his acute eyes focused on the man opposite him. 'But you knew that already, didn't you?'

'No. Why should I? What was he looking for?'

'Raben seems interested in the officers too. I find this all rather . . . disconcerting. An escaped prisoner gets into the ball. Then somehow manages to evade PET on the way out. It's as if he was warned.'

'Really?'

'And then, early this morning, there's a break-in at the personnel office in Holmen. We've got CCTV. It's Raben. He didn't steal anything of value. Just all the files on the officers attached to Ægir. Every last one's missing.'

Jarnvig sat in silence.

'The thing is,' Arild went on, 'we only moved personnel records from Ryvangen to Holmen three months ago.'

He looked into Jarnvig's face and smiled.

'I have to ask myself. Since he's spent the last two years locked up in Herstedvester . . . how the hell did he know where to look?'

'Jens Peter Raben's a resourceful man,' Jarnvig said. 'He always was.'

'But he's only human. Isn't he?'

Another ripped-off car, this time an old yellow VW Polo that felt ready to give up the ghost at any moment. Raben had briefly fled the city, parked in wasteland by the water in Amager Øst. He reached beneath the dashboard, pulled the wires to kill the engine. There was half a tank of fuel. He didn't want to risk buying any more with the scant cash he had.

The documents from Holmen were on the floor of the passenger seat. He scanned the bleak flat land around him, felt confident he'd thrown off PET. Reached down and pulled out the files: identical brown envelopes, each with a mugshot attached.

Familiar faces, part of the jumble of confused memories from that last fateful tour.

One photo was missing. It was from a file on a captain, Torben Skåning. Raben rifled the envelope. There was a typed report inside.

But for the rank it could have been talking about him.

Skåning was sent home from Helmand around the same time. Withdrawn from active service for uncontrollable fits of violent rage and mental instability. Someone reading the report had underlined the most damning parts. There were scribbles, rings and exclamation marks, in different-coloured pens.

Raben closed his eyes, listened to the traffic wheeling into the nearby oil depot.

Skåning.

He'd never heard the name. There was no face to put to it. Yet somewhere in his own head lay the key, buried deep beneath the pain of that last day in Helmand when the bomber hit and the explosion almost killed him.

If he saw the man he'd know him. Raben had told Torsten Jarnvig that and it was true.

He reached down, found the wires, brought the ancient Polo back to life.

Torben Skåning.

A man much like himself. Consumed with rage and fury and violence.

Raben turned the rusty VW back to the main road and trundled on towards the city.

Plough had assembled what information he could glean from the Ministry of Defence. Karina was at her desk making calls. The Security Committee was less than an hour away. Buch had nothing new to tell it.

'Three soldiers died on the mission. Afterwards the Ministry received accusations from a local Afghan warlord. He said a family in the village was executed by Danish soldiers.'

'Was he the kind of man we'd believe?' Buch asked.

'It's Afghanistan,' Plough answered with a shrug. 'Raben's team said they answered a distress call from an officer. They came to relieve him, found themselves trapped. The officer killed the family. According to the judge advocate this was a propaganda effort by the Taliban. After they were questioned the soldiers withdrew their story. All except Raben . . .'

'Why did they change their story?' Buch asked.

Plough frowned.

'It seems no one pressed them on that point. And now they're all dead. Save for Raben. PET seem to have lost him completely by the way. Idiots. König's put up a bad show—'

'Forget König for a moment,' Buch cut in. 'Rossing knew something was amiss. We've got to work on that.'

'He's hardly likely to admit it.'

Karina came in.

'There's a journalist to see you.'

Buch rolled his eyes.

'I don't have time for that.'

She smiled.

'Oh yes you do. I worked all night tracking this one down. She's got an axe to grind with Flemming Rossing. I think you should hear what she has to say.'

Plough took a deep breath and began to knead his brow.

'She's next door,' Karina added. 'Shall I ask her in?'

Connie Vemmer was a tall, striking woman close to fifty, pearl necklace, long tidy blonde hair, elegant top, smart blue jeans, all a little too young for her. She smelled of cigarettes and the faintest whiff of booze.

Buch got up when she entered the room, found her a chair and said, 'Well?'

The woman stretched her long legs.

'I worked in Flemming Rossing's press centre,' she said. 'I was legit before that, though. A real journalist. You can check.'

'We will,' Plough promised.

'Your aide . . .' She glanced at Karina. 'She told me you were interested in the Helmand case two years ago. I was there. On the watch when the accusations came in. I killed them. That's why they never made the papers.'

'Should they have done?'

'Depends on your point of view. On the day the soldiers were buried, when Rossing gave his speech, a fax came in.'

She fumbled in her bag and came out with a packet of cigarettes, lit one.

'It was from Afghanistan. Anonymous. That wasn't so unusual. Do you mind if I smoke?'

'Not in here!' Plough cried. 'It's forbidden.'

'Just the one,' Buch said with a smile.

She lit the cigarette, looked grateful. Karina fetched a saucer for an ashtray.

'It was a medical report from the field hospital at Camp Viking,' Vemmer said. 'That's the part of Camp Bastion we use under the wing of the British. The body parts didn't match.'

Buch's eyes narrowed.

'What do you mean?'

'A hand,' she said with a shrug. 'There was a hand too many. It wasn't from any of the soldiers.'

'You mean it was a civilian's?' Plough asked.

'Seems a reasonable guess. So I passed on the fax to the Permanent Secretary thinking he'd want to look into it. After all it seemed to confirm the soldiers' allegations. But . . .'

A long drag of the cigarette, then she waved the smoke away from her own face, unaware that it was drifting straight towards the horrified Plough.

'Nothing happened.'

Connie Vemmer looked at each of them in turn.

'I checked. No one acted on it. The fax didn't even enter the file. The judge advocate never saw it.'

'I need you to tell this to the Security Committee,' Buch said. 'We meet in half an hour.'

She laughed.

'Are you serious? I signed the Official Secrets Act. I could go to jail just for talking to you.'

'I'm the Minister of Justice.'

'And I'm a freelance hack trying to stay alive. Sorry. If I could go public with this do you think I'd be trying to get you interested? I'd have written the damned story myself.'

Plough retrieved the dying cigarette from her shaky fingers and took it away with the saucer.

'If it's a deal you're after . . .' he said.

'I don't want a deal! What do you think I am? I want someone to look into this case. It stinks to high—'

'If you won't step forward there's nothing I can do,' Buch interrupted. 'We can talk to our lawyers. I'm sure the Official Secrets Act doesn't cover every eventuality. If there's good reason—'

'I doubt Flemming Rossing thinks there's good reason, does he? And from what I read in the papers he's likely to be around a lot longer than you, Buch.'

He smiled at her, said nothing.

She dug around in her bag.

'You can have this,' she said, retrieving some crumpled sheets of paper. 'It's a copy of the fax. I made one before passing it on. Seemed a good idea at the time.'

Three pages. Highly detailed. Buch started to read.

'That's as far as I can go,' Connie Vemmer said.

She let herself out after that. The smell of tobacco hung in the air.

'I don't like this,' Plough moaned. 'We don't know that woman from Adam. She's a journalist, for God's sake. It gives me a bad feeling . . .'

Buch kept reading.

'You can't possibly put that in front of the Security Committee,' Plough insisted.

'Do you have something else?'

No answer.

The Security Committee consisted of the Prime Minister, Flemming Rossing, Gitta Spalding, the Foreign Minister, and Kahn, the ambitious Interior Minister.

Buch had Plough to back him up. That would have to do.

'I'm sorry I'm late,' he said with a smile when he entered Grue Eriksen's office. 'I was delayed.'

No one spoke. Buch dragged two chairs from the side of Grue Eriksen's desk, sat down with his papers on his knee, smiled again as Plough joined him.

'This meeting,' the Prime Minister dictated into a voice recorder, 'has been called to discuss the accusations the Minister of Justice has made against the Minister of Defence concerning some recent past cases. Present are . . .'

Rossing was drinking a cup of tea.

When Grue Eriksen was finished Buch leapt straight in.

'Let me begin two years ago,' he said briskly. 'When an incident in Afghanistan was reported to the Ministry of Defence. I will refer to it as the Helmand case.'

Rossing raised his teacup.

'Very melodramatic, Thomas.'

But he listened all the same.

The office looked like an outpost of Ryvangen itself now. It was full of soldiers dragged in by Strange on her instruction. Men in combat fatigues mainly, unhappy to be painted as anything but heroes.

Madsen came in.

'We've found someone interesting.' He gave Lund a personnel file. 'Peter Lænkholm. They had to pick him up. He didn't come in for questioning like we asked. He was a lieutenant. Got kicked out once Ægir came back to Denmark. Bad apple.'

Peter Lænkholm was in an interview room. He looked a mess. Unshaven, ragged clothes. Dead, unfocused eyes. No money. No life. No hope. One step from the gutter, she thought.

'Why are you bothering me?' Lænkholm said when she started throwing questions at him. He had a droning, lazy voice. Scared too. 'I'm not in the army any more.'

Strange sat at the back of the room. Madsen left them to it.

'You were part of Team Ægir,' Lund said. 'Tell us about Søgaard. Did you like him?'

'Oh!' Lænkholm put on the most artificial of smiles. 'Very much so. Søgaard was great. He trained me at the officers' academy. I learned a lot from him.'

'Is that so?' Strange asked.

'Yeah. He was terrific. I asked to serve under his command. That's how much I respected him.'

Strange flipped through some records.

'You didn't serve very long.'

'I got as far as Afghanistan. How much do you want?'

Lund pushed a report across the table, tapped her finger on one of the passages.

'It says here you were uncooperative. There were disciplinary problems. You and Søgaard don't come across as buddies.'

'I'm not here to slag him off.'

'Listen, mate!' Strange got to his feet, came to the table, planted his fists next to Lænkholm. 'Let me tell you how it is. You've got enough weed in that squalid little pit of yours to put you in jail.'

'It's p-personal. I'm not a dealer.'

'Pull the other one. Tell us about Søgaard.'

'It's personal.'

'Oh for God's sake . . .' Strange looked at his watch. 'I can have you in court by two o'clock.'

'Just tell us what went wrong, Peter,' Lund broke in. 'Do that and we'll send you for counselling. Get you some help.'

'Help?' he laughed. 'You believe that?'

'I believe it's better than jail . . . Søgaard?'

He wiped his mouth with the sleeve of his threadbare, grubby jacket.

'It doesn't come from me, right?'

'It doesn't come from you,' Lund agreed.

'He's fine.' Lænkholm stared at her, alert now, as if the memories brought back a trace of the officer he once was. 'So long as you follow the rules. *His* rules. Do what he says and it's cool. But . . .'

'But you didn't, did you?' Strange asked.

Peter Lænkholm stared at the table.

'You can get weed out there. And worse if you want it. All I did was smoke one fucking joint, for God's sake! I was no more high than the Taliban.'

'And for that he kicked you out?' Lund asked.

He glared at her.

'Søgaard doesn't kick you out. If you fail him it's like you've insulted him. You pay the price. I got the full treatment.'

'What treatment?'

Nothing.

'What treatment?' Strange bellowed in his ear.

'They fetch you at night, when you're asleep. You've no idea it's going to happen. They've got hoods on. You don't know who they really are.'

His shaking hand went for the cold coffee cup on the table. But Lænkholm's trembling fingers couldn't hold it so he gave up.

'They strip you naked and tie you up with cable binders and duct tape. Then they take you outside, shove a flare up your arse and string you up from a post.'

'A flare?' Lund asked.

'A flare. That's what I said. It's not so great, I can tell you.'

Strange was shaking his head, laughing. She scowled at him. He walked to the window.

'Didn't anyone help you?'

'What? And get the same?'

'Couldn't you complain?'

'Jesus. You don't understand what it's like, do you? Out there Søgaard's God. Nobody moves, nobody breathes, nobody takes a shit without his say-so.'

Strange came back, pulled up a chair.

'What about Raben and his squad?' Lund asked. 'How did Søgaard like him?'

No answer.

'Come on,' Strange cried.

'Not a lot. Raben's team used to get into some stuff the rest of us were never told about. There were people around sometimes . . . I don't know what they did. I didn't want to know.'

His head went down again. Lund bent over and tried to look into his glassy, lost eyes.

'Raben was one of them?'

'We all heard the rumours after he was hit. Then this officer got discharged. Me they just let go. But discharged . . .'

Lund shook her head.

'You're losing me.'

'It didn't happen often. You didn't get a formal discharge for smoking a joint.'

Strange pushed a pad onto the table, followed by a pen.

'Name,' he said.

Nothing.

'Peter? Hello? Is there anyone still awake in there?'

'A name,' Lund repeated. 'Then you're out of here. To counselling, not court.'

'His name was Skåning.'

She began to flick through the papers.

'Anything else?' Strange asked.

'No.'

Lund found the file. A photo of a bearded man in a beret. Torben Skåning.

'Him?' she asked.

Lænkholm nodded.

'Great,' Strange said, slapping his shoulder. 'Then we're done, aren't we?'

He grabbed the personnel records off the table, ran his finger down his clipboard.

'Skåning's on the list of men to bring in. Shall we pay him an early visit?'

Lund got up, followed Strange to the door, watched him walk to the circular stairs, never looking back.

She hesitated. After so many days in the dark they seemed to be getting closer to something that might resemble the truth.

That had happened towards the end of the Birk Larsen case too. She was still living with the consequences, and she wasn't alone in that.

You learn from your mistakes, she thought, hearing Jan Meyer's voice in her head, and all the warnings he kept throwing at her, mostly unheeded.

Lund walked to her private locker, undid the padlock, sorted through her things. Got out the 9-millimetre Glock in its leather and canvas holster. Looked it at. Knew she'd always hate the thing.

Caught her reflection in the metal door. Cut over the eye. Bruises. Swelling. But she was still alive, not that she knew how or why.

The gun went into her bag with the gum and the tissues.

'Are you coming or not?' Strange called up from the floor below.

'On my way,' she said and walked to the stairs.

Thomas Buch had prepared what he wanted to say in his head. It didn't change when he delivered his concise and simple speech to the Defence Committee. It couldn't. That was all he had.

'Why was the Folketinget not informed of the accusations? Why . . .?'

'Oh come on, Buch,' Rossing intervened. 'I can hardly go running to Parliament every time the Taliban try to pull a publicity stunt on us.'

'You saw no reason to investigate the alleged killing of civilians? By our own officers?'

Kahn, who'd looked bored throughout, broke in.

'The minister's already answered the question. Whose side are you on?'

'That,' Buch said, 'offends me.'

'It offends me to sit here listening to you question the integrity of one of our most senior ministers. Five seconds in government and look at the mess you've created.' Kahn swore under his breath, stared across the room. 'Do you have anything to support these wild accusations?'

Buch nodded at Plough. The civil servant got up, walked round the room, handed out copies of the fax Connie Vemmer had brought.

Rossing laughed.

'What the hell is this?'

'It's a report from the field hospital in Camp Viking. This fax was sent to you on the day of the soldiers' funeral. Among the body parts was a hand too many. The hand of an Afghan.'

349

'This is a Ministry of Defence document,' Rossing complained. 'I'd like to know where you got it.'

'The doctors' report concludes the alleged killing of civilians must be investigated. You buried this—'

'No, no, no. I called a judge advocate's inquiry. It's all on the record. The case was investigated and to tell you the truth—'

'The truth is you did bugger all!' Buch cried, getting to his feet, a little unsteadily. 'You knew something was wrong and you were determined it wasn't going to get out. You made Monberg keep silent when he found out. And when Anne Dragsholm got wind of it and was murdered for her pains you didn't do shit!'

'You're overwrought, Thomas,' Rossing said idly.

'Damned right I am! Five people are dead.' Buch put up his hand, fingers spread. 'Five lives that could have been spared if you'd done your duty. It makes me—'

'You've made your point,' Grue Eriksen broke in. 'Take a seat. Calm down if you can.' The Prime Minister turned to Rossing. 'Do you have an explanation?'

'Yes. Of course.'

He went through the copied fax again.

'I asked for this to be kept out of the case files because it was inaccurate.'

'Oh no, Rossing!' Buch bellowed. 'You can't get away with this nonsense. The time and place is on the fax. It all fits.'

'I'm sorry you force me to go into such macabre details, Buch. It seems I have no alternative. When the medics in Afghanistan looked into the case further they realized the hand was that of the suicide bomber himself.'

'Not good enough.'

'It may not be good enough for you! But it's in the corrected medical report which was placed on file later.' Rossing glanced at Grue Eriksen. 'I really don't want to waste any more of your time with this. You're all welcome to read the documents if you wish. Had Buch asked for it beforehand I would happily have supplied it. Instead he goes off half cock once more. Really . . .'

Rossing wiped his forehead.

'What with poor Frode's death this has been quite an ordeal.'

'That was all very quick,' Buch snapped. 'How did you know I was going to talk about that fax?'

Rossing shook his head.

'How did you know?' Buch repeated.

'You're prone to conspiracy theories,' Rossing said. 'You ignore expert opinion. You force the police and PET to hound our soldiers.'

Voice rising, he leapt to his feet, jabbed his hand in Buch's face.

'You put pressure on Frode Monberg when you knew he was unwell. You, Buch! And now you dare to make me responsible for your own stupidity and incompetence! Enough.'

He strode to the door, walked out of the room. Kahn followed. Then Gitta Spalding and finally Carsten Plough.

Grue Eriksen stayed in his seat, staring at the wall.

'There's more to this,' Buch said tentatively. 'I promise . . .'

The silver-haired man by the window closed his eyes, rolled back his head, said nothing.

Buch left.

Just after six, icy rain on the windscreen, streets covered with a greasy winter sheen. Lund and Strange driving through Copenhagen still trying to find the missing Torben Skåning.

He lived in one of the old military houses off Store Kongensgade. His wife hadn't seen him all day. They'd checked the local pubs he liked and got nowhere. His one interest outside drink seemed to be the nearby Frihedsmuseet in Churchillparken close to the Kastellet garrison and the Amalienborg Palace. It was a museum dedicated to recording Danish resistance to the Nazis, a small building with a home-built tank from the conflict near the entrance.

Lund stared at the ramshackle vehicle as they drove up outside. It looked like a kid's toy, a large Christiana trike covered in armour, with the message 'Frit Danmark', Free Denmark, scrawled on the front. There were lights on in the building, figures behind the glass drinking wine. A reception of some kind.

She followed Strange into the entrance, told him to talk to the people there, wandered round the nearest exhibits. Lund hadn't stepped inside this place since she was a school kid and barely remembered the stories from those days. War, she recalled once again, was a distant nightmare when she was young. Something that affected other, older people, never her.

Briskly she walked through the exhibition areas, followed the murky, awkward story of how Denmark reluctantly allowed an all-powerful German regime to take control in 1940 then steadily found the courage to resist in the ensuing years.

It was all here. The amateur acts of sabotage by schoolchildren bearing names like the Churchill gang. The more daring and serious attacks by the Communists, aided by secret agents from British special forces. Then, from 1943 on, the terror. The round-up of Jews. Routine arrests, torture, banishment to concentration camps, the execution of those suspected of working with the partisans.

And the response. This part she looked at most closely. Not all Danes resisted. Not everyone stayed neutral. Some joined the Nazis, worked with them, benefited from their patronage. By doing so they risked their lives. When the terror took hold the Resistance formed ruthless assassination groups, published clandestine newsletters with the names and photographs of the collaborators they intended to murder.

Then shot them dead on the street, in their homes, at work.

War was everywhere, in the basement cells of the Politigården where suspects were tortured before being shipped to concentration camps in Germany or, worse, driven to Mindelunden and a quick, brutal death.

Stikke.

That word stared at her from almost every exhibition case, on the underground pamphlets the Resistance printed on their home-made presses, in the newspaper reports, the history books.

Informers. Traitors. Danes who'd lost the right to live.

Everything from that time seemed to be recorded here, in old guns, children's paintings, scraps of newspaper, and score upon score of photos. Dead soldiers in the snow. Home-made pistols and pipe bombs. Mugshots of informers to be shot. Photos of squads like the Lorentzen gang, Danes trained by the Germans to infiltrate the partisans. Bullet diagrams from the shooting of Resistance fighters cornered during raids. Lines of men being rounded up by Nazi guards at the Horserød internment camp near Helsingør, a place Lund knew well since it was now an open prison used for offenders deemed to be of little threat to society.

She'd been an idiot to think that war belonged to history, an accident of the past, something the world had outgrown. Its dark ghost still lurked in the corridors of the Politigården, in the prisons the state now used, in the minds of those who came after her and grew up in a world less secure, less peaceful than the one she'd enjoyed.

Lund stood in front of a shocking display about an attack on a group of Resistance fighters caught unawares, slaughtered without a second thought. Men who'd delivered a similar fate to a Danish *stikke* a few days earlier.

Strange came and stood next to her. He didn't look at the case at all.

'They haven't seen Skåning today. But . . .'

'Is there a picture of your grandfather here?'

Strange shook his head.

'What?'

'I always thought it was so distant. For me it was. But it's not really.' She looked at him. 'Is he here? Haven't you looked?'

'I never knew him,' he said, and seemed offended. 'How could I? My dad didn't talk of him much either. I've only got now. Here. This moment. I don't have time for . . .' He gestured at the display. 'For this kind of stuff.'

'That's what I thought too.'

'You're starting to scare me.'

'Why?'

'I don't like it when you do reflective.'

'Doesn't happen often.'

'Good. Back to the real world. Skåning's wife just called. She said someone else has been trying to get in touch with him.'

Lund turned away from the old photos and home-made guns.

'Who?'

'He didn't leave his name. Just said he was an old army colleague.' He pointed to the door. 'Skåning's still not answering his mobile. His wife says that's unusual.'

'What did the wife say to him?'

Strange frowned.

'Something she never told us. Sunday nights Skåning has a key to use a local library in Nørrebro. He's studying languages there and locks up.'

Two minutes later they were back in the car. Strange took out the blue light as they pulled away from the museum, placed it on the roof, set it going, hit the siren.

*

353

The Yellow polo was the only car outside the little library. Raben had been there the best part of an hour, lights off, slumped in the driver's seat, gun in his pocket. Waiting.

The name troubled him. Skåning. He'd heard it before somewhere. There was a face he thought he could attach to it. Troubled, like his own. Tough and relentless.

Someone who might answer to the name Perk.

In the badlands of Helmand identity meant nothing. All armies had men, sometimes women, who roamed the dangerous terrain behind the front, spoke many languages, wore clothes that disguised who they truly were and where they came from.

The soldiers of Jægerkorpset weren't the only shadows around. There were spooks like the phantom Perk, seemingly beyond the usual command structure, allowed to move freely, unhindered by convention, by rules of battle and engagement, the inflexible norms of the military.

If his head would only work right he'd see this man and know. If . . .

Lights behind. A car drew up. Parked next to his own. Raben stayed low, let his eyes stray to the window.

A bearded man with a hard, unforgiving face. A black beret. Army fatigues.

Raben's mind reeled. He was back in Helmand in that instant, listening to the bombs and the screams, men and women, children too.

Gunfire and flames. Agony and blood.

All these memories raged through his head and he'd no idea what was real, what was imaginary.

The man got out. He was big and muscular. Walked to the library door. Pressed the bell. Shouted, 'Hello. Anyone at home?'

A loud, firm voice. That of an officer.

'Hi, Skåning,' said the man who came out to answer. 'I didn't know if you were coming or not.'

A brief exchange. Raben watched Skåning walk in then climbed out of the yellow Polo.

Felt the gun. Felt something else in his other pocket. Took it out. Jonas's toy, the one he'd left when he got angry at the beach. A toy soldier. Raised sword. Furious face.

Such a small thing. All that was left.

Raben looked at the library, walked to the door. Found it open.

Footsteps ahead inside. Heavy military boots on wooden tiles. He walked through into the main room. Lines of bookshelves, the smell of damp and old wood. A figure just visible in the low security lights, heading for the desks at the end.

He looked even bigger now. Broad and strong. A full head of hair that needed combing. Some heavy hardbacks under one arm. A paper cup in the other.

Torben Skåning placed the books on the last desk, turned on the light above it. Shuffled the titles, took a sip of his drink. Screwed up his lined, haggard features. Yawned.

Arms behind his head. A face like a church gargoyle. Ugly, exaggerated, unkind, with a full ginger beard and wolf-like white teeth.

When he opened his eyes Raben was there.

Buch made the mistake of going back to the Ministry by the public roads. Couldn't face the maze of corridors any more. The briefers had been at work. A mob of reporters and TV cameras hung around the door of the Ministry, under the gaze of the Børsen's dragons.

He strode through them without speaking, eyes ahead, trying to think about everything in his life that was not in Copenhagen. About Marie and the kids. The farms and the cooperative's finances.

It wasn't easy. Wasn't possible.

'Buch,' barked one of the TV hacks. 'The Defence Minister denies all your accusations. Will you apologize?'

On, past the security guards who brought the rabble to a halt at the front door, and let him walk upstairs to his office.

There he sat on the sofa and turned on the TV news. No surprise to see the lead item.

'After only one week in office, the Minister of Justice Thomas Buch faces an uncertain future after what observers describe as an unprecedented political blunder.' Buch sat down and listened. 'The People 's Party is likely to move a vote of no confidence in him tomorrow which, if passed, would seal his departure from government.'

Karina was on her phone again, whispering to someone. He didn't much care who.

'The party expects to press for a more draconian anti-terror package as a result . . .'

355

Plough marched in, turned on her.

'Have you managed to contact this journalist of yours?'

'She's not answering. I left a message.'

'Brilliant! You realize this was all a set-up. Rossing fed her to us and by God we took the bait.'

She didn't answer. Flemming Rossing came on the screen. All three of them watched.

The Minister of Defence was in ebullient mood, smiling, neatly dressed, grey suit, white shirt, scarlet tie.

'No one likes to be smeared,' he said to the interviewer. 'So I'm relieved to hear the Minister of Justice has been asked to withdraw these unfounded and appalling accusations.'

Buch turned off the set.

'This is all my fault. I don't want either of you to think you're to blame. Rossing was right. I pushed Monberg too far. I kept on at him without thinking for a moment about his health. Not for a second.'

'You had good reason to ask him those questions!'

It was Plough who spoke, which surprised Buch.

'I did, but . . .'

'As far as you knew Monberg was recovering,' Plough went on. 'There were serious issues he needed to address. They haven't gone away.'

'But it seems they have.'

'May I call you "Thomas"?' Plough shot a look at Karina. 'She does.'

'If you wish.'

The civil servant took a deep breath.

'You do not have the bearing of a minister. The panache. The guile. The sophistication.' Plough looked visibly upset. 'But by God you're the most honest and decent and open man I've seen hold office in Slotsholmen in all my years here and I will not let those . . .'

His arm shot out towards the Folketinget and the Christianborg Palace.

'Those . . . those *fuckers* do you down if I can help it. I swear to God I won't.'

Buch stared at him. Karina too. Plough was shaking with visible fury.

All three of them were grateful when there was a knock on the door and a pale and puzzled Erling Krabbe blundered in.

'I'm sorry,' Krabbe stuttered. 'Was I interrupting something?'

'Yes,' Buch said.

'Do you have a minute?'

Buch eyed Plough and Karina. They both retreated, still shocked.

He went to his desk, put his big weary feet on the polished walnut, leaned back and relaxed. Krabbe fell into the chair by his side, looked round at the portraits on the wall. A century and a half of Buch's predecessors.

'If you've come to gloat, Krabbe, you chose the wrong moment.'

'Do you mind if I smoke?'

'So long as you don't bore the arse off me with some stupid demands about the anti-terror package. You'll get what you want. And my head on a plate too. Don't expect me to butter you up . . .'

Krabbe pulled out a packet of cigarettes and lit one.

'I will get what I want,' he agreed. 'And I do want rid of you. I don't think you're fit for this job, Buch. You've proved it, haven't you?'

Buch smiled for one brief moment and said nothing.

'How sure are you about your accusations against Rossing?' Krabbe asked.

'Why? I don't see you losing any sleep over it.'

'Do you still believe what you said?'

'What is this?'

Krabbe scowled.

'I'm not an idiot. I don't like being fooled with any more than you do.' He took a drag on the cigarette, blew a cloud of smoke out into Buch's office. 'Rossing seemed remarkably well prepared for all this. Too much so. It makes me . . . uneasy.'

'Of course he was well prepared. He had a reason. I was tipped off about a fax that incriminated him. It looks like he set it up. I walked straight into his trap and he cut off my head in front of Grue Eriksen and the Security Committee. Satisfied? I was outsmarted, Krabbe. I was not proved wrong.'

'You told no one about this fax?'

'Of course not! What do you think? I phoned Rossing to warn him in advance?'

'So . . .' Krabbe was thinking, working something out for himself. 'The only people who knew were your own staff?'

'Krabbe! For heaven's sake, what is this?'

357

'Did you outline to the Prime Minister what evidence you were bringing to the meeting?'

'We had a short conversation. You don't think I'd park my tank on Rossing's lawn without giving Grue Eriksen a clue of what I was going to say, do you? He wants . . .' Buch stopped. 'He wants the truth as much as anyone.'

Krabbe drew on his cigarette, stayed silent.

'You're not suggesting . . .' Buch began.

The door opened. Plough came in.

'We've just had a call from the Prime Minister's office. He'd like to see you later. He suggests nine o'clock.'

'I should go,' Krabbe declared, getting to his feet. 'I won't disturb you any longer.'

He came and shook Buch's hand.

'Thank you for listening. I know you must hate me. I imagine that's inevitable. I'm sorry. If . . .' He looked around for somewhere to dump his cigarette. Plough found him a saucer. 'If you want to talk again do call.'

The two men watched him go.

Plough emptied the saucer into a waste bin.

'What was that about?'

'I honestly don't know,' Buch admitted.

Marriages didn't end with an argument or a dismissive wave of the hand. They were like bereavements. Traces lingered. Physical objects that carried with them memories. Barriers that needed to be removed so a life could move on.

Louise Raben was in her father's storeroom, sorting through the detritus of the life she would now abandon.

Practical material: box files of medical reports, guarantees for cars and washing machines, insurance certificates, receipts and invoices.

Personal things: letters in airmail envelopes from parts of the world she'd never see. Photographs that tugged at the heart. An ancient video camera, unused in years.

There was a cassette next to it. The date on it was a few months before Jonas was born.

The past would not be buried. What happened had happened. It would live with her and carry with it some love, if only in the shape of their son.

And she would not hide from it.

She put the cassette into the video and walked into her empty bedroom, hooked up the cables to the little TV opposite the bed.

Sat down, listened, watched and wondered.

It was Amager Strandpark on a hot summer's day. So unlike the cold, bleak place where she'd finished with him.

Jens, younger, clean shaven, happy and fit. Grinning into the lens saying, 'It's fantastic. Come on! Come on! Get wet, Louise. I dare you . . .'

She blinked. There was a tripod. Still in the storeroom. He liked to set the camera on it and let the film run.

A wavering shot of the beach then it was still. She could see the black shadow the stand made, like that of a stiff mechanical crane.

She was pregnant, wearing the gaudy flowered swimsuit he'd picked for her.

Squealing, 'No! Don't film me! I'm too fat. Too ugly.'

She looked so much younger. It seemed as if nothing could possibly go wrong with the world.

He came into the frame, wagging his finger as if cross.

'Nonsense, young woman,' he said in that firm sergeant's voice. 'You are beautiful, Louise Raben.' She laughed at him. 'You are so beautiful.'

He kissed her. She kissed him. Hands round his rough cheeks, fingers in his hair.

The older Louise watched and felt a tear emerge, roll slowly down her cheek.

She looked at the pile of letters. So many. When she thought about it she felt she could remember every last loving word he wrote, week in week out, however hard the fighting, however remote the place.

A noise behind. She quickly wiped her face with her sleeve. Christian Søgaard was marching in with a box in his arms. More paint. She'd asked for it. He wore combat fatigues. Had that confident officer's face. Nothing like Jens. Never would be.

'I'm sorry I'm late. They kept me at the Politigården all day. Idiots.'

When she wiped away the tears more came. Too many to hide.

'OK,' Søgaard said softly. 'Bad time. I'll come back later.'

'No. Stay.'

She froze the video. It captured the two of them in each other's arms, crackly lines running across the screen as if this love between them was already broken, gone for good.

Søgaard glanced at the picture, looked away.

She removed the cables and the cassette. Placed it in the box with the letters. Turned off the TV. Put the box on the floor then kicked it away with her foot.

'Is Jonas at home?' Søgaard asked.

'No. He's staying over with someone from kindergarten.'

A friend she wanted to say. Except it wasn't that. Jonas had none really.

She couldn't take her eyes off the dead TV.

Søgaard put down the paint, sat next to her, took her hand.

'Louise. You didn't let him down. You put up with more than most women would. You held out. You fought. I know. I watched.'

'Did you?'

'Every minute.'

He looked ready to leave. She didn't want that. There was a break to be made. A decision to be faced.

'What are you going to do now?' she asked.

Hands in his pockets. He looked embarrassed. Hopeful.

'Not much.'

She laughed.

'All alone?'

'As usual.'

'Me too,' she said. 'You want some wine?'

'Wine's good.'

'And a bonfire?'

He looked at her, baffled.

Louise Raben picked up the box with the letters, the video, all the memories.

'I want to burn some things. I want a witness.'

She paused, felt a decision closing in on her.

'I want it to be you.'

The library was at the end of a dark cul-de-sac. Barely a light inside. Lund made Strange turn off the blue light and the siren then stop the car some way from the entrance. There were two vehicles out the front, both old and battered.

360

She walked up, shone her torch through the windows of the first. An old Ford. Nothing. Then the second. In the footwell of the yellow Polo was a pile of manila folders. Army logo. Personnel records with the stamp of the Holmen office.

Lund felt her gun tight against her waist in the holster on her belt.

She called control, got them to run a check on the registration of the Ford. It took a minute.

'Skåning's car,' she said when the operator got back to her. She looked at Strange. 'Do we go in? Or do we wait?'

He laughed.

'You're asking me now?'

'Yes. I am.'

'You did bring your weapon?'

Lund slapped her jacket and nodded.

'Well then you stay back, let me handle the front. We'll take it from there.'

She still wasn't sure. The night Meyer got shot was rattling round in the back of her head.

'We could wait for backup—'

There was a sound from inside the library. A yell. A shout. A scream.

'No,' Strange said, and got out his Glock, checked it, went for the door.

Raben had Skåning strapped to a chair, shirt dragged down to show the officer's tattoo on his left shoulder. He'd punched the bearded man in the gut a couple of times, was getting madder with each failed blow.

This ugly face was familiar. The bent, exaggerated features, the low brow, the broken nose.

'Jesus . . .' Skåning muttered through bleeding lips. 'What do I have to do . . . ?'

'Shut up and listen!' Raben shouted, his voice echoing through the dark empty belly of the library. 'You said your name was Perk. You stole his identity. You were with us in that house . . .'

He whacked his fist into Skåning's face again.

'You had that dog tag. I saw it. I was there, remember? It was you.'

'No, Raben! You didn't—'

Another punch. Blood spattered the blue tattoo on Skåning's arm.

'Admit it, dammit!'

The man in the chair fell forward, retched blood and broken teeth onto his army trousers.

'I know it was you,' Raben snarled. 'We came to your rescue.' He brought up his knee, fetched it hard beneath Skåning's chin.

Another screech. Another howl.

'Leave me alone, for fuck's sake. I never fought in Helmand. I went crazy there. They discharged me.'

A hand whipped round his cheeks.

'I had a breakdown.'

'I saw you—'

'Yeah!' Skåning cried in a high, pained voice close to falsetto. 'And I saw you. On the plane home, with all the other wounded soldiers.'

Raben stood back, felt a sudden, agonizing pang of doubt. A flash of unwanted memory.

'What soldiers?'

'*Your* soldiers! The men who were with you. Grüner and those other guys. They told me what happened. They said you were under siege in a village for two days.'

'You were on that plane?'

'With all of you! I remember seeing you strapped to a stretcher. You were awake, just. But you couldn't talk. They didn't think you'd live. I tried to speak to you. The others told the same story. About some guy called Perk . . .'

One stride closer.

'No!' The bearded man looked terrified. 'No more!'

Raben sat on a chair. Looked at what he'd done. Put his head in his hands. Wanted to weep.

A sound at the back of the library. He turned, reached automatically for the gun in his pocket.

'Raben?' Lund said, walking through the cold, dark hall of the library, seeing two figures silhouetted in the dim light ahead. Two men on chairs, both head down. One strapped, breathing heavily. The other . . .

She wasn't sure.

'Raben!'

She had the gun on him. Held it the way they taught on the range.

362

'Just come with us. It's all going to be fine.'

Strange had disappeared the moment they came into the library, fallen into the shadows. She'd no idea where he was now.

'You think?' Raben asked, head cocked, beard rough and straggly, next to Skåning, wounded and bleeding.

'Just get your hands up and walk towards . . .'

He dashed for the stairs that rose at the end of the hall. Something in his right hand. A gun. No doubt about that.

'Raben!' Lund shouted again and followed him up the wooden staircase.

It was an old library. Had the smell, the feel of a church. At the far end, beyond the tall bookcases, was a circular stained-glass window. Blue with pale figures, scriveners at their desks.

Another shape there. A bedraggled man beneath its soft light, erect by the wall, holding a gun firmly beneath his chin, both hands to the grip.

She put her own weapon back in the holster. Walked on. He was rocking backwards and forwards, eyes closed.

'Don't be stupid,' Lund shouted. 'You've got a wife and a kid. You've got a future.'

A noise came from him and she wondered if it was wry laughter.

'I need your help. We know Perk's real. He's behind this. We know you got framed.'

Still the same motion, to and fro, the gun hard to his throat.

'You're so close to winning,' she said, taking another step closer. 'Do you give up now? You didn't in the army.'

No words.

'Put the gun down,' she ordered. 'Drop it to the floor. Kick it towards me.'

Eyes tight, face wracked with pain.

'You're the only one left! Think about it. If you're dead he's won. If you're dead Louise and Jonas . . .'

The weapon came away. Raben fell to his knees, stumbled forward gasping for breath.

'Come on, Raben. It's easy.'

He looked at her. Blank, exhausted eyes. A man at the end of the road.

'Put the gun down,' she repeated and he did, very slowly, then raised his hands.

A noise from the library below, big shoes on tiles. Raben stayed crouched, close to the weapon.

Lund glanced. Strange was there, staying close to the walls. Gun raised, ready.

'It's just my partner. You're safe with us. Walk away from the gun.'

Strange's footsteps got closer. His silhouette was emerging from the gloom.

Raben could see the shape of him now. His fingers crept back to the weapon, clutched it, raised it.

'Leave the gun alone!' Lund barked at him. 'Come over here.'

Three more strides and Strange emerged from the darkness, stood on the floor beneath them, Weaver stance, Glock ready, pointing.

'Put it on the floor,' he ordered.

She watched so closely. Couldn't work out why this was going wrong. Raben was getting to his feet, the weapon in his right hand again, a look of astonishment and horror on his haggard, bearded face.

'Perk . . .' he murmured.

'Put the gun down!' Strange shouted. 'Do as I say or I fire. Now!'

Lund wondered if she'd heard right.

'Do as he says,' she said. 'Please—'

'Perk, you bastard!' Jens Peter Raben roared, racing to the balustrade, weapon up, at the ready.

She screamed something and wasn't sure what. Saw the bright light burst out from beneath her, heard the single gunshot burst through the darkness, echoing off the old brick walls.

Jens Peter Raben flew back, thrown hard against the wooden shelving, tumbled to the ground in a sea of falling books.

She was there first, had a hand to his chest, feeling for breath.

Torsten Jarnvig couldn't get the conversation with Arild out of his head. Ryvangen was his dominion. What happened to the men there mattered. And now he felt he was in ignorance. Had been kept that way.

Søgaard's phone was off, the man was nowhere to be seen. Jarnvig pulled in Said Bilal and talked to him instead. Bilal was something of a mystery. A loner who didn't mix much, didn't drink, didn't do anything except his job.

Jarnvig had the papers from two years ago in front of him.

'Raben said the officer they were relieving was called Perk. Yet Søgaard had attended Perk's funeral three months earlier. Didn't he think this was strange? There's nothing in the report . . .'

'It couldn't be the same Perk,' Bilal replied. 'Why would Søgaard think anything of it?'

'Because he was in charge.' Jarnvig knew how he'd have approached such an investigation. There would have been questions. Plenty of them. 'What about the radio call Raben said he received? He said it was from a Danish unit in trouble.'

'We didn't pick up any radio call.'

'Would it have been in range from that village?'

'We're on a really tight schedule, sir. Could I suggest we postpone these questions—'

'Do you? Till when? For ever?'

'But there was no officer!' It was the loudest he'd ever heard Bilal speak. 'We had no troops in that area.'

'True,' Jarnvig. '*We* had no troops. It doesn't mean there wasn't someone there. Perk—'

'Perk was a myth. An excuse.'

'I want a transcript of all radio communications. Ours. Other Danish units. Any allied logs you can get hold of.'

'And our schedule, sir?' Bilal said wearily.

'Ask Army Operational Command to send it. I want everything on my desk tomorrow.'

The young officer said nothing, went for the door.

'Oh, and Bilal?'

He stopped.

'Mum's the word,' Jarnvig ordered. 'This is between the two of us. No one else.'

A corridor in the surgical wing of the Rigshospitalet. Raben on a gurney. Oxygen mask, lines in his arm. Blood. A surgeon dictating to a nurse as they raced him towards the theatre.

'Bullet wound, shoulder. If we're lucky it hasn't punctured the lung.'

Lund followed, saw the wounded man open his eyes.

'Has he eaten recently?' the surgeon asked.

'We don't know. He's been sleeping rough.'

The surgeon wore a green mob cap, mask pulled down over his chin.

'He's lost a lot of blood. Do you know if he's allergic to any drugs?'

'We've sent through his medical records,' Lund said. 'The army had them on file.' She hesitated. 'He was badly wounded in Afghanistan two years ago.'

'Well he's badly wounded now,' the man said in a curt, low voice. Then louder, 'Get me a suction drain! Let's get on with this!'

The theatre doors opened. One of the nurses put a hand to Lund's chest.

'What do you think you're doing? You can't come in here.'

She stood outside, watched the door close, wished she could still the furious thoughts in her head.

Strange was a few steps behind, coming off the phone.

'We've brought Skåning in for questioning,' he said. 'They want to know whether to start or wait for us.'

Her wrist was still bandaged from the night before. Her head was starting to hurt. She couldn't think straight and answer his question.

'Is he going to be all right?' Strange asked.

'They didn't say. He seemed pretty bad.'

'I had to shoot. You saw that, didn't you? He was waving that gun about. Looking crazy.'

She flexed her fingers. They still hurt from the fall.

'Why the hell didn't he drop it?' Strange went on. 'If he'd done that we wouldn't be here.'

'He seemed scared, didn't he?'

Strange blinked.

'Of what?'

'I don't know. He did put the gun down. Then he saw you approaching. And . . .' She watched him closely. 'He seemed to think you were Perk.'

Ulrik Strange didn't seem the same man at that moment. He looked angry, unpredictable.

'Oh for God's sake . . .' he muttered.

A voice from behind.

'Where is he?'

Brix in a damp raincoat. Unhappy.

'In theatre,' Lund said.

'What the hell happened?'

The three of them began to walk down the corridor, towards the waiting room. Strange first, silent and angry.

'He took Skåning hostage,' Lund said. 'Beat him up. He had a gun. He took off and wouldn't put down his weapon.'

'Who shot him?'

'I did.' Strange shrugged. 'I aimed for his arm as best I could. It was dark. He was upstairs.' A glance at her. 'So was Lund. I was worried.'

'I want armed guards on the room. No one has access to him unless they come through us.' He stared at Strange. 'Well?'

'OK.'

He walked off to make the calls.

'Is he going to pull through?' Brix asked.

'Maybe.'

'Why the hell didn't he put the gun down?'

A couple of nurses raced down the corridor pushing some equipment into the theatre. Strange was gone through the double doors. She was glad of that.

'I don't know,' she said.

It had been so long she'd almost forgotten what it was like to have a man, to take him to bed, to get so close she could taste his sweat and feel his strength inside. Christian Søgaard lay back grunting, eyes closed, face for once suffused with pleasure. Louise was above him, back arched, thrusting, not too quickly, trying to make it last.

To make him happy the way she once did for Jens. He liked it this way too. Liked to give over some of his power, if only for a short time and then life could go back to normal.

But Søgaard wasn't Jens and it was more curiosity that drove her. Curiosity about herself.

Another man, the first in thirteen years.

How did she feel? Elated? Ashamed? Or just plain dead?

He was getting there. She could sense it, hear it. And she felt nothing at all, but mirrored his growing rhythmic grunts and cries anyway because that was what you did.

Too long? Too short?

She didn't know. Didn't care. With Jens there was something else.

Beyond the physical. A bond between them, a mutual shared mystery that bore the name of love. With Søgaard . . . nothing except his desperate need to have her. Which, like the good army woman she was supposed to be, she'd acknowledged, acceded to. Taken him to her lonely bed and given him what he wanted.

He moaned. He thrust at her. A damp warm feeling.

Louise Raben rolled off him, sweating, head spinning, wondering where the pleasure was and if it turned up whether it would outweigh the pain.

She didn't feel guilty. Jens had seen to that. But she did feel bad, and that somehow was worse.

Sweating, gasping, his arm around her, clinging to his new possession, Christian Søgaard lay on her crumpled bed sheets, eyes closed, content.

This was one more of his battles, she thought. Another victory. Another piece of the world claimed.

Neither of them spoke. It seemed unnecessary. As she rolled from him there was a rap on the door. Loud and urgent.

She dragged on her nightgown, the one she used to go to Jonas when he had the terrors, went to answer it.

Her father was there. He could see inside she was sure. At that moment though he didn't seem to care.

'Something's happened,' he said in a nervous, worried voice. 'The police called. I . . .'

'What?'

'You need to go to the hospital now.'

A sound behind her. Søgaard coming towards them. She moved the door to block the sight of him. A big man, with the officers' tattoo on his arm.

'What is it?' she asked.

'Jens has been shot, Louise.' Her father cast a glance at the tall figure in her room. She couldn't read it. 'They need you there now.'

Thomas Buch felt hungry. He needed a drink. There was a late-night reception at the South Korean Embassy that evening. Music, art and food. He loved kimchi even if it did smell foul.

There was just the meeting with the Prime Minister to get out of the way first.

Grue Eriksen was at his desk going through some papers. He didn't look up as Buch marched in and apologized for being late.

'There are developments. The soldier we were searching for has been shot.'

'I know.' Grue Eriksen smiled at him. 'Would you like a drink?'

'No, thank you. I'm anxious to find Rossing so we can talk things over.'

'Talk about what?'

'I realize I was a bit rash in what I said. I'm new to government . . . I'm sorry about the misunderstanding. I'll offer him my apologies.'

Grue Eriksen smiled and shook his head.

'I hope we can continue our working relationship,' Buch added. 'And Krabbe too. The anti-terror package has put us under pressure. But I'm determined . . .' He rapped the desk with his knuckles. 'Absolutely determined to put this right.'

'Very noble.'

'If I can just have a talk with Rossing. I'm sure—'

'Thomas. You've been a minister for six days. God created the world in just one more. And you've destroyed everything.'

Buch nodded, listened.

'I was never made for the spotlight, Prime Minister. Never sought it.'

'All these accusations have left you damaged,' Grue Eriksen continued. 'I listened to you. I tried to believe a little of the fantasies you were spinning. But honestly. They're incredible. You've picked up a tiny thread of rumour and woven it into the most ridiculous of fairy tales.'

Grue Eriksen pushed a piece of paper across the desk.

'You have to resign. There's no alternative.'

'But I'm not ready to resign,' Buch said as if the idea were ridiculous. 'There are far too many loose ends for one thing. I defy anyone else to pick them up. How did Rossing know I'd mention that fax?'

'The fax?'

Buch laughed. Started to get mad.

'The fax I briefed you on! About the medical report and the surplus hand.'

'Don't shout.'

'Don't shout?' Buch roared. 'How else do you get someone to listen to you in this damned place? It was so convenient Rossing knew, wasn't it? And I didn't tell him. So who did?'

The Prime Minister seemed more amused by his anger than offended.

'You want me to call Rossing over here? Would that make you happy? If I indulge you one last time?'

Buch hesitated.

'No,' he murmured.

He looked at the sheet of paper in front of him. Times for meetings. Everything set out.

'This is your final agenda,' Grue Eriksen said. 'Tomorrow we pass the anti-terror package. With Krabbe's amendments. Then you call a press conference to announce your resignation. Tell them . . .' He waved a dismissive hand. 'Say you want to spend more time with your family. No need to be original.'

Buch glared at him.

'Don't worry, Thomas. We've short memories around here. In a few years you can come back. Not to justice, of course. I'm not sure you have the temperament—'

'Did you pick me because you thought I'd be useless?' Buch asked straight out. 'Amenable. Pliable. Someone like Monberg who'd do as he's told?'

The Prime Minister laughed.

'I picked you because I liked you. I still do. Give it time. You'll see.' He pointed to the door. 'But right now your career's over. Go home and think of what you'll say.'

Grue Eriksen saw him out.

Home.

That was in Jutland, which seemed a million miles away. The invitation to the embassy was in Buch's pocket. Music. Art. Beer and rice wine.

And kimchi.

Plough and Karina were waiting on a bench seat downstairs. Something on their long faces told him they knew his fate already.

'Thomas . . .' Karina began.

'I need some time to myself,' Buch said quickly.

Then left the Christianborg Palace, walked out into the chill, open space of Slotsholmen, thinking of the places he used to linger back before he became a minister. When he was free.

Lund waited as close to the operating theatre as the hospital staff would allow. Strange went back to the Politigården to interview the badly beaten Torben Skåning. Brix stayed to talk to the medical staff.

After an hour Strange called.

'This doesn't work. Skåning's got an alibi. He had a nervous breakdown in Afghanistan. He flew home with Raben and the wounded soldiers. He says Raben recognized him from the flight but didn't remember it.'

'Check that out. I'm coming in.'

She was about to leave when the double doors opened and Louise Raben walked through, pale-faced and anxious.

'What happened?' she demanded.

'He just came out of surgery. You need to talk to the doctors.'

'I asked what happened!'

'He took a soldier hostage. Your husband had a gun. He tried to escape. Then . . .'

Lund didn't want this conversation. She tried to get past the woman. It wasn't possible.

'Why the hell did you have to shoot him?'

She tried to recall what had happened, to get it clear in her own head. It wasn't easy.

'He had a gun. It was dark. He looked crazy. I'm sorry—'

'Jens isn't like that.'

'You weren't there. He put the gun to his chin. We thought he was going to take his own life. Then he changed his mind . . .' She shrugged. 'For some reason. He wouldn't put down the weapon. We didn't know . . .'

'That isn't Jens . . .'

'But it was,' Lund insisted. She pulled out a plastic evidence bag. 'He had these with him. We don't need them.'

A pair of gloves. A toy soldier, sword raised. The woman took them, stared at the little figure.

Brix was at the end of the corridor.

'Excuse me,' Lund said and went to see him.

'Any news from Strange?' he asked.

'They questioned Skåning.'

'I know. Skåning's alibi checks out.'

'It's got to be him. We've been through all the other officers on Ægir. The rest of them are clean.'

'If he was from Ægir . . .'

'If he wasn't God knows where we start. What did the doctor say?'

'Raben's stable. We can interview him tomorrow.'

Brix took a deep breath, looked around, made sure they were on their own.

'We've got a problem. Raben was talking before he went under. He claimed the policeman who shot him was Perk. Strange.'

Lund kept quiet.

'The surgeon said he was delirious,' Brix went on. 'But we can't ignore that. It's got to go on file. There'll be an inquiry into the shooting. You know what they're like, don't you?'

Oh yes, she thought.

'I need to hear this from you, Lund. Is your report accurate?'

'Of course.'

He watched her, interested. Brix didn't like swift and easy answers.

'What exactly did the surgeon say?' she asked.

Brix waited. He knew.

'OK. Something wasn't right,' she admitted. 'When Raben saw Strange he called him out as Perk. I heard that. I thought—'

'You're sure of that?'

'He's crazy, isn't he? A couple of minutes before he'd been beating the life out of Skåning thinking he was Perk. Then he had a gun to his own throat. You can't believe—'

'It has to go on the record. It has to be in the report.'

'Yes! Yes! I know. Raben was in a state. He didn't know what he was doing. I need to get back to the Politigården.'

His hand caught her arm as she tried to leave.

'Listen for once, will you? When we took on Strange a year ago I read his CV. He was in the army for a long time.'

'Yes! I know. He told me. At Vordingborg. He had back trouble. He was a squaddie. Hardly a suspect.'

Brix scowled.

'He wasn't a squaddie at Vordingborg. He was Jægerkorpset. An officer. He came over to us on a transfer programme. He's got weapons training. Lots of . . . skills we probably don't know about.'

'No . . .'

A figure striding down the corridor towards them.

Strange came and stood next to Brix, looked at both of them.

'I thought I'd come and fetch you,' he said. Hands in pockets, mild face miserable and tense. 'I never shot anyone before. How is he?'

'He'll live,' Brix said. 'We need to talk.'

Back in the Politigården. Strange in a chair on his own. Lund, arms folded, next to Brix in his office.

'How long did you serve with the special forces people?' Brix asked.

Strange took a deep breath, looked at both of them.

'Is this serious? Come on . . .'

Brix stared at him.

'Serious? What do you think? You shot a man. He identified you as Perk. Every firearms incident gets an inquiry. In circumstances like these . . . We have to know where we stand.'

'This is crazy,' Strange complained. 'I was in the army. They asked me if I wanted to serve with Jægerkorpset for a while.'

'Why did you lie to me?' Lund asked.

'Because we're not supposed to say! Look. I served. I got sick of it. I wasn't tough enough for that shit frankly. So I quit and applied for the Police Academy.'

'But you went back?' Brix said.

'Yeah. After 9/11 they came and said they needed people. I had a boring job in the drugs squad. They seemed desperate. So I gave it another go.'

He frowned.

'Great idea. Cost me my marriage. I finally quit eighteen months ago and came here.'

He looked around the place.

'I think this suits me better. Maybe you two don't agree . . .'

Lund asked, 'Were you in Afghanistan?'

It took a while for him to answer.

'These things are supposed to be classified,' Strange said. 'But yes. Three times. Not with Jægerkorpset. And I wasn't with Ægir either. I was demobilized six months before they left.'

He leaned forward, stared at both of them.

'You're clear on that? I wasn't there when any of this happened. I never met Jens Peter Raben till tonight. I mean . . .' He tried to laugh. 'Don't you think I'd have told you?'

'You could have said something,' she threw at him.

'What? I hated those last few years. It destroyed things . . . things that mattered to me. I just want to forget about the whole damn business.'

'You could have said.'

It was Brix this time.

Strange threw back his head and looked ready to howl.

'My life came apart while I was pissing around playing boy soldiers out there. My marriage. My kids. I lost them all. It's taken me a long time to get back on my feet. I like it here.'

'Very good,' Brix said and picked up his notebook. 'According to Skåning, Raben seemed interested in a tattoo. A logo with a message. *Ingenio et Armis*. With wisdom and weapons.'

'We're wasting time,' Strange sighed. 'Let's talk to Skåning some more. He's got a tale to tell—'

'He's not the only one,' Brix cut in. 'We sent him home. He's got an alibi remember?'

'Then there's something we're missing. Something we've overlooked.'

Brix pointed.

'Take off your shirt. Let's get it over with.'

Strange shook his head. Removed his black sweater. Pulled up the arm of the T-shirt beneath.

The tattoo was there. A red-handled sword stabbing through a crest. The motto *Ingenio et Armis* in blue lettering.

Lund stared at him. Brix made a note.

'Before you cuff me,' Strange said, 'you ought to check how many officers have got that tattoo. Skåning has it. I'd place a good bet you'll find it on Søgaard too. We all did. It was part of the induction, part of—'

'I need your gun,' Brix ordered, holding out his hand. 'And your ID. We're going to hand you over to the inquiry team. After that you'll go home and stay there until this is cleared up.'

Ten minutes later the inquiry team had Strange in a room. Brix was looking through the glass, Lund and Madsen by his side.

'This is where we are,' he told the young detective. 'I'm suspending

Strange until we get to the bottom of this. You're taking over his assignment. You report to Lund and me.'

'We need to talk to the army,' Lund said. 'Get a list of officers who worked for special forces in Afghanistan two years ago.'

'Good luck,' Madsen said. 'My cousin was with the spooky people for a while. They won't tell us a thing. Those guys barely talk to each other.'

Madsen nodded at the glass.

'If Strange was one of them he won't give you the time of day. Not that you can trust anyway. It's part of the code.'

'Ask for it,' Brix ordered. 'If they object let me know.'

'If it was Strange I'd have known,' Lund said, watching him, arms folded, waiting patiently.

Brix shook his head.

'The case is connected to the army. He should have told us. You know that.'

That was too easy, she thought.

'We didn't know that to begin with, did we? It was all about terrorists.'

'When he shot Raben . . . was there really no alternative?'

'It was dark. Raben was behaving unpredictably. He had a weapon.'

Brix stared at her.

'Were you with him when those people died?'

'Yes. I mean . . .'

She'd been trying to think this through.

Myg Poulsen and Grüner were dead when they turned up. She didn't know what Strange was doing in the hours before they were murdered. And Helsingør . . . He could have got to Torpe's church in Vesterbro before she did, with the traffic and her indecision along the way.

Brix turned to Madsen and said, 'Look into it. Until I see something that says otherwise he's a suspect. Lund?'

She was lost somewhere, trying to fit together the pieces of an impossible jigsaw.

'Lund!'

He took her arm.

'Either Raben's crazy or Strange's lying. I'd rather believe the former. But until we know, we do this by the book.'

*

Louise Raben sat in the hospital corridor watching the doctors and nurses come and go. There were two uniformed cops outside her husband's room. They didn't want to talk which was fine by her.

An awkward, hurtful memory stuck in her head like grit under an eyelid. Christian Søgaard grunting and panting beneath her. She didn't feel ashamed. Didn't even feel guilty. Just stupid. Boredom and an infantile curiosity had tempted her to take him to her bed. Not even a mindless desire.

It was Jens she wanted really. Had all along. The idiotic adventure with Søgaard was her way of punishing him. Ridiculous. Pointless.

No one had spoken to her for the best part of an hour. She was beginning to doze off when a young woman doctor came up, stethoscope round her neck, green surgical gown beneath a white coat, and tapped her shoulder.

'How is he?' Louise asked, getting up.

'Drowsy. He'll probably sleep until tomorrow.' She hesitated. 'But we're pretty sure he's going to be all right. He's healthy. He's young.' She smiled. 'He's lucky.'

'No he isn't. Not at all.'

'He was lucky tonight. You can go and see him if you want.'

It felt wrong. After Søgaard . . .

'I can come back tomorrow. Will someone look after his things?'

'He might wake up,' the woman said in a hard, cold voice. 'It's important he feels there's someone there. Someone who cares for him.'

She had very large, keen eyes. Like the policewoman, Lund.

'I can show you the way,' the doctor said and it wasn't an offer to be refused.

Five minutes later she was alone with him in the private room. Machines on stands. Monitors. Louise Raben was a nurse. She could read these things, understand the clipboard at the foot of the bed. He was fortunate really. It was much worse two years before when he came back from Helmand.

He lay half beneath the sheets in white hospital pyjamas, chest open, shaved in places for the sensors. Lines and drains and monitors. Cannulas in his arms and hands and neck.

Unconscious on the single hospital bed, crooked at a slight angle, he looked at peace for once. They'd cleaned him up. Maybe even trimmed his beard. Like this he was the man she remembered. The one she'd fallen for so deeply.

She looked at him and said, in a low, certain voice, 'The doctor told me I should talk to you.' Her hands fidgeted. She felt nervous and, finally, guilty. 'And I don't know what to say.'

The image of Søgaard refused to leave her head. It shouldn't, she thought. That vile picture was there to remind her. To guide her towards a place she needed to find.

'I saw an old video this evening,' she said, watching the lines on the monitor, listening to the machines click and whirr. 'You and me at the beach, just before Jonas was born. Remember?'

Why ask a sleeping man? She'd no idea. The video was molten plastic and burned tape in an old dustbin in the garden, alongside the ashes of their letters. Gone for ever. Except in her head . . .

'I was fat and ugly and we couldn't think of a name for him. You remember that?' She laughed, couldn't help it. 'We wrote such a long list and they all seemed wrong.' Her voice fell to a whisper. 'In the end you wanted to go for a swim.'

This memory wasn't on the video. It went deeper than that. Was still real.

'But I didn't because I thought I looked like a whale.' She closed her eyes, felt the tears start. 'And you took me in your arms. You carried me, big fat me, all the way to the sea. You kissed me.' Another quiet moment of laughter. 'Then you said you knew what his name should be. Jonas. Because Jonas was inside the whale. And then set free . . .'

Alone but not alone, she found the tears running down her cheeks.

'What a piece of shit I am,' Louise Raben whispered.

Then stood up. Touched his still fingers. They were warm. Life there. Hope there. Love still. He'd never lost that. Never would and now she knew.

Took them away. Wondered. Looked at the man in the bed, eyes closed, shallow breathing. Hurt and damaged by so many things. And now she was among them.

Then she touched his fingers again and knew she wasn't mistaken. There was the faintest of responses. A flicker of movement as she took his hand in hers.

'I'm so sorry, Jens,' she murmured, her voice breaking, then leaned over him, kissed his rough cheek, placed her head next to his on the soft hospital pillow.

There was only one place to be and it wasn't with Christian Søgaard. This difficult, damaged man was all she wanted, with his faults, his troubles, his pain.

Her cheek brushed his rough beard. Her fingers tightened on his. Somewhere outside a siren sounded. Through the glass door she could see the tall cops in their blue uniforms.

Here, at least, he was safe.

Carsten Plough and Karina Jørgensen were back in the Ministry of Justice, desperately trying to track down Buch. His mobile was turned off. He'd gone walkabout after leaving the Christianborg Palace. Even the hot-dog stand hadn't seen him.

The phones kept ringing constantly, media mainly, screeching for a statement.

'We've no comment,' Karina told the latest, the political editor of one of the dailies. 'There's nothing to say. Nothing at all . . .'

She put down the phone, looked at Plough.

'The driver's not seen him. He's been gone for an hour now. How can he do this to us?'

She tried his mobile again.

'It's still on voicemail. I called his wife. She's not heard from him either.'

'The rumours are flying!' Plough said anxiously.

'Forget the rumours. Let's hear it from Buch directly, shall we? Maybe he tracked down Connie Vemmer and had a word with her.'

'Maybe, maybe, maybe,' Plough grumbled. He phoned security. 'Hello? Plough here. Our minister's missing. I want you to find him.'

Nothing.

'Is there a committee meeting or something?' Karina asked. 'Does he have any invitations?'

Plough raised a finger. They walked to Buch's desk, found the diary.

It was scribbled in there for the evening. The address of the South Korean Embassy. And a single word, seemingly written with enthusiasm.

Kimchi!

She called, talked to someone there.

'Oh crap,' Karina muttered as she came off the phone.

Kimchi.

There was lots of it. And skewers of beef. And things he didn't recognize. Beer too. Rice wine. Whisky. Thomas Buch had his jacket off, his tie halfway down his neck. Sat on the floor like a fat Buddha, sweating heavily, only half-listening to a woman in traditional costume play some kind of oriental harp.

He'd no idea whether the semicircle of people in front of him understood a word of what he was saying. A Chinese woman. A kindly but puzzled-looking young black man who wore some kind of African dress. A Korean in a grey suit and some others who didn't seem happy at all.

'I was so . . . so very angry,' he went on in a slow, slurred tone. 'Because I thought there was an extra hand in the coffin. And it was proof. But . . .' Buch's voice rose, as if volume might bring sense to what he was saying. 'But it wasn't an extra hand, you see. Oh, no. There was another medical report.' His fingers gestured through the air, then the right one found his strong beer. A swig of it. 'And it was the hand of the suicide bomber.'

He raised his glass.

'What happened was . . .' He puffed up his cheeks. Said very loudly, 'Boosh!'

Buch nodded.

'Boosh. And there it was.'

He stopped. There was movement at the back of the room. Someone there, a very serious-looking individual who had the appearance of security, had been eyeing him for a while. A blonde woman marched in. Karina. Then the tall figure of Carsten Plough.

'Hello! Hello!' Buch called. 'Come, come! Have beer. Try kimchi!'

The two approached.

'I was telling my new friends about the hand.' His fat, bearded cheeks puffed up again. 'Boosh!'

He waved at the semicircle of silent people on chairs in front of him.

'These are my colleagues. Plough and Karina. Kimchi!'

Plough smiled and gestured with his hand, fingers waving towards himself.

'What?' Buch asked.

'Come, Thomas,' Karina said. 'Time to go home.'

Buch struggled to his feet, smiled, brushed himself down.

'One more beer and a bit of kimchi,' he said and struggled to the buffet.

The two of them came over.

'We need to go back to Connie Vemmer,' she said.

'Kimchi,' Buch replied, forcing a small plate of fermented cabbage on her.

'I don't want kimchi!' she said very loudly. 'Rossing set you up, remember?'

'Oh Karina,' he moaned. 'I'm not cut out for all this intrigue. Haven't you noticed?'

'This isn't finished,' Plough said.

'But it is. And so am I,' Buch whined.

'Thomas!' Karina's voice was hectoring and insistent. 'They've got Raben in custody. He's been shot but he'll live. We can look into this—'

'No!' Buch cried. 'I'm resigning tomorrow. For God's sake let me go quietly, will you?'

Carsten Plough made him sit, then took the chair next to him. Tidied Buch's tie. Stared into his sweating face.

'Give up? Give up?' he said in a low and caustic voice. 'How can you possibly say that after all we've done?'

'Something's amiss,' Karina added. 'You know it.'

Plough picked Buch's jacket off the floor and returned with it.

'We're in this together, Thomas. We have to keep calm. Behave responsibly . . .'

Buch shook his big head, got to his feet, angry all of a sudden.

'Stop it. The truth is we weren't up to it. We were out of our depth—'

'No,' Plough interrupted. 'That's not justified at all. Let's go back to the office and discuss this.'

'Fuck the office!' Buch roared. 'Fuck Slotsholmen. Twice over.'

The room fell into silence.

'The truth is you'd no idea what Monberg was up to! He was a loose cannon. And you . . .'

His finger jabbed at her.

'You even slept with the man. Bloody hell!'

Buch blinked, wondered why he'd said such a stupid thing.

'Oh don't leave,' Buch cried. 'I apologize. Come here, won't you? Please . . .'

He fell back into the chair, grabbed for the glass. Wondered if he could manage more kimchi.

The one who looked like a security guard came up. He had a coat in his hand. Buch realized it was his.

It was cold outside and Buch wasn't exactly sure where he was.

Then remembered something. Erling Krabbe. He lived nearby.

In a nearby cafe he drank two large cups of espresso. Close to midnight he went to Krabbe's house and let his finger rest on the doorbell.

It took a while but eventually he heard a familiar voice cry, 'All right! I'm coming, dammit!'

'Hello?' Buch yelled, peering through the spyglass.

Eventually he saw an eye on the other side.

'What in God's name are you doing here?'

'We've got to talk, Krabbe. Honestly. It's important.'

Buch paused.

'Also . . . I need to use the toilet.'

Krabbe let him in, showed him the bathroom, then took him into a smart modern kitchen, gave him a glass of milk, put out some food. Cheese and biscuits.

'Dig in!' he said. 'You look as if you need it.'

Buch was too drunk to be sure but a part of him thought Erling Krabbe was mildly amused by his condition, and not in a cruel way either.

There were photos on the fridge. An attractive Asian woman with a couple of kids. Thai maybe.

Glass of milk in hand, Buch stared at them.

'We talked about that too. Me and my wife.'

'Talked about what?' Krabbe asked, neatly dividing up some coffee cake.

'Getting an au pair.'

'That's my wife,' Krabbe told him.

Buch gulped at the milk. Wondered when he'd be able to open his mouth without saying something deeply stupid.

He sat down.

'May I ask,' Krabbe said, 'what exactly you're doing here?'

Buch looked at him and ate some cheese.

'I'm sorry if I left you confused,' Krabbe added.

He was in a T-shirt and pyjama bottoms and wore a heavy pair of glasses. Must use contacts during the day, Buch guessed. He was different like this. Less robotic, more human. Krabbe munched on a piece of cucumber and got himself some carrot juice.

Buch stared at the glass of orange liquid as if it were poison.

'I wondered why you came to see me,' he said. 'That's all.'

'It was nothing.'

'Didn't look like nothing.'

'Buch. I'm sorry. I didn't mean any of this personally—'

'Oh no! Listen, Krabbe. I had the Prime Minister's confidence. Then you march in there.' He raised a fat forefinger. 'I demand to know what you talked about. I demand it. I'm still a government minister, you know. Maybe not for much longer . . .'

Krabbe sipped at his carrot juice.

'After that stunt of yours at the press conference I was furious. All the work with Monberg on the anti-terror package was in ruins.'

Buch kept picking at the food, listening.

'Because of you . . .' Krabbe shook his head as if this were somehow hard to believe. 'I had to call a meeting of the executive committee.'

'Big deal.'

'It might have been. But on the way there I got a call from Grue Eriksen's office. They said the whole thing had been investigated and Rossing was in the clear. That was it. You were going to be hung out to dry and the package was up for the vote tomorrow.'

'Wait, wait.' Buch was struggling to work this out. 'You're saying they told you that before I'd even gone in front of the Security Committee?'

'Exactly. I couldn't understand that either. But I think I get the picture now.'

'Going to share this revelation with me?'

Krabbe rolled his eyes.

'What does it matter if Grue Eriksen had prior knowledge? They knew your accusations were false. They were just calling me in advance to make sure I didn't stir things up. They'd lost confidence in you.'

Buch raised his glass of milk in a silent toast.

'So Rossing made a fool of you. It doesn't mean Grue Eriksen was a party to the whole thing, does it? Surely he's above this kind of back-stabbing.'

'Krabbe,' Buch said, aware his mind was starting to clear. 'This isn't about a political row in Slotsholmen. It's to do with murder. Conspiracy. Maybe an army atrocity—'

'I spoke to the Prime Minister this evening. I'm fine on this. We vote tomorrow and put it all behind us. I'm sorry, Buch, but I'm glad he gave you the push. You're not up to the job.'

He pointed to the clock on the wall. Half past midnight.

'Shall I call you a taxi?'

'Are you happy now?' Buch asked.

'I've got what I wanted.'

Buch got up, looked at the photos on the fridge. The pretty Asian woman. The kids.

'Funny, isn't it?' he said. 'We're different people when we step outside that place. When you throw all those fixed positions to one side and talk about things without all that . . . crap around.'

'A taxi,' Krabbe repeated.

'Are you happy?' Thomas Buch asked again. 'Truly? Honestly?'

Lund got home at close to one in the morning, a pizza going cold in her hands. Her head was hurting again. The wound above her eyebrow itched. Walking up the stairs on the way into Vibeke's apartment her phone rang. Madsen with the latest on Strange.

'We need to know exactly when he came out of the army,' she said, listening to his excuses. 'He claims it was six months before Raben's squad got hit.'

'They won't give us that information, Lund. Once it's about some-one who's been in special forces—'

'Tell them we've got to have it! This is a murder inquiry.'

'They're sending some top brass guy to see us tomorrow morning. General Arild.'

'They can send who they like. We still want that information. And Strange's CV. All the personnel information we got when he trans-ferred to the police. Send me that too, will you?'

She put the pizza on the step and hunted for the door keys in her bag.

'Lund,' a low, miserable voice said out of the darkness near the lift.

She jumped as Strange walked out of the gloom.

'How the hell did you get in here?'

'I waited till someone turned up and said I wanted to see your mother. I'm not breaking in, for God's sake. This is for you . . .'

He had a plastic wallet in his hands.

'You shouldn't be here. What's that?'

'Reports on the soldiers who died on Raben's mission. I left them in the car. You should have them now you're taking over.'

'Thanks,' she said and took them.

He'd been home and changed. Nice brown coat, clean shirt, scarf. He didn't look worried at all. Just pissed off.

'You know you shouldn't be here . . .'

'I don't care what Brix thinks.'

'Jesus, Strange. We can't talk about any of this. You're suspended. There's an inquiry—'

'What do you think? That's all I want to know. What do you believe?'

She looked at him, wished she didn't have to face this.

'You should have told me. I had the right to know.'

He nodded, as if he took the point.

'Why? Did you tell me about every last thing in your life? About the Swede you were going to live with? About the cop who got shot?'

'It's not the same . . .'

She tried to push past. He took hold of her. Wouldn't let go.

'The guys in the Politigården said you went nuts and that's why Jan Meyer wound up in a wheelchair.'

'Did they?'

'I told them to shut up. I stood by you, all the time, and you didn't say a damned word. Offer me a thing either.'

The communal light was on a timer. It flicked off at that moment. Just as Ulrik Strange's face came close to hers.

Lund punched the switch and got the light back on.

He waited for an answer. When he didn't get one he swore in a whisper and set off down the stairs. Turned after a couple of steps.

'I told my kids about you,' Strange said. 'They were asking why I looked so happy. I said . . .'

She wanted to yell and scream at him but didn't.

384

'I told them I'd met someone at work. And maybe they'd meet her too one day.'

'Stop it,' Lund whispered.

So quietly he didn't hear.

'Maybe,' Strange said and then was gone.

Nine

Monday 21st November

9.15 a.m.   General Arild was a cocky, ginger-haired man who looked Brix and Lund and Madsen in the eye the moment they called him into an interview room. Early fifties, Lund thought. Short but muscular, confident as he stood by the window, laughing at the conversation. She could imagine him as a soldier in the field, looking for the nearest fight.

'Cooperation?' Arild asked when Lund questioned the responses she'd been getting from the military. 'You think we haven't helped you already? You've been all over Ryvangen. Interrogating our officers while they prepare for the next tour. Goodness . . .'

He wore an immaculate blue uniform covered with ribbons and medals.

'Did you have special forces operatives in the area in question, two years ago?' Lund asked.

Brix stood by the filing cabinets, listening.

'I wouldn't normally answer a question like this,' Arild said. 'But since you seem to think it so important, yes, we had officers there.'

'While Team Ægir was in place?'

'Didn't I just answer that?'

'And Ulrik Strange was demobilized six months before this incident in Helmand?'

'Too far,' Arild replied. 'You know I can't discuss names.'

'I want a list of who was there!' Lund insisted.

He laughed at her.

'You don't want much, do you? Do you understand the kind of people we're talking about? The work they do?'

'Not really,' Lund replied.

Arild's confident, smiling face fell.

'We're fighting animals who'll decapitate their own daughters for wearing the wrong clothes. Hang a man in the street for listening to the radio. Geneva's a long way from Helmand. They know it. We do too.'

He didn't like women, Lund thought. Except in their place.

'I want that information, General.'

'I'm not at liberty to disclose anything about individual officers. What I will say is this. No one from Jægerkorpset or any other special forces unit was involved in that particular incident. It happened without our involvement and our knowledge.'

A knock on the door. Someone asking for Brix. He left the room.

Arild came a step closer.

'I'm trying to help you,' he said. 'We don't go around murdering innocent civilians. Here or in Afghanistan. Now . . .' He picked up his cap. 'You must excuse me.'

'These officers were deployed too,' she said, passing him the latest list of soldiers attached to Ægir from other regiments. 'I want what you have on them. They're not special forces. You've no reason to object—'

'The ramblings of a traumatized soldier do not merit this nonsense,' Arild barked, close to losing his temper. 'And how is it Jens Peter Raben could elude PET so easily? Tell me that. I thought you people had him under surveillance . . . You've no idea what you're getting into, woman. Any more questions before I leave?'

She wanted to ask if he dyed his hair but didn't. Instead she folded her arms, gave him a jaded look and said, 'If you stand in my way I'll go public. You'll have every hack and TV crew in Denmark banging on your door demanding answers. Your choice.'

He didn't like that.

Brix came back. Arild marched with him to the black marble corridor outside.

'What information we can provide,' Arild said very deliberately to Brix alone, 'I will send you. You'll hear from my office this afternoon.'

Then he left.

'What changed his mind?' Brix asked.

'Female charm.'

'How are you feeling?'

The wound didn't hurt any more. The bruise was just a red weal.

'Fine,' Lund said.

'Raben's conscious. He wants to talk. Doesn't mind whether a lawyer's present or not.'

Lund got her keys.

'Take Madsen with you,' he called as she left.

But Madsen was on the phone. Lund walked on without him.

Buch had brushed his teeth four times already that morning. But he could still taste stale kimchi in his mouth. He'd called together the most senior staff in the Ministry, stood in front of them in the reception area outside his office.

No energy for a tie. Just a clean suit, a blue sweater and a white shirt that was in need of an iron.

Plough and Karina stood behind him looking mutinous.

'I'm sorry my ineptitude embarrassed you all,' Buch said. 'The newspapers are telling everyone I'm just a simple farmer from Jutland.'

Karina muttered something.

'It seems,' Buch went on, 'they were right. Which is a shame because I enjoyed working with you greatly. You deserved better. I trust my successor, whoever he or she turns out to be, will bring you that.'

Plough led the applause. Karina took it up. Soon they were all clapping him, which made Buch feel rather odd. As if he'd touched these people, not that he understood how.

He went back into his office. Plough and Karina marched in behind, closing the door.

'Today's schedule,' she began, placing a sheet of paper on his desk. 'The Prime Minister's office will vet your leaving statement and arrange a suitable exchange of letters.'

Buch put a couple of headache pills in a glass, topped them up with water, swilled them around.

'About Raben,' she began.

'Oh, forget it, Karina,' Buch cut in. He looked at her, at Plough. 'Please. I'm really sorry for last night. It was inexcusable. Can you draft a letter of apology to the poor Koreans?'

They said nothing.

'You've both been so kind. So supportive, from the beginning. And all I did was foul things up.'

'Thomas . . .' she began.

'No. Let me finish. This is the best solution for the government and the Ministry.' He thought of the difficult, strained conversation he'd had with Marie that morning. All she knew was what she'd read. It was hard to explain over the phone. 'For me too. I want to go home. I need to. Here . . .'

He reached beneath the desk and pulled out the bottle of expensive Armagnac he'd picked up for Plough.

'I wish you all the best, Carsten. And for you . . .'

He handed Karina a box of chocolates.

Plough's phone rang. He excused himself and walked away to take it.

'Was it the wrong Armagnac?' Buch asked, watching him go.

'It's fine.' She looked at Carsten Plough, talking in low tones in the corner of the room. 'He's got worries of his own.'

'What worries?'

She took a deep breath.

'He's been called to a meeting in the Prime Minister's office. There seems to be some kind of reorganization on the cards.'

Buch gulped at the headache pills and the water. He'd offered his own head. It was never part of the deal that Grue Eriksen would take others too.

'They want to appoint Plough to an EU consultant's post in Skopje.' She shrugged. 'If they're going to pick on Plough then I'm gone too. But that's fine by me.'

'This is wrong . . .'

'It's the way things happen. Connie Vemmer called. She wants to explain . . .'

'Oh no . . .'

'She says she needs to speak to you personally. Only you. I really think . . .'

Buch tried to smile, took another sip of the water.

'We lost, Karina. It's done with. I'll talk to Grue Eriksen about your careers. It's quite unacceptable that you should pay for my incompetence and stupidity.'

'Don't say that!' she shouted. 'It's not true.'

'I'll put this right. If I can.'

Lund sat next to Raben's bed in the private ward, amidst the racket of the medical machinery, listening to his firm and insistent voice.

She left the recorder running, took no notes. Raben claimed he was starting to remember more of what happened in Helmand. There was a decision to be made here: who to believe?

'We were in the Green Zone. We got a message at nine thirty in the morning,' Raben said. 'It was on an emergency frequency. It said a Danish unit was under fire.'

His shoulder had a fresh dressing. The doctor said some of the lines from the night before had been removed. Raben was a hard man. He recovered quickly.

'We crossed the river to help. Did Thomsen tell you what happened?'

'I want to hear it from you.'

'The bridge was mined. I left her to sort it out. We made it into the village.'

He looked at her from the pillow.

'There was no Danish unit. Just one officer who'd got himself trapped in there with the family and didn't dare come out.'

'What made you think he was called Perk?'

'He told me. I saw his dog tag.'

'Did you know him?'

'No. He hadn't been through Camp Viking. I'm sure of that. But the special forces guys came from all over. Kabul. Direct sometimes. He said he got cut off from his squad.'

'You didn't believe him?'

Raben clutched his injured arm.

'I didn't know what to think. He said he'd been on a mission and the Taliban had caught wind of it. They were hounding him. He was waiting for backup.'

She folded her arms and waited.

'We weren't supposed to ask men like that what they were doing,' Raben said eventually. 'It wasn't our business.'

'Do you have any idea?'

'No. But he was scared. We all were. Just five of us left. Myg, HC, David, Sebastian and me. And Perk. Dolmer got hit by sniper fire on the way in. Dead. Grüner's leg was shot to bits. He needed help. There were Taliban in the village. Too scared to come for us but that wasn't going to last. We'd left the radio with Thomsen.'

'What about Perk's radio?'

'He said it got hit by fire after he called for us. I didn't see it. I didn't . . .' His head went from side to side on the pillow. 'I don't remember too clearly. Perk was an officer. It was like he was in command straight off. He said we had to wait. Not try to fight our way out. There were too many of them.'

Raben swore, closed his eyes for a moment.

'We should have just gone for it. The family were getting really jumpy. We couldn't let them leave.'

He stared at her.

'Grüner was screaming. The place stank of shit and blood and . . .' A moment of pain and bewilderment. 'I kept thinking they'd come for us but they didn't. Perk was getting madder and madder. Then he decided we had to get out, whatever.'

Raben went quiet.

'And?' Lund asked.

'It's in here!' Raben shrieked, tapping his forehead.

'Tell me what you can.'

'He said . . .' Raben spoke very slowly, as if unsure of himself. 'He told me he wanted the father to help him get hold of a radio. If we got that we could call in a helicopter and backup. But the father was just a villager. He didn't have one. He didn't have anything.'

He wiped his face with the sleeve of his hospital gown.

'Perk didn't believe him. So he grabbed one of the kids. A little girl.' He shuffled on the bed, dead eyes, face full of pain. 'Put his gun to her head. He said the father had to decide. Was he with the Taliban? Or with us?'

Head thrust back into the pillow.

'Then he shot her right in front of us. Seven years old. Eight maybe. Just gone like that.'

'You remember this? You're sure?'

'I remember!' Raben shrieked, eyes open, full of shame and fear. 'I watched him grab hold of the mother and he shot her too. He was crazy. The man held his son. He was crying, screaming. Begging Perk to spare them. But he just blew them away, there in the room. In front of us.'

She waited till he took hold of himself.

'There was one kid left. A little girl. Four maybe. I held her. I didn't think he'd shoot. Perk just snatched her from my arms and blew her head off.'

'And the others?'

'They were shouting. Sebastian was crying.'

She checked her notes.

'That's Sebastian Holst?'

'Yeah. The youngest. He was more interested in his camera than his gun. Wanted to be a press photographer when he came out. I put my arms round him. Made him calm down. It got dark. Suddenly we heard the sound of a motorbike outside. Some guy drove into the courtyard and blew himself up. They said Søgaard had almost found us by then. He came into the village, got us out of there. I don't recall.'

'And Perk?' she asked. 'Where was he?'

He shrugged.

'I don't really know what happened after that. Perk was a clever guy. I think he maybe found a way out before Søgaard came in. Either that or . . .'

'Or what?'

'Or someone helped him. We were just ordinary soldiers. He was higher up the food chain.'

Another look at her notes.

'Søgaard filed a report. He said there was no sign of any civilians. No bodies.'

'Yeah. Well . . .' A sour expression on Raben's bearded face. 'Maybe Perk got rid of them. Or someone didn't look too hard.'

He stretched up, gazed into her eyes.

'They were there. I'm telling the truth. Ask Perk yourself. He's one of yours.'

'Raben . . .'

'He's the one who shot me.'

She put the notebook to one side.

'What makes you think that?'

'I remember!'

'You said you don't remember well. You said Skåning was Perk. That man you kidnapped two years ago. He was a librarian—'

'I remember now!'

Lund frowned.

'Clearly?' she asked. 'Everything?'

Raben closed his eyes, looked desperate.

'Not everything. No. But I know he's Perk. He killed those people. I saw that. He's got a tattoo on his shoulder. He's—'

'Skåning's got the tattoo. So have lots of officers.'

She pulled out a set of photographs. Black and white mugshots from the files. Men she didn't know.

The moment Ulrik Strange's face appeared Raben picked the photo and thrust it in her face.

'Him,' he said. 'That's Perk.'

Brix and Hedeby were talking when Lund got back from the hospital. They listened to what she had to say. But Hedeby wasn't interested in Raben at that moment. She wanted to know about Strange.

'So now you're telling me one of our own officers killed these people?' Hedeby asked. 'Seriously?'

'I don't know,' Lund admitted. 'Raben's got good reason to tell a tale like that. He's facing criminal charges. I guess he might get off more lightly if he can throw the blame on us.'

Hedeby muttered a quiet curse.

'We need Strange cleared by name,' she said emphatically.

'We won't get it,' Lund said taking a seat.

'Raben's mentally unstable,' Brix added. 'We've got proof of that. He could easily have confused Strange with someone else. He's done it before. Besides . . . Strange has been an active member of the team here. He didn't have time to invent nonsense like the Muslim League.'

Lund sighed.

'There are gaps in his movements,' she said. 'He says he was at home on his own before we found Myg Poulsen. Grüner was killed by a bomb detonated by a mobile phone placed in advance. Same thing. No alibi.'

'Lund—' Brix began.

'He left me in Sweden while I was talking to Lisbeth Thomsen. He was gone for two hours looking for Raben. We were in his car, not mine. He was at the barracks the night the explosives were stolen.'

'And when you found the priest Strange was in Helsingør,' Brix added.

'He was there,' Lund said. 'No one knows what time he left.'

She got her coat.

'I'm going to see Sebastian Holst's father. Raben said he used his camera all the time. It was never found.'

'And Strange?' Hedeby said. 'What do you propose we do with him?'

'Same as we'd do for anyone else,' Lund told her. 'Put him in an interview room and throw some questions his way.'

When she was gone Hedeby turned on him as he knew she would.

'The people upstairs are asking why you took him on in the first place.'

Brix tried to control his temper.

'I didn't appoint him, Ruth. He came with the police reforms. When the Ministry of Defence dumped all those people on us they didn't want on the payroll any more.'

'Someone let him in here.'

He pointed at the ceiling.

'They did,' Brix said. 'And they can wash their hands of him if they like.'

The anti-terror bill was in front of the Folketinget. Three readings and then it was through. TV teams stood outside the Parliament building, reporters delivering live to camera. Someone, from Grue Eriksen's office Buch assumed, had briefed the media already. They were expecting his resignation once the measure was through.

He walked out for some fresh air during a break in the debate, looked round the lobby.

Grue Eriksen and Flemming Rossing were in a huddle by one of the pillars. Buch hadn't bothered with a tie. His career as a minister was over. No need for protocol any more.

He walked over, interrupted the two of them, asked Grue Eriksen for a moment of his time.

A public place. The Prime Minister was all charm.

Rossing stayed there, listening in his smart grey suit, checking his phone for messages from time to time.

'It's about Plough,' Buch said. 'I gather he's being moved side-ways. It must be a mistake—'

'It's no mistake. That department was unfit for purpose when Monberg was there. We all know it now. It's time to signal a new beginning.'

'He's a good man!' Buch said, voice rising. 'A decent, hard-working civil servant. You shouldn't punish him for a politician's errors. Mine and Monberg's . . .'

Rossing pushed his way into the conversation. That big beak nose looked triumphant.

'The Prime Minister tells me you've apologized, Buch. I'm glad to hear it. No hard feelings.'

'Yes, yes. About Plough . . .'

The two of them stared at him. A team, Buch thought. Maybe they had been all along.

'Did you see our draft for your speech at the press conference?' Grue Eriksen added. 'Put in a little personal touch if you want. But don't change anything substantive. I mean that. Now . . .'

Buch was flapping, losing him.

'I've got to talk to someone,' Grue Eriksen said, dashing off. And Rossing was gone just as quickly too.

Buch's phone rang. Plough.

'Everything's ready for the press conference,' he said. 'We can do it whenever the package is done with.'

'Fine . . .'

'Also your wife's turned up at the Ministry. Karina's looking after her.'

'What?' Buch exploded. 'Marie? Who's looking after the kids? Her mother goes to yoga on Mondays. I mean really . . .'

A long silence on the phone.

'I said you'd meet her outside,' Plough responded in an arch, distanced voice. 'Perhaps you'd better ask her.'

Buch marched out of the Parliament building, through the quiet centre of Slotsholmen, past the statue of Kierkegaard, out into the narrow street in front of the Ministry. It was a fine bright day for the moment. The weak winter sun made the twisting dragons opposite look sad and comical.

Karina stood by a black official car near the steps. She wore a black coat and looked dressed for a funeral.

Buch stumbled across the steps.

'Where is she?' he asked, panting as he turned up. 'I don't understand . . .'

He walked up to the big estate. Connie Vemmer was hanging out of the passenger door, long blonde hair blowing in the stiff winter wind, cigarette in hand, coughing smoke out of the window.

'Oh no,' Buch groaned, turning on Karina. But she smiled at him, shrugged, walked off.

'Don't be an arse,' Vemmer barked at him from the car. 'Just listen to me, will you? Get in and let's go for a drive. We need to talk about those medical reports.'

'You cost me my job. What in God's name . . . ?'

He turned and started to walk back towards the door.

'Buch! Buch!' She moved more quickly than he expected, was by his side, tugging at his sleeve. 'Do you think I was running errands for that bastard Rossing? He's the man who fired me.'

Still he kept walking. She hung on his arm like an importunate beggar.

'If Rossing knew about that fax in advance someone must have tipped him off.'

Buch marched on.

'OK. Let's leave that for now,' Vemmer suggested. 'Here's the truth. The evidence you wanted was sitting right under your nose all along.'

They were at the door. Buch was opening it.

She let go, swore at him.

'Hey, genius! Why didn't you check the dates on those two medical reports? Why—'

Buch slammed the heavy wooden door behind him.

Connie Vemmer stood out in the bright cold street, finished her cigarette, threw the butt into the gutter along with a few coarse epithets.

The door opened. Buch came out, eyed her.

'What dates?' he asked.

Sebastian Holst's father lived in a half-finished apartment not far from the Amalienborg Palace. Modern paintings everywhere, on the walls, on the floor. Suitcases and building materials. An old building on the way up. Still some distance to go. Walls to be plastered, ceilings to be painted.

He made Lund a coffee and sat next to her at a table by the window.

'I believe Sebastian always had his camera with him,' she began.

He was a hefty man not much older than she was. Bright-blue shirt, hair long and unkempt.

An artist, she guessed. Or an architect. He never said.

'He was always taking pictures. That kind of thing runs in the family. We see the world through our eyes. Why not try to record it?'

'Everything?'

'Everything he could. He took lots of pictures in Afghanistan. The army kept them. They said they were theirs.' Holst frowned. 'You mean you haven't seen them?'

'Did the army tell you why his camera was missing?'

'Who told you that? He sent it home a couple of weeks before he was killed. He'd broken it. Sebastian was always a bit clumsy. I was going to get it repaired. Or buy him a new one.' Holst sighed. 'Probably the latter.'

He got up, went to some boxes beneath a line of gaudy paintings. Took out an old-looking camera.

'Film only,' Holst said. 'He was very fastidious about some things.'

'Were there more pictures?'

'No. Only the ones the army have as far as I know. They wouldn't let him post stuff like that back here, would they?'

It was a slender hope and now he'd dashed it.

'I guess not. I'm sorry I bothered you,' Lund said, picking up her bag.

'I heard you'd found his squad leader, Raben. I suppose that whole business is going to get dragged up again.'

'What business?'

Holst stared at her. He was no fool.

'Please,' he said. 'I never believed all that bullshit. About there being an officer. Raben made that up as an excuse. He wanted to go into that village anyway. It was his fault Sebastian and the others got killed.'

He was turning the old camera in his hands. A Leica, she saw. Expensive. Marked and worn. His mild, plain face was suddenly wreathed in anger.

'Sebastian said something was going to happen.'

He walked back to the table unsteadily and Lund saw now that everything was a mask, an act of subterfuge. Inside Holst was breaking, weeping.

'I've lost both my sons to a war I don't understand,' he whispered, falling heavily onto a chair near the door. 'One came home in a coffin. The other's not the same.'

He rubbed his eyes with the backs of his hands.

'What did we do wrong? Why did they deserve this?'

The room was quiet except for the low murmur of traffic beyond the window. These walls would stay unplastered, unfinished for a long time. This man was lost in a limbo created by a distant conflict that was beyond him.

His hands played fondly with the old, battered Leica. His mind seemed somewhere else.

'I'm looking for answers,' Lund said.

Holst snapped awake. His sad, dark eyes fixed on her.

'Answers,' she repeated. 'And it's hard.'

'No one asked me any questions before. They just came here to tell me things. What to do. What to say. How to feel.'

'I'm struggling, Holst. People don't talk to me. They want to bury things . . .'

He was frightened. She could see that.

'If there's something you haven't told us—'

'This stops with me,' he said quickly. 'Don't blame anyone else. Not Sebastian. Frederik.'

'Frederik?'

His eyes went to one of two photos on a nearby rollup desk. Two young men in uniform.

'If he doesn't come back God knows . . .'

'It won't go any further,' Lund told him.

Holst got up, shambled back to the boxes, picked up a tiny pocket video camera.

'He had this too. He used to sneak off and keep a diary. It came back hidden inside the Leica.'

He pressed some buttons. Nothing happened. Her heart was in her mouth. Holst rifled through the boxes, found some batteries, put them in the thing.

Flicked a switch. A face came on the tiny screen.

It didn't take long. When she'd finished Lund called Madsen.

'Is Raben fit for questioning?' she asked.

'He's in hospital. How hard can it be?'

'I mean,' she said patiently, 'is he fit to be brought into the Politi-gården?'

'Wait a minute.'

She did.

He came back.

'The hospital says we can bring him in here for an hour or two. He'll need to go back afterwards. His wife was coming to see him. I guess we can tell her to come here now.'

'She can see him first. Then it's a full interview. I want Brix there as well.'

'That's generous of you.'

She watched the tiny picture on the screen.

'Not really,' Lund said.

They put Raben in a secure waiting room with a uniformed guard. When Louise arrived, mad with the police and fearful about the meeting, she found him waiting for her, standing, arm in a sling. No blood, no visible sign of hurt.

She stayed at the door, didn't know what to say.

'Can we get a bit of privacy?' Raben asked the officer in the room.

'Sorry,' the man said. 'I have to stay.'

'For God's sake . . .' he pleaded.

The officer stared at him, leaned against the wall, watched.

'Let's sit down, Jens,' she said, and they took two chairs at the far end of the room.

He didn't look bad at all. There was something dogged, relentless about this man. The more they threw at him, the harder he came back.

His fingers reached over, took hers. She was cold from waiting outside and didn't respond.

'It was just . . .' He was staring at her in that importunate way he had. The one that said: *forgive everything*. 'I was beside myself.'

He held her more tightly. The familiar smell of hospital soap and medication.

'It won't happen again,' he promised.

She didn't speak.

'I know I said that before. This time—'

'Let's not talk about it now.'

His eyes were on her, pleading, insistent.

'I let you down. You and Jonas. I know that. I was a rotten husband. A rotten father. If I could turn back the clock I would.'

She saw the previous night in her head. Søgaard beneath her. A physical act, nothing more. But one that haunted her.

His voice rose, a note of hope in it.

'Things are looking up. They're listening to me now. They know I was telling the truth. You and Jonas . . .'

'Two years,' she whispered. 'All that time on my own. Even when I came to see you. Even when they left us together in Herstedvester. You scarcely touched me. You just talked about yourself. About the army. About what happened . . .'

'We can put this back together.'

It had to be said. She couldn't bear it any more.

Eyes on his, words forming already in her head.

'No we can't. I slept with Søgaard.'

The shock on his face hurt her. He looked like a child who'd seen something real, something terrible for the first time.

He didn't speak. She slipped her fingers out of his.

'I'm sorry. It didn't mean anything. I was just . . . lonely. I missed you, every single day. I knew you weren't coming back. Not after all this. I just couldn't stand it any longer. Being alone.' She wouldn't cry. That wasn't right. 'Can't you see? It's no use. It's never going to happen for us now. They won't let it.'

His eyes fell to the floor.

'You won't let it, Jens.'

The door opened. The detective she knew as Madsen strode in.

'Sorry,' he said, 'but this meeting's at an end.'

'We're talking,' Raben shot at him.

The uniform cop came and stood next to them. Ready for trouble.

'This is important,' Madsen insisted. 'We need you now.'

Lund had Holst's video on her laptop. Raben opposite her, Brix next to him.

'Do you want to see a lawyer?' she asked as she worked the keyboard, finding the file.

'No.' A surly, juvenile tone in his voice. 'I want to see my wife.'

'Sebastian Holst sent his father a video diary not long before he was killed. Did you know about that?'

400

Raben shook his head.

'He shouldn't have done. Against regulations.'

'Lots of things are against regulations,' Lund said, turning the laptop round so he could see the screen. 'But he sent it all the same.'

A face there. A young man with a beard and curly hair. He wore a white T-shirt and looked tired and scared. A bare wall in the background, crude plastering and a tourist poster of Copenhagen.

'. . . Don't get worried, Dad,' Sebastian Holst said in a quiet voice, 'but something's not right in our squad.'

Raben watched, caught by the dead man on the screen.

'Why do I have to see this? He was one of my comrades . . .'

'. . . Raben's the worst.' Holst's voice was clear and unmistakable in spite of the tinny speaker. He shook his head, blinked, looked terrified for a moment. 'He's going crazy. He sees Taliban everywhere. All he thinks of is killing. Like there's one round every corner and we've got to shoot them first. Christ . . .'

The man in the blue prison suit went quiet, eyes locked on the screen.

'. . . He runs so many risks. We do things we shouldn't. Sometimes . . .' Holst's voice was close to breaking. 'Sometimes he makes up radio messages just so we can get out there and kick ass. This morning . . .' There was shame on Holst's face, alongside the fear. 'We crossed the river to raid a village for the third time. Raben thinks one of the men there's Taliban.'

Holst's hand went to his head.

'They're farmers or bakers or something. Maybe they're running dope. Maybe they're bribing someone. Who isn't here? We still took the place apart. Raben yelled at the guy, called him an informer. Poked a gun in his face. I thought he was going to shoot him.'

'Turn it off,' Raben said, reaching for the laptop.

'No,' Brix said, and pushed back his hand. 'You need to hear this.'

'. . . The kids were screaming,' Holst went on. 'The mother and the old women were crying. They thought we were going to kill them all. Raben's running wild, Dad. He wants to do it all over again tomorrow. It's like he's in the Wild West or something. I talked to the others. They say it's going to be OK. We're back home in a couple of weeks.'

Holst didn't look at the camera.

'They don't want to cross him. They're scared. Me too. But I guess . . .' A nod of his head. 'I guess he knows what he's doing. He's the boss. Good guy when the shit hits the fan. Someone gave him that job. We're just . . .'

A smile. He was trying to pull himself together for home.

'Anyway,' Holst said. 'That's me done moaning. Raben says I do it all the time. In a couple of weeks we'll be back in Copenhagen. I can't wait to see you.' He shook his head. 'I'm not coming back here. That's a promise.'

A broader smile.

'I miss you all. I'll see you soon. I'll give your love to big brother when I see him. Bye.'

The dead man in the white T-shirt reached out and turned off the camera. Lund closed the laptop lid.

'Is it true?'

A knock on the door. A call for Brix. He went out to take it.

'Is it true?' Lund asked again.

'Sebastian was only there because his older brother enlisted. It was like a competition between them. He wasn't up to it.'

'He said you broke orders. Threatened civilians.'

'It's war! Not a game! This isn't about Sebastian. It's about Perk.'

'The family he mentioned. Are they the ones you say Perk killed?'

'He murdered them all right.'

'So you and the rest of the squad had been in the house before?'

'The bastard was a crook. Selling dope. Feeding our movements to the Taliban. Scum . . .'

'And you were determined to go back until you proved that?'

Raben shook his head wearily.

'You're not listening to me. What I think's irrelevant. We got that radio call. Perk must have been sent there because whoever was running him knew too.'

'It's not irrelevant, Raben. There's no record of any radio traffic calling you to that house. There was no officer called Perk.'

He swore and there was a look in his face she couldn't quite read. Unless it was defeat.

'What I've told you is the truth. I can't . . .'

Lund was getting mad. She took out some scene of crime and autopsy photos.

'Look at these,' she insisted, spreading the pictures across the table. 'Five people have been killed.'

Anne Dragsholm. Myg Poulsen. Grüner. Lisbeth Thomsen. The priest. Savagely murdered. Still torn corpses caught for ever.

'I've done everything I can to track down that officer,' she told him. 'If you're lying to me and he doesn't exist . . .' Her voice was cracking. 'For pity's sake tell me now and let's bring this nonsense to an end. I'll do my best to help you. That's a promise, and it's more than you deserve.'

He seemed calm. Calmer than her.

'It was my decision to enter the village. The others didn't want to go.' He stared at her. 'They were right. I should have listened to them.'

'You should—'

'But there was an officer. We got that radio message. His name was Perk.' He paused, made sure she was looking at him. 'He's the man I saw. The one who tried to kill me.'

The door opened. Brix came back, sat down.

'We just received documentation from the army,' he said. 'It shows beyond any doubt that the police officer you accused yesterday . . .'

Brix shuffled the photos on the table, glanced at them.

'He wasn't in Afghanistan at the time. He wasn't Perk. Couldn't be.'

The man in the prison suit swore and shook his head.

'What about Sebastian's older brother?' Lund asked. 'Do you know him?'

'Not really.' His voice was low and miserable. 'He was a doctor working out of Camp Viking.'

'An army surgeon? Frederik?'

'Why ask me?' Raben shot back at her, punching his head with his fist. 'I'm just crazy, aren't I?'

Then he stamped hard on the pictures of the mangled corpses in front of him.

'Someone killed these people, didn't they? And that wasn't me.'

'We need to talk to Frederik Holst,' Brix said. 'Fix it.'

The debate on the anti-terror package had dragged on into the early evening. Birgitte Agger's MPs were doing everything they could to stall it. Buch had spent an hour driving round Copenhagen with Connie Vemmer, watching her smoke, listening all the time.

When he marched back into his office Karina and Plough were waiting for him. In the room outside a desk was set up for the resignation press conference. Microphones in place already.

'I'm sorry I tricked you,' Karina told him as he marched to his desk. 'You needed to see her.'

Buch took his chair. It felt familiar. Comfortable. Right.

'We know you can't tell us everything,' Plough added. 'But if you felt able . . .'

He had a set of papers inside a yellow document folder. Buch read the top page again, absorbed in what Vemmer had said.

'Even if you don't act upon it, Thomas,' Karina added, 'I thought you deserved to hear what she had to say.'

Still Buch kept quiet.

'I'm resigned to going to Skopje,' Plough added. 'It's in Macedonia apparently.'

Buch stared at the microphones.

'Thomas,' Karina added quietly. 'If you're going to do something you need to do it—'

'When does the vote start?'

'Soon.'

'And Krabbe's there?'

'Of course.'

He grabbed the yellow folder from the desk and got up.

'But Krabbe's got nothing to do with it!' she cried as he bustled for the door.

'He's a decent man,' Buch cried as he left. 'Not my type but . . .' He waved the papers. 'Krabbe is all I've got.'

The Folketinget before a vote was like a theatre between acts. An interval was in place, men and women in serious business suits conferring in whispers in the anterooms outside the chamber.

Buch saw Krabbe chatting to one of Grue Eriksen's aides at the far end of the room. Then he disappeared into the toilets.

No one at the urinals. Buch walked up and down the stall doors, saying, 'Krabbe? Are you here? You are. I know it. I saw you come in. Krabbe?'

He paced the length of them, looking for the red locked sign and feet underneath the door.

Only one appeared occupied. Yellow folder in hand, Buch hitched up his trousers, got down and placed his bearded face against the cold tiles to peer through.

'Krabbe? Is that you?'

All Buch could see were two black trouser legs down around skinny ankles, some shiny shoes and a very colourful pair of underpants.

'Bloody hell,' said a disgruntled voice inside. 'This really takes the biscuit. If you want to talk to me, Buch, call my secretary. I'm enjoying a private moment if you please.'

'The medical report about the extra hand was faxed in August,' Buch said, squinting beneath the door. 'But the revised report didn't arrive until October!'

'Is that so?' Krabbe sighed.

Buch pushed the yellow folder beneath the door.

'So you see the implication?' he said, thrusting the documents towards the hidden Krabbe. 'First there's one report suggesting civilians have been murdered.'

A hand came down from above and took the folder.

'What a pathetic attempt to cling to office!'

Buch got up, wondered how hard it would be to force the door open.

'This is nothing of the kind. All I want is the truth and so do you. You see what I mean? In spite of the initial report nobody did anything for two months. Two whole months!'

His hand was banging on the door. Buch regretted that but he was getting mad again.

'There was no need for any urgency, was there?' Krabbe called. 'It was the hand of the bomber.'

Before Buch could reply the door opened and the man inside walked out, marching for the sink.

'Why did no one say anything in all that time?' Buch asked. 'What were they up to?'

He followed, watched Krabbe wash his hands in a very precise and punctilious fashion, plenty of soap and hot water.

'When the first report arrived Grue Eriksen was proposing additional funding to get more troops in Afghanistan.' Buch jabbed at the papers in Krabbe's hands. 'Here and here. See for yourself. The money was promptly approved when the Folketinget came back from recess in October.'

Krabbe was reading the sheets in front of him.

'You and your party voted for that,' Buch went on. 'So did I. Would we have been so keen if we'd known our troops had been accused of a civilian massacre?'

'This proves nothing. It's just speculation.' Krabbe passed the folder back to Buch. 'I can't believe Grue Eriksen would manipulate things—'

'That's what happened, dammit! See for yourself.'

Krabbe looked at his hands and thrust them under the dryer.

'Go ahead and push for a stricter anti-terror package if you like. But you'll be picking on an innocent party. Those pathetic immigrants didn't kill our people. It was someone—'

'Who?' Krabbe asked.

'I don't know. Someone closer to home. I'm asking for your help. I think—'

'We've worked so hard for this . . .'

'Krabbe!' Buch's voice was high and hard. 'Let's be candid. What you believe in mostly I abhor. You feel the same about me I'm sure. But this I know . . .' His fat forefinger waved in Krabbe's narrow pale face. 'You don't like being lied to. And you don't like being used.'

Buch took the yellow folder and waved it in front of him.

'There,' he said. 'We've something in common. Now the question is . . .'

Krabbe was listening intently.

'What are we going to do about it?'

The farewell ceremony for the new detachment was over. Torsten Jarnvig stood outside the Ryvangen Barracks hall watching the men and their families saying goodbye. Søgaard was there too.

'I think they're going off in a good mood,' he said as Jarnvig approached.

'You never told me we'd got radio traffic five days before Raben started shrieking.' Jarnvig threw the documents on the bonnet of Søgaard's G-Wagen. 'I've been through every last one of the traffic logs. I saw this . . .'

He was still mad. The bitter look on Søgaard's face didn't help.

'What?' he asked.

Jarnvig slammed his hand on the papers.

'We got a message. August, two years ago. When I was in Kabul.'

Søgaard picked up the logs.

'Five days before the incident.'

'So you said,' Søgaard muttered. He flicked through the pages.

'It was from a special forces unit. No ID in the records. No names.'

Søgaard shook his head.

'I don't understand. What are you implying?'

'Implying?' Jarnvig bellowed. 'It's here in black and white. We had a unit operating just thirty kilometres from the village where Raben's squad ended up.'

'I never saw any of this.'

He put the papers back on the bonnet.

'You were officer in command in my absence. Every message comes through the office—'

'I'm telling you. I never saw it.'

Jarnvig's fist pummelled the vehicle.

'It's in the file, Søgaard. Even if you were half asleep on duty, which I doubt, you investigated Raben's claims. He said someone from special forces was in the vicinity. We didn't believe him because you . . .' Jarnvig's hand went out. 'You told us no one was there.'

Nothing. Not a word.

'You said they were seeing ghosts.'

'They were. This doesn't prove he wasn't lying.'

'It proves he could be right! And you never mentioned it.' Jarnvig took a step closer to the tall precise man in the neat dress uniform. 'Why was that? Come on. Out with it.'

'I've no knowledge of this. I never saw the message. I never knew special forces were in the area.'

'It's here!' Jarnvig roared, waving the papers in his face.

'If there's an official complaint being filed I'd like to see the details. I want Operational Command informed. General Arild's team was involved in the investigation too.'

Jarnvig stared at him, waited.

'Look,' Søgaard pleaded. 'I don't have time for this now. I've got to go to the airport. We're due to fly in five hours.'

'You're going nowhere. I'm suspending you from duty as of now. I've got someone to take your place on that plane. You're confined to barracks until I know what the hell went on there.'

'I'm due in Helmand!' Søgaard shouted.

'Not this time,' Jarnvig told him. 'You're staying here.'

Forty minutes later, after eating supper with a silent Louise and a tired Jonas, Jarnvig retreated to his office. Jan Arild was waiting for him.

Jarnvig tried to smile at him. It was obvious what had happened. Søgaard had been on the phone.

'I'm glad you came,' he said, taking a seat opposite the general. 'I was about to call you.'

'You've been unreachable all day, Torsten,' Arild said, leaning back in his chair, hands behind his head.

'I was checking out the hunting,' Jarnvig lied. 'We ought to pick up on that again. Get out of these uniforms once in a while.'

'I told you,' Arild said with a scowl. 'I don't have time for that any more. Not your kind anyway.'

'That's a shame.'

'Not really. Those days are long gone. I went somewhere, Torsten. You just . . .' He looked round the little office. 'You just served, didn't you?'

'Raben could have been right,' Jarnvig said, ignoring the taunt. 'There was radio contact with a Danish special forces unit five days before his squad was attacked.'

Arild, in his green uniform, cap on the desk, ginger hair perfectly combed, looked bored.

'We must tell the police,' Jarnvig said.

'Aren't we putting up with enough shit from them already? Why invite their attention any more?'

'Because Raben could be telling the truth!'

'The man's mad,' Arild declared. 'A shame. He was a good soldier once, or so I gather. We're the army. We don't need civilians to come and tell us what to do. I don't understand why this concerns you so much.'

'It's possible Søgaard withheld information. Covered up what went on. I was in Kabul at the time. He was in sole command. He says he never saw the radio traffic. That can't be true. It came across my desk every single day.'

'That's a very serious accusation.'

'I know.'

'And you're right,' Arild agreed. 'Something is amiss.' He stared at Jarnvig. 'But it isn't Søgaard, is it?'

Torsten Jarnvig looked at Arild's smiling face and knew this was going wrong.

'You're a rotten liar,' the general said with a laugh. 'Always were. Let me prove it. Look me in the face and tell me. Did you help Raben escape PET the night of the ball?'

'What do you mean?'

'It's a simple question. So simple I already know the answer. I told you in confidence he was under surveillance. Yet he still got out of the building. Someone saw you go into a side room. Raben was in there, wasn't he?'

'What happened in Helmand is important, Jan. We need to investigate.'

'Don't use my name, Colonel. Twenty years ago that might have worked. Not now.'

Arild picked up his cap.

'You're a small man. With limited ideas and meagre ambitions. Dammit!' Arild's voice rose in sudden fury. 'You can't even lie to save your own skin.'

'Can't we leave the personal issues to one side . . . ?'

'Come on!' Arild urged. 'Just answer, will you? Look me in the face and say it. Did you see Raben or not?'

Torsten Jarnvig took off his glasses, stayed silent.

Arild threw back his head and laughed.

Then was serious in an instant.

'I've called the military police. You'll go with them. Don't make a fuss.'

'This . . .' Jarnvig brandished the documents from Operational Command. '. . . will not go away.'

Arild smiled.

'But it has. And so will you.'

He looked at the down-at-heel office Jarnvig had occupied for the best part of a decade.

'This place can be Søgaard's now. It needs a lick of paint if you ask me.'

*

Lund spent the best part of an hour trying to track down Frederik Holst. It seemed hopeless. Then Brix walked in, something in his hand.

She finished the call, thanked Holst's father who was playing scared and ignorant again.

'No one wants to talk about Frederik Holst,' Lund told Brix. 'Even his relatives.'

'Maybe they've got good reason. I got through to someone in Operational Command. We just missed him. Holst's back in Afghanistan. He's been on home leave in Copenhagen for a month. It seems he was renting a short-term apartment in Islands Brygge, not far from where Grüner died. Maybe he didn't tell anyone.'

'Why would he do that?'

Brix showed her a plastic evidence sleeve. A photograph inside.

'We found this in the rubbish he left when he cleared out.'

An army picture. Soldiers in a brief moment of relaxation. Raben's team set against the Danish flag, cans of beer in their hands. Happy. Drunk. Sebastian Holst was at the front shouting, arm raised in the air. Behind the rest of them. Myg Poulsen. Lisbeth Thomsen. Grüner. The others.

Combat fatigues. A table full of food and drink. A moment off-duty.

There were cross marks in black felt pen through all the faces except one: Jens Peter Raben.

Lund walked to the desk, checked her calls, her papers. The idea had been nagging her for a while.

'You can get us on the soldiers' flight tonight.' She thought for a moment. 'If I need my passport I'll have to go home first.' Lund looked at him. 'Will I need my passport? It's Danish territory, isn't it? We've got jurisdiction.'

Brix was so surprised he couldn't help but laugh.

'What the hell are you saying?'

'We've been running round in circles.' Lund pulled out some files she thought she might need. 'Frederik Holst saw his brother's video diary. He sent the camera back. The father confirmed it.'

'Lund—'

'Frederik was at the field hospital when they brought in his brother's body. If he was here we'd be bringing him in for questioning right now. We can't let it go just because he's in Helmand . . .'

'I need to talk to Hedeby. There are avenues to go through. The permission . . .'

It was her turn to laugh.

'Come on. That'll take days. We can't wait on paperwork.'

'There are procedures.'

'Don't give me that.' She kept her eyes on him, wouldn't let go. 'You pulled that information about Holst out of Operational Command when I couldn't. You know the people to talk to.'

She picked up the files, asked one of the desk officers to check some medical reports.

'I can't get you on the army flight,' Brix told her. 'It's too late.'

'There's nowhere else left to look.'

'It's a war zone!'

She gazed at him and knew it had to be said.

'If this was Ruth Hedeby's show I'd be back in Gedser already. I don't know what you've got over her and I don't care. Just do it, will you?'

He was wavering.

'You can't go into Afghanistan on your own.'

'I know that.'

'So what . . . ?' Brix went quiet for a moment. Knew what she was thinking. 'Is that a good idea?'

'Fix the flights and the paperwork. Leave the rest to me.'

Brix was on the phone straight away. This would happen, she thought. There'd be a brief chance to see the distant, enclosed world of Helmand. Then home, with answers.

The last stamp in her passport was for a holiday in Mallorca with Mark two years before. Her son had moped most of the time. Lund had hated it.

She walked down the black marble corridor, found the interview room, kicked out the uniform man deputed to watch Strange.

When he was gone she sat next to him on the bench seat. Jeans and a T-shirt. Tattoo just visible on his shoulder. Strange looked like the kind of man who could go anywhere at the drop of a hat.

He puffed out his cheeks, sighed, said nothing.

'My old partner . . . Jan Meyer,' Lund said. 'We got to this warehouse.'

Strange stopped staring at the floor, looked at her instead.

'It was dark. I went inside. I didn't think there was anyone in the building.' Lund's hands wouldn't keep still. This was so hard to say. 'Then Meyer came in too. He knew someone was in there with me.'

Strange's eyes wouldn't leave her.

'I shouldn't have gone in on my own. It was all my fault. We found the man who shot Meyer.' She wiped her mouth with the sleeve of her black and white Faroese jumper for no reason. 'What good does that do? He's still stuck in a wheelchair.'

A pause. She didn't know whether to say it or not.

'Sometimes I wonder if he wishes he was dead. He looked that way when I saw him in hospital. But—'

'People can change. Get better,' Strange said.

'Sometimes,' she agreed. 'Sometimes they're who they are for ever.' Another moment of hesitation. 'Like me.'

He watched her, hands on knees, that odd, calm, angular face interested as usual.

'I shut myself down. I got that job in Gedser and I told myself . . .' Her voice was firm and unwavering. 'If you can't feel anything then it can't hurt you. Gedser suited me fine.'

Strange raised an eyebrow.

'I wanted to stay buried there for ever. If you hadn't turned up I would have done too.' She fidgeted a little closer to him, looked into his eyes. 'Not happy. Not sad. Not anything.'

The eyebrow went down. A ghost of a smile on Strange's stubbly face.

'I'm sorry,' she said, staring directly into his grey-blue eyes. 'It's hard to trust people if you can't trust yourself sometimes. Do you understand?'

A moment of indecision. It could go any way.

Then he laughed, that low, self-deprecating chuckle she'd come to like.

'Yeah,' Strange said. 'I always pick the difficult ones. Now what?'

Closeness.

It frightened her. Always would.

'We have to leave.'

'Where to?' Strange looked at his T-shirt and jeans. 'They didn't even let me get my jacket when they dragged me in here.'

She slapped his leg, got up.

'We'll pick it up along the way. And your passport too.'

Ulrik Strange sat on the bench seat, mouth wide open.

'Are you coming or not?' she asked. 'We've a plane to catch.'

One hour later. Kastrup airport. Brix had organized for the scheduled flight to be held for fifteen minutes so they could make it. He walked with them down the gangway. Passed over a folder.

'There's Frederik Holst's personnel details and a warrant for his arrest. Some contact phone numbers in Afghanistan. Here . . .'

A satellite phone in a case with some instructions.

'This should work anywhere you're going. If the army give you trouble call me. Strange?'

He had his jacket back, and his swagger.

'Yeah?'

'According to your file you speak Pashto.'

Strange laughed.

'Don't shoot. Where's the toilet? Can you get a beer round here? That good enough?'

Brix wasn't in the mood.

'You've got military experience. Lund hasn't. I want you to take the lead on the ground.' The chief looked at her. 'You hear that? You do what he says.'

Strange laughed again and shook his head.

'It's three hours to Istanbul,' Brix said. 'The visas and authorities have been sent ahead by fax. When you get to Turkey the army will meet you and put you on board one of their flights to Camp Bastion. Five hours. You'll be there in the morning our time. Midday theirs. Try to get some sleep.'

'You haven't been on an army plane,' Strange told him.

The door was open. The flight attendant was beckoning them on board.

'You're under military control for the duration,' Brix added. 'Don't go wandering off. You've got one day there only. You come back the same way. The flights are fixed. You'll be in Kastrup thirty-six hours from now. Any questions?'

Neither of them spoke.

Brix sighed.

'For God's sake take care,' he said.

Then watched as they got on the plane.

*

413

When Brix got back to his office there was a string of messages from the army. Operational Command, Ryvangen and more distant branches too.

He ignored them, called together the team, told them to dig up everything they could on Frederik Holst. Phone records, credit card activity while he was on leave. A full profile.

'I want his movements day by day, from the moment he got off the plane to when he got back on it. Where was he at the time of the murders? What does his father know?'

Hedeby was standing in the shadows at the end of the room, close to the corridor that led to her office. She didn't need to beckon him. The summons was in her face.

Brix read through some notes Madsen had made after talking to Holst's neighbours in the rented flat in Islands Brygge. They didn't amount to much but he took his time over them. Then, when he was ready, he followed Hedeby into her room, took a chair, watched as she closed the door behind her.

She was furious. She often was since Lund had returned to the Politigården. Hedeby was once a reliable detective. Promotion had turned her into a civil servant, a manager of budgets and resources and she never even noticed.

'I've had a call from the Ministry asking for an explanation,' she said.

'Understandable,' Brix agreed.

'Along with half the army.' She stood by the window, looked down at him.

Brix shrugged.

'It happened very quickly. Strange was cleared and Lund picked up this lead . . .'

She walked to the filing cabinet, slammed her fist on it. Brix tried not to laugh.

'I don't give a shit about Lund and Strange! What the hell—?'

'We found a suspect. He's just returned to Helmand. His brother was in Raben's squad. One of the men who died.'

'And no one told me?'

'The brother, the one we're looking at, is called Frederik Holst. He'd been tracking the members of Raben's squad.' Brix offered her some of the papers Madsen had given him. 'He's a doctor at one of the field hospitals in Lashkar Gah.'

414

She seized the sheet, looked at it.

'Holst has a motive. He was here in Copenhagen when the murders occurred, so he had the opportunity too. We couldn't ignore—'

'Dammit, Lennart,' she bawled at him. 'You know this has to go through me.'

Brix leaned back in the chair, put his long arms behind his head, thought about his answer.

'But you'd have said no, Ruth. So what was the point?'

For once she seemed speechless.

'You'd have pushed some papers around the desk,' he went on. 'Called someone in the Ministry who wasn't there. Waited until morning.'

No answer. Just those wide, wide eyes.

'I hate waiting,' Brix went on. 'I don't much appreciate being lied to either. Holst looks like our man. There was a flight going. I managed to rush through the visas and the authorizations—'

'I can't believe you'd do this to me. After all that—'

'The plane's gone. They're in the air. It's done,' he said with a shrug. 'That's it.'

Brix got up, made for the door. Madsen was there, holding a phone.

'It's the Ministry of Justice,' he said, looking at Hedeby. 'They want an update.'

Brix went to see Raben in the interview room. Tired, arm still in a sling, moaning for painkillers, not that he looked as if he needed them.

One of the younger detectives was trying to get him to talk. Raben glanced at Brix as he came in. A look that said: is this the best you've got?

'Tell me about Frederik Holst,' the young cop said.

Raben yawned.

'What was your relationship like?'

'We didn't have one. He was a doctor. Didn't mix with the troops unless he had to.'

Brix sat down, said, 'How's it going?'

'It's not. He just sticks to the same stupid story.'

'Maybe that's because the same stupid story's the truth,' Raben said wearily.

'Smart arse,' the cop replied. 'You just start coming up with something or you're here all night.'

'All the time in the world,' Raben said with a smile.

'Leave us,' Brix ordered and waited for the two of them to be alone.

Raben didn't look quite so confident then.

Brix sorted through his papers, glanced at him across the desk.

'I talked to Herstedvester. Frederik Holst wanted to visit you there. Phoned five times. You said no to each one.'

'I want to see my wife.'

'We found several letters in Holst's flat. They were addressed to you.' He pushed a folder across the table. 'He posted them to the prison. You sent them back.'

'Why are you telling me things I already know?'

'Holst was angry with you. He saw that video. He blamed you for his brother's death.'

'Ask Holst about that. Not me.'

'We plan to. Lund's on her way to Helmand now.'

Raben's tired eyes opened.

'This isn't going to stop until we get to the bottom of it, Raben. Until we know what happened. It's in your interests to help us—'

Raben's free hand thumped on the table.

'I did help you! I told you the truth!' His face was stern and fixed. His eyes on Brix. 'An officer executed that family. He brought the Taliban down on us. Not me.'

'You said it was one of our men. But we checked. He wasn't even in Helmand at the time. How can we believe—?'

'I want to talk to my wife.'

Raben's eyes were on the table.

'You need to reconsider the statement you gave us. The one that incriminated Ulrik Strange. Do that and we can try to move things forward. I'm telling you. It can't have been him.'

Raben was starting to get mad.

'Talk to Colonel Jarnvig. He believes me. It's all there in the files. You just have to look in the right places. You've got to ignore their lies.'

'Whose lies?' Brix wondered.

'The special people,' Raben yelled. 'The spooks. The ghosts. The guys . . .' His hand jerked towards the door. 'The guys who come and go and you never even know their name. That's who. Ask Jarnvig.'

'Jarnvig's under arrest. The military police are questioning him. They say he helped you get out from under the noses of PET.'

Nothing.

'You've got a preliminary court hearing tomorrow. Do yourself a favour.'

'You mean do you a favour?'

'Just come up with a story we can believe, will you?' Brix looked at the man across from him. 'Is there anything I can get you? Some medication? A doctor?'

'I told you already. I want my wife.'

Brix got up from the table.

'I called her before I came in here. Trouble is . . .' He sighed. 'She's got more than you to worry about now.'

Christian Søgaard was in Jarnvig's house, going through his papers in the study with Said Bilal.

'Let me get this straight,' he said, looking at the young officer squirming in the seat opposite. 'Jarnvig came to you and wanted details of all the radio traffic from two years ago?'

'That's right,' Bilal said.

'Why didn't you tell me?'

Bilal blinked.

'He said no one else was to know.'

'Why?' Søgaard asked. 'What did he think was going on?'

'I don't know! The colonel didn't seem to be himself. He was . . . asking all kinds of things.'

A noise behind. Søgaard glanced and saw Louise Raben, jeans and leather jacket, as if she was ready to go out somewhere.

'Quiet,' he said to Bilal and got up from the desk.

A big smile for her. Søgaard felt more than a little awkward.

'Hi,' he said. 'How's things? Going somewhere?'

'Where's my father? I've been looking all around the camp. Isn't he back yet?'

Søgaard perched on one of the chairs. Jarnvig's house. Soon it could be his. And all it contained.

'Your father's been taken in for questioning. The military police are holding him.'

She blinked, looked at him, said nothing.

'He talked to Jens at the cadets' ball. Helped him shake off PET.'

'That's a lie,' she said straight off. 'I was with him. You were there too.'

'He went off on his own when we were dancing. Someone saw him.'

'Who?'

'I don't know,' Søgaard said. 'But they told General Arild. Your father confessed immediately. You know what he's like. He wouldn't . . .'

His voice trailed off.

'Wouldn't what? Lie? Try to hide things?'

'He wouldn't do that,' Søgaard agreed. 'I'm sorry but . . . it's serious. He's been acting strangely ever since this began.'

A shake of his blond head.

'Tonight he was accusing me of things . . .'

'What kind of things?'

'He seems obsessed by the murders.'

'What kind of things?' she repeated.

A noise behind. Søgaard could see Bilal in his green uniform trying to stay out of sight.

'He said I'd been concealing radio traffic from the investigation. It's ridiculous. As if he believes all that crap Jens made up.'

She hugged herself in the black jacket, stared at the living room with its plaques and photos and memorabilia. The debris of Torsten Jarnvig's army life.

'I'll do what I can to help him,' Søgaard said, coming to stand behind her. 'It's a serious charge. He's been under a lot of pressure. With a record like his it won't come to anything—'

'So you're saying he believed Jens? After all this time?'

Søgaard shrugged.

'Sounds like it. The whole idea's crazy . . .' He wasn't used to this kind of conversation. It felt uncomfortable. 'What about you? Jonas? Can I get you some food or something?'

'We can look after ourselves, thank you. I want to see my father.'

'They won't allow that. Not until they're ready.'

'He gave everything he had to the army, Søgaard! How can they treat him like this?'

'Your father talked to Jens. He helped him get away. What do you expect?'

'If you hear anything I want to know. Do I at least get that?'

'Of course.' He touched her arm. She pulled back, glared at him. 'If you and Jonas—'

'I told you. We're fine.'

She was going. He got up, put out a hand to stop her.

'Louise. You don't think I'm involved in this, do you?'

'No,' she said too easily. 'Why would I think that?'

Søgaard watched her go then went back to the desk.

'You should have told me,' Søgaard said. 'I don't give a shit about Jarnvig's orders. I shouldn't have to hear it from Arild.'

He put his fist in Bilal's dark face.

'You answer to me. You did then. You do now.'

Then he looked at the documents on the desk, radio logs, maps, details of troop movements, and brushed them to the floor with a single violent sweep of his arm.

Bilal sat there in silence.

'Now pick it all up,' Søgaard ordered and got to his feet.

Around the time Lund and Strange's delayed flight lifted off from Kastrup, Thomas Buch found himself watching the Folketinget's decision on the anti-terror package hang in the balance.

Krabbe's sudden demands for more information had led Grue Eriksen to postpone the vote. The Prime Minister had summoned Buch to a brief and ill-tempered meeting in his office. There Buch revealed that a police team had been despatched to Helmand to investigate the alleged atrocity. Flemming Rossing had shrieked about being kept in the dark once more and threatened Buch with expulsion from the parliamentary group. Grue Eriksen listened and said little. Slotsholmen was in the midst of a feverish crisis, one Thomas Buch had never witnessed before.

One, he knew only too well, of his own making.

Back in the Ministry afterwards Plough gave him a judgemental stare and said, 'You're not a man for cards, are you?'

'Of course not. Why?'

'It's called overplaying your hand. All we know is the police sent a team to Helmand. We've no idea what if anything—'

'Do they have any idea what the doctor might say about the hand?'

'No!' Plough replied. 'If you'd only allow me to brief you before shooting off your mouth. The doctor's now their prime murder suspect—'

'I need more ammunition by tomorrow. Grue Eriksen won't let this run for ever.' He turned to Karina. 'See if you can get any communication between the military and the Ministry of Defence on this.'

'By tomorrow?' she asked, wide-eyed.

'Don't we have the right of access?'

'Up to a point. It would normally take a week—'

'We don't have a week! Oh for pity's sake . . .'

He marched into his room, sat at his desk, stared at the growing mountain of papers.

Karina pulled up a chair.

'What is it?' he asked.

'Here's a thought. We stop shouting at people. Instead let's try persuading them it's in their own interest they talk.'

Buch pulled out a drawer, found a chocolate bar, bit on it.

'I've no idea what you're talking about,' he said, mouth half full.

'The only one who can deliver you Grue Eriksen's head is Flemming Rossing.'

Plough groaned.

'Even if that's true, Karina, why on earth would he talk to us?'

'To save himself?' Buch suggested. 'If we make Rossing feel he's more to lose by sticking with Grue Eriksen than coming clean . . .'

He scratched his straggly beard.

'If Rossing knows it's all going to come out anyway he's going to want to limit the damage. When will we hear from Lund?'

'They land in the morning,' Plough said. 'They've only got one day. It seems a lot to ask—'

His phone rang. Without thinking he answered it.

Home. Jutland. His wife, Marie, going on about the kids, about how he hadn't called.

She was mad. So was he. The dam burst. All the suppressed rage and misery came out at that moment, engulfing the wrong person, the last one he would have blamed for anything. Thomas Buch shouted at her, called his wife bad names, used words he never liked.

420

When he finished he put down his mobile and stared at it on his desk as if the phone was responsible somehow. Karina and Plough stared at him, embarrassed, silent.

'No more family calls for now,' Buch ordered in a meek and miserable voice. 'Not until I say.'

It was close to midnight. He wondered what the time was in Afghanistan. How the curious and persistent woman he'd met just once, in a banqueting hall kitchen beneath a wedding, would fare in such a distant, hostile land.

Ten

Lund slept on the passenger jet to Istanbul. Slept after they got on the basic, uncomfortable military transport plane from Atatürk airport to Camp Bastion. Halfway through she woke up, opened her eyes, found her head on Strange's shoulder. He didn't know she was watching him. His placid, ordinary face was staring ahead, at nothing at all.

Memories, she thought. He was recalling the army. Perhaps they never lost it. There was nothing to say. So she shuffled her head from him, slumped in the seat, tried to sleep again, was unsure whether she managed it on the long, boring flight into a place she couldn't imagine, let alone picture.

At Bastion airfield they were driven to Viking, the Danish quarter. It looked like a shanty town of mobile accommodation blocks and tents, with constant traffic, the to and fro of men and equipment.

After their documents had been checked a bored, taciturn officer gave them a soldier as a driver then pointed them to some equipment in the corner of the office. Strange helped her. A hard helmet, covered in khaki material. A jacket so heavy and uncomfortable she hated it the moment he started putting it on her.

'Why do I need a bulletproof vest?' Lund asked. 'We're just going to interview a doctor, aren't we?'

The soldier and the officer stared at her.

'Are we going behind the front line?' she asked, shrugging off the thick, heavy vest.

'This is Helmand,' the officer said. 'There is no front line. Put it on or you can go back to Copenhagen right now.'

Strange was gently pulling it over her arms.

'It's called body armour,' he said. 'It isn't magic. But it can stop an AK47 round from distance. Keep you alive if we hit an IED. Block a knife—'

'Not much use if they shoot you in the head. Or blow your legs off.'

'Dammit, Lund. We've got these back in headquarters. You're supposed to wear them whenever you go out on an armed incident. Don't you even bother then?'

She didn't want to tell him: usually a gun was too much trouble.

'Not much need in Gedser,' she said, then let him drag the khaki vest over her slender frame, tried to shuffle to a position that chafed the least.

'Very fetching,' the officer said. 'Your flight out of here is at seven this evening. You will be on it. Even if I have to strap you in myself.'

Twenty minutes later the Land Rover was bouncing along a rough stony track that seemed to lead to nowhere. The terrain was dry and bare and mountainous, the air cold and dusty. Snow covered the peaks of the surrounding hills. No villages. No other traffic. The driver, twenty-five at the most, with sunglasses and a skimpy moustache, seemed to know the way by heart. Travel had never interested Lund much. Helmand wasn't going to change that.

'This is a bad time for us,' the soldier said. 'We had two suicide bombers this morning. Been quiet for weeks. Then the bastards come back.'

They sat next to one another in the back, Strange at home in the body armour and helmet, Lund fidgeting with it.

'The hospital's frantic,' the driver added. 'Buckle your helmet, please. And your vest. Otherwise they're useless.'

Strange sighed, reached for the straps and did them up before she could say anything. The soldier didn't look happy having a woman in the vehicle.

'Do you want to . . . freshen up when we get to the base?' he asked.

'Just take us to the hospital, will you?' she said. 'We want to see Frederik Holst.'

Thirty minutes later they met the first traffic. A truck with locals in the open back. Farm workers maybe. They squatted in the rear, stared at the Land Rover as it went past. Lund saw the driver tense as they got near. Soon there were more vans, a few battered cars, some army vehicles. Troop carriers, jeeps, armoured cars.

After an hour they pulled into a small town. Women and girls walking round a few vegetable stalls, faces hidden inside gaudy burkas. Men by the roadside sipping tea from glasses, watching the army Land Rover with keen dark eyes.

A checkpoint. Soldiers in uniform with the Danish flag, rifles in their arms. They looked at the driver's papers and waved them through.

It was more like a run-down market hall than a hospital. A single-storey grubby brick building; on the side a large red cross crudely painted against the crumbling plasterwork. She thought of the spot-less, shiny corridors of the Rigshospitalet. Copenhagen was a world away. She was a stranger here, a foreigner, unwelcome to locals and soldiers alike.

Lund climbed out of the door. A man in a turban was hacking a side of raw lamb on a wooden table just outside the perimeter fence, flies all round. He watched as she gathered up her clipboard and folders.

'They all look like that,' Strange said. 'Ordinary. Innocent prob-ably.' His calm, intelligent eyes scanned the area, the way they must have done so many times when he was serving here. 'You never know until it's too late.'

There was a sign by the hospital entrance: NO WEAPONS. The driver checked his with security. They had none anyway.

It was dark inside, the smell a fetid mix of medicine and decay. A couple of locals, an elderly man and a young woman, sat in a corner, crouched on the floor, back against the wall, the woman wailing, the man glassy-eyed.

'You couldn't wait, could you?' the soldier at the desk asked. 'We've got casualties. Ours and theirs.'

'No,' Lund said. 'We can't.'

She walked on. Peered in and out of the side rooms where men struggled on crutches, lay moaning on ancient gurneys. Further along three Afghans sat patiently on chairs, their clothes covered in blood, bandages round their hands.

Someone pushed at her from behind, barked an order to get out of the way.

A stretcher, a figure on it, legs just visible. Or the remains of them, flesh and bone.

A look of pain and disbelief in the soldier's face. A nurse was fixing a drip into his arm, feeding what Lund guessed was painkiller into a vein.

A memory: Jan Meyer unconscious, leaping with the electric shocks they gave him in the ambulance when he was shot.

She hated hospitals. This place more than any she'd seen.

'I'm going home in a week,' the man on the stretcher said in croaky Danish. 'Home. You hear that?'

He struggled to get his head up, peered down his body.

Lund looked again. Two stumps where his feet should have been.

The soldier didn't cry. Just puffed out his cheeks in a big, deep breath then lay back on the grubby stretcher pillow and gazed at the ceiling.

Strange was by her side, silent, watching too.

'Let's get this over with,' she said.

The operating theatre was nothing more than a small area closed off with curtains. One circular light, two nurses in white uniforms, a surgeon in green. A body on the table, mask on, eyes closed, unconscious. A gaping wound in his torso. Peeling walls, barely white as if someone had been fighting a losing battle to keep them clean. A ragged piece of fabric at the window, the white winter sun pouring through the holes.

'Holst?' Lund said, when the man in green came away from the table and issued some orders to the nurses. 'We're—'

'I know who you are. Wait outside, fifteen minutes. Then we'll talk.'

They sat in a small room with an arched ceiling and a single light. Strange let her take off the helmet. The body armour stayed. It took thirty minutes then Holst marched in, tore off his paper mask, threw it into the bin, began to wash his hands in the simple basin.

'We want to know what you did in Copenhagen,' Lund said, watching him.

'I was on leave. Three weeks. A month. Something like that.'

He sat down. A big, unsmiling man with the face of a surly

teenager. The faintest resemblance to his dead brother. Frederik looked tougher, more worn by the war. Lund was struck by a thought: he should have been the soldier, Sebastian the doctor.

'So what?' he said and reached for a drawer, took out a packet of cigarettes, lit one, blew smoke towards the window.

'Where were you?' Strange asked.

'What business is it of yours?'

'We've got a warrant for your arrest. Come up with some answers or you'll be on a plane with us tonight.'

He looked surprised.

'I wanted some time to myself. That's all.'

'You didn't talk to your father?' Lund wanted to know.

'Not much. I told you.' He pushed back some boxes of dressings and drugs on the desk, a stethoscope. 'Do you mind telling me who I'm supposed to have murdered? Just out of politeness, you know.'

She took out the photos from her bag: Anne Dragsholm, Myg Poulsen, David Grüner, Lisbeth Thomsen, Gunnar Torpe.

Holst picked up the picture of Dragsholm.

'The rest look familiar. Who's she?'

'Where were you?' Lund repeated. 'What did you do?'

'I'm a surgeon. I spend my life saving people. Not killing them. You could have phoned. I would have saved you the trip.'

Lund placed the photo of Dragsholm back among the others.

'She was the woman who was going to prove they were innocent. Two years ago you tried to save your brother. We saw his video diary. What he said about Raben.' She reached into the case, took out the squad photo with the crosses on it. 'We found this in the rubbish you threw out from the flat you rented in Islands Brygge.'

He looked at the faces, the marks through them.

'You think Raben was responsible for Sebastian's death, don't you? Anne Dragsholm was going to get him vindicated.'

'I don't even know who that woman is . . .'

Holst stubbed out his cigarette. Someone came to the door and tried to talk to him. He waved them away.

'We know you tried to contact Raben,' Strange went on. 'He sent your letters back.'

'Really?'

'Start talking,' Lund told him. 'We've come a long way. We're not going back empty-handed. You'd better believe that.'

'You're wasting your time. I didn't kill anybody. Why—'

Strange bellowed a curse, slammed his fist on the table. The noise was so sudden and so loud it made Lund jump.

'Don't give me this shit! You had their photo. You crossed them out, one by one.'

'Just a game,' Holst said calmly, with a shrug. 'Something to pass the time.'

'You were here when they brought in your brother.' Lund looked round the miserable little field hospital.

He blinked, didn't look at her.

'It must hurt whoever it is,' she went on. 'But your own brother, wounded alongside the rest—'

'Yeah, yeah! You made your point!'

'And then you find out Raben and the others were to blame. They're alive and he was on the slab.'

Holst pointed a long pale finger at her.

'Stay away from heroes,' he said in a quiet, damaged voice. 'That's my advice. They get you killed.'

'So Raben's got your brother's blood on his hands?'

'Oh yes!' he cried. 'And I hope the bastard burns in hell. But . . .'

They waited. It took a long time.

'That's the way it goes,' Holst said in the end. 'Raben was in command. There's no law that said he couldn't force a kid like Sebastian into that hornets' nest. What could I do?'

He laughed.

'Except put a little surprise in there myself. There was another body part in all the pieces they brought in. A hand.'

His eyes were somewhere else. Holst was remembering.

'I thought if I threw that in then maybe someone back in Copenhagen would start asking a few questions. There were lots of rumours going round. How a family had been murdered.'

'You think they did it?' Strange asked.

'Who else? No one believed that fairy story about an officer. I thought . . .'

He reached for the cigarettes, lit another one.

'I thought the army would get to the bottom of it. Check it out.

Find the truth. We don't cover things up. Not like that. But . . .' A grim, brief smile. 'I was wrong there too. The judge advocate dismissed the idea that any civilians had been killed. They walked away scot-free, until Raben got himself locked up anyway.'

Lund checked through the documents.

'The hand belonged to the suicide bomber,' she said.

'It was a hand. I don't know whose.'

'You were pissed off. You worked up a false medical report—'

'The hand came from the village! Someone should have looked into what went on there!'

'You're in trouble, Holst,' she said.

That short laugh again.

'Oh dear. How very worrying.' He leaned forward. 'Sebastian died here, just round the corner. From a punctured lung. That was all. If it had happened back in Copenhagen he'd be walking round now. It's nothing. But here . . .'

His eyes ranged the room, beyond.

'I couldn't save him. I had to watch him die. And that psychopath Raben, the idiot who made him go into that village, had a fancy lawyer who got them off scot-free. It's a wonder he didn't get a medal. Pissed off?'

The anger broke in him. Both hands, straight from the operating theatre, hammered the desk.

'Yes!' Frederik Holst roared. 'You bet!'

Lund waited.

After a while Holst recovered, said in the same low, flat tone he'd used before, 'But it doesn't matter how pissed off I am. It won't bring Sebastian back. So what else can I do? Except try to save him again. Every single day on that wreck of an operating table.'

Holst sniffed, stubbed out the half-smoked cigarette.

'That's all it amounts to,' he said, pushing the photo with the crossed-out faces back across the table. 'Sorry to disappoint.'

They got nothing more out of Frederik Holst. He had work to do. Another patient, a Taliban fighter, badly wounded and screaming at the nurses.

Lund used the satellite phone to call Copenhagen.

'Holst can't account for his movements during any of the murders. Or won't,' she told Brix.

'Never mind that. Did he do it?'

Even over thousands of miles and a satellite connection his anxiety came through clearly.

'I don't think so.'

'Jesus, Lund. Are you telling me this was all a waste of time?'

'I don't know yet.' They were back in the main reception area. Nurses and another doctor were gathered round the soldier she'd seen earlier. The one who'd lost his feet. 'Has Raben said anything new?'

'He's sticking to the same story.'

'Søgaard's name keeps coming up here,' she lied. 'He was commander when it happened. Everything must have gone through him.'

'Just pack your sunglasses and come home, will you? Søgaard's a surly, unhelpful bastard. We've got nothing on him.'

Silence.

Then, 'Lund? *Lund?*'

She couldn't stop herself looking. The nurses round the trolley had moved back. Except one, a young woman with glassy, sad eyes. She was pulling up the green sheet. Covering the face of the Danish soldier who'd only wanted to go home. To escape the maelstrom for another week. To survive.

Strange stood next to her. He walked in front, blocked her view.

'What does Brix say?' he asked.

'He says we should come home.'

Strange picked up her helmet, placed it carefully on her head, did up the strap, looked into her eyes.

'Brix is right.'

Ruth Hedeby was watching from the end of the corridor as he came off the phone. They knew one another well enough by now. She was a smart, sensitive woman. Could read his face.

'For God's sake, Lennart, tell me this whole adventure was worth it. That we're not just taking a shot in the dark.'

Brix walked to join her. He didn't want anyone else listening in.

'Everything's dark to begin with.'

'Don't get cryptic on me. I've got the Ministry, Parliament, PET on my back every minute of the day.'

Brix nodded.

'They think we've made a breakthrough in the case,' Hedeby added.

He smiled.

'Have we, Lennart?'

'I'm sure the Minister of Justice will understand—'

'He's hanging on to his job by a thread. Probably not for much longer.' She had a newspaper under her arm, took it out. A photo of Thomas Buch looking furious, making accusations he seemed unable to substantiate. 'Don't count on him.'

'I'm still working on this.'

'That's not good enough. We're under a microscope here. Everything we do's under scrutiny.'

'What's new?'

'This,' she said, prodding his jacket. 'Do nothing without my knowledge from now on. I want no more surprises. Or I will suspend you in an instant.'

He watched her go, went back into the office. Asked Madsen what had been happening.

Precious little. The trawl of officers had led to nothing.

'If it's not Frederik Holst,' Madsen said, 'we're left with Raben.'

'How could Raben have done all of this?' Brix asked wearily. 'He was in a cell in Herstedvester.'

One of the detectives came over with a new file.

'We've been chasing the things he was buying in Per K. Møller's name. He didn't use a credit card. Just cash, bought second hand from individuals mainly. If a couple of them hadn't sent receipts to Møller's mother we'd never have known.'

'What did he buy?' Brix asked.

'So far,' the man said, reading from a list, 'we've got a video camera, a laptop, and a copy of the Anarchist's Cookbook. A bomb-making manual. They all got sent to a PO box at the same place Faith Fellow used when he set up that box for Kodmani.'

Brix took the sheet.

'Did he use Møller's name to rent accommodation? Storage space somewhere?'

'Not that we can find. But there may be something.' More notes on his pad. 'The mobile we think was used to set the bomb that killed Grüner was stolen. The SIM's active again.'

Madsen came and stood next to him.

'Where?'

'Somewhere near Ryvangen.'

'Inside the barracks?' Brix demanded.

'Don't know, boss,' the detective replied. 'The signal was weak.'

Brix found himself wishing Lund was back already.

'This doesn't add up. Why would he use the phone again? He knows we're looking for it.'

'Everyone makes mistakes, don't they?' Madsen suggested.

Brix thought for a moment then ordered up a team for immediate dispatch. Decided in an instant he wouldn't tell Ruth Hedeby.

'They're having the funeral service there today,' Madsen pointed out. 'For those dead soldiers. The army won't like it.'

Brix snatched a look at his watch. Wondered what time it was in Helmand. Lund had hours to spare.

'I can live with that,' he said.

The Land Rover was back in the rough mountainous hills between the field hospital and Camp Viking. The driver had orders to take them straight to the Camp Bastion airfield for the plane to Istanbul.

'Maybe we could stop by Viking and ask some questions about Søgaard,' Strange suggested as they got bounced around in the back of the vehicle. 'We've got time.'

She wasn't much interested in that idea. The army said what it wanted to say. It seemed unlikely their guard would drop in a war zone.

'Tell me what happens when you're on a mission,' Lund said. 'Special forces.' She looked at him. 'The kind of thing you ended up doing.'

'Such as what?' Strange replied. She'd half expected him to turn cagey.

'How do you operate? How do you communicate?'

He looked at her.

'I didn't do a lot. Honest.'

'Just tell me!'

'It was always a group of five men. We'd go places sane people didn't. Mostly intelligence. Not fighting. That was too risky.'

'Did you stay in contact with other forces? Ours? The British? The Americans?'

He laughed.

'There aren't any Americans around here. And the answer's no. We were undercover. If it turned hot we shot at anything that moved

431

and hoped we'd get out in one piece.' He pointed at the bleak terrain. 'This is no man's land. You don't stop for a conversation. But we always moved five at a time. A team. Besides . . . didn't Arild say there were no special forces in the area?'

The helmet wasn't too uncomfortable. The vest still annoyed her. Lund tapped on the driver's shoulder.

'Can you stop the car, please?'

'Can't you hang on till we get to the airfield?' he said and kept driving.

'No.'

He swore, pulled in by the side of the rough track.

Lund got out and looked around. After a while Strange joined her.

'What's up?' he asked.

The driver got out too, scanning the rocky hills anxiously.

'How far's the village where Raben's team got attacked?'

Strange slapped his forehead.

'You must be joking.'

'I want to see it.'

'We're not tourists on a day trip!'

'I know that,' she said and looked at the driver. 'Can you take us there? How long?'

The soldier shook his head.

'You don't have authorization.'

'What do you mean we don't have authorization?' Lund yelled at him. 'Do you think they sent us all the way from Copenhagen to get ordered around by a driver? We've got arrest warrants and visas. We can go—'

'You can't leave the military zone,' the man said. 'That's that.'

A step closer, hands on hips.

'We've got full authority from the Ministry of Justice. Here . . .' She pulled out the satellite phone. Brix was right. It did seem to work everywhere. 'I'm going to call Copenhagen. I'm going to get through to the minister himself right now and tell him some adolescent squaddie won't let us go where we need to—'

'Lund!' Strange cried.

She stared him down. Started hitting the buttons.

'What's your name again?' She read the tag on his combat jacket. 'Siegler. OK.'

The soldier went back to the Land Rover, started looking through his documents. Lund didn't place the call.

'Does it say we can't go to the village?' she asked.

No answer.

'Well, does it?'

The man was scanning the hills again, looking for movement.

'I've still got to get you back to Bastion on time.'

'Agreed,' Lund told him. 'And call in the local chief of police. He was in the judge advocate's report. I want to talk to him too.'

The police had found Raben a lawyer. A young, doleful woman who looked as if she'd drawn the short straw from that day's prisoners.

'You're going to be charged with burglary, vehicle theft, possession of a firearm, unlawful imprisonment, violent and threatening behaviour.'

She sat at the interview room desk, flicking through the papers.

'That's for starters. How will you plead?'

His arm was still in a sling though the pain was so muted he could move it with some ease.

'Guilty on all counts?' the lawyer asked.

'Has my wife been in touch?'

She shook her head.

'What about the police officers who went to Helmand?'

'Don't expect any miracles there. That story about the officer is doing you no favours.'

'But it's true.'

She gestured at the papers in front of her.

'Things look bad enough as it is. There's no need to make them worse by provoking people.'

He laughed.

'I'm provoking them?'

'You are. This looks like a long sentence. If they decide you're too unbalanced to be allowed out in public it could be indefinite.' She waited for that to sink in. 'You understand what I'm saying? The judge may say you should never be released.'

'Do you know if Louise has tried to visit me?'

'She hasn't.' The lawyer brushed the papers into her briefcase. 'Someone else has. The police allowed it. He's waiting. I don't think they had any choice . . .'

She got up, went to the door, rapped on it to be let out.

'Help me, Raben. Give me something to work with.'

Then she was gone, and a short, active figure was there instead. Blue uniform. Badges and ribbons. Ginger hair, bright, alert eyes, a smile so insincere it ought to hurt.

'No need to salute,' Arild said as he took a seat. 'It's not as if you're in the army any more, is it?'

Raben was at the window, leaning on the sill, looking enviously at the grey world outside.

'Funny, you know. I've heard so much about you. I looked at your records. Quite a story. You don't mind this little visit, do you?'

Arild held out his hand.

'General Arild from Operational Command. This is official business.'

Raben didn't move.

'Ah well,' Arild murmured, giving up. He took the lawyer's chair, made himself comfortable. 'Make things awkward if you want. I understand you feel we've let you down. I can assure you I'm very sorry you feel that way.'

'Really?'

Arild took out some papers.

'You were a good soldier. Loyal, talented.' A glance. 'Ingenious. If you stick to this nonsense you'll be hurting yourself and the military. I can't believe you want that.'

A pen, a sheet with what looked like a space for a signature.

'The solution to this problem lies with you. Sit, for God's sake!'

Raben did as he was told, couldn't stop himself. There was something in the man's tone.

'Let's help one another,' Arild suggested. 'Instead of this pointless fighting—'

'If you want me to withdraw my statement, forget it.'

Arild had a distant, penetrating stare. He tapped the papers on the table to straighten them.

'On behalf of the military I'd like to offer you compensation. We have the option to adjust the insurance policy you took out with your service contract. At our own discretion—'

'Just fuck off out of here.'

Arild stared at the ceiling for a moment, then at the man.

'This isn't for you. It's for your wife and son. If you'd been killed in action she'd have been entitled to a pension. With a little good will on both sides we can change the conditions of the policy.' He lifted the papers, waved them. 'So it also applies to long-term illness.' The bleak, cold smile again. 'That would make life a lot easier for Louise and Jonas. I'm sure you appreciate that.'

Arild brandished his fountain pen.

'All I ask in return is . . .' The man in the uniform shrugged. 'You know perfectly well. It's up to you.'

He picked up the papers, held them out.

'Your decision entirely. Louise is a fetching young woman. I'm sure she could find herself a new husband. An officer, perhaps. Without any form of income . . .'

Arild peered around the room.

'Who could blame her?'

Louise Raben had placed one call to the Politigården to check on her husband's condition. And five to the army custodial facility at head-quarters, trying to talk to her father.

At nine thirty she made another effort to get through to the military police, walking out of the infirmary, standing in the road, coat on, scarf round her neck, dealing with the switchboard, pleading with an officer to talk to.

Finally she got through to the same man she'd spoken to twice that morning.

'You again?' he said cheerily.

'Look. My father's been with you since yesterday. I'd like to talk to him.'

'He's being questioned.'

'Jesus Christ! If he was a common criminal I'd be able to talk to him.'

'From what I gather you're in a good position to know that,' the man said, laughing. 'I'll take your word—'

'He's my father. A good officer. Won't you—?'

'Can't talk individual cases. Not over the phone. When he's allowed visitors we'll let you know.' A pause. 'Didn't I tell you that earlier? Oh, right. I did. And here you are wasting my time again.'

She wanted to scream. Thought of her husband, furious and making things worse.

'I'm sorry I yelled at you. It's difficult here. We've got the memorial service today.'

He didn't say anything. She could see him mouthing at the phone: really?

'Just do me one small favour,' Louise begged. 'Pass him a message. Tell him—'

'No messages. I told you that already.'

'Well, fine! Thanks for nothing. You . . .'

The line went dead. She was mouthing one long, loud curse when a police car screamed through the red-brick barracks entrance arch, blue light flashing on the roof. Three more followed, lights too. And a white van that came to a halt and started to disgorge men.

Søgaard was in dress uniform. Immaculate, ready for the service. He marched over to the tall, taciturn cop from the Politigården as he climbed out of the first car and started barking orders to the men assembling around them.

'What the hell is this?' Søgaard shouted. 'I didn't get advance notice—'

'We don't give advance notice of raids.' He pulled out an ID, flashed it at Søgaard. 'Lennart Brix. Head of homicide. Remember me?'

'There's a memorial service today.'

'We'll try not to get in your way,' Brix said, pulling a sheet of paper from his heavy blue winter coat. He brandished it at Søgaard. 'This is a search warrant. We've reason to believe there's crucial evidence hidden here.'

'If you told me what you were looking for . . .'

The cop was smiling at him.

'I gather you're in charge now, Søgaard. That was a rapid promotion, wasn't it?'

No answer.

'Unless you want an equally rapid demotion don't get in our way,' Brix added. 'I want someone with all the keys. No one's to leave. Not until I say so.'

He tucked the warrant down the front of Søgaard's jacket, walked off and started to direct his men towards the stores complex.

Louise Raben edged closer, interested by the sudden flash of fear on Søgaard's face. She hadn't seen that before.

Said Bilal had joined him. Just as smart, black beret, ribbons. Never a smile.

'What's up?' he asked.

'Get hold of General Arild,' Søgaard ordered.

Bilal was watching the police.

'What do they want now?'

'Just do as I say!' Søgaard bellowed. 'For fuck's sake . . .'

She walked closer, watched him, noted his anger, didn't smile.

'Deal with it, Bilal, will you?' he said more quietly and didn't meet her eye.

Stalemate on Slotsholmen. Karina was working the phones. Buch was desperately waiting for news from Afghanistan.

'Krabbe's getting a hard time from his own party,' she said coming off a call. 'They don't like kicking up a stink.'

Buch was walking round the office cleaning his teeth with a brush she'd found for him. The moving people were in, ready for his departure. Boxes stacked everywhere.

'I'll talk to him. Krabbe wants to get to the bottom of this just as much as I do.'

She winced.

'What is it?' Buch asked.

'One way or another he's going to want some political gain, Thomas. Where is it?'

'Never mind that.' He finished brushing, got a glass of water, gargled with it then spat everything back into the glass. 'Are the police really coming home without any evidence?'

'Plough knows more about that than I do.'

'Then where the hell is he? Why does he always disappear just when I want him?'

She was barely listening. One of the transport people wanted instructions. He went off with two boxes of folders.

'The press have given up on you. Three members of Parliament have accused you of treason.'

'What?' Buch's face lit up with rage. He ran his fingers through his hair. 'Treason? What century are these morons living in?'

Plough came through the door. Grey suit, tie. Always the civil servant.

'We need evidence the Prime Minister shelved that first medical report,' Buch said. 'And where in God's name have you been?'

Plough came and stood in front of him, hands in pockets. The surest sign of rebellion he had. He gestured at Buch's face. Toothpaste on the beard. Karina passed him a napkin and told him to wipe it away.

'All the evidence we've seen,' Plough went on, 'suggests the doctor was happy with the revised report. No one's suggesting Grue Eriksen's murdered civilians. These accusations of yours . . .'

Buch's mind was wandering.

'Thomas!' Plough pleaded. 'At least fight battles you've a hope of winning! We should focus on Rossing. We know he was involved. We know he hid things.'

'Rossing would never do all this on his own. He doesn't have the balls. Where is he now?'

Karina checked the government diary on the nearest computer.

'At the memorial service in Ryvangen. For the dead soldiers.'

Buch went for his jacket, a tie. And, almost as an afterthought, stripped off his shirt from the night before and found a clean one.

'Get me a car.'

Flowers and four coffins draped in the Danish flag set in a line next to the black stone font. A lone trumpet echoing through Ryvangen's tiny chapel. The place was cold. Flemming Rossing shivered next to the biers, staring at the bouquets and the regimental caps by their side.

The service was postponed. The police were searching the barracks. Army personnel had been confined to quarters during the investigation. Only a lone undertaker, black jacket, black tie, white shirt, joined Rossing and the trumpeter in the chapel. The relatives were in the mess hall. If the search continued no soldiers or officers would be able to take part.

The door opened. A large, heavy figure marched through. Rossing turned, saw, took a deep, pained breath.

Buch sat down in the pew behind him.

'More fairy stories to throw at me? What are you doing here? Were you invited?'

Buch's voice was low and croaky.

'I know you don't trust me. But we've more in common than you think.'

Rossing kept his eyes on the coffins and the red and white flags.

'I seriously hope that isn't so. I hear your little adventure in Afghanistan proved fruitless. There's a surprise. No wonder you're stressed.'

A low, muttered curse close to Rossing's ear.

'Don't play the pompous ass with me,' Buch hissed. 'You think you served a higher purpose.'

'I have.'

Buch's heavy arm came up by Rossing's face and pointed ahead.

'Do you think they'd agree?'

'They're the reason. Every coffin reminds me we've got to continue until no death's in vain.'

'That's politician's claptrap and you know it. This wasn't about war, about victory. Not for Grue Eriksen. It was about power and money and votes.'

Rossing turned and stared at him, said nothing.

Buch got up, came and stood in front of him.

'I know you didn't do this on your own, Rossing. You got your orders and you obeyed them. These men . . .' His voice was louder than ever, his bearded face contorted with anger. 'They died because of what happened.'

'You don't know that—'

'Deny it then!' Buch roared. 'You've got a responsibility, for fuck's sake. At least Monberg had a conscience.'

'And it killed him . . .'

Buch threw up his hands in fury.

'And who killed them?'

The undertaker strode towards him.

'You have to leave now. I demand it. This behaviour's quite inappropriate.'

'Inappropriate?' Buch stared at Rossing, shook his head. 'That's a good word, isn't it?'

'You must leave or I will order the guards!' the undertaker said more firmly.

'He'll load the blame on you,' Buch yelled, going for the door. 'Just like he did with Monberg. And me.'

Rossing sat, eyes closed, face stony and grey.

'We need each other,' Buch added. 'If you can find yourself a spine you know where I am.'

Forty minutes into the search, Brix and Madsen were walking through the main officers' quarters, watching the teams go through desks and lockers and filing cabinets.

They hadn't found a single thing.

'Try calling the phone again,' Brix ordered.

'Done that,' Madsen replied. 'Maybe the battery's dead.'

'Have you looked in the basements? The cellars? The . . .'

They went into the entrance hall.

'Big place,' Madsen said, admiring the elegant ceiling and the curved staircase. 'With the men we've got this is going to take a couple of days.'

'I want every inch searched. I don't care how long it takes. There's something here. There has to be . . .'

He stopped. A man was walking down the stairs, blue uniform, ginger hair, sharp, intelligent face hard with anger. General Arild had a phone to his ear and was speaking in a whisper.

'Stop!' Arild said in a voice so full of authority he barely needed to raise it.

He'd put the call on hold, not finished it.

'I know what you're going to say,' Brix told him. 'Don't waste your breath. This is an official police investigation. We're here for the duration. Live with it.'

Arild's bleak eyes fixed on him. He held out the phone.

'For you.'

Brix snatched the mobile from his hand. He knew who'd be on the other end.

'What the hell are you doing?' Hedeby shrieked down the line.

'This isn't a good time.'

'Pack your things and get out of there. That's an order. How dare you . . .?'

Søgaard had come to join Arild. The two soldiers stood next to one another, arms folded, faces calm and confident.

'I'm in charge here,' Brix said. 'I take full responsibility for the situation. Once the search is finished I'll get back to you.'

'Not this time. I've talked to the commissioner. You've no author-ity any more. Get out of there.'

He took the phone away from his ear. Heard her ask quietly, 'Lennart . . . ?'

Arild reached out and removed it from his fingers.

'If you're not gone in five minutes,' he said, 'God help you.'

The coldest of smiles then Arild turned on his heel and left, with Søgaard walking obediently behind.

Brix stood in the chilly hall, unable to think for a moment. He'd suspended officers himself in the past. It was never easy.

His own phone rang.

'Yes?'

'We've got something in the basement. You need to come now.'

Two floors down beneath the officers' hall. Central heating pipes, low lights, dusty and cold. Brix and Madsen put on latex gloves, walked to the team of men huddled by the door at the end of the corridor.

A locker room. Rows and rows of wooden doors, all of them open now. A woman forensic officer was shining a torch into the space of one in the middle. The man with her reached inside.

A phone with a flashing green light.

'It's the number,' the officer said. 'The same SIM used to trigger the call that killed Grüner.'

There was a long red metal box on the shelf below the phone. A small brass padlock keeping it secure.

Brix pointed at it.

'Let's have a look.'

The woman got a pair of bolt cutters and removed the padlock. Brix walked in front of them, bent down, opened the lid with his gloved hands. Someone shone a torch.

He picked up the first thing he found. A glittering piece of metal. Dog tags on a single chain, severed in half, one of them covered in dried blood.

Brix stood up, closed the door. Looked at the name on the locker. Søgaard.

Called Ruth Hedeby.

'Just listen for once, will you?' he said as she began to squawk.

*

It was barely a village at all. Just a collection of wrecked buildings inside a low perimeter wall breached by force and weather. A few houses made of mud and brick, every one reduced to broken shells. A boy of ten or so was feeding a small flock of goats outside what was once a gate. He fled the moment the Land Rover appeared.

Lund got out with Strange. The driver picked up his assault rifle and joined them. The place lay in a long valley surrounded by barren fields. A burnt-out pickup stood by the nearest house. The marks on it, black and ugly, could have been a bomb blast.

Beyond stood a white truck with a blue lamp on the roof. A stocky man in a blue police uniform leaned on the side smoking a cigarette. Two others in long robes, turbans round their heads, sat in the back, rifles slung round their shoulders.

'Salam Alaikum,' the soldier said as he approached them.

The policeman threw his cigarette to the ground, stamped it out, looked into their eyes and shook their hands, Lund last.

He didn't say a word, just grabbed his rifle out of the back then led them inside the compound, with the two men making up the rear.

Strange had the file. It was hard to connect what it contained with the wrecked house the cop showed them. Black smoke stained the front from the suicide attack. The windows were broken and open to the bitter winter blasts. Most of the furniture was gone. Just a few broken chairs and a tiny table in the living room.

Strange led the way upstairs.

'According to the investigation Raben's people got the family up here.'

Three rooms, only one of any size. More trashed furniture. A grubby cooking pot. On the floor broken glass and bullet casings. She picked one up. Strange came and looked at it.

'That's a 5.56,' he said. 'Danish army M-95. This is the place.'

She went into the small room next door. Kicked open an old chest. Tried to rifle through the broken doors and cabinets. The place looked as if a deadly hurricane had hit it.

Back downstairs. A big fireplace, sooty and damp. A rickety kitchen table.

'The soldiers slept in shifts in here,' Strange said, going through the notes.

A single mattress. She picked it up, looked. No sign of blood.

Next to it the entrance hall, behind a door off its hinges.

'This is where the family were killed?' Lund asked.

'According to Raben,' Strange agreed. 'He said the corpses were moved one room along.'

He took out a torch, opened another rickety door. One more empty space.

'So they didn't dare go outside?'

Raben shook his head.

'Not if there were Taliban out there. How could they?'

'But there's nothing here! Just some casings. No blood. No sign of rations. You wouldn't . . .' It felt so wrong. 'You wouldn't think anyone lived here.' She opened the ragged, grubby curtain and looked at the bleak parched countryside. 'Died here either.'

The driver was getting worried.

'Are we done yet?' he asked.

'We've plenty of time,' Lund said. 'I want to talk to the policeman. Can you translate?'

They went back into the big room. The cop was seated on a chair, the two men he came with stood over him like guards. They were all smoking. The man in the blue uniform looked bored and surly.

'Who lived here?' Lund asked.

Waited for the translation.

'A family of five. Some people thought the father was a drug lord who gave money to the Taliban,' the soldier said eventually.

'Does he think they were killed by Danish soldiers?'

The cop yawned, got up, brushed the dirt from his cap, picked up his rifle. Said something slowly.

'No,' the soldier translated. 'He said there was no sign of the family.'

Lund kept her eyes on the man.

'So they just disappeared?'

'People do,' the soldier said. 'Don't push it.'

There was something on the floor. It looked like a big wooden paddle with a handle. Lund picked it up.

'What's this?'

The cop made an eating gesture, said something.

'It's for bread,' the soldier said. 'The family ran a bakery.'

'As well as selling dope for the Taliban?' Lund asked.

'It happens.'

'Where's the oven?'

A long stream of Pashto.

'He says everything was destroyed.'

'In that case show me where the oven was.'

'Lund,' Strange whispered.

'What?'

'We're not welcome here. We need to get back.'

There was a back yard. Some low buildings in it.

'I'm not done yet,' she said.

Buch sat at his desk, watching the boxes move out of the office, listening to Plough whining about the confrontation in the Ryvangen chapel.

'Thomas . . .' Plough began. It was always first-name terms now. 'What could you possibly hope to gain?'

'Rossing's no fool,' Buch said. 'He knows Grue Eriksen may come gunning for him next. I gave him a chance. He didn't take it. I've called in some private lawyers to discuss our options. I want you to sit in with them—'

'We've got bigger things to worry about!' Plough cried.

'Such as?'

'Lund's investigation in Afghanistan.'

'So what?' Buch replied, shaking his head. 'If she's going to go all that way—'

'She's left the military zone without authorization.'

'Then send her some.'

'You've no idea how these things work. Afghanistan's a NATO operation. There are international rules. We've broken them. Operational Command are furious. The British are pissed off—'

'When aren't they?'

Karina rapped on the door. She was dressing down these days, as if her time was numbered too. Red shirt, tight jeans.

'I've got the Minister of Defence outside,' she said, looking more than a little surprised. 'He wants to see you in private. Shall I . . . ?'

Buch clapped his hands, was out of his seat in a moment. Rossing walked in, waited for Karina and Plough to leave.

'If you've come about some trivial clearance issue for the police in Helmand, forget it,' Buch said.

'No,' Rossing said with a wry smile. 'I've given up trying to guess what you'll do next there.'

'Then what can I do for you?'

Rossing took a seat by the window. He looked different. Defeated maybe.

'I've always been loyal to Grue Eriksen. Why wouldn't I be?'

'Congratulations.'

Rossing's hooded eyes looked him up and down.

'Sometimes that meant I had to compromise. On policy. On principles. That's politics.'

'I would have said that was compromise.'

'One week in office and you're lecturing me?' It was said more with sorrow than anger, Buch thought, and that surprised him. 'It's never easy. Never simple. When we heard these stories about civilians being killed . . .'

Rossing looked out of the window.

'There was a lot going on. We needed more money. More soldiers.' He looked weary, jaded. 'One decision always impacts on another. You tip over a domino here. Another falls somewhere else, and then a line with it. The Prime Minister and I agreed to put off the investigation of the hand. I'd no idea where it could lead.'

Rossing leaned forward, looked into Buch's eyes.

'If I'd known for one moment . . . Poor Monberg. All these murders . . .'

Buch sat down next to him and waited.

'Maybe some alarm bells should have been ringing,' Rossing murmured. 'I'm not proud—'

'What bells?'

'The doctors who looked at the hand saw some inconsistencies. We felt it was inconclusive. Military intelligence told us none of the victims were civilians.'

'Rossing. You're the Minister of Defence. You of all people can find out the truth . . .'

The aquiline head went back and Flemming Rossing let loose a long, hearty laugh.

'Oh God. You're such a child sometimes. Do you think I know everything? Do you imagine for one moment they tell me every last detail? Or that I want to hear it? This is war. This is government—'

'What inconsistencies?'

Rossing's face was back at the window, distant, as if he didn't want anyone or anything to witness this. He reached into his jacket and took out some papers, read from them.

'There was a henna tattoo,' he said then passed over the sheet.

Buch looked. A photo of a severed hand. The palm marked by a brown circular tattoo.

'We consulted some experts,' Rossing went on. 'They said it was typical of the Hazara people. They hate the Taliban. Fear them too, with good reason. There's this . . .' He pointed to the second finger. A band of pale metal there. 'It's a gold ring. The Taliban don't wear gold. This is a woman's hand. It can't possibly be that of a suicide bomber.'

There were no words in Thomas Buch's head for a while. Then he dared to ask the question.

'Did the Prime Minister know about this?'

Flemming Rossing closed his eyes.

'It's not on the record.'

'But did he know?'

A brief laugh. .

'Haven't you worked that out yet? Gert knows things he's never been told. Gets favours he's never asked for. That's why he's Prime Minister. The man in charge. The one to whom we're all beholden.' Rossing eyed him carefully. 'Even you if you knew it.'

Then he got to his feet.

'Why are you telling me this?' Buch asked.

'It's what you wanted, isn't it?'

'But why? Why now?'

'Poor Buch,' Rossing said with a shake of his head. 'You can't feel the earthquake coming, can you?' He tapped the papers. 'I'm going now. Those are for you. Do with them as you see fit.'

Buch thought about it for the best part of five minutes after Rossing was gone. Then he called in Plough and Karina, asked them to sit in front of his desk, keep out the moving people for a while.

'What is it?' Plough asked warily.

'A change of strategy,' Buch said, passing them the papers about the hand.

'I didn't like the look on Flemming Rossing's face,' the civil servant grumbled. 'Are you telling me it's you two against Grue Eriksen now?'

'Read what he gave me,' Buch demanded and waited till they'd both looked at the photo with the tattoo and the report attached to it.

'How can you trust him?' Karina asked. 'After all the lies. All the tricks he's pulled? Why would he get an attack of conscience now?'

'This has nothing to do with conscience,' Buch replied. 'He's scared. He's using me to warn off Grue Eriksen. I'm going to talk to Krabbe. Get me something from Lund. Let's find out what we can from PET. The police . . .'

Plough wriggled on his seat.

'Well?' Buch asked.

'Erik König's been summarily dismissed. On the order of the Prime Minister's office.'

'I'm still the Minister of Justice! He's mine to fire!'

'And Grue Eriksen's the Prime Minister. It's done. König's gone.' Plough wrinkled his nose in puzzlement. 'I asked him why and he wouldn't tell me. A replacement will be announced tomorrow. I find this somewhat disturbing . . .'

Brix put Søgaard in an interview room with Madsen. No major's jacket any more. Just a plain military shirt, beret on the table. He didn't look cowed in the slightest.

'This is ridiculous,' Søgaard complained. 'I told you a million times. I haven't used that locker in months. It's just coincidence it's still got my name on it.'

'Coincidence?'

'Exactly.'

'Here's another one.' Madsen was standing by the window, looking down at the man at the table. 'The phone we found there was used to murder Grüner.'

Søgaard shrugged.

'If you say so. It's not mine.'

Brix was getting bored with this game. He opened the folder that had just turned up from forensic. Photos of the severed dog tags found in Søgaard's locker.

'Take a look at these and tell me they're a coincidence. The lab's gone through and examined all the halves.'

Søgaard glanced at the pictures and said nothing.

'Every one matches a half found with the victims,' Brix said, spreading out the five photos: bloody metal and chains. 'This places you in the crime, Søgaard. Start coming out with some answers.'

'Like what?' He barely looked at the pictures. 'I haven't seen these things before. I've no idea how they got there.'

Brix threw a plastic evidence bag onto the table and asked, 'What's that?'

Søgaard loosened his black tie. Picked up the envelope, threw it on the table.

'A key. New to me. I've never seen it before.'

'I'm charging you with all five murders,' Brix told him.

'Then you're making a big mistake.'

'You said you'd never met Anne Dragsholm. That's a lie. You knew she was reopening the old case.'

'God this is tedious . . .'

'You're going to be charged,' Brix repeated. 'You'll be put in solitary pending the investigation. We'll let the army see you when we feel like it.' He scooped up the photos, turned to Madsen. 'Get him out of here.'

'Wait.'

Søgaard didn't look so cocky any more.

'So I did meet the Dragsholm woman. She phoned me at Ryvangen pushing for a meeting. Mouthy cow who wouldn't take no for an answer. I told her Raben's story was a pack of lies. She didn't believe me so I said she could go to hell.' He picked up his beret. 'End of story.'

'You lied,' Madsen repeated.

'I didn't want to get involved. Why would I kill my own men?'

Brix shuffled the photos, listened.

'And if I did,' Søgaard went on, 'do you really think I'd be dumb enough to leave an incriminating phone, switched on, in a locker with my name on the door?'

'Let's see what the judge thinks, shall we?' Brix said.

'No!' Søgaard was getting scared. 'This is all wrong. We didn't care about Dragsholm. Raben's story was just bullshit.'

'We?' Brix asked. 'You mean you and Jarnvig?'

'No. The colonel's too damned nosy for his own good sometimes. I wasn't going to push this in front of him.'

'Then who?'

'Said Bilal. He was my number two when Jarnvig was in Kabul.

He handled all the radio traffic reports when the investigation happened.' Søgaard tapped the table. 'He can confirm everything I say.'

Brix took out a pen and a pad, scribbled a few things.

'How did Bilal react when Dragsholm starting flinging the mud around?'

'Mad as hell. You'd think it was personal. Bilal's a Muslim but he's a Dane first. He hates those fanatics more than anyone. A good man. Operational Command like him. Arild especially. He was the one who saw Raben with Jarnvig and told Arild about it. I guess . . .' Søgaard broke into a sarcastic smile. 'A dark face looks good on the recruiting posters these days.'

'Does Said Bilal have access to those lockers in the basement?'

'Knock it off. He can barely think for himself.'

'Does he have access?'

A memory from somewhere. Søgaard scratched his head.

'He said something a week or so ago about how we weren't supposed to use the place. The ceiling was unsafe or something. Maybe it could collapse.'

'No one mentioned that when we went down there,' Madsen said.

Søgaard was gripping his major's beret, pummelling it nervously.

'I didn't kill anyone,' he said. 'You're wasting your time if you try to pin this on me.'

The lawyer was back. She'd spoken to Arild. That much was clear.

'So,' she said as they walked through police headquarters, towards the car back to the hospital, 'this is all agreed? You'll withdraw your statement about the officer and civilian casualties?'

Three cops with them. Burly men. One jabbed Raben in the chest when he wouldn't walk quickly enough.

He made a low, pained noise. Arm still in a sling. He was limping too.

The lawyer was getting irate.

'You shot this man yesterday,' she yelled at the cop. 'Don't push him around too.'

'We're with him all the way to hospital,' the detective said. 'Once they tell us he's fine to be released he goes to jail.'

They were passing through the main investigation room. Photos on the wall. Bloodied corpses. Weapons. Dog tags.

Raben stared at them, glanced at the three cops.

Sleepy men who thought being tough was all you needed.

There was a huddle of detectives by the photos. The lawyer, a smart, quick woman, he thought, one who never missed an opportunity, told him to wait a moment and went to talk to them.

Raben looked at the cops and smiled. Then held his arm, the one in a sling, and winced.

'Getting shot's no fun. Twice in two years. I must be unlucky.'

'Must be something,' the one who pushed him muttered.

Raben just smiled again. The lawyer came back. She seemed happy too.

'We won't be having a hearing tomorrow.' She glanced at the men around him. 'I'm going to ask for him to be kept in a secure room in the hospital. Until we can get to court—'

'What's the delay?' he asked.

'They think they've got their man. Major Søgaard's in custody, about to be charged. They found incriminating evidence in his locker.'

'Oh for God's sake,' Raben yelled. 'Søgaard? Are you serious?'

She didn't like his response.

'You're a hard man to please. You've been telling all the world someone in the army was involved.'

'It wasn't Søgaard. He wasn't Perk. He couldn't be . . .'

The big cop said, 'Can we go now?'

Then pushed Raben towards the exit.

They took the long way out. Down the black marble corridors, to the tall staircase leading to the front entrance.

'I can't come with you to the hospital,' the lawyer said, looking at the cops. 'You're not allowed to question him without me present. Is that clear?'

No answer.

He was limping again, taking the steps one by one.

'Søgaard might cover something up but he's not a murderer,' Raben went on.

'Why don't you just shut up and walk?' the first detective barked. 'You're boring me.'

'He's an injured man,' the lawyer shrieked at him.

'He's a piece of shit who's been giving us the runaround—'

'Søgaard's not your man!'

'Really?' The cop folded his arms, stopped on the stairs. 'We found the other half of the dog tags in his locker. How do you explain that, smart arse? Now move, will you?'

The gentlest of pushes and Raben almost stumbled, would have done if the cop's arm wasn't through his.

Bottom of one flight of steps. Another ahead.

'My wife and son are at the barracks,' Raben yelled at him. 'This matters—'

'You're really getting to me now . . .'

Raben was screaming. The second cop came in, told him to relax, jabbed him in the back.

The lawyer was shouting again. They watched Raben in his blue prison suit stumble forward on weak legs, one arm flapping, the other trapped in a sling. Over the second flight of steps then down them, tumbling all the way to the bottom.

'Shit,' the big cop said when he got there. He held Raben's head, felt his pulse. 'He needs the hospital now.'

Night in the barracks. Quiet and deserted with the latest troop dispatch headed for Helmand. Louise Raben had spent most of the evening trying to track down her father. Now Søgaard was missing. The place seemed rudderless.

She walked round the empty offices looking for someone to talk to, to nag. Finally found Said Bilal in the weapons store cleaning a service rifle.

He didn't look up as she walked in. Never smiled. Never responded.

'Bilal,' she said. 'What the hell's going on here? The military police still won't tell me when they're going to release my father.'

He cradled the weapon in his arms, stroked the oiled barrel. Glowered at her, said nothing.

'What the hell were the police doing here anyway?' she demanded.

'I don't know,' he said with a shrug. 'The last one's gone. They took Søgaard.'

She crouched down next to him, tried to see into his blank and surly face.

'My father found out someone had concealed the radio messages during Jens's mission. Kept them from the judge advocate.'

He went back to the rifle, took out the magazine, checked it in the dim light of the store.

451

'Who would have done that?' she asked. 'It's got to be a soldier here. Someone who was serving with the unit.'

He stood up, ran his eye down the sight.

'Don't you care, Bilal? Don't you see how important this is? It shows Jens was right. Someone fitted him up—'

'It's war!' Bilal roared and his dark eyes were full of such fury she felt frightened for a moment. 'You've never been there. You don't know what it's like.'

'Don't say that,' Louise Raben said quietly. 'I've seen what it does. Someone set up my husband—'

'There were no messages. No one concealed anything. Raben was a rogue soldier. Just a shame he took others with him.' A fierce glance into her face. 'Not himself.'

She stood her ground.

'That's not what my father thinks, is it? He's got evidence. Maybe the same man put those things in Søgaard's locker—'

Bilal swore. It was the first time she'd ever heard that. Put the rifle back on the table, got up, walked to the boxes of weapons.

'If they found those things Søgaard must have put them there,' he said. 'Who else? He's an idiot. I told everyone to keep out of the place. The ceiling's not safe—'

'Who was running the radio two years ago, Bilal?'

Another rifle was in his hands. He held it the way they all did. As if the weapon was a part of him.

'You're a nurse. Stick to what you're paid for.'

'I'm Raben's wife! Your colonel's daughter. The two men who matter to me most are in shit because of this—'

'There's a computer log!' he yelled at her. 'It's just a list of traffic. That's all.'

She wasn't going to leave this.

'Let's say someone worked out how they could delete messages. I guess Søgaard could have done that. He was in command. Who else?'

He took out the rifle magazine, looked inside, ran a finger across the breach, slammed it back into the body.

'I can't talk about this any more,' Bilal said. 'It's army business. Not yours.'

'Call that bastard Arild! Find out who ratted on my father about the cadets' ball.'

He stared at her.

'What?'

'God you're slow. As soon as my father started digging some-one got him arrested. Why? Because he *was* digging. If we find out who . . .'

He came and stood in front of her, young, foreign face devoid of expression.

'Make the call,' she insisted. 'Tell the police too. They need to know.' She shook her head. 'If you won't do it, I will . . .'

Slowly Bilal pulled his phone out of his pocket. She watched as his fingers ran across the keys.

He wasn't dialling.

'I'm waiting . . .' she began.

He looked round the empty store, put the phone back into his pocket.

Stretched out his hand, gripped her round the throat, squeezed hard.

The driver watched Lund breaking up the shattered tables in the outside bakery. He was getting jumpier all the time.

'I've talked to the base,' he said. 'They want us out of here right now.'

She'd got splinters in her fingers. Cut herself a couple of times. Found nothing at all.

Strange leaned against the doorway, arms folded, silent.

'I want to see this oven,' she said. 'Where is it?'

The Afghan cop called through from the adjoining room. He'd found another fireplace, full of soot and burned logs.

Lund looked.

'That's not an oven,' she said. Stared at the man, said, 'Oven!'

'That's helping,' Strange muttered. A trilling sound. The satphone in his pocket.

The Afghan threw up his hands in despair. Said something she didn't understand but couldn't miss the tone.

Lund marched back into the first room. A pile of timber had been set up at the end. She began to tear at it as one of the Afghans behind her turned his torch beam on the wood.

Finally she saw a stack of broken bricks and boulders. They looked as if they'd been pushed in place to hide something.

The Afghan and the soldier were behind her.

'Right,' she said. 'We have to remove all the debris and see what's behind here.'

The two of them started talking in Pashto. The Afghan put a hand to his head, made a gesture.

'He thinks you're crazy,' the soldier said. 'I'm with him on that.'

'What happened here led to murder!' she yelled at them. 'An entire family.'

'We don't know that, Lund,' Strange said, coming off the phone.

'But we do!' she cried. Finger pointed in the face of the Afghan. He didn't like that. 'If you know something about this tell me now. A family, for God's sake! Mother and father. Three children.'

The soldier was translating again. The cop looked bored.

'I need to know what happened to them!' Lund yelled.

To her amazement the burly bearded cop looked at her and started laughing. He said something to the soldier.

'Families round here die every day in case you didn't notice,' he translated. 'Since when did you people care?'

The Afghan glared at her, lit a cigarette.

Lund shook her head, astonished, furious.

'What the fuck is that supposed to mean? Hey. Hey!'

Strode over, grabbed his arm. Bad idea. He didn't like a woman doing that, had his hand on his rifle. Not that she cared.

'Hey! Mister!' she bawled. 'When people get killed it matters, even here. What in God's name's wrong with you? Don't you give a fuck or what?'

Lund glared at the soldier.

'Translate that, damn it.'

He was saying something. She wasn't sure it was right.

'Tell me what happened,' Lund said, patting his blue chest. 'Or is that uniform just a big fat joke like you? What happened to the bodies? You're the law around here. You must have seen something, heard something.'

He was very still, peering straight into her eyes. Not a pleasant look.

'Did someone bury them? Cremate them? Take them somewhere else?'

Something the soldier didn't translate.

'You don't care, do you?' Lund yelled. 'Don't give a shit. No wonder they're dead . . .'

He was in her face then. Pushing her back with his fat belly. That made her even madder.

Strange was the first to get between them. Hand out, keeping back the man in blue. He said something in Pashto to the cop, then to her in Danish, 'Easy now, Lund. It's their country. Not ours.'

'We came here, Strange! If we killed this family we're responsible—'

'We've been through everything. There's no oven. No bodies. No sign of any anything.'

'It happened—'

Strange held out the phone.

'It's Brix. He wants to talk to you. He thinks he's got his man.'

Lund took the mobile, went outside, heard them making consoling noises to the fat Afghan cop.

'I want you on a plane now,' Brix said. 'I've got the Ministry of Defence and the army all over us.'

'What's up?'

'It looks like it's Said Bilal.'

She stared at the wrecked courtyard, the house reduced to rubble in front of her. A family died here. She knew that somehow. She could still hear their cries.

'Bilal knew Dragsholm was opening the case,' Brix continued. 'We found the other halves of the dog tags at the barracks. He tried to fit up Søgaard.'

'At the barracks? Why would Bilal hide things there? He's not Perk—'

'Bilal's gone missing. Louise Raben could be with him. Just get on the damned plane, will you?'

The line went dead. Lund tried to picture the young soldier. He seemed so subservient. A follower. Not a leader.

The driver seized her arm.

'Now we really are going,' he said.

Buch had called the Prime Minister's office demanding another meeting. To his surprise he got it. Gert Grue Eriksen sat in the centre of the table, Kahn on his left. Buch took the seat opposite. Rossing came and sat next to him.

The Prime Minister watched as his Minister of Defence took that seat. A long, hard stare.

'Plenty to talk about,' Buch began without being asked. He'd found his best suit, a clean blue shirt, a dark tie. His hair was tidy, his beard trimmed. Karina had insisted on all these. 'As you may know, little new has so far come to light in the investigation in Afghanistan. That changes nothing. We have a scandal on our hands. A stain on the history of this party, and our government.'

'Same old, same old,' Kahn cut in. 'That's it? The police have come up with nothing?'

'Not yet. But if I may continue—'

'You've launched a personal attack on the Prime Minister's integrity,' Kahn interrupted. 'I'm not listening to more of your rants.'

'Then why are we here?' Buch laughed. 'If it's not to consider the facts?'

Grue Eriksen shook his head and said, 'For better reasons, Thomas. Please listen carefully. This isn't easy for me. I've received information . . .'

He handed a brown leather folder to Kahn who knew straight away what to do. A set of papers was distributed round the table.

'It's clear the Minister of Defence has deceived us,' Grue Eriksen went on.

Rossing stared at the shiny table as if expecting every word.

'He withheld a certain expert's testimony.'

The papers arrived in front of them. The severed hand with the Hazara tattoo. Rossing stared at it, looked at Buch.

'This testimony suggests the hand found in Afghanistan and shipped here did not belong to a Taliban suicide bomber. This information was suppressed to avoid the suspicion of civilian casualties.'

'That's not true . . .' Rossing began.

'If only I could believe that,' Grue Eriksen replied. He paused, stared at Rossing across the table. 'But I don't. You're dismissed as Minister of Defence with immediate effect. Your actions will be investigated by PET to see if criminal charges are appropriate—'

'Say it, Rossing!' Buch cried. 'Tell Kahn. He ordered you to hide those papers.' A finger pointing across the table. 'This bloody, scandalous trail leads directly to him—'

'With regard to the Minister of Justice,' Grue Eriksen went on, 'the situation is equally grave.'

'Oh for pity's sake,' Buch grumbled.

A shake of the silver head. A politician's look, more sorrow than anger.

'You could have used your talents to benefit your country, Thomas. Instead you abused your office to pursue a misguided and unwarranted personal campaign against me.'

Buch tried to catch Kahn's eye.

'Listen, will you? The Prime Minister instructed Rossing to do these things. For his own reasons—'

'In this prolonged smear campaign,' Grue Eriksen continued, 'the Minister of Justice has been scandalously careless in his handling of confidential and privileged information. He has distributed classified documents to people who should never have seen them. There's an apparent breach of the Official Secrets Act which the new director of PET will be investigating alongside Rossing's actions—'

'Ha! So you squeezed him out to get in your own man! Now I understand. Wouldn't even König do your bidding? Is this the Middle Ages again, Gert? Are you a medieval king who'll march me out into the parade ground for a beheading?'

At a signal from the Prime Minister the clerk got up and opened the door. Police in uniform. Plain-clothes men too. Rossing stood up and buttoned his jacket, as if ready for this. Buch kept yelling abuse at the short, composed figure opposite.

'You won't get away with this,' he barked as someone brusquely took his arm.

'Both of you will leave the building immediately and be taken into custody. You can't take anything with you. I think it's evident you've stepped down now.'

Two of the uniformed cops had hold of Buch's big frame. He was screaming, fighting them.

'Go with dignity, Thomas!' Grue Eriksen cried, raising his voice for the first time.

Buch was a big man. With his two fat arms he threw them off, sent the cops scuttling to the back of the room.

Then he went to the door.

'I can walk on my own,' he yelled and did until they caught up with him, shoved him out into the public area and the media scrum.

He should have guessed they'd be tipped off. Everyone was there. TV, radio, newspapers.

Rossing walked on, head high, silent. Buch followed, sweating, panting, dishevelled again, struggling through the mob.

A microphone in the face. A single stupid question.

'Are you guilty? Buch? Rossing? Are you guilty?'

Marie would see this on the news in Jutland. Their last conversation had not been good.

So Thomas Buch managed to wriggle free from the police officers who'd seized his arms one last time.

Then he got to the nearest camera and said a single word.

'No.'

It was dark by the time the Land Rover got back on the road. Lund was dog-tired, her head full of questions. The body armour felt heavy and unnecessary. But Strange was onto her the moment she tried surreptitiously to loosen it.

There was a bright moon. With the snow on the hills the place almost looked enchanting.

'Why did this happen?' she asked.

He didn't answer.

'Why? If there were no civilian casualties there was nothing for Dragsholm to investigate. Why kill all those people?'

'Jesus, Sarah. You can't know everything. We'll be back in Copenhagen tomorrow. Let's ask Brix then.'

He sighed.

'You shouldn't have talked to the Afghan like that. They don't appreciate it.'

'He didn't give a shit.'

'Maybe he's got more on his plate than you know. This is Helmand. Not Vesterbro.'

'Why would Bilal take Louise Raben with him? You don't think . . . ? The two of them?'

Strange laughed.

'Søgaard had his beady eyes on that one. Didn't you see?'

'Maybe,' she murmured. 'I'm not sure I've seen anything much since you dragged me out of Gedser.'

'Well then,' he said grandly. 'We must get you home. And there . . .' His arm swept the moonlit horizon ahead of them. 'Vicepolitikommissær Lund will ensure all is revealed. The bad guys get their comeuppance. The world will be one again . . .'

'Sarcastic bastard,' she said but she was laughing.

He smiled.

'No I'm not. I mean it. You pick up things that aren't there. You know where people come from when they don't know themselves. What makes them. What hurts them. On top of which you're the most stubborn, awkward, infuriating—'

It was automatic. She reached out, squeezed his hand. Looked into his eyes. Then let go.

'There's something wrong at that house,' Lund said. 'I'm telling you—'

'Shit!' the driver cried as he stomped on the brakes so hard they were thrown against one another in the back. 'Now we're screwed.'

Lund leaned round his shoulder and stared.

A white pickup blocking the narrow dusty road between two rocks. Five men, long, heavy Afghan robes, rifles in their arms, walking towards them.

One yanked open the Land Rover door, the other two kept their rifles on them. A torchlight flashing over the interior. Words she couldn't understand.

Orders. They had that sound.

'They want you two.' The driver had his hands up. He looked terrified. 'Best do as they say.'

Fifteen minutes down a track so rough she wondered how the truck stayed upright. Then somewhere ahead there were lights. Another pickup. Lund's night vision was adjusting.

They were back in the wrecked enclosure, in front of the house.

'Go,' one of the Afghans ordered, picking up an ancient oil lantern, putting a match to it.

The fat police chief sat on the one good chair, beaming.

'So?' he said in broken English. 'Did you get a surprise, angry woman?'

Lund stayed quiet.

'Lots of surprises here.' He grinned then said something in Pashto to the others, made them laugh. 'Some not so nice.'

He got up, stood so close to her she could smell something sweet on the man's breath.

'I didn't want you to leave empty-handed. So I got a little present for you. Come! Come!'

Someone pushed her in the back. Lund walked out to the court-yard behind the house. Strange followed.

Two more men there. They'd been removing the bricks and rubble from a filled-in hole at the back. To reveal a large, blackened space.

Two lanterns on the floor cast their waxy beams into the hole. The cop walked forward. The men got out of his way without a word. He bent down, looked inside, came out with something in his hands.

Lund felt cold and scared and a very long way from home as he gave it to her with all the slow ceremony that might come with a treasured gift. It was a child's skull. Blackened with smoke and flame. A ragged tear in the temple from a bullet wound.

'This make you happy?' the cop asked in his lilting, half-tuneful English.

Lund took the lantern from him, walked to the oven. Peered inside.

More bones. Ribs. A hand. And something metal in the dust.

She picked it up with a pencil. Old habits died hard.

It was a dog tag, stained with smoke. A name: *Per K. Møller* and a number, 369045–9611.

The cop had a bag in his hands. Made of raffia. A little battered, but with a pretty pattern on the side.

'Take home what you want,' he said. 'It's yours now.'

Ten minutes to the Rigshospitalet from the Politigården. Raben stayed in the back, eyes flickering, moaning, breath ragged.

Just the cops with him now. Worried men.

They got out when the police car pulled into the ambulance area, blue light flashing, ran into the emergency area shrieking for help. Doctors. A stretcher. Something to save them.

He waited till they were out of sight then let himself out of the passenger side away from the hospital. Half walked, half hobbled out into the damp night, keeping in the shadows all the way.

From the trees he heard them screaming, looked back briefly. Saw nurses with a gurney, doctors in green coats, the puzzled cops yelling curses.

But didn't wait.

He had things to do.

Eleven

11.04 a.m. The flight from Istanbul took them straight back to a busy Kastrup and a world Lund knew. Strange picked up a newspaper the moment they stepped onto Danish soil. The headline said the government was in crisis. Rossing, the Defence Minister, had been fired for covering up an atrocity in Afghanistan. Buch was in custody accused of a breach of the Official Secrets Act.

Lund glanced at the stories, said nothing. The battered raffia holdall hung from her right hand, a collection of blackened bones, a child's skull and a dead soldier's charred dog tag inside.

Strange was busy on the phone all the way into Arrivals. She was glad of that.

'Bilal's taken an army Land Rover,' he said when he'd talked to headquarters. 'We've got an alert out for him. With the border guards too.'

'He thinks he's more Danish than we are. Bilal's not going abroad. What about Louise?'

A frown. He didn't look tired. Didn't look upset or surprised by what they'd found either.

'Seems he snatched her from the barracks. Raben's gone missing again.'

'Oh for pity's sake . . .'

She wasn't feeling well after the long, difficult journey. Too many thoughts running round her head.

That shrug again.

'He gave our guys the slip when they took him to hospital,' Strange said. 'It's no big deal. In his condition . . .'

461

'He trained with Jægerkorpset. Special forces and God knows what else. He thinks he's immortal.'

She couldn't stop herself looking at him when she said that.

'I never did,' Strange replied with that same, self-deprecating innocence. 'But I guess I wasn't in Raben's class. I put a bullet in his shoulder. We'll have him before long.'

Out into the Arrivals lounge. The bag felt heavier than it was.

'They found a key in Søgaard's locker,' Strange went on. 'Bilal had rented an industrial unit where he planned all five murders. There's a machine for making fake dog tags there. Other stuff—'

'Where's Brix?'

'I'm not his keeper.'

He was starting to sound angry and that was unusual.

'I need the bathroom,' Lund announced.

She didn't. Just some space. But she walked off towards the toilets anyway, and Strange followed her.

'Sarah?' he said, catching up. 'What's up? You've hardly said a word to me all the way back.'

She stopped, looked at him, tried to think of something to say.

'I'm tired. It's a long journey . . .'

'That's it?'

A familiar, unexpected voice close by shrieked, 'Yoo hoo! Hello there!'

Lund felt the earth was falling beneath her feet. Her mother and Bjørn were beaming joyously as they walked arm in arm from another gate.

'How sweet of you to come and meet us,' Vibeke said and kissed her.

Her mother smelled of perfume. Lund guessed she didn't.

'Where did you go exactly?' she asked, shaking her head.

'Prague! I told you.'

'Living it up!' Bjørn added, making a drinking gesture with his right hand.

Vibeke put her arms round Lund, held her closely, whispered in her ear, 'What have you been up to, Sarah? I had a terrible nightmare in the hotel. I dreamt you were all alone somewhere, lying lifeless. Nothing I could do would bring you back to life.'

'Mum—'

'I was crying! Mark was crying! It felt so real.'

462

Strange said he'd get the car. Her mother pinched her arm.

'I'm so glad you're not mixed up in that horrible job any more. You should leave that to the men. Bjørn and I have decided we're going to visit you in Gedser. There must be lots to see there.'

She told Strange she'd take a cab with her mother and Bjørn.

He didn't move.

'You're sure?'

She shrugged.

'Why not? You take the car.'

'Oh!' Vibeke cried. 'What a lovely bag! So pretty. Where did you get it?'

Her fingers were on the top, reaching inside already.

'It's nothing,' Lund said and snatched it away. 'Honest. Shall we go?'

Lund let them sit in the back of the taxi, tried to talk as quietly as possible from the front. Brix was busy. Satisfied for once by the sound of it.

'Why did your friend leave?' Vibeke asked from the back.

Lund turned and pointed at the phone.

'I like him,' her mother declared. 'He seems a nice man.'

Lund went back to Brix.

'We found the remains of two adults and three children.'

'This is definite? No mistake?'

The raffia bag was between her legs on the floor of the taxi.

'It's definite. They'd been burned in an oven. Someone covered it up with debris afterwards.'

'Well done.' He sounded impressed. 'I passed on your initial report.'

'There's a bullet hole in the child's skull. It looks like an execution, not a firefight.'

'Did you pick up anything on Bilal?'

'No. We found Møller's dog tag. Raben was telling the truth. Did we get a list of active special forces officers from the army?'

'That doesn't matter any more.' The old impatience was back. 'I told you. We're looking for Bilal. Any killings in Helmand are for the army to investigate.'

Her mother was listening intently from behind. There was no way of hiding this.

'We can't leave it at that. Bilal wasn't there pretending to be Perk. He was in the base, handling the radio traffic. Maybe he was part of the cover-up but he didn't kill this family.'

'The army—'

'It was like a ritual killing, for God's sake. Like the ones here.'

'Bilal—'

'Bilal's not your man. It's someone else.' A pause. It had to be said. 'We need to look at Strange again. He was so . . .' This was what had kept her awake all the way back from Helmand and she had to face it. 'So at home. Like he belonged there.'

She could hear the instant anger in his voice.

'Arild told us categorically that Strange was never in Afghanistan when this happened.'

'You think you can believe him?'

A long pause on the line.

'I'm going to forget you said that.'

He gave her an address in Vesterbro, told her to come when she could.

'Brix. Brix!'

Then he was gone. Vibeke's street was coming up.

'We need to tell the driver where to stop,' Bjørn said from the back.

Her mother was pale. No longer smiling.

'Mum,' Lund said and put a hand to her cheek. 'It was just a dream. Everything's all right. This is just work. What I do.'

'I don't know what you do, Sarah. I don't want to.'

The quickest of showers, a change of clothes. Then a cab to the place they'd found. It was near the Det Ny Teater close to Vesterbrogade. Brix met her at the door.

'Bilal left the key in Søgaard's locker with the mobile phone,' he said, leading her through the grubby entrance into a small workshop. 'Along with the broken-off halves of the five dog tags.'

A large room, white tiles, yellow markers everywhere, bright winter light filtering through the high windows.

'This is a starter building for small businesses,' Madsen said, padding along in blue forensic shoe covers. 'No one else has moved in yet. He had it to himself.'

A laptop on the table. Anne Dragsholm's terrified bloodied face frozen there.

'Shouldn't we wait for Strange?' Brix asked.

'Let's get on with it.'

She lugged the raffia bag with her as they talked.

'We've got the camera he used,' Madsen said, pointing at the long work table by the window. 'The computer. Traces of explosives. Ryvangen personnel records on the hard drive.'

Six mobile phones in a neat line. Instructions for making explosives.

'They all match the evidence from the killings,' Brix said.

Books on the Taliban and Islamist extremism. Terrorism and secret forces.

'Knives.' Madsen held up a plastic bag. Two blades inside.

So much evidence, so neatly laid out.

'Bilal's a Muslim,' Brix went on. 'But everyone says he hates Islamists.'

Lund looked at the sharp curving blades, the bloodstains.

'Why—?' she began.

'Because he saw Raben's squad as traitors,' Brix cut in. 'Bilal thinks he's a loyal Dane. Raben's accusations would damage the reputation of the army by incriminating officers in the killing of civilians.'

She turned on her heels, looked round. Five forensic officers in white suits going over everything.

'And he did all this? On his own?'

Brix pointed to the wall. Printouts from Kodmani's website.

'He invented the Muslim League. He was Faith Fellow. We've got the emails on the laptop. He was trying to frame Kodmani.' Brix stared at her. 'Might have done if it wasn't for you.'

It didn't feel like consolation.

There were photos near the printouts. Old pictures, some she recognized. Executions of traitors during the war. Hunted down by the partisans, shot in the street. The same pictures she'd seen in the Frihedsmuseet in Churchillparken when they were chasing Skåning. Bodies curled up and bloodied on grubby cobblestones. Notices giving warning of the next *stikke* on the list.

'I guess he knew his history,' Brix said watching the way she stared at them. 'That's why he took Dragsholm to Mindelunden.'

Lund hated false logic.

'They didn't kill traitors at Mindelunden. They murdered heroes. That doesn't add up.'

He glared at her.

'Dragsholm was his first victim. She wanted to reopen the case. They met a few months ago.'

More photos. The three original stakes in Mindelunden. A victim in South Africa, incinerated by a tyre around the neck. A young man, a woman about the same age, both staring at nothing, looking bored, unconcerned, as a Nazi officer placed a noose round their necks beneath a makeshift gallows.

Then army mugshots of the soldiers in Raben's squad and a snatched photo of Dragsholm walking down the street.

'Bilal rented these premises not long after.'

'You know that?' Lund demanded. 'You can place him here? Fingerprints? DNA? Documentation?'

'Give us time, for God's sake,' he replied wearily. 'The man's fled Ryvangen. He's taken Jarnvig's daughter hostage. We've enough evidence . . .'

She was sick of looking at the walls. There was a determined, obsessive mind at work here. She just wasn't sure whose.

'Did anybody see him here?'

'The building's empty. Who's going to see him?'

She walked up and stood in front of the tall homicide chief.

'So the only proof you have this belongs to Bilal is the key at the barracks?'

'Lund!' He was getting mad again. 'First he gets the colonel fired because he was investigating the old radio messages. Then he snatches Louise Raben and takes off God knows where. Do they sound like the actions of an innocent man?'

'He's scared. Did Jarnvig trace those radio messages?'

He folded his arms.

'So you're telling me Bilal's of no significance? And no one else can see this except you?'

'He's significant,' she agreed. 'He can help us find that officer. But it doesn't make him the killer. Why would Bilal hide a key and a mobile phone at the barracks? Who got you to search there in the first place?'

'You were in Afghanistan—'

'Dragsholm said she'd found the officer. The one pretending to be Perk. That's what kicked this off. Bilal was at base when Raben went into that place, fixing the radio logs. It couldn't have been him.'

Lund's hand swept towards the table, the photos on the wall.

'This proves nothing. Raben's been right all along. We should have listened to him. He accused Strange—'

'We double-checked Strange!' the chief bellowed at her. 'He was demobilized long before the incident. He wasn't in Afghanistan. It can't be him. What the hell is wrong with you?'

She picked up the raffia bag, emptied it onto the table. A tiny blackened skull with a bullet hole. A skeletal hand. Dry, sooty bones.

'That's what's wrong with me.'

The forensics officers were torn, staring at her, staring avariciously at the bones. Then at the door.

Lund sighed. Knew what she'd see there.

Ulrik Strange. Hair freshly washed. Stubble newly shaved. Face perky and innocent. Clean clothes. Ready to start again.

She still felt grubby, even after the shower. And a little guilty. But not so much.

Brix said nothing.

Strange said nothing, just turned his back and walked outside.

A bright day, chilly. Not much different from Afghanistan. It was the same sun after all. He was leaning on his black Ford. She took off her blue shoe covers and plastic gloves, walked straight up to him.

Leaned on the car too, hands in pockets.

Strange was watching her. Hard to read his expression. Sorrow? Disgust? Anger? His face seemed so calm, so impassive that extreme emotions simply passed it by.

'What's the matter with you?' he asked in a quiet, calm voice. 'Why do you do these things?'

She coughed, shrugged.

'I didn't sleep all the way back. Jet lag. I don't know.'

He watched a uniformed officer take in some equipment, dodging beneath the Don't Cross tape.

'It's like the whole world's guilty until you prove it innocent.' He caught her eye. 'You. No one else.'

That wasn't such a bad observation, Lund thought. Or a bad idea.

'Sometimes,' Strange went on, 'I get the feeling you like a few things about me.'

'I do!'

'You've a damned funny way of showing it.'

'True.'

She waited for him to say more. There was nothing.

'So,' Lund said and clapped her cold hands. 'Now we've cleared the air—'

'Jesus!' Strange cried, so furiously one of the cops guarding the building turned and stared.

'I'm sorry. OK?'

'You're sorry?' He nodded. 'That's all there is to say?'

Lund frowned.

'What more do you want? I'm sorry. I was wrong. My head's somewhere else. I'm trying to get it straight.'

Nothing.

'OK?' she asked.

Still nothing.

'OK? Or do I go and see Brix and ask for a bus fare back to Gedser?'

'As if,' he said with a low laugh she couldn't interpret. 'So what now?'

'Isn't that obvious? We need to find Bilal.'

As she spoke Lund was looking round the neighbourhood, trying to picture a soldier coming here. Even out of uniform.

'We need to talk to Søgaard about the radio messages too.'

She crossed the street, looked at the posters in the immigrant bookshop opposite.

'Bilal must hate the extremists,' Strange said, following her. 'He sent the video just at the end of Ramadan.'

'Is that significant?' she asked.

'I don't know. Maybe he's kind of an extremist in reverse.'

Lund pointed at the walls. Posters for a rabble-rousing preacher, in Danish and Arabic.

'If it was Bilal he didn't have far to look for inspiration.'

There was an old book in the window. *Muslimsk Liga.* Muslim League.

'Hello!' Brix cried. He was coming out of the building with

Madsen and some of the others. 'Bilal took a military G-Wagen from Ryvangen. He's been seen heading west. Let's go, shall we?'

She couldn't stop staring at the shop window.

'Lund!' the chief yelled. 'That means you too. Doesn't it?'

'It does,' she said and followed Strange to the car.

The army let Torsten Jarnvig out of custody at midday. He went straight back to Ryvangen. The place was crawling with police. No one was complaining any more.

'Any idea where your daughter is?' a young detective asked when Jarnvig got to his office. Søgaard had begun rearranging things already. Filing cabinets. The computer.

'No. She was looking round for things. She believed Raben from the start. Maybe I should have . . .'

Her picture was on the desk. Søgaard must have made the decision to leave it there.

Jarnvig was in plain army fatigues. No signs of rank any more. Maybe they were gone for ever. It didn't feel such a loss at that moment.

'We need to go through all the places Bilal kept things.'

'To hell with that!' Jarnvig shouted. 'My daughter's missing. What are you doing to find her?'

The cop didn't seem interested in answering.

'Do you think Bilal was hiding more than we know?'

'Ask Operational Command,' Jarnvig barked. 'Ask Arild. Bilal was the general's pet.'

The detective frowned.

'Yelling at me won't help. Do you have any idea where he might go?'

Jarnvig glared at him, furious.

'Do you specialize in stupid questions? Of course I don't. If I did, I'd be there.'

The faintest of raps at the door. Jonas was there in his winter coat and scarf. He looked forlorn.

'Are we done here?' Jarnvig asked the detective.

'Were you aware that Bilal hates Islamists?'

Jarnvig rolled his eyes.

'Oh for God's sake. He's done three tours fighting the Taliban. He knows what these people can do. What do you think?'

'I was asking you.'

'I think . . .' It was a good question, not that Jarnvig wanted to acknowledge that. 'I think he always seemed the perfect soldier. Conscientious. Loyal. Obedient.' A pause. 'Obedient to a fault sometimes. He'd never get any higher than he was. He wasn't great at thinking for himself.'

Another cop came in from Bilal's quarters, said, 'Look at this. I broke open his locker. Interesting stuff.'

Clippings from the papers. All five victims, with photos, glued to card. Dozens of them.

'Perfect soldier,' the first cop said and laughed. He waved the clippings at Jarnvig. 'Make sure you let us know if you hear anything. The same goes for Raben. He's got plenty to answer for too.'

Jarnvig watched them go. When they'd left Jonas marched across the polished floor, hands swinging. Just like a soldier.

'You've got your jacket on,' Jarnvig said, bending down and doing up the top buttons. 'Have you been playing outside on your own?'

No answer. The usual blank look.

'Joakim and his parents are coming to take you to the cinema. That's good, isn't it?'

'Where's Mummy?'

Jarnvig smiled. It always seemed necessary when you lied to a child.

'I bet she'll be here by the time you get back.'

Another false grin and he realized for the first time it didn't work at all.

'That's what Daddy says,' Jonas told him in a low, hurt voice.

The boy leaned into Jarnvig's face, whispered in his ear, glancing all the time at the two cops down the corridor.

'It's a secret, Grandpa. He's waiting for you by the fence at the back. Where the tower is.'

Two young, accusing eyes.

'You won't tell, will you?'

Jarnvig tugged the boy's jacket.

'I won't tell, Jonas. That's a promise.'

He was waiting in some bushes by a fire exit close to a little-used guard tower. Jarnvig unlocked the gate, walked through, had Raben in his face straight away.

'Do the police have any idea where he took her?'

'They don't know a damned thing.'

He was in a grubby blue jacket that looked as if it might have been pulled out of a rubbish bin. He held one arm awkwardly.

'You shouldn't be here, Jens. You're sick.'

'I'm not helping in a hospital, am I? Where could he have gone?'

'We've checked all the army bases we can think of.' A pause. 'You're normally full of ideas. Where do you think he is?'

Raben shook his head.

Jarnvig put a hand on his shoulder.

'People get hurt when you're around. I don't want that to happen to Louise. Stay clear of this.'

'We're equal now. We've got to help each other.'

'This is all your fault!' Then, more quietly, 'Louise kept trying to help you. Asking questions. Doing things she shouldn't.'

'I told you the truth all along. Why didn't you believe me?'

Jarnvig closed his eyes for a moment.

'Because I didn't want to. There. Are you happy now? Can we put this to one side and think about Louise?'

Raben looked happy with that admission.

'Bilal used to go camping on an old military site near Hillerød. We can start there . . .'

'You have to stay away.'

'And leave it to you and those idiots in the police?'

Jarnvig gave up, walked back to the gate and his green Mercedes G-Wagen. The phone rang. He answered so quickly he almost dropped the thing.

'Hello? Hello?'

A soft voice, faintly accented, distant and detached.

'We must stick together against the enemy.'

Jarnvig tried to picture the location. No traffic noise. Just the faintest sound of birdsong.

'We're not the enemy!' Said Bilal said, his flat, monotonous voice rising. 'We never were . . .'

'Where are you?' Jarnvig demanded. 'I want an answer.'

'You're not my colonel any more. They took that away from you, didn't they?'

There was a strange mix of fear and fascination in his voice.

'Where are you?' Jarnvig asked again, aware Raben was next to him now, eyes shining, face full of curiosity.

'I did my duty. That was all. I did what I was told. Like a soldier should.'

'Where's Louise? She's nothing to do with this.'

The shortest of laughs.

'I won't take the blame. Never . . .'

The line went quiet.

'Bilal! Come back.'

'You turned against me. After all I did. All the work, all the loyalty. I still wasn't good enough. Just because of what I was—'

'No one turned against you! The police found evidence—'

'I didn't put it there. Someone's trying to frame me. Can't you see?'

A brisk wind was whipping up around this forgotten corner of Ryvangen. The sun was disappearing. Rain was on the way.

'You've got my daughter. Let her go. We can talk about this. I can make sure—'

'You can't do anything,' Bilal broke in. 'You're finished too. Tell General Arild. Say he's got to get me out of this. If it wasn't for—'

'What in God's name are you talking about?' Jarnvig cried.

A sudden movement. Raben's good hand snatched the phone from Jarnvig's hand.

'Let me speak to Louise,' he said in a low, calm, determined voice.

'I'm talking to Jarnvig. Not you!'

'Nothing happens until we hear from Louise, Bilal. Nothing . . .'

Said Bilal walked to his stolen Land Rover, opened the back door.

She was where he'd left her the previous night. Duct tape over her mouth. A military sock wrapped round her eyes as a blindfold.

Bilal ripped off the tape, didn't mind when she yelled at the pain.

The colonel's daughter. She looked down on him just as much as the rest of them.

He put the phone to her ear, underneath the blindfold.

'Louise?' Raben said.

Straight away, 'We drove for an hour and a half. A place underground—'

Bilal snatched away the phone, punched her hard in the mouth. Then again for sure.

He watched her hurting, listened to her screams. When they died down he put the phone back to his ear.

'Don't touch my wife,' Raben muttered in a low, hard tone.

'Too late.' Bilal looked around. This was a place he knew. They couldn't find it, not from what she'd said. 'I'll call again this evening. Get Arild. Talk to the police and I'll kill her.'

He opened the back of the phone. Took out the battery, threw it on the ground.

Louise Raben's nose had started bleeding. One red line down into her mouth.

She said in a cracked, pleading voice, 'Bilal. Let me go. What's wrong? I never hurt you.'

The young officer slammed the door on her, looked around, saw nothing but flat, bare grassland in all directions. Walked to the front of the vehicle, got in and started to drive.

Buch had been kept in an interview room in the Politigården all night, interviewed by a succession of surly PET officers who barely listened to a word he said. Around six in the morning they let him call home to Marie. That went almost as badly as the interrogations.

Now it was the middle of the day and a new shift, one young officer, one middle-aged, had turned up. They wore dark suits and blank, uncaring expressions. Neither of them sat down much. Buch had the impression they were biding their time. Wasting his. He wasn't a lawyer but he didn't believe for one moment he'd done anything that could lead to a prosecution.

'Tell us again,' the nearest PET man said.

Buch wiped his sweaty forehead with his right hand.

'This is a political issue, not a criminal one. Not yet. The Prime Minister was aware I had evidence of misdeeds on his part. The Defence Minister was ready to confirm this. Somehow Grue Eriksen knew. So the Prime Minister tried to shift the blame to us.' Buch smiled at each of them in turn. 'Through you. How does it feel to be used?'

'The trouble is,' the younger PET man said, 'Rossing won't confirm your story. He's been released without charge.'

'That's because Grue Eriksen's got to him. Offered him a deal I suppose. It doesn't change the facts—'

'How could the Prime Minister know you were going to do this?' the second officer asked.

'Because someone warned him! Isn't it obvious? You've detained me all night for no reason.'

'National security's no reason?' the young one asked.

'I've done nothing to jeopardize national security. Quite the contrary. I've been defending it.'

There was a folder on a desk by the window. Both of them went to it, took out some papers.

'Let's see,' said the old cop. 'A confidential PET memo gets leaked from your office.'

'Not by me,' Buch insisted.

'You met with a suspended police officer, Sarah Lund. What for?'

'I was Minister of Justice. Lund was suspended only briefly. I believe she's back in service now. What's the problem?'

They didn't want to push that one.

'You visited your predecessor, Monberg, who took his own life.'

'Tell me how I acted illegally, please.'

'Your secretary accessed data without authority.'

'My secretary! Not me!'

'You obstructed PET's investigation. You defended Islamist organizations and their rights. You've been in contact with a journalist who provided you with confidential information she obtained while working for the Ministry of Defence . . .'

Buch felt like putting his head on his hands and going to sleep.

'Oh for pity's sake. Am I being subjected to an all-night interrogation because you and your new boss, whoever it is, doesn't like the cut of my jib?'

'We're at war!' the young one said and finally took a seat. 'There's a word for undermining our government and our democracy. It's called treason.' He waved his hand. 'Doesn't matter whether some Afghans got killed here or there. Treason. The betrayal of your own country.'

Buch groaned, closed his eyes, covered up a yawn with a tired, grubby hand.

'Are you going to persist with your accusations against the Prime Minister?'

'No.' A long, serious nod. 'Is that what you want to hear?'

'It's a start,' the young cop said, smiling at his colleague.

'Good,' Buch added. 'I intend to go even further. Grue Eriksen's the traitor. If you weren't the spineless, gutless creatures you are, you'd have him in here, shining a light in his eyes. Keeping him awake all night. Hoping to break him. He's the traitor, and you nothing but his quislings . . .'

A knock on the door. Someone outside announced a lawyer had arrived. A tall, grey man came in and spoke quietly with both the PET officers out of Buch's earshot.

'Hello! What's going on here?' Another slam of his fists on the table. 'Am I invisible suddenly?'

The quisling crack was a touch too far, Buch thought. He might apologize for that one.

But then the older officer turned to him and said, 'There's someone outside for you.'

'Someone I'm allowed to see?'

'Sure. You can go.'

Karina and Carsten Plough were waiting in the circular vestibule by the Politigården stairs.

'I must say,' Plough declared archly as Buch came out, 'this is the first time I've ever had to spring a minister from jail.'

'First time for everything,' Buch declared. 'Besides, I'm not a minister any more.'

'Nor me a Permanent Secretary,' Plough added miserably.

'Well, you're free,' Karina said. 'That's something, isn't it?'

'Yes,' Buch agreed. 'But why?'

'Lund found something in Afghanistan.' She had a folder full of photographs. 'Take a look.'

A small skull with a bullet hole. A dog tag stained with smoke.

'That's what she was looking for when she went off limits,' Plough said. 'The police are chasing a Danish soldier now. He committed the recent murders to prevent the case being reopened.'

'And the officer who killed these people in Helmand?'

'The army say they're taking care of that,' Karina said with little enthusiasm. 'Though since they never found the bodies in the first place . . .' She looked at him. 'You can't win every battle, Thomas.'

This pair had stuck with him throughout. Damaged, perhaps ruined their own careers through nothing except an innate sense of justice.

'Thank you,' Buch said very earnestly. 'Is it too much to ask you to call a meeting of the parliamentary party? Without Grue Eriksen.'

'We can try,' Plough responded.

That note of caution never really left Carsten Plough's voice.

'Say what you mean, will you?'

'You've got nothing on Grue Eriksen,' Plough insisted. 'I told you before. It's Rossing you should aim for. We know he was lying. We can prove it.'

Buch laughed.

'Ah. That old story . . .'

'It was the Prime Minister who got you out of here,' Plough added.

'Since he threw me in here in the first place that seems appropriate, don't you think? Can you arrange that meeting?'

Plough didn't move.

'I don't want you to snatch defeat from the jaws of victory, as they say. Think carefully . . .'

'I will,' Buch promised. 'Now can we get out of this grim hole, please?'

By the time Buch got to the Folketinget the word was out with the media. A full pack of reporters and TV crews blocked the entrance.

'Are you back in the government?'

'Do you support the Prime Minister?'

'Are you being charged?'

'Do you maintain your accusations?'

He knew now to do nothing but smile and push his way through. The experience had changed him. Perhaps made him a politician at last.

Kahn was waiting for him in his old office, still unoccupied ahead of the coming reshuffle.

'Where is everyone?' Buch asked.

'They asked me to come alone,' the Interior Minister said. 'Best not to make too much fuss.'

Buch realized he'd been so preoccupied he'd forgotten to brush his teeth. So he went to the desk, took out the brush he kept there and the little tube of toothpaste, poured himself a glass of water. Plough and Karina watched in silence from the bookcase near the door.

'I apologize for the mess,' he said, seating himself on his desk. 'I left in rather a hurry as you may know.'

Then he started brushing his teeth.

'We were hasty yesterday,' Kahn said. 'We didn't know the full facts. We had to protect the party.'

'At all costs? At the expense of the truth?'

'Fine, fine. Bawl me out. You've got to admit. It was a pretty tall tale. We're all sorry. OK?'

'Accepted,' Buch said. 'Now we must act quickly. There are only two options.'

Kahn glanced at Plough and Karina.

'Either Grue Eriksen resigns,' Buch said, 'or we force him to do so. Let's have a private conversation first and see if he'll do the decent thing and fall on his own sword.'

'There'd be a general election. One we'd lose,' Kahn said wearily.

'That's a reason for not doing the right thing?' Buch asked.

'Listen to me, Thomas,' Kahn pleaded. 'The Prime Minister wants to see you. He's appointing new ministers. You're looking at promotion.'

Buch turned to the window and the twisting dragons, walked to the door, pointed at it with his toothbrush and said, 'Get out.'

'You like being a minister!' Kahn cried.

'Out!'

Kahn walked through the door, sour-faced again.

'Krabbe and the Prime Minister are of one mind on this. Rossing won't help you. It's time to grow up.'

'Wait till I put Krabbe right on a few things. Thank you! Thank you! Goodbye! Chop, chop!'

Buch slammed the door behind him. Karina and Plough watched, wide-eyed and speechless.

'Well?' Buch asked. 'What else could I do? Krabbe!' He raised a fleshy finger. 'Let's find him.'

Carsten Plough put his hand to his eyes, shook his head, then wandered slowly outside.

Søgaard was still in the Politigården. Brix's personal decision. He didn't like the man and was in no rush to let him go.

The major now wore the blue suit of a prisoner and faced being charged as an accessory. Lund and Strange sat in the interview room watching him walk nervously up and down by the window. He was finally starting to look scared.

'Tell us about Bilal's contacts,' Lund began. 'Friends? Family?'

Søgaard dragged a seat to the table, sat down, glared at her.

'I was his commanding officer. Nothing more. Why in God's name am I still here?'

She tapped the pile of evidence in front of him.

'There's clear proof in the radio logs that some messages were deleted. You investigated.' Søgaard picked up the sheet and looked at it. 'Why didn't you find any of that?'

He didn't answer. Lund nodded.

'You didn't look into this yourself, did you? Too menial. So you delegated it. Let me guess—'

'Of course I asked Bilal to check them! He was the officer responsible for that area.'

Strange threw up his hands and laughed.

'So you asked him to investigate himself? Give me strength . . .'

She showed Søgaard the new photos from forensic. The skulls and bones she'd brought back from Helmand.

'We know for a fact these civilians were killed. No point in denying it now. An officer was there. Raben told the truth.'

'Raben was talking like a madman—'

'He told the truth! Bilal concealed those messages. Your men were witnesses to an atrocity. I don't believe for one minute you'd no idea something bad went on.'

'No.' He kept looking at the radio logs. 'I was assured nothing happened. I never knew about the messages. We never found anything at the house.'

'That's because you didn't look,' Lund threw at him. 'This isn't going to go down well with the next promotions board—'

A knock on the door. Strange went to deal with it.

'I can't answer for Bilal.' Søgaard leaned back, looked weary. 'Ask him.'

'You knew about the message five days before. The one that told you special forces were heading for the village. Who were they?'

A hand to his head.

'I never saw that message!'

She got up from the table, stood by the window, hands on hips, staring at the rain running down the pane.

'You really weren't much in command at all, were you?' Lund asked, looking at the grimy glass.

'You don't know what it's like . . .'

'Listen to me, Søgaard. What future you've got in the army

depends on the answers you give me now. The man who murdered these people used Per K. Møller's identity. Did Bilal know Møller?'

It took him a while to answer.

'No reason why he should.'

'Was Bilal there when the real Møller died?'

'I don't think so.'

'Was anyone from special forces . . . Jægerkorpset . . . any of these people around when that happened?'

'No. He was on his own when there was an explosion. He went straight to the nearest field hospital in Lashkar Gah.'

Lund turned and looked at him.

'Was he wearing his ID?'

'Why wouldn't he be?'

She picked up the photos, showed him the charred dog tag she'd picked up in Helmand. All in one piece.

'Explain that.'

'I'm not going to try.'

Lund didn't take her eyes off him.

'If you had a special forces officer come to you and say he needed a new ID for a covert mission—'

'Never happened, Lund! Don't go there.'

'*If.* You could just look through the recent deaths. Pick a name. Get a new dog tag made.' Her hand went to her head, ran through her long dark hair. 'Maybe Møller's did get lost. Or someone took it. If this is a covert mission they'll give him a new one anyway. Like a fake passport.'

Søgaard was rigid in the seat opposite her.

'But an order like that's above your pay grade, isn't it? Above Jarnvig's too I guess. It would need someone back here.'

'I never did anything like that in my life. I was never asked.'

'If you were?'

No answer. A knock on the door. Strange there.

'They've found Bilal's G-Wagen outside Hillerød. No sign of him or the woman. He must have stolen a new vehicle.'

She got up to leave.

'What about me?' Christian Søgaard shouted as she walked for the door.

'You can wait,' Lund said.

*

479

Outside the office was buzzing as Brix gathered a team. They'd placed a tap on Jarnvig's phone and captured the conversation with Bilal.

'What did he say?' Lund asked. 'This still doesn't—'

'He claims he's been set up. He wants Arild to get him out of this.'

Lund sat down next to an officer at a computer.

'Bilal's never been anything but a soldier. He's going to want somewhere military to hide. The place he left the G-Wagen—'

'There's nowhere military in that area,' Brix said. 'We checked.'

'Nowhere now,' Strange said. 'During the Cold War we had lots of places up there. We thought the Russians were going to walk straight in, remember?'

Lund ran her finger over the screen, not minding how much this annoyed the woman detective perched in front of it.

'What kind of facilities?'

'All sorts,' Strange said. 'Underground barracks.' His mild face hardened. 'We were supposed to hide there and wait. Just sixteen Danish soldiers died when the Nazis invaded. The Russians weren't going to get off that lightly.'

'I imagine not,' Lund murmured, thinking. 'Have we checked for abandoned facilities?'

She got up, went to the wall, looked at the evidence photos. A blackened skull from Afghanistan now alongside the bloody photos of Anne Dragsholm and the four members of Ægir.

'I want someone to get hold of Frederik Holst,' she said to the nearest detective. 'He's an army surgeon in Lashkar Gah.'

There was a photo of the smoky piece of metal she'd dragged out of the oven the Afghan cop had uncovered at the back of that sad little house.

'Get through and ask him what happened to Per K. Møller's dog tag.'

A buzz of excitement ran round the office.

'Lund!' Strange yelled from the exit. 'We've got somewhere. Grab your coat. We're going.'

'Ask him if there were any special forces officers in the hospital at the time,' she added. 'Get me names. Is that clear?'

'Sure,' the young officer said. 'Will do.'

She got her donkey jacket from the locker. Looked at the gun in the locker, took it. Strange was right. She knew there'd been body armour sitting on the second shelf. It had been there ever since they took her back. No one mentioned it. No one ever told her how to use the thing. Not that she minded. She knew now.

The woods north of Hillerød were dense and dark. The green army G-Wagen moved slowly down the narrow lane. Jarnvig at the wheel. Angry.

'This is ridiculous. We can't keep looking.'

'Bilal used to come here,' Raben said. 'He told me about it. You could break in. Go underground. See all these places they used during the Cold War.'

He waved at the broken wire ahead. Flat green land beyond it, forest in the distance. No buildings. Not even a sign.

'We should call the police,' Jarnvig said again.

There was a shop along the road.

'Keep driving, will you?' Raben said.

'I'm taking orders from you now, am I? We could get hold of Arild. Bilal worships him. If anyone could cut a deal . . .'

The roadside shop was for local campers. Fruit and vegetables. Gas. Clothing. General supplies.

'Let's ask someone,' Raben said.

He told Jarnvig to stop the jeep. The two of them walked into the ramshackle store. A short bearded man stood behind the counter.

'Can I help? We've got fresh potatoes—'

'We're from the army,' Jarnvig said. 'Looking for a deserter. Probably in fatigues. Acting a bit scared. He's—'

'He's sick,' Raben said.

'What kind of sick?' the man asked, reaching for something underneath the counter.

'A bad kind. He's young-looking. About twenty-eight. Dark hair. Dark skin. Immigrant. He'd probably want to buy food or . . .'

The bearded shopkeeper pulled out a double-barrelled shotgun, held it loose in his arms.

'Don't get many people this time of year. Those you do get . . . sometimes they act funny.' He looked at them. 'What kind of bad?'

'We can deal with it,' Raben said.

The man nodded at Jarnvig.

'You're the second squaddie who's walked in here with a gun on his belt. I'd get arrested if I went round like that.'

'Where did he go?' Raben asked.

He laughed.

'Come into a shop and you've got to buy something. It's only polite. Everyone knows that.'

Jarnvig muttered something, nodded at the cigarette stand and threw fifty kroner on the counter. 'Give me twenty Prince.'

'Prince cost a hundred out here, mister,' the shopkeeper said with a big grin. 'It's the transport, you see.'

Raben was getting furious. Jarnvig threw another note on the counter.

'Where . . . ?' Raben started.

'Go left. A couple of hundred metres down he took an old track into the woods. Not seen that used in years. You ought to find him just from following the tyre tracks.'

'He had a woman with him?' Jarnvig asked.

'Not that I saw. You want to buy something else?'

But by then Raben was hurtling back towards the Mercedes.

Torsten Jarnvig sat in the passenger seat, shaken by Raben's crazed driving as they careered along the overgrown trail.

There was only one set of tyre marks ahead. He could have followed them. Would have done too. But Raben was a *jaeger*, just like Jan Arild all those years before in the Gulf, the Balkans and places they never talked about. Like dogs after a scent, they didn't pursue a quarry. They chased it down.

The woods were coniferous, thick and dark, even in winter. From the state of the ground it looked as if only one vehicle had been this way all season.

A crossroads. Raben didn't even stop before taking the Mercedes into a hard left swing, rounding the corner at such speed the vehicle almost toppled over. Jarnvig clung to the door handle, didn't say a thing. There was no point.

The track narrowed. There was open space ahead. At fifty kilometres an hour they burst into a clearing. An old black Land Rover was parked on a concrete pad. A rusty, low watchtower to the right. Raben stamped on the brakes, kept the wheels bursting in and out of lock, brought the vehicle to a halt in a dead straight line.

No one in the Land Rover. Behind it was an ancient fence topped with rolls of barbed wire. A yellow sign, rickety, now at forty-five degrees: MILITARY AREA. KEEP OUT.

Raben stretched out his hand. How long did Torsten Jarnvig think about this? As long as he did in the Iraqi desert, when he was alongside Jan Arild, wondering how to stay alive.

He took the army handgun from his belt and handed it over.

'Call the police,' Raben said.

'Do you want me as backup?'

That was a look Arild gave him from time to time too.

It said: *Are you kidding?*

'There's space enough for a couple of thousand soldiers underground here,' Raben said. 'Their radios won't work. They won't know where I am.' A sour, hurt expression on his face. 'I'd rather not get shot again. Tell them that too.'

Then he worked his way through the wire.

It took a minute to find the entrance. Cold War. Built to shelter from a nuclear blast. They'd been mothballed by the time Raben came into the army. But the word was they were never totally out of commission. Some bright spark had realized the end of one conflict, even a half-century stand-off between the world's great powers, didn't spell peace on earth. The time might come again . . .

Raben remembered this as he edged through the open heavy iron door set into what looked like a derelict guardhouse surrounded by blackthorn and elder bushes. He had a torch but he didn't need it. The place was lit up like Strøget at Christmas. Two lines of bulbs in a whitewashed ceiling led down a stone staircase that seemed to go on for ever. The place had power. Was still breathing, alive.

Jarnvig's P210 pistol sat steady in his hand. He took the steps one by one, moving slowly down this steep artery into the earth. There was nowhere to hide in this freezing, dank refuge beneath the ground. Not for him. Or Said Bilal.

Buch found Erling Krabbe on the main staircase in the Folketinget.

'I left you some messages . . .'

The People's Party man looked even more evasive than usual.

'I was about to call you back. After my next meeting. Look . . .'

MPs and civil servants were wandering up and down, glancing at them. Krabbe walked down to the next landing, disappeared into the shadows of a corridor. Buch followed.

'Just tell me,' he begged. 'Will you join the Opposition in bringing down Grue Eriksen?'

Erling Krabbe bit his bloodless lower lip, said nothing.

'Dammit!' Buch barked. 'You know he's not fit to stay in office. The man's as guilty as hell. They found proof that family was murdered in Helmand.'

'You only have Rossing's word for that and he's chosen to take the blame . . .'

'Rossing's the scapegoat! And a happy one too. He won't get prosecuted. He'll be back in government in eighteen months. It was the truth. You know it too.'

Krabbe glanced at his watch so quickly Buch knew he hadn't even checked the time. Then he started to walk off.

Buch's hand came out and grabbed his arm.

'What the hell's going on here?' Thomas Buch demanded. 'I've got a right to know.'

Krabbe peeled Buch's fat fingers from his arm.

'I'm not going to get into bed with Birgitte Agger without thinking it over. You don't honestly believe it's justice she's after.'

'This isn't about politics. It's about right and wrong . . .'

Erling Krabbe was staring at him, as if he'd seen something new.

'It really is that black and white for you, isn't it?' He laughed. 'I suppose it was for me once. But it isn't and it never will be.'

He went back to the staircase, started to walk down the steps.

'So it was you who spilled the beans, was it?' Buch bellowed, his voice echoing off the walls, making heads turn everywhere. 'When I told you Rossing had confessed. You went straight to Grue Eriksen like the lapdog you are?'

Krabbe came back, astonished. Hurt, Buch thought.

'What on earth are you talking about?'

'You're the only one I told!'

Erling Krabbe folded his skinny arms and waited.

'Apart from . . . my own people,' Buch said more quietly. 'People I trust, naturally.'

Krabbe laughed at him.

'Oh honestly. Did your week as a minister teach you nothing? There's no one you can trust in this place.'

A pat on the arm. A look that seemed almost kindly. He held out his hand.

'I'll call you when I've decided,' Krabbe said.

Buch shook his dry, cold fingers then watched him go.

Back through the endless corridors, into the Ministry of Justice, mind racing all the way.

Karina was at her desk alone.

'The Prime Minister's office called wanting a meeting,' she said when he marched in. 'I declined. I hope that was right.'

'I suppose.' Buch walked to his desk. 'Who prepared the documents yesterday? After Rossing came in here and I asked someone to make a note of what I told you afterwards?'

'Plough,' Karina said. 'I offered but he insisted.'

'Who typed it? Which secretary?'

She tugged on her blonde hair.

'Plough did it himself. He said they were busy with other things.'

'Could someone have seen his report and warned Grue Eriksen?'

'No! He printed it out and gave it to me. Then he went over to the Prime Minister's office . . .'

Buch looked at her.

'Oh for God's sake, Thomas! It was about that post in Skopje. You'd intervened on his behalf, hadn't you?'

'And the office called him in?'

'I don't remember. Ask him when he gets back.'

'Where is he?'

'I don't know. Now can we . . . ?'

He went through more papers, scattering them everywhere.

'Who leaked that memo to Birgitte Agger? Did we ever find out?'

She folded her arms.

'Plough looked into it. He didn't get anywhere.'

Buch went to the nearest document mountain, started sifting anxiously through it.

'Where's the information on the military squad? Ægir?'

'Thomas!' Karina cried in a high, piercing voice. 'What's going on?'

Nothing in the papers. Buch picked them up, launched them at the sofa, watched them flutter round the room.

'Calm down,' she ordered. 'I won't talk to you if you're going to be like this. I'll walk right out of here . . .'

He kicked a pile of box files, stumbled to the desk. It was there all along. A list of the soldiers in Raben's unit. Mugshots, profiles.

She followed, trying to reason with him.

'Listen, Thomas. I know Plough was angry with Rossing. He's never liked the man. But he didn't want you to go for the Prime Minister because he thought you couldn't win.'

Buch flicked through the pages. Myg Poulsen. Raben. Lisbeth Thomsen. Photos, brief service records and a few personal details.

A head shot he'd never really looked at before. There'd been no reason.

'Does Plough have a son?'

She groaned.

'He did. He died last year. Plough took it very badly.'

'In a traffic accident, right?'

She nodded.

'Plough lives in Nørrebro? What street?'

'Baggesensgade. What's this about?'

'If I've still got a driver,' Buch said, heading for the door, 'tell him I'm on my way.'

'And if not?'

Buch ran his fingers through his pockets, checked the wallet there.

'Maybe you could lend me some money for a taxi?'

Karina Jørgensen handed over two hundred kroner then went to the desk and retrieved the file.

It was open at the squad member no one looked at.

Hans Christian P. Vedel. Killed in a car crash on the Øresund bridge. Suicide, the police said.

A picture of a serious, plain young man, gloomy eyes staring straight at the camera.

An address in Baggesensgade.

'Thomas . . .' she started, but Buch was gone.

Lund and Strange were in the first car to meet Jarnvig outside the underground facility.

The heavy iron door was open. A long staircase, lights all the way.

'They're in there. Raben went after him,' Jarnvig said.

'Is he armed?' Strange asked.

The colonel nodded.

Lund got out her gun, Strange did the same. More cars were arriving. Two cops from the first ran over.

'There are going to be more exits than this one,' Strange told them. 'See if you can pull up a plan or something. Make sure every one's covered. Tell Brix nobody's to enter until we've checked it out.'

The first officer looked uncertain.

'If you wait a minute you can tell him yourself . . .'

'My daughter's in there!' Jarnvig yelled.

Lund set off down the long stairs, gun ahead of her, listening. The place smelled like a gigantic mouldering tomb, the air stale and fusty.

Strange was soon with her. They half-ran down the first flight of stairs, stopped at the bottom. The place changed here. The floor was cracked and damp in places. The walls looked as if they'd been hewn from the native rock. At regular intervals there were doors that must have led to subterranean offices, barracks, storerooms.

'How big's this place?' she asked as Strange went forward, looking left and right.

'God knows,' he murmured. 'How the hell—?'

A distant sound. Footsteps, loud and rapid, hard to pinpoint as they echoed off the walls.

Strange looked round, listened, pointed to the right and they began to run.

Raben was deep in the bowels of the underground camp, checking every door. The ones he met were open. And then he got to a closed one. Red paint and the number forty-four on the outside.

Put his good shoulder to it, felt the old iron creak then move under his weight.

Through, gun in one hand, low and ready.

There was another section here, rooms and corridors. All part of the hidden tide of fury waiting to loose itself on a Russian army that would never come.

A noise not far away.

Her voice. Crying with pain and fear.

Raben leaned against the damp wall, brick here, not rock. Then he edged slowly, quietly forward, got to the end, saw bright lights beyond in what looked like a wide room to the right.

One brief moment of reconnaissance. His head flew round the door, flew back.

In that fraction of a second he saw them. Louise on her knees, hands tethered. Bilal standing, a gun to her head. The place was a generator room. Vast antiquated machines down one side. Places to run for cover.

Not that it mattered. Bilal was a good soldier too. The moment Raben stuck his head round the door he knew he'd been spotted.

After a while Bilal yelled nervously, 'Step forward so I can see you!'

Raben stayed where he was.

'Get out of there or I'll blow her head off now.'

Raben walked straight out, hands down by his side, gun pointed at the floor.

Louise looked up at him with tired, terrified eyes. Her nose was bloody and bruised. Bilal's fingers wound into her hair, his pistol hard against her scalp.

Said Bilal didn't even seem frightened. Short dark hair, boyish face, regulation fatigues. Model soldier.

'Put down your weapon,' he ordered. 'Drop it!'

Straight away Raben crouched down, placed the black handgun on the tiles, then pushed it across the floor, hard enough so it came to rest in front of Louise's feet.

'Where's Arild?' Bilal asked. 'I told you not to come looking for me.'

'Sometimes things don't work out,' Raben said with a shrug. 'Let her go. You've got me now. Whatever it is you want. Take me. Not my wife . . .'

The gun came away from her head, pointed straight at his face.

'If only you'd kept your big mouth shut! None of this would have happened.'

'But it did.'

'They weren't civilians! They were Taliban informers. Bankrolling the bastards.'

'The kids weren't doing that—'

'Don't you lecture me about the kids! Don't . . .'

Raben's heart leapt. Bilal's gun hand was steady as a rock. Then there were more footsteps and they were close.

*

Lund got there first. Walked to Raben's side, watched Bilal's gun turn to face her.

'Stop this,' she said as calmly as she could. 'Put down the gun. Let her go. You can't—'

His fingers wound more tightly into Louise's greasy black hair. The pistol went straight back to her head. She shrieked with terror and pain.

'No!' Lund yelled, took a step in front of Raben, gun out, two hands on the butt, aimed straight at the man in the army fatigues. 'Walk out of here. We can talk this over. I want to hear—'

'You're not army,' Bilal spat back at her.

'What's this to do with Louise?' Lund cried. 'Leave her out—'

'You're not army! I did my duty. What I was told.'

One more step towards him. Gun steady. She was a lousy shot. Maybe he could tell.

'I believe you, Bilal. I can help. But you have to let Louise go.'

Another step and Raben was edging towards him too.

Then the door on the far side burst open and Strange was walking through, weapon up, face taut and determined.

Bilal looked left, looked right, looked up for an instant, then at Lund. His fingers relaxed in Louise Raben's hair. His knee pushed her forward.

'Go,' he ordered.

Lund didn't watch as she half-stumbled to her feet then fell into the arms of her husband.

Something wasn't right here.

'Get her out, Raben,' she ordered. 'Get her upstairs and . . .'

Bilal was sweating. Weeping now. Strange had got in front, checking him over, gun steady all the time. Not taking his eyes away for a minute he edged round to stand next to Lund.

'I just did my duty,' the young officer repeated standing erect by the ancient generator.

'Which was what exactly?' she asked.

'You're not army,' he said again but more softly this time.

He held his gun loosely by his side. No real threat. Lund walked closer.

'They were just little things, Bilal. You deleted some radio recordings. Someone told you to. Who was the officer involved? What did the radio messages say?'

489

Without being asked he leaned down and let the gun fall to the floor. Then back to the stiff soldier pose again.

'Good . . .'

He wasn't listening any more. His eyes were ahead. Somewhere else altogether.

'Lund,' Strange said. 'I don't like this. Something's wrong.'

'Nothing's wrong,' she insisted, not that she believed it. 'Come on, Bilal. Let's get out of here. We can go back to headquarters. You'll be safe. I'll get you a lawyer. We can talk . . .'

He was unzipping his jacket. She watched and felt her blood run cold.

A belt there. Wires and packets. Pink sticks of explosive like fireworks. The familiar pineapple shape of a grenade.

Strange didn't say any more. He raced away from the soldier, grabbed her by the jacket, almost picked her up as he pushed and shoved her back towards the exit.

A voice behind. Loud and certain. The words of an army man reciting a long-cherished refrain.

'For God, King and Country!' Said Bilal chanted.

The red door was getting closer. She could read the number forty-four. They were turning towards it.

The bellow of an explosion. The world turning the colour of fire. Something lifted her and Strange off their feet altogether, threw them into the corridor outside until gravity beckoned and the hard damp tiles bit at her body, her face and hands.

When she came to his arms were still over her, fingers holding down her head, shielding it, his body wrapped above hers like protecting armour.

Sparks flew around them. There was the smell of cordite and explosive. And behind that the fresh, sharp tang of blood.

Plough's house was as inconspicuous as the man himself. A plain detached bungalow down a long drive, almost invisible from the street. Thomas Buch realized he'd no expectations of what it would be like. No idea how Plough, a quiet, introverted solitary man, lived.

The lights were on downstairs. The front door was open. He knocked then walked in.

A kitchen with half-washed dishes and empty cartons of microwave food. Then a chaotic living room full of packing cases. A map of the world on the wall. Shelves of books.

Two boxes stood open on the desk. Medals inside. Military, from service in Afghanistan.

A set of photographs in frames. Mostly the same face, a young man growing from schoolboy to manhood. Smiling, not the surly, uncertain figure in the army mugshot.

There was a resemblance there, Buch thought, as he picked up the nearest photo. If Plough smiled easily he'd look like this. Perhaps he did once. Long before Frode Monberg, Flemming Rossing and – it had to be faced – Thomas Buch entered his life.

It was hard to let go of the picture. Buch thought of his daughters, wondered if either of them would want a career in the army. It was safe money these days and there wasn't much of that about. A way of paying off your debts to get through college. Security of a kind.

He heard familiar soft footsteps behind, turned and faced Carsten Plough.

'I'm sorry,' Buch said, putting the picture back on the desk. 'I knocked but no one answered. The door was open.'

Plough was in a green and blue plaid shirt and jeans. He looked different.

'Hans Christian Plough Vedel. Vedel was my wife's name. In the army they always called him HC.'

The tall civil servant came over and looked at the photo.

'He was the only one in the squad who got out unharmed. It was a miracle, or so I thought.'

Plough's calm and gentle face creased with sorrow. He picked up some paperback books from the desk, tidied them into a neat pile.

'Hans told us there'd been some kind of incident in the village. There'd been an officer, and some civilians were killed. Then the judge advocate came along and called him a liar. A lunatic, like that Raben fellow.' A caustic smile, one Buch had never seen before. 'It wasn't possible, was it? A Danish soldier would never do such a thing.'

More books. Buch wondered if the man even knew what he was packing.

'He changed his statement when the army leaned on him. But I think that made it all worse. You see.' Plough tapped his head. 'In here he knew he wasn't mad. He was sure of what he saw. But the army said otherwise and the army didn't lie. So I believed the army too, and Hans became sicker and sicker.'

There was a grand piano by the window. He picked some sheet music off the stand, tossed that into the box.

'Then, a year ago, he drove the wrong way down the motorway to the Øresund bridge. And that was that.'

He went through the pictures one by one, shook his head as if to say, 'Later.'

'It was the end of my marriage. Things hadn't been good since Hans came back.' The shortest, most bitter of smiles. 'I was a civil servant, you see. I was bound to side with authority. So afterwards I buried myself in work, even more than before. And then . . .' A bright, vicious note in his voice. 'One day Anne Dragsholm turns up asking for Monberg. My minister.' A possessive finger pointed at Buch. 'Mine. She knew Hans wasn't lying, any more than Raben. Because Dragsholm had done something all the clever people in Operational Command couldn't. She'd found the officer.'

More books. Then Plough carefully closed the lid.

'I won't forget that day. I sat outside on a bench eating my sandwich, drinking my bottle of water. Thinking I was the most loathsome, most despicable man on earth. Because my son had needed me and I'd thought him a lunatic and a liar. When all the time he was simply telling the truth.'

He lifted the box and placed it on the floor. Got another empty one. Fetched some more books from the cases.

'I'm a loyal, gullible man. So I believed Monberg when he said he'd look into it. But then Dragsholm was killed, and still he did nothing.' A cold laugh that seemed out of character. 'Instead, like a coward and a fool he tried to take his own pathetic life.'

'And then you get me, the new boy, dumb and innocent, waiting to be fed a line,' Buch said, alarmed by the venom in his own voice.

Plough looked offended.

'What else could I do? I'd tried Monberg and he let me down. I had to lead you to the case. So I leaked the PET memo. Yes! Me! Quiet as a mouse Carsten Plough, the most discreet and reliable civil servant in Slotsholmen. I made sure Karina found Monberg's private diary. I laid a trail of breadcrumbs for my fat sparrow and you followed them, Buch, every last one. More enthusiastically than I could ever have hoped.'

'For God's sake! You could have gone to the police!'

That bitter laugh again.

'Eight days a minister and still so much to learn. Of course I couldn't. Rossing had been pulling Erik König's strings for years. The two of them were in cahoots long before any of this happened. König answered more to the Defence Ministry than he ever did to us.'

'Then the Politigården . . .'

'Who would have turned the case over to PET in an instant. Give me credit. I know the system. I invented half of it.' The books had been forgotten. 'But I had no proof. Not till yesterday. And then . . .' The broadest, happiest of smiles. 'I gave it to the Prime Minister.'

He beamed at Buch.

'There was no hesitation on Grue Eriksen's part. He didn't dither, like you.'

Buch closed his eyes and groaned.

'Of course not! He had his own skin to save.'

'No. Monberg as good as told me. He had a meeting with Rossing. As soon as he returned, the case was closed. There and then.'

Buch picked up a paperback on the desk. A cowboy story. It looked familiar.

'Thanks for giving me that,' Plough said. 'But it's not to my taste.'

'You should have told someone.'

'Who would have believed me?' Plough touched his arm, an odd and unexpected gesture in such a man. 'Not you. Not in the beginning anyway. Thomas . . . I'm genuinely sorry for the way things turned out. But you and Karina will do all right.'

Another book. A guide to Manhattan.

'When we talked the Prime Minister asked me whether I really wanted to go to Skopje. If there was anywhere else I'd prefer. So I said . . .'

Plough went through the photo frames, picked up one, showed it to Buch whose heart fell instantly.

'New York. Of course.'

A younger Carsten Plough. Dark hair. A pretty, happy wife by his side. A son with them, tall and smiling, no more than twelve or thirteen. They stood on the observation deck of the World Trade Center. Clothes from a different time. Everything from a different time.

'It was the most expensive holiday we ever had,' Plough admitted. 'I wanted it to be something we'd remember for ever.'

He gazed at the picture: lost faces, lost world. Lost family.

'There's nothing wrong with dreaming, is there? You'll be the crown prince now, Thomas. Karina can be your right hand—'

'All this time, Plough, all these years of service! And still you don't see how it works, do you? Monberg was screwing with you! What else are you hiding?'

A furtive look and that too was new.

Buch walked round the desk, tapped Plough on the plaid shirt.

'Tell me dammit or I'll take you down with them.'

'I'd like you to go now, please.'

The prim tone was back in his voice.

'Jesus.' Buch wanted to scream. 'You did just what they wanted all along. You helped the wrong man. You sucked up to the bastard who caused your own son's death—'

It came out of nowhere. A slap across the face. Like a challenge to a duel. Or a spat between children. Buch felt his cheek. It barely hurt. Not physically.

'The right people have been punished. I owed that to my son.' His arm stretched out to the door. 'You will leave now. I demand it.'

There were tears behind the staid horn-rimmed civil servant's glasses.

Thomas Buch picked up his old Western novel from the table, wondered why he'd given it to Plough in the first place. Even he wouldn't like these stories any more. Too many heroes and villains. Too much black and white and never a hint of grey.

'Goodnight,' he said then let himself out into the dark chill street.

Raben was back in a Politigården interview room, facing the same lawyer he'd seen the day before. He couldn't work out whether she was mad with him for fleeing the cops at the hospital or pleased he'd been proved right.

Either way it didn't matter. Louise now sat by his side. There was a deal on the table, a better one, though it still came with conditions.

'I don't think there's any doubt they'll accept your story this time,' the woman said. 'That doesn't change everything. You still need to drop your accusations against the police officer here.'

His arm was in a fresh sling. They'd cleaned up Louise's face. He didn't say a thing.

'It's clear your other allegations were correct. That means you've served two years in custody for something that should never have happened. Whatever penalty you get for the crimes you've just committed I can argue the time you've served already covers that.'

'You mean I'm free?' he asked. 'I can go home? See my son?'

'You can see your son. But you'll have to be in custody until we can get in front of a judge. It'll take a week or two at the most.'

He glowered at her.

'You've waited a long time, Raben!' the woman cried. 'For God's sake be patient now. I've talked them into giving you a place at Hørserod. It's an open prison. As pleasant as jail gets.' She glanced at Louise. 'You'll have family quarters there. The three of you can live together. Just a week, two or three at the most. Then I'll get you released. On bail at first. But they won't get away with opposing that. I can't believe they'd even try.'

'Jonas,' he whispered.

'And I advise you to sue for damages. You'll win. Big time.' She placed a piece of paper on the table. Raben looked at it. His original witness statement naming Strange as the officer in Helmand. 'But please . . . you need to sign a formal statement withdrawing that accusation against the policeman. As long as that's hanging over us . . .'

He looked at Louise.

'Can we have a moment to ourselves?'

'Of course,' the lawyer said then left the room.

He turned to the battered, tired woman next to him, didn't see the dirty clothes, the blood, the bruises.

'If we want . . .' he began.

Her head fell on his shoulder. Her hand found his. He brushed her dark and grubby hair with his lips.

'I'll do anything they ask,' he whispered. 'Whatever they—'

'So long as you come home I just don't care.'

His soldier's fingers found her cheek. They were too rough for her. Too coarse, too soiled by the work he'd done. But she never minded, and didn't now. She lifted her mouth, held it close to his, waited.

It was a brief and awkward kiss. The only kind he had. What was good between them came from her alone and she never even knew it. All he had to give was himself, his love, his dedication. And they'd failed somewhere along the way.

Not now though, he thought, as he held her, smelled the mud and mould of that underground hell they'd left behind.

Raben kissed his wife again then got up, moved his pained and aching frame to the table, and ripped the statement there to pieces, scattering the shreds across the floor.

Jarnvig was back in place in Ryvangen. Reinstated as colonel by Operational Command. Søgaard had been sent on leave ahead of an inquiry into his conduct towards those under his command. A new major, a genial man from the south, had taken his place.

They hadn't had much time to talk. Jarnvig had been on the phone constantly, to Camp Viking in Helmand, to contacts in Denmark demanding an immediate reopening of the investigation into the incident Raben had reported.

A distant voice in Afghanistan was listening to his orders.

'I want a military police team sent back to that place immediately. Look under every stone. Interview that Afghan officer Lund found. I can't believe she uncovered more in one day than we managed in three months.'

'I wasn't here then, sir,' the man said dryly.

'Well you are now, Major, and you've got a job to do. Get on with it and make sure I'm kept informed.'

He finished the call. The new man stood in front of his desk. Not stiff and severe like Søgaard. He looked more like a civilian who'd found a uniform somewhere.

'Any news about General Arild?' Jarnvig asked. 'I need to talk to him.'

'Not yet. We've got a new team arriving tonight. If it's OK I'd like to welcome them myself . . .'

'No, no,' Jarnvig said, not looking up from the pile of papers on his desk, most of them to do with the original report into Raben's claims. 'Thanks but I can manage.'

'I thought ... Your daughter's back. She wants to see you. She looks ...' He grimaced. 'She looks worn out. Really. If you need me ...'

'Then I'll let you know. Show her in.'

The new man nodded at the window.

'She's in your house right now. Packing her things. I think she's called a cab to Hørserod.'

Jarnvig took off his reading glasses.

'Hørserod?'

Two soft bags full of clothes. Jonas trying hard to stuff his plastic sword into the second.

Ryvangen was a castle, a fortress of a kind. It protected her. It enclosed and trapped her too. Like family. A trade-off between security and freedom. She'd come close to making a bargain that carried too high a price. The bed beyond the door. Søgaard beneath her ...

It was nothing to do with him. Nothing to do with Jens much. It was about being an army wife and mother. Another loyal servant inside the tribe. There was a time for that, and a time to break free, wrap your arms around the ones you loved, the people who truly mattered. And leave.

She'd stopped packing, was still staring at the unmade bed when her father walked in.

A smile for him. She knew what was coming.

'We've got to go now, Dad.'

'May I ask where?'

'Hørserod. To visit Jens. They're giving us family quarters.' She picked up a scarf, put it in the bag with some of Jonas's shirts. 'It's easy enough to come and go. I can still be in the infirmary.'

She'd spent so long in the shower, washing off the filth and the memories of the place Bilal had taken her. The bruises were healing. There was a light ahead of them, dim and shapeless, but one she recognized. It had a name she hadn't heard in a long time. The future.

'We've got to get away from Ryvangen.'

'To live in a prison camp?'

'It won't be for long. The lawyer said Jens will be out in two or three weeks at the most.' She patted Jonas on the head. 'We can wait for that, can't we?'

497

He was more focused on his toys than their conversation, still trying to cram as many as possible into the bag. Plastic dragons, more swords.

She got up, went to her father, took the door keys out of her bag, handed them over.

He looked like a man betrayed. Deprived of something that belonged to him.

Soldiers, she thought. Good men. Decent men. Clinging to the things they loved for strength and confidence.

'Dad . . .' She put her arms round him, kissed his rough cheek. 'I'll see you tomorrow. The day after that. The week after that.' She touched his face, looked into his hurt eyes. 'We're not leaving you. Just Ryvangen.'

'Right,' he whispered.

Men were always lost for words when emotion raised its awkward head.

Jonas walked up and gave Jarnvig something. A warrior with a shield and a sword. Wrapped the colonel's wrinkled fingers round its body.

'The car will be here,' she said and kissed him again, very quickly. 'I'll call. Come on, Jonas.'

The two of them left, didn't look back. Jarnvig watched them go, clutching the toy soldier Jonas had given him.

Then he sat at the dining table trying to imagine what the house would be like without their presence. Bereft of Louise's energy and warmth. Of Jonas's childlike curiosity and games.

Dead, Jarnvig thought. One more brick box in the warren that was Ryvangen.

His phone rang. It was Søgaard's replacement.

'You wanted me to find General Arild,' he said.

'Yes . . .'

'Well he's here.'

Arild was in his office, smoking as he went through the papers on the desk. Jarnvig could only smile awkwardly as he walked in.

'Oh come on, Torsten,' Arild said. 'You're not going to play hurt with me are you? Like a little girl?'

Jarnvig took his chair. Arild grabbed the one opposite.

'I don't know what you mean.'

Arild gestured at the office.

'You're back here. Running Ryvangen again. The colonel. Louise came to no harm. Things aren't so bad. I could have put you in front of a court if I'd wanted.'

'Raben was right.'

Arild smirked.

'So what? He was a criminal on the run and you helped him escape PET. But what the hell? Water under the bridge.'

Jarnvig nodded, said nothing.

'What a business!' Arild added, still grinning as if it was all a game. 'Young Bilal running rings round us to make sure we never found out what really happened in Helmand.'

'You knew, didn't you?'

'Me?' Arild threw back his head and laughed. He looked like a young man sometimes. So fit he could go out on active service tomorrow if he wanted. Perhaps did. 'How could I? I'm a pencil-pusher in Operational Command. My life's even more boring than yours.'

Jarnvig watched him, becoming more convinced with every easy gesture, each casual denial.

'You do believe me, don't you?' Arild asked.

'No,' Jarnvig said with great certainty. 'I know how it goes with engagements like these. I worked them with you once . . .'

'That was a long time ago. These are different days.'

'Nothing on paper. No trails to entrap you. No footprints . . .'

'This is a fantasy,' Arild insisted.

'If you've got something to tell me, General, say it now. You can't cover it up any more. The police are involved. The Ministry. Tell me and I'll do everything I can to clear up this mess. I don't want to harm the army . . .'

'What a smug little cretin you've become,' Arild declared then blew smoke at the ceiling. 'Your horizons really don't stretch beyond these miserable barracks, do they? You've no idea how complicated the world's become.'

'A Danish officer massacres an innocent family. What's so compli-cated about that?'

'Lots,' Arild said. 'We have to protect our own.' His fist banged the desk. 'Our own! No one else will. The politicians play armchair generals in Slotsholmen. The media snipe from the sidelines looking to belittle and blame us at every opportunity. And every year we send more men . . .' A shrug. '. . . and a few women to their deaths. For reasons we forgot ages ago, even if we ever knew them.'

'Either you lied to the police or you didn't.'

'Did I? Even if I did . . . so what?'

'I can't believe I'm hearing this . . .'

'Believe it, Torsten, or by God I will have you in front of that court. Yes, the police came to me. They had the name of a special forces officer. A man who served with courage and dedication.'

Jarnvig folded his arms and waited.

'They suspected him,' Arild continued. 'I told them I'd looked at the records and he'd been demobilized six months before.' His knuckles rapped on the desk. 'He wasn't even in Afghanistan at the time.' The short, muscular man flexed his shoulders, eyed Jarnvig. 'That wasn't strictly true. He was there. Not that you'll find that in the records.'

'That was our zone,' Jarnvig insisted. 'We should have been told.'

'It was none of your business. Why do you think I ordered Bilal to delete those radio messages? It was important there was no trace—'

'He killed this family!'

'You don't know what happened!' Arild yelled. 'He was a trained special forces commando. Not a hothead. Or a war criminal.'

Jarnvig grabbed a pen and a pad, began to write.

'Don't bother with that,' Arild ordered.

'There's going to be an investigation.'

'It won't go any further than the last one. The family who died weren't innocents. The father was funding the Taliban through drug shipments. He was an informer, a crook and a murderer.'

'There will be an investigation,' Jarnvig repeated.

Arild swore, shook his head, laughed more loudly than ever.

'You stupid little man,' he said, wiping his eyes. 'You never really understood, did you? You thought all there was to being a soldier was to listen and obey.'

'Get out,' Jarnvig said, staring at him.

'And you're right, for most of them,' Arild went on. 'But it's a shitty world out there. The Taliban don't play by the rules. If we do, then more fool us.'

'Get out!'

Arild didn't move.

'Do you know why I stopped going hunting with you?' he asked.

No answer.

'Because you didn't get that either. You used to wait for the prey to come to you. You thought it was enough to hide somewhere and hope it would come along.'

Arild stood up. Wiry man, active, general's uniform, handgun on his belt. He got his heavy winter coat from the stand.

'That's not what hunting's about,' he said. 'A *jæger* tracks his prey. Follows it. Identifies it. Gets to know it. Then . . .'

A hand as a gun, a finger as a barrel, aimed straight at Torsten Jarnvig's head.

'Boom!'

'Never show your face in here again. Never come near me or my men . . .'

Arild thrust his hands into his pockets and smiled.

'Do I make myself clear?' Jarnvig barked.

'You're overwrought. The strain I imagine. Take a week off. That's an order. When you come back I expect you to make the next team as strong and as ready as the last one. I'll be around to check—'

'No—'

'Torsten. Do I have to spell it out? Are you really so idiotic you can't take a hint?'

Arild patted his handgun, buttoned his coat, pulled on a pair of leather gloves, then looked at the man opposite him.

'Fuck with me and I will eviscerate you,' he said simply. 'Fuck with me and you'll wish you and your sorry little family were never born.'

A noise from the phone in his pocket. Arild looked at a message there then put it away.

'And now,' he said, 'you must excuse me. I have more interesting company to keep.'

She hated it when people started drinking at work. There were places for alcohol and the Politigården wasn't one of them.

Lund watched them gather as she sat at the desk she'd shared with Strange. He had a can of Coke, was moving from officer to officer, all genial smiles and relief. Brix was the leader, proven right

501

in the end, a glass of whisky in his hand as if to show it. Ruth Hedeby hung on his every word, even though her elderly husband stood alone and bored at the other side of the room, silent next to one of the junior detectives who was too gauche and shy to mingle.

She followed Brix telling a joke, Hedeby giggling, gulping at her glass of wine, eyes glittering, never leaving his rugged face. There was something going on between those two. Lund just knew it.

Strange caught her eye, grinned, his ordinary face, so full of pain and uncertainty once, now happy, satisfied.

'Come on,' he mouthed, waving her in with his hand.

She smiled, said, 'In a minute.'

Then sipped at the bottle of beer Brix had forced on her and turned her back on them all.

The photos of the dead were still on the walls. Anne Dragsholm and Lisbeth Thomsen. Myg Poulsen, David Grüner and Gunnar Torpe.

No pictures yet of Said Bilal, blown to pieces in that underground warren outside Hillerød. No photos of an Afghan family murdered in their own home two years before. They would never get that dubious privilege. And soon the rest would be gone.

Case closed.

Madsen walked up.

'We need to take the files. Brix says best we get them in store before midnight.'

'Sure,' she said with a shrug. 'Why not?'

He nodded at a uniform man to come and start taking the boxes.

'Did anyone get through to Frederik Holst like I asked?'

Madsen looked guilty. A nice, quiet, decent unambitious man, she thought. The kind who always did as he was told.

'Someone gave him your number and asked him to call. Got a bit busy to chase. Sorry. Do you want me to . . . ?'

'No.'

There was one other thing she'd asked for and that had turned up. Two sheets of paper from intelligence, records so old she didn't even recognize the design of the Politigården stamp. Lund read them as Madsen and the uniform man went to and fro with the boxes.

When they came back for the last one she stopped him.

'You were there when we searched the barracks a few days ago, weren't you?'

'Yeah,' Madsen laughed. 'What a place. Didn't they love us?'

'Why didn't you see anything in Søgaard's locker then?'

'Nothing to find. We looked. Bilal must have put that stuff there later, when he was getting desperate.'

The oldest intelligence file dated back to 1945. She couldn't imagine Copenhagen then. Or the Politigården making the difficult transition from being a part of the Nazi machine, struggling to be Danish, to be free once more.

'So we searched everything?'

'Dead right! Are you coming drinking with us or what?'

'I am, I am.' She watched him fill one of the few remaining boxes. Time running out. 'Did we ever work out how Dragsholm tracked down that officer? You know.' She tried not to sound sarcastic. 'The one the army are going after.'

'No.' Madsen frowned. 'I went through her case files. That was one angry woman. You could tell the way she wrote. We were all bastards. She had meetings with her soldiers. With other lawyers. With us supposedly.'

Lund stared at him.

'With us? Here?'

'No. Just one meeting,' he corrected himself. 'There was a diary note about talking to an officer in court.'

'That's how she contacted us?' she asked very carefully. 'Before she was killed? By going up to someone she met in court?'

He was getting bored with this.

'It's one line in her diary, Lund. I checked it out this end. There was nothing to confirm it. She never called here, that's for sure.'

'But she must have done. When she was looking into the case—'

'No,' he said firmly. 'She hired her own private investigators. Besides . . .' He shrugged, looked enviously at the crowd beyond the door. 'What could we have told her? We didn't even know something happened in Afghanistan until you came along.'

There was one last box file. She realized she had her hand on it.

'Can I take that one too? Then get you another beer?'

She held out the black box.

'Who was in charge of the first search at Ryvangen? Looking at the lockers and the rest?'

'Hell, I don't remember! We've all been working twenty-hour days. You've been to Afghanistan and back. Let's go . . .' He made a gesture. 'Glug, glug.'

'Was it Ulrik Strange?'

He had his free hand on the box.

'Right,' Madsen agreed. 'Strange. Why?'

Lund was thinking. He tugged at the box.

'Can I?'

'Take it,' she said and watched him go.

Holst's number in the hospital was still on her pad. Alone at the desk she dialled it, got through first time, said, 'This is Lund. When I ask you to call me I expect you to do it.'

'Sorry,' said the bitter drawl on the other end of the line. 'Things got in the way. Bombs. Bullets. Bodies. You know the kind of thing.'

'What happened to Møller's dog tag?'

Silence.

'This is important, Holst. What happened to his dog tag?'

'What do you think? I did what I always do. I cut it in half and put both pieces in the body bag. Is this important?'

'His parents never got a tag.'

'I put it in there, Lund!' he yelled from three thousand miles away. 'If it didn't turn up in Copenhagen someone took it.'

And made a new one, which was now in an evidence bag, stained with smoke from a baker's oven once full of human bones.

'Could they have taken it in Afghanistan?'

'What is this?'

'It's a question. Could they have taken it before the body bag went on the plane?'

'Not likely, Lund. We treat our dead with respect. More than they get alive sometimes. If someone got caught stealing a dead man's dog tag . . . I can't imagine.'

'Thanks,' she said.

The beer was empty. It was time to mingle.

It had to be Brix. No one else really listened to her. Not that he did all the time.

She wandered through the sea of bodies. Uniform men sweaty from the long day. Women from forensic. A few call handlers. It was turning into quite a party. Someone shoved another bottle of beer in her hand and she didn't even see who.

One side of the room finished. She was about to start on the other when a hand came out and stopped her.

Lund looked. Polished nails. Manicured fingers.

Ruth Hedeby was smiling for the first time Lund could recall in a while. It was a worrying sight.

'The people upstairs wanted me to tell you, Lund. Well done.'

She tried to walk on. Hedeby was having none of it.

'We got there in the end,' she said, keeping her hand on Lund's arm. 'No small thanks to—'

'You think?'

'I do!' The woman was loyal. Reliable. A drone. 'I must admit . . .' A flash of naughty regret as she fluttered her eyelashes. 'I had my doubts. When Lennart . . . when Brix sent for you. It seemed rash.'

The superior stare. She'd been hitting the wine.

'Seemed even more rash when I met you,' Hedeby added. 'First impressions matter. You should remember that.'

'What matters is looking until you get to the truth.'

Hedeby so wanted to be thanked. To share in the glory being distributed around this room.

'There's a good chance you won't be sent back to Gedser.'

'I like Gedser,' Lund lied. 'Lot of birds.'

'Birds?'

Lund's hands swept the ceiling. She made a tweeting noise.

'In the sky. Excuse me . . .'

Brix was talking to a burly man from upstairs. One of the suits who ran the place and never usually deigned to dirty their fingers with the troops.

'Can we talk?' Lund asked, carving straight into the conversation.

The suit went quiet, glared at her and walked off. Brix looked . . . disappointed. Again.

'What is it?'

'The day Strange went to the refugee centre in Helsingør. When I chased the man who killed Gunnar Torpe. Did someone check his alibi?'

'Yes,' he said with a pained look.

'He was with another officer?'

'No. They'd split up earlier. What is this?'

She looked round the busy room.

'Where's he gone?'

'Working,' Brix answered with a shrug. 'I don't know why. I could have found someone else.'

'To do what?'

'Escort Raben to Horserød. They're downstairs in the garage.'

Horserød. A picture in her head. The childlike drawing from the museum. Sad figures, starving, shuffling through the snow. Lund couldn't stop herself glancing round the room, wondering what this place was like back then.

'Have you been to the Frihedsmuseet?' Lund asked and watched Brix's interesting face crease with puzzlement. 'The Germans tortured people downstairs.' She shrugged. 'Some Danish cops did too. Then took them to Mindelunden and those stakes . . .'

'I do know that, thanks,' he said. 'Not now, Lund. Have a drink. Try to . . . I don't know. Wind down a little. If you can.'

A breezy voice over her shoulder.

'Lennart!' Hedeby all smiles. 'You must come and say hello to my husband.' She beamed at both of them. 'He's dying to meet you.'

'I bet he is,' Lund muttered then walked through the sea of bodies, out to the lockers beyond.

Downstairs. White police motorbikes, blue patrol cars. A warren of rooms and corridors leading off. She'd never thought about it much before but now it seemed obvious. This subterranean labyrinth was bigger than the sprawling Politigården itself, tunnelled underneath the street outside, the buildings beyond.

Seven decades before no one would have heard the screams. But they surely knew they were there.

Skinny, starving figures in Horserød. Ghostly voices in a dusty, stinking car park. The past didn't die. It lingered.

Lund walked on until she heard voices. Strange was there, next to his black Ford. A uniform man was helping Raben into the back. Couldn't help but push down his head along the way. Old habits . . .

'You can go now,' Strange said. 'I can take care of it. Have a beer for me.'

She watched from the shadows. The uniform man scratched his head.

'You're sure? There's supposed to be two of us.'

Strange laughed.

'He's got one arm in a sling and he'll be free as a bird in a week or two. I don't think we'll get any more trouble from this one.'

Strange banged hard on the roof of the car, kept smiling at the cop. 'Will we?'

No answer from inside.

'Save a beer for me!' Strange cried, pointing at the uniform man. 'I'll be back in an hour or so.'

'No way,' the cop laughed. 'Every man for himself.'

Strange grinned at him. Watched him go. Looked surprised when she walked out from the darkness and said, 'I'm coming with you.'

A long pause.

'Why?'

'Because I am.' She held out her hand. 'We need to talk. Let me drive.'

'What is this, Lund? You're missing the party.'

'I'm not in the mood. Give me the keys.'

He grunted something, threw them over, climbed into the passenger seat. Lund got behind the wheel and looked in the mirror. Raben's bearded face was watching their every move. He had his seat belt on. The doors were reinforced and locked. He wasn't going anywhere.

'What is this?' Strange asked again.

'Horserød,' she said.

'It's inland not far from Helsingør.'

'I know where I'm going, thanks.'

She took them up the ramp, out into the busy night traffic, glad to get away.

Five minutes in and Strange was getting restless.

'That car's following us,' he said as they struggled to get out of the city centre.

'What car?'

'The one behind. That's following us.'

Raben hadn't said a word since they left.

'You're paranoid. It's traffic. Everyone's following somebody.'

'Yeah, well.' He looked at the dashboard. 'What about some music?'

He didn't wait for an answer. The radio was set to a classical station. Opera. Must have been his choice. It was his car. He wasn't an ordinary cop.

She listened for twenty seconds then turned the music off.

'So what do you want to talk about?' he asked.

'I'll get to that.'

They weren't far from Østerport Station.

'And why are we going the long way round?'

She glanced at him.

'I want to show you something.'

A little further down the road Lund turned off.

'Oh come on,' Strange cried. 'Horserød's straight ahead.'

'Won't take long.'

They were close to Ryvangen. Another piece of history came back from the museum. The Danish Army had long used the barracks before the Nazis swept in and seized it as their base. The shooting range of Mindelunden was a practice area for soldiers, not a killing ground for the Germans. Only the railway track now separated the barracks from the memorial that Mindelunden had become. Soon they were on the park side, turning into a quiet dead end lane next to the long rows of graves, the statue of the mother with her fallen son, the three stakes in the ground.

'What the hell's going on?' Raben asked, worried from behind. 'My wife's waiting for me. My son—'

'You just stay where you are,' Lund ordered, then turned into the empty car park, killed the engine, got out and stood beneath the bare winter trees.

Clear night, half-full moon. Frost forming on the ground. The place was silent though beyond the memorial park she could see lights in the low wooden buildings of the adjoining schools.

Strange got out of the car. Lund used the remote and double locked it. He came and stood next to her.

'Something's wrong,' she said. 'It's Brix. He's covering up for somebody.'

He'd got a blue polyester vest beneath his light jacket. Probably felt cold. Not happy anyway.

'Brix?' Strange asked, shaking his head.

A train went past like noisy metallic lightning rumbling through the night.

'There's something you need to see,' she said when it was gone

508

then walked over and forced open the wooden side door into Mindelunden.

'Bloody hell, Lund,' Strange complained. 'We're supposed to be taking a prisoner to Horserød. What is this?'

Past the long lines of names, past the graves and the frozen mother and son.

The moon was brighter than it should have been. Nothing here escaped its rays.

'Much as I'd love to be alone with you,' he went on, following her as she walked, 'this isn't very cosy. Can't we go for pizza and a beer or something? After we've dumped off chummy back there?'

'This is a memorial park for the Danish Resistance.'

The place it all began while she was chasing smuggled dope and immigrants in Gedser.

'I know that.'

The firm, hard sound of her footsteps rang up from the footpath.

'They were war heroes. Said Bilal saw himself as a patriot too. He would have worshipped them.'

He caught up, looked at her.

'Sadly we can't ask him now, can we?'

'Bilal would never have left Anne Dragsholm in a place like this. A graveyard for martyrs? She was a *stikke*, wasn't she? A turncoat. A traitor. Someone who wanted to drag the army . . . Denmark down into the gutter.'

He waved his arms in front of him.

'At the risk of repeating myself . . . we can't ask him now.'

She kept walking.

'Bilal erased those radio messages. Helped cover up what happened in Helmand. He didn't kill her. Or the others.'

He stopped, hands in pockets, a jaded look on his face.

'Then why did he take the Raben woman hostage?'

She shook her head.

'God you're slow sometimes. He wanted the army to come in and save him from being fitted up for something he never did. Fat chance . . .'

Lund turned and stared at the trees and the pale memorial stones.

'They were murdered by someone who felt differently about this place.'

'What's all this got to do with Brix?'

They were approaching the old shooting range, with the three sacred stakes.

Walking, walking, never looking at him.

'Brix is protecting the real killer.'

They looked like shrunken totem poles. Or relics from a lost Stonehenge. Part of a ritual, a ceremony most had forgotten, and those who remembered only dimly understood.

'Stand there,' she said, and got him to stop by the middle pole.

'What is—?'

'Dragsholm was terrified. She knew someone was going to come for her. Her house was full of alarms. She'd ordered sensors for her garden. She'd hired her own security guards.'

It was too dark down here beneath the branches of the overhanging trees. She needed the moonlight.

'Come,' Lund ordered and they walked up the steep bank behind the stakes, the buffer that once took the stray bullets that never hit their intended target.

Stopped at the top, a little breathless, looking around.

Then Lund stared at his plain face caught in the moonlight.

'But she never went to the police. She thought someone was going to kill her. And she never once called us.'

Strange shrugged.

'Maybe she wasn't sure.'

'She was sure.'

'Then—'

'She found him. She knew who the officer was. He'd been given Møller's identity deliberately by someone in Operational Command. They even forged a new dog tag.'

Strange hugged himself in the cold, kept quiet.

'Dragsholm knew he was working in the Politigården. She told Monberg. He did nothing. There's no other explanation.'

'Lund—'

'Nothing else fits. And then suddenly we find all that incriminating evidence at Ryvangen. Even though we'd searched the same place only a few days before. Don't you see?'

He stared at the frosty grass and shook his head. Lund came up to him, touched the front of his jacket.

'Someone planted that during the search.'

'I was in charge of the search. I didn't plant a thing.'

'Then . . .' She shrugged. 'It's got to be somebody on the team.'

His hand went to her arm. He peered into her eyes. She wondered about the expression there. It looked like sympathy. Pity even.

'This is what happened last time, isn't it? With Meyer. You won't let go, even when it's over.'

'That wasn't over. It still isn't.'

'Maybe not.' His arms gripped her firmly. 'But this is. Please let it die. For God's sake . . .'

Lund pulled herself away.

'Have you talked to Brix about this?' he asked.

'Not yet. Do you think I can trust him? He's going to send me back to Gedser.'

'We can stop that! Let's have a talk with him. Both of us. You're not going back to Gedser. But . . .'

His grizzled head lowered, his bright eyes bore into hers.

'You can't rock the boat for ever. We drop off Raben. We go back to the party. We have a few beers. Then tomorrow . . .' She remembered the time they'd almost kissed. He looked like this. Young and vulnerable. 'Tomorrow you decide. About everything.'

'Tomorrow,' she murmured.

'Can I have the keys? Can I drive?'

She looked back towards the graves and the memorial plaques with their endless lines of names.

'I couldn't find your grandfather on the wall.'

Strange blinked. Shuffled on his feet.

'I couldn't find his name in the memorial yard in the Politigården either,' Lund added. 'And that's odd. Every police officer who died under the Nazis is there. Even the ones who went abroad to the concentration camps.'

She looked up into his face.

'Why is that?'

No words. And his eyes were different. The way they looked in Helmand. Another Ulrik Strange was with her at that moment.

'I wasn't asking out of curiosity,' she added. 'I know the answer. I just want to hear it from you.'

*

Buch couldn't work out why he still had a ministerial car. But there it was waiting for him when he came out of Plough's house, Karina sitting in the back, arms tightly folded, face furious.

'Maybe we should get a taxi,' he said, sticking his head through the door.

'Why?'

She wasn't in a good mood. That was obvious.

Because this belongs to them, he thought. Like everything else. There could be a bug in the roof. Something that relayed everything he said straight back to the silver-haired man, the father of the nation, seated in the old king's office over the muddy riding ground where the horses went round and round. Just like him. Going nowhere.

'Just get in, will you?' she said.

He did and sat silent for ten minutes, thinking as they moved slowly through the night traffic. Then told her what Plough had said.

'That can't be true,' she cried, next to him in the back. 'You know Plough. He wouldn't leak a damned thing. It's not in his genes. Besides—'

'He did it, Karina.'

'I was with him every single day.'

'He did it! He told me!' The residential streets were long behind. This was the city now. Lights and noise and people. The grey island of Slotsholmen where Absalon once built his fortress and created a city called Copenhagen was getting closer. 'He was proud of it.'

'For God's sake why?'

There was a kind of logic there. Buch had to admit it.

'Because all he wanted was revenge. In his own head Rossing was to blame. Never Grue Eriksen. Not the grand old man.'

She howled with fury.

'He's not that stupid, Thomas! He must know something that implicates the Prime Minister. Something—'

'He doesn't.' Buch's gloomy stare silenced her. 'And even if he did he wouldn't say. Plough's part of the system. It brought him up. Made him what he was. It's hard enough to tear down one little part of it. To ask him to pull the rug from under everything . . .'

Buch put his hand on her arm, tried to make her see.

'We haven't been up against Rossing. Or Grue Eriksen. Certainly not Plough. We've been fighting . . .'

Slotsholmen. There it was beyond the windscreen. All the buildings, the ministries and the Folketinget, the little converted houses for the civil servants, the garden with its statue of Kierkegaard.

'We've been fighting that,' Buch said, waving his hand at the grey shapes ahead. 'Plough thinks he did the right thing. He was loyal. To the system to begin with. To his son in the end.' He glanced at her. 'And what were we?'

She was a smart, ambitious, dangerous young woman, Buch thought. He hadn't spoken easily with his wife Marie in days. A part of him, a part he hated, had looked at Karina, thought of Monberg, and wondered . . .

'Thomas,' she said very slowly. 'We know for a fact the Prime Minister was involved in a conspiracy that killed people. Killed them!'

'True,' he agreed as the long black car pulled into the Ministry entrance.

'We can't let him get away with that. How could you live with yourself?' Her hand fell on his, soft and gentle and warm. 'I know you well enough now . . .'

Buch took his fingers away, looked at the door he'd never walk through as a minister again.

He liked that job. He was good at it.

'I don't give a damn about my career,' she whispered, watching him, every expression on his jowly, bearded face.

The car stopped. The driver was waiting for instructions.

'I'm not giving up!' he said, too quickly. 'Believe it.'

'Good.' She patted his knee. 'So what do we do?'

Buch got out. The night was cold but there was no rain and the twisting dragons he'd learned to live with looked as if they were dancing in the clearest moonlight he'd seen in weeks.

He walked to the entrance, opened the door for her.

'What's Grue Eriksen up to now?' he asked.

'Talking to people about the reshuffle. He wants you there. To get your reward for keeping quiet.'

'How soon can you put a press conference together?'

'If I've got something good to dangle on the hook . . . thirty minutes.'

'Do it, please,' Buch said, then turned right to begin the long, interior march through the labyrinth of Slotsholmen, right and left, up and down until he found himself in the Christianborg Palace. There he asked a couple of questions. Found the room.

The Prime Minister was on his own. Slightly hunched, shoulders rounded, not that Buch had noticed before. Face so familiar most of Denmark seemed to have grown up with it. Benign. Dependable. Indulgent. A man to be relied upon.

Gert Grue Eriksen smiled when he walked in.

'Hi, Thomas.' He gestured at the seats round the table. 'Take one, will you? We've fences to mend, haven't we? I want this reshuffle fixed this evening.' Hand outstretched, Buch took it without thinking. 'I'm glad we've got the chance to talk first like this. That trouble with PET . . .'

The Prime Minister frowned.

'I'm afraid those officers became a little overenthusiastic. They seemed to blame you for König's dismissal. Which is unfair and now they know it.'

For some reason Buch found himself staring at his hand after shaking Grue Eriksen's. Sweaty, ugly, fat fingers marked by the scars of his early farming days. The hand of a labourer, not a politician. Cautious, common men who didn't shake with anybody, not without looking them up and down first. As he had once.

'I owe you an explanation,' Grue Eriksen said as Buch sat down.

'Why can't you let things go?'

Strange stood in front of her, back to how he'd looked in Helmand now. A soldier. A man of duty. Forcing all emotion from himself. Getting ready to serve. To fight. To rage.

'I can let them go when they're finished.'

'Some things never finish, Sarah. It's best to walk away.'

'Your grandfather wasn't a hero. He was a *stikke*. He worked for the Nazis. He was the one torturing them in the basement of the Politigården. Bringing them here so they could be tied to these stakes and shot.'

Strange folded his arms and nodded.

'And then one day,' Lund went on, 'a group of Resistance fighters called the Holger Danske caught up with him outside Central Station. Gunned him down in the street.'

He didn't move, didn't speak.

'It's all there in the Politigården records,' she said. 'Not the Frihedsmuseet. I checked. So I guess . . .'

Thinking. Imagining. This was what she was good at.

'I guess one day a young police cadet comes in for work experience. He thinks his dead granddad was a hero. Because that's what his father told him. So he decides to look up the records for himself.' She moved closer to try to see into his eyes. 'And when he finds the truth he goes home and does what any kid would. He spills it.'

'You're not normal,' Strange murmured.

'This isn't about me. It's about you. Who you are.'

The eyes did flicker then, stared hard at her.

'It doesn't hurt any more. Sorry.'

'Did your father lie to himself too? Did he pretend . . . ?' she asked.

'We all want heroes. We just don't like to think of the cost.'

'And then you run away to the army. God . . .' She shook her head. 'They must have loved you. All that inherited guilt. Talk about someone with a point to prove. An army man from an army family and what a secret to live with. When you brought Dragsholm here did it make it even? One *stikke* for another? How did it feel when they said that wasn't enough?'

Nothing.

Lund went back down the slope. He slunk after her.

'Come on, Strange. You said it yourself. You're a foot soldier. Not a leader. Someone put you up to this. Someone gave you the code to the munitions store in Ryvangen. Fixed that forged dog tag. Told you to kill those people and make it look so hellish we'd think some fake terrorist gang murdered them—'

'Cut it out.'

'You didn't enjoy that part, did you?' she went on. 'Torturing Anne Dragsholm. Cutting Myg Poulsen and the priest to ribbons. Locking a man in a wheelchair inside his own—'

'Give it a fucking rest for once!' he yelled at her, alive and jumpy.

Lund went quiet. Scared. At him in part. But more at her own growing fury.

Slowly, like a cat stalking its prey, he came over, walked round her once, returned to look in her face.

'You're not right in the head,' he said.

She didn't blink. Couldn't have done if she wanted.

'About this I am. Why did you go along with it?'

His hand came up, touched her cheek, ran across her dry lips, brushed the soft lines of her throat. Left her.

'Why?' Lund asked again.

'Because sometimes things come back to bite you.' He looked at the stakes, the little ramp above them. His voice had turned soft. He sounded younger. 'I was at a court hearing last summer. It was hot.' A shrug. 'I had a short-sleeve shirt. The Dragsholm woman came over wanting to talk about Helmand. Halfway through she saw the tattoo. All these questions. She must have looked in my face and . . .'

Strange nodded.

'She was like you. She wasn't going to give up. She knew. I knew. We all thought that nightmare had been buried. But . . .'

Lund got out her phone.

'You need to come in now. I'm calling Brix—'

He snatched the mobile from her fingers, flung it down on the grass below.

'You don't know what happened! Don't think for one moment you do.'

'I know five people got murdered. That's enough for now. I know you didn't do this on your own. Someone put you up to—'

'You don't understand a fucking thing!'

'Just tell the truth, Strange,' she said calmly. 'How hard's that?'

'I told my father the truth once. He didn't want to hear it either. Look where that got me . . .'

'Five people dead—'

'Every one of them a *stikke*!'

The noise, half shout, half scream, echoed around them in the little grove of Mindelunden. She couldn't think for a moment. Not even when she saw he had a gun to her chest.

'Don't you shoot me in the head?' Lund asked, looking him in the eye. 'Isn't that the way they teach you?'

No movement. No expression on his plain and ordinary face.

'You couldn't kill me before. You're not doing it now.'

She pulled away from him, turned her back. Aware he wasn't moving. Looked through the grass for the glint of an LCD screen. Found the phone, picked it up. Walked towards the three upright stakes.

No sound from behind. She put the phone to her ear.

Glanced to the end of this small open space in the Mindelunden trees.

Another figure there, where the riflemen would once have been. A body position she recognized. Legs apart, arms outstretched, a weapon held with both hands.

Lund was listening to the centre operator talk in her ear when it happened. Yellow flash of fire first, then the sound.

From behind a shriek of pain. She turned.

Ulrik Strange was on his knees. Hands to his chest. Mouth oozing blood.

Another explosion. He bucked back with a movement so violent it was like a puppet getting jerked on a piece of string.

The phone fell from her fingers.

Lund wheeled round.

One flash and when the shot hit her it was so powerful she staggered back, fell against something that could only be the first stake, stopped there, pinioned like a target under the bright silver moonlight.

Gasping for breath. Struggling to think.

Then another vicious burst of fire, an impact that threw her wheeling round clutching at her chest, leaving the stake for the thick cold grass, the darkness, the stink of grass and mud and death.

'No.' Buch shook his head angrily. 'I don't want to hear it. I've had enough of this. You can keep your ministerial offices. Your bribes.'

Grue Eriksen's eyes registered that news.

'I know Plough gave you the ammunition to blame everything on Rossing. One more puppet for you to manipulate, huh?'

The weakest, most political of smiles appeared on Grue Eriksen's face. He walked over to the door, closed it, made sure they were on their own.

'Do you think you can get away with anything?' Buch yelled. 'You can't bury this one. I'm calling a press conference. I'll tell them everything. Then I'll tell it to the Folketinget, the police, PET. Anyone who'll listen.'

'Thomas . . .'

Grue Eriksen thrust his hands into his trouser pockets, looked exasperated.

'I've got the documents,' Buch went on. 'I'll distribute them. Lock me up for breaching the Official Secrets Act if you want. The damage is coming . . .'

'Please—'

'You've been covering up for murder. People died because of you.'

'I'm the leader of this country. We're at war. The same war that killed your brother—'

'Jeppe died in Iraq!'

'Same war,' Grue Eriksen said quietly. 'It just goes on and on.'

Buch was thrown for a moment.

'Don't give me that shit,' he said. 'Don't . . . I know you were behind all this. I can prove it.'

He got up, went for the door.

'Do you really want to walk out of here without knowing why?' the Prime Minister called as he left. 'I find that hard to believe. You're such an inquisitive man. God knows we've all learned that . . .'

Buch stopped, fingers on the handle.

'I've been fed so much bullshit.'

'You have,' Grue Eriksen admitted. 'And much of it from me. It seemed right at the time. Perhaps I was mistaken. But . . .'

Buch started to leave.

'We weren't covering up the killing of civilians,' Grue Eriksen said in a loud, insistent voice. Enough to stop him, make him turn.

The Prime Minister frowned, folded his arms, leaned back to sit on the polished table behind him.

'Ordinary people die in war,' he said ruefully. 'Sometimes it happens by accident. Sometimes by mistaken design. But in the end . . . people forgive. They understand.'

'What then?' Buch demanded, marching back towards him.

'The problem was the officer. You see . . . he wasn't there.'

'Riddles, riddles . . .'

'That's just what they are,' Grue Eriksen agreed. 'Exactly. Do you think I sit at my desk in there and watch the whole world pass by in front of me? That I say yes or no to everything? Even with the domestic agenda I'm at best a distant captain, delegating to good men like you. As you delegate to others—'

'Don't flatter me, please.'

'I wasn't. The officer wasn't there. He was working on a secret mission. It hadn't been cleared with the Security Committee.'

Buch's finger rose.

'You have to do that. It's the law.'

'It's the law,' Grue Eriksen concurred. 'Tell that to the men and women we've got on the ground in Helmand. Let's say . . . they know a certain minor warlord is bankrolling the Taliban. Providing information, weapons, funds.' He looked at the ceiling, as if inventing all this. 'Let's imagine we get word that he's about to flee. He knows we're onto him, you see. So our forces have maybe a day, two at most to get in there. Interrogate him. Take him into custody. Well?'

'Well what?'

'When Operational Command comes to me what do I say? Do I tell them to wait until we've managed to check through all our diaries, ticked off our committee meetings, our lunch dates? Our evenings at the opera? In Monberg's case his assignations with his various mistresses? Do I say to these brave men and women fighting a hopeless war in a brutal distant land . . . wait a week or so, and maybe then I can get back to you with a yes or no?'

Buch said nothing.

'What would you do, Thomas? The moment a secret decision's committed to paper here it's a day away from the streets of Kabul. That I guarantee.'

'You knew who that officer was all along . . .'

'No, I didn't then and I don't now. Do you listen to what I say at all? I don't want to know. I wouldn't ask. All I understood was I had a decision to face. We were short of money. Short of troops.'

'You could have done something to stop it. When Anne Dragsholm was murdered—'

'This is the real world!' Grue Eriksen barked at him. 'Not the one we'd like. Denmark's at war and we're losing. The Taliban gain strength all the time. They exploit our every weakness. If we hand them a scandal on a plate . . . what do you think they'd do? Sit round the table and look for a solution? How do you think the mothers and fathers of soldiers coming home in a coffin would feel? Would they thank you for this? Or me?'

He pulled a chair from the table, sat down, briefly put his head in his hands. Gert Grue Eriksen looked old and tired for a moment, before the politician returned.

'When I first became a minister I was like you. Keen as mustard. Determined to do the right thing. To see justice done. But God . . .'

His clenched fist hammered the polished wood. 'Nothing's as simple as that. It's a dangerous, fractured world we live in. Serve here long enough and you'll see it. One day someone will tell you there's something bad round the corner. So bad you don't want to hear.'

He opened his hands.

'And then what do you do? You ask for a report and options. And they say . . .' Grue Eriksen closed his eyes briefly. 'They say it's best you didn't hear. As you once said to me . . .'

Buch recalled uttering those very words. It seemed a lifetime ago.

'If we're not responsible,' he asked, 'who is?'

'Everybody,' Grue Eriksen answered in a soft, damaged voice. 'Nobody. You.' A brief, humourless laugh. 'Me, when it's late at night and I can't sleep. Conscience is a wonderful thing. Yours especially.' His hand clutched at Buch's arm. 'We need it here. To remind us when we go too far—'

'People died!'

'I know. And sometimes you have to tell that virtuous, nagging voice to shut up. To put democracy aside in order to fight for democracy.' The hand tightened on Buch's arm. 'I thought you of all people would understand that. If that brother of yours were here today—'

'Don't throw the dead at me,' Buch yelled. 'I've got enough of them in my head already.'

'Not as many as I have,' Grue Eriksen said in a voice close to a whisper. 'And they all know me by name.'

He looked round the grand room.

'We make a deal with the devil when we cross the bridge into Slotsholmen. You're learning that the hard way. I need you, Thomas. I need your intelligence, your innocence.' He laughed. 'Your infuriating naivety too.'

The Prime Minister got up, placed a firm and insistent hand on Buch's arm.

'If I make mistakes, you must tell me. Help me govern better. Make sure—'

'You must be out of your mind,' Buch said, removing himself from the man's grip. 'When I tell Krabbe and Birgitte Agger you're finished. You'll be gone by the morning.'

'Still not quite there, are we?' Grue Eriksen smiled. 'Still that childlike stubbornness holds you back—'

'I've had enough of this . . .'

'There's nothing to tell and no one to hear it. This secret's shared already. Come . . .'

Two large black double doors with star adornments stood at the side of the room. Grue Eriksen marched towards them like a little soldier himself.

'Meet those who've heard my tale already, Thomas. And agreed that the most important thing of all is to continue the good fight.'

'These games . . .'

'No game,' the Prime Minister said quickly. 'No sides either. When it comes to war we're as one. The way you always wanted it.'

The doors went back slowly. A gathering beyond. Buch came and stood to watch, breathless, sweating, knowing what he would see.

Erling Krabbe was there. Birgitte Agger too. The leaders of the minority partners. Every member of the cabinet. The political royalty of Slotsholmen, foes on paper, gathered together in unison.

Gert Grue Eriksen walked in, stood in their midst, turned, beckoned with a hand.

'Thomas!' shrieked a high-pitched voice from behind.

Buch didn't move.

'Thomas.' Karina Jørgensen marched in and stood by him. She was the one tugging at his arm now. 'The reporters are here. They need you. They're waiting.'

He broke the passenger window on Strange's car with his Neuhausen pistol, freed the lock, dragged out the handcuffed man inside. Took him through the shattered wooden door into the memorial park, back to the firing range and the stakes.

Two still bodies on the ground. He'd need the keys to the handcuffs. Strange would have them.

He'd need a plan, a story too, and that was halfway there already.

Raben rolled on the grass, cursing and shrieking.

A boot in the gut, another under the chin. Then the Neuhausen in the face. That silenced him.

'Ungrateful piece of shit,' he said, and fetched him another kick, hard in the groin this time.

Wiped the weapon with a cloth from his pocket, crouched down over the wheezing man, squeezed the gun into his fingers, fired two rapid shots into the body a couple of metres away.

Watched Strange's corpse jump and twitch with the impact. The woman hadn't moved since he shot her. Too far for this trick. She could stay where she was for now.

A plan.

He'd brought two guns. Threw the one he'd just fired into the grass by the stakes. Took out the second Neuhausen, stood over the gasping, choking shape on the ground.

'You put him up to it,' Raben muttered then wiped his blue sleeve across his mouth, cleared away some grass and blood. 'They'll find you . . .'

He laughed

'No they won't. Do you think shooting a worm like you counts for anything? Besides . . .' The man above Raben relaxed for an instant. 'You really don't remember, do you? I thought it was an act. But it's not . . .'

'Remember what?'

He crouched down, looked.

'You're the one who started all this. You shot that first kid. Strange was a good officer. Sound man. He'd kill anyone but not without a reason.' A shrug. 'You never put it in your statement. But Strange told us. So did your own men. Why do you think they were so scared of you?'

He rolled back his head. Laughed at the moon.

'All this time you spent chasing the monster, Raben. And you never knew. The monster's you.'

'Liar, liar . . .' Raben's voice was a low, frightened sound in his throat. 'You fucking liar . . .'

Two steps closer. The black barrel of the Neuhausen to his temple.

'Why would I lie? I'm about to shoot you. The way you shot her. The other kids. The mother.' A glance at the body behind. 'He got the father. But then the bastard was a friend of the Taliban so what the hell?'

'Shut up—'

'You started this. You and your fury. You murdered those kids because you just . . .' Free hand to head, finger whirling. '. . . lost it. And everyone was to blame except you. Come on . . .'

The barrel prodded at Raben's skull.

'Remember now? You were a snivelling wreck afterwards. All grief and regret. The good men we lost—'

'Arild—'

'Call me "General". For once in your sorry life act like a soldier.'

He went to Strange's body, rifled through the jacket, got a set of keys that looked good for the handcuffs. Came back and waved them at the figure on the ground. Raben was starting to weep, to choke and shake.

'Finally,' the man with the gun said. 'We've unlocked that memory, haven't we? A little late I guess . . .'

He took out his phone, called the Politigården, got through to what sounded like a party.

'Brix? Are you drinking?'

A caustic answer.

'Well, you can stop,' Arild said. 'I got a call from Raben asking me to meet him at Mindelunden. He said one of your cops was trying to kill him.'

Arild let that sink in.

'Raben's got a weapon from somewhere. He's shot them both. The lunatic's loose here.' A pause. 'I think he wants me next.'

'Stay where you are,' Brix ordered.

He snapped the phone shut, looked at the trembling man on the ground. Raised the gun.

There was a noise from somewhere.

A dog maybe. An urban fox.

A train went past, lights flashing. Arild raised the gun. Then something hit.

She hurt.

Hurt more when she crashed the police handgun hard into Jan Arild's head, sent him grunting to the floor, his weapon scuttling into the grass.

Lund coughed.

Looked at the still, sad, familiar shape lying there.

No movement. No breathing. That was clear in the bright moonlight.

It felt as if a horse had kicked her in the chest. Sick of the thing, she undid her jacket, stripped off the body armour she'd taken out of her locker for the first time that night, on the way to the car with Strange, fixing in her mind what she'd say.

It isn't magic.

She wondered when his gentle, inquisitive voice would leave her head.

Stopped when the man in the heavy military coat in front of her came to on the ground, began laughing, looking.

He had the face of a fox. Long sharp nose. Beady eyes. On her now.

'Raben,' she said quickly. 'Find the bastard's gun, will you? *Raben?*'

The figure in the blue prison suit was hunched up, a mess, drawn in on himself. Broken, maybe for ever.

Lund had heard every word of the exchange between these two, felt the fog clearing in her head as she did so. Strange was a special forces soldier. Capable of anything, provided duty and an officer above him called for it. But he didn't kill kids for fun. Only the enemy. And anyone who merited the name *stikke*, a curse that was too close to home.

Still no movement.

'Raben! There's a gun here somewhere. I'm on my own. I'm not . . .' What was the word? Her pained head hunted for it. 'I'm not good at this. You've got to help—'

'He can't, you stupid bitch,' Arild laughed back at her from the grass.

His fingers were probing the wound in his ginger hair. Blood, black in the moonlight. Not a lot.

'Thanks for that,' he said in his cruel, laughing voice. 'It all adds to the story.'

His head was off the ground. Arild was looking round. Right hand out, grasping.

Raben's moans were starting to get to her. The man was gone. Back in that room in Helmand, killing a kid because he felt like it, starting a bloodbath that would never leave him.

'You won't get away with this,' Lund said. She held the gun in both hands. Kept it on him, not steady. That wasn't possible. 'Stay where you are.'

Arild grinned at her.

'This is nothing. I've buried better before. Better than you.' He wasn't afraid. Not for a moment. 'Who do you think you are? What?

You're like him . . .' Arild nodded at Raben, rocking back and forth, eyes full of tears. 'One more pawn getting shoved round a chessboard you can't even see. I . . .'

He was on his knees, looking around him.

'I push you. Like I pushed Strange. And somewhere else . . . someone I can't see pushes me.'

A black shape glittered in the grass back towards the stakes. Within his reach. They both saw it. Arild watched her, head to one side.

'Your fingers are unsteady, Lund. Your arms are shaking. You don't even hold the gun right. You're a disaster, woman. You have been from the very start.'

'If you don't stay where you are I swear . . .'

But he was on his way already, quick as a wild animal on the hunt, rolling towards the black gun, the talisman he owned.

Now she saw it, felt it. The red roar rising in her head until there was nothing there except fury and hate, savage and raw.

The first bullet caught him in the shoulder. Arild bellowed with pain, skewed to one side, lay back on the grass, clutching the wound, staring at her, furious.

The second hit him in the chest and Lund didn't even know she'd pulled the trigger.

On the ground. Blood pumping from his gaping mouth.

She didn't count the rest. Lund fired and fired until the gun clicked on empty. Listened to Raben's howls then threw the hot, spent weapon into the damp thick grass.

Stood there, close to Strange's body and Arild's shattered, torn corpse. Sweat going cold beneath her jumper. Two bruises gathering where the bullets had smashed hard into Kevlar.

Sirens from somewhere. Blue lights on the distant road.

She walked towards them, eyes on the path. Out of Mindelunden not looking at the graves and the long lists of names. Or the mother with the dead son in her arms.

A shape ahead and she barely looked. Brix was there. Madsen too. Strange ought to be with them, face calm, eyes concerned, telling her to get in the car. To go home. To sleep. To forget.

To forget.

'Lund,' Brix said as she walked past, eyes on nothing but the night. '*Lund?*'

*

Torsten Jarnvig ignored Arild's final order and was welcoming troops for the next dispatch. Watching them stand to attention outside the Ryvangen barracks hall. Drilling into them the rules and rigours of the army.

In a warm and comfortable family apartment at Horserød open prison, Louise Raben sat on a sofa, Jonas half asleep on her lap, wondering when her husband would get there. Stroking the child's soft fair hair. Smiling at the thought of the future that lay ahead of them.

By the long line of marble slabs that listed the distant dead, Raben slumped in his grubby prison suit, mind gone, turned in on itself, capable only of tears, too afraid to go near the truth.

And on Absalon's island of Slotsholmen Thomas Buch stood in front of an open room, Gert Grue Eriksen beckoning to him. Birgitte Agger too. Krabbe, Kahn and all the others. The king and all his princes, friend and foe, half-smiling, arms open with only Karina's soft insistent fingers to hold him back.

He didn't look at her as he removed her hand from his jacket. Didn't look at her as Grue Eriksen closed the long black doors and led him into the crowd where glasses chinked, small talk ruled and no one spoke of a past that would soon be buried and forgotten.

There was nowhere else to go and now he knew it.